QUINN'S 11TH REGIMENT

by

MICHAEL IRELAND

Published by
Bronsdon Publishing LLC
1st American ed.
http://quinns11thregiment.weebly.com
ISBN: 978-0-615-72732-5

About the Author

Quinn's 11th Regiment is Michael Ireland's first novel. His world observations and interest in history inspired him to set down his research tucked inside a ghost story. His findings show that the history of evil has been manipulated, with events having been turned upside down and inside out. Ireland brings his readers along his path of discovery, as he sets the record straight.

PROLOGUE

BEHOLD I HAVE TOLD IT TO YOU, BEFOREHAND.
Jesus to his Disciples
Matt. 24:25

This is a story of good vs. evil throughout mankind's existence. It is the story of the Israelites, those of antiquity and those of the 21st century. Their bloodline still exists today, but the description of their traits, their very identity has been hidden from them. Only those who stole their identity know who they are, for they continue to enslave the Israelites through education, the media, through legislation, through every facet of their lives. This is of God's design, but not yet forever. As the end times approaches, the Israelites are beginning to wake to the realization of their enslavement, but not of who they are. Here, the story of evil is exposed. For make no mistake, Satan walks among you. But only the brave dare read this history of evil. Now, let us begin with the nature of the slavery.

"The individual is handicapped by coming face to face with a conspiracy so *monstrous* he cannot believe it exists." J. Edgar Hoover, FBI Director, 1935-1972; (Henry Makow, Ph.D., www.henrymakow.com/000166.html)

"For we are opposed around the world by a *monolithic and ruthless conspiracy* that relies primarily on covert means…on infiltration…guerrillas by night…It is a system which has conscripted vast human and material resources into the building of a tightly knit, highly efficient machine that combines military, diplomatic, intelligence, economic, scientific, and political operations…its dissenters are silenced…no secret is revealed…Those who make themselves our enemy are advancing around the globe…It is my obligation to inform and alert the American people to make certain that they have all the facts that they need and understand them as well." President John F. Kennedy, April 27, 1961

The coming of a *world state* is longed for, and confidently expected, by all the worst and most distorted elements. This state, based on principles of absolute equality of men and a community of possession, would banish all national loyalties. In it, *no acknowledgement would be made of the authority* of a father over his children, or *of God over human society*. If these ideas are put into practice, there will inevitably follow a reign of unheard of terror." Pope Benedict XV, 1920

Chapter 1

She knew that war was coming, everyone on the Internet talked about it. One day soon, they all said, the United Nations troops will be marching in the streets of America. It was exactly what Heinz Messinger, former U.S. National Security Advisor and Secretary of State, had promised in his speech to the secretive Leachburg group back in 1991. Messinger cried in a soft, thick German accent, "We can decree that there's an outside threat. Some kind of UFO alien invasion. Or we can send out our fighter jets with foreign insignias painted on them and have them blow up a few cities. Americans will beg us to bring in U.N. troops to protect them."

Patriots deduced that they'd use an extraterrestrial invasion. The Internet had broadcasted that the U.S. government had their own UFOs, which they had back-engineered from the two UFOs they had shot down in the 1950s. That's what had been going on in Area 51; the building of U.S. spaceships. The claim was that the U.S. Government could take ET home. We had our own superluminal flight. Patriots clamored, they'll fly a few impressive circles around the earth, maybe bomb a third-world country, so that the United Nations could announce that earth was under attack by space aliens. That was the kind of outside threat that could threaten mankind's very existence.

That was the kind of threat Messinger said was needed to make Americans "beg us to deliver them from. We just need to give them and overwhelmingly, powerful enemy, to scare the shit out of them. Americans are a stiffnecked, proud people. It's the only way we'll get them to willingly relinquish all their individual rights. We need Americans to cooperate. Give up their guns readily. Otherwise, we'll have an uncontrollable revolution on our hands. And we'll lose."

Maggie paused in reading the website article, "These idiots are telling us how to defend ourselves. They need Americans to cooperate before the World Government can openly assert themselves. So, we don't cooperate; we don't get scared of anything that they throw at us. We screw with their minds!" She shook her head, "They messed up their own plans by selling computers and Internet services to Americans. We learned quickly how to communicate with each other across the country. Across the world!"

Maggie recalled, "It was just before Tsaeb was elected that gun sales increased by 400%. Now, the media is reporting that gun sales are "exploding." People are getting ready for his re-election. They know he's intentionally destroying the United States. America's greatest enemy terrorist conquered the Office of the Presidency!"

Dennis Knickerbocker had admitted in his book, *Memories*, that he and his family were establishing a new world order. They had begun to set up Federal Reserve central banks in every country. The elite international banking cartel was quickly becoming the slave masters over the citizens of the world. Countries that refused found war at their door. Knickerbocker asserted, "All we need is the right major crisis and the nations will accept our New World Order."

The plan was to create an economic crisis. Destroy nations' currencies and establish a world currency, regulated by the World Bank.

There was no way to stop them. They had it all worked out. Even to their creating weapons that shot sound-wave frequencies that inflicted paralyzing pain in the victim, a white noise that scrambled the brain. Maggie wondered how does one protect themselves against sound and radio waves, or biological weapons sprayed over farmland, towns, and cities that spread diseases among the citizenry. Or the spraying of chemicals that put people to sleep or psychogenic drugs that caused hallucinations. While Americans are spaced out, UN troops come in and carry them off to FEMA camps. How do we fight that!? Maggie thought for a moment - we need our own military to work with the patriots. We can't do it without them.

Besides all the YouTube videos of FEMA trains, tank movements, UN vans, the most significant sign that the thugs in charge of the U.S. Government are planning war against American citizens is that the elite had begun been moving out of America to Russia and China, and hidden islands around the world.

Fear was building among the Patriots. Israel was saber rattling of its planned attack against Iran. The only question was would they attack before the presidential election. President Tsaeb had been leaking top secret special ops missions for months, warning Muslim countries. Was it Tsaeb who would give the order to the 35 Muslim paramilitary training camps along the eastern and southern coasts, from Springfield to Malibu, to attack American cities and towns – enough to provide the excuse for Tsaeb to declare Martial Law. President Putin of Russia had sent a nuclear sub to the Gulf of Mexico. A Texas judge had called for increased money to hire and arm more police to defend against an invasion; he warned that Tsaeb was about to turn the country over to the UN troops.

Maggie shook her head, "I just can't see Tsaeb walking out of office. He'll never do that."

Patriots had begun to realize that no matter how many times they shut down the Capitol's switchboard with complaining phone calls, Congress and the President were going to implement the laws that would destroy the United States. The elites had planned, and were on course, to dismantle the United States. Intuitively, Maggie knew that Americans were preparing to mount their own offensive. And that this would be bigger than any war Americans ever fought. She knew that the world was in the end times.

She prepared as much as she could. She bought one gun at a time and now owned a 300 mag. Browning Winchester with scope; a 30-06 with a hair trigger and scope; a 20-gauge shotgun; a 22 cal. rifle; a 9 mm. police special; and for her purse, a triggerless .38 cal. pistol. With her 300 mag.

she could take out the enemy at 5 miles; with the shotgun, she could take them out in a home invasion. With the .38, she planned to protect herself against rapist known as the UN Beasts. They had raped and prostituted the women and children they were sent into countries to protect from the invading enemy.

Maggie bought boxes and boxes of cartridges for each of her guns. Her Internet group had told her that Americans personally owned more than one *trillion* rounds of ammo for all types of guns. And that was before the latest "explosion" of gun sales. Americans privately owned more guns than any people of the world throughout the history of the world.

She had set aside warm, dark clothing and black overalls made of tough material, so she could survive crawling along a wintered forest floor to fight for her country. She bought a gas mask with filters, and made hazmat clothing from plastic sheeting with an undercoat of aluminum, sealing the seams with aluminum tape. She bought knee-high rubber boots and rubber gloves. She sold her gold jewelry to buy medical supplies to treat gun wounds, dried food to eat in caves and on the edges of battlefields. A tent and sleeping bag, map, compass, toolbox with a hatchet, a knife, a crowbar, 25 feet of nylon rope and metal clips, wooden matches and Bic lighters, steel wool to start fires, batteries, a large tarp to keep off the rain, a lantern, a container for water, another for gasoline and a hose to siphon gasoline were stored in the trunk of her car. She stocked up on canned and dried foods, large bags of rice and others of barley, and MREs. She was ready to survive wherever the fight took her. And then she waited.

But she knew that the only reason they had not yet sent U.N. troops out in the streets of America was because the elite knew they couldn't take down the Americans. If they thought that they could beat us, they would have moved on us by now, she thought to herself. I don't care how many Chinese troops are in Canada. Most of all, she knew that they wouldn't use nuclear bombs, or any kind of chemical that would permanently contaminate the land, to maintain it for their use after the war. Patriots knew that all the gas stations, now mostly owned by Muslims, were likely wired to explode by remote control once the fighting began, destroying Americans' ability to be mobile against the government or escape from being rounded up. As a result, patriots had begun to store gasoline in mobile containers.

She knew that Senator Sean Merry of Massachusetts had presented a bill to give foreign Muslims training and jobs as teachers and city planners of city infrastructure, and of underground gas and electrical lines. Merry was asking for legislative authority to give to Muslims, America's sworn enemy, the maps and underground access to blow up American cities. One criterion of his bill was that the Muslims must be 21-40 years old, the same as military enlistment age. Sean Merry, Maggie knew, was a member of the Craniums and Erects and the Foreign Relations

Private Council, two groups known to be Satan worshipers. But his colleagues knew that such a law would be too revealing of their intent to destroy America, and Merry's bill failed.

Everybody knew what the other side was doing; it was just a matter of igniting the war. The only question - which side would be the one to do that.

Maggie asked aloud, "What other power would an enemy have over a people, if they defeated them in military combat - than the power former President Schirf had put into the hands of the Director of Homeland Security and his/her designate - and that power President Tsaeb had now put into the hands of two devout Muslims."

Maggie couldn't take herself away from the Internet. It was, at once, informative, depressing, uplifting, defeating, and inspirational. She had formed a group, and those individuals had formed other groups, and so on and so on, so that she was connected with Americans from across the country. All of them were trying to save the America that they had grown up in that no longer existed, as the internationalists had entered the home stretch of their endgame. Americans came together like never before, one on one, north to south, from sea to shining sea.

They informed each other of the Chinese troops in Canada and Chinese troops in Mexico, along with the Russians, Hezbollah, Hamas, Al Qaeda, Cubans, Iranians, and Mexican Militaries to the south. All these armies are waiting for the order to invade America.

President George Erbert Wake Schirf, German-born, a/k/a George E.W. Schirf, served in the German navy, and was instrumental in merging Nazi (SS) intelligence with the OSI to form the CIA with "Wild Bill" Davidson and Allen Dulleston. Schirf was part of the CIA mind control experiments, MK-ULTRA. During his presidency, Schirf invited U.N. troops onto U.S. Military bases, and they have been here ever since. They're also in national park lands, increasingly taken over by the federal government. Today, there are more than a million U.N. troops unconstitutionally on American soil, on U.S. Military bases, or in UNESCO biospheres scattered across 650 million acres, or 29% of the United States.

And if Tsaeb failed to call for Martial Law, the United Nations Charter, Chapter VII, Article 43, allowed the United Nations to order troops to quell "riots" inside America, if the UN Security Council deemed that there was a *breach of peace* in the United States. If the president and congress were killed in revolution, the UN would take control of the United States - the unconstitutional continuity of government that the elite had put in place would still carry on. And this was just one of the purposes of the UN Military, to destroy revolutions against their New World Order. They were determined that an annoying revolution would not stop the endgame of the very secret elite from gaining control of the world.

The UN Charter treaty is the supreme law of the land in the U.S., in spite of any state law to the contrary. Nothing can stop the U.N. troops from taking control of America. They are already here, prepared to take control. The only hope that the American Christian Militias had was that Jesus Christ will rescue them from the evil of the world.

The leaders of America had signed the pact with the Devil, and the UN Charter was the result. President Franklin Roosevelt and British Prime Minister Winston Churchill presented their Atlantic Charter, in August of 1941. President Roosevelt knew of Japan's plans to attack Pearl Harbor, so he made sure film crews were on the ready, so the American people could see and become outraged and cooperate with his declaration of war. The United States entered WWII, after the attack on Pearl Harbor on December 8, 1941, by August 1941 - 8 months later; the Atlantic Charter was presented to the allied nations.

In agreeing to the terms of the Atlantic Charter, the World War II alliance of 26 nations signed the Declaration of a United Nations, in 1942. In that Declaration, Roosevelt first coined the term, United Nations. They met in Washington, D.C., in 1944, at the Dumbarton Oaks estate and drafted a charter for the United Nations. The Soviet Union, China, United States, and the United Kingdom, ratified the United Nations Charter on October 24, 1945. It replaced the President Woodrow Wilson's League of Nations, which failed because the U.S. Congress refused to sign on. Failure came because the U.S. didn't fund it. Today, the U.S. funds 22% of the United Nations' budget - not counting the cap and trade taxes on their way to every American household. The United Nations Charter fulfills Biblical prophecy.

The main architect of the UN Charter, President Franklin D. Roosevelt, was a 32nd degree Freemason; he put the "seeing eye" on the dollar, a symbol of the eye of Satan. Roosevelt was also a member of the Order of Nobles and Mystics. The Order was founded by the descendants of Muhammad, who was the descendant of Ham, who was the descendant of Satan. The Order's symbol is a crescent moon, engraved with a pyramid, an urn, and a pentagram; the crescent hangs from a scimitar (curved Islamic sword). The moon represents the Universal Mother worshipped in ancient times as Isis. Her other name was Astarthe, the idol Solomon worshipped that brought us under the control of Satan. To become a member of both the Freemasons and the Order of Nobles and Mystics, the initiate must choose hell over heaven.

Winston Churchill was the other architect of the UN Charter and a grandson of Leonard Jacobson, who was a business partner of August Belmont, Rothschild's main American representative. Churchill became a Freemason in 1901 and was installed into the Albion Lodge of the Ancient Order of Druids at Blenheim Place, 15 August 1908.

Churchill said, "You must understand that this war (WWII) is not against Hitler or National Socialism, but against the strength of the German people, which is to be smashed once and for all, regardless whether their strength is in the hands of Hitler or a Jesuit priest." The largest nationality group of U.S. citizens is German. The second - the Irish. The largest group of Christians in the world is in America.

It has been said that the Jewish Holocaust was a planned excuse to establish the State of Israel, so that the world would be so moved with compassion as to support an independent State of Israel, and therefore, the British government led the prohibition of Jewish refugees from escaping Nazi Germany.

But when WWII began with Hitler's first annexing Austria and then his occupation of Switzerland, then Czechoslovakia, between 1938-1939, the world did nothing. When Hitler published propaganda that German speakers were being persecuted in Poland - an excuse to attack Poland - and that Germany found that outrageous, Poland began to prepare for war. The day before Hitler attacked Poland, Poland and Britain signed a treaty that Britain would aid Poland against German aggression. Britain told Poland to stop a general call up of its troops, until Britain could attempt a peace accord with Germany. That failing, Germany marched on Poland, because Germany was intent on providing living space, territory, for the German people. Having made an agreement with the Soviet Union that, if the USSR remained uninvolved, Germany would split the territory of Poland with them. But in June 1941, Germany attacked Russia and seized all of Poland. In German Nazi concentration camps, which were much like the FEMA camps in the U.S. today, 3 million Polish Jews were exterminated. Britain never helped Poland, except to fire upon German ships, which only kept them away from Britain, not Poland. Where was Churchill's resolve to smash the strength of the German people, then? Or did he literally mean people and not the German Military?

France only attacked along its border with Germany and completely stopped all assault, when Warsaw was surrounded by Hitler's army, when the Polish government leaders and Polish military commanders fled the country. Hitler's Luftwaffe, air force, was a superior air force and immediately took out all Poland's air bases. Hitler moved with a strategy of Lightning War - bombing cities indiscriminately, just to terrorize the Polish people. Polish military commanders sent out their troops to confront a larger, better trained German military, even using their horse Calvary against German tanks. Poland never had a chance with such a poor military strategy. Their men were captured or killed in quick fashion.

Today, Americans know that the Chinese are blocking all escape routes to the north; the Russians, Iranians, Hezbollah, Hamas, and Mexican militaries are blocking the escape routes to the south. Christian Americans are trapped within the U.S. as were the Israelite-Jews in Germany. FEMA exterminations camps await Americans just as the extermination camps of Treblinka, Auschwitz, Belzec, and Chelmno had awaited the Polish Israelite-Jew. The Zionists-Jews had left Germany one and two years prior to WW II breaking out - just as today, where Zionists-Jews and their rich Muslim counterparts have left the U.S.

Different in the analogy is that the Americans are not the WW II

Israelite-Jews. Americans still had the memory of stories from fathers and grandfathers who fought in WWII; had seen the films of the Nazi concentration camps. They saw the FEMA camps and the millions of blue coffins on Internet YouTube. They knew what was coming, unlike the Poles. And Americans are irreverent sons-of-bitches who bow to no one, and no one will take their guns or their freedom of movement. This is the Super Bowl of American ingenuity with no holds barred. And Americans will fight this war covertly, from behind every tree and rock - not by marching out to confront better equipped militaries - but by sniper attacks. Constant, repetitive, kill and run, kill and run, to and from every direction against the United Nations military, and wherever possible, taking out their commanders - this will be the military strategy of the American citizens.

Maggie knew that each side was waiting for the other to make the first move. The thugs in control of the government passed one unconstitutional law after another, as if goading Americans in to uncontrolled anger that would flare out onto the streets, giving Tsaeb the excuse to call for Martial Law and put Americans into FEMA extermination camps. Under the Homeland Security Act, this closed, military-controlled venue would allow the Director of Homeland Security and the two Muslims appointed to the DHS, to order biomedical experiments, vaccinations, and thereby, order the torture and murder of millions of Christian Americans - as a category of people - stipulated in the Homeland Security Act that the Muslims could experiment on. The Homeland Security Act laid out the legal instrument to allow the repeat of the Angel of Death, Dr. Mengele's medical experiments in the Nazi concentration camps, but now here in American FEMA camps.

Maggie also knew that the Director of Homeland Security was a member of the Foreign Relations Private Council. She was the front for Muslim control of DHS.

Americans know that this will be a war of selection, not against our own citizens charged with keeping the peace, but against the select few giving the orders to the thugs holding high government positions. This will be a surgical revolution against the two heads of the Illuminati - the Zionists and the Muslims, against the seeds of Satan that are about to take control of the world. This will be a war between the Sons of Light and the Sons of Darkness.

She also thought of the notion of universal knowledge - that Americans had telepathically communicated to each other that rushing in to the streets was not the method of fighting this war. Not this war. The stupid open-field battles of the Civil War, WWI, and WWII, proved that to be folly. No, she thought, Americans know they need to strike the way the Special Ops do it. Spring up from holes in the ground, from hidden places, to strike by surprise and overwhelm the elite trying to destroy our country from within. They knew enough to take down the elite through accident or illness before any more of them could leave the country.

Maggie was filled with questions. Why were patriots saying that we were in the end times - end of the world? How can that be; what happened to life? She grew up watching her grandparents grow old, her parents buying a house, her playing out in the yard with her friends. Life was about doing well in school. About going to Mass on Sunday. Growing up and getting married, having children. Growing old gracefully. Watching the Ed Sullivan show on Sunday evenings. When in God's name did we turn that corner and come in to the end times. Why was this happening? These people - the real elite that no one sees, they are trillionaires - they can break any law and buy their way out of jail! They could buy countries; they've bought the souls of our leaders! Why do they need a New World Order, why? She searched the Internet for an answer.

She found on YouTube Project Camelot - a series of interviews by Kerry Cassidy. One was with Bob Dean. Bob Dean had experienced his first spiritual rescue at the age of three. These people seemed to have been watched over all their lives. Maggie thought of the guardian angels she had been told about in her girlhood. Dean told of being invited numerous times to visit the aliens and was taken by them through portals. They can manipulate your awareness, unless there's a trigger mechanism; he's now suffering total recall. The aliens can manipulate time and matter - they can take you for six weeks, but when they return you home, only ten minutes has passed. The good aliens told him to talk, to help people handle what is coming down the road. After we go through what is to come, the human race will have a greater expansion of consciousness. He said - Americans don't care what's going on. The U.S. Government is lying to them. The U.S. Military are working with the aliens, but the aliens are calling the shots. There's been a battle going on in D.C., as to whether to tell people of the aliens and what their agenda is. People aren't ready to hear; this is too big, one side argued. There are aliens who are so spiritually evolved as to be angels. There was something about types of civilizations, three layers of differentially-evolved civilizations.

Dean told of FEMA concentration camps and of Continuity of Government underground facilities that are located all over the country that are massive. The underground facility at Fort Huachuca, AZ, is luxurious and for the politicians. Maggie looked it up and found that the fort is under the command of U.S. Army Installation Management Command; it's located 15 miles north of the Mexican border; the 19th Cavalry Regiment is stationed there. Dean said that there is an official-level relationship between the U.S. Government and the aliens.

Maggie was stunned by what Dean said next: The Aerospace Command that used to be in Colorado Springs is now located in orbit as an international unit. Dean told of hyper luminal, speed of light, flight used to travel out of our solar system. He had been told by U.S. Military - "We can take ET home!" Los Alamos, Dean said, is doing time travel.

The one thing Dean said that stuck out in Maggie's mind - the aliens won't tell where they are from. The other: "We do have a future and it's glorious." There will not be a nuclear war; the higher aliens will not allow it. The flora and fauna of the earth are too precious. There is a struggle between two alien groups still going on out there. There's a hierarchy of alien groups, and some groups have their own agenda, predominately spiritual. The angelic level of aliens slapped around the level between them and us. Synthetic beings will be arriving from another planet. (*See,* Project Camelot, Bob Dean; www.youtube.com/watch?v=CxkQU_JYXl w&feature=relmfu.)

Maggie put the pieces together with what she knew, mumbling to herself, "These reptilian aliens are Satan's army! So, are the good aliens from Michael the Archangel's army?"

Maggie searched for another Project Camelot interview. She found one with Dr. Pete Peterson, a physicist who has invented and built things for the U.S. Government, from the age of 13 he was "picked up" to work on projects for the government; he calls himself a problem solver, a maker of instruments that can see and hear. He comes from genius inventors on both sides of his family. He talked of 9/11 and of a building that was "not involved; why did it come down; it didn't even have ashes fall on it; it was out of the wind pattern; why did that building come down?" Peterson asked. He then said, "It had massive amounts of gold in it, and the gold disappeared...Anyone that goes looking for it will find an early grave."

Peterson built a machine that would detect the aura around a human's body and organs, to detect diseases. It worked on 85% of people, but not on 15%. And those 15% have common genetic characteristics within their group, but which are not found on earth. Later he found that the 15% had alien DNA. He thought that he had alien DNA in him. He said that mind control will work on 85% of people, but not on those 15%. Those people with 15% alien DNA are found in all races and cultures.

Peterson said that the Vatican Library is stuffed with documents that are contrary to the beliefs we've been taught; he thought the documents were remnants of the Library at Alexandria. People "in the know" told him to get to a safe hiding place. Europeans are moving into his hiding area of the U.S. Peterson said that movies about aliens are partially funded by the U.S. Government; they want the movies to inform Americans of what's to come. He said that the coming economic failure will bring anarchy and chaos; under the Great Depression people had morals and ethics, today's 20-somethings do not. And they have no idea what's to come. Store food for six months. Peterson said that there is no survival in an urban setting. When your neighbor smells you cooking a steak on an outside grill, and he hasn't had food for two weeks and his two kids are telling him they're hungry, what do you think is going to happen? There is climate change, but it's getting colder, not warmer. A lot has been done to dumb down the population. He knows of a U.S. Government program to remove intelligence from people. Rely on self, no one else; prepare mentally, Peterson warned. We have the ability to heal, using our minds.

"Leaks on the Internet, in early 2009," Peterson had said, "were claiming that Congress had a closed session for the first time in history; there is talk of Congress, for the sake of their health and safety, will move someplace else, *when the American people find out what they did to them*." Peterson said he won't contradict the leaks. He also stated that the Founding Fathers later wrote that the Second Amendment was put into the Constitution for Americans to use in order to fight a corrupt government, not to go hunting. And that superdomes were built to lock in people until they died. He talked of the "very large" concentration camps and the government plans to shift people around; and microchips can be injected through hypodermic needles. They are geolocators. The collapse of the dollar is intended to bring about the global currency and it will be tied to microchips.

In Peterson's second interview he talked about SRI buying by the thousands, devices to put on the head while teaching the brain to move things. His interviewer, Kerry, said it's used "to teach remote influencing." Peterson replied, "Don't say that! You will be visited, and it won't be nice."

In a third interview, Peterson talked of how to protect against microwaves used remotely in mind control - that the President and diplomats wear a device to protect themselves against mind control. But people can learn "to use their mind to generate a benevolent electro-magnetic field frequency around themselves." www.youtube.com/watch?v=ooSRh7V68uk.

Maggie immediately thought of how she called on the Holy Ghost to White Light her, to protect herself. And that remotely, she asks the Holy Ghost's White Light to cover her children and grandchildren and their homes and animals. Most of what she had heard in the interviews was tangential to what she already knew, but coming from people who had firsthand knowledge, inside knowledge, was overwhelming by its confirmation of what she knew or what she thought. It was emotionally draining. She decided to continue on with UNESCO and found that the Wildland Project is "a plan to designate ONE HALF of the United States of America as 'protected areas where special measures need to be taken to conserve biological diversity.'" *See,* Phyllis Schlafly Report, *Supra.*

Maggie thought to herself, "Satan's army is corralling us." Then the thought occurred to her, putting the Project Camelot interviews together with UNESCO's biosphere reserves, "Are these the future land areas that the aliens are planning to live in once they arrive en masse?"

Chapter 2

There it was again. That strange feeling that an intruder had quietly slipped in undetected. Its essence now hung over her rooms. She hated it. There was no defense against it. And whom do you call for protection against a spirit? How do you describe the feeling that you aren't alone, yet no one is there?

She tried to ignore the feeling of being watched. She exhaled heavily; ruffled her blonde hair vigorously, as if to wipe the recognition from her mind. Finally, she got up from her computer, deciding that the best idea was to move around. It's not going to take over my apartment, she thought to herself. Instead, she decided to invade its space. She turned on lights, as if to expose all the dark crevices where it hid in her rooms.

She walked into the kitchen to make a cup of coffee. But just as she stepped in front of the sink, something brushed up against a bare toe. She quickly pulled her foot back. She looked down and saw a long screw roll out from under the kitchen cabinet and pass her feet. As she watched, the screw continued to roll slowly and steadily over the black rubber mat in front of the sink. Without thinking, she bent over to pick it up, but it escaped her grasp. Intent on not letting it get away from her, or perhaps intuitively trying to stop the paranormal display before fear set in, her hand attacked it in a quick assault, grabbing the two-inch long screw covered with old white paint. She examined it closely. It certainly had been used, but not by her. And how did it get under the cabinet; she had swept the floor many times; and why did it suddenly roll out now? And how did it roll across a texture rubber mat? The floor is not slanted, not there.

A foreboding feeling came over her. How does a screw slowly roll 18 inches across a flat, textured surface without being pushed or kicked or anything else - by her? What's Newton's theory, she asked herself, an object remains at rest until a force is acted upon it? If she hadn't applied the force, what the hell did?

She looked up at the refrigerator in the corner of the small kitchen, remembering the week before. Again, she made note of the objects on top of the appliance. Sitting in front of the microwave was a coffee maker, a bottle of Fish Eye Pinot Grigio, a new bottle of Jim Bean whiskey, and a jug of Tullamoore Dew. Except for the whiskey, the others had sat there for more than a year. She made close note of their positions, as she had done the week before.

It was just a week ago that she had picked up the Jim Bean and considered making herself a drink, but decided against it. She had bought it solely for gunshot wounds that would occur during the coming war - she bought it to clean out wounds and deaden the pain. It was after she had thought of opening it for simple pleasure that she had noticed that the bottle had moved - on its own. She made the excuse that she had not replaced it in alignment with the other bottles - that it was she who had left it in a conspicuous position close to the edge of the refrigerator when she had decided not to make herself a drink.

But now, as she looked, after picking up the screw, she saw that the bottle of Jim Bean had again been moved out of position. She let out a quiet moan. She so wanted to ignore the evidence before her. The screw moved on its own on a flat surface without prodding from her. The bottle of whiskey that she knew she had deliberately placed up against the microwave was now sitting five inches away from it.

Okay, she thought to herself, it's an old building; what could I expect? It had been a munitions factory for more than a century. Maybe the spirits hung around after the renovation into apartments. Did the spirit want her to open the bottle of whiskey? Maybe he wanted to drink the whiskey, smell the vapors of whiskey as she poured it into a glass for herself. Who the hell knows! All she knew for certain was that she had placed the bottle up against the microwave along with the other bottles, and those bottles had not moved - from vibration or anything else.

Again, she placed the whiskey bottle up against the microwave and made a note to herself - all the bottles are touching the microwave.

She decided to pretend that she was alone. She walked into her dark bedroom and up to the windows overlooking the front terrace and lawn four stories below. On the side of the room were two more large windows, making the entire corner of the large room open to the sky. She often thought of her bedroom as an eagle's nest high in a treetop.

The old munitions factory consisted of two separate buildings that sat perpendicular to each other, joined by glass-enclosed corridors. Maggie's building was one story taller and she had the corner apartment. She could see past the rooftop of the other building for miles beyond, and together with the front view it gave her a 90-degree view over treetops to four towns. She loved to look out, especially at the night sky when all her neighbors in the next building were asleep and wouldn't notice her standing at the windows of her darkened room. The buildings were two blocks from the small town square where there was always a car passing through even in the dead of night. It gave her a sense of not being totally alone. Life was always in flux before her.

The old street lamps of the square lighted enough of the night so she could only see the brightest of stars and largest of planets in the sky. But at its regular intervals a full moon would pass across the sky and set behind the treetops of the horizon. Since spring, she had left the windows open; a constant breeze flowed throughout her rooms.

Outside her bedroom was an alcove where she had set up an office with a desk and bookcases. As she sat at her desk, she could turn to the side and look at the sky through two large windows. She loved the evening breeze caressing her skin as she typed on the keyboard of her computer. The setting was perfect for her; life was close by, but not intrusive upon her solitude.

Chapter 3

They had met online, on a conservative website, exchanged photos and telephone numbers, and every night they discussed the state of the union. Quinn had been an Army Special Ops, trained in five different combat martial arts. He had been sent on killing missions in Columbia, Peru, and Venezuela. On one mission, from a mile away, he shot and killed a drug cartel leader lounging in his back yard. The bullet hit before it was heard. But Quinn regretted killing unarmed men. Maggie thanked him for it. "They were leaders of drug cartels," Maggie had admonished.

"Everyone says that they can kill, but they don't know - when they go down they scream. You shoot them twice in the chest and then you walk up to them and shoot them in the head. A lot of people can't do that, not while they're screaming on the ground."

"Yes, I could," Maggie argued. "First, I would never pick up a gun and aim it at anyone unless the life of my family or myself were in danger. And if I picked up the gun, it would be to kill. Better the drug dealer screaming on the ground than my grandsons! Their drugs are killing our children! Better they should be dead!"

Three times a week, Quinn and Maggie met on the gun range. He taught Maggie how to shoot and clean her guns. He had reset the alignment of her 9-mm. He showed her how to kill with a small knife, "cut into the side of the neck and outward to prevent the noise of gurgling blood or a cry to warn others of the kill; then wipe the knife across the trouser leg to clean off the blood." He taught her how to take a tank with a knife. "Hide in the environment and wait for the tank driver to come out to take a piss, then cut his throat; and wait for another to emerge and do the same - then climb into the tank and fire upon the enemy." He showed her the hand signal to get down, "two fingers pointing down"; and the hand signal for get the fuck down!, "show the back of a closed fist and pull it down quickly."

His idea of bragging was to shoot holes in the target's narrow circular lines; with bullets, he made them into paper cut outs. Maggie smiled. She was indeed impressed. He competed in bow and arrow competition at the range where he had shot seven Robin Hoods. He was the man they made movies about, and Maggie fell in love with this man she had been looking for all her life. She had given up hope; she thought the man she wanted didn't exist. But, now, there he was standing before her. She told him, "When I listen to you; when I watch you, I feel as though I'm looking at my male counterpart. And when you say you feel guilty for shooting an unarmed drug boss, I want to hit you upside the head with a two by four! I thank you for what you did for our country!"

He was pensive for a while and then leaned closer to her, with a smile, "Do you really think that I would let you hit me with a two by four?"

Maggie grinned, "Ahh, No!" But that was the best part of him, she thought to herself; that he wouldn't put up with being pushed around.

He was an independent thinker, his own man, who wouldn't take crap from anyone, including Maggie. But with all that Quinn was a gentleman, thoughtful, and respectful of Maggie's feelings. He truly was an honorable man. And Maggie didn't want to change any part of him.

Chapter 4

They had finished eating dinner and Maggie put the dirty plates up on the shelf of the large pass-through between the kitchen and dining room. She got up, picked up the plate of roast beef and bowl of mashed potatoes and took them into the kitchen. She covered them and put them into the refrigerator and began drawing water into the sink to wash the dishes. When she turned to the pass-through shelf to get the dishes, she saw that the salt and pepper were on the shelf, too.

"Thanks, Quinn," Maggie said.

"I didn't do anything," Quinn responded.

"Shit!" Maggie mumbled quietly under her breath.

"What?" Quinn asked as he entered the kitchen, picking up a dishtowel.

"Why did you swear?"

"It's the ghost," she said quietly. "He put the salt and pepper up on the shelf of the pass-through."

"You have a ghost? Quinn's interest peaked. Have you ever talked to him?"

"No. I've been told that it's not good to talk to them because you give them energy. Power."

After Maggie related the paranormal events she had experienced, they quietly finished the dishes. Afterwards, Quinn put down the dishtowel and went back and sat down at the dining table. "Have you ever heard of the LISA project?"

Maggie joined him at the table. "No. Why?"

"Well, you've heard of the Large Hadron Collider - they call it LHC, at Cern, Switzerland."

"Yes, I've heard of the collider - it was also the primary motivating factor in the book, Angels and Demons. They were trying to create the God-particle."

"Well, you have to understand scientists and their constraints of thinking; for a theory to be accepted, such as, God created the universe, a scientist must be able to follow a formula and recreate the same result."

"Oh, much like following a cake recipe - the ingredients must be precise," Maggie teased.

Quinn smiled, but ignored the euphemistic comparison, "While they call it creating the God-particle, what the accelerator does is try to smash particles together to break open the protons to see what emerges. They are trying to see how the universe was created; what was the formula. What were the ingredients used. Actually, they think the universe created itself, the Big-Bang theory, without God."

"Like the ingredients of a cake?" Maggie pushed with a playful grin.

Quinn nodded in consent, but continued, "And likely, they will create matter using the same formula - that is, once they discover the ingredients and how they interact with each other to come into being as a universe. That's the big question, what was actually created, at the subatomic level. They've been looking for the quarks and also the Higgs bosons that they have only predicted to exist. They just announced that they found the Higgs bosons, the God particle. While the accelerator is smashing the protons, they track these particles," Quinn explained.

"Back up a minute here. The particles are the protons, but the Higgs bosons. What are they?"

"Let me back up even further. In the Fermilab, near Chicago, there is a particle accelerator, once the largest in the world, where they discovered the quark. But that accelerator doesn't have the necessary power to detect the Higgs bosons that they had theorized existed. So they spent around $100 billion to build the accelerator in Cern, Switzerland, that they expect will create enough power to smash the protons and detect the Higgs bosons and other things like the muons and tauons."

"Stop there! Don't get too deep for me or you'll lose me," Maggie cried. "I remember from high school that electrons and protons have negative and positive charges, respectively. And the neutrons have no charge. What you seem to be saying is that the accelerator can manipulate the charged particles of protons, but not the neutrons."

"Correct. Free neutrons are produced in nuclear fission and fusion; they produce nuclear power and bombs."

"Is the breaking open of the protons going to suffice to complete the formula?"

"That I can't answer. It's one discovery at a time. My guess is that something drives the protons; if their internal structure is made up of quarks, and now claim house Higgs bosons, it is likely that the quarks and Higgs bosons play a part in the movement, the energy charge of different atoms. Something causes the protons to adhere to neutrons, but what? Gravity, more than likely. And if gravity, what is creating the gravity, protons? Or are their electrical charges being controlled by their substructures, the quarks, Higgs bosons, muons, or tauons, or whatever else they might find inside these particles."

"Okay. And the quarks?" Maggie asked.

"At this point, it gets more technical than I can explain. But it has to do with the idea of taking the smallest known element of matter and smashing it open - like a walnut, to see what's inside. They detected quarks inside these particles. But quarks can't exist on their own for prolonged periods of time. They only exist in groupings. For instance, a proton has three quarks with each having its own electrical charge. The quark is an elementary particle, without a substructure. It's the basic building block of the universe from which all other particles are made. And they have theorized that Higgs bosons also exist, but they can't detect them. They can measure a particle's spin as a fundamental property such as the scalar boson whose spin equals zero. The interesting thing is that quarks have properties of electric charge, color charge, spin, and mass.

But the Higgs boson is believed to be even smaller, its spin and even its detection is yet to be measured. It seems that as soon as these Higgs bosons are released that they self-destruct in a nano-second."

Quinn continued, "Well, what they have discovered in the tracking of these protons is that some disappeared and then reappeared."

"How can they be sure it's the same proton coming back, re-appearing?"

"Each has its own path; some are spirals, wider or tighter spirals. Others have a straight path that veer left or right; some arch. Think of a snowflake each having its own pattern; our fingerprints are all unique."

"So, each proton is unique in identifying characteristics, one of which is its path, another its electrical charge?" Maggie surmised.

"That's right. But it has been theorized that these particles are not the smallest element of matter."

"Okay. So what does that have to do with the salt and peppershaker being moved by the ghost in my apartment?

"He's able to move things," Quinn replied.

"Yes, that's correct."

"You also said you saw a ghost in your son's house. You saw a solid form of her skirt?"

"Yes, as she was leaving the doorway, I could see the bottom portion of her skirt. It was solid, made of lace. It was golden in color."

"Taking all these things into consideration, how do we apply it to your ghostly experiences? In the basic format, some ghostly activity is only repetition. They are known as the insane ghosts, thinking that the same activity will one day change and result in whatever it is that they want to change."

"I'll buy that that is insane."

"But the ghost who can fuck with our minds," Quinn smiled, "move things, hit us, travel, follow people to wherever they move - it is thought that they exist in a different dimension."

"Dimension?" Maggie questioned.

"We live in the fourth dimension. We have knowledge, awareness of the universe in one of time, and three of space dimension - that is, depth, height, and width. But physicists think that other beings live in higher levels of dimension - as many as 11 dimensions. It's a mathematical reality in measurement of gravitational wavelength."

"Soooo." Maggie pondered, "If we can see the height, width, and depth of something, during a specific time period, it exists in our dimension, the 4th. Then there are other beings in another dimension that can see things that are invisible to us?"

"Not only that, but these beings are invisible to us. They exist; work on the level, the plane, of the invisible. Let's go back to the collider in Cern," Quinn leaned forward, resting his elbows on the table. "The protons that they have tracked and which have disappeared only to reappear they think are made up of the smallest elements, quarks."

"Right," Maggie followed Quinn's connecting of the dots.

"Okay, now these quarks, once activated somehow, disintegrate immediately. But the question is, when they are not activated, opened, or whatever, how are they expressed? Quarks are the smallest of matter that exists, but at what level of awareness to us? They are too small for us to see even with our optical instruments."

Maggie frowned, "Is this when energy is given off - I mean, when something is burned it changes its mass from one state to another, giving off energy when it does? Like boiling water. The solid water turns in to a gas, steam. When the energy given off during this change of mass is harnessed, it can drive an engine."

"Yes and no; we can still see the steam in large quantities or when light reflects off the vapor. Think more in terms of when a body dies and the soul leaves it. We don't see the energy expressed in the change of state of the mass, the body. And we don't see the soul. The soul is invisible regardless of lighting, but they have weighed the body at the time of death and there is a measurable drop in weight of the body when the soul leaves it. They think that souls, or ghosts, exist in a dimension where the soul, made of quarks, can be seen. They know those quarks are invisible in the fourth dimension, but if they reappear, they were not destroyed, so where did they go? What changed to make them invisible and visible, again?" Quinn gestured the question with his hands. "And maybe. Somehow. The soul controls the quarks of other matter; other things."

"Whoa," Maggie contemplated the possibilities. "What do you mean, control?"

"When we see ghosts, we see them dressed in uniforms or fashions they wore when alive."

"Yeah."

"Do they control the matter of the clothing that they wear, or is it our imagination that creates their appearance in a fashion of dress?" Quinn asked.

"I think they control the dress - the matter of the clothing - it's also made up of neutrons, atoms. Clothing is matter as much as the body is matter. Maybe they take the quarks of the clothing's matter when they leave the body. That is, some portion, some percentage of the clothing's quarks."

"Okay. Let's suppose they control the matter of the clothing they appear in - when they want to appear. In other words, they have the ability to control the quarks, electrons, protons, neutrons that make up matter and they control all that to enter and disappear from the fourth dimension in which we live - in which we have awareness."

"Gees," Maggie sighed. "It's scary as well as fascinating. All right. Is this why people say to acknowledge them gives them energy, or claims of batteries dying in their presence - are they taking the energy to collect more quarks, increase protons, to make themselves seen to us?"

"That could be," Quinn replied, "But let's continue with the overview for a moment. Let's give them the ability for the sake of argument to control clothing."

"Okay."

"In the same method of controlling their clothing, whatever method that is, they have the ability to move the salt and peppershaker, or any other object, regardless of its size or weight."

"Regardless. Is that because these objects exist in the fourth dimension and the ghost exists somewhere in the 6th through the 11th dimension?"

"Perhaps. We don't know if any of this is true, although it touches upon Einstein's general theory of relativity."

"Yeah, sure," Maggie laughed.

Quinn laughed, "Let's proceed."

"I'm listening, Quinn," Maggie said. "What else can these souls do, telepathic messaging?" Maggie laughed with sarcasm.

"Yes!"

"Oh, shit!" Maggie cried.

"Did you hear about the USS Hornet?"

"Yes. WWII."

"It was an aircraft carrier that they were going to scrap after it was decommissioned, but someone saved it, and I think it is now berthed in San Diego, California."

"Doesn't matter, what about it?" Maggie wasn't sure she wanted to know, but her curiosity was peaked.

"After it was berthed it suddenly became haunted. In all its history there weren't any reports of ghosts, but now they say it's haunted with hundreds of dead seamen, including its commander. People have seen them, appear and disappear. I think maybe someone even talked to one of them."

"Wow. Okay. And it's meaningful that it was after it was berthed that these ghosts came to haunt." Maggie offered, "Maybe they heard it was going to be scrapped."

"That's right. And maybe they were the ones who stopped it from being scrapped. Spoke in the ear of those who finally bought it and berthed it. How did these hundreds of ghosts know that the USS Hornet needed them? They came together, these souls, from all over the country, to take up the guarding of their old ship. But how did they know?"

"Telepathy," Maggie suggested.

"I think so," Quinn said.

"How did these souls come to exist in these upper dimensions?' Maggie asked. "What are the ghost remnants - what did you call them, the insane ghosts? What or how is there a difference?"

"They think that to get into the upper dimensions that one is allowed or granted that ability, or that souls choose to live on those planes. Maybe some people, when they die, feel they still have something to contribute, still want to protect our country that they died for. We'll never know these things, for sure."

"Dante's Inferno. Nine levels of hell." Maggie mumbled.

"Maybe it's more like levels of existence. Edgar Casey wrote about the progression of souls."

"Well, let's not digress," Maggie cautioned. "Let's just accept that souls exist on levels that we cannot see or have awareness of." Maggie grew quiet a moment. "How is it that some people have psychic powers? They can see the future, or see other people when we are not with them, or hear what others say to themselves? If we don't exist outside the fourth dimension, how can we do things that souls do on the upper dimensions of existence?"

"Those telepathic skills, psychic skills are usually through a bloodline, inherited through the generations. I bet there are other members of your family who have psychic abilities."

"My great-grandmother read tea leaves; my younger son is definitely psychic about future events. When they were children, my son saved my daughter's life with his psychic ability. And my older son has heard the ghosts of children laughing in his house in Rockport. One night he heard a child's voice ask, 'should we wake him up?' I know these children's laughter; they woke me up one night when I was staying there over a weekend. At first, I just thought it was kids in the neighborhood until I realized that there were no kids in his neighborhood.

One night he called me after hearing a knock on his bedroom door. That door closes off a suite of rooms. There are two small rooms off of the bedroom; one he uses as his office. At night, he'll close the bedroom door so the rooms get warmer during the night. He had been in his office reading when he heard five distinct sounds of knocking on the door, from outside the bedroom suite. His dog even started barking. It scared the hell out of my son. So, he called me, asking me what I thought of it. What he should do. I told him to go check everything in the house, to make sure he shut off the stove, for instance. Maybe the ghost was trying to warn him of some kind of danger."

Maggie paused a moment, "He hates to talk about the ghosts; he just bought the house a few years ago and he absolutely loves it and the town. But he admitted that one morning he closed the door tightly to his bedroom, leaving Dakota. Dakota is his dog. Leaving him inside so he wouldn't tear up the house. When he came home that night, Dakota greeted him at the front door. My son checked the bedroom door; it was still shut tightly just as he had left it that morning. There is no other way out of the bedroom suite, except to the deck outside, but then Dakota would have been outside the house. The only explanation is that the ghost let Dakota out of the bedroom and shut the door, again."

"Is that son psychic?" Quinn asked.

"Yes. He's been leery of it; he tries to ignore it. But I told both of my sons that they have to accept it and develop the skill." Maggie grew quiet. "My daughter doesn't have any psychic ability and isn't interested in the least; I mean she won't even talk about the subject. But both she and my younger son refuse to spend the night at my elder son's house in Rockport." Maggie thought for a moment, "Well, actually, my daughter took photos of her two sons sitting on a bench on the front porch of my son's house. But she tore them up because she thought there was a ghost inside the parlor looking out the window at her. Is that ability? To feel that a ghost is near, looking at you? Or can everyone detect a ghost's presence? I don't know."

After relating the story, Maggie grew quiet, again.

"What are you thinking about?" Quinn asked.

"I never added up all the encounters that I've had with ghosts or voices. Not before now. I don't know why, but they all seem to be flooding into my head."

"Like what?"

"When I was married and we were having problems. I couldn't sleep."

"You seem to have a lot of problems getting to sleep," Quinn smiled.

"Yeah. It's when the world is quiet and I can think. It's usually my favorite pastime, sitting in a quiet room, thinking. But there was a night that I was very worried, upset about the marriage, our financial problems, the usual stuff, I guess." Maggie looked at Quinn, "As I had lain in bed, wondering what was going to happen, I felt a hand stroke my brow, twice. It was trying to comfort me. But it scared me. I thought to myself, please don't touch me. And it stopped, just like that. Another night two male spirits were standing across the bedroom. I heard one ask the other, should we let her know we're here? And, again, I thought, No! Go away! And it seemed as though they did. I couldn't feel them in the room after that."

"Are these all the same ghosts that you see, hear, or feel?" Quinn asked.

"Not that I'm aware of. I did a psychic reading from my apartment on the ghosts in my son's house in Rockport. They are a family, a man, woman, a boy and a girl, from the 1800s. Just a family, nothing scary. She loves the orange Venetian plaster in the dining room. I think that's why she was making all the noise, so I would finish it. When I was up there another time, I was stretched out on the sofa. I heard the woman talking to the man, her husband. She said, 'Look how long she is!' I could feel them standing across the room, looking at me.

"Well. I would have to agree, Maggie, being six feet tall would make you look very long lying down." Quinn smiled, trying to lighten up Maggie's mood.

"It hasn't been all bad," Maggie nodded. "When we were in high school, a group of us headed for Nantasket; on the way we stopped and bought some booze. I was 17, but looked 27. So, I would buy. They never carded me; and I acted as though it was an everyday event, nothing out of the ordinary. It's kind of amazing how far you can get by standing up straight and acting like a lady."

Quinn smiled, quietly listening, trying to picture Maggie as a 17-year-old girl.

"Well, we drove to Nantasket Beach. There's an old underground fort nearby that they used during WWII. The problem was we didn't know it was there; we only saw rolling mounds of grass where we could go and drink without being disturbed before going back to the beach. I can't remember where they came from, but the next thing I knew there were five boys coming over to talk to us while we were sitting on the grass drinking, looking down at the inlet waterway. The night grew dark and we grew happy. Life was wonderful, expectant. We sang and ran around the mounds of rolling grass. Some of us rolled down the grassy mounds; one almost fell into the water." Maggie started laughing. "My God! We were so drunk. And stupid! And for whatever reason, each of us girls took the hand of a boy, and we ran around for the hell of it. Talk about tiptoeing through the tulips!" Maggie laughed again and then sighed. "I was holding a boy's hand and we were running; it was pitch dark now, no moon. And I heard a man's voice a few feet above me; it seemed to float along in the air over us as we ran."

"What did it say," Quinn asked.

"It said, 'Sit Down.' In my head, I said to the voice, 'They'll all think I'm crazy, if I sit down because a voice told me to!' So, I kept running. And then the man's voice yelled at me, 'SIT DOWN!' Without saying anything, and knowing the boy would continue to run while holding my hand and then cause me to go flat on my face, I tucked my elbow into the fold of his elbow and fell backwards, bringing him down on his butt next to me. I heard the other kids call out, 'Are you okay?' And then someone said, 'Hey, watch out for that!' I was sitting there on the grass with my legs in front of me, the boy next to me. Then I realized that my heel was leaning against something. It was a sidewalk. I got up on all fours and crawled over to the sidewalk. The boy next to me doing the same thing. The other kids walking onto the sidewalk, cautioning each other. I crawled to the other side of the sidewalk and looked down. There was a cement stairwell, 20 feet below. If we had continued running we would have either dropped 20 feet and then down cement steps, or dropped 20 feet and smashed onto the cement terrace on the other side of the stairwell."

"Jesus Christ! You would have been dead!" Quinn exclaimed.

"That's the conundrum in all this experience, while they scare the hell out of me; they have saved my life more than once. And I think you're right when you say that we, I, communicate with them telepathically. I never gave it a thought until now. And come to think of it, I think they spoke to those who purchased the USS Hornet, to get them to buy it and save it from being scrapped."

"I had a strange experience once," Quinn mumbled.

"Before you get started, do you want some coffee?" Maggie asked.

"That would be great," Quinn said, sitting back in his chair.

As Maggie prepared the coffee, she talked to Quinn through the kitchen's pass-through opening. "When did you experience communicating with the dead?"

"When I was married. We were at a family gathering and my wife did something that really upset me. I was sitting at the dining table, talking with an old woman at the time. I was controlling my anger over what my wife had done, when suddenly the eyes of the old woman changed. They turned gray and strange looking, and then she looked at me and said, 'Let it go, Amigo!' No one except Shooter ever said that to me, called me Amigo, that is."

Maggie came over to the pass-through and rested her elbows on its shelf, "It seems as though your dead friend took possession of that woman's body to communicate with you. Is possession one of the abilities that souls on the upper dimensions can do?"

"I think you're right. And yes, the souls in the upper dimensions can take possession of our bodies. I've read that sometimes we're not aware of it, sometimes we are - we allow it, or we can't stop it. They take possession and live our lives."

"That's the part that I don't like. That's when I call on the Holy Ghost to protect me - to White Light me; cover my body with God's essence so no evil can touch me."

Maggie brought the coffee cups to the dining table and sat down. "So, where are we now? The ghost that moved the salt and peppershaker lives on a higher dimension of existence, and has control over the smallest of elements of existence, the quarks. And somehow people who live in the fourth dimension have some of the abilities of those living in the six through eleven dimensions - telekinesis, telepathy, but not possession. The one thing those of us in the 4th dimension cannot do is possess the bodies of others."

“Oh," Maggie suddenly remembered, "Did you ever have an out of body experience? It's called astral projection."

"Let me guess, you have," Quinn responded with a smile.

"I was sleeping. Concerned about someone, and I guess more than I was aware of at the time. Before I knew it, I was flying over the treetops at night and as I was flying I looked down and behind. I saw a very thin silver thread coming from someplace on my body that drifted behind me in the air. I had no idea what it was, but decided to leave it alone. It was as though I was instructed that nothing must happen to it. In a few minutes, I got to a house that I had never been to before and hovered outside the second story window and looked in. I saw the person walking around their room, and I could see that they were okay."

Maggie became pensive, "You know, it's not as though I had awareness of where I was going. That is, I didn't know that the person I was concerned about was in that particular house, or in that particular room, although it was the only light on in the house. I had no previous knowledge that a soul could leave the body like that and go off and fly, or hover above the ground. There was no conscious thought, 'gee, I think I'll go fly.' There was only the concern for the person, and suddenly I was on my way to see them - it was an automatic activity. I did think about knocking on the window and decided that it would frighten the person and so I didn't. I know I left the window, but can't remember flying back. I do remember passing through the structure, the walls of my house. Then suddenly it felt as though I fell from the ceiling of my bedroom and onto my bed. It was such an impact that it woke me; I felt my body hitting the mattress."

"It wasn't your body that was hitting the mattress, it was your soul re-entering your body, your arms and legs being hit by your soul," Quinn advised.

"I guess you're right," Maggie took a sip of coffee. "Well, I went to the library. I don't remember how I found it, how I began the research, but I found a book on astral projection. And yes, my soul had left my body and the silver thread was the connection of my soul to my physical body. And if that thread breaks, you can't re-enter your body." Maggie paused a moment with a sudden realization, "Jesus Christ! You said that these souls have the ability to possess a body and that the person doesn't always know, or can't prevent it?"

"Yes," Quinn replied.

"Does the soul doing the possessing know that they have taken possession of another person's body?!" Without thinking Maggie had asked the question, but she didn't want to tell Quinn that she had just remembered that one time she heard a voice inside her head, a soft helpless voice cry, 'Help Me!' Maggie's mind raced, trying to figure out if she, herself, was in possession of another's body. How would she know, she wondered, but she decided to figure that out on her own another time.

She shook her hands, as if to erase the question from the air it lingered upon. "Well, never mind that; how come some people experience astral projection, but most do not? Bloodline?"

"Yes. That would be my guess. But, knowing you, Maggie, I don't think you are of Satan's bloodline. I think you are descended from Adam." Quinn lit up a cigarette, blowing the smoke away from Maggie, then continued, "Maggie, there is a retired colonel who runs an institute that accepts volunteers to teach them these skills. Telepathy, astral projection, telekinesis. They might even teach how to kill someone through focusing their mind on the subject."

"You aren't suggesting that I look him up!" Maggie charged.

"Only if you are interested," Quinn answered.

"Don't think that I am, Quinn. But the subject is fascinating. It takes a certain kind of courage to face these dimensions because you are on your own - it's a personal experience, just like being born or dying. One-on-one sort of thing. And you never know who you're going to meet up with. I don't think I have that kind of courage."

"I don't know," Quinn said, "Just imagine seeing all the people you knew that have died. You could see them again; communicate with them. And if you think about it, maybe they could help us in the fourth dimension of existence."

Maggie laughed, "You mean pick out the lottery numbers for us?"

"Well," Quinn was thoughtful, "What if some of these ghosts that hang around military bases, war memorials, Civil War forts - what if these soldiers who were killed in action, what if they can fight in the coming war?"

"What do you have in mind?"

"Everyone knows, both sides. We all know war is inevitable. It's only a question of when. Consider the idea of what they could do, if they fought for our country?"

"Fight as ghosts!"

"Yes!" Quinn became focused, determined. "They could go behind lines, walk up to the United Nations troops and slap them around. Kill them! No one could see them. But the greatest thing is that the enemy can't kill them, they're already dead!"

The idea was so outrageous that Maggie didn't know whether to laugh or get scared, scared to see fighting units of ghosts. But the idea had limitless potential. "Do you think that you could pull them into a fighting unit?"

"I could if we could talk to them. If they are willing."

"Hmmm." Maggie's mind began to race from one military strategy to another. Then she thought of the inevitable question, what happens to these fighting ghosts after the war? What kind of a world would we have after organizing military ghosts, energizing them? Would they try to control live souls?

Quinn interrupted her reverie, "Remember the history of WWII; they used the Navajo Indian language that the Japanese couldn't break, to send messages. They used Comanche code talkers in Europe. This would be a similar, unique weapon - that no one has ever considered before. I mean, has anyone ever used ghosts to fight? Besides Michael the Archangel?"

"Do you think the research our government is doing with the LISA project has something to do with invisible weapons?" Maggie asked.

"The Pentagon will always be looking over the shoulder of this type of research, you can count on that!" Quinn replied, "We know that the ghost in your apartment can move things," Quinn added. "He moved the screw, the bottle of whiskey, and now the salt and pepper shakers. Why couldn't he use a knife or a gun? The point is, while he's somewhere in the 6-11 dimensions, invisible to us, he is moving objects in our 4th dimension!"

Maggie argued, "But even if the Pentagon took research from the

LISA project to form an invisible army, they would be live soldiers, albeit invisible, a gun or bomb could injure them, so they're not as good as if you had 11th dimensional soldiers - they're already dead."

"But if the live soldiers are invisible, can they be killed, that's the question," Quinn responded. "They are invisible because they manipulated the quarks of their body - manipulated their own matter. When invisible, is there enough density to their matter to injure?"

"I just had a thought," Maggie paused a moment. "Souls can manipulate matter, but objects cannot. There seems to be a missing element here. What I have always noticed about life - that is, Maggie's first principle of life," Maggie laughed, "is that the universe is consistent. If the soul in leaving the body causes the death of the body, and its removal begins the decay, the soul is controlling the matter of the body. There is something that no one is considering in their pursuit of the God-particle, or the recipe for the creation of the universe."

"What's that?" Quinn asked.

"Under the consistency principle, if we have a soul, God has a soul; it's his Holy Ghost. His soul controls the life and death of the universe. If the Holy Ghost leaves the universe, the universe will decay the same way the body decays after the soul leaves it. If God created the soul separately from the physical, with the soul having an infinite existence and the physical having a finite existence the soul cannot be recreated by smashing protons of the physical."

Maggie leaned in toward Quinn across the table, "Do you see, Quinn? The invisibility factor comes from the soul - not of the objects, our bodies, the moons, planets, and stars of the universe!"

"I think you might have something there, Maggie," Quinn replied. "And if God's soul is controlling the protons that are disappearing and reappearing, then the Holy Ghost is the living dynamic energy keeping the universe alive. Then the existence of the universe is proof that God exists and is present with us."

"That's right!" Maggie replied. "And the movement of the proton into another dimension of the invisible can only occur through the function of the soul of the universe, through the Holy Ghost."

Quinn laughed, "Are you saying that God is screwing with the scientists?"

"Why shouldn't He!" Maggie defended, "Look what they are doing to Him, they dismiss His existence!"

"Well, they are just a tad egomaniacal," Quinn conceded. "The Big Bang theory is widely accepted in the science community as true, but it's all conjecture. Why do they accept it when they can't prove it, while at the same time claim there is no God because it cannot be proven that He exists? They theorize that the expanded universe will consist of such a large amount of matter that the universe will collapse in on itself and nothing will exist thereafter. With this claim, they are saying that energy has a finite existence. And, yet, that is in direct countenance of their other theories. They are creating inconsistent theories to prove God does not exist. And talking about inconsistency, the greatest scientist of today said that he does not believe that God exists. In other words, he has faith that there is no God."

"Humph!" Maggie exclaimed, "Ironic, isn't it?"

"Well, he says that there is no proof that God exists. He believes, therefore, that God does not exist. Isn't that faith – to believe that God doesn't exist? He could just as easily say that God does exist even though there is no scientific evidence - one way or another. Just as he's claiming that the Big Bang theory is true even though there is no scientific evidence to support his claim."

"I see the dichotomy," Maggie snide. "God asks us to have faith that He does exist, but this super brain scientist chooses to have that same measure of faith that God does not exist - the method is the same, the outcome different."

"Remember, scientists don't know what is going on," Quinn advised. "They throw out ideas, claiming as true - misleading us with their junk-in-junk-out science. They want you to have faith in them, the demigods, that what they theorize is true without them proving the theory to you. Take global warming. It's all theory and those scientists who claimed it were found to have falsified their data. The U.N. based its claim on a high school student's science paper."

Maggie sighed, "Everyone knows the global warming thing is a scam, an excuse for taking more of our money for the cap and trade stock exchange. It's not worth discussing. We were talking about objects of and by themselves do not appear and disappear. It seems to indicate that objects have no control over matter. An object at rest tends to stay at rest unless a force is applied against it. It's the soul that moves the body to apply the force on the object. A dead body cannot do that. Therefore, it's not the body but the soul that controls the matter."

"We are left with the soul," Quinn said. "If God creates an infinite soul, it would seem that to do so, He would have to be infinite, also. No human has ever created a soul."

"What about in vitro fertilization?" Maggie asked.

"They physically brought together an egg and a sperm and introduced it into a woman's body for growth. When an egg and sperm join - is the joining accomplished by God adding a soul? Who is to say that God doesn't add the soul to bring about further growth, eventually bringing the body to term and birth? The baby moves inside the womb; that's a sign that a soul exists and is moving the baby's body inter utero. Or, if He doesn't, and the embryo dies."

"But we don't know what the military are doing in those underground labs," Maggie argued.

"I don't see how they can create a whole human being to live without a soul. If they are creating a body, maybe the evil spirits of the 11th dimension are taking possession of those bodies. But more than likely they are taking volunteers and surgically adding parts to their bodies, parts that are super-human, or they manipulate their genes. Or combining animals with humans. Isn't that what happened to cause God to flood the earth? The fallen angels were breeding with human women, creating the Nephilims - hybrids. I think the military underground labs are creating hybrids, so the human "volunteer" already has a soul."

Quinn took a sip of coffee then asked, "How is it that the scientists are ignoring the soul? Why are they dismissing the existence of God? They are using the Big Bang theory, which they cannot prove by their own standards, as proof that God does not exist. They are conning us over global warming, and it seems conning us over the Big Bang theory." Quinn was pensive for a moment then quietly mumbled, "What the fuck are they up to!?"

"Off the top of my head," Maggie offered, "if they convince people that God does not exist, people will be pressured to leave the faithful worship of God, leading them to feel hopelessly alone - and more likely to worship the Antichrist. I can see their plan to use the weapon of political correctness to drive people to laugh at those who believe in God, claiming that He is a pagan god. That's the propaganda they'll put forth next - He didn't create the universe; it's a scientific certainty just like global warming! And stop thinking about a soul! That's ancient thinking. Ghosts are only seen by crazy people.

Quinn, do not underestimate the political correctness weapon that they have developed over the last four decades. It is a weapon given to the most ignorant of us to defend their ignorance and lack of reasoning ability. It is tantamount to an intellectual Napoleonic complex of the minds whereby the stupid emerge as being correct, by shutting people up. Don't counter me, the political correctness weapon warns, if I can't intelligently argue my point then I will call you a name - you'll be labeled! And being called a name is the worst thing you'll ever suffer - society will cast you out - they promised us! Lazy minds, the unthinking, they love it - it's a trump card that titillates their self-esteem. Political correctness Nazis become orgasmic when they can silence those more intelligent than they. It silences reasoning and speech, and therefore, allows the elite to divide and conquer all of us. But the ignorant are too busy bathing in the titillation of self-aggrandizement that they don't realize that after we are divided by labels, the elite will bring about their endgame, which is to force us to worship Satan!

Quinn, did you ever read Freud's book, *Future of an Illusion*? Basically, he claims that our parents are our first gods, they feed us, clothe us, comfort and protect us; they are our gods. And when we grow up, we look for a god to do these same things for us; make us feel safe the way our parents did. Every culture throughout time has worshipped something as a god, which proves Freud's theory. So, if we accept the Big Bang theory that God did not create the universe, and we are led to believe that scientist know more than we because they have gifted intelligence, so they must be right, and if we doubt, we must be wrong. When it comes to that point - we're really screwed. Freud claims we need to believe in a god, but scientists say God does not exist, so who should we worship? Who should we pray to protect us in this world? We are being set up to accept their next step - putting an anti-Christ in front of us to hang our hopes on; to rescue us from our fears."

Quinn took a sip of coffee, and with a pensive expression, took a drag on his cigarette. Then finally, "It could be that the LISA project has nothing to do with trying to prove that God did or did not created the universe with a specific formula. I don't think they give a shit about how the universe was created at all! They assert an unproven theory of the Big Bang without God's hand. There isn't an intellectual curiosity about the subject. There is no noble, philosophical inquiry of creation. The government only wants to know how to make things invisible. How to reach the dimension that the protons go to when they disappear. How can they make soldiers and weapons invisible," Quinn concluded, "That's their true objective. I'm convinced of it. And if they discover that technology, and they convince people that God does not exist; and if people turn to some anti-Christ and the government uses this invisible technology against us - we are royally screwed! I think we should try to talk to your ghost. We might need him."

"I don't know," Maggie retreated. "I don't like that idea at all."

"Why not? What harm can there be in talking to them; making contact?"

"I can tell that you've never experienced a ghostly encounter. Yes, it might have been a spirit who took possession of that old woman that spoke to you, and even though you can't be sure, he did seem to be your friend, not the spirit of a stranger. There were a lot of other people around. You felt safe. It was a parlor game level of interaction, if, indeed, it was an interaction with someone from another dimension. Do you really believe in the dimensions, in ghosts, or is it just intellectual curiosity that attracted you to learn all you've told me about."

"You have to admit, it is a fascinating subject," Quinn admitted.

Maggie sighed, and then softly, slowly, she tapped her fingers on the table, wondering whether to tell Quinn. She never thought it wise to expose one's deepest fears to another. What she had noticed in life was that such exposure was a handing over to another person a weapon to use against them at a later time when they were most vulnerable. During a heated moment of anger, without thought, all the known vulnerabilities would be assaulted. Only when love is so resolute can one rely that the lover would control their desire to maim. Everything was in degrees, the degree of love was proportional to the experiences shared and time lovers had spent together, proportional to individual maturity, proportional to the want of each to be with the other for life. It was a tentative navigation around the scars each carried. It was a matter of quality of soul each possessed. There was a relationship between them, but not yet fully developed, not sufficiently where Maggie could judge any of these characteristics necessary to trust. But she had to make Quinn understand that this ghost business was nothing to play around with. Perhaps a little information at a time, she thought, to see what he did with it. For her, it was taking a big step in their relationship, and these kinds of steps can't be retrieved. Once taken, forever vulnerable. She looked across the table at Quinn. The two quietly looking at each other. She wondered, could I handle his attack of my fear? What was the true quality of his soul, whether or not love developed between them, would his soul be compassionate or would he leave her with added injury that deepened her fear?

"Quinn," she began, "What is the quality of your soul?"

"What!" Quinn was taken aback.

"What is the quality of your soul? Beyond all that your life's experiences have taught you, and beyond that experience forming the nature of your personality - what is the quality of your soul?"

"Shit! Maggie. That's not an easy thing to answer," Quinn replied.

"Think."

Quinn sat back in his chair, his eyes looked up at the ceiling, as his hand stroked his beard. After a few moments, "I feel so vulnerable."

"I know, but it's important at this point," Maggie gently explained.

"Ok. I'll be honest with you, Maggie. Overall, I'm a nice person. I don't look to hurt anyone. I don't feel delight when another suffers, even my enemy. I like to be left alone. If someone hurts me, I walk away. The way I look at it, if someone you love hurts you badly, don't hold on to the pain; walk away from the lover. It wasn't love to begin with, but a façade. I talk regularly with God in my own way. My kids are the most important part of my life; I told you that. And I would kill anyone who hurt them, or any kid. I guess you could say that my soul is a protective one. When I get angry, I wait. I like to think about the situation before I open my mouth."

Quinn looked at Maggie, penetrating her eyes, "I would never intentionally hurt you, Maggie. You have my respect, and if we ever fought, I would want you to tell me how you are feeling, tell me what I did wrong. I don't want you to try to change me - what you see of me here and now is what I am. I did some exceptional things in life, but I'm just a regular guy. I hope you will accept that you can't change me in to something else."

Maggie smiled, "Good. And no, Quinn, I don't want to change you. I like you just the way you are."

Quinn leaned forward and reached across the table and took Maggie's hand. "What's going on?"

Maggie took a deep breath and sat up straight, gearing up to expose her fear. "Quinn, I told you about seeing the skirt of the ghost at my son's house."

"Yes. And there's more?"

"There were several other experiences I had and I think from several ghosts that live in my son's house."

Quinn sat back in his chair, a frown on his face, intently listening.

"One night, up there for the weekend to work on the dining room, I couldn't sleep. I could feel something standing next to my bed, staring at me. I didn't dare open my eyes for fear that I would see something. I would have awoken the entire neighborhood, screaming. I could feel it standing only two feet away from the bed. Finally, I couldn't take it anymore and thought it better to be close to the outside door where I could run out of the house, so I went downstairs to the great room. I sat in a chair near the door as I was listening to TV. I had the sound turned down very low because my son's bedroom suite is above the great room. His dog, Dakota, always stays in my room with me or follows me around the house. This night, I was sitting in a leather chair. Dakota came over to me and put his front paws up on the arm of the chair, so I would pat him. While I was patting him, I looked into his eyes; he wasn't looking at me, but over my shoulder. Staring at something over my shoulder, behind the chair, for the longest time. He looked as though he was trying to tell whatever it was that he was looking at not to hurt me. I tried to ignore it, so I picked him up and put him on my lap where he went to sleep. I was watching a movie when suddenly the clock in the parlor started charming, then dong three times. It was 3am in the morning. The clock was sitting on a shelf in the inset china cabinet next to the fireplace in the parlor. The parlor door to the great room was open."

"So, what was wrong with the clock charming the time?" Quinn asked.

"The next morning, I asked my son, when did you get the clock fixed? He said, 'I haven't.' I explained to him that it charmed the time at 3am. My son asked, very seriously, 'three o'clock this morning? In the morning?' I confirmed that I had checked out the time displayed on the TV - it was 3am. He seemed hesitant, concerned. So, I asked him, why? He explained to me that there is a legend that between 3am and 4am is the time that the devil does mischievous things. But don't worry about it, it's only superstition."

Quinn listened quietly, as Maggie continued, "My son took the clock down from the cabinet and placed in on the table in the center of the parlor, took off the back of the clock, and proceeded to pull out newspaper that he had packed inside to prevent movement of the charms when he moved into the house two years previously. He asked me what did it sound like, so I hummed the charms and the dongs. Then he somehow got the clock to charm for one time, but then the clock stopped. I told him, that's the sound I heard, but somehow it was in a vacuum," Maggie shook her head. "I couldn't find the words to describe the filter. The sound was perfectly clear, but as if behind some sort of a wall."

"What did your son think?" Quinn asked.

"He was upset. A little shaken. He related the story of the clock. When he visited a friend years ago in Germany, I forget how he met her, but she was German and she gave him the clock. She told him that during WWII the Germans dug holes in the street and buried their families' treasures so the Nazis wouldn't take them. Her family had buried that clock under a German street during the war and later dug it up. I wondered why she would give away a family heirloom to him. I told my son that when I heard the charms that I had gone to the doorway of the parlor and saw that the hands were on mid-night, three minutes past midnight. I thought it curious that it charmed 3am, as the TV had displayed the time, yet the hands were on three past midnight."

Maggie took a sip of her coffee, now cold, and continued, "Later that day, I was up in bed, after being up all night, taking a nap. The clock began to charm, again. It woke me up; I got up and went downstairs, expecting to find my son trying to repair the clock. He was working at a counter in the kitchen, just three feet away from the parlor doorway and the china cabinet. The clock was still on the shelf in the cabinet. I was taken aback to find that he wasn't working on the clock. I asked him if he had just finished working on the clock. He said, no. I explained to him that I just this minute heard it; it woke me up. He said that he had been only three feet away from the clock for the last ten minutes and didn't hear anything."

"That sounds a little scary," Quinn comforted.

"There are more incidents like that. I had been working on refurbishing the walls and ceiling of the dining room, teaching my son how to plaster. We did a Venetian plaster of the walls in the dining room. I went up there most weekends for about six months. The dining room was a mess during that whole time. There were two tarps covering the wooden floors, a ladder, cans of paint and plaster, sander, and rags, paintbrushes, and trowels. The room was a mess. But the house is so big; my son could just close off the room. We ate at the kitchen table, and when company came over we ate at the round table in the parlor."

"It sounds like a big house," Quinn remarked.

"It's very big and very old, and it's 300 feet from the ocean, in Rockport. It needed some cosmetic work, especially in the dining room. The previous owners had painted the dining room walls dark purple. It was horrorable, but it hid the cracks of the plastered walls. The room had a fireplace on one wall, but my son put in a pellet stove in the opposite corner, so the heat would radiate out of the dining room into the foyer in the opposite corner and the kitchen off to the right. Besides, he doesn't trust the old chimneys; every room in the house has a fireplace. But the dining room is large enough to handle the pellet stove, even when the formal dining table is extended.

Well, six months in to the effort of restoring the walls, sanding and burnishing the plaster - it was really coming out beautiful. It feels like cool, polished marble. He picked out orange, and after applying a thin coat, I told him that he needed two other colors to give depth and design. I picked up gold and cream-colored plaster to blend with the orange. I told him, look at each wall as a pallet and make large and small strokes with the trowel, using it like a paintbrush, blending and highlighting the three colors. Well, we were almost finished. I had finished plastering and sanding the cracks in the ceiling; just needed another coat of paint. And on this particular weekend, I took my niece up with me. It was a nice time, she was cleaning out his refrigerator, while my son and I were sanding and polishing the dining room walls. We'd chat between the two rooms; had a few laughs, remembering when they were kids; it was all very memorable.

On Monday morning, my son went to work, my niece decided to take Dakota for a walk along the beach, and I decided to take a nap for an hour or so before getting to work in the dining room," Maggie sighed, "another night of not being able to sleep. Well, I was upstairs in bed, in the room that I usually stay in; my niece stayed in another bedroom. She had gotten dressed and went downstairs to go for her walk with Dakota. I was trying to fall asleep when I heard a noise coming from the dining room. I ignored it. A few moments later, I heard more noise; I ignored it, again. I figured that it was my niece getting something out of the dining room, or maybe she decided to work instead of going on the walk. Then suddenly, there was loud prolonged banging, as though paint cans were being thrown around the room and the ladder was being dragged across the tarp on the floor with the ladder banging down as it was dragged over the folds of tarp. The noise got so bad that I threw off my covers, talking out loud, 'What the fuck is going on!' I went downstairs into the foyer; the dining room door was closed on the left, the parlor open to the right. I went into the parlor and looked across into the great room to see that my niece was standing in front of the mirror, putting on lipstick. I went in and asked her, 'What's all the noise?' She was surprised, 'what noise?' she asked me; 'all I can hear is the TV.' No, no, I told her. It was coming from the dining room. She followed me into the parlor, into the kitchen, heading for the dining room. At the doorway to the dining room, I stopped short in my tracks. I was terrified of going into the room."

"Was it a mess," Quinn quickly asked.

"NO! That's what was so terrifying. Nothing was out of place. Everything was as I had left it the night before after working on it. I mean it was a mess as I described with all the paintbrushes, rags, and tarps, and so forth. But the noise indicated that cans had been thrown across the room, bouncing off the walls. I expected to see spilled paint cans; the ladder overturned - that kind of mess. But there was nothing like that! I couldn't go into the room. My niece did. She looked around and came back to me, 'Aunt Maggie, you probably heard a ghost.' 'Okay, that's enough,' I told her. And she mentioned ghosts two more times until I screamed at her to 'shut up!' Quinn, I can't explained to you how it feels to hear things like that when there is no physical proof that the sound happened, or that no human made those sounds."

Maggie began to tremble at the memory.

Quinn stood up and went over to her and took her hand, lifting her up from her chair to his embrace.

"There's more, isn't there, Maggie?" Quinn held her, slowly rubbing her back to comfort her. "You need to tell me the rest. What are you scared about?"

Maggie gently pulled away from Quinn's embrace, walked toward the windows of the living room and looked up at the full moon, now high in the sky. She turned back toward Quinn, standing next to the dining table at the other end of the large room. As she walked back toward him, she asked, "What do you know of bloodlines, Quinn?"

Quinn held out his hand to her, "Come over to me." As she reached out, taking hold of his hand, Quinn reassured her, "Maggie, I don't think there are necessarily bloodlines of good and evil. Too many centuries have past to have kept bloodlines separate. The other thing is - when did they teach at Mass or in the Catechism that there are Satanic bloodlines?"

Maggie objected, "How can you ask that when you know they control our Christian religion? We know that the government has threatened every Christian church that they will lose their tax status unless they preach from the pulpit that parishioners must do what the government tells us to do - that it's our Christian Duty to shut up and comply! I paraphrase Jane al-Celosini."

Upset, Maggie sat down at the dining table and lit up a cigarette, mumbling to herself, "Those sons of bitches!"

"Do you want another cup of coffee?" Quinn asked.

"Yeah. Please."

Maggie continued, "I read Genesis 1. It said that God created man and sent him out to multiply and subdue the earth. Then He created the Garden of Eden, then Adam, and then Eve. God told them not to touch the Tree of Knowledge of Good and Evil. I read elsewhere that 'to touch' meant in those days, to lie with a woman. To have sexual intercourse with her, so when the Bible talks about Satan telling Eve that it's okay to touch the Tree, he is seducing her in to having sexual intercourse with him. Eve became pregnant with Cain. When God came looking for Adam and Eve in the Garden, He told Satan that he was condemned to crawl on his belly and eat dust for the rest of his life. That's a pretty harsh punishment, if it's only because Satan seduced Eve to eat an apple, giving her intellectual knowledge. That's what we've been taught. But it seems fitting punishment, however, for having impregnated Eve. The Church doesn't teach Satan's impregnation of Eve.

Then, one has to question the word knowledge, as in the Tree of Knowledge of Good and Evil. And, by the way, I was always taught that it was only called the Tree of Knowledge. Other chapters of the Bible," Maggie paused in recollection, "I think it's Genesis 19, where it says that the men in the city of Sodom asked Lot to bring out the men, who were actually angels, bring them out that we may know them! The archaic, Biblical definition of 'to know' meant sexual intercourse. The Tree of Knowledge of Good and Evil is about sex! Not intellect! Not about knowledge!"

Quinn took their coffee cups into the kitchen, asking, "Are you saying that the Tree of Knowledge of Good and Evil is a clue about the bloodlines? That Eve had evil sex with Satan and then righteous sex with Adam?"

"Yes. Exactly! And depending on which version of the Bible you read, the story is a little different, but they tell of Eve having both evil sex and righteous sex. In one version, Adam was with Eve when she took from the tree of knowledge, took sexual intercourse with Satan. Then she offered the fruit, she offered herself...she offered sex, to Adam."

Quinn came back with the hot coffee and sat down across from Maggie.

Maggie continued, "Another version of the Bible said that God then told Eve to go desire her husband, have intercourse with him. The timing is significant. The two sexual events happened on the same day - while her body continued to be ready to conceive. The commonality between the two Biblical versions of events is that Eve first had sex with Satan and then with Adam. She became pregnant with Cain and then Abel, respectively, on the same day! Cain and Abel were twins, Cain coming out first. The scriptures are pointing out the timing, not only of conception, but also of birth. One Biblical version says that after giving birth to Cain, Eve continued to labor and then Abel was born. Scripture is telling us that Satan fathered Cain and Adam fathered Abel. These two bloodlines are significant, important in the struggle of life. And when Cain killed Abel, it's a warning that Satan's bloodline will murder Adam's bloodline."

Quinn offered, "We were told not to read the Bible that we would not interpret it correctly. That it was all allegory."

"They didn't want you to figure out the truth of the bloodlines because we might look for them today. Because they, in fact, exist today!"

"Go on. What else did you get from reading Genesis?" Quinn asked.

"We were taught, 'Don't eat from the Tree of Knowledge.' I hadn't heard that the full name is Tree of Knowledge of Good and Evil until a few years ago. We had been taught that the Tree of Knowledge was forbidden because to eat its fruit would give one the same intellectual knowledge as God. To eat from this tree amounted to an intelligence competition with God, and this is the only reason why it was wrong. The notion of intellectual competition with God completely misdirects everyone away from looking at the creation of Satan's bloodline. They don't want Christians to know about it."

"Who are they?" Quinn asked.

"Satan's bloodline! They control everything!" Maggie responded. "In Genesis 3:15, God says to Satan that He will put enmity between Satan and the woman, and between Satan's OFFSPRING and her offspring; Adam's and Eve's offspring will crush Satan's offspring's head - the head of the snake! And Satan's and Eve's offspring will strike the heal of Adam's and Eve's offspring. Well, you can read about the Kenites, who were the descendants of Cain, yelling for the crucifixion of Jesus. The Kenites had helped the Israelites when they came out of Egypt, so the Israelites thought the Kenites were friends. When they heard the Kenites calling for Christ's crucifixion the Israelites joined the Kenites in calling for His crucifixion, also. When Jesus was crucified, His heel was struck with a spike into the cross. Jesus came through the Chosen People, the Adam and Eve bloodline. Right there you have God's statement in Genesis 3:15 fulfilled."

Maggie looked at Quinn, "Remember when Jesus was dying and He asked His Father, forgive them; they know not what they do? He meant that the Israelites didn't know that the Kenites were descendants of Satan, not friends advising, but an enemy deceiving them to kill their own Messiah."

"And you're saying that Satan and Eve had a bloodline and Adam and Eve had a separate bloodline?" Quinn asked. "And that these bloodlines exist today?"

"That's what I'm saying," Maggie said. "Think about it. How many times have you asked yourself, when you saw horrendous acts man had perpetrated against man, how could anyone do that? How could they even think of such an act! It's because those who committed those acts were descendants of Satan. Only then do those horrific actions make perfect sense."

"I have wondered that," Quinn nodded, "That makes sense, now."

Maggie hypothesized, "I think God set all this up ahead of time, knowing what Satan would do. God created mankind and sent them out to multiply and subdue the world; afterwards he created Adam and Eve to be the ancestors of His Son, Jesus. Adam and Eve are God's chosen people. God created the enmity between good and evil, and He came down as Jesus to speak to us directly, asking us to follow Him. The conflict between good and evil is to test us - either by putting us directly under attack by Satan's descendants, or as a witness to their evil. The test is how do we respond to that evil, that enmity, of those evil descendants striking the heel of the good, disabling them unto death. And don't forget about mankind that He created first."

Quinn listened intently.

Maggie pursued, "When Cain killed Abel, God sent him out of the Garden. Cain said to God, 'But when THEY find out what I've done they will kill me!' So, God made a mark on Cain's forehead to warn his potential killers that their punishment would be sevenfold. I think that means that because the potential killer would have killed Satan's *only* progeny, Satan's only chance for a bloodline with Eve. Satan, not God, would punish Cain's killer sevenfold."

"The 'they' that Cain feared were the people God created before

Adam and Eve, and who God had sent out into the world to multiply and subdue the earth?"

"That's right, Quinn. They are the witnesses to the good and evil that was later to begin in the Garden. I think that Adam and Eve are the 'Chosen People' that we always hear about. It's not the Zionist Jews. DNA tests show Zionist Jews have no genetic connection at all to Israel, but to Central Asia - where Cain went and began his family, who worshipped Cain, the Son of Satan! Archeologists have found the Garden of Eden as described in the Bible, it's located in Turkey, and Cain left and headed east of Eden to Nod. He took a wife - who might have been a daughter of Adam and Eve - or he married one of those first people. In either case, Cain fathered children and built the first city of the world.

Adam and Eve had another son, Seth. And when Adam and Eve had been evicted from the Garden, it is said that they went to Haran. This is the place mentioned in Genesis 11:31 in which Abraham settled for a time after leaving Ur. It was where Abraham's father, Thare, died, Gen. 11:32. Haran is in the modern day district of Sanliurfa, Turkey. It's one of the oldest settlements known in the world, and has been continuously inhabited for at least 6000 years, therefore, it sounds likely it was the place Adam and Eve went to live when they left the Garden. It's just inside Turkey on the Turkey-Syrian border. And not far from where Noah's Ark came to rest on Mount Ararat."

Quinn interrupted, "This is quite a history lesson, but how does it apply to today?"

"Oh, it's very pertinent to what we are enduring today. We have come full circle in creation - from the Garden of Eden to the final battle between the descendants of Satan and the descendants of Adam! That is our test, do we fight on the side of Jesus, or on the side of Satan. Then comes the battle between Jesus and Satan."

"We are fighting for our souls? Not against the elite of America, the progressive communists?" Quinn asked.

"That's what I'm saying. This Second American Revolution that is to come is a fight for our souls! Do we choose Heaven or hell?" Maggie answered.

Quinn pursued, "You are saying that the coming American Revolution is actually the Armageddon?"

After a pause, Maggie replied quietly, "If America falls, the world falls with it. Our country was the strongest super power that civilization has ever known. Americans are the most independent people the world has ever known. And we are the most armed people that mankind has ever known. If they take us down, nothing and no one will be able to stop them. America is the only obstacle to the New World Order."

Maggie took a sip of coffee, then asked, "Consider this premise, Quinn, the Bible doesn't mention the time span between the first people God created before creating Adam and Eve. Those first humans, Homo Neanderthal, could have existed from the time of 180,000 years ago up to the time of Adam and Eve, which was sometime around 5400 years ago, give or take. Studies were done on mitochondrial DNA, using differing methods to determine a single mother of all living humans of today, but no one agrees with anyone. The disagreement comes from the varying hypotheses of what the rate of mutation of the mitochondrial is; it cannot be determined with certainty. And this rate of mutation is key. They theorize the cyclical rate of mutation shows up in one in 600 generations, or one in 300, or some other ratio of generations. The rate of mutation - its number, multiplied by a generation, 20 years, controls the outcome in determining how old humankind is. The varying theories of rate of mutation produce various outcomes of these calculations. In other words, there is no scientific proof of any of these theories. Our theories are as good as theirs."

Quinn asked, "What's the difference between DNA and mitochondrial DNA?"

"What I have read is that the mitochondrial DNA, or mtDNA, is smaller than the regular DNA. It's round in shape while the DNA chromosome is a rod shape. The mtDNA lies outside the nucleus of the cell, in an organelle, or little organ, which is bound by membrane. Its own compartment, if you will, inside the cytoplasm of the cell. It is the source of energy power of each cell, especially cells of muscle tissue. The mtDNA converts nutrients into energy among other things. There are many copies of it in every cell. This is in opposition to regular DNA chromosomes that are a single set inside the nucleus, on the mtDNA chromosome, and it can only be transferred by mother to all her children regardless of whether they are male or female."

"But all genetic code is female chromosome - Is that why all fetuses are female until developing into a male child later in pregnancy?" Quinn asked.

"That's plausible reasoning. It might also cause homosexuality, if during that development from female to male, mutations occur in the mtDNA, or enzymes prohibit the completion of the process. Or maybe the process goes too far, and a lesbian results. The Y-chromosome determines male, the lack of the Y-chromosome determines female. But those chromosomes compliment the mtDNA. In other words, an embryo has a Y-chromosome, but the mtDNA over responds, and a homosexual male is produced. The important thing to note is that all genetic risks for diseases come from female mtDNA," Maggie offered.

Maggie lit up a cigarette and sat back in her chair, "mtDNA chromosome, like the Y-chromosome, does not mix, that is, does not recombine in human reproduction the way that regular DNA chromosomes do. In regular DNA, we get half of our mother's genes and half of our father's genes. Those particular genes, or chromosomes, combine to give us uniqueness, while all of us carry the same mtDNA of our mothers. Boys carry the same Y-chromosomes of their fathers - unchanged throughout the generations. I think that's the way it works, if I understand this stuff correctly," Maggie took a drag from her cigarette.

"So, what does this have to do with the Bible?"

"Oh, sorry. I got ahead of myself. It means that the bloodline of Adam and Eve can be traced to today. In other words - the bloodline of Satan and Eve can be traced to today!"

"You're losing me here," Quinn replied.

"The human genetic code is the genome and only 1% of it differs between the races of humans alive today. That 1% determines eye color or disease risk and the like, of specific races. This 1% difference in genetic code among the races points to the fact that there are, indeed, genetic differences between the races. Some of this 1% DNA can mutate, and that mutation gets passed down to descendants. These mutations show whether one individual shared the same ancestor as another. They can tell who contributed to a person's genetic code. Bloodline!" Maggie paused, "The mtDNA Eve is a theory that claims that all humans descended from a single mother."

"How so?" Quinn asked.

"If the Bible says that Satan had offspring, and according to the scientific proof that the Y-chromosome does not recombine, but remains intact through all descendants, it means that Satan and Eve have their own traceable bloodline. The mtDNA Eve theory is a lineal bridge claiming that all women descended from Eve, but that an unbroken lineage could only come through Adam and Eve and their daughter and with every generation thereafter having a daughter. By the way, the Bible said that Adam and Eve went on to have other sons and daughters after Abel and Seth. And the unbroken chain of daughters having the same mtDNA proves that Eve had a daughter. Eve only had intercourse with Satan one time in the Garden of Eden, and that union produced Cain. So, if a woman can have her DNA tested and finds that she belongs to that unbroken chain that's proof beyond a doubt that she is a descendant of Adam and Eve through their daughter. She's not of Satan. And it is consistent with the scientific theory that all living humans today have the same mother. We just can't measure the broken female lineage through Satan and his son, Cain. So, too, if there were no daughters in any descending generation then we can't measure that broken female linage as descending from Adam and Eve through their daughter. But Adam's sons and their male lineage would carry Adam's Y-chromosome."

"Hold it right there!" Quinn laughed. "Are you telling me that there actually are daughters of Satan!?"

Maggie laughed, "That I am, indeed!"

"That would make sense when thinking back to some of the women I've known in my life."

"Okay, to continue," Maggie said, "There is some disagreement over whether or not the son passes his mother's mtDNA on to his children. If a woman has no daughter and the son cannot pass on his mother's mtDNA to his children, the sons are possibly marrying women who are carrying Eve's mtDNA. It's difficult to follow. Let's suppose the guy across the street has the same ancestral mother as you, but he carries the Y-chromosome of Satan, from about 5400 years ago. Satan's lineage cannot be calculated through the matrilineal line because Satan had no daughter with Eve, but his lineage can be traced through the patrilineal line of descent. I disagree with the theory that all men are descended from Adam's Y-chromosome. I believe that there is a biological difference between the Y-chromosomes of Adam and of Satan. There has to be, God created those two separate from each other, and Genesis speaks to Satan having offspring. So, there has to be two types of Y-chromosomes out there among the men living today. God created two separate bloodlines! And don't forget, Satan was created as the quintessential angel. Adam as a man. Their Y-chromosomes must be different!"

Quinn interrupted, "I remember years ago that they did studies on criminals' DNA and found that they had two Y-chromosomes, one smaller than the other, or maybe it was that their Y-chromosome was oddly shaped. I can't remember, now. But there was something abnormal about their Y-chromosomes! These men were all bad. Sociopaths who felt no guilt for the mutilating deaths that they had committed."

"Descendants of Satan!" Maggie concluded. "Because they have proven that today's human is not descended from Neanderthals; there was no evolution as Darwin theorized."

"No, some of the sick stuff some people do, mostly men, is not in the realm of the ignorant barbarian, but in the sadistic realm of evil," Quinn agreed. "So, where does this take us now?"

"Well, I'm considering the idea that of all mankind, there are those who came from Adam and Eve and their offspring, Seth, and their other sons and daughters. Then there are those who came through Satan and Eve and their offspring Cain, and those whom God created first and were not of the lineage of either Adam or Satan, but those people were killed in the Great Flood."

"You think that Satan's seed and Adam's seed survived the Flood in Noah's Ark?"

"Yes. Satan knew what God was planning, creating a bloodline through which He would come with the birth of His Son, Jesus. Satan wanted to mess up that plan, by literally inserting himself into part of that bloodline. But an omnipotent God would know this, first. So, it's almost as though both God and Satan acted in concert in setting the battlefield in which they would war over our souls. That's why we're here! Our lives are a test in that battle between God and Satan! It's not just a matter of how we live our individual lives, but how we respond to the evil that we see in the world."

"When you think of it," Quinn added, "If there were no active evil in the world, how would God know that a soul was worthy of Heaven, or belonged in hell? The test of character is adversity. Put us under the gun and give us free will." Quinn paused a moment, "But if God is omnipotent, doesn't He already know which we'll choose?"

"Well, yes. But consider it this way. If a man gives a woman free will to choose to be his lover, his wife, even though he knows that she loves him and will submit to him eventually, isn't her final submission that much sweeter if the man knows that he didn't compel her, didn't force carnal knowledge on her, but she chose willingly to submit to him? That freedom to choose to be one with the man makes that union the perfection of love. It's a union of complete surrender of mind, heart, and body. Freedom to choose, especially when the woman's love has been tested, is the only way that that kind of union can be achieved. And I don't care what men say, that's what every man is looking for. They just don't trust that it will happen to them, and many times they take a different approach to force the union, immediately causing it to fail. When you see the Buddha, kill it!"

"So, God's test to choose Him rather than Satan is to prod an awakening in us," Quinn replied. "He knows, but do we know how we'll respond. The adversity we endure is what causes us to think, to contemplate life and God. He wants us to look at Him and decide if we love Him, not out of tradition, but love Him because He is loveable. Do we accept Him in spite of the hardships that we endure in life that He has the power to stop, but doesn't?"

Quinn paused, "You know, Maggie, I think when you see a good person suffer, one who is close to God, yet still suffers, their example of continuing to trust in God during their suffering, I think, means their suffering is only for the purpose of teaching others about faith. Many of those people ask others to pray for them. The others then examine that faith; it causes them to look at God. Their suffering brings others to God."

"I think you're right," Maggie responded, "And to appreciate God. How do you know if something is great unless you examine it? Not look outwardly to judge God, but to achieve understanding of Him in relation to ourselves. He wants us to examine why He loves us and why we love Him. It's a call to a love affair."

"Except the sex?" Quinn smiled.

"Yeah, without the sex," Maggie laughed, "But the passion to be with, talk with, keep company with the lover is the same."

Maggie and Quinn remained quiet for a long time, finally, Maggie offered, "You know Quinn, love is very difficult to find in this world. I'm not talking about people telling you quickly and easily that they love you. I'm not talking about telling someone you love them to capture them. You do know that in the telling, it is a way to capture someone, for how can you leave someone, not help them, not be there when they need you, when they have told you that they love you. Between a man and a woman it's a way the teller of the love can ease in to, even force, their way in to a marriage. You cannot leave me now; I've told you that I love you! You have to marry me; I love you! Are you going to knowingly choose to break my heart?! You'll be labeled a bastard by my friends and family - and perhaps even the captive's friends and family. I said it, it's a done deal - now ask me the big question - will you marry me!"

Quinn listened to Maggie, knowing she was right, but wondering what she was leading up to.

Maggie continued, "What is love? The big question. Is it a smooth-working interweave of neurosis? Is it co-dependency, I'll not nag you for your drinking because I'm an alcoholic, too? A Socratic symposium will not solve the question. But why is it so difficult to answer? Everyone experiences love, in some form or fashion. Everyone wants it; it's a goal humans must achieve in their lives or their lives are deemed sad."

"I don't know," Quinn replied. "We humans are flawed. We cannot function outside of our neurosis, so neurosis becomes part of all our relationships."

"Love," Maggie began thoughtfully, "Is only felt by very few. Only the truly unselfish can know, can feel love. Others use the term selfishly, to get, to take, to possess, to protect only themselves. In that sense, love is an alliance of two against the world; a pledge to keep the other's back in protecting them. So we won't be alone. There is a difference between that façade and actual love. Therefore, only the brave, the unselfish, really know what love is, and they give it wisely for it can only be given to another who is equally brave and unselfish."

"Are you brave and unselfish, Maggie," Quinn asked.

"I don't know."

After a quiet moment, Quinn asked, "What are you thinking?"

"I've been divorced 29 years, Quinn, but I have been alone all of my life. Truly alone in the world. The only one who ever had my back, who protected me, who was always there for me was Jesus Christ, His Holy Ghost, and His Father. When I think back to the people that passed through my life, my natal family, the only way I survived them was through God's love of me. There is no other way to explain how I survived all those who worked at hurting me, or stood by and watched without helping me, during times of absolute vulnerability."

Maggie shook her head as the memories passed through her mind. "How vulnerable I was. How vulnerable were my children, I just can't believe it."

"Have you never looked back?" Quinn asked.

"Not like tonight," Maggie smiled at Quinn. "It's the discussion of God, His creation." Maggie lit up a cigarette and sighed the smoke out from her lungs. "They say that a person will survive if there is one person in their life who guides them, shows them love. The kid only needs one person and they can survive all that the world throws at them. I didn't have anyone, Quinn. Looking back from here, not one person ever had my back. But I always had a love relationship with God, His mother, His Son, His Ghost. God is the only love that guided me. And certainly protected me from the snakes and my natal family."

Quinn leaned back in his chair, "When I went into the Army, our drill sergeant lined us up and yelled, 'I'm not your mama!' Then he walked up to me, nose to nose, and asked if I thought I was tough enough to survive the Army. I was 17; the day after my high school graduation I enlisted. I told him, 'Yes, Sir! I can take it, Sir.' He yelled, 'Are you sure, boy! I ain't your mama!' 'Yes, Sir, you don't know my mother, Sir!'"

Maggie smiled, but then frowned, "In other words, your mother was worse than any Army drill sergeant could be."

"That's right. My point is, I understand what you're talking about. Freud is wrong in his assumption that a parent is viewed as a god by the child."

"Sometimes, the parent is viewed as a Satan!" Maggie added. "Which brings us back to the bloodline of Satan."

"Are you thinking that because your natal family was so evil that you are in the bloodline of Satan?" Quinn asked.

"Well, how do we know?" Maggie replied, "How do we really know? If the horrendous indignity put upon us is from those who allegedly love us, how does one answer that? How can you think that your siblings and parents are evil, but at the same time, consider yourself from a different bloodline than theirs? That you are not of an evil bloodline, but they are! You share their blood, their genes!"

"I can't answer that," Quinn sighed. "But I think that we can look at that choice thing, again. The freedom of will is given to each of us. For the sake of argument, let's presume that both you and me - and I'm thinking of the evil of my own mother - what if both you and I are from the bloodline of Satan? Both our families have the genes to do evil. Genetically predisposed to do evil. Obviously, some of us went with our genes, and obviously some of us did not."

Quinn lit up a cigarette and blew the smoke up to the ceiling, "Free will. Do you have a conscious thought of resisting the desire, the genetic will urging you to reciprocate evil for evil?"

Maggie laughed, "Are you kidding? And with my imagination! Let me tell you, some of my evil thoughts to get revenge on some of 'em have been off the chart, brilliant!"

"And what did you do with those thoughts?"

Maggie sighed, "Oh, sometimes I wrote them down just to get them out there; looked them over and then I tore up the paper. But no, I let go of the evil thoughts. I knew that I couldn't live with myself if I carried them out. And I don't like the idea of jail, either."

"But you had considered evil and decided not to function with evil!" Quinn surmised.

"Yes. I decided against evil," Maggie nodded. "Especially as I have matured with experience."

"It seems to me that even if you had Satanic genes, you controlled your desire to expound upon them. You wisely control your desire."

"Plato," Maggie mumbled, as she lifted her coffee cup and took a sip. "I'm a philosopher king!"

Quinn smiled, "Yes, you are!"

Maggie put down her cup and folded her arms on the table in front of her, "Why are you here, Quinn?"

"I like you."

"Why?"

"You're intelligent, interesting, easy to talk to, and funny. And you're absolutely gorgeous!" Quinn smiled.

"Ah shucks! You're gonna turn my head," Maggie grinned.

"Why did you invite me?"

"I like your company. You bring a vitality of life to everything you do, and you bring it to me. I don't see any down side to you and I've been looking for it. Everything I know about you is good," Maggie smiled, "Okay, and yes, you're good-looking with that graying beard and those beautiful brown eyes. And that body of yours is very nice."

"No, it's not anymore. You should have seen me when I was a Special Ops."

"I can imagine. If you were able to carry your buddy over your shoulder and run for five miles, you must have been something to look at. But you still have a strong body, nice broad shoulders, very muscular arms." Maggie's face suddenly turned red as she looked back up at Quinn's eyes and saw him smiling at her.

"Ahhh. Okay." Maggie said, trying to break the quiet of the moment. "So, ahh, you think it's a good idea to talk to the ghost that moved the salt and peppershaker?"

"Yes, I think we need to ask him if they can help us in the coming war," Quinn replied.

Just then a loud crashing bang came from Maggie's bedroom.

Maggie looked at Quinn, "Oh shit! I think the ghost has been listening to us. I think he might have just answered you."

Quinn got up from the table and went into Maggie's bedroom; he turned on the light next to the door and looked around the room. There on the floor in front of the armoire was a gun, Maggie's 9mm pistol.

Quinn called out, "Do you want to fight with us?"

Maggie hid behind Quinn, cringing as she held her breath, waiting for an answer.

The gun moved slowly across the floor toward Quinn. "Does he want you to pick it up?" Maggie asked.

Quinn bent over and retrieved the 9mm from the floor. He held the gun for a moment, waiting to see what the ghost might do next. Just then the door to the armoire opened and the box of cartridges moved to the edge of the shelf.

"I think he wants you to load the gun!" Maggie whispered.

Instead, Quinn walked out of the bedroom and over to Maggie's desk, picked up a pad of paper and a pen, then went back to the dining table and sat down. Maggie followed him.

Quinn spoke to the room, "Do I know you? Can you speak, or can you write your name on this pad of paper?"

The pen resting on the table where Quinn had placed it rose up from the table and wrote the name, "Col. Will Booker."

"Do you want to fight?" Quinn asked the ghost.

Again, the pen moved on its own, "YES!"

"Do you know others who will fight?" Quinn pursued.

"Yes!" the pen wrote.

"How many?"

"Which war?" Booker wrote.

Quinn and Maggie looked at each other with incredulity. They recognized that an entire new world had just opened up to them. Maggie whispered to Quinn, "Are they God's legions of angels?"

"I don't know," Quinn answered, but thought, with these spirits winning the coming war is now possible. The known vulnerabilities of the country were now outweighed. The armies of the world brought against Americans by their own leaders would be defeated. Trained patriots living in the invisible world assured that victory. They must be God's legions of angels.

Quinn straightened up, his mind racing with military possibilities and logistics never before considered. His heart pounded, "Ok. Let's see, ahhh, the Gulf War?"

"Yes," the pen scribed.

"The Vietnam War?"

"Absolutely!" the pen quickly scribbled. "the World Wars, the Civil War, and the Revolution."

"How many are we talking altogether?"

"Many millions of angry American soldiers!" Booker wrote out. "The elite are destroying the country we died to protect! They are intentionally destroying our civilization!"

Maggie couldn't keep still any longer, blurting out her question to the ghost of Will Booker, "Do you know about the New World Order?"

"Yes. We have been in their boardrooms, secret meetings, we know who is connected and how they are involved. And we know who the Anti-Christ is."

"Oh my God!" Maggie gasped. "Oh my God!" as she reached her arm across the table, grabbing Quinn's arm.

Quinn looked at Maggie as he asked the invisible spirit of Booker, "Who has sent you to fight?"

"Jesus Christ, our Lord and Savior. Evil has been destroying our country. We have been under attack for more than a century by the descendants of Satan's son, Cain. We want to join with the living to fight until Jesus' judgment of the living and the dead. We guard the country from what you call purgatory. We call it the 11th dimension."

Maggie cried. "This is really it, isn't it, Quinn?"

"Yes," Quinn answered coolly. "This is the final battle between good and evil. We're in the end of times."

Maggie and Quinn sat quietly for a moment, thinking about the enormity of the moment. Finally, as the two looked at each other, Quinn asked Will Booker, "How do we proceed?"

The pen moved across the page, "We will be in contact with you. Be prepared."

Chapter 5

On the drive home from Maggie's apartment, Quinn had a strange feeling that he couldn't identify. At first, he dismissed it as residue of the discussion he and Maggie had that evening that ended with them communicating with Will Booker. Suddenly, Quinn cried out, "I can't believe I communicated with a Civil War spirit! A dead man! I talked to a dead man!"

Quinn was fascinated by the 11th dimension possibilities, especially the astral projection. But how does one wrap their mind around it as real - as part of everyday life, he wondered. Nice movie, but reality? At the same time, he couldn't help think that astral projection could be a way for him to fight in the coming Armageddon. It had worried him that he was beyond middle age, and that he couldn't realistically count on having the physical strength and energy for sustained combat. He had to wage an intellectual strategy rather than the physical side of combat. At least, until the young of America were brought in to the battle, until they opened their eyes and learned of the legislative seizure our country had been suffering for the last century from the conquering elite. Yet the elite controlled their education, the media, and had been actively indoctrinating them to accept communism - how were they to learn of the conquering? Of their loss of freedom until it was too late? They had already accepted the political correctness weapon that shut down freedom of speech. They don't even know what it was like without it.

And how could he even begin to strategize any military offensive? He didn't know all the weaponry at his disposal or the army that would be available for him to command. And he confessed to himself that he didn't have the education to be commander of an entire war. Will booker had told him about the veteran spirits that were waiting to fight with the living American patriots. But he couldn't build a strategy just on Booker's word. Not on one interaction with one spirit soldier. He had to see for himself; he had to look over the troops. And who was the 'we' that would be contacting him? Did they have strategic military planning experience? How and who was going to do all that was necessary to wage a war? A war against all the armies of the world?

It wasn't a long distance from Maggie's apartment into the next town where he lived. But his mind was so engaged that he had driven the route without thought and before he knew it, he found himself driving down the long private way to his house, set at the edge of eleven-acres of woods. Funny, he thought to himself, he would fight with soldiers of the 11th dimension and he owned eleven acres of woods; strange how numbers come together, reflect and repeat themselves. As he got out of his car, he began to recollect Maggie quoting Genesis 3:14. In trying to think of the words, his mind suddenly realized, "Wait a minute!" he cried out loud, "3:14 written another way is 3.14; isn't that pi?"

As soon as Quinn got inside his home, we went directly to his

Bible and looked up Genesis 3:14 and read: "'And the Lord God said to the serpent: Because thou hast done this thing, thou art cursed among all cattle, and beasts of the earth: upon the breast shalt thou go, and earth shalt thou eat all the days of thy life.' That's talking about Satan deceiving Eve to have intercourse!" Quinn said aloud.

He continued to read, verse 15: "'I will put enmities between thee and the woman, and thy seed and her seed: she shall crush thy head, and thou shalt lie in wait for her heel.' Genesis 3:15 is telling that a Satanic bloodline was created! More proof that to eat of that Tree meant sexual intercourse; that Eve gave birth to Satan's son, Cain."

He looked up from the Bible, staring at the world map on the wall above his desk and thought, "Maggie was right, but I don't think she knows how right she really was. This is a flashing neon sign to us!"

He read further in Douay-Rheims, until he came to Genesis 4:1, and read: "And Adam knew Eve his wife: who conceived and brought forth Cain, saying: I have gotten a man through God."

Quinn whispered aloud, "We know that 'knew' means intercourse. Satan knew Eve and that's why they were banished from the Garden. Now we're told that Adam also knew Eve! But when Cain was born - she said 'a man through God.' Did she think that Satan had been a god - Cain must have looked like Satan. As soon as Cain was born, Eve immediately connected the two.

Satan had told Eve, Gen. 3:5: 'For God doth (does) know that in what day soever you (if you should ever eat) shall eat thereof, your eyes shall be opened: and *you shall be as Gods*, knowing good and evil.' Satan was talking as though he knew the rules of the Garden; as though he had already eaten from the Tree of Knowledge. Eve saw Satan, the most beautiful angel that God had created, and figured that he must be a god. That he must have become a god by eating of the Tree of Knowledge of Good and Evil - 'you shall be as Gods.' Eve had no way of knowing how many gods there were in the Garden - she had just been created!"

Quinn read on, verse 2: "'And again she brought forth his brother Abel.' Why didn't Eve then say, 'another man through God'? This is significant," Quinn concluded. "Eve must have thought that Satan, the most beautiful angel, was a god - and she could see that Adam was not an angel, not a god - because he was human, like her. Abel looked like Adam - Cain looked like Satan! There had to have been a readily visible, very prominent difference between the two babies. She said she got a man child - a boy - through God, even before Abel was born. Therefore, Cain could not have looked like Adam or herself. It had to be that Cain's skin was a different color - to make him immediately identifiable with Satan as opposed to Adam. Hair or eye color would not present the evidence to convince Eve that Cain was from Satan. Satan could not have been White, as Adam and Eve were. We know that Noah descended from Adam and Eve, and Noah was White, as was Sem. Noah's alleged sons, Ham, was Black and, Japheth, was Yellow. Therefore, Satan was either Black or

Yellow, or both, but not White.

Quinn went back to the word, again, 'and again she brought forth his brother Abel.' That doesn't indicate a year later! Cain and Abel were twins! Especially, within the same verse, Gen. 4:2, 'Abel was a shepherd, and Cain a husbandman.' That indicates the same age. Gen. 4:4 'Abel also offered of the firstlings of his flock...." Abel was capable of slaughtering a sheep - a boy can't do that - he's not physically big enough, or strong enough, knowledgeable enough to accomplish such a killing. Were it a baby sheep, its mother would have rammed Abel to stop him. As a boy, he might not have survived a mother sheep's attack."

Quinn sat down at his desk and turned on his computer. Talking aloud to himself, he browsed for pi and its numerical value, 3.1415. He was looking for the compilation of the Biblical chapter 3 and verses 14 and 15 and its relation to pi. All at once, questions flooded his mind, "pi is infinite, isn't it? It's a mathematical symbol used to measure the area of a circle - perhaps there is some significance - Maggie's explanation of the mitochondrial DNA of a woman - it's round, circular - it's located in a organelle, little organ. Maggie said it was located outside the nucleus of every cell, bound by a membrane - circular shaped - it's passed down to all female descendants, intact. The regular DNA is shaped like rods."

There has to be significance between the number of Bible chapter and verses and the round mtDNA of Eve, both are so unique, Quinn thought. "The Biblical chapter 3, and its 14th verse tell of God condemning Satan, the serpent, to crawl on his belly and eat earth FOR ALL THE DAYS OF HIS LIFE!"

As he put the pieces of the puzzle together, Quinn yelled out loud with excitement, "Pi is an infinite number! Satan's existence is infinite! Pi measures the area of a circle. Eve is the mother of all living today, identified by her unique circular-shaped mtDNA. Measuring that circular-shaped mtDNA you have to use pi, 3.1415; the Bible chapter and verse: 3:14-15 tells of Satan's bloodline exists among us, even to today! Satan is the infinite, constant enemy of mankind!"

Quinn sat back in his chair, as if hit by a ton of bricks. This is why we're told not to read the Bible! We would discover that there is a Satanic bloodline today. The ancients were warning us! He thought of calling Maggie to tell her, but when he looked at the clock on the corner of his desk, it displayed 1:00 a.m. I'll call her in the morning, he thought to himself. If this isn't a sign, I don't know what is!

He quickly became consumed by the significance of pi. He got up and paced around his office, talking aloud to make it all sink in, to make it real to his mind. "It's like a neon sign - Look here! Look here! The Biblical passage is flashing to its readers. Satan and his bloodline is among you throughout the centuries!"

But just in case, he researched the Dead Sea Scrolls on Genesis 4:1; it read:

> And Adam knew his wife Eve, who was pregnant by

> Sammael (Satan), and she conceived and bare Cain, and he was like the heavenly beings, and not like the earthly beings, and she said, I have gotten a man from the angel of the Lord."

Quinn mumbled, "Satan is the angel of the Lord!"

He then looked up #202 Targum and Midrash, the Targum being the Aramaic version of the Bible:

> "And Adam knew that his wife Eve had conceived
> from Sammael the angel [of death] (sic)
> and she became pregnant and bore Cain.
> And he was like those on high and not like those below.
> And she said:
> -- "I have got a man from the angel of the LORD."
> Targum, pseudo-Jonathan on Genesis 4:1

Quinn kept searching for more proof. He found in the Epistle of St. Paul to the Hebrews, 1:6, "And again, when he (God) bringeth in the first begotten into the world, he said: 'And let all the angels of God adore him.'" It seemed to Quinn that in this specific verse that the first begotten into the world was Adam, and that there were angels in the Garden of Eden watching God create Adam. And one of those angels seduced Eve. And God cursed that angel to become a serpent, crawling on his belly. From that point on, the angel was called what God had turned him into, a serpent, a Devil, a viper! Satan!

Quinn went back to Gen. 1:26. "And he (God) said: Let us make man to our image and likeness: and let him have dominion over the fishes of the sea, and the fouls of the air, and the beasts, and the whole earth, and every creeping creature that moveth upon the earth." This was the power given to Adam.

Quinn had always been curious that God had said, "Let us," who was he talking to? After reading Hebrews 1:6, it seemed that God was creating with His angels watching him. But if there were angels watching God create the earth and the creatures, then God must have created a heaven and angels, first. Quinn searched for the evidence. In Nehemiah 9:6 (2 Esdras 9:6), "Thou thyself, O Lord alone, thou hast made heaven, and the heaven of heavens, and all the host thereof: the earth and all things that are in it...." Quinn thought to himself, this verse indicates numerous heavens.

In Psalms 8:4, "For I will behold thy heavens, the works of thy fingers: the moon and the stars which thou hast founded." Quinn thought this meant the Universe. The Universe was to thank God for its existence.

There seemed to be three parts to existence that God had created, which was confirmed in Psalms 148:1, "Praise ye the Lord from the heavens...(4) Praise him, ye heavens of heavens...." Quinn concluded that the Father dwells in the superlative heaven of heavens with his angels; the universe was the second heaven. In Gen. 1:8, "And God called the firmament (earth), heaven...." So that would make the waters above the heaven, earth and its atmosphere, the third heaven. There are three levels of heaven, three levels of existence.

In Matthew 6:9, was Jesus' sermon on the mount. Quinn sneered at the thought of Tsaeb's criticism of Christ's Sermon on the Mount, laughing as he said that Sermon was so radical that it was unlikely that the Defense Dept. could carry out its order. In the Sermon on the Mount, Quinn found The Our Father, which is recited by every Christian. In verse 9, Jesus said, "Thus therefore shall you pray: Our Father who art in heaven, hallowed be thy name."

Quinn couldn't help pity Tsaeb's soul for such mockery against Jesus and His Father. Pity for Tsaeb's attempt to dissuade Americans from saying the Our Father prayer; that it was so radical as to be absurd. Tsaeb's laughter, as he spoke, was the enchantment of a deceiver. He laughed at people who pray the Our Father, as though it is the act of a fool. Therefore, anyone who follows Jesus is a fool. Tsaeb is like Satan, provoking Americans to turn away from worshiping the Father of Jesus. Tsaeb is implying that there is something else that Americans should worship, (Matt. 4:3) "And the tempter (Satan) coming...(9) "And said to him (Jesus): All these will I give thee, if falling down thou wilt adore me." Is this how Tsaeb became president, Quinn wondered, he sold his soul to Satan!

But Tsaeb wasn't mocking just the Israelites, the Christians, he was also threatening the Jews and Muslims - do not turn to Jesus, or His Father! He is not the god of the Jews and Muslims! But in Matthew 15:22, Quinn found that Jesus came to save the souls of those who had faith in Jesus and his Father. For a Chanaanite woman, of the evil bloodline, came to Jesus, crying: "Have mercy on me, O Lord, thou son of David: my daughter is grievously troubled by a devil." The disciples wanted Jesus to send her away, because she was of the evil Chanaanite bloodline, but Jesus told them (Matt 15:24), "I was not sent...(only) to the sheep that are lost of the house of Israel." Quinn realized that Jesus came to save all who believed in Him, not just to save the Israelites, His bloodline. But also to save the bloodline of Satan, if.... A very big IF - they believed in Jesus.

Quinn knew that the Heavenly Father wanted us to worship only Him and no other. To love Him only, and that we should tell that to all His people. Ask for forgiveness for your sins, and go and sin no more. For He is to come, He who is the I AM. Behold the Son of God is with you. My Son will condemn those who sinned against Me.

This is what Satan is trying to prevent, with the help of President Tsaeb. Just as Satan was jealous of Adam's power to name all the creatures of the earth, Satan is jealous of Jesus' power to judge the living and the dead. It was this pride of Satan, once God's most beautiful angel, that he, Satan, should control the earth and that he, Satan, should judge the living and the dead. And this is what caused his fall.

In Isaias 14:11, "Thy pride is brought down to hell...(12) How art thou fallen from heaven, O Lucifer, who didst rise in the morning? how art thou fallen to the earth, that didst wound the nations?"

Quinn analyzed that Satan and the angels were created by God, first, and that they dwelled with Him in the highest levels of the three heavens, until God made Adam. The statement that Lucifer rose in the morning means that he rose into existence - into being - as one of the first things that God had created. After God created the highest level of heaven, He then created the angels - Satan. Then He created the second level of heaven, the Universe. Then God created the third level of heaven, the earth and the atmosphere of the skies above earth. And on earth, He created the Neanderthals, first. But when God created Adam, while the angels and Satan watched, God gave to Adam, Gen. 2:19, "the Lord God having formed out of the ground all the beasts of the earth, and all the fowls of the air, *brought them to Adam* to see what he would call them: for whatsover Adam called any living creature the same is its name." This, Quinn thought to himself, is when the trouble began.

It seemed to Quinn that Satan became jealous of Adam being given the gift on controlling the earth and the creatures on it. For to give something its name, is to be master over it, Quinn reasoned. That's why, when Satan appeared to Eve in the Garden, not as a snake, because God had not yet cursed him, but as a beautiful angel, wise, a divine enchanter, she was indeed seduced by him. For one thing, he seduced Eve to show that Adam had no control over her to keep her from touching the Tree of Knowledge of Good and Evil - to keep her from having unlawful, evil sex with Satan! To show that Eve controlled Adam. Adam listened to Eve instead of God. Gen. 3:12, "And Adam said: The woman...gave me of the tree, and I did eat." And through this chain of control, Satan took control of the earth and all the creatures in it, including Eve, and most especially Adam, regardless of to whom God gave that control.

Quinn recognized that Satan's seduction of Eve was to show God that He was wrong in giving Adam control of the woman and the earth. And Satan was sadistic in taking his revenge against God by intruding himself into the lineage that He had created specifically for Jesus. This betrayal of God, who created Satan, is where Dante states in the Inferno, in his *Divine Comedy* - that the lowest level of hell is saved for those who betray their benefactors. For those who committed malicious sins, as Satan did commit against God. Satan betrayed his benefactor, his creator, God the I AM.

The competition between Satan and Adam to control the earth would continue to this day between the descendants of Adam and descendants of Satan. Between the followers of Jesus Christ and the New World Order of the Zionist Jews and Muslims, and of Tsaeb. Suddenly, it hit Quinn, as he cried out, "This is why they want a New World Order! They are carrying out their father's, Satan's, wishes!"

And like a tremor of an earthquake's aftershock, a deeper level of realization hit Quinn, not just as a researcher looking for the truth - out of curiosity, out of suspicion, out of intrigue, but as a Christian. He sat back in his chair and softly mumbled, "Oh my God! They really are going to turn the world over to Satan! This is really real! This isn't crazy talk. It's not a conspiracy theory. It's not the United Nations, per se taking control - the UN is only the conduit of control, through which Satan will exact upon mankind and all the creatures of the earth! This is a true reason for the return of Jesus Christ!" And from a deeper level still, Quinn realized, "Jesus Christ is going to return. He's actually going to return. We're going to see Him!"

Quinn's heart raced with excitement and joy. Then he quieted himself and thought, I should prepare my soul for His coming.

After a few moments, he looked down at the Bible on his desk before him, mumbling, "Satan wanted to control the earth from back to 6764 years ago, in the Garden of Eden. That's where the New World Order began. Satan's descendants have been working towards that end ever since, and more recently through their Federal Reserve Banks. A more deceitful way - the seduction of 'let us control the money and the banks and we will keep the U.S. from depressions and economic failure' - the bank failures that they caused in the first place! Through the Rothschilds; Lazard Brothers, Israel Moses Sief, through Kuhn, Loeb & Co.; Warburg & Co.; through Lehman Bros.; Goldman, Sacks; and through the Rockefellers, these private owners control America. These people are working for Satan! ACTUALLY working for Satan! That's the only thing that makes any sense. These people are trillionaires, they can buy and sell countries, they can buy and sell the United Nations; why else would they want a New World Order, but to finally deliver Satan's desire to him. Control over the whole earth!"

Quinn speculated, most of those owners are foreigners, so they targeted the U.S. because that's where Adam's descendants are now. America is their target because it is the largest Christian nation in the world - not just because its citizens have the most guns and can fight back and block the United Nations from controlling her. America is the new Israel where the Israelites have been gathered together, again. America is the battlefield for the Battle of Armageddon! The battlefield on which the kings of the world come together - they gather inside the United Nations building in New York City. The land it sits on was given to the UN for its headquarters, given by the Rockefeller family. America is where the United Nations troops will go against American Christians. Revelations 16:13, "And I saw from the mouth of the dragon, and form the mouth of the beast, and form the mouth of the false prophet, three unclean spirits like frogs. (14) For they are the spirits of devils working signs, and they go forth unto the kings of the whole earth, to gather them to battle against the great day of the Almighty God....(16) And he shall gather them together into a place, which in Hebrew is called Armageddon."

Quinn concluded aloud, "The United Nations, where Satan, the Antichrist, and false prophet go before the kings of the world to gather them to battle Christians and create a New World Order. As did Tsaeb appear, and each of the Popes since the UN's beginning."

The question suddenly hit Quinn, is the seat of the Presidency the Antichrist - that whoever sits in it is the Antichrist? For other U.S. presidents have committed treason against America, too. And the Papacy, is that throne the seat of the false prophet; during the Middle Ages, Popes ruled with iron fists. Pope John XXIII immediately established an official connection of the Papacy to the newly formed United Nations. Pope Paul VI and Pope John Paul II, Pope Benedict XVI, all spoke before the United Nations - all of them calling for a New World Order! And with the New World Order comes a new world religion - which is not Christianity! They all met with other kings on the battlefield of Armageddon!"

Quinn then looked to the prophecy in Revelation 12:1. "And a great sign appeared in heaven: A woman clothed with the sun, and the moon under her feet, and on her head a crown of twelve stars." Quinn figured that this was Eve, clothed with the sun because she was naked in the Garden. The moon symbolized her being in the fertile phase of her monthly cycle when Satan seduced her there. The crown of twelve stars symbolized her mothering the Twelve Tribes of Israelites, the holy nation. Exodus 19:5, "If therefore you will hear my voice, and keep my covenant, you shall be my peculiar possession above all people: for all the earth is mine. (6) And you shall be to me a priestly kingdom, and a holy nation. These are the words thou (Moses) shalt speak to the children of Israel."

Quinn considered the alternative, but decided that this could not be the Blessed Mother, the mother of Jesus, not with what followed in Revelations. The Blessed Mother was immaculate, born without original sin, because she has been protected from Satan from the time she had been conceived. If Satan went near the mother of Jesus - he would have been extinguished immediately. Annihilated from all existence. Satan knew his boundaries.

In Revelation 12:5 "And she brought forth a man child, who was to rule all nations with an iron rod: and her son was taken up to God, and to his throne." Quinn thought that the "man child" was Cain, as in the Dead Sea Scrolls, the Midrash, and Gen. 4:1 "I have gotten a man through God." Eve referred only to her first delivery as a "man child," not so of Abel. And this man child of Revelations is not referring to Jesus Christ, who gave mankind free will; who gave the gentleness of the Sermon on the Mount. And Jesus did NOT "rule all nations with an iron rod." Jesus was the Lamb of God. Therefore, the woman is not the Blessed Mother Mary. Quinn noted that there is a colon in the verse; it separates two births, two sons. The colon denotes a difference between Eve's two deliveries; one was a man child who looked like, according to the Dead Sea Scrolls and the Midrash, "heavenly beings" and did not look like earthly beings, and the other delivery was her *son*, Abel - the son that Cain killed – that God took up to Heaven.

In Rev. 12:4, where the "dragon stood before the woman who was ready to be delivered: that, when she should be delivered, he might devour her son." Cain was delivered first and outside her body "before" - as in front of her, as she delivered Abel. And Cain, in fact, did kill Eve's son. This is telling that Cain was the son of Satan, because before Cain's birth, Satan was cursed to be a serpent, a dragon.

In Rev. 12:3, Quinn thought the "red dragon" descriptive meant anger, as when someone is so angry that they see red - the blood rushes to their head, their eyes. This anger, Quinn reasoned, is towards Adam, his son Abel, and the woman, Eve, for causing Satan's fall. Gen. 3:14, "upon your breast shall you (Satan) go, and earth shall you eat all the days of your life," because he deceived Eve into having intercourse, telling her that she would not die if she touched the Tree of Knowledge of Good and Evil. Anger because Satan was no longer the most beautiful angel in Heaven.

In Rev. 12:5, "and her son was taken up to God, and to His throne."

Between verses 4 and 5 many years passed; enough for Cain and Abel to grow up, and Cain kill Abel. But verse 6 is in immediate response to the killing of verse 5. In Rev. 12:6, "And the woman fled into the wilderness, where she had a place prepared by God, that there they should feed her a thousand two hundred sixty days." Quinn mumbled to himself, "Eve fled from Cain after Eve realized that Cain killed Abel. It was the first murder of the world, that's something to fear and to run from. For Eve knew that Cain was fathered by the "angel of the Lord," Satan, as stated in both the Dead Sea Scroll and the Midrash.

For more than 3.5 years she hid in the wilderness, and if that place was "prepared by God," then the "they" that "should feed her" could be angels, who also protected her from Cain coming after her, killing her other children to prevent Adam's descendants from coming into existence, the Israelites and Jesus. That would be reason for God, Himself, to prepare a place for her.

Quinn looked up Gen. 4:25: "Adam also knew his wife again: and she brought forth a son, and called his name Seth, saying: God hath given me another seed, for Abel whom Cain slew." It was from Seth that Noah was descended, later Abraham, later King David, and later Jesus Christ. Gen. 5:1-30, lists the names. If Seth, which means substitute, and Genesis says "for Abel" - Seth was born after Cain murdered Abel. It was during those 3.5 years when God gave Eve shelter that she gave birth to Seth.

Sometime between when Cain had murdered Abel and Eve fled, the next verse in Rev. 12:7, relates, "There was a great battle in heaven, Michael and his angels fought with the dragon, and the dragon fought with his angels: (8) And they prevailed not, neither was their place found any more in heaven." The verse states that after that battle, Satan is then no longer in heaven, which means that he had been able to go into heaven as a serpent-looking angel, after the Garden seduction of Eve. His sin against God occurred because he was beautiful; his beauty seduced Eve. So, the punishment fits the crime. Quinn concluded that God's punishment was the taking of that beauty, but not the taking of Satan's supernatural powers of an angel, not until he was cast out after the battle with Michael the Archangel. But when did that battle occur? What had Satan done to deserve being cast out of Heaven once and for all?

Rev. 12:9, "And that great dragon was cast out, that old serpent, who is called the devil and Satan, who seduceth the whole world: and he was cast unto (to) the earth, and his angels were thrown down with him...." This is Satan being put into the bottomless pit.

But between this verse 9 and verse 13 are 1000 years. Verse 13 talks about after Satan is released from the pit: "And when the dragon saw that he was cast unto (to) the earth, he persecuted the woman, who brought forth the man child...."

It was after his release that Satan, in Rev. 12:17, "And the dragon was angry against the woman: and *went to make war with the rest of her seed, who keep the commandments of God, and have the testimony of Jesus Christ*." Obviously there are many years between Satan beguiling Eve, impregnating her - and the testimony of Jesus Christ.

Quinn noted the descriptive, "old serpent" of Rev. 12:9, indicated that he had been a serpent for a long time, and during that time he "seduceth the whole world." Satan's descendants have been all over the world, ruling all nations with an iron rod. Satan is ticked off at the woman, blaming her for the loss of his beauty, loss of his status as the greatest of angels when they were back in the Garden of Eden. Imagine, Quinn thought, of having the beauty of the most perfect angel and being turned into a serpent, a snake. That's big time trauma. But there's even more than that - its Satan's seed striking the foot of Eve's seed that she had with Adam.

Quinn reasoned that the "great battle" of Rev. 12:7 seems to be sometime after the testimony, that is, the sacrifice of Jesus Christ. So, it is sometime after Jesus' testimony on earth that Satan attacks the "rest of (Eve's) seed." If Adam and Eve were created 6764 years ago, minus 2000 years since Jesus. At the time of Jesus, Satan had been a serpent for 4764 years. That would make him the "old serpent.'" Quinn paused a moment. Then asked out loud, "The battle in heaven - was that after the temptation of Jesus in the desert?"

Matthew 4:3-11, "And the *tempter* coming said to him...Again the devil took him up into a very high mountain, and shewed him all the kingdoms of the world, and the glory of them…And said to him: All these will I give thee, if falling down thou wilt adore me…Then Jesus saith to him: Begone, Satan: for it is written, The Lord thy God shall you adore, and him only shall you serve…Then the devil left him; and behold angels came and ministered to him."

It seemed to Quinn that since God "hath given his angels charge over thee" meant that Michael the Archangel and God's army of angels proceeded to battle Satan to protect Jesus - protect His ability to carry out His mission. For God had sent His only son to die for the sins of many. Matt. 26:28, Jesus said at the Last Supper, "For this is my blood of the new testament, which shall be shed for many unto remission of sins." It was after this coming of Jesus and His sacrifice and His testament for the remission of sins that Satan attacked Eve's seed, directly. Jesus is the seed of Eve and Adam! Jesus was the testament, the Gift.

Satan, according to Rev. 12:13-18, worked directly, himself, against the descendant of Adam and Eve, Jesus Christ. Satan wanted to prevent the sacrifice of Jesus! To keep His sacrifice from saving the souls of those who believe in Jesus, the God I AM. When Satan couldn't, because he was thrown to earth, into the bottomless pit, after being defeated by Michael the Archangel, his descendants wanted to get rid of Christians' knowledge of the sacrifice of Jesus. Hence, his descendants went after and persecuted the Apostles. They corrupted the Popes. They corrupted the liturgy; the respect and reverence shown by kneeling when receiving the Eucharist - the symbolic Body of Christ - was taken away. They stopped the priests from making the sign of the cross prior to giving the Eucharist. These changes were made by Vatican II. Communion with God - as a reminder of Jesus' sacrifice for our sins, now eventually, becomes only a symbolic community supper - and God is forgotten over the next generations.

Satan's descendants want to prevent today's Israelites/Christians from finding out that they are of the bloodline of God's chosen people. The identity of which the Pharisees stole from them back in Babylon. After thousands of years - few would know the details of Ezra's lies, threats, and theft - of the Israelites identity and Persian gold. The Zionist Jews, the descendants of the Pharisees, know that they are not God's chosen. They know it!

For after the battle with Michael the Archangel, Satan, the "dragon," was cast out of heaven, as Quinn read in Rev. 12:10-13, "And I heard a loud voice in heaven, saying: Now is come salvation, and strength, and the kingdom of our God, and the power of his Christ: because the accuser of our brethren is cast forth, who accused them before our God day and night. And they overcame him *by the blood of the Lamb*, and *by the word of the testimony*, and they loved not their lives unto death. Therefore rejoice, O heavens, and you that dwell therein. *Woe to the earth, and to the sea, because the devil is come down unto you*, having great wrath, knowing that he hath but a short time. And when the dragon saw that he was cast unto the earth, he persecuted the woman, who brought forth the man child."

It seemed that Satan had dwelled in the heaven of angels as a serpent-looking angel, complaining day and night that he was better than Adam, and then, better than Jesus - that he, Satan, should rule the world; and he, Satan, should judge the living and the dead. Michael and God's army of angels defeated Satan "by the blood of the Lamb." Jesus is the lamb of God. They defeated Satan by Jesus' crucifixion! When the angels came to minister to Jesus, after He sent Satan away, the rest of the angels went with Michael to battle Satan, knocking him out of the heaven of angels.

Satan was defeated "By the word of the testimony." At the Last Supper, Jesus used the words "of the new testament," Matt. 26:28. As in Last Will and Testament, as in a document gifting personal property to heirs. Quinn concluded that the blood of Jesus was the gift, "my blood of the new testament." Jesus is the Word, the legal document, in which He carried His blood that would be shed for many. This had to happen; Jesus' crucifixion had to happen for the salvation of man. And this was the very thing that Satan did not want, this is why Satan himself tempted Jesus in the desert - trying to prevent Jesus from giving up His life. It was necessary for God and Michael the Archangel to defeat Satan, before Satan could stop the crucifixion.

God couldn't chance Satan telling the Kenites, Satan's descendants, not to demand Jesus' crucifixion. God couldn't risk that the Kenites would not instigate the Israelites to cry out for the crucifixion of their Messiah. Otherwise, the crucifixion would not have taken place and "the many" would not be saved by Jesus' death. Satan wanted those souls. When Michael the Archangel defeated Satan, God told Michael to put Satan into the pit - this occurred immediately after Satan tempted Jesus in the desert and before Jesus was crucified.

This was the only cause worthy of the battle between Michael the Archangel and Satan. Satan had to be stopped before he interfered with Jesus' crucifixion. Satan had approached Jesus in the desert, and Jesus sent him away. What would he have tried next? And if left alone, Satan could have won all the souls of the Israelites. To Quinn, Satan being cast out of the heavens also meant that Satan no longer had supernatural, angelic powers. Only the power of deception of the fool who would listen.

Quinn was convinced that Satan was jealous of Jesus, because the Son of God would judge the living and the dead. In Acts 10:42, Peter said, "And he (Jesus) commanded us to...testify that it is He who was appointed by God, to be judge of the living and of the dead."

When reading the Book of Revelations, Quinn found that the chapters were out of sequence. The sequence of events occurred:

In Rev. 12:7-8 it tells of the battle.

Rev. 12:9 Satan is cast out of Heaven and to earth.

Rev 20:1-2 Michael the Archangel chains Satan and puts him into the bottomless pit - for 1000 years.

Rev. 20:3 *Warns* that Satan *must be loosed a little time* - after the 1000 years is up.

Rev. 9:1-2 Satan is let out of the pit.

Rev. 20:9 Satan is cast into the pool of fire forever.

Rev. 12:11 Satan was defeated by the blood of the Lamb - Jesus is the Lamb of God; Satan was defeated by Jesus' crucifixion - this is how and why Michael the Archangel chained Satan in the pit. To keep Satan from stopping the crucifixion; by dying Jesus saved the souls of many (Matt. 26:28). Otherwise, Satan would have gotten those souls.

Rev. 12:12 This event is when Satan is loosed. This event occurs after the 1000 years is up - after the lock up in Rev. 20:1-2. Satan is freed from the pit, and he has a short time. This is when Satan goes after the woman. The woman is Eve, it was Eve who gave birth to the man child, (Gen. 4:1), Cain. But Satan is going after the descendants of Eve and Adam (Gen. 3:15).

Rev. 12:14 The woman is given two wings of a great eagle, so she can fly in to the desert, to her place, where she is nourished for a time and times, and half a time, away from the face of the serpent. This Rev. 12:14 verse happened after Rev. 20:1-2.

Quinn muttered to himself, "Chapter 20 verses are out of sequence, too! They should go before some of Chapter 12 verses. Rev. 20:7 occurred after the battle with Michael the Archangel in Rev. 12:7-8.

In Rev. 20:7 Satan is loosed: 'And when the thousand years shall be finished, Satan shall be loosed out of his prison, and shall go forth, and ***seduce*** the nations, which are over the four quarters of the earth, Gog and Magog, and shall gather them together to battle, the number of whom is as the sand of the sea."

This comes in the final days - after he goes after Eve's descendants of Rev. 12:17.

Quinn wondered who it was that rearranged the chapters and verses – and why? Was it done to confuse the reader – to allow the claim that scripture is allegory – a myth! Don't read the Bible, you won't understand it. Or – was it a code to ensure its publication, so it could be unlocked in the end times?

In exasperation, Quinn cried aloud, "And the time and times, and a half time of Rev. 12:14 - is talking about *EVENTS*, not 3.5 years, which is mathematically irrational. To think that "times" is only double of "time" is a false premise, when "times" could mean an exponential multiple of time - ten times time, 40 times time, or whatever number times time. Talk about deceiving!"

Eve was nourished in the desert, a wilderness, kept from the face of Satan while events occurred elsewhere, Rev. 12:14. If Satan was put into the pit immediately before Jesus' crucifixion, which was in A.D. 30. After 1000 years, Satan was released in A.D. 1030. Then in A.D. 1030, Satan went after the descendants of Adam and Eve, (Gen. 3:15).

Quinn was aware that all dates were subject to historians carrying forward the correct dates, but also in comparing one event in history to another was vulnerable to approximations. On an historical timeline, 23 to 48 years between events could have actually occurred at the same time.

He wondered, what happened in A.D. 1030, or just before? Eric the Red, a redhead, was exiled from Norway (around A.D. 960) and from Iceland (around A.D. 982) for three years. He sailed west and found Greenland, which was void on inhabitants. The rich soil and trees allowed Eric and his family to be well-nourished and sheltered. After three years, he returned to Iceland and told of the green land and its resources. Families followed him back to Greenland. His son, Lief Ericson, was tall, strong, large and imposing, redhead, usual of the Viking-Norway bloodline, who later discovered North America. Lief, on his first adventure, sailed to Norway, his family's homeland, around A.D. 1000. King Olav Tryggvasson greeted him warmly, so Lief and his men stayed one winter and learned Christianity. Before they left, Lief and his men were baptized, returning in the spring to Greenland. He brought with him Christian priests and converted everyone in Greenland, except his Father, to Christianity. But his father built a church for his wife and the people to worship in. Lief later travelled to Labrador and Newfoundland, which he named Vinland, about A.D. 1002. Both places were without inhabitants - a total wilderness. Lief and his men built a large house on Newfoundland/ Vinland, returning in the spring to Greenland. When Eric the Red died, about A.D. 1003, Lief stayed and took over his father's farm in Brattahlid.

In about A.D. 1005, Eric the Red's son, Thorvald, and his 35 men borrowed his brother's ship and for two years travelled the same coastline route Lief had sailed, but going further they found America, about A.D. 1007, where they met Native Indians - the descendants of Japheth. Thorvald was killed in a skirmish with the American Indians, and his men buried him in America. A year later, the 35 men left Newfoundland and returned to Greenland. The Christian Viking society of Greenland lasted 500 years; cause of its disappearance remains a mystery. www.greenland.com/en/about-greenland/kultur-sjael/musik.aspx.

Quinn realized that the description of King David matched the descriptions of Eric the Red and his son, Lief. They were all redheads, exceptionally tall, and built for war. Therefore, they were descendants of Sem, of Adam and Eve. And Satan's descendant, Japheth, father of the Native American Indians - were carrying out Genesis 3:15, the enmity that God put between Satan's seed and Eve's seed - Eve's seed "shall crush the head" of Satan's seed - and Satan "shall lie in wait for her heel." This was one event - of many to come.

Quinn went back to Rev. 12:17, "And the dragon was angry against the woman: and went to make war with the rest of her seed, who keep the commandments of God, and have the testimony of Jesus Christ. (18) And he stood upon the sand of the sea." The Native Indians of America killed the brother of Lief Ericson, and Thorvald had the testimony of Jesus when Lief brought Christianity to Greenland. Since Lief's brother was sailing along the coastline, the skirmish with the Native Indians was likely, as noted in Rev. 12:18 - "And he stood upon the sand of the sea." It was in America that this first occurred - between Satan's and Eve's descendants and Adam and Eve's descendants, almost at the time Satan was loosed from the bottomless pit.

But is this only representative of the beginning and the end - that the last battle will occur in the United States. When Satan was about to be let out of the pit - the first European reaching the United States was a Christian, Thorvald, of the bloodline of Adam and Eve - and he was killed in warfare, by Satan's descendants.

Is this first event symbolic of the last event - to show where and who will fight the Battle of Armageddon? The largest Christian nation in the world is the United States. It stands in the way of the New World Order religion – worship of Satan. Rev. 16:16 says: "And he shall gather them together *into a place*, which in Hebrew is called Armageddon." Armageddon is a *place*! Can Armageddon mean America?

Rev. 12 points to the beginning of the conflict - between Satan and Eve and their descendants. Were the verses put together out of chronology for a purpose, and what was that purpose? The beginning and the end, the alpha and the omega - represents God. He is the beginning and He will be the end.

Rev. 20:7 shows the end of that conflict - pointing to Gog and Magog and his UN troops attacking American Christians. It's pointing to American Christians because they are the largest group in any country of the world - and are armed to the teeth. They are the formidable target. When they fall, the world of Christians will fall - to the worship of Mother Earth! The New Age religion!

The UN Secretary General controls all the militaries of the world - and his office is in the UN Building, on the East River! On the sand of the sea, of Rev. 12:18, just as Native Americans stood on the sand when they attacked Thorvald and his 35 men, all Christians.

The UN Conference on Environment and Development called for a Global Biodiversity Assessment. Chapter 12.2.3 states: "It is a world view that is characterized by the denial of sacred attributes in nature, a characteristic that became firmly established about 2000 years ago with the Judeo-Christian-Islamic religious traditions." Judaism began with Ezra in 457 B.C.; Christianity began with Jesus in A.D. 30; and Islam began in A.D. 632. The United Nations is blaming Christianity for the denial of sacred attributes in nature - denial of the worship of trees and rocks - the end of idol worshipping.

1 John 2:22, "Who is a liar, but he who denieth that Jesus is the Christ? This is Antichrist, who denieth the Father, and the Son." That would be the Pharisees, founded by Ezra, and its Chief Priest Caiphas, who condemned Jesus to death for the blasphemy of saying He was the Son of God.

That would make Ezra and his Pharisees and Caiphas, along with UN Secretary General Yoon Won-Skik the Antichrists of their respective time and times, and a half time.

Quinn found on the Internet that Yoon Won-Shik will not disclose his religion. Quinn also found that 46% of South Koreans do not have any religion; Christianity (Protestantism and the Catholicism) was next in percentage of So. Korean population; Buddhism was the next popular religion, from ancient times. Buddhism worships the Dragon as the most important divinity of Korea; the Dragon is shown on the walls of Korean temples. The Black Dragon with four toes is a thousand years old, and he could wield the Yeouiju, an orb that fell from Heaven, therefore, he was blessed with abilities of omnipotence and creation at will. (http://ftp.buddhism.org/Publications/IABTC/Vol08_06_Hye-young%20Tcho.pdf)

Quinn thought of his grandfather's words - if you aren't with me, then you're against me. They were the words of Jesus Christ, Matt. 12:30. If Yoon Won-Shik did not profess his Christianity to the world, then he wasn't a Christian - therefore, against Jesus. If Yoon Won-Shik is a Buddhist, then he worships its most important god - the Black Dragon - one who can create at will. "That sounds like Satan to me," Quinn mumbled softly.

1 John 4:3, "And every spirit that dissolveth Jesus, is not of God: and this is Antichrist, of whom you have heard that he cometh, and he is now already in the world."

2 John 1:7, "For many seducers are gone out into the world, who confess not that Jesus Christ is come in the flesh: this is a seducer and an antichrist." Quinn mumbled to himself, "That means the Zionists and the Muslims are the seducers and the antichrists, too. There are multiple antichrists!"

The Beast of Rev. 20:9, in the end, is thrown into the pool of fire and brimstone, along with the devil and the false prophet. Quinn mumbled to himself, "The beast, the Antichrist, is the Secretary General of the United Nations, as commander of the United Nations Blue Beret BEASTS. The Antichrist must sit on a seat of power, if he is to control people. And the Secretary General of the UN already controls the world by controlling the militaries of 193 member countries under the UN Charter, under UN Agenda 21 blueprint of indoctrination of our children. And under the Law of the Sea Treaty - Yoon Won-Shik controls 70% of the earth, and under UNESCO's biosphere-land takings - 650 million acres, or 29% of the United States."

Quinn went back to the "two wings of a *great* eagle," Rev. 12:14, it has to mean the United States, a superpower, beyond the other nations that used the symbol of an eagle, like Nazi Germany.

Quinn looked at the world map hanging on the wall above his desk, "The descendants of Japheth, the Asian-Native American Indians, could have sailed along the coastline - along the Japanese, Kuril Islands, to the Aleutian Islands to North America. Then even down the west coast of the United States to Mexico, to Peru and Chile. It's the same type of coastline sailing that Lief Ericson did to find Newfoundland; the same that his brother, Thorvald, did when he came onto the United States. These were not dangerous sailings for either the Asians or the Vikings. They could stop and forage for food. They didn't have to do a 3-month open Pacific or Atlantic crossing.

The American Indians coming to America would make it their "unto her place," if they are symbolized through their mother, Eve. As in the seed of Satan and Eve - the Asians. Not the seed of Adam and Eve - the Vikings. Many Native Indian nations lived peaceful lives, especially when they first came to the United States - when it was a wilderness, and their tribal nations were not as large. Not as large as when the Europeans moved in on them and they numbered in the millions. Yet, some tribal nations were incredibly brutal against each other, as well as against the white man. Then again, who was the alleged white man who killed off the Indians - European descendants of Japheth!? The Spanish! The JP Morgans! It's the same as the Sunni and Shite Muslims killing each other - in greater numbers than the Christian Crusaders did.

Quinn continued on, trying to summarize Revelations.

Rev. 12 gives a capsulated description of the beginning in the Garden of Eden, to the end and the Battle of Armageddon. From Eve, to her giving birth to Cain and Abel. Abel being murdered by Cain. God preparing a place for Adam and Eve, where Eve gave birth during that time to Seth and his other siblings. Then Rev. 12 describes Satan being defeated by Michael the Archangel, and Satan is chained in the pit, let loosed, had a little time, and persecuted the woman, Eve, who gave birth to the man child. This is Satan, after 1000 years, going not to Eve, but to her seed with Adam. Rev. 12:14 is pointing to the Armageddon - it is to be fought where the great eagle returned Eve's descendants to its home - the United States. Native Indians lived in North and South America for centuries before the descendants of Sem, Ham, and other descendants of Japheth came to the United States. Centuries before Thorvald Ericson came to the "great eagle" of America. During those centuries Japheth's descendants, Native Indians, lived in America for a time, and times, and half a time - hidden from the face of their father, Satan. They were hidden until the Christian, Thorvald, first found them, to when the Christian, Columbus, 400 years later announced their presents to the world and took their lands for Spain; to the Christian Pilgrims who came and settled, ending their private sanctuary, once and for all. Time and times and half a time - events of Native Indians growing in to large tribal nations, to events that destroyed them.

But more than that, Rev. 12:14 is pointing to where Armageddon will be fought. In the United States. It is in the United States that the Antichrist lives. Quinn read, Rev. 12:15, "Its talking of the Antichrist, UN Secretary General Yoon Won-Shik, who controls 70% of the planet - the oceans, seas, and inland waterways - the Great Lakes - Yoon Won-Shik is trying to destroy the United States, by controlling its water through both UNESCO and the Clear Water Act connecting the U.S. to the Law of the Sea Treaty - as in verse 15 says - the serpent cast out of his mouth after the woman, symbolized by the Statue of Liberty - which is also under Yoon

Won-Shik's control through UNESCO (whc.UNESCO.org/en/list/307). Yoon Won-Shik poured out of his mouth the Law of the Sea Treaty - water as it were a river - that it might carry her away.

But in Rev. 12:16, the earth helped the woman, opening her mouth, and swallowed up the river. Quinn reasoned, "It's talking about an earthquake that will bring down the UN building that sits on the edge of the East River, New York City. The earth will rumble and the UN building and the East River - will be sucked down into hell, taking the Antichrist with it." Quinn continued to mumbled aloud, "The earthquake will come from the 125th Street Fault line that runs across northern Manhattan from the Hudson River to the East River. Scientists are worried because there has been no activity along that fault for 200 years - it's due to blow."

As he turned the pages of the Bible, Quinn read, "Jesus told his disciples of the end times," his finger drawing down through the verses "here it is, - Matt. 24:6, 'And you shall hear of wars and rumours of wars. See that ye be not troubled. For these things must come to pass, but the end is not yet. (7) For nation shall rise against nation, and kingdom against kingdom; and there shall be pestilences, and famines, and earthquakes in places....(21) For there shall be then great tribulation, such as hath not been from the beginning of the world until now, neither shall be.' Yeah, swallowing up the UN Building and the East River would be the largest earthquake that I ever heard of. But it won't be just the UN Building, millions of people all along the river would die; the rotting bodies would cause great sickness - plagues as in pestilence.

He continued to read, verse 27, Jesus is saying, 'For as lightning cometh out of the east, and appeareth even into the west: so shall also the coming of the Son of man be.' Quinn thought for a moment, I always wondered why they called Jesus the Son of man; He's the Son of God. Then it came to him, Son of *man* means, Son of Adam. Jesus came through the bloodline of Adam and Eve, not the bloodline of Satan and Eve. Adam was the first *man*. He re-read the verse and said, "Jesus will come very suddenly." But the next verse in Matthew intrigued him, "'(28) Wheresoever the body shall be, there shall the eagles also be gathered together.' What does that mean? Is that the body of Jesus? Does this mean that He will be where the eagles are gathered - in the United States? But too many countries use the eagle as a symbol, so from this particular verse, it could mean any of those countries, not the United States. Or," Quinn smiled, "It could mean all of the many countries who use the eagle as a symbol for their armies are included in the 193 countries - are members of the United Nations. United Nations troops are now in the United States! The eagle-heralded armies of the world are gathered under the banner of the UN peacekeeping BEASTS! Never before in history, have all the armies of the entire world been gathered under one commander - General Secretary Yoon Won-Shik, descendant of Japheth, a man from the east, Korea. Korea's Buddhism religion holds the Dragon as their most important god."

Quinn went back to Rev. 12:17, 'the dragon was angry against the woman: and went to make war with the rest of her seed...' and Eve's seed are those 'who keep the commandments of God, and have the testimony of Jesus Christ.' This verse is talking of after Satan was released from the pit; talking of Satan going after only the Christians. This is the Battle of Armageddon - because in verse 7, the dragon was defeated by Michael the Archangel. In verse 12, the dragon is put into the bottomless pit. In verse 13, the dragon defames Eve. And in verse 14, the woman is hiding out for a time and times and a half time from the dragon - while he's in the pit! In verse 15, the dragon is now called a serpent who spits out a river to carry away the woman. In verse 16, the river that the dragon cast out of his mouth is swallowed up by the earth - an earthquake. By verse 17, there is nothing else left, but the Battle of Armageddon! Earthquakes have swallowed rivers. But this earthquake, this swallowing of a river, is symbolic of ending the Law of the Sea Treaty and Yoon Won-Shik's control over 70% of the planet - all its water. And there's never been a war against America's Christians. Not until openly admitted by Bill Maher on his show following Constitution Day, (http://www.jeremiahproject.com/prophecy/warxian.html).

Quinn listened to the video of Maher, to his laughing audience, when Maher made the statement: "People who are against this war from the start were a minority. But the majority once believed that the world was flat. If you believe that today you'd be packed off to Bellevue.' Hmm," Quinn sighed, "doesn't President Tsaeb use that expression to discredit and mock his political opponents, that they are like those who once thought that 'the world was flat.'" Quinn continued to listen to Maher's video: “It's okay for a presidential candidate to believe that 'Jesus survived His own death and will return during an Osmond concert in Branson...At the end of the day, is magic underwear much crazier than a giant ark, virgin births, talking bushes...you're either a rationalist or you are not...there are enough rationalists to stop being shy about expressing the opinion that we're not the crazy ones!'” “He's implying that anyone who believes in Jesus Christ is crazy." Quinn shook his head, "Maher and his audience remind me of Sodom and Gomorrah."

He went on to read the article, "Countries who have waged war on Christians: China, Sudan, Saudi Arabia, Egypt, Turkey, Burma, Greece, Ethiopia, Vietnam, Cuba, Laos, and North Korea. In those countries, Christians are being beaten, tortured, imprisoned, and murdered by those hostile to their faith in Jesus Christ. Never before in American history have Christians experienced being hated for following Jesus Christ as they are today, in 2012. In America it is called secularism - hatred of God and Jesus Christ." Quinn sighed, "I guess Maher was right - there is a war going on, and people seem to be taking his advice and becoming boisterous. And Maher's kind of intolerant bashing of Christians will increase with propaganda, until Christians are completely shunned - like cigarette smokers and those who don't go green."

Quinn burst in to uncontrollable laughter. An image had flashed into his head of little barking dogs, like Maher, who think they have unstoppable power, when in the image, suddenly the silent majority of Americans jumped up and smashed them to smithereens! It was the suddenness of it all. In one quick pounce, the little barking dogs were silenced. When he finally stopped laughing, he murmured the words: secularism, my enemy a secularists.

Quinn's thoughts then went back to the Native Indians. Some are Christians. He wondered, right after the crucifixion of Jesus, the Qumran religious sect - the strict Monastic followers of the Law of Moses, the Essenes, who lived around Qumran near the Dead Sea, they disappeared. It is claimed that they wrote the Dead Sea Scrolls. The Essenes and Pharisees hated each other; the Essenes chose to live apart from the Pharisees, well outside Jerusalem. The Pharisees sentenced Jesus to die; the Roman Governor, Pontius Pilate, had to approve all death sentences of the Pharisees' Sanhedrin Court. But Pilate saw no wrong in Jesus, so he left it up to the people, who cried for the Roman version of death - crucifixion. Likely, the Essenes feared that the Pharisees would come after them, next.

Quinn tried to remember an article he had read, of a Decalogue stone found that was used by the Essenes. "It was found in Ohio," he mumbled to himself. "It had the name Moses and an abridged version of the Ten Commandments inscribed on it." Quinn wondered if the Essenes came to America after the Native American Indians. And maybe the Essenes, being a monastic group, taught the word of God to the Indians. "I know that 4% of Native Americans are Christians. I know that the incense that they use in their religious ceremonies is considered sacred. The smoke from the burning incense brings their prayers up to God. Just as the incense that God gave to Moses, Ex. 30:34, God said was sanctified. Only to be used on the altar, for prayers to Him.

"In any case, Quinn concluded, "Satan had been put into the bottomless pit in A.D. 30, just before the crucifixion of Jesus and then released in A.D. 1030. Besides Thorvald, brother of Lief Erickson, there were the Middle Ages, from A.D. 800 to A.D. 1500. Tyrannical Popes of the Middle Ages ruled with an iron hand; then there were 200 years of European Witch Trials and the Age of the Pricker; the Spanish Inquisition and its Iron Maiden, administered by the Jesuits. To today, to Pope John XXIII creating a liasion with the United Nations; to Pope Paul VI negotiating with the Zionist Rabbis during Vatican II to change the liturgy, to release them from the guilt of sentencing Jesus to death, and to omit five prayers at the end of Mass, one being for Michael the Archangel to protect the Catholic Church. And to when John Paul II decided to 'continue the policy of secrecy' of priests raping altar boys - only moving the priest to another venue to continue his raping.

And, since Satan was loosed from the bottomless pit for a short time, as on June 8, 1967, the Zionist Jews/Israelis slaughtered their unarmed Egyptian POWs and then attacked the American non-combatant USS Liberty, murdering 34 and wounding 174 crew members of the intelligence ship that was sailing in international waters, to hide the murder of their POWs. To today, where UN Troops put a boy into a metal drum until the hot African sun baked him to death; where UN Troops prostituted young girls in the villages where they were assigned to be 'peacekeepers.' Satan had shown his hand time and times and a half time. In America, where ten-year-old girls wear jelly bracelets of different colors, each representing a sexual act that the girl will perform on a strange boy or man who can wrestle the bracelet off her wrist - including oral anal sex. And the daytime, doctor-talk show, teaching how to use a remote-controlled, clitoris-stimulating sex toy. It was the culture that the Zionist-Jew-owned media had brought to America, stripping America of its Christian culture and values."

Quinn thought to himself, "That's what Jesus meant: 'But woe to you scribes and Pharisees, hypocrites; because you shut the kingdom of heaven against men, for you yourselves do not enter in; and those that are going in, you suffer not to enter', Matt. 23:13.

Quinn mumbled softly, "But the Zionists are not alone. Vatican II brought on the great apostasy of clergy and lay people alike, such that Church attendance has dropped to the point of closing down parish churches all over the country."

What Quinn found next in his research made him sick to his stomach. The Croatian Ustachi movement beginning in 1930, a pre-WWII terrorist movement that became the rulers of the puppet state of Nazi Germany, led by Croatian fascist dictator Ante Pavelic, the Independent State of Croatia. Fanatic Catholics, holding that Catholic and Muslim faiths as the only religions of the Croatian people. Croatian Cardinal Stepinac and his Nazi Ustachi group forcibly converted thousands of Orthodox Serbians to Catholicism and massacred thousands who refused. Cardinal Stepinac was beatified by Pope John Paul II, (www.northuistandgrimsayfcc.org.uk/The_Papacy_is_the_Antichrist.html)

They are responsible the for WWII holocaust of Serbs, Jews, and Romanis in Croatia, with their own concentration camps. They left for the Nazis occupational troops to discover between the villages of Vlasenica and Kladani - children who had been impaled upon stacks. The Catholic priest, Juric, said: "Today, it is no longer a sin to kill a child of seven, should such a child be opposed to our movement of the Ustachi."

Quinn found this one act alone to be proof that Satan walked the earth. He mumbled aloud, "If you're going to kill a child, why not a bullet to its head, so he's dies quickly. Why not minimize its suffering? Why is it necessary to inflict unmerciful pain on a seven-year-old child? This is pure evil. Juric, allegedly a Christian priest, agrees with this evil! How in God's name does anyone follow someone like the fascist dictator, Pavelic, or a Catholic priest like Juric - who think this evil is acceptable. A people who accept this are aiding and abetting such evil, thus, belong in hell!

This is the same as Solomon sacrificing infants to be burned and roasted on the arms of the idol Moloch. Or Americans who follow the tearing off of arms and legs from infants in their mother's womb with abortion." It suddenly hit Quinn, the pain inflicted upon children has increased over time. Although burning a baby alive, intentionally, has to be the worst of it all. I can see why God destroyed the nation of Israel.

The more he researched the more abominations he found: Peter Brzica, Franciscan educated, a member of the Catholic organization of Crusaders - won a competition on August 29, 1942. The wager was, who could kill the most inmates (Serbs, Jews, and Gypsies) of Jasenova concentration camp. Brzica sliced the throats of 1360 prisoners with a butcher's knife. He was awarded: a gold watch, silver service, and roasted suckling pig and wine; and the title of King of the Cut-Throats. He did all this under the authority of Franciscan monk Miroslav Filipovic, Camp Commandant - where children prisoners were starved to death.

At Nevesinje, the Ustachi rulers, who impaled seven-year-olds, captured a Serbian father, mother, and their four children. Separating out the father, the mother and children were starved for seven days - without water. Then the Ustachi rulers served them a roast with water. After the mother and children devoured the food and drink, the Ustachi told them that they had just eaten their father and husband. Quinn said aloud, "This can only come for a Satanic bloodline. Who else would even think to do such a thing?"

What Quinn discovered next was equally troubling. That Hitler, Mussolini, Franco had all signed concordats with the Vatican, and the claim that the Jesuits controlled the Gestapo and set up WWII, which coincided with Churchill's words: "You must understand that this war (WWII) is not against Hitler or National Socialism, but against the strength of the German people, which is to be smashed once and for all, regardless whether it is in the hands of Hitler or a Jesuit priest." Hitler's war machine was financed by the Vatican. The claimed motive was that the Vatican wanted the entire world converted to Roman Christianity. Cardinal Pacelli, later known as Pope Pius XII, signed a concordat, an agreement, with Germany. Thus, the German government leaders became part of the government of God. With the signing of the concordat the Vatican intends to stabilize the government leaders who sign with them; give it divine and international protection.

Quinn thought a moment, "This sounds like Ezra threatening the Persian Kings, Cyrus the Great, Darius, and Artaxerxes - give me all your gold and power over the Israelites or the God of Abraham is going to get you the way he did the Egyptian Pharao in the Exodus. And if you do, then the God of Abraham will protect you."

But Quinn wasn't convinced of the claimed conversion to Catholicism motive of the Vatican's involvement with Germany. He continued his search. What he found was that when Cardinal Pacelli became Pope Pius XII, he surrounded himself with what they called the

"German Mafia." Cardinal Augustin Bea, a Jesuit, was a forcible influence after being appointed Pius' confessor. Before he succeeded Pius XII, Pope Paul VI directed the Rat Line through Bishop Hudal, an Austrian, who became the Vatican connection for the Nazi 'Rat Line.' The Rat Line was a process of preparing false documents, giving money, and providing escape escorts or routes for Nazi officers out of Germany when it appeared that Germany would be defeated.

A German Nazi officer, Reinhard Kops, stationed in Rome, gave identity cards to escaping Nazis such as Josef Mangele, the Angel of Death at Auschwitz, and Adolf Eichmann, who organized and managed the logistics of the mass deportation of Jews to concentration camps - latter kidnapped in Argentina by the Israeli Mossad and taken to Israel for trial, was hanged in 1962. Others helped by the Vatican to escape were Franz Stangl, who was the Commandant of Treblinka concentration camp; Klaus Barbie, the Butcher of Lyons; Ante Pavelic, the bloody dictator of Croatia. And Erich Priebke, who had beaten inmates with brass knuckles and shot 335 in the massacre of Rome, killing 15 to 70-year-old men, 70 were Israelite-Jews.

Quinn was angered by what he read, but what peaked his attention, as well as his temper, was reading that *Nazi Kirt Waldheim, also escaped through the Rat Line, and later became Secretary General of the United Nations*. A post-WWII War Crimes Commission marked him as a suspected war criminal because he had been an intelligence officer in the Nazi German Wehrmacht - the unified armed forces of Nazi Germany. He held two terms as Secretary General of the UN, 1972-1981, and then became President of Austria in 1985.

Opus Dei, a Catholic/fascist secret group, assisted the Vatican by murdering, laundering money and assets that were stolen by the Nazis and washed through the Vatican Bank then sent on to the Nazis in Argentina, United States, England, Canada, Australia, and other countries.

Opus Dei also dealt in drug peddling, arms trafficking, concealment of WWII loot, embezzlement, and manipulation of financial markets. The Vatican, engulfed in the German Mafia, with Bishop Hudal specifically setting up an underground railroad that went from Germany, over the Italian Alps, using Franciscan convents and monasteries to hide the likes of Mangele, Eichmann, Ante Pavelic, and Otto Skorzeny, a leading force of the Rat Line. Once inside Rome, Nazi Reinhard Kops provided them with false identity papers, then these Nazis needed a witness to certify to the Red Cross their claim of the false identity papers were true. The Vatican used Croatian Catholic priest, Krunoslav Dragonovic, to witness the false identities. Croatian dictator Pavelic was hidden in Rome by the Vatican, driving around with Vatican diplomatic license plates.

It is said that Hitler wrote that he learned much from the Jesuits and greatly admired the organizational structure of the Vatican. The Vatican had copied the hierarchal structure from the Roman Army. Walter Schellenberg, Chief of Nazi counter-espionage said: The SS organization had been constituted by Himmler according to the principles of the Jesuit Order. Spanish Dictator Franco wrote that Hitler, a son of the Catholic Church, died defending Christianity. The Vatican put Hitler in charge of Germany to get rid of their rival - the Israelite-Jews.

The United States called it Operation Paperclip; they worked with Dragonovic in bringing in Von Braun the rocket scientist; Reinhardt Gehlen, a chief SS officer and assassin, to the U.S. Otto Skorzeny was Hitler's bodyguard and SS spy/assassin, and another who came to the U.S. under Operation Paperclip. George Schirf, of the German Navy came through Operation Paperclip, helped in the merging of Nazi SS intelligence with the OSI to form the CIA; he later became the 41st President of the United States.

Quinn thought back to Winston Churchill's words: "You must understand that this war (WWII) is not against Hitler or National Socialism, but against the strength of the German people, which is to be smashed once and for all, regardless whether it is in the hands of Hitler or a Jesuit priest." Quinn focused on the phrase: "strength of the German people, which is to be smashed once and for all...."

He set out to find who the German people were descended from - he found the Biblical Assyrians. In Gen. 10:22, Sem fathered Elam, Assur, Arphaxad, Lud, and Aram. The Germans descended from Assur, the Assyrians. The Israelites descended from Arphaxad.

"The Germans and the Israelites are of the same bloodline - they are cousins!" Quinn cried. He realized that God used the Assyrians to conquer the idol-worshipping (4 Kings 17:7) Ten Tribes of Northern Israel Kingdom (4 Kings 17:6) and took them back to Assyria, in 721 B.C. Assyria was located on the coast of the Black Sea. The Greeks referred to the Assyrians as the whites or blonds. At the time of Christ, the Assyrians lived north of the Black Sea. Many of the Assyrian tribes were in constant conflict with the Roman Empire, therefore, the Romans, 2000 years ago, named the Assyrians - Germans - which means: war men. Around A.D. 100 and 200, these Germans migrated from the Caucasus and countries around the Black and Caspian Seas - into Central Europe. At the time of Christ, the Israelites of the southern Kingdom of Judah, who Ezra captured from the Babylonians under penalty of death, were still living under the control of Ezra's established Pharisaic leaders. These Israelites were scattered by the Romans in A.D. 70, when the Romans destroyed Ezra's Second Temple and Jerusalem. The whites or blonds, as the Greeks called the Assyrian/Germans are cousins to the whites or blonds of Ireland, Scotland, England, Vikings, Norwegians, Sweden - who all have collected together in the United States of America. The Germans and Irish being the two largest ethnic groups in the U.S.

With the Treaty of Verdun, A.D. 843, the grandsons of Charlemagne divided his empire into three parts. The eastern part became Germany; the western part became France; the middle part never coalesced in to an independent state, becoming the battleground of Germany and

France. Otto I took over Germany and was crowned Emperor by Pope John VII (955-964), in A.D. 962, in Rome, therefore, the name Holy Roman Empire was applied to the realms which Otto I ruled. But it was a German kingdom, not holy, not Roman, and not an empire, but a collection of tribal duchies barely held together, (http//faculty.ucc.edu/egh-damerow/holy_roman_empire .htm).

Days after his coronation, Otto I and Pope John VII signed the Privilegium Ottonianum, which gave Emperor Otto I the power to ratify papal elections. On three occasions Otto I marched on Rome - to depose Pope John VII and set up Leo VIII as pope - Otto suppressed the Roman revolt against Leo VIII. Upon Leo's death, Otto appointed John XIII for pope, but the Romans expelled John; Otto marched on Rome and stayed there, A.D. 966 to 972; Rome was subdued, (www.britannica.com/EBchecked/topic/434895/Otto-I).

German bishops, appointed by the Emperors, during the Middle Ages became thoroughly intertwined with the feudal system. They were given sizeable territories from the King as a fee; they were expected to provide military service. Between 1024-1556, the Catholic Church was in danger of losing its spiritual mission (http//faculty.ucc.edu...*Supra*). Sometime around A.D. 1030 - Satan had been loosed from the bottomless pit for a short time.

Between A.D. 1024 and 1125, a great power struggle erupted between the Popes and the Holy Roman Emperors - called the Investiture Struggle. Who should appoint the bishops in Germany, the Emperor or the Pope? This struggle climaxed between Emperor Henry IV (1056-1106) and Pope Gregory VII (1073-1085). The papacy worked to undermine the power of the German Emperors. Frederick II came close to breaking the independent power of the Papacy, but he suddenly died of an illness in 1250. Thus, the popes fought against the Emperors giving their power to their sons, as hereditary rights. After 1273, the position of German Emperor of the Holy Roman Empire became strictly an electoral system, in which a small group of powerful princes elected the Emperor. In 1356, Emperor Charles IV issued a Golden Bull delegating his electoral power to seven imperial electors. These feudal lords never elected an emperor that was the most powerful candidate. The popes, the free cities, and feudal lords had triumphed over the Emperors.

Napoleon finally abolished the Holy Roman Empire in 1806. It became a weak confederation of independent little states. Neither Italy nor Germany were unified till the 1860s, (*Ibid.* at http//faculty.ucc.edu).

After all this research, Quinn decided to take a break. He went and made himself a cup of coffee. When he came back to his desk he decided to return to Revelations.

Rev. 12:3, 4, and 5, are talking about Satan waiting the delivery of his son, Cain, and Cain would later kill his twin, Abel. But the description of the dragon, identified as Satan in Rev. 12:9, having seven heads and ten horns, seven diadems was a specific description possibly to make it specifically relevant and akin in character to the first beast described in Rev. 13:1, "And I saw a beast coming *up out of the sea*, having seven heads and ten horns, and upon his horns ten diadems, and upon his heads names of blasphemy.

These descriptions are telling that Satan, the father of Cain, is the same beast - in the next Revelations chapter. The dragon of Rev. 12 is the same as the first beast of Rev. 13:1. It suddenly occurred to Quinn, had these verses been written more directly it would have been easier to understand - but then, they would have been destroyed centuries ago by the descendants of Satan.

Rev. 13:2-4, "And the beast, which I saw, was like to a leopard, and his feet were as the feet of a bear, and his mouth as the mouth of a lion. And the dragon gave him his own strength, and great power…And I saw one of his heads as it were slain to death: and his death's wound was healed. And all the earth was in admiration after the beast…And they adored the dragon, which gave power to the beast: and they adored the beast, saying: Who is like to the beast? and who shall be able to fight with him?"

Quinn stopped to consider the words: "and one of his heads...were slain...and his death's wound was healed." He sighed heavily, thinking, the League of Nations failed because it had no power - even though the whole world loved the League of Nations, it had not been ratified by the United States Senate. President Wilson wanted the League of Nations, but the Senate said, no. This is describing one of the heads of the beast were slain to death. But the death wound was healed (Rev. 13:3).

The death of the League of Nations that was established as a result of the Treaty of Versailles, in 1920, lasting until 1946, died because the U.S. Senate refused to sign on. And the League of Nations did not have a military force to impose the 'peace.' But Roosevelt and Churchill got together and brought forth the Atlantic Charter, which turned into the United Nations Charter, emerging in 1945, taking on the same goal as the League of Nations of controlling the world. The United Nations Charter's main architect was U.S. President Franklin D. Roosevelt, a 32nd Degree Freemason, and member of the Islamic Order of Nobles and Mystics, for which Roosevelt chose hell over heaven.

Quinn laughed to himself, "I'm sure FDR got his choice and is burning in hell to this day."

He looked at the first beast of Rev. 13:1, coming up out of the sea, Quinn saw as the United Nations. Under the United Nations' Law of the Sea Treaty (LOST), the United Nations controls all the oceans of the world, 70% of the earth's surface. The U.S. Congress couldn't get LOST passed because Americans knew its provisions, so Tsaeb issued an illegal Executive Order, 13547, "Ocean, Coasts, and Great Lakes," requiring a task force to develop a plan for conservation must be consistent with the United Nations' Law of the Sea Treaty. The Clear Water Act, July 30, 2010, made Tsaeb's Executive Order a congressional law and mandates,

Sec. 106, the U.S. joining the Law of the Sea Treaty. It gave the United Nations jurisdiction over America's coastline, its Great Lakes, and its waters out to the international line.

"Not only that," Quinn mumbled to himself, "the UN Headquarters building is on edge of the East River - donated by the Rockefeller family. As noted in Rev. 12:18, Quinn read: "And he stood upon the sand of the sea."

Quinn reviewed each verse: Rev. 12:15, "And the serpent cast out of his mouth after the woman, water as it were a river, that he might cause her to be carried away by the river." Tsaeb cast out of his mouth his Executive Order, that the United States would be carried away by the United Nations controlling the flow, the use, the economy of America's waterways. Thus, carrying away America to destruction. The Clear Water Act will certainly carry the United States away in to oblivion.

Rev. 12:16, "And the earth helped the woman, and the earth opened her mouth, and swallowed up the river, which the dragon cast out of his mouth." Quinn paused, trying to figure out what could save the United States from Tsaeb's Executive Order, the Clear Water Act, and the Law of the Sea Treaty. An earthquake along the 125th Street fault line toppling the UN Building, would be a good start.

"Could the description of the first beast, Rev. 13:2, be an indicator? There were four nations that met to draw up the Charter of the United Nations, Mao Zedong of China, who brought Marxism-Leninism to China, is represented by the leopard. Joseph Stalin, Premier of USSR, a communist, is represented by the feet of a bear; and Prime Minister Winston Churchill of England and President Franklin D. Roosevelt (FDR) - who were cousins, are represented by the mouth of a lion.

The populace didn't know that FDR and Winston Churchill were Satan worshippers. Or that both FDR and President Truman, who was the U.S. signatory of the UN Charter, were 32nd degree Freemasons, whose symbol is the dragon. Joseph Stalin of USSR and Mao Zedong of China were both leaders of the Communist Party in their respective countries. Stalin and Zedong, therefore, did not worship God. These powerful leaders created the United Nations.

Quinn sighed, as he read Rev. 13:4, "And they adored the dragon, which gave power to the beast." Those leaders were all Satan worshippers - they adored the dragon. And the dragon/Satan possessed the Secretary General - giving power to the UN, the first beast.

But the next verse troubled Quinn, Rev. 13:5, "And there was given to him [the first beast] a mouth speaking great things, and blasphemies: and power was given to him to do two and forty months." Blasphemies can mean the act of claiming for one self the attributes and rights of God. This is the power, claimed under the UN Charter, by the Secretary General - Yoon Won-Shik. He claims control of the world and every person and animal walking on earth - the right of God. The two and forty months is 3.5 years. Yoon Won-Shik is going to do terrible things to the people for 3.5 years. What would set him off?

If Yoon Won-Shik is a Buddhist, he worships the dragon deity - does he speak profanity during that worship against God, as noted in Rev. 13:6? If he has control of countries, why doesn't he stop the persecution of Christians around the world? I guess he doesn't want to stop their persecution.

Quinn sighed as he read, Rev. 13:7, "And it was given unto him to make war with the saints, and to overcome them. And power was given him over every tribe, and people, and tongue, and nation." This can only refer to UN Secretary General Yoon Won-Shik, and therefore, he is allowing China, Sudan, Saudi Arabia, Egypt, Turkey, Burma, Greece, Ethiopia, Vietnam, Cuba, Laos, and North Korea - to murder Christians. Even though the mission of the UN Charter is to be an international peacekeeping security organization.

Chills ran down Quinn's spine when he read, Rev. 13:9-10: "*If any man have an ear, let him hear*...He that shall lead into captivity, shall go into captivity: he that shall kill by the sword, *must be killed* by the sword. Here is the patience and the faith of the saints." Quinn assumed that the saints were the Christians being murdered around the world - as well as American Christians.

President Tsaeb has waged war against them, with supporters like Bill Maher. Tsaeb had ordered FEMA to conduct a National Level Exercise (NLE) with the militaries of Mexico, Canada, Australia, and the United Kingdom - on U.S. soil for 'terrorism prevention and protection.' Tsaeb was setting up the battlefield to slaughter the Christians.

In Rev. 13:11, Quinn read of a second beast that he saw as the *Blue Beret Beasts* of the United Nations Military, an army that kills on land. "And I saw another beast coming up out of the earth, and he had two horns, like a lamb, and he spoke as a dragon." We are told, Quinn thought to himself, that the UN Military are only used as peace keepers - like a lamb, but in fact, they murder, torture, and rape the helpless in the countries in which they are peacekeepers, therefore, the UN Military speaks like a dragon that devours those who do not obey/adore the United Nations Secretary General, the "former beast."

Rev. 13:12 "And he executed all the power of the former beast." This is the United Nations Military that executes the orders of the UN Secretary General Yoon Won-Shik. "And (the second beast) caused the earth, and them that dwell therein to adore the first beast, whose wound to death was healed."

Quinn sighed heavily when he read, Rev. 13:15, "And it was given him (the second beast - the UN Military *Blue Beret Beasts*) to give life to the image of the (first) beast (UN Secretary General Yoon Won-Shik), and that the image of the beast should speak; and should cause, that whosoever will not adore the image of the beast, *should be slain.*"

"Shit!" Quinn mumbled under his breath - "the image of the beast should speak!" A microchip "speaks" to the machine that reads its number.

The "image" is the microchip. "The image of the (first) beast" - the microchip belongs to Yoon Won-Shik. The UN Beasts - "give life to the image" - they force the injection of the microchip - and "whosoever will not adore the image" - whoever refuses to take the injection of the microchip - will be slain - murdered!"

Messinger's speech flashed through Quinn's mind, and Messinger telling the elite that they need to create an unknown threat that would cause Americans "to plead for UN troops to protect them," to get Americans to allow UN troops to march in their streets. And in *Memories,* Dennis Knickerbocker said that he and his family were establishing a new world order, "All we need is the right major crisis and the nations will accept our New World Order." That could be an economic crises. Destroy nations' currencies and establish a world currency, regulated by the World Bank. That currency will likely be a microchip, used both as a geolocator - tracking the whereabouts of every citizen, but used as a bank account.

Quinn mumbled, "You couldn't buy toilet paper and go into the woods to take a shit without them knowing about it." Quinn then thought of the FEMA camps and the millions of plastic coffins stacked therein caused him to have a heavy heart. "There really, truly, is going to be a war with these degenerates."

He continued on, determining that Rev. Chapter 12 gave the history and identity of Satan, the dragon, the devil, ending the chapter with him standing on the sand of the sea - the edge of a body of water. That location is significant - it determines the site of the Satan's throne - is the United Nations Building.

Rev. Chapter 13 tells of two beasts that provide a physical expression of Satan's power. The UN Charter was established by the leopard/China, bear/Russia, and lion/England & U.S. (President Franklin D. Roosevelt was a cousin of Prime Minister Winston Churchill). The UN Charter established the seat of power in the position, the physical body, of the Secretary General, the Commander and Chief Executive Officer of the UN Assembly - the first beast. The Dragon/Satan gave his own strength and power to this first beast - when he possessed the body of the Secretaries General. And those who adored this first beast, Satan, their names were not written in the Book of Life of the Lamb/Jesus, Rev. 13:8.

The second beast of Chapter 13, coming up out of the earth - is the UN Military, the Blue Beret Beasts.

Only the United Nations had the organization and the treaty ability to invade, at their will, its military into any country per the UN Charter that 193 member nations had signed and agreed to. That is, except the Vatican. The United Nations had the ability and its organization was the perfect vehicle for Satan to control the earth and force the citizens of the world to take the mark of the beast. Rev. 13:17, "And that no man might buy or sell, but he that hath the character, or the name of the beast, or the number of his name."

Quinn considered aloud, "This is why they are destroying the U.S.

Dollar, so they can call for a world currency controlled by the United Nations, allegedly to stabilize the markets - that they destabilized. And then with such control the United Nations would require the mark be placed on everyone's hand, or use a special card for an account to which the individual's wages or welfare check would be automatically deposited. There would be no actual currency. And if they refused, they wouldn't be able to buy food, or medical, dental care, or clothes, or rent an apartment, or buy a house, for the only financial system in the entire world would be through the mark of the beast."

Quinn read, Rev. 13:18, "*Here is wisdom. He that hath understanding, let him count* the number of the beast. For it is the number of a *man*: and the number of him is six hundred sixty-six."

Quinn read that the United Nations has *six goals*: International law; international security; economic development; social progress; human rights; world peace. And it has *six principle organs*: General Assembly; Security Council; Economic and Social Council; Secretariat; International Court of Justice; Trusteeship Council. It has *six languages*: Arabic; Mandarin Chinese; English; French; Russian; Spanish. Quinn wondered, "Would it be too presumptuous to see that as: 666? Otherwise, how come it doesn't have more than six languages, what about Japanese, Norwegian, Cantonese, why stop at six, there are 193 member nations." Then he sighed, "None of these things are certain. And that goes to the deceit of it all."

While Quinn read again Revelations, the Apocalypse, he became more confused, not in the understanding of each verse, although they were obvious brain-teasing puzzles, but the sequence of their layout. The entire book of Revelations is out of sequence – not just a few chapters. Finally, he wrote out the chapter numbers and beside each he wrote a sentence of what the chapter was about - he read them over and over - "They're out of order! They don't make sense, God defeats the beast and they glorify God, but in the next chapter the angels pour out the vials of plagues. Why?" he asked. He then went back over the list and re-ordered them to what seemed to make better sense to him.

Following Chapters 1-7, which he kept as it, Quinn listed Chapter 11 should follow Chapter 7, and the two witnesses - for now, he wasn't sure who the two witnesses were. At the time of John writing the prophecy of Apocalypse, Revelations, the destruction of Jerusalem was about to come. John wrote Revelations about 64 years after the Lord's Ascension, and the Romans destroyed Jerusalem in A.D. 70. In Rev. 11:7, it talked about the two witnesses. "And when they shall have finished their testimony *the beast, that (had) ascendeth out of the abyss*, shall make war against them, and shall overcome them, and kill them." Quinn reasoned, "These witnesses come then after Satan is released from the bottomless pit - sometime around A.D. 1000. And their death occurs in the "the great city, which is called spiritually, Sodom and Egypt," Rev. 11:8. In other words, Quinn thought, in sinful cities of the world, such as 'where their

Lord also was crucified' - Jerusalem, controlled by the Pharisees. New York City! Washington, DC, are sinful cities!"

Quinn wondered, "What two people died in a sinful city sometime after A.D. 1000?" Suddenly, it hit him, "Eisenhower and Kennedy!!! They are the witnesses! Eisenhower died in DC, and Kennedy was living in DC when he was murdered in Dallas - a sin city? Both presidents had lain in state for three days, in the U.S. Capitol Building. Rev. 11:11 'And after three days and a half, the spirit of life from God entered into them. And they stood upon their feet, and great fear fell upon them that saw them.'"

Quinn mumbled to himself in analyzing the verse, "If they both had lain in state for three days, and then 'the spirit of life from God entered into them' - this could mean that the spirits of Eisenhower and Kennedy were standing at their own grave sites. Maybe some of those visitors actually saw their spirits and were scared." He paused a moment, "I feel certain that these are the two witnesses. Their testimonies relate to today."

Quinn went to the Internet videos and played President Eisenhower's Military-Complex speech of January 17, 1961. He heard Eisenhower saying American makers of 'plowshares' could, with time...make 'swords.' "This is a sign! No one used the term plowshares in 1961. Eisenhower is warning us through a code - so his speech won't be destroyed. Eisenhower is referring to Joel 3:10. In Joel 3:10, God commanded: "Cut your ploughshares into swords...." This passage alludes to the end times battle; where God will judge all nations in the valley of Josaphat.

Eisenhower also said that "3.5 million men and women are directly engaged in the defense establishment." "This is another sign," Quinn said, "- 3.5!" He searched Douay Rheims online, he found in Joel 3:5, "For you have taken away my silver and my gold: and my desirable and most beautiful things you have carried into your temples." That could mean, Quinn reflected, the Federal Reserve - controlled by a handful of those who carry out Satan's orders - who bankrupted the U.S. within 20 years, and had required payment in only gold. That same elite of the world orchestrated world wars - "taking away the most beautiful things" - the children of America, who died for their profit.

Eisenhower continued his warning, "The total influence...*even spiritual*...is felt in every city, every State House, every office of the Federal Government..." This is exactly the method used by UN Agenda 21, to carry out the orders of the Secretary General Yoon Won-Shik - to change the zoning laws, ordinances of towns and county level governments, up through putting his people into federal government positions.

Eisenhower stated, "*we must not fail to comprehend its <u>grave</u> implications*. Our toil...all involved, so is the very structure of our society....*The potential for the <u>disastrous</u> rise of misplaced power exists and <u>will persist</u>*....We should take nothing for granted. Only an alert and knowledgeable citizenry can compel the proper meshing of the huge industrial and military machinery of defense with our peaceful methods and goals. So that security and liberty may prosper together."

Quinn reckoned, these industrial corporations are now international, not American, not necessarily. And the military machinery - is that of Yoon Won-Shik as Commander of the UN military machinery "peace keepers." The UN military machinery - is a system of conscripting soldiers from 193 member countries! Eisenhower is specifically separating those corporations and military machinery - from "our peaceful methods." He's not talking about the U.S. Military!!

Quinn thought - this speech - this testimony is worthy of a Biblical witness, for it came from a WWII hero, a beloved and respected president, who had worked for the containment of communism - and he is telling of his witnessing in both his military career and from the inside knowledge of the presidency, and he is giving dire warning to all of America, at once, just three days before leaving the White House that our personal freedoms are in grave danger. Quinn mumbled to himself, "This is definitely one of the end-times witnesses."

Quinn searched the Internet videos of President John Kennedy's monolithic conspiracy speech: "The very word secrecy is repugnant in a free and open society....*there is very grave danger that an announced need for increased security will be sieged upon by those anxious to expand its meaning*, to the very limits of official censorship and concealment. *That I do not intend to permit*....For *we [Americans] are opposed around the world by a monolithic and ruthless conspiracy* that relies primarily on covert means for expanding its sphere of influence, on infiltration instead of invasion, on subversion instead of elections, on intimidation instead of free choice, on gorillas by night instead of armies by day. It is a system which has conscripted vast human and material resources in to the building of a tightly knit, highly efficient machine that combines military, diplomatic, intelligent, economic, scientific, and political operations. It's preparations are concealed....*It's dissenters are silenced*...No secret is revealed....I am asking your (newspapers) help in the tremendous *task of informing and alerting the American people* for I have complete confidence in the response and dedications of our citizens when they are fully informed....No Republic can survive. That is why the Athenian law maker...*decreed it a crime for any citizen to shrink from controversy*...the First Amendment...specifically protected by the Constitution...to inform, to arouse, to reflect, *to state our dangers...to indicate our crises* and our choices...to educate and sometimes even anger public opinion...it means greater...analysis of international news for *it is no longer far away* and foreign, *but close at hand and local*.... So it is to the printing press, to the recorder of man's deed, the keeper of his conscious, the courier of his news that we look for strength and assistance, confident with YOUR help *man will be what he was born to be, free and independent*."

Quinn immediately recalled the words of Jesus, Matt. 23:8: "all you are brethren," not the slaves of the Pharisees.

Quinn was also struck by both of these witnesses using the same word 'grave' to the point that he looked it up in the dictionary: "death or extinction," not just serious. But Kennedy's speech stating that the conspiracy is highly efficient goes directly to the essential ability of the Jesuits. And their Superior General, Alonso Negrete, the 30th Black Pope. Quinn thought, how many orders are there in the Catholic Church, why do the Jesuits alone need to be headed by a General? A military arm of the Vatican?

In Kennedy's speech, to the Greater Houston Ministerial Association, before he became president, on Sept. 12, 1960, Houston, Texas: "I believe in an America where the separation of Church and State is absolute...where no public official either requests or accepts instructions on public policy from the Pope, the National Council of Churches, or any other ecclesiastic source....no president must be humbled by any religious group...his religious views are his own private affair...This is the kind of America I fought for in the South Pacific and my brother died for in Europe...This is the kind of America for which our forefathers did die when they fled here...when they fought for the Constitution, the Bill of Rights, the Virginia Statute of Religious Freedom...at the Shrine of the Alamo...side by side with Bowie and Crockett fought and died Fuentes, McCafferty, and Bailey, Bedillo, Carey, but no one knows whether they were Catholics or not, for no religious test there....Judge me...(on my) declared stand against an ambassador to the Vatican....The Church does not speak for me."

In September 1960, when Kennedy said these words, the Rabbi Heschel and Pope John XXIII had been working towards the convening of Vatican II, in 1962.

In describing these two witnesses, Rev. 11:6: "These (witnesses) have power to shut heaven...they have power over waters to turn them into blood, and to strike the earth with all plagues as often as they will." These two presidents had that power - as the "Commander in Chief of the Army and Navy of the United States...." U.S. Constitution, Art. II, sec. 2, cl. 1.

And John wrote in Rev. 11:12, "And they went up to heaven in a cloud: and their enemies saw them." As their spirits were ascending to Heaven; an evil spirit would be able to see another spirit. Spirits can see, not only our dimension, but see in the 11th dimension.

Quinn noted, that after their ascent to Heaven, in verse 14, "*The second woe is past: and behold the third woe will come quickly*." Quinn saw that the first woe was the crucifixion of Jesus Christ and a thousand years later the release of Satan from the pit; the second woe as the death of the two witnesses, Eisenhower and Kennedy.

Quinn also noted in verse 13, following the ascent to Heaven of the witnesses in verse 12, and before the passing of the second woe in verse 14: (Rev. 11:13) "And at that hour there was made a great earthquake." When Kennedy was assassinated, Quinn reasoned, the world shook in its foundation; kings and presidents of the world walked behind his horse-drawn caisson. But the murder of such a beloved president put the fear of God into these leaders - if a highly protected President of the great United States, protected by the Secret Service, CIA, FBI intelligence - could be murdered, then no world leader was safe. "And the rest were cast into a fear, and gave glory to the God of heaven."

Quinn thought back to the organization of the Chapters of Revelations.

Rev. 20:1-2 - Satan is bound for 1000 years.

Rev. 5:5 - Jesus, the Lamb that was slain, of the tribe of Juda, the root of (King) David - is in Heaven, and opens the Book of Life - and opened the seven seals of the book.

Rev. 9:1-2 - Satan is loosed from the bottomless pit.

Rev. 9:12 - One woe is past.

Rev. 10 - A mighty angel brings a small book to John
- John is told by a voice in Heaven not to write what the seven thunders had said;
- the mighty angel swore by God - that "time" shall be no longer;
- that the mystery of God shall be finished;
- John is told to eat the small book; and
- John is told to prophecy, again - to many nations.

Rev. 11:14 Describes the two witnesses,
- after their death - the second woe is past - the third woe is to come -

Rev. 12 Gives the history of Satan - it should have come before Chapter 5. Chapter 12 tells of the Satanic bloodline created with Eve in the Garden. But this placement connects Satan to Chapter 13 that describes the third woe, without calling it the third woe. It's here!

Rev. 13 Tells of the Antichrist, the United Nations, and the UN military machinery
- of the forcing of the mark of the beast.
- no man can buy or sell unless he has the image/microchip of the beast.

Rev. 13:12-14 - People should make the image/microchip of the beast, which had the wound (the League of Nations' death that healed and became the United Nations), therefore, the microchip of Yoon Won-Shik, Secretary General of the United Nations.

Rev. 14:9-10, warns that the wrath of God will come upon anyone taking the mark of the beast - that the UN military machinery will impose on citizens, under penalty of death, as noted in Rev. 13:15. The message: It is better to resist and die at the hands of the UN Troops than to take the mark of the beast, which is the United Nations Secretary General, the Antichrist! For those who had resisted and had been murdered by Yoon Won-Shik's UN military machinery went to Heaven, Rev. 15:2-3. And those who took the microchip, felt the wrath of God, Rev. 14:9-10. In Rev.

14:7-10, an angel warns that the hour of judgment is come, he is followed by another angel who reminds people of the fall of Babylon - that angel is followed by another angel who warns not to take the mark of the beast. The memory of Babylon equates Ezra taking the Israelites, the remnants of the tribes of Benjamin and Judah held captive in Babylon, which Ezra forced back to Jerusalem under threat of death, to take the mark of Ezra's brand of the mark of the beast - to obey his new religion - Pharisaism, to worship idols. As Jesus said, Matt. 23:15, "Pharisees...you make him the child of hell twofold more than yourselves."

Quinn saw the verses as connecting Ezra's new religion with taking the mark of the beast - just as the UN and its military machinery will require all of today's world to take the mark - and Quinn connected them to the Rabbi Heschel and Popes John XXIII, Paul VI, John Paul II as forcing their new religion onto Catholics - as the taking the mark of the beast. Pharisee Chief Priest Ezra and Rabbi Heschel - were of the bloodline of Satan and do their father's will - deliver the souls of the Israelites, yesterday's and today's, into hell.

Quinn researched further and found that Heschel wasn't the only Zionist Jew that was out to change the Catholic Church in to another religion. Rabbi Marc Tanenbaum, 1925-1992, was an international activist for social justice; the buzz world for New World Order. He was founder and co-secretary of Joint Vatican International Jewish Consulative Committee. "He supervised an initiative which addressed negative portrayal of Judaism in Catholic textbooks and in the liturgy. It included concrete steps to alleviate tensions and reduce prejudice." (Cited with permission: Tanenbaum Moving Beyond Differences website, http://67.20.95.173/old/mission .html)

"Shortly after joining the AJC (American Jewish Committee), Tanenbaum used his American contacts to gain access to certain key members of the hierarchy and through them, to the Vatican office handling a draft text on the Jews. In this, he was ably assisted by the AJC's European representative, Zach Shuster, who relayed information on the progress of the draft text and conveyed the sentiments of Tanenbaum and the AJC leadership In New York to the officials in the Secretariat for Promoting Christian unity, which was then charged with developing the draft text. Tanenbaum knew that the SPCU's head, Cardinal Augustin Bea, was going to be the most important person with whom to make contact, but he relied on Shuster to cultivate as many allies in the newly constructed Secretariat as possible....No one, including the Pope, had foreseen any discussion by the Secretariat on Judaism or anti-Semitism, but that changed on June 13, 1960, when Jules Isaac met with (Pope) John XXIII, who awareness and motivations were heightened to include some statement on Judaism. In September of that year, Pope John communicated to Cardinal Bea that a declaration should be drawn up dealing with the Jewish people and the staff set to work....When

Tanenbaum began to work there (at AJC) in early 1961, he moved quickly to allay any reservations among those in Rome who were meeting behind closed doors. He contributed the AJC's own research to those private discussions as a friendly gesture. The first of several large memoranda sent by the AJC to Cardinal Bea was entitled, "The Image of the Jews in Catholic Teaching," dated July 13, 1962, and presented to him by representatives of the AJC on that date. The second (memorandum) was "Anti-Jewish Elements in Catholic Liturgy," and dated November 17, 1961." (Citation with permission: "The Virtues of Dialogue Thomas Stransky, CSP, and Rabbi Marc Tanenbaum on the Making of Nostra Aetate," by Patrick J. Hayes, Ph.D., from Bulletin 78, January 2007. Monastic Interreligious Dialogue, http://monasticdialog.com/a.php?id =809)

"Tanenbaum was present on the final day of *Second Vatican Council in 1965 - which decreed that Catholics could not blame the Jews for the death of Jesus...*Tanenbaum believed Jews needed to take an active role in U.S. politics in order to prevent marginalization and anti-Semitism. He became involved in Washington politics." (Citation with permission: "Tanenbaum Moving Beyond Differences"; http://67.20.95.173/old/mission.html)

Quinn also found:

Nostra Aetate: Latin for "Declaration on the Relation of the Church with Non-Christian Religions on the Second Vatican Council," promulgated (to proclaim, to put a law into force or effect) by Pope Paul VI, on October 28, 1965. "Pope Paul VI who shepherded through the council, promulgated, and implemented the most radically transforming document on Jews and Judaism to have ever been produced by the Catholic Church...Nostra Aetate was the Jewish Declaration - a unilateral peace treaty...Nostra Aetate, Ch. 4 states: 'We (Christians and Jews) are children of Abraham by faith, and since by definition a Jew is a child of Abraham...(the Church) draws sustenance from the root of that well-cultivated olive tree onto which have been grafted the *wild shoots, the Gentiles'*...Nostra Aetate, Ch. 5 states 'That all men are created in God's image, and that it is contrary to the teaching of the Church to discriminate against, show hatred towards or harass any person on the basis of colour, race, religion, condition of life and so on.' (1985 "Notes" followed by "The Correct Way to Present Jews and Judaism in the Teaching and Catechesis of the Roman Catholic Church in 1985")...'*All this is based on a recognition of the validity of the covenantal claims of Jews to be God's people*, for God 'does not repent of the gifts He makes or the calls He issues'...." (Citation with permission: By Gerald Darring, "Pope John XXIII, Pope Paul VI, The Second Vatican Council, and the Jews," http://www.shc.edu/theolibrary/ resources/IIJohn.htm)

Quinn continued his analysis. Rev. 12 discloses that a Satanic bloodline exists, and thereby, identifies the characters who are to be fought in the end time - they come from Satan's bloodline. Rev. 13:7, "power is given to the beast over every tribe, and people, and tongue, and nation." UN Secretary General Yoon Won-Shik has that power, today. No other time in the history of mankind has anyone person held such power; and with U.S. legislation handing over 650,000 acres, 29% of the U.S. and all U.S. waters and coastlines to Yoon Won-Shik - as have all the 193 UN member countries, Yoon Won-Shik has been given control over 70% of the earth under the Law of the Sea Treaty.

But it was in Rev. 15, Quinn found, that the third woe begins with plagues. Rev. 15 is a turning point in the Book of The Apocalypse. Those who had been murdered for resisting the mark of the beast were in Heaven, Rev. 15:1-5. There was a thousand years between the one woe identified as Satan being loosed from the pit (A.D. 1030), as Rev. 9:12 states, one woe is past and two more woes to come. And the second woe, identified the two witnesses and their deaths (A.D. 1963 and 1969), Rev. 11:14: the second woe has past - and the third woe will come quickly. This implies that the third woe is the actual end time because there are no other woes to follow. Revelations does not say that the third woe has passed; not as it did with the one/first and second woe. Rev. 13 identifies the Antichrist, the Beast, and the False Prophet, and their armies gathering for the Battle of Armageddon. Rev. 14 warns of God's wrath for taking the mark of the Beast, the United Nations - the hour of His judgment has come. So the correct sequence leading up to the end time, third woe: Rev. 12, 5:5-8, 20:2, 9:2, 13, 14, 15.

Quinn then realized - this is where the prophecy of Daniel comes in, when the angel Gabriel was sent to Daniel in response to his passionate prayer during the time of the Israelite captivity in Babylon - during the time that Ezra was establishing his new religion - Pharisaism.

Quinn read: Daniel 9:11-27, "And all Israel have transgressed God's law, and have turned away from hearing God's voice, and the malediction, and the curse, which is written in the book of Moses (Deuteronomy 28:15) the servant of God, is fallen upon us, because we have sinned against Him...And he has confirmed His words which he spoke against us, and against our princes that judged us, *that he would bring in upon us a great evil, such as never was under all the heaven, according to that which has been done in Jerusalem (destroyed Jerusalem because Solomon and Israelites worshipped idols)*... Seventy weeks are shortened upon thy people, and upon His holy city, that transgression may be finished, and sin may have an end, and iniquity may be abolished; and everlasting justice may be brought; and vision and prophecy may be fulfilled; and the saint of saints (Jesus) may be anointed...Know you therefore, and *take notice*: *that* from the going forth of the word (God's curse), to build up Jerusalem again (by Ezra, 457 B.C.), unto Christ the prince, there shall be seven weeks, and sixty-two weeks: and the street shall be built again (Nehemias, 444 B.C.), and the walls in straitness of times...And after sixty-two weeks Christ shall be slain: and the people that shall deny him shall not be His (of His bloodline). And a people (Romans) with their leader that shall come, shall destroy the city and the sanctuary: and the end thereof shall be waste, and after the end of the war the appointed desolation…And he (Jesus) shall confirm the covenant with many, in one week: and in the half of the week the victim and the sacrifice shall fail (die): and there shall be in the temple the abomination (idols; Judaism) of desolation: and the desolation shall continue even to the consummation, and to the end."

Just short of 40 years after the crucifixion of Jesus, the Romans destroyed the Second Temple. But Daniel is also talking about the abomination of desolation continuing until the consummation. The word abomination is a noun - the name of a person, place, or thing - it is name of the Pharisees. The Pharisees are the abomination. Abomination meaning someone who elicits abhorrence. The Pharisees murdered the Son of God, causing them to be greatly disliked. Desolation is also a noun, meaning ruin, a state of being wretched. The Pharisees are named an abhorrence of wretchedness. These Pharisees, these despicable people will continue throughout time until the consummation, and to the end. After the Romans destroyed the Second Temple in A.D. 70, the Pharisees arose under the name of Rabbis. Pharisaism and the Talmud arose under the name of Judaism. In Matt. 24:15, when Jesus described the consummation of the world, 'When therefore you shall see the abomination of desolation, which was spoken of by Daniel the prophet, standing in the holy place: he that readeth let him understand.' Jesus is warning of the Pharisees standing in the holy place - the Catholic Church is the holy place. The Rabbis wielded great influence in Vatican II!!!

The continual sacrifice was taken away by Popes Pius XII, John XXIII and Paul VI, and *Rabbi* Abraham Joshua Heschel - but especially by Cardinal Augustin Bea, a German Jesuit, born in the Black Forest of Germany - they '*set up* the abomination unto desolation.' Pope John XXIII was elected pope on October 28, 1958 and appointed Bea in 1960 as Secretariat for Promoting Christian Unity, and established the Central Preparatory Commission for Vatican II on June 5, 1960; Bea invited very involved 'observers.' Bea drafted the Nostra Aetate the most important declaration of Vatican II Council, which passed after years of fighting and resulted in the exoneration of the Pharisees for their demanding of Pontius Pilate that he agree with the Pharisees' condemnation of the death of Jesus. Today, the Pharisees are called Rabbis of Judaism.

Rev. 16:12, noted the 'great' Euphrates River, Quinn saw it as the Rio Grande. Naming the river the Euphrates only indicates those countries east of the Euphrates. In the Biblical verse, to "*dry up the water thereof,* that a way might be prepared for the kings from the rising of the sun" - the east - they would be the kings of China, Iran and Afghanistan - the Iranian Military, Hamas, Hezbollah, and Al Qaeda. That's what the verse was disclosing, but those militaries are waiting in Mexico, across the Rio Grande, the 'great' river - along with the Russian Military, while the Chinese Military are also on the northern border of the U.S. All countries east of the Euphrates are now south of the Rio Grande. U.S. Intelligence found that Iran has targeted 800 sites inside the United States: electric grids, water and food supplies, and bridges. Muslim student groups here in the U.S. on student visas are part of the planned attack.

And after the first woe is passed, Rev. 9:14 "Loose the four angels, who are bound in the great river Euphrates. (15) And the *four angels were loosed, who were prepared for an hour, and a day, and a month, and a year: for to kill the third part of men*." It had to connect to each other, but out of sequence. Rev. 16:12, the dried up water, preparing the way for the kings from the east, should have come first. And in Rev. 9:14, which takes place one thousand years AFTER Satan had been released from the pit in Rev. 9:11, comes the releasing of the four angels, 'who are bound in the great river Euphrates.' The four angels: Iranian Hezbollah, Hamas, Al Qaeda - are all bound by the Rio Grande - in that they cannot cross it until given the order - but 'who were prepared for an hour, and a day, and a month, and a year' - to cross - to be released from the river into the United States - to kill the third part of men - a third part of Americans! That limitation of time in preparation of attack, a year, month, day, hour, supports the Rio Grande theory, as opposed to the Euphrates because Iran has been east of Israel since the beginning of time. But Iran is also east of the U.S.

Quinn searched for answers - the Rio Grande, 1896 miles long beginning in Colorado and emptying into the Gulf of Mexico - *but at Presidio, Texas, it is dried up*. Down river, tributaries feed it, again. But Quinn noted that *Presidio means garrison, fortress.* Was this Biblical prophecy fulfilled - to prepare the way for the kings of the east?

Quinn then searched for the Deep-water Horizon oil spill in the Gulf of Mexico, which began April 20, 2010 and dead dolphins washed ashore in April 2011. But the death of sea life, marshes, and the loss of fishing, along with the Corexit 9500 spraying killing people and sea life - was that an indication that Rev. 9:15, 'for to kill the third part of men' had been fulfilled? Or was it yet to be fulfilled by the invasion of the four armies of the east, lying in wait for the order?

This, Rev. 16, 3 spirits like frogs, to Quinn, was clearly Tsaeb, the UN Secretary General, and the Pope 'working signs' as in a portentous event - an indication of something calamitous is about to occur; presage - a warning of a future event - as in red flag. As in - give up your right to privacy so that the federal government can make you secure - as in Patriot Act! As in the TSA groping screaming children and old ladies - all in the name of national security because something calamitous might happen if they aren't allowed to molest people. As in the National Defense Authorization Act of 2012 that allows Tsaeb to lock up American citizens without charges, without appearing before a judge, for the duration of hostilities that are not identified, simply on Tsaeb's suspicion that an American might be a terrorist - for as long as Tsaeb wants to imprison the American citizen.

These three devils, Tsaeb, UN Secretary General, and the Pope, collude under the guise of peace, but all are in agreement to use any and all military force against the United States, where there is the largest collection of Christians; a country whose citizenry owns the largest private collection of guns and a trillion rounds of ammo. The UN demanding a list of names and addresses of all those American gun owners; an international registry of gun models, and the UN demanding that the U.S. legislate the banning of automatic guns. Their argument: a pistol satisfies the 2nd Amendment. What they want is to be able to use AK-47s against a five-chamber, individually loaded, .38 special. The Pope offering his 'full support and cooperation' to 'mechanisms for prevention, reduction, accountability, and control' of guns. The Pope's support of the UN's demand to create a system of marking, tracing, and record-keeping of guns; his support of mechanisms for collecting and destroying arms in peace processes, and more. What these devil spirits are attempting to do is to disarm as many Americans before going into battle; before sending in the UN troops to murder Americans. An efficient method of disarming your enemy before going in to battle, a trademark of the highly efficient Jesuits.

But in Chapter 17, the prophecy provided another puzzle, but mostly because it should have come before Rev. 16:14. In Rev. 17:1, 'the condemnation of the great harlot, who sitteth upon many waters.' Quinn mumbled to himself, "That has to be Rome, Italy, that stretched out peninsula that seems to be sitting upon *many* waters."

Quinn checked his world map hanging on the wall above his desk. "Italy is surrounded by the Tyrrhenian Sea, the Adriatic Sea, the Ionian Sea, and the Mediterranean Sea. *Many* waters. No other country in the world, except possibly England, could fit such a description of appearing to be sitting 'upon many waters,' as opposed to the one water of the Pacific Ocean, or the Atlantic Ocean. But Rome seems more of a whore than London because of the claim that the Vatican itself has made: to be the home of the Vicar of Christ, the Pope - all the while the Pope and Vatican Council II gave away the continual sacrifice of Jesus - as they took away the kneeling rail before the sanctuary that brought congregants to their knees in respect of receiving the Body of Christ - the Eucharist. And as they took away the priest making the sign of the cross before placing the Eucharist on the tongue of the worshipper, for out of respect of the holy symbol of the Body of Christ, the worshippers were never to touch the Eucharist. The priest making the sign of the cross was to remind the worshipper of Christ's sacrifice for the remission of the sins of many, Matt. 26:28. It was all too sacred a moment - between God and those who love Him - for the Pope and Vatican Council II and the Zionist-Jews - to allow to continue. And the Pope and Vatican Council II did away with fasting after mid-night before receiving the Eucharist at the next morning's Mass/Liturgy. Directly countering God's own words: Joel 2:12, "Now therefore saith the Lord: Be converted to me with all your heart, in *fasting*, and in weeping, and in mourning." And the Pope sold dispensations and indulgences, setting aside Canon Law for those who paid, because the Pope is considered above Canon Law; he acts outside the law instituted by the Catholic Church. And the Pope and Vatican Council II set up of collegiality - the sharing of authority among the bishops, instead of sole authority resting on the Pope - the Pope and Vatican Council II - took away the rock on which Jesus Christ built his Church - Matt. 16:17-19, "Blessed art thou, Simon Bar-Jona: because flesh and blood hath not revealed it to thee, but my Father who is in heaven. (18) And I say to thee: That thou (you) art Peter; and upon this rock I will build my church, and the gates of hell shall not prevail against it. (19) And I will give to THEE (YOU) the keys of the kingdom of heaven. And whatsoever THOU (YOU) shalt bind upon earth, it shall be bound also in heaven: and whatsoever THOU (YOU) shalt loose on earth, it shall be loosed also in heaven." And they did all this - to become acceptable to the Zionists-Jews, devil worshippers. Quinn reasoned, all this devastation of the Church of Jesus would make the Pope a whore.

Quinn read, Rev. 17:3-4, 'a woman sitting upon a scarlet coloured beast, full of names of blasphemy, having seven heads and ten horns. (4) And the woman was clothed roundabout with purple and scarlet, and gilt with gold, and precious stones and pearls, having a golden cup in her hand, full of the abomination and filthiness of her fornications.' This," Quinn said, "is describing the ornate robes of the Papacy, the gold cup is a chalice, and her abominations," Quinn shook his head, "God only knows what they have done, besides financially aiding the rise of Hitler, providing escape of Nazi war criminals who killed the Israelite-Jews."

Quinn paused a moment - it wasn't for the conversion to Catholicism or for heresy that the Jesuits administered the Spanish Inquisition, but for the property of the wealthy; nor was it to create a Roman Catholic world that Jesuits set up WWII. But above all of these things, no one realizes - no one considers - that these acts allowed the bloodline of Satan to murder the bloodline of Eve. There were Zionist Jews who were able to escape Germany before the war started - BEFORE the war started - how did they know? And how did Zionist Silverstein know that he should *not* carry out his daily routine of going to the top of the World Trade Tower for his breakfast - on the morning of 9/11? Satan is on earth, killing the seed of Eve.

The Illuminati Jews, a/k/a the Zionists, a/k/a the Pharisees, a/k/a the Rabbis caused hatred against Semitic Israelites - whose lineage produced King David and Jesus Christ. The Zionist did it to obtain the world's consensus to turn a blind eye against the murder of Israelite-Jews. To keep countries from taking in the Israelite-Jews as their citizens. So they would have no place to go. So that the only answer was to give them their own country after WWII. Their slaughter during WWII and the Zionist's theft of their heritage, as with Ezra in 457 B.C., gave the Zionists power in the world with their own country. Franklin Roosevelt knew of the slaughter of the Israelite-Jews and did nothing to stop it, for the

Zionists-Jews were out of Germany, out of harm's way. And the Holocaust was to bring about the sympathy of the world to allow and support what they were told to give the Israelite-Jews their own country. But, in fact, Israel was carved out for the Zionist-Jews - the descendants of Japheth - NOT the descendants of Sem.

That is, to finally bring about the previous mandate of the League of Nations (whose Rev. 13:3's death wound of the beast was healed and it rose again as the United Nations). "Israel's juridical birth certificate is the pre-Holocaust League of Nations Mandate for Palestine of 1922 - based upon the pre-existing 'historical connexion of the (Israelite) Jewish people with Palestine and to the grounds for reconstituting their national home in that country.' (Mandate for Palestine, Preamble, Paragraph 3) (http://www.rosenblit.com/CREATE %20ISRAEL.html.)

After WWII, the United Nations General Assembly issued Resolution No. 181 of 1947, the Palestine Partition Plan, giving all lands west of the Jordan River to Zionist-Jews as their own state. And the world sighed relief, dismissed their guilt, for the hated Israelite-Jews left their country to inhabit their own country state.

Quinn turned next to Rev. 17:4, specifically describes the robes later adopted by the Popes - "the woman was clothed roundabout with purple and scarlet, and gilt with gold, and precious stones and pearls, having a golden cup in her hand, full of the abomination and filthiness of her fornication." This is a prophecy that identifies the popes through their purple and scarlet garments and their holding of the Eucharist golden chalice.

Rev. 17:6 - "drunk with the blood of the saints, and with the blood of the martyrs of Jesus" - this is where the Catholic Church gets its power. The world's great admiration is for the blood of the martyrs of Jesus, not for the Papal Tiara-crowned, coronated kings of the Catholic Church.

Quinn read further: Rev.17:7-8, "I will tell thee the mystery of the woman, and of the beast which carrieth her, which hath the seven heads and ten horns...The beast, which thou (you) sawest, was, and is not, and *shall come up* out of the bottomless pit, and go into destruction...." The beast in this case, Quinn knew, was Satan, not the United Nations Antichrist. Michael the Archangel defeated Satan and then locked him up in the bottomless pit, therefore, he 'was' and 'is not.' Satan - was - when he walked the earth until Michael defeated him; then Satan - is not - on earth because Michael locked him in the pit for 1000 years; and Satan will come out of the pit and do destruction. Only a woman is called a whore, but in this case, Rev. 17:2 is referring to the Pope, who sits upon Satan, and Satan has finally destroyed the Church of Jesus with Vatican II. The Popes of the Catholic Church are the False Prophets, noted in Rev. 20:10.

But Quinn noted a difference in the language between Rev. 9:1, "and there was given to him the key of the bottomless pit. (2) And he opened the bottomless pit...." This verse tells of the completion of events that stemmed from the crucifixion of Jesus when Satan was put into the pit; 1000 years had passed, and then he was released.

But in Rev. 17:7, the language is of the future; that Satan *shall* come up out of the bottomless pit. While Chapter 9 states that he is released; Chapters 9 and 17 are out of sequence.

And added to that confusion, Quinn found, is Rev. 20:1-2, "And I saw an angel coming down from heaven, having the key of the bottomless pit, and a great chain in his hand...And he laid hold on the dragon the old serpent, which is the devil and Satan, and bound him for a thousand years." Then in Rev. 20:9-10, "And there came down fire from God out of heaven, and devoured them; and the devil, who seduced them, was cast into the pool of fire and brimstone, where both the beast...And the false prophet shall be tormented day and night for ever and ever." Within Chapter 20, alone, Satan is put into the pit - and nine verses later, without being released, God cast Satan into the pool of fire and brimstone! It's as though, Quinn thought, that these verses should interweave through Ch. 9 and Ch. 17.

Rev. 17:7 tells of the future of Satan coming up from the pit. Rev. 9:11 Satan is released. Rev. 20:2 Satan is put into the pit. Rev. 20:9 Satan is cast into the fire and brimstone *for ever and ever*. The proper sequence of these chapters of Revelations should be: Rev. 20:2, Rev. 17:7, Rev. 9:11, and then Rev. 20:9.

Satan was bound into the bottomless pit just before the crucifixion of Jesus, then he was released around A.D. 1030. While he was bound, the early popes presided over councils, not countries. And the *people of Rome* voted to elect the pope; Christians in other cities elected their bishops. But in A.D. 1059, Nicholas II issued a decree at the Council in Lateran that, instead of the people of Rome, the cardinals and bishops would elect the pope (www.rosarychurch.net/answers/qa022003b.html). Then, popes became temporal rulers of the city of Rome and surrounding regions. Then, popes raised and led armies, imposed taxes, and *decided where people could live.*

In the 10th and 11th centuries, the papacy fell into one of its darkest, most disgraceful periods. The debasement resulted from the increasing secular control of the papacy and the use of its powers for political purposes. Popes became less spiritual leaders and more temporal rulers (www.bible.ca/history/eubanks/ history-eubanks-20.htm)

And when around A.D. 1030, Satan was set loose from the bottomless pit, the Christian Church split - west from east, in A.D. 1052, because the Norman rulers insisted that Greek Churches in Italy conform to Latin practices. The Patriarch of the Greek Church in Constantinople demanded that the Latin Churches in Constantinople conform to the Greek practices; when they refused, the Patriarch shut down the Latin Churches.

In A.D. 1073, Pope Gregory VII changed the Church, making it unrecognizable to the previous 1000 years of Christians. He made the Church a "legal institution" (Yves Cardinal Congar, http://crossfaith

ministry.org/papacy.htm). In the first 1000 years, the Church was in communion with ministers serving God and people. Under Pope Gregory VII, the Church became a monarchy, and the Pope became a king with power over society, (Richard P. McBrien, *Lives of the Popes: The Pontiffs from St. Peter to John Paul II*). This was the turning point of the papacy, shortly after Satan was released from the pit. Corruption now extended beyond Rome and in to Europe. In the 1500s, the Church split off, again, with the Protestant Reformation as the result of such corruption, crime, and claims of violations of basic principles of Christianity. Martin Luther argued that the Bible, not the pope, was the central means to discern God's word, and salvation was granted by faith alone (www.u-s-history.com/pages/h1136.html).

As with Ezra's Talmudic interpretation of the Hebrew Old Testament, and his interpretation allowed the sacrifice of children to the idol Moloch, the Pontifical Biblical Commission presented, "The Interpretation of the Bible in the Church," on March 18, 1994. This commission followed the dogmatic constitution created by the Second Vatican Council, along with the pontifical document, "Dei Verbum," of November 18, 1965, stating that their interpretation was the right way to understand Holy Scripture. Vatican II's ecumenical movement seeks to restore the unity of what they consider to be God's people, and that unity is based in ecumenical interpretation of Scripture. The ecumenical translations of the Bible can only be achieved by the adoption of the same method of analysis, resulting in the same interpretation of Scripture. In such ecumenical Bibles, the Vatican II interpreted word appears, not the actual word once written by Moses, Matthew, Mark, Luke, or John. Ecumenism is the unity of diversity of *all* religions (www.ewtn.com/library/CURIA/PBCINTER.HTM). It hides the truth. It blends the *Talmud* and the Pharisees with Jesus' opposing message, so that Jesus' sacrifice for the salvation of many is destroyed - with the intent that in time it would be completely forgotten, when all but the ecumenical Bibles will no longer exist.

Quinn realized that since Satan had been released from the pit, these major changes in the Catholic Church was Satan's influence and his going into destruction of the Church of Jesus. Quinn continued reading.

In Rev. 17:9-10, "the seven heads are seven mountains...and they are seven kings…Five are fallen, one is, and the other is not yet come: and when he is come, he must remain a short time."

Quinn cried out, "If this isn't a brain-teaser, I don't know what is." He researched the Popes, beginning with Pius XII, who died in 1958 - it was he who appointed Cardinal Augustin Bea, a Jesuit, as his advisor; it was Pius XII who internationalized the Roman Curia - the Curia being the administration office of the Holy See - the governing body of the Catholic Church. "This was the set up," Quinn said. "This is the first of five who have fallen - died. And the one that is, is the current Pope Benedict XVI. And the 'other is not yet come,' Quinn mumbled, "that must mean Satan has not yet been revealed - and after being revealed, 'he must remain a short time." Quinn had remembered Rev. 12:12, 'Woe to the earth...because the devil is come down unto you...he hath but a short time.' Quinn reconciled the two verses as identifying Satan as the one who only has a short time.

Pope John XXIII came next after Pius XII, and it was he who called for the Second Vatican Ecumenical Council, known as Vatican II - it was he who brought together Jesuit Cardinal Augustin Bea and Rabbi Abraham Joshua Heschel - a descendant of prominent European rabbis on both sides - a dynasty - Rabbi Heschel taught the *Talmud* - he was a professor of Jewish mysticism - or Kabbalah, which has become the mainstream Jewish theology - the true meaning of Judaism. *It was Rabbi Heschel who persuaded the Pope to eliminate or modify passages in the Roman Rite Catholic Mass, effectively destroying the rite by taking away the sacrifice of Christ*. He persuaded the Pope to no longer expect or pray to Jesus for the conversion of the Jews; and to stop blaming the Pharisees/Rabbis for demanding the crucifixion of Jesus. (www.jewishjournal.com/world/article/nostra_aetate_20051021/)

While on the cross, Luke 23:34, Jesus asked his Father to forgive the Israelites who were deceived in to following the Kenites, the Pharisees, in crying for the crucifixion of Jesus, "for they know not what they do." (www.jewishjournal.com/world/article/nostra_aetate_20051021/)

Heschel had asked the question: "Is it God's will that there be no more Judaism in the world?"

Quinn responded aloud to the question: "YES!

In Matt. 23:13-15, Quinn read the words of Jesus Christ…But woe to you scribes and Pharisees, hypocrites; because you shut the kingdom of heaven against men, for you yourselves do not enter in; and those that are going in, you suffer not to enter…Woe to you scribes and Pharisees, hypocrites: because you devour the houses of widows...For this you shall receive the greater judgment. ..Woe to you scribes and Pharisees, hypocrites; because you go round about the sea and the land to make one proselyte (convert); and when he is made, you make him the child of hell twofold more than yourselves."

"Yes," Quinn smiled, "Yes, I think God would like to end Judaism, the religion of the devil. Heschel," Quinn said, "must have been descended from the Pharisees, the non-Israelites, if he came from a dynasty of Rabbis."

Quinn grew quiet, his thumb tapping on his desk, finally he wondered aloud, "How is it that Popes John XXIII and Paul VI would allow a Zionist Rabbi to take away the continual sacrifice; the altar rails and the kneeling down on two knees to receive by mouth the Holy Eucharist - and Jesuit Cardinal Bea 'brilliantly' reconciling biblical evidence to the Vatican II Council's declaration, Nostra Aetate, that exonerated the Pharisees and Rabbis. How did these two Popes give up the religion of Christ - for a Pharisee? This Rabbi Heschel and the Jesuit

Cardinal Bea fundamentally ended the Catholic Church. They created a new religion! Just as Ezra had created Pharisaism/Judaism, Heschel created another religion - and it's not Christianity. Cardinal Bea, a Jesuit, was the confessor of Pope Pius XII, the Pope who set up Bea for the powerful position of ushering in Rabbi Heschel's demands through Vatican II Council. Bea certainly had secret knowledge of Pius' sins; did Bea use them against him? While FDR and Churchill were crafting the initial UN Charter that internationalized nations; a charter that collected the nations of the world under a centralized, consolidated government - the United Nations, it was Pius XII who was internationalizing the Papacy. Pius XII set up the destruction of the Church.

Vatican II Council created the Lumen Gentium, the Dogmatic Constitution on the Catholic Church. Lumen Gentium means 'Light of the Nations.' A Jesuit priest remarked of the Lumen Gentium: It 'deserves to be called the *most imposing achievement* of Vatican II.' Quinn read its first paragraph:

> By her relationship with Christ, the Church is a kind of sacrament or sign of intimate union with God, *and the united of all mankind. She is also an* instrument *for the achievement of such union and unity.*

In #9 of the Lumen Gentium, Quinn read:

> Christ instituted this new covenant, the new testament... in His blood, calling together a people made up of Jew and gentle, *making them one*, not according to the flesh but in the Spirit. *This was to be the new people of God.* For those who believe in Christ, who are reborn not from a perishable but from an imperishable *seed* through the word of the living God, not from the flesh but from water and the Holy Spirit, *are finally established* as a chosen race, a royal priesthood, a holy nation, a purchased people...*who in times past were not a people, but are now the people of God.*

Quinn sat back, "The language is brilliantly crafted and can only be the work of Jesuit Cardinal Augustin Bea, who also crafted the Nostra Aetate that exonerated the Pharisees/Rabbis. But, still, this is another way of admitting that Cain was fathered by Satan and Adam was created by God - and that it was Adam that God created to be the patriarch of His Chosen people. The Zionists are not from Adam's bloodline - so they want people to stop thinking about the Satanic bloodline. Ignore it; bury it somewhere in the past as a myth by changing the words of Moses and Jesus Christ. The Vatican will tell us how to think, how to read and interpret - and will take away all references of original text that we might interpret ourselves. Vatican II changed the words of Jesus Christ and instituted a different meaning altogether. This is the Satanic hand of Rabbi Heschel in Vatican II Council! They are erasing the distinction between God's lineage - the Israelites - and the Satanic bloodline of the Pharisees, the Rabbis, the Zionists-Jews, and 'making them one.'

In Babylon, Ezra stole the identity and heritage of the Israelites of the Kingdom of Judah. Rabbi Heschel has done the same thing, destroying the identity of separate bloodlines. Only Adam's bloodline are God's Chosen People. And Heschel's demand: let's forget that God created Adam as His Chosen patriarch and let's just DECLARE that there is a NEW Chosen People - which includes US, the SEEDS of Satan!"

Quinn turned back to Matt. 22:14, when Jesus told the parable of the marriage feast: "'For *many* are called, but *few are chosen*.' This counters what the Lumen Gentium is saying here: ALL are called - and this is why they changed the words of the liturgy - to now falsely quote Jesus at the Last Supper; changing His words from 'shed for many' to 'shed for all' - the change intentionally disguises their Satanic bloodline!" Quinn muttered to himself. "This is why they did it! This is exactly what they were talking about when they said that Rabbi Heschel demanded changes to the Roman Catholic Liturgy. 'To modify passages in its liturgy that demean Jews.' That can only mean: demean the Pharisees by not including them in the sacrifice. But Jesus did not include them in His sacrifice for the remission of sins. Jesus sacrificed for the Israelite Jews and those of Satan's bloodline who believed in Jesus. In Matt. 18:1-4, when the disciples asked Jesus, who do you think is the greater in the kingdom of heaven, and Jesus answered: "unless you be converted, and become as little children, you shall not enter into the kingdom of heaven... *Whosoever* therefore shall humble himself as this little child, he is the greater in the kingdom of heaven."

But the Pharisees and the Rabbis did not believe in Jesus. And the Zionist Jews, the Rabbis, and Rabbi Heschel still do not believe that Jesus is the Son of the God of Abraham. Nothing has changed! By Vatican II's changes in the liturgy, today's Zionist Jews are told that they should NOT convert to believe in Jesus as the Son of God - and for Catholics to pray for such conversion to Jesus is "demeaning" to the Zionist Jews. The Pharisees/Rabbis, as in Heschel, still suffer the people not to enter the Kingdom of Heaven, as in Matt. 23:13: "But woe to you scribes and Pharisees, hypocrites; because you shut the kingdom of heaven against men, for you yourselves do not enter in; and those that are going in, you suffer not to enter.

But Jesus came, as stated in Matt. 15:24, "I was not sent but (only) to the sheep that are lost of the house of Israel," God's Chosen People. Jesus was also sent to convert such people as the woman of Canaan, a descendant of Ham, of the bloodline of Satan, (Gen 10:6). Jesus cured the woman's daughter, Matt. 15:28, "O woman, great is thy (your) faith: be it done to thee (you) as thou (your) wilt (will): and her daughter was cured from that hour."

Quinn realized that to Jesus, bloodline didn't matter, only the faith that Jesus is the Son of God.

And Quinn read that Jesus told the Pharisees, "For I came not to call the just, but sinners," Mark 2:17. Quinn mumbled to himself, "And regardless of bloodline, we are all sinners."

Before Satan was put into the pit, Ezra, father of the Pharisees, stole the Israelite identity to take control of the Israelites, so he could destroy their faith in the God of Abraham and force his new religion on them. God's only Chosen People were the Israelites, but Ezra was not an Israelite. His theft was the work of his Satanic bloodline. And the Pharisees couldn't see, refused to see, that Jesus was the Son of God because they were not of God - Heschel is not of God, either! So why would Jesus sacrifice Himself on the cross to save the evil Pharisees; they hated Him; they denied Him as the Son of God; they destroyed His Body. And Heschel and Jesuit Cardinal Bea destroyed the Sacrifice of Jesus with Vatican II. Heschel tried to destroy others' faith in Jesus.

Quinn yelled at his computer screen, as his rage boiled over from their attempt at deception that was so blatantly satanic, "Through Vatican II Council, Heschel demanded and Jesuit Cardinal Bea responded by convincing the Council to agree that the Zionist Jews and Gentiles are the NEW Chosen People of God - because THE PHARISEES/RABBIS WERE NEVER THE CHOSEN PEOPLE OF GOD! They are BURYING GOD'S ADAMIC BLOODLINE!"

Quinn turned back to the Lumen Gentium, promulgated by Pope Paul VI and voted on by all the Bishops of Vatican II Council, paragraph 22:

> The order of bishops is the successor to the college of the apostles in their role as teachers and pastors....Together with their head, the Supreme Pontiff...*they have supreme and full authority over the universal Church*...that the office of binding and loosing which was given to Peter, was also assigned to the college of Apostles united to its head.

Quinn knew that this was absolutely counter to the words of Jesus, as to be totally dismissive of Him. He looked again at the Bible, Matt. 16:17-19, where Jesus said, "Blessed art thou, Simon Bar-Jona: because flesh and blood hath not revealed it to thee, but my Father who is in heaven…And I say to thee: That thou art Peter; and upon this rock I will build my church, and the gates of hell shall not prevail against it…And *I will give to thee* the keys of the kingdom of heaven. And whatsoever *thou* (you) shalt bind upon earth, it shall be bound also in heaven...." Quinn reasoned to himself, the other Apostles were right there with Simon Peter and *Jesus gave nothing of authority or power share of His Church to those other Apostles* - only to Peter.

This can't be more clearly stated than with the dialogue between Jesus and the Apostles - and there was a purpose to that dialogue. There was a reason Jesus gave authority to ONLY Peter: Matt. 16:15-18:

> Jesus saith to them (Apostles): But whom do you say that I am?...Simon Peter answered and said: Thou art

Christ, the Son of the living God... And Jesus answering, said to him: *Blessed art thou*, Simon Bar-Jona: because flesh and blood hath not revealed it to thee, *but my Father who is in heaven...*And *I say to thee*: That thou art Peter; and upon this rock I will build my church.

"The purpose of that dialogue," Quinn said, "was to show that Jesus gave only to Simon Peter the authority of His church - and no one else! The Vatican II Council threw out the Church of Jesus Christ!"

Quinn thought for a moment, "The Lumen Gentium is a manipulation of the words of Jesus Christ. It changes the very power structure of Jesus' Church that Jesus Himself instituted. Vatican II created their own Church! Or, at least, they instituted chaos in the Catholic Church. Satan's influence, a step toward breaking up the Church of Jesus with all the Bishops laying down their own laws of administration all over the world."

Quinn searched for the Homily of Pope Paul VI, the Ninth Anniversary of the Coronation of His Holiness, Homily of Paul VI, Solemnity of Saints Peter and Paul, Thursday, June 29, 1972:

> (Referring to the situation of the Church today, after Vatican II)...'*from some fissure the smoke of Satan has entered the temple of God*....No one trusts the Church...(Satan) entered the doubts of our minds, and came to the windows who were to be opened to light....It was believed that after the (Vatican II) Council there would be a sunny day in the history of the Church. It came instead, of clouds, storm, darkness, research, uncertainty...His name is the devil, this mysterious being which also makes allusion in the Epistle of St. Peter.'

(http://www.vatican.va/holy_father/paul_vi/homilies/1972/documents/hf_p_vi_hom_19720629_it.html)

Quinn mumbled aloud, "It sounds as though Pope Paul VI had a change of heart. Wishing he didn't vote for collegiality, sharing his Papal power with the Bishops. Now, I remember reading the book by Karol Wojtyla, Pope John Paul II, *Alle fonti del Rinovamento*, who was at the First Session of Vatican II under John XXIII, he wrote: 'The principle of collegiality (Bishops sharing authority with the Pope) demonstrates the principle of the primacy (foremost in rank) in that both come forth from the institution of Christ.'"

Quinn sat back in his chair and thought aloud for a moment, "This is an outright lie! If the Pope is the figurehead rather than the boss of a group of Bishops, he cannot act alone, but only with the approval of the Bishops, who can gang up against him and vote against his decree - and that is not what Jesus said to Simon Peter. The Apostles were right there; Jesus did not make them equal partners in power or authority over the Church. Jesus said nothing to them! He gave all authority; He gave the keys ONLY to Peter! That was the point of Jesus' question to all the Apostles, 'who do you say that I am' - because Jesus knew that God the Father would choose who was to head His Church - and put the answer into that Apostle's mouth - that selection was evident by Simon Peter's answer. Simon Peter was the only Apostle who gave the answer, hence, only he was given the authority in the Church. Otherwise, all the Apostles would have said something to the same effect. The singular gift of authority to Peter was signified by the keys - only Peter was given the keys to the Kingdom of Heaven! The Vatican II shitheads even admit that it "was given to Peter." And not one of the Apostles - who were there and witnessed what Jesus had said to all of them and wrote down what He said - and they did not write that they "*also*" were assigned the "supreme and full authority."

Vatican II and John Paul II are liars! They were under the influence of Satan!"

Quinn found John Paul II's *Redemptor Hominis*: "We are...dealing with the...real, "concrete," "historical" man. We are dealing with "each" man...Every man comes into this world through...his mother's womb and being born of his mother, and precisely on account of the mystery of the Redemption is entrusted to the solitude of the Church...The object of her care is man in his unique unrepeatable human reality, which keeps intact the image and likeness of God himself. The (Vatican II) Council points out this very fact when speaking of that likeness, it recalls that "man is the only creature on earth that God willed for itself. Man is "willed" by God, as "chosen" by him from eternity and called, destined for grace and glory - this is "each" man, "the most concrete" man, the "the most real"; this is man in all the fullness of the mystery in which he has become a sharer in Jesus Christ, the mystery in which each one of the...human beings living on our planet has become a sharer from the moment he is conceived beneath the heart of his mother." (www.vatican.va/holy_father/john_paul_ii/encyclicals/documents/hf_jp-ii_enc_04031979_redemptor_hominis_en.html)

"This is such bullshit!," Quinn cried out. "I don't think John Paul II understood Matt. 26:28, 'my blood of the new testament, which shall be shed *for many* unto remission of sins.' The 'for many' is NOT every human conceived beneath the heart of his mother.' The language is seducing - beneath the heart of his mother - what romantic, manipulative bullshit! John Paul II used loaded words, heart and mother, to seduce the world in to believing that everyone is from the same parents - they are not! Some were fathered by Satan. John Paul II was part of the cover up!"

Quinn noted that only the mother was spoken of, not the father - no one gets into this world without having a father, either! And why all the quoted references of the real concrete man, the historical man, and each man?

Quinn paused a moment, "I think he's referring to the Garden of Eden - the historical man! He's obliterating any thought that Satan fathered

Cain in the Garden of Eden. He's covering up Satan's bloodline! They are shrouding the idea that Jesus died to redeem "many" not their claimed "all" - they are claiming mystery of redemption when there is none. There's no mystery about Jesus sacrificing Himself for the remission of sins for the many. Quinn shook his head in disgust. Here was the Pope aiding and abetting in the destruction of Jesus and His church.

Quinn continued on to analyze Rev. 17:9-10, "the seven heads are seven mountains...and they are seven kings…Five are fallen, one is, and the other is not yet come: and when he is come, he must remain a short time."

"Yes," Quinn mumbled, "Gregory VII made the papacy a monarchy - its head would be a king. This is definitely talking about the papacy - the False Prophet!" He continued to analyze.

"Number two of the prophesized 'fallen five' was Pope John XXIII. In his last Encyclical, he clearly exposed himself to be a communist, therefore, an atheist: '(7) Men's common interests make it imperative that, at long last, a world-wide community of nations be established.....(11) But first we must speak of man's rights. Man has the right...to...food, clothing, shelter, medical care, rest...social services....right to be looked after in... disability...old age....(13)...natural right to share in the benefits of culture...a good general education...a system must be devised for affording gifted members of society the opportunity of engaging in more advanced studies with a view to their occupying... positions of responsibility....(22)...the right to own property entails a social obligation as well....(25)...when there are just reasons in favor of it, (a man) must be permitted to emigrate to other countries and take up residence there. The fact that he is a citizen of a particular State does not deprive him of membership in the human family, nor of citizenship in that universal society, the common world-wide fellowship of men....(35)...[man must be] animated [to inspire to action] by such love [manipulation] as will make them feel the needs of others as their own, and *induce* [persuaded] them *to share their goods with others*....(53)... men...*must harmonize* their own interests with the needs of others, *and offer their goods and services as their rulers shall direct*....(54) The attainment of the common good is the sole reason for the existence of civil authorities...therefore, the authorities must...*adjust their legislation to meet the requirements of the given situation*....(63)...most exalted task...to bring about true peace in accordance with divinely established order. We must include the *task of establishing new relationships* in human society, under the mastery and guidance...between individuals, families...." (www.vatican.va/holy_father/john_xxiii/encyclicals/documents/hf_j-xxiii_enc_11041963_pacem_en .html)

Quinn remembered the dictionary definition of Communism: "Economic system with collective ownership of property and the organization of labor working for the common good."

Quinn murmured to himself, "This is why children must now

volunteer their service before receiving Confirmation in the Catholic Church - to get them used to sharing their hard-earned efforts with others. The purpose is to institute a mindset in these children; the mindset of slavery. And the U.S. Congress passed the Americorp Act, sec. 120, which *mandates* 'volunteerism' from every socio-economic group in the United States. In 2009, Tsaeb sent home applications to high school students in Ohio, getting them to sign up to 'volunteer,' and one venue in which they could volunteer and meet their legislated mandate would be on Tsaeb's own presidential campaign. The new relationships of families is straight out of the UN's Agenda 21."

Quinn wondered if this Pope John XXIII was the Antichrist of his day - 1958-1963. "He published this garbage two months before his death, and ironically called it: 'Peace on Earth.' He was ready willing and able to work with Heschel, but he died, on April 11, 1963, after the First Session of Vatican II. Pope Paul VI followed and recalled the Council and finished Vatican II and the destruction of the Catholic Church."

After Pope Paul VI, came Pope John Paul I. "He was the one who visited with one of the girls who saw the vision of the Lady of Fatima, and came away saying that he would implement the consecration of Russia - but they murdered him before he could. They poisoned him after 33 days of his becoming pope."

Quinn continued, "Then came Pope John Paul II. He sat in on the First Session of Vatican II when it first opened under Pope John XXIII. After the Vatican II Council passed, in 1965, John Paul II implemented its mandates. John XXIII and Paul VI changed the Church by softening the monarchy of the church, allowing the power sharing of collegiality on every level - and changed Christianity to Zionist Satanic worship, reaching out to bring in other religions. That's why Jesuit Cardinal Bea invited and allowed participation in Vatican II of more than 2000 religious observers - sucking them into being controlled by the Vatican."

Quinn looked at Rev. 17:9-10, again, "And here is the understanding that hath wisdom. The seven heads are seven mountains, upon which the woman sitteth, and they are seven kings…Five are fallen...." Quinn talked out his analysis: If it began with Pius XII, John XXIII, Paul VI, and I'm not going to count John Paul I, because they murdered him - how did he get elected, anyway? Then there was John Paul II, and now Benedict XVI. But if I count all of them - as an identification of the kings - then there are six kings, five have fallen - died, and one is. And one is to come."

Quinn mumbled, "All the popes refer to the Church as "her" - the Catholic Church is the woman sitting on the mountain - which are seven kings - the popes from the time of Vatican II!

Quinn paused, "That would mean that Benedict XVI, who is 83, who has had a stroke and is on heart medications, will soon be replaced by the 'one is to come.' If Revelations is only counting these seven kings - and the Papacy is a monarchy, therefore these are kings, it would indicate the Battle of Armageddon will take place during the reign of the next pope."

What Quinn read next troubled him, Rev. 17:11, "And the beast which was, and is not: the same also is the eighth, and is of the seven, and goeth into destruction." Quinn thought a moment, "'the same also is the eighth,' what could that mean?" He couldn't help wonder why Revelations was written with such codes, puzzles. Was it encoded so they would publish it, and Apostle John, its author hoped that someday someone would figure it out? This verse could mean anything. The beast which was and is not is clearly Satan, but 'the same also is the eighth' - could that mean that the next pope will be Satan, or that the Black Pope - who is of the seven by being popularly identified as a pope - that he's Satan? He is among us, but hidden. But so is the next pope, he just hasn't been elected yet. Whoever he is - he goes 'into destruction.'"

It is after that, in Rev. 17:12, Quinn found, that the 'ten kings, who have not yet received a kingdom, but shall receive power as kings one hour after the beast.' These," Quinn reckoned, "are the ten kings that we don't know who they are. These kings are separate from the kings of which 'five have fallen, one is, and the other is not yet come.' Those kings were represented by seven heads. In this verse 12, those kings are represented by 'ten horns' - they are a separate group who are given power 'one hour after the beast.' Rev. 17:13, 'These have one design: and their strength and power they shall deliver to the beast.'"

Quinn tapped his thumb on his desk, again. "I wonder if they are the presidents of the unions...that could be it...the UN has a plan to section off the continents, a Roman Empire-type layering of power, controlling the world under the United Nations Secretary General, the Antichrist.

Quinn researched the list and found that the proposed continental unions are: 1. Asia Cooperation Dialogue; 2. Association of Southeast Asian Nations; 3. Central American Integration System; 4. Central Asian Union; 5. North American Union; 6. Pacific Union; 7. Organization of Eastern Caribbean States; 8. Arab Union; 9. European Union; 10. Community of Latin American and Caribbean States. Each of those unions would require a president - a king. The European Union is the first to have a president - Jose Manuel Durao Burroso, President of European Commission Union for Peace, Prosperity, and Partnership.

Quinn quickly remembered that U.S. President George Wake Schirf signed an amendment to the North American Free Trade Agreement called Security and Prosperity Partnership, SPP. It institutes new regulations that so far are secret. The documents were signed by the leaders of the United States, Canada, and Mexico, joining the three countries together with laws written by a handful of representatives from those three countries - sitting behind closed doors in the Dept. of the Treasury. They are creating new courts from which no one can appeal, effectively eliminating the U.S. Supreme Court. The three countries are being merged without U.S. legislative bodies involved. By attaching the

SPP agreement as an amendment to the NAFTA treaty that our Congress already approved, therefore, Pres. Schirf claimed, he didn't need to go through Congress to change our laws.

On the provincial government website of Manitoba, Canada, Quinn found: Manitoba...a key part of the Mid-Continent Trade Corridor, connecting Canada to a Central North American market of 100 million people. And in a press conference in January 2010, Canadian Prime Minister Stephen Harper officially announced the creation of Canada's inland port and transportation corridor that will serve as its trade hub for the NAFTA Superhighway project. Harper described the system: a four-lane divided, high speed transportation corridor.

Quinn also found a statement by Mexican Vicente Fox: he sought a convergence of U.S. and Mexico, 'a convergence of our two economies ...on the basic and fundamental variable of the economy... convergence on income of people, convergence on salaries.'" Quinn mumbled to himself, "This is why so many Americans are being put out of their jobs - to destroy the middle class to bring it down to the level of Mexico's citizens, a third world country.

Quinn searched more and found that U.S. President Tsaeb and Canadian PM Harper will finalize the establishment of a common security perimeter, or New Border Vision, that began with President George Wake Schirf's signing of the Security and Prosperity Partnership. Tsaeb and Harper will do this in 'the Fall of 2011.'

Quinn didn't bother to look further as to the status of the completion of the other continental unions. It seemed that if they take control of the most difficult union, the North American Union, that they could easily force the others to fall in to line in quick succession.

These unions will have presidents, 10 kings of 10 country-unions, Rev. 17:13, 'and their strength and power they shall deliver to the beast.' These kings are part of the hierarchy of Satan's control of the world. So, does this mean that Satan will sit on the throne of the papacy or the United Nations?

It suddenly dawned on Quinn that the fighting in Libya, Egypt, Yemen, Jordan, Syria - this is not for independence - it's to collect these countries in to the Arab Union! "The fighting that we are witnessing is Biblical prophecy occurring before our eyes!"

And according to Revelations, 17:12, these kings will 'receive power as kings one hour after the beast.' If Tsaeb is going to finalize the Security and Prosperity Partnership this Fall 2011, that means that Satan will be revealed sometime thereafter, but before they appoint a president of the North American Union. How soon is anyone's guess. The European Union had been established and working a number of years prior to the instituting of the position of President of the European Union Commission. But that was a trial test, I think we can assume that they will use that paradigm to institute presidents of these unions within the next year. And they are working furiously to take down all those Arab nations; some fell quickly.

Quinn sighed, "It would seem that we have awhile to go, perhaps. If Tsaeb has already moved forward with the finalizing of the North American Union's Security and Prosperity Partnership Amendment, will he become a king over Canada, U.S., and Mexico in the November 2012 election? Will they suddenly announce it to the world? Will Tsaeb suddenly announce that the United States has been completely taken over by the United Nations? Or will Yoon Won-Shik, the Secretary General of the U.N. make the announcement?

Quinn looked further at Revelations, as it referred to the ten kings. Rev. 17:14, "These shall fight with the Lamb, and the Lamb shall overcome them, because he is Lord of lords, and King of kings, and they that are with him are called, and elect, and faithful."

"Shit!" Quinn mumbled, "The country-union kings/presidents are going to use all the militaries of the world against Jesus Christ - against the Christians of the world! This isn't going to be just the United States under attack by some NATO force, or a million terrorists pouring over our borders."

In Rev. 17:15, Quinn read, "'And he said to me: The waters which thou sawest, where the harlot sitteth, are peoples, and nations, and tongues.' This must be talking about the Mediterranean Sea - all the different nations, peoples, of those countries that border Rome, Italy."

In Rev. 17:16, he read, "'And the ten horns which thou sawest in the beast: these shall hate the harlot, and shall make her desolate and naked, and shall eat her flesh, and shall burn her with fire.' These are the kings/presidents of the country-unions, who hate the harlot - the Catholic Church. These kings, presidents, are going to destroy the Catholic Church. That would seem a reasonable next step, since they have already given the Vatican over to Satan."

In Rev. 17:17, Quinn read, "'For God hath given into their hearts to do that which pleaseth him: that they give their kingdom to the beast, till the words of God be fulfilled.' The Zionists, the Muslims, the Popes, the ten kings of the country-unions - they are the ones referred to here. They are the ones doing what pleases "him," and him means Satan. They are all giving the world to Satan."

In Rev. 17:18, Quinn read, "And the woman which thou sawest, is the great city, which hath kingdom over the kings of the earth."

"Now this is interesting," Quinn said, "If verse 17 says that the Vatican will be burned, who is *this* woman, 'the great city, which hath kingdom over the kings of the earth'?"

Quinn did more research and found that the United Nations complex of four buildings: the Secretariat, General Assembly, Conference Building, and the Dag Hammarskjold Library, along with a small park, sits on 18 acres of land donated to the UN by the Rockefeller family - *has been officially converted to <u>international</u> territory* - it does not belong to the United States." Quinn yelled, "It's a fucking sovereign city state! The UN has its own laws, its own courts! The woman of verse 18 is a different woman than the previous verses. She cannot be the Vatican, the Catholic Church, because the Vatican doesn't have kingdom over the kings of the earth! But! The United Nations does! The great city that has kingdom over the kings of the earth is the United Nations!"

"Shit!" Quinn mumbled to himself after reading Rev. 18:6, 'Render to her as she also hath rendered to you...(7) As much as she hath glorified herself...so much torment and sorrow give yet to her...(8) Therefore shall her plagues come in one day, death, and mourning, and famine, and she shall be burnt with the fire; because God is strong, who shall judge her.' This is telling the reader to destroy the United Nations! And the UN Building complex will burn in one day! This has to be at the hands of Americans revolting!"

Quinn continued to read, Rev. 18:9, "'And the kings of the earth, who have committed fornication, and lived in delicacies with her, shall weep, and bewail themselves over her, when they shall see the smoke of her burning: (10) Standing afar off for fear of her torments, saying: Alas! alas! that great city Babylon, that mighty city: for in one hour is thy judgment come.'"

But Quinn became confused, the verses following seem to describe the Vatican, Rev. 18:16, "'that great city, which was clothed with fine linen, and purple, and scarlet, and was gilt with gold, and precious stones, and pearls.' It seems to be describing the vestments, historical treasures of the Vatican. And in Rev. 18:18, 'what city is like to this great city?'" Quinn shook his head - nothing is like either Vatican city or the United Nations city! But one is the center of spirituality and the other of administration, to the world."

Quinn found that Rev. 18:23 was the most confusing, 'And the light of the lamp shall shine no more at all in thee; and the voice of the bridegroom and the bride shall be heard no more at all in thee: for thy merchants were the great men of the earth, for all nations have been deceived by thy enchantments.'"

Quinn thought out the words: "The voice of the bridegroom and the bride indicate the popes, the Church. It would seem that the Vatican will also be attacked, burned, and prayers will be silenced. In Matt. 9:15, Jesus referred to Himself as the bridegroom: 'Can the children of the bridegroom mourn, as long as the bridegroom is with them? But the days will come, when the bridegroom shall be taken away from them, and then they shall fast." Jesus' words were once read by the popes, but their voices and Jesus' words shall be heard no more! But 'All nations have been deceived' - that indicates the United Nations.

Quinn sat back in his chair, wondering aloud, "Is this conflation of description indicating that the Vatican and the United Nations are one in the same power? Or does the Vatican indicate the False Prophet and the United Nations indicate the Antichrist?

In Rev. 18:24, 'And in her was found the blood of prophets and of saints, and of all that were slain upon the earth.' That one sentence describes both the Vatican and the United Nations! They both rose in power on the murder of prophets and saints, with the United Nations' acts of murder having spread further across the earth. There definitely looks as though the Vatican and the United Nations are the two entities that must be destroyed - that will be destroyed. And only then will there be the salvation of Rev. 19:2, 'For true and just are his judgments, who hath judged the great harlot which corrupted the earth with her fornication, and hath revenged the blood of His servants, at her hands. (3) And again they said: Alleluia. And her smoke ascendeth for ever and ever.'"

Quinn sighed pensively, "The Vatican is the throne of the False Prophet, and the United Nations is the vehicle that the Antichrist uses to control the earth. They are extensions of each other. Both are necessary for Satan to rule the earth - his desire since the Garden of Eden! The Church of Jesus must be destroyed for Him to rule without hindrance."

Quinn moved on and continued his search of Satan's bloodline. In Gen. 2:7, he found the descriptive of God creating Adam, "And the Lord God formed man of the slime of the earth: and breathed into his face the breath of life, and man became a living soul." Quinn noted that when God created the first humans, Gen. 1:26, God did not breathe life into "male and female" before He sent them out into the world. Did that mean that they did not have souls? Were these the Homo genus Neanderthals? Does it mean that these soulless people would become part of Satan's lineage, interbreeding with Cain after God sent him out of Haran - when Cain went east of Eden?

Quinn got up and went to the kitchen and got a beer and returned to his office and sat back down at his desk, talking aloud as he wrote, "If you consider Abraham lived about 5000 years ago, or 3000 BC. And Abraham came 20 generations after Adam and Eve, counting both Adam and Abraham. And if we accept the Biblical ages of those men back then when they became fathers," Quinn added up the ages of the 20 generations, "There are 1764 years covering those 20 generations to Abraham's birth.'

Quinn pursued, "Noah was 10 generations descended from Adam. He would be able to remember oral teaching of his ancestors. After surviving the flood, he probably thought it a good idea to write down the events. Answer the why of the flood. If nothing else to memorialize his ancestors as part of the earth that was erased. It was so catastrophic that someone had to have thought to write this stuff down and record the generations leading up to the flood. If not Noah, maybe one of his children or their household."

Quinn took a sip of his beer and lit up a cigarette. He decided to read the why of the flood; he found it in Genesis 6:5: "God saw the wickedness of the human race and ever inclination of thoughts of the human heart was only evil all the time." Quinn wondered, who was the human race at that time. There were those God created first, those of Adam and Eve's descendants, and those of Cain's descendants; they were the humankind that God saw as wicked. Quinn wondered, also, of the Satanic influence of that evil. The Y-chromosome carried down through his son, Cain. How much intermarriage took place? Did the interbreeding of these three groups signify hybrids among humans? It suddenly hit Quinn, "One must be born of the Holy Ghost to be saved. If the Neanderthals didn't have souls and they intermarried with Cain's descendants - did they have any soul at all - would they need to be baptized of the Holy Ghost?"

Quinn read on: "God regretted that He made human beings on earth…I will wipe them from the face of the earth…that I have created…for I regret that I have made them."

Things had to have been very bad, Quinn thought, look what's going on today and we still exist! But in the re-reading it seemed that God meant the witnesses, too; those that he made before Adam and Eve, for they were destroyed, also. Along with Noah's extended family. Only Noah was saved; only a direct descendant of Adam. But what of his three sons, Sem, Ham, Japheth, and their wives - did one of their wives descend from Eve? What happened to Cain and his descendants? According to scripture, they all would have been killed in the flood. If all had been wiped out except Noah, a descendant from Adam, and Noah only had sons then Eve's mtDNA stopped with those three sons.

"How does this compute with Maggie's research that only mothers can pass on Eve's mtDNA?" Quinn wondered how he could construe all these facts to prove that Maggie was right. He looked at the total of ages, 1764 years account for 20 generations from Adam to Abraham's birth, and added that to Abraham living 5000 years ago and Quinn found that Adam and Eve were created 6764 years ago, or 4764 BC. I'll accept that as a given, Quinn thought.

Now, how does Satan's Y-chromosome and Eve's mtDNA survive the flood if only Noah, his wife, their three sons and their wives are on the Ark? Quinn turned to the Bible, again. He couldn't find any evidence of the lineage of the wives of Noah's sons. He did find in Genesis 3:20 that Eve would become the mother of all the living, and he knew that today's scientific findings support the Bible. Quinn mumbled to himself, "That is consistent with God wiping out all mankind with a flood, even those he created before creating Adam and Eve in the Garden of Eden. They were all killed in the flood. But he had also read that Neanderthal genes were in some populations of today. That would be consistent of Cain marrying Neanderthal women when he went east of Eden."

He pursued, looking for supporting evidence of that statement. He found Genesis 5:4. After Seth was born, Adam lived 800 years and had other sons and DAUGHTERS. Quinn continued to read down through Adam's descendants, Genesis 5:7-30, and each generation had daughters. That is, until Noah; Noah only had the three sons. That's strange, why only three children?

Quinn took another sip of beer and lit another cigarette. He had to solve the problem of Satan's bloodline. Quinn reasoned, Adam and Eve started in the Garden of Eden - in Turkey; they were expelled from the Garden and went to nearby Haran - in Turkey - sounds reasonable that they didn't see other humans than their own family, therefore, the sons and daughters of Adam and Eve intermarried. The first humans that God made before Adam and Eve in the Garden of Eden had to have been the Homo Neanderthals, who Cain feared when God "cast me out...every one, therefore, that findeth me, shall kill me." (Gen.4:14) This is telling that Adam and Eve lived apart from the Neanderthals who were outside Haran, Turkey. Therefore, Adam and Eve and their descendants did not interbreed with the Neanderthals. If Neanderthal DNA is in some populations of European and Asian populations, today, that means they came through Japheth, allegedly Noah's third son. This could mean that they did interbreed with Cain before the Great Flood. Cain was part serpent, part homo sapien, and married Neanderthals, Quinn concluded.

He hypothesized, "Ok. This is how it went down: Cain went out of Haran, east of Eden, therefore, towards the Tigris River that flowed out of the Garden of Eden. He took the Tigris down to Eridu in southern Iraq, bringing with him the culture and technology of Adam and Eve, and he interbred with Neanderthals. And they worshipped him as a god, and he built the first city of the world, Eridu. To build a city implies a large population would use it. No other people existed except those from the Garden of Eden and the first humans, Homo Neanderthals. If today's scientists are finding Neanderthal DNA in some populations, it means that Cain's descendants survived the Ark. And if Neanderthal DNA is found in Asian and European bloodlines - they came through Japheth. It also means that Japheth was not Noah's son, since the descendants of Adam and Eve lived apart from the Neanderthals!"

Quinn continued on, thinking to himself, if there was Adam, Seth,... eventually, Noah. Likely, there was Adam, daughter,...eventually, wife of Noah. They all lived for centuries in the same area of Turkey, therefore, interbreeding throughout the Adam and Eve lineage for 10 generations, down to Noah. That would put Eve's mtDNA on the Ark. What about Satan's Y-chromosome? How did that get onto the Ark? Quinn wanted more than Neanderthal DNA to prove that Satan's Y-chromosome came through the Ark.

He looked at the sons of Noah; scripture talks about their fathering nations. Down through Noah's son, Sem, came Abraham, Genesis 11:10. Quinn decided to hold out Sem as carrying Adam's Y-chromosome and Sem's wife, Eve's mtDNA, and passing them along to Abraham's son, Isaac, whose son was Jacob renamed Israel, and Israel's 12 sons fathering the Twelve Tribes of Israel, the Israelites.

Quinn came up against another stonewall, Abraham only had sons, Ishmael and Isaac. Both Ishmael and Isaac should have received Abraham's Y-chromosome, intact. Quinn mumbled a swear under his breath, "Only the first born son is listed!" Quinn sighed, "I can only assume that one of Noah's daughters-in-law, or Abraham's daughters-in-law carried the Eve mtDNA. Shit! Damn assumptions! So easy to dismiss, but they could be right."

Quinn asked, again, in frustration, "How did Satan's Y-chromosome get onto the Ark! If I can't figure that out, the whole argument of Satan's bloodline existing today, fails." He carefully read Adam's direct line down to Noah. The lineage says that Noah carried Adam's Y-chromosome. Done.

Noah had three sons. Quinn thought it strange that while the scripture gives more detail to each descendant, it only states that Noah fathered Sem, Ham, and Japheth. "Hmmm," Quinn mumbled. "This is far less information than any of the other preceding descendants, including Adam. Are they hiding anything here? Were the sons triplets and the reason that they recorded all three names? Could it have been another Garden situation - Noah impregnated his wife, but that she was seduced or raped within a day and impregnated with Ham and Japheth? Did the rape keep Noah from knowing his wife ever again and having more children? He lived another 350 years after the flood - he had to have been healthy enough for sex. Nothing is said of his wife dying. But if one were to consider that Noah's wife had evil sex with a descendant of Satan, whether forced or willing - men rejected their wives after intercourse with another man. It wouldn't matter if the man beat the living hell out of the woman, only that she had intercourse - even today men will reject their wives after they've been raped by a psychopath. Is this what happened? Did Noah reject her and that's why he only had three sons and no other children?

Quinn sat back and thought for a moment. Finally, he mumbled aloud to himself, "What if, in the place where Cain settled outside Haran, Eridu in southern Iraq, that Cain married two of those first-created humans; maybe a Black and an Asian woman. Let's assume he did. Let's assume that two descendants of Cain, of the tenth generation visited the old homestead, Haran, and found Noah and his wife and son, Sem. There was enough evil in the world that God brought on a Great Flood. How farfetched would it be to assume that that evil came into the house of Noah. If those descendants of Satan's bloodline raped Noah's wife and she was impregnated with fraternal twins, one part Black and one part Asian, then Ham and Japheth would carry those Y-chromosomes of Satan down through Cain. That would put three races into the world after the Flood. That makes genetic sense rather than saying that Noah fathered three genetically-different races; a physical impossibility.

Now, if God's plan is to test who we choose, Jesus or Satan, and God allowed Satan in the Garden, God could also let Satan in the house of Noah. It brings good and evil into the world, which would be necessary for the test. It would be necessary to set the battlefield for God and Satan to fight for our souls.

Quinn read further that after the Flood, Noah was asleep from the wine of the vineyard he grew. Ham saw his father naked and went out of the tent and told his brothers, Sem and Japheth. For one thing, Quinn reasoned, it meant that Noah and his family lived together in Turkey where the Ark settled, at least long enough to grow those vines, ferment the grapes.

Sem and Japheth held a blanket over their shoulders and backed into the tent, dropping the blanket onto Noah to cover him without seeing him naked. In Genesis 9:24, Quinn read: "And Noe awaking from the wine, when he had learned what his younger son had done *TO* him," (25) He said: Cursed be Chanaan, a servant of servants shall he be unto his brethren. (26) And he said: Blessed be the Lord God of Sem, be Chanaan his servant. (27) May God enlarge Japheth, and may he dwell in the tents of Sem, and Chanaan be his servant."

What caught Quinn's eye was that Noah blessed ONLY Sem's God, not the God of Ham or Japheth, as though they had different gods because they were from a different father. As though Noah knew Sem was his son, and that Sem's God was Noah's God. It also caught Quinn's attention: "when he (Noah) had learned what his YOUNGER SON had done TO him." Noah's youngest son was Japheth, Gen. 5:31, "And Noe...begot Sem, Ham, and Japheth." Or could 'younger son' mean grandson? Or could 'young*er*' son have meant Ham, while Japheth was Noah's young*est* son. Quinn finally cried out, "This is so maddening!"

But it nagged at Quinn, it was Sem and Japheth who covered Noah, so they did not commit a sin. If Ham raped Noah, did Noah curse his son, Chanaan, to make it more painful for Ham? Why didn't he curse Ham? Why curse Ham's son? It doesn't say that Ham undressed Noah. Gen. 9:22, "Which when Ham the father of Chanaan had seen...his father's nakedness was uncovered, he told it to his two brethren without.' It's saying Ham saw. He didn't undress Noah. He watched.

He had read that Chanaan was a blood drinker and a cannibal, if he could do that, was sodomy so out of the question? Quinn persevered and finally found in Leviticus 18:1-7, "And the Lord spoke to Moses, saying…Speak to the children of Israel, and thou shalt say to them: I am the Lord your God…You shall not do according to the custom of the land of Egypt, in which you dwelt: neither shall you act according to the manner of the country of *Chanaan*, into which I will bring you, nor shall you walk in their ordinances...No *man shall approach* to her that is near to kin to him, *to uncover her nakedness*. I am the Lord…Thou shalt not uncover the nakedness of thy (your) father, or the nakedness of thy (your) mother: she is thy (your) mother, thou shalt not uncover her nakedness."

Quinn read on, the entire chapter spoke of marriage in relation with the marital sex act expressed as nakedness, and it was prohibited with close kin. Leviticus 18:17, "Thou (you) *shalt not uncover the nakedness... such copulation is incest*." Uncover the nakedness meant sexual intercourse! Ham saw Noah's nakedness was uncovered. The rape had been completed.

Quinn cried out in a soft voice, "Chanaan raped Noah! And Ham watched and laughed at the rape, and then told his brothers about it!" Then suddenly, it hit Quinn, "Wow!" he whispered, "Chanaan was Black. Is this why Blacks were enslaved throughout time, throughout the world, even until the Civil War? Because of Noah's curse that Chanaan be the servants of Sem, the White race!"

Quinn moved on. He found in the Book of Judges 1:16-21, "And the *children of the Cinite* (Kenites/Cainites), the kinsman (in-laws) of Moses went up from the city of palms (Egypt), with the children of Juda...and *they dwelt with him*...But the sons of Benjamin did not destroy the Jebusites that inhabited Jerusalem: and the *Jebusite hath dwelt with the sons of Benjamin* in Jerusalem until this present day."

From the time when Josue led the 12 Tribes of Israelites into the Land of Chanaan and divided up the land and gave to the tribe of Benjamin part of the city of Jerusalem - the Jebusites, descendants of Chanaan, descendants of Cain (Cainites) controlled Jerusalem until King David conquered the Jebusites, taking control of Jerusalem and renaming it the City of David.

Douay Rheims Commentary: This city of David, Jerusalem, was divided into two; one part was called Jebus, the other Salem: the one was in the tribe of Juda, the other in the tribe of Benjamin." Quinn reasoned, Benjamin and Judah were the sons of Jacob/Israel, a direct descendant of Adam. And the Jebusites, direct descendants of Chanaan and of Satan, lived among them.

Douay Rheims Commentary: "The Cinite, Jethro the father-in-law of Moses was called Cinacus, or the Cinite (Kenite/Cainite); and his children who came along with the children of Israel settled themselves among them in the land of Chanaan, embracing their worship and religion. From these the Rechabites sprung of whom see Jeremias 35."

Quinn realized that the children of Adam were constantly surrounded by the children of Satan. From when they built the Golden Calf while Moses was on the Mount of Horeb receiving the Ten Commandments, to the Egyptian and Edomite wives of Solomon seducing him to worship idols and conjure demons, to the Kenites seducing the Israelites to cry out for the crucifixion of their Messiah, Jesus Christ. Each time the Hebrews/Israelites were seduced to turn away from their God. The Israelites were constantly bombarded by the seduction of the children of Satan. As they are today seduced by political correctness to turn from Christianity: Happy Holidays instead of Merry Christmas; Winter Holiday Tree instead of Christmas Tree; to taking out of the Roman Rite Mass the continual sacrifice for many, to no longer making the sign of the Cross when a priest hands out the Eucharist - a symbol of the body and blood of the New Testament. Adam's descendants, the Hebrews, Israelites, Christians, have been seduced throughout time. But faith must be unquivering. Faith requires the constant obedience to do God's will.

God said to the Israelites, Exodus 19:5-6, "If therefore you will hear my voice, and keep my covenant, you shall be my peculiar possession above all people: for all the earth is mine...And you shall be to me a priestly kingdom, and a holy nation. These are the words thou (Moses) shalt speak to the children of Israel."

But Quinn found that for their obstinacy, their sin of being seduced, they would be punished. God spoke to the Israelites. Jeremias 7:23-34, "But this thing I command them, saying: Hearken to my voice, and I will be your God, and you shall be my people: and walk ye in all the way that I have commanded you, that it may be well with you...But they hearkened not, nor inclined their ear: but walked in their own will, and in the perversity of their wicked heart...Because the children of Juda have done evil in my eyes, saith the Lord. They have set their abominations (idols) in the house in which my name is called upon, to pollute it...And they have built the high places of Topheth...to burn their sons, and their daughters in the fire (to sacrifice to the idol Moloch): which I commanded not...And I will cause to cease out of the cities of Juda, and out of the streets of Jerusalem, the voice of joy, and the voice of gladness, the voice of the bridegroom and the voice of the bride: for the land shall be desolate (destroyed)."

Quinn knew that Solomon had built an idol for his Egyptian wives to worship Baal, upon which they would roast infant babies as a sacrifice to Baal, to their god, Satan. When Bethseba married Uriah, the Hittite, she took up deceit to obtain the throne of David for her son, Solomon. In the House of Judah, King Mannaseh had even roasted his own babies.

The infiltration of Satan's descendants among the Israelites continued, 1 Chronicles 2:55 (1 Paralipomenon 2:55) "And the *families of the scribes* that dwell in Jabes (Jerusalem), singing and making melody, and *abiding in tents. These are the Cinites, who came of Calor (Hamath) father of the House of Rechab*."

Quinn, therefore, realized that the Kenites were descendants of Ham, Satan's descendant," Quinn cried allowed, "The Kenites were the SCRIBES IN JERUSALEM! The Kenites tried Jesus in their Great Assembly/Sanhedrin, then turned Jesus over to the Roman Govenor Pilate to be crucified. The Kenites are the Pharisees, who, after the Romans destroyed Jerusalem and the Second Temple, called themselves Rabbis! And still do today! And it is today's Rabbis who corrupted the Second Vatican Ecumenical Council and pushed the bishops to take away the continual sacrifice of Jesus. Today, the new priests are no longer trained to say the Roman Rite, the Tridentine Latin Mass. When the generation of priests who were trained in the Roman Rite, the youngest now around 50 years of age, die off, the Tridentine Mass will die with them. And Satan and his Zionist Jews will take complete control of the Catholic Church. And absolute control over the earth."

The Israelites had been corrupted, worshipping false idols - idols of the Kenites of the House of Rechab, the descendant of Chanaan, who was the son of Ham. And Ham's grandson was Nemrod, whose kingdom was Babylon, Gen. 10:10. Babylon, the place of the Israelite captivity,

Babylon where Ezra, who was not an Israelite, who forced his *Talmud* religion of Satan on to the Israelites. Idols had been brought to the Israelites in Jerusalem, to the tribes of Benjamin and Judah - the Kingdom of Judah. Just as their descendants, the Rabbis, brought Pharisaism/Judaism to the Second Vatican Council, and the Catholic Church.

What Quinn read next seem to be a defining moment between God and Satan in fighting for the souls of mankind. It began back in Haran, Turkey, at least 5400 years ago. In Gen. 4:11-12, God cursed Cain for murdering his brother, Abel: 'Now, therefore, cursed shalt thou be upon the earth, which hath opened her mouth and received the blood of thy brother at thy hand…When thou shalt till it, it shall not yield to thee its fruit: a fugitive and a vagabond shalt thou be upon the earth.'

Quinn connected those verses to Jeremias, 35:2-10, when God told the holy prophet, Jeremias, "Go to the house of the Rechabites...bring them into the house of the Lord...give them wine to drink....And they answered: We will not drink wine: because Jonadab the son of Rechab, our father, commanded us, saying: You shall drink no wine, neither you, nor your children, for ever:…Neither shall ye build houses, nor sow seed, nor plant vineyards, nor have any: but you shall dwell in tents all your days, that you may live many days upon the face of the earth, in which you are strangers….Therefore we have obeyed the voice of Jonadab....Nor to build houses to dwell in, nor to have vineyard, or field, or seed:…But we have dwelt in tents, and have been obedient according to all that Jonadab our father commanded."

The latter scripture echoes the first, Quinn thought. God's curse upon Cain, became God's commandment to Cain. And it was sent through his family, down through Cain's descendants, his family through to Ham, down to the House of Rechab, down through to Rechab's son Jonadab and Jonadab's people; that through all the generations they accepted God's curse as a commandment that the people of Jonadab obeyed.

But as to the Israelites, Quinn continued to read Jeremias 35:15-19, "And I have sent to you all my servants the prophets...saying: Return ye every man from his wicked way, and make your ways good: and follow not strange gods, nor worship them, and you shall dwell in the land, which I gave you and your fathers: and you have not inclined your ear, nor hearkened to me…So the sons of Jonadab the son of Rechab have constantly kept the commandment of their father...Therefore thus saith the Lord of hosts the God of Israel: Behold I will bring upon Juda, and upon all the inhabitants of Jerusalem all the evil that I have pronounced against them, because I have spoken to them, and they have not heard: I have called to them, and they have not answered me...Therefore thus saith the Lord of hosts the God of Israel*: There shall not be wanting a man of the race of Jonadab the son of Rechab, standing before me for ever*."

Quinn understood that this offshoot, the people of Jonadab, of the family of Rechab/Ham was the only one that God extended this promise.

And not to their cousins, the Pharisees. It seemed to Quinn that Cain was repentive for the murder of his brother, Abel, when in Gen. 4:13, 'And Cain said to the Lord: My iniquity is greater than that I may deserve pardon.' Certainly, God had reason enough to smite Cain for committing murder - an eye for an eye retribution. But Cain served a greater purpose, to bring the lineage of Satan in to the world. Yet along Cain's lineage was carried the commandment of God, as though the one good thing that Cain had instilled in his descendants was that they would be forever vagabonds upon the earth. Through Cain's descendant, Jonadab, his people followed God's commandment.

Ham, and his descendants, the Kenites, the Rechabites, Nemrod and his Babylonians were all Black. Ham's son, Chus, fathered Nemrod and the beginning of Nemrod's kingdom was Babylon. Nemrod rebelled against God. Nemrod was a "hunter of men," Gen. 10:9, meaning that men were prey to be hunted like animals. Nemrod through deceit and tyranny in his Kingdom of Babylon caused the multitude of people to follow him, rejecting God and worshipping Nemrod. Thus, Nemrod was the enemy of the Kingdom of Judah, into whose hands God would deliver the inhabitants of Judah, the Israelite-Jews for their idol worshipping.

A chill went down Quinn's spine as he read it, thinking to himself, we Americans have turned away from Christianity, we live in a land of fornicators, we've turned away from Christianity and the Catholic Church, now controlled by Satan. Quinn shook his head - we are so royally screwed! How can we ask for God's help in overthrowing the Zionist Jews who deceive us through their media, movies, instigated and financed the drug revolution, and woman's movement that demanded a woman's right to abortion, to seduce us to let go of our Christian faith and values and become fornicators? The whole country must repent!

Quinn saw that God's curse upon the inhabitants of Jerusalem and all the evil that He pronounced against them was carried through by the Babylonian King Nebuchadnezzar. At its height, under King Nebuchadnezzar, the Kingdom of Babylon destroyed Jerusalem, the First Temple, and took what was left of the Israelites, the southern Kingdom of Judah, captive. Ham's descendants, Nebuchadnezzar had destroyed the Israelites and held the remnants captive. And in Babylonian captivity, Ezra, the scribe, arose and brought them captive, under penalty of death, into Jerusalem and ruled them by the Ezra-created *Talmud.*

In Jeremias 8:8-19, God said, "How do you say: We are wise, and the law of the Lord is with us? *Indeed the lying pen of the scribes hath wrought falsehood*…The wise men are confounded, they are dismayed, and taken: for they have cast away the word of the Lord, and there is no wisdom in them… Therefore I will give their women to strangers, their fields to others for an inheritance: because from the least even to the greatest all follow covetousness: from the prophet even to the priest all deal deceitfully...For behold I will send *among you* serpents, basilisks, against which there is no charm: and they shall bite you, saith the

Lord...<u>*My sorrow is above sorrow, My heart mourneth within Me*</u>...why then have they provoked Me to wrath with their idols, and strange vanities?"

Quinn sighed heavily, thinking of the sins that he had committed in life, reading the words of God through the prophet Jeremias, his heart was heavy with guilt for the broken heart that he had brought to God. He wondered if he and the rest of America could be forgiven their sins. Would we be scattered across the earth? He got down on his knees and prayed for forgiveness for offending God. And after a few minutes he got up and continued his research. He looked for how the Kenites were able to get so close to the Israelites.

He found that so deceitful were the Kenites that Saul protected them, (1 Kings 15:5-6) "And when Saul was come to the city of Amalec, he laid ambushes in the torrent...And Saul said to the Cinite (Kenite): Go, depart and get ye down from Amalec: lest I destroy thee with him. <u>*For thou hast shewn kindness to all the children of Israel, when they came up out of Egypt.*</u> And the Cinite departed from the midst of Amalec."

Quinn had found the evidence that the seed of Satan, Cain, and Cain's descendants, through Ham, through Chanaanites, through Rechabite scribes, scribes becoming the Pharisees, the Pharisees becoming the priests and creators of the Oral Law, those sitting on the Sanhedrin court, through that entire lineage came the Pharisees, chief priests: "And straightway in the morning, the chief priests holding a consultation with the ancients and the scribes and the whole council, binding Jesus, led him away, and delivered him to Pilate...And Pilate answered them (the Israelites), and said: Will you that I release to you the king of the Jews? (Do you want me to release Jesus to you, the Pharisees?)...*For he (Pilate) knew that the chief priests (of the Pharisees) had delivered him up out of envy.* <u>*But the chief priests (Kenites/Pharisees) moved the people*</u>, that they should rather release Barabas to them...And Pilate again answering, saith (said) to them: What will you then that I do to the king of the Jews? (What do you Pharisees want me to do with Jesus?)...*But they again cried out: Crucify him...*And Pilate saith to them: Why, what evil hath (has) he done? *But they cried out the more: Crucify him.*" (Mark 15:1-14)

After following Ham/Chanaan's lineage, Quinn continued his search of Noah's other alleged grandchildren through Ham.

Ham's son, Mesram, fathered the Egyptians, who held the Israelites captive. And Mesram fathered Chasluim, who fathered the Philistines. The Greek name for Philistines is Palaestina, Palestinians. The Philistines were at their height, living on the Mediterranean seacoast, when the Israelites were unorganized after coming out of Egypt. The Israelites lived on the eastern Philistine/Palestinian border. This is when the fighting began between the Israelites and the Philistines, a/k/a Palestinians, began; when the king of the Northern Israelite Kingdom, Saul, "fought against all his enemies...the Philistines...." (1 Kings 14:47)

The Philistines constantly attacked the Israelites, and at one time took the Ark of the Covenant when they defeated the Israelites (1 Kings 4:11), for which God sent the Philistines a plague of mice, and with "an exceeding great slaughter" of men, and those who lived were smote (hit) with "emerods (hemorrhoids) in their secret parts." The people told the lords of the Philistines to take back the Ark of the Covenant to "its own place." But it wasn't until after numerous battles that David, the shepherd boy who killed Goliah, the Philistine; the same David of the family of Bethlehemites, who later became King David, went and took back the Ark. It was King David who went up to Cariathiarim to fetch the Ark of the Covenant (2 Kings 6:12) and brought it into Jerusalem, the City of David.

Quinn surmised in his mind that from the descendants of Ham came those who would try to destroy the Israelites. From Ham's family came the Philistines, Hittites, and Nemrod, who began the kingdom of Babylon that later destroyed Jerusalem and the First Temple, Solomon's Temple, in 586 BC under King Nebuchadnezzar, and took the people of the Kingdom of Judah, the southern two tribes of Israelites and other people who dwelled among them, into captivity. It was in captivity that the Kenites/Pharisees, who were among the Israelites of Judah taken into captivity, rose to power and created their own law, the *Talmud,* imposing it onto the Israelites.

In Babylonian captivity, all peoples who were captured in the fallen Kingdom of Judah were called Jews. Included among those other people were the Edomites, descendants of Esau, twin of Jacob, grandsons of Abraham. Esau married into the Chanaanites, descendants of Ham/Cain/Satan, and lost their souls to idol worshipping. When the Persian King Cyrus the Great conquered Babylon, he freed the Israelites and the Pharisees from their captivity. Cyrus would not allow the Israelites to re-establish a monarchy; there would never be another King David. This decree opened the way for the Pharisees to grow in power, taking over the teaching of their Oral Law/*Talmud,* a bastardized version of the Law God gave to Moses.

The Pharisees became dominant authority over the Second Temple. Ezra and his scribes and sages were the ones who first developed the Oral Law in Babylon, refusing to write it down, keeping the people dependent on the scribes and sages.

Quinn found, "*From the group of scribes and sages emerged the Pharisees*." (1 Chronicles 2:55)Therefore, the Pharisees wrote the tort, criminal law, the governance, the sacrifices and rituals that the people were forced to follow through their Oral Law. Their religion was their government and their government was whatever their religious leaders determined - as with Islam. The Pharisees established themselves as the Sanhedrin that passed judgment on the Israelites. It was the Pharisees' rigid restrictions of alleged traditional Oral Law that Jesus condemned. The Pharisees refused to write down their Oral Law, so that it might be interpreted without opposition, for the result they desired. Thus, no one could interpret the Law of Moses' Torah, except the children of Satan.

"How ironic," Quinn mumbled to himself, "the Pharisees weren't even Hebrew or Israelites, yet they controlled the Israelites through their created Oral Law. And after the Romans destroyed the Second Temple, AD 70, the Pharisees emerged under the name of Rabbis; Pharisaism emerged under the name of Judaism. And they still control the 3% of the world's actual Israelite-Jews, who actually came from the House of Judah - from the lineage of King David and Jesus Christ. The Rabbis today are Kenites, not Israelites. The Rabbis of today are descendants of Satan!"

In the letter the Apostle Paul sent to the converted Christians of Philippians (3:2), in which Paul warned, "Beware of dogs (false teachers), beware of evil workers, beware of the concision (separation)." Quinn thought Paul was writing in code, for he was writing from the prison in Rome. Concision meant separation, as does the word Pharisees mean separation. Thus, Paul is warning: beware of the Pharisees.

Paul went on to instruct in Philippians 3:18-19, speaking of the Pharisees, "For many walk, of whom I have told you often (and now tell you weeping), that they are enemies of the cross of Christ... Whose end is destruction: whose God is their belly...."

Paul was warning the Philippians about the Pharisees' Oral Law, *Talmud.* They are the enemies of the cross of Christ, whose end is destruction. Quinn immediately thought of the money-changers in the Second Temple that caused Jesus to become outraged. The Chief Priest of the Pharisees set up the Oral Law that no one could buy an animal or bird for Temple sacrifice, unless they purchased the sacrificial animal with the coin of the Temple. The Chief Priest set up the tables of the moneychangers and profited on the interest charged in the exchange of the money. His system was like today's Federal Reserve System, where a handful of mostly foreign owners order the U.S. Treasury to print the dollar, for which the Feds charge the U.S. Taxpayer interest on each dollar for issuing the order to print, payable in only gold - in order that Americans can use their own money. The Federal Reserve System put the U.S. into bankruptcy within twenty years (1933), which is still being managed today. The Federal Reserve System controls the economy of the United States, by regulating the value of the dollar - a Constitutional responsibility of Congress. No Constitutional Amendment was made to give that handful of foreigners the authority, power, to regulate the value of the U.S. dollar.

The descendants of Satan, the Kenites, a/k/a Pharisees, a/k/a Rabbis, Paul is warning, are out to destroy the Church of Jesus Christ! And those Pharisees changed their name after the Romans destroyed Jerusalem and the Second Temple, in A.D. 70, as if that event had killed all the Pharisees and history might record that they no longer existed. But those Pharisees became Rabbis! Pharisaism became Judaism, and the Rabbis have maintained control over the Israelites' identity and heritage! The Rabbis and Zionist Jews of today are the enemy of Jesus Christ and His followers! Rabbi Abraham Joshua Heschel, the evil hand of Vatican

II, fulfilled this prophecy of Paul's.

Quinn turned to Ham, allegedly the second son of Noah, carried the Y-chromosome of Satan; and that Mesram, Ham's second son, who was the first inhabitant of Egypt and his Egyptian descendants enslaved the descendants of Jacob/Israel and the Twelve Tribes of Israel in Egypt. Therefore, like the Kenites, the Egyptians were the enemy of the God of Moses, of the 3% of Israelite-Jews of the world, and Christians.

It made geological sense to Quinn. It has been proven by geologists, archeologists, volcanologist, and the Douay Rheims all saying the same thing about Exodus. It actually happened. And scientists found that it occurred around 1500 BC. And according to the Bible, God told Moses: "I am come down to deliver them out of the hands of the Egyptians, and to bring them out of that land into a good and spacious land, into a land that floweth with milk and honey, to the places of the Chanaanite, and Hethite (Hittite), and Amorrhite, and Pherezite, and Hevite, and Jebusite." (Exodus 3:8) The Land of Chanaan, the son of Ham.

Quinn then decided to search Noah's alleged son, Japheth; the youngest son. They left the messa of Turkey after the Ark came to rest and migrated down to Judea and to Greece, Italy, Spain, and into Europe.

Gen. 10:2, The sons of Japheth were: "Gomer, and Magog, and Madai, and Javan, and Thubal, and Mosoch, and Thiras." Gen. 10:5, "By these were divided *the islands* of the *Gentiles* in their lands, every one according to his tongue and their families in their nations." [Douay Rheims Commentary: [5] "'The islands' So the Hebrews called all the remote countries, to which they went by ships from Judea, to Greece, Italy, Spain, etc."]

Quinn noted that these descendants of Japheth were known as the Gentiles. "That would also mean that Ham's descendants, the Egyptians, the Muslims are Gentiles, too. As well as the Edomites, Ezra and his Pharisees, today's Zionist Jews – are the Gentiles."

From Ezechiel 38, Quinn read, "Gog shall persecute the church in the *later days*. He shall be overthrown. (1) And the word of the Lord came to me, saying: (2) Son of man, set thy face against Gog, the land of Magog, the chief prince of Mosoch and Thubal: and prophesy of him, (3) And say to him: Thus saith the Lord God: Behold, I come against thee, O Gog, the chief prince of Mosoch and Thubal. [Douay-Rheims Commentary: This name [Gog], which signifies hidden or covered, is taken in this place, either for the persecutors of the church of God in general, *or some arch-persecutor in particular: such as Antichrist shall be in the latter days*. See Apoc. 20:8.] Quinn realized that this secret, or hidden person, was the Antichrist that was among us today. From Japheth came the sons whom God would destroy in the latter days.

Before Quinn turned to Apoc./Rev. 20:8, he read Apoc./Rev. 20:6, 'Blessed and holy is he that hath part in the first resurrection. In these the second death hath no power; but they shall be priests of God and of Christ;

and shall reign with him a thousand years.' This, Quinn realized was about the death of Jesus, the first resurrection, and the apostles who were murdered for His sake. They have reigned with Jesus for the last 1000 years, which meant that Satan had been bound at the time of the crucifixion and had been let loose and had been walking the face of the earth since, Quinn figured sometime around A.D. 1000. Through the Medieval times, during the corruption of the Popes, Satan has been walking among us. Persecuting the woman who gave birth to his child, which seduction Satan was changed in to a serpent. While the Medieval, Middle Ages, was taking place, the Essenes were hiding out in America, Rev. 12:14, from the time of the crucifixion until 1620, when the first Europeans arrived.

Quinn turned to Ezechiel 38:4, "And I will turn thee (Gog) about, and I will put a bit in thy jaws: and I will bring thee forth, and all thy army, horses and horsemen all clothed with coats of mail, a great multitude, armed with spears and shields and swords." This seemed to Quinn to be the Antichrist leading his military that God will defeat.

Ez 38:5 "The Persians, Ethiopians, and Libyans with them, all with shields and helmets." This signified the United Nations military fighting for the Antichrist.

Ez 38:6-8 "Gomer, and all his bands, the house of Thogorma, the northern parts and all his strength, and many people with thee…Prepare and make thyself ready, and all thy multitude that is assembled about thee, and be thou commander over them…After many days thou shalt be visited: *at the end of years* thou shalt come to the land that is returned from the sword, and is gathered out of many nations, to the mountains of Israel which have been brought forth out of the nations, and they shall all of them dwell securely in it."

This, to Quinn, talked of the United States, of all the different nationalities, and Americans living securely, having never been attacked on its soil by foreign armies, until the end times.

Quinn continued to read, Ezechiel 38:9-20, "And thou (Gog) shalt go up and come like a storm, and like a cloud to cover the land, thou and all thy bands and many people with thee...Therefore, thou son of man, prophesy and say to Gog: Thus saith the Lord God: Shalt thou not know, in that day, when my people of Israel shall dwell securely?...*And thou shalt come out of thy place from the northern parts*, thou and many people will thee, all of them riding upon horses, a great company and a mighty army…*And thou shalt come upon my people of Israel* like a cloud, to cover the earth. Thou shalt be in the latter days, and I will bring thee upon my land: that the nations may know me, when I shall be sanctified in thee, O Gog, before their eyes…Thus saith the Lord God: Thou then art he, of whom I have spoken in the days of old, by my servants the prophets of Israel, who prophesied in the days of those times that I would bring thee upon them…And it shall come to pass in that day, *in the day of the coming of Gog upon the land of Israel*, saith the Lord God, that my indignation shall come up in my wrath…And I have spoken in my zeal, and in the fire of my anger, that *in that day there shall be a great commotion upon the land of Israel*…So that the fishes of the sea, and the birds of the air, and the beasts of the field, and every creeping thing that creepeth upon the ground, and *all men that are upon the face of the earth, shall be moved at my presence:* and the mountains shall be thrown down, and the hedges shall fall, and every wall shall fall to the ground.....(Ch. 39:3-8) And I will break thy (Gog's) bow in thy left hand, and I will cause thy arrows to fall out of thy right hand…Thou shalt fall upon the mountains of Israel, thou and all thy bands, and thy nations that are with thee...Thou shalt fall upon the face of the field: for I have spoken it, saith the Lord God…And I will send a fire on Magog, and on them that dwell confidently in the islands: and they shall know that I am the Lord…And I will make my holy name known in the midst of my people Israel, and my holy name shall be profaned no more: and the Gentiles shall know that I am the Lord, the Holy One of Israel…*Behold it cometh, and it is done, saith the Lord God*: this is the day whereof I have spoken."

Quinn sat back and looked again at the words of God, "Behold it cometh." No matter what, Armageddon would come to America. It seemed overwhelming to him. "I guess that solves the mystery of Japheth, he and his lineage were just as evil as Ham's." He gathered himself together and searched Noah's firstborn, Sem.

In Genesis 11:10-27, Quinn read that Sem fathered Arphaxad; Arphaxad fathered Sale; Sale fathered Heber (Hebrews); Heber fathered Phaleg; Phaleg fathered Reu; Reu fathered Sarug; Sarug fathered Nachor; Nachor fathered Thare; Thare fathered Abram/Abraham. Later, he read that Abraham had Ismael and Isaac. Isaac fathered twins Esau and Jacob, and Jacob was renamed Israel by an angel. Quinn accepted that Jacob/Israel fathered the Twelve Tribes of Israelites.

Quinn decided that if Adam and Eve were the chosen people, created separately and apart from the mankind God created first, and if through direct lineage from Adam came the Israelites, then the Israelites were the chosen people. And that meant that the Zionist/Pharisaic Jews were NOT the chosen people of God. Quinn mumbled to himself, "The Zionist Jews claim of being the chosen people of God is just another deceit of Satan!"

Quinn noted that through Abraham's son, Isaac's lineage, came Kings David and Solomon, and finally, Jesus. Quinn decided that Adam's Y-chromosome came down through Noah, Sem, and eventually Abraham, and to Jesus Christ through the lineage of the Israelites.

Again, Quinn was frustrated, Esau the Edomite, he read, took Hittite wives; Hittites were the descendants of Chanaan. Esau was the twin of Jacob, one evil and one good. And many generations after King David came Manasseh, from the Tribe of Joseph, who was the 'most wicked king of Judah'. How are these people coming from the same bloodline!" Quinn grew frustrated. "Unless, as in the Garden of Eden, the bloodline of good was corrupted by the bloodline of evil. Esau came from a good bloodline, but mingled his bloodline with the Satanic bloodline of the Chanaanites. He sold his birthright and sold his descendants to Satan. It says that even from a good bloodline, one can choose evil. Free will, again, Quinn thought.

Quinn tried to look at the big picture and write the historic events on a time line. The Egyptian Empire broke up around 1500 BC; God brings Moses and Israelites out of Egypt, gives them the Ten Commandments, tells them how to build the Ark of the Covenant to carry them in; while they wander the desert for 40 years, Moses writes the five books of the Torah, Genesis, Exodus, Leviticus, Numbers, and Deuteronomy; these are the Laws of Moses. Just as the Egyptian Empire is breaking up, Moses dies and Josue leads the Israelites into the Promised Land of Chanaan, which the Israelites conquer; the Israelites form themselves into two kingdoms, with Saul as the king of the Northern Israelites, and David as the king of the southern Kingdom of Judah, later, king of the combined two kingdoms.

"Okay, so far, so good," Quinn thought. He continued: David can't build the Temple because he has blood on his hands in causing the death of Uriah, husband of Bathsheba. Solomon, his son, becomes king and builds the First Temple, 960BC; Solomon begins to worship his Egyptian wives' pagan god. As a result, God brings dissention on the Nation, but not in Solomon's time; half the Israelites refuse to follow Solomon's son; the kingdom is weakened with the division of the kingdom in two, the Northern Israelite Kingdom and the southern Kingdom of Judah. The Assyrians destroyed the Northern Israelite Kingdom in 722BC; Assyrians deport most of the Ten Tribes of Israel. Meanwhile, in the southern Kingdom of Judah, there comes King Manasseh, the longest-ruling king of the Israelites, 687-642BC; it's the only kingdom left of the remaining Israelites; and this dude, Manasseh worships Satan, sacrifices his own children to Satan, divines demons, uses wizards who possess occult knowledge; Manasseh puts idols in the Temple - when the Ark of the Covenant is in the Temple!? This is all in 2 Chron. 33:6, and in 2 Kings 21:6. After 22 years of rule, Manasseh is attacked by King Ashurbanipal, the last Assyrian king. Ashurbanipal drags the chained Manasseh, a ring pulled through his upper lip; he's humiliated, but Ashurbanipal finally released him from captivity. Manasseh is repentant and gives up the worship of Satan; he's restored to his throne for many years. But his son, Amon, does not give up idols, and his reign is over in two years, assassinated by his officers, 642-640 BC. The Israelites make his son, Josiah, king at the age of 8, 642 BC - 606 BC. Josiah fights the Egyptians trying to attack Assyria, and he gets wounded at Megiddo; is taken home to Jerusalem and dies, 606 BC. Babylonians take the Kingdom of Judah, 605 BC; Israelites rebel, 600 BC. Babylonians capture Jerusalem, 597 BC, but the Israelite stage an insurrection, 588 BC. And then, then the Babylonians, under Nebuchadnezzar capture Jerusalem, 586 BC; they destroy the city and the Second Temple, and take Israelite population captive. Likely, the Babylonians take the Ark of the Covenant, but it wasn't listed on the accounts of war treasure. And when Josiah had the temple renovated around the time he was 20 years old, 630 BC, his High Priestess Hilkiah found a scroll in a cave. How or why is it that the finding just occurred simultaneously to the renovation? The scroll was the Torah that Moses had written. It had been in the Ark of the Covenant. Who took it out? Who put it in a cave? Was the Ark of the Covenant in the Temple at that time of the renovation, or had Manasseh taken it out because he was worshipping Satan? When Josiah told the scribe to read the scroll, the first thing his eyes set upon was Deuteronomy. It was Deuteronomy that warned of heavy punishment for the Israelites if they failed to follow in God's ways. Josiah knew what had happened to his grandfather, Manasseh, and how he had repented. He knew of his father, Amon, and how he was murdered after a two-years reign. It was the Passover; Manasseh had ruined the Kingdom of Judah, and all the Israelites were worshipping idols, the Passover had not been celebrated for generations, not since the days of the Judges of Israel when they first came out of Egypt, before King Saul, the first Israelite King. If they took the Torah out of the Ark, did that same person or persons take the tablets God had written the Ten Commandments on?

"Shit!" Quinn cried out. It hit him suddenly - the Knights Templar, the precursors to the Illuminati! Could the Templars have found something when they established their headquarters at Temple Mount in Jerusalem? Was their actual goal to obtain access to the site because it was built over the ruins of King Solomon's Temple? The Templars had secluded access with time to explore the depths of the underground Temple Mount Hambers. Maybe they found something belonging to pagan worshipers, Solomon or Manasseh. Could Manasseh have written about the conjugations of demons, how to contact them? Or wrote of the rituals of sacrificing his children? Isn't that what today's Bohemian Club members do? The Illuminati do? Maybe just other people's children are sacrificed. The thought gave new meaning to the news of missing children across America over the years. Never found.

Quinn continued his research, finding that the Templars were charged with obscene rituals, heresy, and idolatry. I know King Philip IV owed money to the Templars; easy way to get out of that debt is to torture the Templars into submission. But, still. They also possessed the head of St. Euphemia; who does that? Why wouldn't you bury a head in a nice crypt in a church? The Templars build a lot of buildings, churches. Why didn't they bury the saint's head in one of them? Quinn couldn't help think of the Skulls & Bones allegedly digging up the head of Geronimo to use in secret rituals. Did the Templars use the head of St. Euphemia for secret rituals?

He sighed heavily, and continued on with the timeline: "God probably allowed the Babylonians to conquer the southern Kingdom of Judah because the Israelites had run amok under Manasseh." Quinn shook his head, "The Israelites lost the Ark of the Covenant through their own undoing. There had to have been interbreeding of the bloodlines, or individuals choosing Satan over God. That's the only thing that makes sense. Just as in the Garden, God allowed Satan to impregnate Eve; God had to have allowed Satan the corruption of good seed. Then, there's free will. It would seem that regardless of your bloodline, you have a choice to be good or go along with your Satanic genes, or go against your good genes the way that Esau had done. Control desire for the sake of the Kingdom of Heaven!

Quinn wondered about the Greek influence and perhaps the disclosure of Plato's writings of controlling desire to become a wise philosopher king. Plato lived from 428 BC - 348 BC. He wrote that injustice corrupts and withers the soul; the soul itself becomes more unjust and unholy. Quinn thought to himself, I remember that Plato mentioned a myth about the many-headed beast. But I'm getting far afield, here. The bottom line, control your emotions; two sins against faith are despair and presumption." Quinn wondered about the pressure the Israelites faced under Manasseh's long reign of demonic worship, especially finding that he sacrificed his own children. Quinn wondered, was that a lesson to Americans today, regardless of the governmental pressure, do not despair, stay faithful to the God of Abraham. And protect your children from the United Nations takeover of them.

Quinn decided to look back over the centuries to follow the lineage from Abraham who only had two sons. Where is Eve's mtDNA in that lineage? What about the lineage of the Muslims, beginning with Ismael. He read Gen. 12 when God sent Abraham and his family out of Haran into the land where Chanaanites dwelled and God promised that land to Abraham. Because a famine came over the land of Chanaan, Abraham took his family to Egypt where he told his wife, Sarai - who was his niece, to tell them she was his sister. Quinn stopped and considered, Sarai being Abraham's niece brings Eve's mtDNA down through Sarai. Sarai was a descendant of Adam and Eve.

Quinn read verse 16: "And they used Abram well for her sake. And he had sheep and oxen, and he asses, and men servants and maid servants, and she asses, and camels."

Quinn read that Sarai was taken into the Pharaoh's house. God cursed the Pharaoh with sickness and the realization that Sarai was Abram's wife, so the Pharaoh gave Abram back his wife and sent him out of Egypt. Quinn noted that in the Dead Sea Scroll it said nothing of men or women servants.

Quinn deduced that it was in Egypt that Abram had gotten the handmaid for Sarai, since Agar was Egyptian. And if the Pharaoh gave so much other property, including gold and silver, to Abram that the Pharaoh likely gave him servants. In any case, they brought back Agar with them from Egypt. It is likely that one of the Egyptian men servants was close to Agar. Abram takes everyone back up into Chanaan and from Bethel, God gives Abram all the land Abram can see to the north, south, east, and west. And they settle in for the next ten years.

Then Quinn read something that he had never heard of before: Douay-Rheims Bible: Genesis 16:1-5:

> Now Sarai the wife of Abram, had brought forth no children; but having a handmaid, an Egyptian, named Agar…She said to her husband: Behold, the Lord hath restrained me from bearing: go in unto my handmaid, it may be I may have children of her at least. And when he agreed to her request,…She took Agar the Egyptian her handmaid, ten years after they first dwelt in the land of Chanaan, and gave her to her husband to wife…And he went in to her. But she, perceiving that she was with child, despised her mistress… And Sarai said to Abram: Thou dost unjustly with me: I gave my handmaid into thy bosom, and she perceiving herself to be with child, despiseth me. The Lord judge between me and thee.

Quinn mumbled to himself - "Sarai and Abram are arguing that Agar was pissed that she had to wife - have sex with - Abram because Agar PERCEIVED HERSELF TO BE WITH CHILD - Agar was ALREADY PREGNANT before she went into the tent of Abram! Shit!" Quinn cried, "Abram WAS NOT the biological father of Ismael! Does anyone know this? Why haven't I heard of this!? I heard that the Muslims claim a link to Ismael, and therefore, to Abraham. Is that why I've never heard of this - it's been covered up? But this is a pointed discussion between Sarai and Abram. Sarai is pissed at Abram because he did not impregnate Agar - she was already pregnant! Now, Sarai has no claim to Ismael as her child without Abram having intercourse with Agar! It sounds as though Abraham didn't have intercourse with Agar at all. But if he did, and she was pregnant with her lover's child, that would really piss off Agar! Agar and an Egyptian man servant were likely lovers who were in Bethel for ten years together, living as servants in the Abram household. I don't think servants were allowed to marry; likely they just had their own private life together. Maybe they were married, but Sarai and Abraham certainly didn't know about it beforehand. Now, Agar can't continue to be with the man she loves and with whom she conceived a child. That's something for Agar to be pissed about!"

Quinn read on, Genesis 16:6-10:

> And Abram made answer, and said to her: Behold thy handmaid is in thy own hand, use her as it pleaseth thee. And when Sarai afflicted her, she ran away… And the angel of the Lord having found her, by a fountain of water in the wilderness, which is in the way to Sur in the desert… He said to her: Agar, handmaid of Sarai, whence comest thou? and whither goest thou? And she answered: I flee from the face of Sarai, my mistress…

> And the angel of the Lord said to her: Return to thy mistress, and humble thyself under her hand…And again he said: I will multiply thy seed exceedingly, and it shall not be numbered for multitude.

Quinn cried out, "Whoaa! The angel said: *I* WILL multiply thy seed! How can an angel multiply thy seed? That's God's job - only God tells people that." A chill ran down Quinn's spine, "Who's this angel? An angel of God could be the fallen angel of God, which was Satan. Wait a minute," the language of 'angel of the Lord' struck Quinn, "It was the name used in the Dead Sea Scroll, Genesis 4:1, quoting Eve after giving birth to Cain. And that verse said Eve was pregnant by Sammael (Satan) - the angel of the Lord is Satan in Eve's quote and in this passage where Satan is talking to Agar. Satan might have the power to multiply her seed by killing off those who go up against that seed, or is deceitful enough to lead her to believe it.

Does this mean that Ismael will be treated and viewed as the son of Abram, and not as a servant, so don't tell anyone that Ismael was fathered by an Egyptian male servant? Was the angel promising Agar that everyone would view Ismael as the son of Abram even though he isn't? Was Agar running away before they found out that Abram wasn't the father? She couldn't look at Sarai's face because she was ashamed of her pregnancy! Sarai knew Agar was unwed; and thought she was not pregnant and that's why Sarai thought she could have sex with Abram. Didn't servants and concubines ever marry the master. Didn't they have sex with the master and bare him children. Wasn't that a normal course of events, but to have a child out of wedlock was not acceptable. It was shameful and Agar couldn't face Sarai now that she knew. And is that why Sarai afflicted Agar, because Agar became pregnant by an Egyptian before Abraham could do the job? It would benefit Sarai to keep Agar's secret; the tradition would give the child to Abram and Sarai, as was Sarai's goal in the first place. But that's why Sarai did not want Isaac to share in the estate of Abram, because Ismael wasn't Abram's son, but an Egyptian's! That's why Abram finally agreed to get rid of Ismael!"

Quinn read on: The angel of the Lord said to Agar, Gen. 16:11-13:

> And again: Behold, said he, thou art with child, and thou shalt bring forth a son: and thou shalt call his name Ismael, because the Lord hath heard thy affliction…He shall be a wild man: his hand will be against all men, and all men's hands against him: and he shall pitch his tents over against all his brethren…And she called the name of the Lord that spoke unto her: Thou the God who hast seen me. For she said: Verily here have I seen the hinder parts of him that seeth me.

Quinn was struck by the language, "Thou the God who hast seen me." Is Agar referring to a god who saw her praying to him? Egyptians were pagan worshippers. Egyptians were descendants of Ham's second son, Mesram. Ham's son, Chus, fathered the Sudanese, the Ethiopians; Ham's son, Chanaan, fathered the Libyans, the Hittites, Amorites, Sidonians, Perizzites, and Zemarites. All carried the Y-chromosome of Satan.

Quinn searched on the Internet for a god worshipped by the Egyptians and the name of the well located between Cades and Barad. Quinn found that a local goddess was considered the protector of the Pharaoh, called the Eye of Ra. She was a cobra goddess symbolic of the land of Egypt.

Again, Quinn was struck by the language: "The COBRA goddess!" As in a snake; as in serpent; as in the Garden of Eden. Who tempted Eve to have intercourse with him, Satan. And the Egyptians worshipped her! Agar was raised to worship her. The cobra goddess was the God of Agar!"

Quinn concluded that if Agar had been living within the camp of Abram and Sarai for ten years before becoming pregnant - and not by Abram - that she had to have been very young when the Pharaoh gave her to Abram as a handmaid to Sarai. Agar had been from the household of the Pharaoh; she had to have been taught of the goddess protecting the Pharaoh, and likely prayed to that goddess for protection of her going into the foreign land of Chanaan without her family.

Quinn noted, in verse 13 that Agar said that she had seen the hinder parts of him who seeth me. Was the god obstructed from Agar's view because she was no longer in Egypt where god icons and images were within the household, especially in the Pharaoh's house. The goddess was part of the land of Egypt - Agar was hindered from seeing the land of Egypt. Agar says, 'here have I seen' - from Bethel - is the 'here' of her location in Chanaan and the distant location from Egypt had obstructed her view of her Egyptian god, an icon, a carved image of a pagan god. It was well known that Abram did not allow these idols in his camp. Therefore, Agar's view of her idol cobra goddess was hindered, obstructed, by the distance between Egypt and Chanaan.

Quinn concluded that the 'angel of god' who appeared to Agar was not the Lord God of Abram, but was Satan. Just as Eve had referred to him when she delivered his son. And that it is Satan that promised to multiple the seed of Agar's son, exceedingly - and it 'shall not be numbered for multitude.' Quinn was troubled by the language, and again, tried to analyze it's meaning, "Would it fit that it means Satan's seed will not carry the mark of the beast, but only the brethren that Ismael will go against, set his tent over against"? Quinn read, again: '[12] He shall be a wild man: his hand will be against all men, and all men's hands against him: and he shall pitch his tents over against all his brethren.'" Quinn thought it a strange description of a single man - his hand will be against all men - how can that even be allegory? And all men's hands against him - is this a way of warning that Ismael will be so evil that he is against all men and all men will be against him? Quinn wondered how such an evil Ismael could be the son of Abraham, but he found that Ismael was not Abraham's son.

In Gen 15:3-4, Abraham speaks with God, "And Abram added: But to me thou hast not given seed: and lo my servant [Ismael], *born in my house*, shall be my heir…And immediately the word of the Lord came to him, saying: *He shall not be thy heir: but he that shall come out of thy bowels, him shalt thou have for thy heir [Isaac]....*" This passage was proof that Ismael did not come from Abraham; Ismael did not carry the Y-chromosome of Adam.

Suddenly, it all seemed to fit together, at once, and Quinn sighed, "Jesus Christ protect us. The New World Order! Satan's descendant, Ismael - will pitch his tent over against all his brethren - one tent over all mankind! It can only mean the One World Order. One man's single hand will rule over the rest of mankind - who will have their hands against him, as opposing slaves forced to wear the mark of the beast micro-chipped on their hands. The Satanic Y-chromosome of Satan will come through Ismael, too! And he will be a 'wild man,' did that mean a wild BEAST!?" Would the Antichrist be a Muslim?

Quinn researched for the Y-chromosome descended from Ham, his son Chus, who fathered the Sudanese and Ethiopians and found that the Ethiopians and Kenyans shared the same Y-chromosome, the haplogroup L0 clades, and that it was rare or absent in other African populations. It all fit with the theory that Ham brought the Y-chromosome of Satan onto Noah's Ark, and into modern day America through the genes of the current President of the United States!

Dread flowed over Quinn's body. He had to get up and walk around and shake it off. A foreign Muslim, a descendant of Ham, the genetic descendant of Satan held the power of the Presidency of the United States!

Quinn suddenly laughed out loud, "Gees, I expected that Satan would have had a more intelligent descendant than Tsaeb. Or at least a head that is bigger than the size of a baseball." He continued to laugh as he sat back down to do more research.

But the whole story of Abraham and Sarah and Ismael, and its revelation nagged at him; he decided to look at the Torah, at the same passage to see if it said the same message about Agar's pregnancy without intercourse with Abraham.

Quinn read the Genesis 16:4-10: "And he went in...(to) Hagar (Agar), and she conceived: and when she saw that she had conceived, her mistress was despised in her eyes…And Sarai said unto Avram 'My wrong [be] upon thee: I have given my maid...(to you)...and when she saw that she had conceived, I was despised in her eyes...Malak (angel) said...(to Hagar/Agar) I will multiply thy (your) zera (descendants) exceedingly, that it shall not be numbered for multitude." (www.ishwar.com/ judaism/holy_torah/book01/book01_016.html)

That sentence contradicts itself, Quinn thought. The angel will multiply Agar's descendants, (not Ismael's descendants) and descendants is in the plural, yet goes on to say that 'it' - meaning singular descendant. Verse 12: "And he will be a wild man; his hand (will be) against every man, and every man's hand against him; and he shall dwell in the presence of all his brethren." Hand is singular. Quinn couldn't help equate the passage with a warning. The New World Order microchip would only be placed on one hand. And dwelling in the presence of all his brethren completely disguises the 'pitching of tents over against all his brethren.' The pitching of tents over and against all his brothers is the power that the New World Order would exact against all mankind.

Verse 13: "And she called the name of YHWH [God] that...(spoke to)...her,...(you) Elohim/God...(see) me...Have I also here looked after him that...(sees) me?" Agar is asking if the god who is talking to her is the same god that she looked for in Egypt - and also in Bethel, from the house of Abraham.

Douay Rheims never named the word of the god she called, but the Torah says she called him the name of the God of Abram. Why? She didn't worship him; certainly not from Egypt before she met Abram and Sarai. Why would she expect the God of Abram to appear to her? The Torah said it was a Malak, an angel who appeared to her, but then the Torah also says Agar called the angel YHWH! It's saying that Agar called the angel, God. The Torah is contradicting itself within the verse. Verse 15: 'And Hagar bare Avram a son....' If Abram didn't allow pagan idols in his household and forced her to worship his God, why would the angel, or God, be hindered/blocked to her in Bethel? Surely, Abraham's God, YHWH could be seen in Bethel where Abraham dwelled. Only the Egyptian god would be obscured to Agar from Bethel."

Quinn talked out loud to himself, "How could she call the name YHWH, which means God, when it was an angel of the Lord who was talking to her?" Quinn was confused; all of it seemed confusing. All of it was deceitful.

The deceit continued in the International Version of the angel's description of the type of man that Ismael will be a 'wild donkey of a man.' That only implies that he'll be stubborn as a donkey; he'll be a jackass and this is the reason for the hostility toward his brothers - he's a jackass, ignore him!

The other exception to these verses was in Gideon, after the word exceedingly, 'so <u>they</u> shall not be counted for multitude.' Quinn could only conclude that it supported the message that Ismael's lineage will be countless!

Quinn found that the International Standard version of the Bible, the King James, and the Gideon Bibles quoted the Torah verbatim. He also noted that the Gideon carried the symbol of the Unitarians, a chalice with a flame. And that these biblical storylines are irrational. Only the Douay Rheims story made sense of the emotions that Sarai, Abram, and

Agar had expressed. Quinn reasoned, I don't believe a woman would want to have intercourse with a man while she is pregnant with another man's child. It seems as though it would disrespect the child or expose him to health risks, or even miscarriage, and a mother would be protective of her child. And from Abram's point of view, Quinn reasoned, I don't think a man would want to knowingly have sex with a woman he knew for ten years and who was pregnant with another man's child. Only a rapist or sexual deviant would find that acceptable.

Quinn was disturbed by the differences between the Douay Rheims Bible and the other Bibles and decided to search the history of the Douay Rheims Bible. "The original (publication) dates back to 1582 for the New Testament and 1609-10 for the Old Testament. It was written for the faithful of England and Europe. And it was written in response to controversial editions translated by Protestant reformers. By the end of the 16th century, there were nine English Bibles and a few other New Testament translations in English. Much of the Protestant translations included controversial and biased translation, used in polemical ways to support Protestant schism. The Douay-Rheims is a literal translation of the Latin Vulgate Bible, word for Word. Initially translated by St. Jerome and found authoritative by the Council of Trent. Not bending word meanings to fit biases."

Quinn decided to accept the Douay Rheims version of the Bible, written before Vatican II novus ordo seclorum, as the best account that modern day man would ever be able to count on for unadulterated first works. While Moses wrote the Pentateuch/Torah, numerous edited revisions had occurred since the time of Moses. Today, those revisions are verbatim texts that also appear in the International Standard Version. And the International version translated a conclusion, not the original text. Quinn figured that the International Version of the Bible was written or approved by the United Nations, so that the five books of Moses had probably been bastardized by the elite. This was the New World Order people attempting to corral, to indoctrinate the 3% of Israelite-Jews descended from the Israelites and the Christians, to disguise Satan's descendants living among them today.

Quinn found, that in 722 BC, after the Assyrians attacked the Northern Kingdom of Israel, some Israelites who fled to the southern Kingdom of Judah found differences between the northern and southern Torahs, so that the Northern Kingdom edited their copy to match Judah's. The second editing of the Torah occurred when the Levites filled in gaps of genealogy. A third time when Josiah refurbished the temple and was given the scrolls found in a cave, i.e., Deuteronomy. The fourth time that the Torah was edited was by Ezra; Ezra the non-Israelite. In Ben Zion Bokser's book, *The Wisdom of the Talmud: The Forerunners of the Talmud*, 1951, www.sacred-texts.com, Bokser wrote:

"In Biblical times the work of supplementing the written Torah was in the hands of the priests, Levites and community elders.

When the second Jewish commonwealth was founded by the returned Babylonian exiles, that function was taken over by the sopherim. That term sopherim has...been translated as scribes....The pioneer of the sopheric [scribe] movement, was Ezra who came from Babylonia in 459 BC with the ideal of directing the reorganized Jewish settlement in Palestine toward the principles and institutions of the Torah...*They [Ezra and scribes] re-edited the Biblical text [Torah] bringing it in to greater conformity with their developed religious and literary sensibilities*...The successors of the sopherim who carried on the interpretation and development of the Torah during the Maccabean times, were called the Perushim or Pharisees....*The Pharisees supplemented the written Torah with new legal formulations.* They taught...the immorality of the soul...and an extensive angelology. They elaborated the Temple ritual with new ceremonies ...All these...measures adopted by them were grounded in the recognition that the written Torah must be supplemented by a continuing new tradition...."

Quinn decided that Ezra and the scribes and those who followed them had hidden behind the Torah to create their new religion, Pharisaism, which today is called Judaism.

But Quinn wanted more proof before declaring that the descendants of Ismael were the enemy to mankind, and specifically to the United States. He began with Douay Rheims:

> Genesis 22:1-22 After these things, God tempted Abraham, and said to him: Abraham, Abraham. And he answered: Here I am…He said to him: Take thy (your) only begotten son Isaac, whom thou lovest, and go into the land of vision: and there thou shalt offer him for an holocaust upon one of the mountains which I will shew thee…And he said to him: Lay not thy hand upon the boy, neither do thou any thing to him: now I know that thou fearest God, and hast not spared *thy (your) only begotten son* for my sake.

Quinn found more evidence that specifically stated that Ismael was not the seed of Abraham. Genesis 17:4-21: God spoke to Abram:

> And God said to him: I AM, and my covenant is with thee, and thou shalt be a father of many nations…And I will establish my covenant between me and thee, and between thy seed after thee in their generations, by a perpetual covenant: to be a God to thee, and to thy seed after thee…And I will give to thee, and to thy seed, the land of thy sojournment, all the land of Chanaan for a perpetual possession, and I will be their God…Again God said to Abraham: And thou therefore shalt keep my covenant, and thy seed after thee in their generations… This is my covenant which you shall observe, between me and you, and thy (your) seed after thee: All the male

kind of you shall be circumcised:...And you shall circumcise the flesh of your foreskin, that it may be for a sign of the covenant between me and you...And my covenant shall be in your flesh for a perpetual covenant...God said also to Abraham: Sarai thy wife thou shalt not call Sarai, but Sara...And I will bless her, and of her I will give thee a son, whom I will bless, and he shall become nations, and kings of people shall spring from him...And he said to God: O that Ismael may live before thee...And God said to Abraham: Sara thy wife shall bear thee a son, and thou shalt call his name Isaac, and I will establish my covenant with him for a perpetual covenant, and with his seed after him...*And as for Ismael I have also heard thee. Behold, I will bless him, and increase, and multiply him exceedingly: he shall beget twelve chiefs, and I will make him a great nation...* But *my covenant I will establish with Isaac*, whom Sara shall bring forth to thee (you) at this time in the next year.

It was clear that the God of Abraham was not including Ismael in His perpetual covenant with Abraham's descendants. It said two things to Quinn: The God of Abraham and Father of Jesus Christ was not the god of Ismael and Ismael's descendants. And that supported Quinn's determination that the angel of God that appeared to Agar was the fallen angel of God, Satan, who made a covenant to multiply Agar's seed, if she would return to Sarai and lie that Ismael was the son of Abraham. If she did that, Satan could pull off the deceit - lying to the world - that Ismael came from the seed of Abraham when, in fact, Ismael did not. In spite of Satan's deceitful lie to Agar, God answered Abraham's prayer to multiply Ismael's seed. For the God of Abraham knew of the coming need to afflict the seed of David. Ismael's descendants would be instrumental in carrying out that punishment.

Research proved to Quinn that Agar worshipped the serpent god of Egypt as she was raised to do. He concluded that an Egyptian male servant that the Pharaoh gave Abraham impregnated Agar. That Ham brought Satan's Y-chromosome into the Ark, and Ham passed it on to his sons. Mesram, Ham's second son, fathered the Egyptians, and the Egyptian Agar making a covenant with the angel of the Lord coincided with the Dead Sea Scrolls' account of Eve referring to Satan as the angel of the Lord. The Egyptians were of Satan.

Ham's second son, Chus, fathered the Sudanese and Ethiopians, that science proved were genetically tied to the Kenyans, and that President Tsaeb's father was a Kenyan, making Tsaeb literally the seed of Satan.

And Quinn's research of the House of David, King Manasseh in particular, also indicated two things. One, that God mixed, or allow to be mixed, Satan's evil seed with Adam's good see. The second thing was that control of one's emotions, desires, regardless of genetics either led a person to Satan or to God. It was their free will to choose. Those of the evil bloodline, even Tsaeb, could choose Jesus right now, and his soul would be saved.

Chapter 6

As if in some cosmic affirmation, the dawn pierced the darkness of night just when Quinn's research enlightened him of the status of Ismael being the descendant of Satan. Therefore, every Muslim who claimed Ismael as an ancestor is an enemy to the Christian nation of the United States of America and every Muslim is working towards its destruction.

When he heard the birds outside his office window, he looked out and wondered aloud. "Where did the night go!" He got up and stretched his body, stiff from sitting for hours at his computer, and headed in to take a shower. While he brushed his teeth, he thought of what he had discovered. He couldn't shake the fear that chilled his spine. It was an ominous, furtive sense that an unleashed fury might strike him at any moment, and he had no way of defending himself. It made him feel helpless for the first time in his life. But he needed to tell Maggie as soon as he could. She needed to know how right she was. It would confirm her fear, but at least she would no longer feel isolated and paranoid in that fear.

His body was exhausted from the lack of sleep. And he realized that he too, now had to learn how to handle the fear. "It's the damned sense of helplessness, it's stressful," he mumbled to himself. "What is among us; what is before us?" He felt driven to shout the news out to the world - the descendants of Ismael carry the Y-chromosome of Satan - they will try to kill every Christian in America! The whole mess that the country was in now had a defined enemy. It is a deliberate, intentional destruction of a Christian nation. He was now absolutely sure of it. His research proved that our country has been under siege by evil forces. But it wasn't just the Muslims, the Zionist Jews, the Asians, the Blacks - all of them who were not Christians - all hated White Christians and Israelite-Jews. A whole new dimension of the attack against America was brought to light. It wasn't a matter of throwing out the corrupt politicians or hang them for treason. As a nation, Americans were about to engage in war with the descendants of Satan. "We can't do that alone!" Quinn mumbled.

He made himself a cup of coffee and took it back into his office to call Maggie.

When Maggie answered, her voice was filled with the grogginess of having just fallen asleep.

"Did I wake you? I'm sorry," Quinn said.

"No. No. That's okay, Quinn. I just got into bed; I'll fall back to sleep easily enough. What's going on?"

"Well, how come you were up all night?" Quinn asked.

"Did you ever read the Art of War? It was written in 500 B.C. by a Chinese general. They still follow the strategy today. I figured it was a good idea to know the strategy of the enemy."

Quinn laughed, "I am beginning to realize just how much alike you and me are."

"Why?" Maggie asked, "Have you been up all night, too?"

"Yes. And I had to call you. I just got through researching the Satanic Y-chromosome. I am convinced that Ismael carried Satan's Y-chromosome."

"That would certainly explain why the Muslims hate us, and while hating us are moving into our country in droves! Why would such a huge immigration of Muslims move into a country that they hate?"

"To destroy it," Quinn exclaimed. "But I don't want to keep you up. I just wanted to say that you were right about the Satanic Y-chromosome living among us, living today all over the world through the descendants of Ismael. That is, along with the other descendants of Japheth and Ham, as well."

"We live among the spiritual world far more than we know, Quinn. In ancient times, it was part of their everyday experience; American Indians know; Puritans used the Bible to teach their children how to read and about the sacred. But we were not taught about good and evil in the coexisting forums. We were taught that the Bible were fables; lessons on morality only. We were told not to read it; we wouldn't understand it. They taught us that it was called the Tree of Knowledge, only, and that Adam and Eve ate the apple to obtain the knowledge of God, thus they sinned. Sex never entered in to the instruction. Good and evil is taught today from only the perspective of obeying our government - you are good when you keep your mouth shut and obey the government. The last Speaker of the House threatened Christian Churches that they would lose their exempt-tax status, if they did not preach from the pulpit that parishioners should obey the government! You are sinners, if you don't! Evil if you speak out against communist policies being shoved down our throat."

"I agree, but that policy, that political correctness weapon used on us, it's for the purpose of masking the enemy. It's not nice to criticize Islam, and they will soon make it illegal to speak our opinion against Islam, but only Islam. While the Muslims will continue to criticize Christians. The Relations for American Theological Studies and Islamic Council, alias RATSIC, has been working on getting that legislation through."

Maggie sat up in bed, becoming more awake with the feeling of dread coming over her. After Quinn's supportive response the night before to her confession of the fear she felt from encounters with ghosts, she decided to tell him more.

"Quinn, there are two other experiences that I had that I think you should know. It has to do with what you're talking about. It's not the Y-chromosome, and it's not a dimensional ghostly encounter, but something far beyond any of that."

"What is it?"

"Many years ago I worked in a nursing home, in the administrator's office, and one day they took me on a tour of the different departments and to see the patients."

Quinn listened intently, wondering where Maggie's story would take him. A nursing home seemed so harmless, so unexpected a setting for something Maggie said was more serious than the Y-chromosome.

"Go ahead. You were taken on a tour."

"Yes. And near the end of the tour, the last patient we visited was sitting on a geriatric chair. Oh, she was well cared for, well dressed, hair combed and so forth. The patient was okay. But her spine was bent forward with osteoporosis, her hands rested on the wide arms of the chair. I had spoken to patients as we toured, just to say hello."

"Okay. Go on."

"Well, this particular patient, a woman, bent forward in her chair so that she was facing down, looking at her lap. They told me she never lifts her head and rarely talks. I felt badly for the woman, so I took her right hand and cupped it between my hands and I bent down to her and looked into her face and said, hello."

Quinn listened quietly.

"Suddenly, the woman lifted her head to look at me. And I smiled and looked into her eyes. They were strikingly beautiful; her eyes smiled back at me, but she said nothing. As I looked, I thought how beautiful her eyes were, and then suddenly I realized that those were not the woman's eyes looking back at me."

"Shit," Quinn mumbled.

"Tremendous fear overcame me and I straightened my body, sucked in air, opened my mouth ready to scream my lungs out when suddenly I saw this golden ray come from a small circular area in the ceiling and descend down, widening over the old woman and me. As it passed down over my body, a tremendous feeling of peace overtook me, and I quietly breathed out the air that I had sucked in."

"That was Jesus Christ, Maggie," Quinn cried.

"Absolutely," Maggie replied. "But that's not all. Years later, my daughter and I were driving home after dropping off my elder son at college and we stopped at a comfort station on the New Jersey Turnpike. I don't know if I ever mentioned that my daughter is 5'11" and I'm 6'1" - we look like two confident Amazons that can take care of ourselves, and no one has ever messed with us on these road trips down to Virginia.

It was late, I can't remember exactly, but sometime around 11pm when we stopped. We parked the car and started walking up the small slope of the walkway, talking with each other about what we would get to eat. I was looking at my daughter as we talked, but when I saw a figure coming down the steps toward us, I looked up at him," Maggie stopped and sighed.

"Was he a thug coming toward you? Mafia?"

"He was nothing that I had ever seen before. And he was something that caused me more fear than I had ever experienced in my life. I have to tell you, Quinn, I grew up with two older brothers, and we had fistfights every day. We were all athletes, and they were 6'7" and 6'4"; and they taught me how to fight, but more importantly, they taught me that I could take a beating."

"Jesus, Maggie," Quinn responded.

"No, Quinn, I look at it now that it gave me the courage to raise my three kids on my own. There is no man that I fear. I don't fear the world. And that is worth a lot. I'm not afraid of a Hell's Angel; don't fear the Mafia, and I've met one or two of both of them. I don't fear Black men and I don't fear Mexican drug lords. I wouldn't be stupid enough to go looking for trouble, but if they came after me, they would know that they had been in a fight for their lives. I'm not saying that I'd win; just that I would knock the shit out of them before they killed me. I have no problem with any of that. And if they ever came after one of my kids, they would be dead."

"My God! Who was the guy you met on the pathway on the New Jersey Turnpike?" Quinn asked.

"For a split second I looked up at him and I immediately knew he was evil. It literally took my breath away. I'm not talking about a killer or a psychopath; he wasn't a rapist or druggie. I mean he was evil. The awareness was shocking. In my head I was yelling at myself, don't look at him! My eyes never landed on him - they glanced across his face - that's how immediate the fear came over me - fear that he would look me in the eye. He was at the top of the stairs, and I saw that he looked over our heads, as though my daughter and I were not on the pathway in front of him. He never once recognized our presence; it was as if we were invisible to him! He started down the center of the small stairs with obvious intent to walk straight down the middle of the pathway, as though he owned it. The arrogance was palpable. He would have walked either between my daughter and I, or ploughed through us. But he was not going to move from the center of the pathway."

"What did you do?"

"We were within steps of each other. I had to move quickly, so I stepped off the pathway as fast as I could, to get out of his way and give him a wide berth, and thinking he would pass my daughter without incident. I didn't have time to grab her and pull her with me because he would have banged right into her, if I had tried. And there were bushes on the other side of her, so I couldn't push her away. But my daughter had seen him at the same time that I did and she jumped behind me and grabbed the back of my jacket. Both of us were completely off the pathway and standing in the flowerbed; our left shoulders pressed against the building's wall."

"What did he look like? How big was he; what was he wearing? How old was he?"

"He was my height; thin. Had he been any other man, I could have snapped him like a trig! He was dressed all in beige except his jersey, which was white. The colors struck me as ironic. He wore a hat that had a turned-down rim that encircled the hat - like some kind of rain hat that an old man might wear, or a fly fisherman would wear. He had a white turtleneck jersey, khaki pants, and a London Fog raincoat that was open, and as he walked the wind flared it open. In my head, I heard a voice warning me, "Don't let his coat touch you. Don't let it touch you!" I was terrified. I watched the corner of his coat fly up; I pulled back from it - but still, it was only an inch from me. I saw him out of my peripheral vision as he passed. He never looked at us, not once. It was as if we had been invisible to him. It wasn't normal. His face was average looking; nothing out of the ordinary; no scars; no marks, no mustache or beard. He looked to be around 45 to 50 years old and definitely from the city."

"What did your daughter think?"

"My daughter was shaken. After he had passed, she asked me, 'Did you see that guy?' I said, 'Yes! Get the hell inside!' I grabbed her arm as she started to turn back to look at him, 'Don't talk; don't look back at him; just get the hell inside around the people.' We walked quickly up the steps and into the comfort station, trying to get lost among a bunch of people. I told my daughter, 'we're going to wait 30 minutes by the clock before we leave. I want him far beyond us in case he's heading north. But from that particular station, he could have gone either north or south."

"I don't think two Amazons can get lost among a bunch of people!" Quinn said.

"Yeah, I know and that's what scared me. I didn't want to say anything to my daughter; I just pretended that we could."

"Then what happened?"

"We got back on the highway, heading north, watching to see if any cars seemed to be following us. But the thing that freaked me out - this guy was absolute evil. It's really hard to describe, and I really don't want to think about it long enough to find the words. But I don't throw around that term easily. There are bad people in the world, murderers and thieves, and other descriptives - but evil is in a category of its own. And what terrified me was the thought that his kind of evil had to have supernatural powers. I was terrified that his powers would tell him where we lived. For six months, I kept waking with nightmares that he would find us. I mean I would bolt upright from a deep sleep, gasping. My daughter had nightmares, too."

"That's one hell of an experience," Quinn said.

"Look at the two experiences together. One told me that God was among us, the second told me that Satan was walking the earth."

"Yes. I guess you're right, Maggie."

"It goes to your research, Quinn."

"After the research I did during the night, I look at the Bible as literal, and not at all allegory or myth. And I understand now that Satan's descendants work and walk among us today. That was hard enough to contemplate, to accept. But how the hell do we defend ourselves against them?"

"You know, Quinn, after our discussion last night after dinner, and looking back at the New Jersey Turnpike incident," Maggie explained, "I wonder if the Holy Ghost actually made my daughter and me invisible to that thing."

"You mentioned last night that you White Light yourself and your loved ones," Quinn said.

"Yes. When you White Light someone, you call upon Jesus Christ and His Holy Ghost's White Light to be within your mind, your heart, and on your lips that you may speak God's will. You ask God to protect you within the sphere of His Ghost's Light. I ask it all the time, and in my mind's eye I picture my kids, my grandchildren, their homes and their animals, and imagine the Light of God covering all of them. Then I know they are safe."

"You didn't have time to ask God to White Light you on the New Jersey Turnpike," Quinn argued.

"I think God knows where Satan is walking and keeps close tabs on him to keep him from harming those who believe in and pray to Him and His Son, Jesus. I'm sure God was there on the pathway of the New Jersey Turnpike rest stop. I'm sure of it. Think of it! Why else would the voice tell me not to let his coat touch me. If it had, he would have known that we were there. He never showed any sign of seeing us on that pathway. I'm convinced that we were made invisible to him."

Chapter 7

After Quinn's call to Maggie, she had hung up the phone and lain back in bed. Her eyes were weary after spending the night reading The Art of War and taking notes. She had been asleep only a short time when she began dreaming of Booker. He spoke gently of needing her to watch over Quinn's body. The idea that something was wrong with Quinn caused her to wake with a start. Still in the haze of sleep, she sat up in bed and looked around. When she went to brush the hair out of her eyes, she felt a hand take hold of hers. She spoke out to the room, "Is that you, Will? Show yourself to me, Will. Is there something wrong with Quinn?"

Suddenly, standing next to her bed, was the apparition of Will Booker, smiling at her, "It's okay. Quinn is okay. You need not worry, ma'm."

"What's going on?"

"I'll be taking Quinn astral projecting, and you need to protect his body while his soul is out of his body. He has to meet with General Eisenhower."

"What!"

"The Quinn's Regiment. They're having a meeting at the Pentagon."

"At the Pentagon! Quinn is going to astral project to the Pentagon! I just spoke to him! He didn't say anything about meeting with Eisenhower."

Maggie was disoriented and stunned. "Give me a second here to wake up. I mean, this is just incredible!"

"Yes, well, he doesn't know yet, ma'm. Right now he's sleeping. It'll be a surprise to him, I'm sure. But we need to go to his house, now. I need to bring his spirit to the Pentagon. They're waiting for him. It only takes a few minutes to fly there. I'm a mighty fast flying spirit, ma'm." Booker's lighthearted attitude was disquieting to Maggie's sense of incredulity of the topic of their conversation.

"Booker, you can't just come in here all smiles and funny; you're about to take Quinn's soul out of his body! Oh my God! Oh my God!" Maggie jumped out of bed, pulling clothes from bureau draws and closet. Before she realized it, she was fully dressed. She had been so concerned for Quinn that she didn't think of Booker being in the room, as she took off her nightgown and put on a sweatshirt and pants.

Booker explained what was going on and that the Regiment would be going to the Montana Territory to do 11th dimensional training. Maggie was excited for Quinn, but worried about how she could protect his lifeless body.

Maggie drove her car with Booker's solid apparition sitting next to her giving directions. When they got to Quinn's house and walked up to the porch, Maggie asked, "How am I going to get inside. I'm sure it's locked!"

"I can take care of that, ma'm," Booker answered and then passed through the front door, turned the doorknob, and unlocked the lock.

"I have to say, Booker, you're really handy to have around."

Maggie entered the house, passing through the living room, she whispered, "Where is his bedroom?"

"Upstairs," Booker said.

When Maggie reached the top of the stairs, she looked into the first room across from the steps, but there was no Quinn.

"Down here, ma'm."

Maggie followed Booker to the room at the end of the hallway and looked in to see Quinn in his bed.

Slowly walking over to the side of his bed, she looked down at his sleeping body.

"What do I do?" Maggie whispered to Booker.

"Just watch that nothing gets in him."

"You mean, as in another spirit?!" The hair on the back of Maggie's neck prickled.

"Yes, ma'm," Booker smiled.

"And how do I stop that!?"

"Tell it to go away in the name of Jesus Christ our Lord and Savior."

"Okay," Maggie mumbled.

Booker looked at Maggie, "I'm going to call his spirit. He might not notice you, but that's okay. Don't worry and don't speak and startle him. Okay?"

Maggie swallowed hard, "Okay," she whispered.

"Quinn should be back in about seven hours."

"Seven hours!"

"Shhh," Booker cautioned. "They'll be going from the Pentagon to the Montana Territory. There's a lot of training, Maggie. You'll be okay."

After Quinn had gotten off the phone with Maggie, he had gone to bed, exhausted from being up all night. His brain felt fried from all the information that he had absorbed. He had found himself thinking of his relationship with Maggie, the events happening within the country, and the actual significance of the Y-chromosome exposing Satan's bloodline. Life appeared to him as it never had before. It was a strange existence, yet weirdly familiar. All his life-long questions were being answered. Life seemed to be fuller, all inclusive of every aspect of existence. He began to think of his soul and how he felt a new, deeper relationship with God. He made a conscious choice to fight for Jesus; willingly giving unto God's will whatever God showed him to do.

As sleep had overcome him, he mumbled, "I'm ready God to be your servant. Your will be done." He drifted deeper in to sleep, feeling a peace deep inside his bones.

He hadn't been asleep long when he began to dream of the night's discussion, of ghosts, of his Special Ops team members who had been killed on missions. The same question always entered his dreams – had they been set up? His sleep had been restless till finally sitting up, suddenly awake, his body sweating, he had looked around the room to get his bearings. The sunlight peeked along the edges of the closed window shades. He sighed. His hands stroked his head down to the back of his neck. He tried to clear the memories of seeing his buddies being overwhelmed in a surprise encounter with the Columbians. "How the fuck did they know we were going to be there," he asked. He had lain back down, punching the pillow into a comfortable cradle for his head and he had drifted off again.

He lay quietly in a peaceful dream of Maggie and her gentleness, when Booker's voice called him, "Quinn?" He continued to dream of Maggie, her kiss goodnight, when again the voice came, "Quinn!"

"Whatttt!" he cried out, still asleep.

"Quinn, would you like to fly?" the Civil War spirit asked.

"Is that you Booker?"

"Come with me, Quinn. Come with me."

In a dream state, Quinn turned over, "Booker?"

"Yes. It's me. We need to go to the other leaders. To the spirits who protect the country. They're waiting for you, Quinn."

Quinn sat up and looked at the foot of the bed; there stood the apparition of the young Civil War veteran, Will Booker.

"Booker? I can see you!"

"Get up, Quinn. Take my hand. We're going to fly to the leaders."

Quinn stood up, reached out for Booker's extended hand. As he did, he saw that his hand looked the same as the spirit of Booker, vague, and without color. He looked back at the bed and saw his body, lying outstretched on its back. He saw Maggie, sitting on a chair next to his bed, blessing herself in prayer.

"She's going to protect your body while you're gone, Quinn."

Quinn began to call to her, but Booker interrupted, "She won't be able to hear you, Quinn."

Maggie felt a strange essence moving near her, but before she could turn around, Booker and Quinn were gone. And then the feeling was gone. She assumed that Quinn's soul had left his body. She turned back to his body, watching his face for a few minutes and then remembered that she had brought a cross and brown scapular to put around Quinn's neck. She placed them carefully over his head and adjusted the pillow to keep his head supported. Then she took holy water and anointed his body.

Before he knew it, Quinn and Booker were flying above the treetops. Quinn thought of what Maggie had told him about the silver thread. He looked down at his spirit and saw the thread trailing behind him. He looked down at the houses, the trees, and the streets, flashing by faster and faster under them. He and Booker were accelerating in speed, holding each other's hand. The freedom of flying exhilarated Quinn. There were no obstacles; nothing restricted their flight. There were only the stars above and the land below. Quinn was mesmerized by the beauty, the peace of it all, the solitary quietude. If this is death, he thought, I'm okay with it. The pain of arthritis that had started to settle in his knees from jumping out of helicopters was now gone. He was completely free of all pain. His spirit was totally relaxed. It was glorious. All he had to do is think the thought and his spirit flew in that direction.

Soon they reached the Pentagon in Washington, DC. Will Booker held tighter to his hand and directed them to the inside courtyard where they came to a stop, hovering outside a thick wall of the Pentagon. Booker explained to Quinn, "This is going to seem weird; the walls are thicker than your house. Don't worry; you won't get stuck. Just don't let go of my hand or you might get lost."

"Okay," Quinn swallowed hard. "I'm ready."

"After they passed through the exterior wall they encountered plumbing pipes, and electrical and cable wires. It was dark, and out of reflex, Quinn held up his arm in front of his face. He became disoriented and confused, not sure what his soul was passing through, not knowing where the other side of the wall was. They passed through layers of different matter. Maybe Booker was wrong. Maybe he would get trapped. Yet he could tell that they weren't just going through the walls, but down through the floors of the building. He grabbed tightly to Booker's hand, knowing Booker would pull him through. Then suddenly, they came out into a room.

Quinn was dazed for a moment. He looked around the room and at the long table in its center. There were no windows; air was pumped in from wall vents; at the end of the long table were red and black phones. Sitting at the long table were spirits dressed in various uniforms. Quinn looked at each one of them. The uniforms indicated high-ranking officers from the various wars fought by Americans, mostly in foreign lands.

Chapter 8

Quinn was incredulous, there he was standing in a meeting room of the Pentagon, and there before him were the leaders of the 11th dimension ghost soldiers, sitting at the long conference room table. He looked down at his own hand to remind himself that he, too, was a ghost. At least until his soul returned to his body. Astral projection was, to him, an unbelievable adventure.

Will Booker stood next to Quinn, "General Eisenhower, this is Quinn, Army Special Ops.; he's come to meet with you to discuss a military strategy for the war."

Without thought, Quinn snapped a salute.

General Eisenhower stood up, returned Quinn's salute and walked up to him and shook his hand and gestured, "Please have a seat, Quinn."

Quinn sat down slowly. He was still in a daze, as he looked at the spirits and looked at his own body just as vague and without mass.

"Just take a minute there, son," Eisenhower said to him, "After a while you'll get used to it. In the meantime, let me brief you on our activities."

Quinn nodded.

Eisenhower began, "We know that Maggie was up reading the Art of War, Quinn. We ask that you read it, also."

"How did you know that she read it?" Quinn was stunned.

"One of the tasks we assigned to our troops, our deceased troops, is to go around the country and examine Americans that we can use in the fourth dimension to fight with us."

"You send out scouts?" Quinn continued to be stunned.

"Yes. We reviewed your service record, as well. You were quite a soldier, Quinn. We expect that you will serve exceedingly well in the coming war."

"Yes, sir!"

"We have been all over America. Sent scouts to the Tea Parties and listened in on phone conversations, read blogs. By the way, those allegedly patriotic websites, many of them have been infiltrated by communists and progressives. One is run by a CIA agent."

Another astral projecting leader sitting at the conference table interjected, "That CIA agent is collecting a list of names. But we're keeping our eyes on those alleged patriots. And there are two Muslim sons of Satan running the Department of Homeland security; the Director is just a figurehead. Why do you think she hasn't closed the border – she's not in control. The Hezbollah, Hamas, Al Qaeda Muslims are pouring over it and into the Muslim training camps. And Muslims own all the gas stations. Why do you think that is, Quinn!" Before Quinn could answer, the angry leader told him, "Those gas stations are bombs! If they own the franchise, no one can enter their property without a search warrant, but in the meantime, those gas stations are all rigged, and no one knows about it. As soon as the shit hits the fan, they'll set off timers, or use their cell phones to blow up those underground gas tanks, killing Americans and destroying neighborhoods. And how the hell are we going to fight in the fourth dimension, if we have no gasoline! Americans won't be able to get to where the action is."

"Yes, sir!" was all Quinn could manage to say when Eisenhower took over.

"We asked Will Booker to contact you, Quinn. Well, we knew that Maggie was a sensitive, a translator of the spirit world, so we brought you and Maggie together. We had Booker whisper in her ear to invite you to dinner and then had Booker provoke the conversation using the salt and peppershakers. We wanted to introduce you to Booker through Maggie. That way you'd be open to Booker when he appeared to you in your sleep and asked you to come with him to meet with us."

"Yes, sir!" Quinn croaked out. The trauma of astral projection flying into the Pentagon and meeting Eisenhower's spirit and all the 11th dimension leaders left Quinn otherwise speechless.

"Booker told you that we have all the dead soldiers of all wars fought in defense of America. There are some that were too exhausted, too broken; they wait in the fifth dimension. But that's okay; we have millions and millions of spirits waiting to fight, including 4Fs, which doesn't matter in the spirit world. We've been gathering intelligence. And you should know, Quinn, there are enemy, evil spirits who will be fighting against us."

"Yes, sir. Excuse me, sir, may I ask a question?"

"Yes, son. Go right ahead," Eisenhower replied.

"How do we defend against dead evil spirits with all kinds of power? They are invisible to us in the fourth dimension."

"We have that same power, Quinn. They are not stronger than you, not while you're in the 11th dimension. Oh. That reminds me, after this meeting, Booker is going to train you on those powers. When needed, you will astral project out of your body and into the 11th dimension."

"Yes, sir." Quinn was excited with anticipation of learning how to use the powers of invisibility, possession, telekinesis, and telepathy.

"One of our concerns is the underground military labs. They will be our first priority, Quinn. Always attack your enemy's strength, first. Two things are going on in these labs. They are manufacturing hybrid humans; corrupting the DNA of men with that of animals and doing transplants. They are also mass-producing diseases, plagues, but most of the plagues and poisons are being created at Grayard University, in Cambridge, Massachusetts. They are poisoning our population with the chemtrails; killing some, weaken the majority, and sometimes spraying chemicals that create euphoria, so we won't fight back. They have set up multiple fronts in attacking Americans. The Corexit 9500 on the Gulf of Mexico is poisoning that seafood supply and all land vegetation in the surrounding states. Jesus Christ," Eisenhower exclaimed, "The people down there are bleeding internally from breathing in the toxic air dumps.

The fellow that ordered that chemical spraying is Tony Faywood; he's a member of the Scottish Freemason satanic-worshipping group. He refused to stop the spraying after two weeks when our EPA told him to stop. President Tsaeb refused to involve himself. The Coast Guard Ret. Admiral Chad Mellon who took control of that cleanup is a member of the Foreign Affairs Private Council. Anyone who is a FAPC member is a Satan worshipper and an enemy to America.

They're all in on the destruction of America. The START treaty, that Congress consented to, prevents the United States from defending against missile strikes from Venezuela and Iran. That is, through this treaty, Congress agreed to destroy and not produce enough defense missiles that one day we will need to aim at Venezuela and Iran, or any other country. They are making us completely defenseless against the world. The War in Afghanistan is for the drugs, heroin for the elites to peddle. Another reason Congress hasn't closed our southern border; they're profiting from the drug sales. Congress has intentionally put us in tremendous debt through wars in the Middle East that Schirf started and Tsaeb has continued. They're making themselves rich while destroying America, that's their method in breaking the backs of the American people.

In the meantime, China has leased 600,000 acres of prime gas and oil fields in southeast Texas and pumping oil off our Florida coast. We'll be in too much debt, without resources to defend against the Chinese and Russian invasion that is planned. Diana Elfeinstein and Bea Carboor are turning the greatest fertile land in our country into a dust bowl and destroying fruit trees. What those daughters of Satan are doing is destroying our food supply; they are setting up Americans to starve to death."

"Sir, may I ask a question?" Quinn asked.

"Go ahead."

"How do we reach these people? I mean from the 11th dimension."

"That's going to be a fight in itself. The elite are protected by evil spirits, both dead and alive evil spirits. Elfeinstein and Carboor, along with Celosini, Dier, Brockworst, MacSham, and Tsaeb worship Satan and do his bidding. Satan, in turn, protects them with his legion of evil spirits. The best way to fight them is through the 11th dimension where those evil spirits exist. While they haven't reported it on TV, living patriots have tried to kill these people. Those patriots were murdered instead of being arrested; some were reported as druggies or socio-paths, committing suicide and whatnot," Eisenhower explained.

"Where do we begin to fight? How do we pull these 11th and 4th dimension good spirits together?"

"That's why we called you here today. There are spirit generals from past American wars that are strategizing the entire war as we speak, but you and these leaders," Eisenhower gestured toward the spirits sitting at the conference table, "will lead the actual fighting. Each of you will have your own regiment."

"Yes, sir."

"We asked the other live, astral-projecting leaders to wait in another room. We wanted to explain things to you first, before we introduced you to them. We didn't want to overwhelm you." Eisenhower looked across the table to Booker, "Colonel, will you call those leaders?"

While Eisenhower continued to talk, Booker used telepathy to call in the leaders from down the hall, waiting in another meeting room of the Pentagon. Quinn's attention was on Eisenhower, not thinking of how Booker would call the other leaders. It only appeared to Quinn that Booker wasn't moving at all. But what had been ordinary in the 4th dimension was obsolete in the spirit world. And what was extraordinary in the 4th was ordinary in the 11th. Booker didn't use a cell phone or landline, yet suddenly Quinn began seeing spirits pierce the thick walls of the Pentagon and fill the room to capacity. It was mind-boggling to Quinn. Many wore the black Barrett of the Special Ops that had no insignia.

He quickly scanned the faces, looking for his fallen buddies. There among the group was Shooter, Falcon, and Braverman. They all shared with Quinn the same eagle tattooed on their left shoulders. Quinn wanted to run over to them, but knew he was at attention even though he was seated. He couldn't move away from Eisenhower's instructions.

"Quinn, you're going to train with these spirits on the powers of the 11th dimension. The deceased soldiers will train you and the other live patriots that we handpicked from across the country. You can tell the difference by the silver thread. The deceased soldiers do not have the silver thread. The live soldiers astral projected just as you did for this meeting."

"Yes, sir."

"We're going to give you a month to perfect your skills," Eisenhower was now addressing all the fighting spirits that answered Booker's telepathic call. "We are planning a late spring attack. While we spirits can fight regardless of time of year, the live patriots who will be fighting with you will do better in the spring, after the snows of winter have passed. We're going to infiltrate the 4th dimension enclaves of patriots and delay their plans, which were to begin war in late winter."

Quinn looked at the spirits sitting at the large table and standing around the room, taking them in more clearly now that his mind began to accept all that had happened. But still, Quinn felt overwhelmed, how did we get to this point in our country, he wondered.

What he didn't realize was that each spirit could hear his thoughts. Eisenhower answered his question, "It's been a relatively slow steamroller, crushing every aspect that is America."

"What?" Quinn asked.

"You wondered how our country got to the point that we're at today," Eisenhower said.

"Yes, but…." Quinn replied.

"Your thoughts are open to all of us, Quinn."

Eisenhower turned to face Quinn directly, "Let me try to explain a few things. You remember the assassination of President John Kennedy?"

"Yes, sir," Quinn answered.

"Well, they did that because Kennedy realized what they were doing – the Federal Reserve System, etc. So, Kennedy issued an Executive Order 11110, to take control of the printing of our currency – the one dollar silver certificate – since Congress had given up that power, as the Constitution provides – and take it away from the owners of the Federal Reserve Banks. You see, Congress never passed a Constitutional Amendment to give the printing and regulating of our money to a private group of people. Kennedy sieged that power through Executive Order. Under the Federal Reserve Act, the Feds decide how much money to print, the US Treasury does the actual printing, and we pay the Feds interest on how much money is printed. If that doesn't tell the American people how corrupt the U.S. Congress is, nothing will. When Kennedy signed that Executive Order and ordered the Treasury to print silver certificates – over $4 billion worth were printed – that's when the Jesuits knew that they had to get rid of Kennedy. The only purpose of that central banking system is to financially enslave Americans – through the interest they charge running up a national debt that could never be paid off. And the Feds directly control the recessions."

Eisenhower cleared his throat and continued, "Kennedy made a speech that referred to the secret cabal of the Jesuits who are supported by the likes of David Knickerbocker and the central banking internationalists trying to take over the entire world. The danger is not just within our country. Every citizen and nation is under attack. They want to corral us by controlling our food, our healthcare, our education, our jobs, so they can force us to worship Satan. That's their endgame!"

Eisenhower paused, then added, "They did this to Lincoln, as well. When Lincoln tried to stop them, they assassinated him. They are pure evil and have infiltrated every office of the federal and local governments. I don't think people understand that they have infiltrated local governments, too. The United Nations are directly instructing local leadership through their Agenda 21 Sustainable Development. It won't be long before they actually announce that they have conquered the United States. But before they make that announcement, they have to take our guns!"

Quinn listened to Eisenhower and recalled Kennedy's speech on secret societies. He had memorized its chilling words that were all the more striking because they came from a man who had learned of the conspiracy first hand and suffered the consequence of its opposition. Quinn had also noted the trepidation in Kennedy's voice as he spoke. It was as if Kennedy knew that they would later kill him for his exposing words. Kennedy had warned: "There is a very grave danger that an announced needed increase of security will be seized upon by those anxious to expand its meaning to the very limits of official censorship and concealment…Today no war has been declared…(but) those who make themselves our enemy are advancing around the globe…(and) no war ever posed a greater threat to our security…(they are a) clear and present danger…The danger has never been more clear…its presence has never been more imminent. It requires a change in outlook…by the people…For we are opposed around the world by a monolithic and ruthless conspiracy that relies primarily on covert means…on infiltration…(and by) guerrillas by night… it is a system which has conscripted vast human and material resources into the building of a tightly knit, highly efficient machine that combines military, diplomatic, intelligence, economic, scientific, and political operations…its dissenters are silenced not praised…no secret is revealed…My obligation is to inform and alert the American people to make certain that they have all the facts that they need and understand them as well…."

Quinn reasoned that both Kennedy and Messinger, the former U.S. National Security Advisor and Secretary of State, had said the same thing about the conspiracy: that it will claim a need for national security. But Messinger was instructing the Foreign Affairs Private Council that they should create a fear of attack to warrant an increase in national security - to get Americans to plead for the UN Troops to march in their streets.

Quinn wondered about the covert means Kennedy mentioned that they have used to expand their power. Kennedy had warned that they had infiltrated every institution of the United States, which to Quinn included the US Supreme Court, the FBI, CIA, NSA, and other agencies so secret that no one knows of their existence; they had infiltrated every state legislature, the US Congress - and the Office of the Presidency. Quinn sighed when he remembered Kennedy saying that this ruthless conspiracy controls the U.S. Military. He sometimes wondered if the missions he and his team had been sent on was part of the ruthless conspiracy's way to use fear against others to get them to do their will - or just kill them to get them out of their way. Kennedy said that they silenced their opposition. And Quinn and his men had been sent to assassinate drug cartel leaders, but the drug leaders' opposition were allowed to live.

Quinn surmised that the intelligence and wherewithal of the mind it took to conceive and bring together such a conspiracy could never have come from anything less than Satan's mind. Therein lies the enemy of the world that all the world must fight. Quinn thought of the angel of God that spoke to Agar, telling her that the hand of her son, Ismael, would be against all men, and all men's hand would be against him. Quinn had concluded that Ismael was a son of Satan, and his bloodline lives on today and has brought that hand against America.

Quinn turned to Eisenhower, "Sir, I need to know. Weren't you a member of the Foreign Affairs Private Council? Weren't you working to conquer our country when you were president?"

Eisenhower took a seat at the head of the table. "Quinn, I won't lie to you," Eisenhower replied. "Yes, I was a member of the FAPC. But when you first join, you don't know all the players. They pick you and convince you that you are needed to advise the government leaders on how best to run the country. They convince you that it's a patriotic thing to do. You are taken in by broad verbiage that sounds honorable. You listen from your principles, while they are referring to their evil principles. Have you ever heard a president say that he believes in God?"

"Yes," Quinn responded.

"But Presidents Jeffers, Schirf senior and Schirf junior, and Tsaeb are not talking about the God of Abraham; they are talking about their god, Satan. You listen from your perspective, not realizing that they have another. And after you get into the White House, then you realize the power of the military complex, and that they're causing wars for their profit. They convince you that war is necessary, but what I didn't know, at first, was that those corporations, the Rothschilds, the Knickerbockers, the Morgans, and their ilk hired people to commit atrocities in foreign countries to convince Americans that war was necessary. I didn't know about the Illuminati in the beginning, or that the Jesuit General Black Pope controls every intelligence agency in the world. The senators and congressmen that Americans vote for do not win elections; the elections are fraudulent. At least, the key seats like Barry Dier, Fred Brockworst, Celosini, Carboor, and MacSham are fraudulent. Those races were bought and paid for long before the elections. For president, they don't take any chances. They pick candidates for both sides, Democratic and Republican candidates. Those candidates are just two sides of the same coin of corruption. They hand pick candidates, groom them, and sell them to the American people. And the American people fall for it every time, or they see that they are given no other choice. Americans vote against the most offensive, not for the best. Stanislaus Nazwisko handpicked Timmy Tercart; those two joined David Knickerbocker in establishing the Triple Commission, as a front for the evil FAPC. And the FAPC is only a front for a smaller group of 13 who orchestrate everything for Satan. At the top of that heap of inhuman dung is the Jesuit General Black Pope, the False Prophet."

Eisenhower lowered his head, "Quinn, I didn't know how bad the attack on our country was until it was too late. Then they threatened that they would kill my entire family. That they would use my grandchildren in their satanic rituals."

Eisenhower paused for a moment, looking down at his hands folded on the table, he continued, "I thought they were just corrupt, and that even if they were corrupt, they provided manufacturing jobs for Americans. They caused me several heart attacks; the office of the presidency doesn't offer protection from them - presidents are only protected from Americans. To keep Americans from hurting their front man, but you know what they did to Lincoln and Kennedy. Their protectors assassinated them! When I was leaving office, I tried to warn Americans with my outgoing speech. Today, they call it my military-complex speech. I'm here now using my military training from West Point to counter what I helped them to set up in destroying our country."

"I understand the position you were placed in, sir. I've been researching the evil that these people come from. That evil is horrendous and it truly exists all around us."

"Thank you, Quinn," Eisenhower replied. The men stood and shook hands. "Now, we're going to begin your training."

"Yes, sir," Quinn said and saluted Eisenhower; Eisenhower returned it and turned to Booker, "Booker, take these fighting leaders with you and begin training in the use of 11th dimension powers."

Quinn interrupted, "Sir, one more question."

"Yes, Quinn."

"Is it true that Ismael and his descendants are descended from Satan? That Islam is a religion that worships Satan?"

"Yes, to both questions, Quinn. And all Muslims are planning to kill every American and take our country. Do not trust any Muslim, Quinn!" Eisenhower responded, and then putting his fists on his hips, added, "But don't forget the Zionist Jews are also descended from Satan. These two lines are the forbearers of the two heads of the Illuminati. We will be fighting both. The Zionist Jews conquered and captured the U.S. in 1913 with the Federal Reserve Act; now the Muslims have invaded and are fighting the Zionist Jews for that control. Americans haven't owned their own country for the last 99 years, but most don't know that. We are witnessing the covert battle between the Muslims and Jews over who will finally conquer the U.S."

Eisenhower looked at Will Booker, "Stand at ease soldier. I think my discussion here will take a little longer."

"Yes, Sir!" Booker saluted then turned and walked away.

Eisenhower turned back to Quinn, "Quinn, have you ever read the *Talmud*?"

"Just a bit of research, Sir," Quinn said.

"Take a seat for a moment, Quinn." The two sat down at the table, and Eisenhower pulled the computer closer to him. At the top of the page he read, Vol. I History of Talmud, Book 10, Chapter 1, "Origin of the Name Talmud," (www.sacred-texts.com/jud/t10/index.htm):

"The name Talmud...designated all the commentaries of the sages on the Scriptures which the Pharisees had begun to interpret *figuratively*...The literal interpretation of the text (Torah) which in the opinion of the Pharisees, was falsified by them [Samaritans], or from that of the Macedonian conquest of Judea, when the term 'Great Assembly' was changed to the Greek 'Sanhedrin.' It (Oral Law was the)... instruction of the Law, of ordinances relating to clean and unclean, to property, to crimes. All sages who interpreted the biblical passages figuratively, unlike the Samaritans, were called 'Pharisees'...*At last* Janai Hyrcanus the First, overcame them [Samaritans], burned their temple, divested their city, and *compelled them by force of arms to conduct themselves according to the doctrines of the Pharisees....*"

Eisenhower came back to Quinn, "Finished? All right, I want you to read this - it's very important that you understand this next Chapter of the *Talmud.*" Eisenhower found Book 10, Chapter VIII, "Islam and Its Influence on the Talmud," (www.sacred-texts.com/jud/t10/ht111. htm). When he found the paragraph, he slid the laptop over in front of Quinn. "Read this:"

"In (A.D.) 622, the Hebrew religion gave birth to a second daughter Mohammedanism - founded by Mahomet (Muhammad) of Mecca...When Mahomet arose to say that through Gabriel, the angel, the Lord had destined him to confirm the truth of the Divine revelation previously (given) to Abraham, Isaac, and Jacob, Moses and the rest of the saints who had been on earth, he (*Muhammad*) *borrowed only the foundation of his idea from the Hagada of the Talmud.* Likewise, he borrowed many sayings, *traditions*, and historic legends from the same (Talmudic) source, and these materials served him as the foundation of the principles he prescribed for the guidance of his people. All the Hebrew plants succeeded speedily on the Arabian soil, as if they had been native...When the Jewish tribes of Arabia...had refused to believe in the inspiration of the new prophet, Islam arose on its parent Judaism, as Christianity had done before, persecutions, massacres, blood and fire and exile were visited on the adherents of the *Talmud.* As long as Mahomet had entertained the hope of gaining Jews for converts, his treatment of them was favorable and he enjoined in the *Koran* not to be inimical to adorers of one God...Islam gained few Jewish converts, he (Muhammad) turned the enemy of the Jews and became wroth against them ('The Vision of the Cow,' a chapter in the *Koran*) and persecuted them with fury and bloodthirstiness as infidels. But at his (Muhammad) death his hatred and intolerance died with him...In Egypt, Syria, Fez, and Morocco, wherever Islam dominated, Jewish communities flourished."

Quinn sat back in his chair and turned to Eisenhower, "The Muslims and Pharisaic-Zionist Jews have the same religion, the same principles, the same traditions!"

"That's right, Quinn, and it is *not* the Law of Moses. While the *Talmud* states that Christianity arose on its parent Judaism - that is a direct lie. Christianity has a foundation in the Law of Moses and was established by Jesus with His new testament. Christianity is God-created. Judaism is the man-created Pharisaic religion, which Islam copied. Therein lies the great deceit. Neither Islam nor Judaism are of the God of Abraham and not of His Son, Jesus Christ.

The Pharisees destroyed the religion of the Israelites; today, the Zionist-Jews are destroying Christianity. Throughout history, Satan's children have attempted to destroy God's children, and sometimes they have succeeded to come between God and His people.

As you can see by their *Talmud*, the Pharisees claimed that the Law of Moses had been corrupted. This claim gave the Pharisees the excuse to create their own religion. They used the *Torah* as a cover. The other deceit is that the Pharisaic/Judaic Zionist Jews and Muslims are each other's enemy. They are not! Except in who gets control of the U.S. and the world, to turn it over to Satan. They are two 'daughter(s),' one Mohammedanism and the other Judaism, vying for THEIR father's blessing."

Eisenhower paused a moment before continuing. "There's a book called *Constantine Porphyrogenitus De Administrando Imperio*. The Greek text was edited by Gy. Moravcsik. The English translation was by R.J.H. Jenkins, 1966, Dumbarton Oaks, 2008. The treatise was compiled 1000 years ago by Roman Emperor Constantine VII, A.D. 905-959. It is basically a letter from father to son, from Constantine VII to his only son, Romanus. 'Hear now, my son, those things of which I think you should not be ignorant, and be wise that you may attain to government,' p 49."

Eisenhower sat back in his chair, his arms folded casually over his chest. "The letter was a father's personal advice to his son, not the world, to give Romanus the background and insight of world-known individuals that had brought the world to where it was and that he would encounter – and that could have an impact on the Roman Empire when Romanus became the emperor. It is in this book, p 77 as I recall, that Constantine tells Romanus of the background of Mahomet, now called, Muhammad. Constantine wrote to his son:

> "The blasphemous and obscene Mahomet…This Mahomet, being destitute and an orphan, thought fit to hire himself out to a certain wealthy woman, his relative, Chadiga by name, to tend her camels and to trade for her in Egypt among the foreigners and in Palestine. Thereafter by little and little he grew more free in converse and ingratiated himself with the woman, who was a widow, and took her to wife. Now, during his visits to Palestine and intercourse with Jews and Christians he used to follow up certain of their doctrines and interpretations of scripture. But as he had the disease of epilepsy, his wife, a noble and wealthy lady, was greatly cast down at being united to this man, who was not only destitute but an epileptic into the bargain, and so he deceived her by alleging: 'I behold a dreadful vision of an angel called Gabriel, and being unable to endure his sight, I faint and fall.'; and he was believed because a certain Arian, who pretended to be a monk, testified falsely in his support for love of gain. The woman being in this manner imposed on and proclaiming to other women of her tribe that he was a prophet, the lying fraud reached also the ears of a head-

> man whose name was Boubachar. Well, the woman died and left her husband behind to succeed her and to be heir of her estate, and he became a notable and very wealthy man, and his wicked imposture and heresy took hold on the district of Ethribos. And the crazy and deluded fellow taught those who believed on him, that he who slays an enemy or is slain by an enemy enters into paradise, and all the rest of his nonsense. And they pray, moreover, to the start of Aphrodite, which they call Koubar, and in their supplication cry out: 'Alla wa Koubar,' That is, 'God and Aphrodite.' For they call God 'Alla,' and 'wa' they use for the conjunction 'and,' and they call the start 'Koubar,' and so they say 'Alla wa Koubar.'"

Quinn had listened intently and when Eisenhower was finished, Quinn asked, "Are you, or rather, is Roman Emperor Constantine VII telling his son that Mahomet, the Prophet Muhammad, told everyone that he saw the angel Gabriel to cover up his epileptic seizures?"

"That's correct," Eisenhower replied. "Muhammad was never visited by Gabriel. He was covering for the epileptic seizures that he was having. Now, in Constantine's letter to his son, he wrote:

> 'And the deluded Jews at his (Mahomet) first appearance had taken him for the Christ whom they expect, so that some of their leading men approached him and received his religion and forsook that of Moses who beheld God. But when they saw him eating camel's flesh, they realized that he was not what they had thought him. But they taught him to do nefarious crimes against the Christians and continued in his company. These are they who taught him to accept some parts of the Law, both the circumcision and other matters, which the Saracens observe,' p 81.

So, you see," Eisenhower said, "both the *Talmud* and Constantine VII are saying that Mahomet, Muhammad, took traditions, laws, from the Ezra Jews. From the *Talmud.*

Constantine wrote:

> 'The first to come after him (Mahomet), then, was Aboubachar, who had proclaimed him (Mahomet) to be a prophet and was for that reason left behind to succeed him. And his heresy prevailed in the district of Ethribos, at first in secret ten years, and at last through war another ten years, and openly nine years (p 81-82). This Aboubachar first took the city of Gaza and all the territory around about it. And the same Aboubachar died after ruling as emir three years, and Oumar succeeded to the rule and governed the Arabs twelve years. This Oumar marched against Palestine (Israel), and laid siege

in it and blockaded Jerusalem for the space of two years, and took it by guile. When Spohronius, bishop of Jerusalem saw him (Oumar), he said: 'Of a truth this is the abomination of desolation spoken of by Daniel the prophet, that standeth in the holy place.' He (Oumar) demanded the temple of the Jews that Solomon built, to make it the place of worship of his blasphemy. And it is so to this day,' p 83."

"Is that the Dome of the Rock," Quinn asked. "Omar built the Dome of the Rock."

"Yes. And Omar and his followers were Sunni Muslims. The problem within Islam comes from the conflict between the two divisions of Islam, the Sunni and the Shiite. 'The most critical issue following Mohammad's death was his succession. The forbearers of the Sunnis followed the tribal tradition of having a council of elders select as the head of the Islamic community the individual most qualified to lead. The forbearers of the Shiites on the other hand believed that Mohammad's heirs should rule the Islamic community. The conflict came to a head in the Battle of Karbala in (A.D.) 680…when the Sunnis forbearers massacred the prophet's grandson Husayn and his followers…the victors carried Husayn's head to Damascus and paraded it there. Is it any wonder that for the next thirteen hundred years, there has been hatred and recurring warfare between these two sects within Islam who differ radically in their religious practices?" (Allan Topol; www.military.com/opinion/0,15202, 120282,00.html)

"Iran is ruled by a Shiite government, as is Iraq Shiite. Al-Qaeda and Hamas are both Sunni," Eisenhower explained.

"So, there is warring between two Islamic sects and warring between Islam and Judaism, Zionist Israel. And all of them are against Christians!" Quinn surmised. "What a nest of snakes!"

"That's right. Now, son," Eisenhower said, "let's get back to the *Talmud*."

Eisenhower pulled the laptop toward him and clicked on (www.sacred-texts.com/jud/t08/t0810.htm) the *Talmud's* Book 8, Chapter VII, Rules and Regulations Concerning the Four Kinds of Death Prescribed...Mishna VIII: "If one *gives one of his children to Molech, he is* ***not*** *guilty unless* he had transferred him to the servants of Molech and let him pass through the fire. If, however, he had *transferred* and not passed through the fire, or vice versa, he is not guilty. Gemara: The Mishna speaks of idols, and mentions Molech. Said R [Rabbi] Abiu: Our Mishna is *in accordance with him who says* that Molech is not an idol *at all."*

Quinn sneered, "Sounds like Satan in the Garden telling Eve, 'No, you shall not die the death,' (Gen. 3:4)." He turned to Eisenhower, "Who's the 'him who says that Molech is not an idol'?"

"We can't be sure, but if Ezra created the *Talmud* in Babylon, my first guess is that Ezra said that Molech is not an idol, when, in fact,

Molech is an idol."

Eisenhower took up the Bible, "Quinn, here is what the God of Abraham told Moses, in the Torah, Leviticus 20:1-5, "And the Lord spoke to Moses, saying:...If any man of the children of Israel...give of his seed (children) to the *idol Moloch*...: the people of the land shall stone him...And if the people of the land neglecting...(do not prosecute) the man that hath (has) given... his seed (child) to Moloch, and will not kill him...I will set my face against that man, and his kindred, and will cut off both him and all that consented with him, to commit fornication with Moloch, out of the midst of their people."

Eisenhower looked up from the book, "You can see that the Pharisees are twisting these words of the Old Testament, Leviticus, to permit idol worshipping and to deceive the Israelites and get them to worship an idol. It's a deceitful way to capture their souls for Satan. Now, I want you to remember this Pharisaic rule when we look at Ezra. Ezra established the *Talmud* and the Great Assembly that forced this doctrine on the Israelites. This is God's punishment - the dung in the faces of the Levi priests. The Pharisees brought the Israelites into captivity in Jerusalem, led by Ezra, from 457 BC to AD 70. Enslavement under the Pharisees was longer than their captivity in Egypt."

Eisenhower continued to read Matt. 23:13, Jesus said to the Pharisees, "'But woe to you scribes and Pharisees, hypocrites; because you shut the kingdom of heaven against men, for you yourselves do not enter in; and those that are going in, you suffer not to enter.'"

Quinn replied, "And this is why the Pharisees wanted only their figurative interpretation. So they could mangle the Law given to Moses, to capture the souls of the Israelites for Satan."

"That's right, son." Eisenhower continued reading from Mark 7:6-9, "Jesus said to the Pharisees, 'Well did Isaias prophesy of you hypocrites, as it is written: This people honoureth me with their lips, but their heart is far from me...*teaching doctrines and precepts of men...For leaving the commandment of God, you hold the tradition of men*...And he said to them: *Well do you make void the commandment of God, that you may keep your own tradition*."

Eisenhower closed the book, "And according to the *Talmud*, this is also what the Muslims believe, having adopted the Pharisaic religion for Islam. The *Talmud* is exposing as a lie, Muhammad's claim that an angel of Allah appeared to him and gave him the religion of Islam. When, in fact, Muhammad copied the Pharisaic religion of idol-worshipping. From the beginning, this is the very point of contention between the Pharisees and Muhammad. Now, between the Zionist Israelis and Muslims. Muhammad took his religion from the Ezra Jews, but demanded that they follow him!"

Quinn added, "The Zionist Jews follow their own religion, and the Muslims follow that same man-created religion. And this is why the Pharisaic/Judaic/Zionist Jews were up in arms over the publication of the translated *Talmud* online. It exposes the fact that the Zionist Jews do not worship the God of Abraham!"

"That's right. Now, please read the next chapter. I think you'll find it interesting after your research last night."

"You know of my research?"

"Well," Eisenhower smiled, "Will Booker was waiting for you to go to sleep. He was with you from the time you left Maggie's apartment."

It was sinking in slowly with Quinn that the world was a much different place than he had been taught. He was beginning to realize that the world had been deceived for 6000 years, beginning in the Garden of Eden. Later, with other significant events: the creation of Pharisaism/Judaism in 586 B.C.; the creation of Islam in A.D. 632; and in A.D. 1073, Pope Gregory VII changed the Catholic Church, making it a legal institution; the Church became a monarchy and the Pope became a king. The corrupt Popes from Medieval days who pursued the Israelites to America under the Spanish Inquisition, to take them back to torture them in such things as the Iron Maiden, to get them to convert to Christianity. And, now, to present day Second Ecumenical Vatican Council, whose members handed the Catholic Church to Satan. Now, all three groups, the Zionist Jews, Islamic Muslims, and Catholic Cardinals and Popes were worshipping one god, Satan. All the while under the disguise and deceit of claiming to worship the God of Abraham.

They all had collectively created a world turned upside down wherein a lie is held as the truth, and the truth is disparaged as a lie. Only now was the fog of confusion lifting, thanks to the Internet connecting Americans and the world, and everyone is teaching each other. And Quinn realized that he had come a long way from those first teachings by patriots.

Quinn looked at the computer where Eisenhower had brought up (www.sacred-texts.com/jud/t08/t0807.htm) Book 8 of the *Talmud*, Chapter IV, Rules and Regulations Concerning Examinations..."

Eisenhower explained, "This next section of the *Talmud* reveals what is actually going on and reveals their satanic bloodline.

Quinn read: "Rabbis [Pharisees] taught that: "Adam the First was created singly, and why? *That disbelievers should not say there were many Creators* in Heaven. And another reason is because of the upright and the wicked, that the upright should not say: We are descendants of an upright man; and the wicked should not say: We are descendants of a wicked one (hence we are not to be blamed)...*As we see that when only one man was created there are quarrels of rank*, how much more (quarrels of rank) if many original Adams had been created."

Eisenhower explained, "The Talmudic phrase: 'many Creators in Heaven' is referring to the Garden of Eden, Gen. 1:8, "And God called the firmament (earth), Heaven...."

Quinn asked, "How would God creating many original Adams indicate multiple creators? God created male and female, Gen. 1:27. Then, inside the Garden, God created Adam, Gen. 2:7, and then Eve, Gen.

2:18. There were at a minimum of four people created - not Adam singly.

"Well, the *Talmud* is not talking about the male and female that God first created and sent out in to the world. They were the Neanderthals. The *Talmud's* argument only concerns the Garden of Eden."

"What about Eve?" Quinn asked.

"Zionist Jews think very little of women, as do the Muslims. To them, women are only a necessity of procreation and sexual pleasure, otherwise, they are nothing, therefore, not counted in this Talmudic verse."

"Even still," Quinn argued, "using the Pharisees' reasoning, why are they concerned that the creation of Adam should indicate singularity of a creator, yet the creation of the heavens and angels, the universe, the earth and all the creatures on it – how does all that not suggest more than one creator?"

Quinn turned to Eisenhower, leaning next to him, as they read the passage. "Sir, this doesn't make any sense, it's the reasoning of a child. Anyone can see right through their deceit."

The two men sat up straight, looking at each other. Eisenhower offered, "Gen. 3:9-14, proves that only God, Adam, and Satan were in the Garden at the same time when Adam was created. But while God created Adam, the *other* 'creator' was Satan. It was Satan who created/fathered Cain, therefore, multiple creators. It's the only logical explanation for the notion that there might have been many creators. Adam didn't create Cain - God didn't create Cain - so who did? The *other* creator! Who else was in the Garden - Satan!"

Quinn replied, "And the Pharisees who wrote this don't want people talking about or looking at Satan as a 'creator.' This is a deceitful attempt to keep people from knowing that Satan fathered Cain.

Eisenhower added, "But the Pharisees expose themselves by acknowledging that there were quarrels of rank - as in, who would control the earth. If there was no other person in the Garden, besides God, Adam and Eve, and Satan - and Eve wasn't trying to control the earth - she just wanted sex with the angel of the Lord, and then with Adam. And God wasn't competing. He's the one who gave that power over the earth to Adam. And Adam had the power, so he isn't quarreling with anyone over his rank.

So, who are the Pharisees talking about? Who is quarreling with Adam over his rank - over his power - and why did it matter to the Pharisees that disbelievers should be prohibited from saying there were many creators in Heaven, specific only to Adam? Who are they protecting? The Pharisees, at the time of their creating this Oral Law, were in control over the Israelites - the Persian King Cyrus the Great had set free the Israelites, after they had been captured by the Babylonians, the descendants of Ham. It was during that Babylonian captivity when Ezra rose in power. It was Ezra who created the *Talmud*, the Oral Law by manipulating the Law of Moses."

Eisenhower added, "It's been hypothesized that Ezra paid off King

Cyrus to issue the decree that the Israelites were no longer to have a monarchy, because it was Cyrus' decree that paved the way for the Pharisees rise to power. They would not have achieved their totalitarian power over the Israelites, if they had a King. The tribes had been scattered, the priestly tribe of Levites had been taken with the Assyrian conquest and the rest by the Babylonian conquest. The Levites had been in charge of the Torah, the Law of Moses, and the Ark of the Covenant, that is, until the political Pharisees took control of the Second Temple. Cyrus gave that control to Ezra and his Pharisees. Cyrus' parents were both descendants of Japheth; Cyrus was not Semitic. But then, neither were the Pharisees, nor are the Zionist Jews of today, Semitic. And after all, the Pharisees used the military force of Cyrus and his successor, King Artaxeres, with his decree of death to the Israelite who did not return to Jerusalem under Ezra's control.

When they returned to Jerusalem, the Pharisees then used King Hyrcanus the First to overcome the Samaritans, so the Pharisees could compel the Samaritans to 'conduct themselves according to the doctrines of the Pharisees,' (Book 10, Vol. 1, Ch. I, Origin of the Talmud; www.sacred-texts.com/jud/t10/ht104.htm). And this is their own Talmudic description of events! The Pharisees turned Jesus over to the Roman Governor Pilate to be crucified by the Roman soldiers. How unreasonable is it to believe that the Pharisees paid off Cyrus for his decree prohibiting an establishment of a monarchy? The Pharisees, politicians first, didn't want another King David, a priestly king! The Pharisees wanted to win that quarrel of rank between the Pharisees and a king, to control the children of the God of Abraham, before that quarrel got started. And the Pharisees/ Rabbis have held that rank of control ever since."

Eisenhower continued, "After giving the Israelites alleged freedom, the Pharisees immediately claimed control over the Temple and the Scriptures - the *Torah*, which they dismissed and created their own Oral Law, the *Talmud*. And what disbelievers are they talking about?"

Quinn answered, "The disbelievers of their Pharisaic religion - which is not the religion of the God of Abraham! The disbelievers were the Israelites who knew the *Torah* and the God of Abraham."

"That's correct," Eisenhower said, "Ezra's Oral Law - the *Talmud* - controlled the education of the future generations of the Israelites that he dragged back to Jerusalem. Ezra didn't want questions raised about the other creator in the Garden of Eden. Ezra was covering for Satan fathering, 'creating,' Cain - and the satanic bloodline – Ezra's bloodline. It would blow there cover of destroying the Israelite religion and creating a satanic religion."

Quinn gestured toward the computer, "Ezra, and today's Zionist Jews are covering up the fact that Satan got to Eve first, therefore, Satan was the other creator, besides God, who was in the Garden.

And if Adam was given control over the earth, who was competing with him for that position, that rank? The quarrel began, '*As we see that when only one man was created there are quarrels of rank*' after God gave power over the earth to Adam," (*Talmud*, Book 8, Ch. IV, *Supra)*.

Quinn pointed to the computer's screen and looked at Eisenhower, "Note the present tense indicative plural - 'are' - - there are numerous quarrels, not just the seduction of Eve. It indicates that Satan not only quarreled over who would get Eve first, who would father the first-born of Eve, but also, who would control the earth. And, in fact, those quarrels continued from the Garden to, at least, the day of the Pharisees. I read in John 12:19: 'The Pharisees therefore said among themselves: Do you see that we prevail nothing? behold, the whole world is gone after him (Jesus).' They quarreled with Jesus over rank.

Then there was the quarrel between the Pharisees and the Samarians on the proper interpretation of the Law of Moses; and the quarrel the Pharisees had with Jesus for the souls of the Israelites. And if the quarrels continued through those thousands of years, why not to today?"

Quinn paused a moment, "But are they exposing themselves as the wicked? Deliberately? They are specifically setting up a puzzle that can be easily solved. Here it is - but don't look here!" Quinn smiled, "It sounds like that cartoon character saying, 'whatever you do, don't throw me into' that bush - he said it because that was exactly what he wanted his captives to do, so he could escape. I mean, sir, why say anything at all? It's as though they want to brag about being descended from Satan without their admitting it."

Just then, Quinn remembered the phrase that he found the night before in 1 Chronicles 2:55, about the Pharisee scribes being the Kenites, and that the Kenites were of Ham; Ham was the father of the House of Rechab, Ham was descended from Cain. The Rechabites had defied the God of Abraham out of loyalty to their father's orders. And Quinn remembered reading John 8:44-47, when Jesus said to the Pharisees: "You are of *your* father the devil, and the desires of your father you will do. He was a murderer from the beginning, and he stood not in the truth; because truth is not in him. When he speaketh a lie, he speaketh of his own: for he is a liar, and the father thereof...He that is of God, heareth the words of God. Therefore you hear them not, because you are not of God."

Quinn mumbled under his breath, "They really are. They really are from the same genetic pool, the same Y-chromosome - the Pharisees - the Rabbis, Zionist Jews, all of the same genetic pool as Satan!"

Quinn continued his analysis of the Talmudic phrase, "'The wicked should not say: We are descendants of a wicked one (hence we are not to be blamed),' While on the surface it seems to be instructing that the wicked should not shirk from responsibility of their actions, it's actually an instruction to the wicked to keep silent about their bloodline. Because the other side of that coin is: if one is admittedly wicked, they will not be given any power.

Disguised as the Chosen upright bloodline, the wicked Pharisees were able to enslave the Israelites, defeat the Samarians who read the Law of Moses as literal, and they were able to murder Jesus Christ. The Samarians got their temple burned down and were forced to accept the doctrine of Pharisaic/Judaic figurative interpretation of the Law of Moses. The Pharisees had the Israelites convinced that they were so upright that the Israelites joined the Pharisees in demanding the crucifixion of their own Messiah, Jesus. The Pharisees/Zionist Jews had picked up their father's – Satan's – gauntlet of 'quarreling over rank.'"

Quinn looked at Eisenhower, "But their teaching in this paragraph is that they don't want you to know that they are quarreling. Otherwise, their plan to control the world will be stopped. The Talmudic writing of the phrases: the 'upright should not say' and the 'wicked should not say' exposes themselves. No wonder they didn't want the *Talmud* published on the Internet!

This Talmudic teaching continues to today with the true upright bloodline being controlled by political correctness - that weapon is the same as this Pharisaic teaching - the 'upright should not say.' Political correctness forces acceptance when you are told that it's not nice to speak against the picked-on, abused, sacred Zionist Jews of Israel. One is a racist if they speak against them or recognize them as a satanic bloodline. And they also teach that the worst thing that could happen to someone is to be called a racist; society is immediately expected to hate you. All of society is called upon to reject you. Banish you. It's mob rule to silence speech, to silence knowledge of who they are.

And the upright should go to war to protect the State of Israel from the Muslims, their cousins, those who share their religion. The United States has been giving the State of Israel multiple billions of taxpayer dollars each year since their formation, in 1948, even though they steal our military weapons secrets and sell them to Russia. Even though the Israelis spy on the U.S. Our government leaders say that we must be their ally. Yeah," Quinn grew sarcastic, "at least, until they have control over the earth. Have instituted the New World Order, enslaving the upright. The Pharisaic message of 2586 years ago is the same as the Judaic message of today, 'Let's just all blend together in one humanity.' All the while the world is still compelled to think that the Zionist Jews are the 'Chosen' of God's people, hence, to go against them is to go against the God of Abraham. Nothing could be further from the truth! They've turned the world upside down! The Zionist Jews call today's Israelites, Gentiles. When, in fact, the Zionist Jews are the Gentiles, who do not worship the God of Abraham. It's only the Christians of the world who worship the God of Abraham. And they are the only ones who do!"

Eisenhower read Luke 21:24, "And they shall fall by the edge of the sword; and shall be led away captives into all nations; and Jerusalem shall be trodden down by the Gentiles; till the times of the nations be fulfilled." Eisenhower explained to Quinn, "Gentile means a nation, or a race, or a people who are specifically non-Israelite. And 'the Gentiles' is interchangeable with 'the nations.' That is to say, until the time of the Gentiles be fulfilled! Since neither the Zionist Jews nor the Islamic Muslins are Israelites, therefore, they are both the Gentiles. So Luke is telling us, until the time of the Zionist Jews and Muslims is fulfilled. And both have been controlling the United States."

Eisenhower said, "The Assyrians were descendants of Sem, Gen. 10:22, and God sent them to punish the Northern Israel Kingdom after the Israelites followed Solomon in worshipping Satan. The Assyrians were of the same Semitic bloodline, but cousins of the Israelites. If a Gentile is someone who is not an Israelite, then technically, the Assyrians were Gentiles. They conquered, captured, and deported the Northern Kingdom, who then became the Ten Lost Tribes of Israelites, 'led away captives into all nations.' This is when the Israelite diaspora began.

The later Gentiles were the Babylonians, descendants of Ham through his son Chus who fathered Nemrod (Gen. 10:6-10). The Babylonians conquered and captured the Israelites of the southern Kingdom of Judah. From that captivity rose Ezra and the Pharisees, the descendants from Cain/Ham/Kenites. It was the Babylonians who destroyed Jerusalem and Solomon's Temple, the First Temple. But the Apostle Luke is talking about the coming destruction by Gentiles - the Romans. 'Jerusalem shall be trodden down by the Gentiles.' Luke is talking about the final diaspora of Israelites after the Romans destroyed the Second Temple and Jerusalem, A.D. 70. It was after this that the Pharisees called themselves Rabbis and Pharisaism was called Judaism, which exits today.

There are three basic races in the world, those who descended from the White race, King David/Jacob-Israel/Isaac/Abraham/Sem/Noah/ Adam/ who God created; those descended from the Black race, Ham/Cain/ who Satan created, and those descended from the Yellow race, Japheth/ Cain/who Satan created. If the Biblical text refers to Gentiles, goyim, as a race of non-Israelite people - then the Gentiles are from Ham and Japheth - Satan. The Zionist Jews have stolen the ancestry of the Israelites as a cover for Pharisaism/Judaism, and they are the Gentiles who continue Luke's warning of Jerusalem being trodden down by the Gentiles – by the Zionists and Muslims!"

Quinn nodded.

Eisenhower continued, "The 1913 Federal Reserve Act conquered, captured, and enslaved the Israelites, the majority of whom are now collected together in the United States. The Federal Reserve Act gave eight, non-Israelite private families control over the American Israelites/ Christians. The time of the Gentiles continues. Satan's quarrel over control of the earth continues. God's punishment of the Israelites continues - until, as Matt. 24:15 warns, 'you shall see the abomination of desolation.' The ancient use of the word abomination meant 'idol.' This phrase of Matthew's means: when you see the idol of destruction. That is to say, until you see Satan – 'standing in the holy place: he that readeth let him understand.' The holy place is the Catholic Church. The Rabbis and the Jesuits control the Catholic Church and changed its dogmatic constitution. This was their plan from the last decades of the 19th century, the 1880s-1890s – to implement Modernism, the Jesuit Liberation Theology. It is based on Marxist revolutionary principles and its goal is to establish a world-wide Communist system of government – with no place for God, because their idea is that each man is a god. And this idea was held by radical Jesuits who rose up through the ranks of the Society of Jesus and either was imposed on their Jesuit General and the Popes who then complied, or the Jesuit General and the Popes elected were of their mission. Only God knows the answer. Today's Jesuits had declared war against the mission of the founder of the Society of Jesus and against the Pope, who they had previously vowed to obey without question."

"Sir, if I may ask, what exactly is the Society of Jesus? And how powerful are they today?

Eisenhower nodded his head, "The mere title of Jesuit immediately indicated a brilliant mind. The Jesuit is also immediately recognized as a person of absolute self-control, and willing to do whatever the Pope asks of him, hence they have always been considered the 'Pope's Men.' The Society of Jesus was founded by Ignatius of Loyola in 1540. No single organization has rivaled the Jesuits throughout the history of mankind, (Martin, M., The Jesuits, The Society of Jesus and the Betrayal of the Roman Catholic Church, Simon and Schuster, NY, 1987, p 26).

The Jesuits were the first body of Catholic Scholars who became pre-eminent in secular sciences and arts…The list of inventions and scientific discoveries had filled endless numbers of volumes in the most diverse fields. The list numbs the mind by its all-inclusive variety of study. Their manuals, textbooks, treaties, and study were authoritative in every branch of Catholic and secular learning. They were giants but with one purpose: the defense and propagation of papal authority and papal teaching (*Ibid.* p 29).

They had a special vow of obedience to the pope in whatever they did – and through that vow the entire society has been silenced by their leaders. At the height of their efforts, 200 years after their founding, the Jesuits had a formative and decisive hand in the education and science of practically every country in Europe and Latin America. They had a part to play in every political alliance in Europe – an influential post with every government, an advisory capacity with every great man and each powerful woman. They drafted treaties, negotiated peace pacts, mediated between warring armies…lived where they were not welcome as underground agents of the Holy See. They passed as pig farmers in Ireland, businessmen in Prussia, clowns in England, merchant seamen in Indonesia, beggars in Calcutta, swamis in Bombay. There was nothing anywhere they would not undertake for the 'greater glory of God.' The worldwide power of the Jesuits became so great that their Jesuit Father General was called the Black Pope, after the black cassock of the ordinary priest. They represented the papacy (*Ibid.* pp 30- 33).

In the 1950s, Jesuit influence on papal policy was never before greater. Their prestige among Catholics and non-Catholics was never higher. Yet, some inner rot was corroding both Jesuits and the Catholic ecclesial body. Some hidden cancer planted decades before within these bodies had gone neutral, but not benign. The 1960s brought about a violent change in both. This is why the Lady of Fatima wanted the Third Secret revealed by the Pope of 1960. The Third Secret was about the apostasy, the fall of faith in the hierarchy of the Church. The Pope of 1960 refused to reveal the secret against the wishes of the Mother of Jesus. This tells us that the Blessed Mother wants us to look at that Pope of 1960 – John XXIII. And the Blessed Mother told the Pope of 1960 – God knows what you are doing!

It was in 1965, Vatican II had ended, and Pedro de Arrupe was elected by the Jesuits to be their Jesuit General, the Black Pope. It was in 1965 that the Society of Jesus, the Jesuits, openly changed rather than existing as some festering cancer hidden from the world. This new outlook, their new mission was antipapal and sociopolitical that had been flourishing in a covert fashion for over a century was now espoused by Arrupe and the Society (*Ibid.* p 35). Arrupe was the one man responsible for the turnabout of the Society.

Arrupe and the Jesuit Superiors denigrated the pope, deceived him, disobeyed him, and waited for each pope to die in hope that the next pope would leave them with a free hand. As a Jesuit policy, they were violently against papal authority. (*Ibid.* p 79)

The Jesuits controlled the Vatican Bank; Pope John Paul I was about to investigate that bank. He also knew of the enthronement of Satan on the Throne of Peter. He was about to issue a decree to disband the Jesuit Order when he was murdered. John Paul I had finalized his speech and the Papal Bull on September 27-28 regarding his disbanding the Society of Jesus. On September 29, 1978, Arrupe was the last to meet and have a glass of wine with John Paul I; hours later he was found dead. Arrupe made all arrangements; he ordered the cleaning up the crime scene – the apartment of the Pope, after he murdered the Pope; he ordered the wine glasses to be washed, the furniture wiped of fingerprints; he ordered the body embalmed without an autopsy.

Pope John Paul II, elected in 1978, 'tried everything, including calling a conference with six of the most powerful Cardinals to discuss how to proceed with John Paul I's Papal Bull of disbandment of the Jesuits – (*Supra at* Martin, *Jesuits,* p 79) in April 1981. On May 13, 1981, Arrupe had arranged for the KGB to use a hit man, Mehmet Ali Agca, to kill John Paul II. For if the Jesuits had been disbanded, the way was clear to perform the ceremony to reverse the Enthronement of Satan. Arrupe's agents brought John Paul II to a local hospital instead of the one prepared to care for the Pope, including storage of good blood. At the local hospital they transfused bad blood, giving the Pope hepatitis. That local hospital is under Jesuit control. Later, Arrupe suffered a stroke and resigned; some say John Paul II removed him from office (http://one-evil.org/people/people_20c_Arrupe.htm).

But Jesuits had murdered before. Pope Clement XIII was preparing a Papal Bull to disband the Jesuits, February 2, 1769. The night before the Bull was due to be enforced Jesuit General Lorenzo Ricci had Pope Clement XIII murdered. Ricci spent the rest of his life in prison, dying on November 24, 1775. The Bull was only valid in countries in which it had been promulgated."

Eisenhower paused for a moment, "It's been claimed that the Jesuits assassinated Presidents Lincoln and Kennedy; that the Jesuits control the global drug trade; and started the Vietnam War in order to make Asia Roman Catholic. Who knows if all of that is true, but they have the organization and the necessary brilliant minds to carry out such missions. We are talking about a collective of individual brilliant minds who are ruthlessly passionate about their mission, and damn the world – they will carry out their mission. We must never underestimate their individual abilities and their organizational network; it is worldwide in every place of power, explicitly and covertly. There is nothing in this world like them. Nothing! They are our most formidable enemy.

In 1965, their mission openly became the change of the Church through Vatican II documents that the bishops never dreamed of. The 'Spirit of Vatican II' blew the roof off the Catholic Church. Their plan was to change the Church of Jesus in to the People of God Church. The Jesuits 'had become modernists,' (*Supra* at Martin, p 480). Their mission of instituting modernism is that 'the hierarchical structure of the Roman Church must be 'adapted' to this modern view of the modern mind and of modern conditions. The prerogatives of the Pope – his teaching authority and his personal infallibility – as well as the dogmas and moral rules inherited from the recent and remote past of Catholicism – all of it could and must be changed. Abandoned,' (*Supra* at Martin, p 478). And so Vatican II brought about collegiality, the sharing of papal power with the Cardinals and Bishops of the Church. While the Pope maintained authority to act alone and the Bishops could not, the Jesuits spoke openly against the Pope when he went against the Bishops' desires. Key, is that there was dissension and disunity among the Bishops, as in Adam Weishaupt's Illuminati notion to 'bore from within,' to destroy the Church. What the Jesuits did in 1965 through Vatican II was nothing short of a coup d'etat, a revolution that took control of the Roman Church. And this is separate and apart from Satan being Enthroned. Once they opened Vatican II under John XXIII, they took control, prepared for the enthronement, and once Paul VI was elected, they instituted the ceremony that gave the Church to Satan. Then they continued with Vatican II and changed the Church's constitution that legally installed Satan as the head of the Church.

What the Jesuits have done in this war that they declared on the papacy is to bring two ancient adversaries onto the final battlefield. These cosmic powers are Intelligent Good (God) and Intelligent Evil (Satan). The Jesuits have locked God and Lucifer in a struggle for the allegiance of all human beings. And it is on that cosmic plane that the war is being fought' (*Supra* at Martin, p 37). While the Jesuits were joined in this war by many groups, such as Rabbi Abraham Heschel, a representative of American Jews at Vatican II, the Jesuits blazed the way. There were also the Illuminati and Adam Weishaupt's promise to infiltrate the Vatican. And the KGB, the Soviet Secret Police, financed by the Rothschild family, 'and other Warsaw Pact intelligent services, saw their opportunity to penetrate the Vatican's central administration, deploy new intelligence assets throughout Catholic institutions in Rome and a way to tighten their own grip on Catholic populations behind the Iron Curtain' (www.firsthing.com). 'Catholicism and Communism offered the world two radically different visions of human nature, human community, human origins, and human destiny. These visions were fundamentally incompatible…someone was going to win and someone was going to lose.' (*Ibid.*)

Pope John XXII insisted that two prelates from the U.S.S.R. attend Vatican II, so he made a deal with the Devil – the Soviets would allow two priests from the Soviet Orthodox Church to attend Vatican II, if Pope John XXIII would agree that the Vatican would never again say anything against Communism and the Soviet Union. Pope John XXII agreed because then he could not carry out the wishes of the Lady of Fatima, consecrating Russia to the Blessed Mother, for it would be tantamount to saying that the Soviet Union and its Marxist dictator, Nikita Khrushchev, were criminals. While Pope Pius XII, John's predecessor, had consecrated the 'entire world' in 1942, and the Peoples of Russia in 1952, the country of Russia had not yet been consecrated to the Blessed Mother. Pope John XXIII hid behind his assumption that the Soviets would retaliate by killing millions throughout the Soviet Union. But there is the little known fact that John XXIII was a Communist. His insistence of having the two Soviet Orthodox Bishops attend Vatican II was a ruse to bring about the devil's agreement. His whole purpose was to silence future popes against Communism. And the Moscow-Vatican Pact of 1962 was written by Jesuit Cardinal Augustin Bea, and this document would forever silence the Vatican speaking out against atheistic Communism – 'for how could the Vatican complain about the Jesuits for their support (in arming, funding, and fighting with) Marxist thinkers and Communist guerrillas in Latin American without explicitly condemning the Soviet Marxism and its Communist surrogates?' (*Supra* at Martin, p 83)."

"They get a Communist elected as Pope John XXIII, who almost immediately calls for Vatican II, and claims that it is absolutely necessary to have two Russian Orthodox Bishops attend Vatican II, and all this is an excuse to silence future popes from speaking out against Communism inside the Church. And Vatican II allows the Jesuits to take control of the

Vatican, and destroy the pope's power through collegiality. They are, indeed, very brilliant men these Jesuits," Quinn said.

After pausing, Quinn asked, "But this modernist approach of the Jesuits, what exactly is that? Why is it significant?"

Eisenhower nodded, "It comes down to the new Jesuitism openly throwing considerable weight of the Society of Jesus against democratic capitalism and economic capitalism as the great evils to be scourged from human society, and this remains today (*Supra* at Martin, p. 481). It means that the Jesuits are against the structural foundation of the United States. Arrupe's successor, elected by the Jesuits to be their General, Kolvenbach, stated, that the 'negative aspects' of John Paul II's stance against Liberation Theology are regrettable, certainly social activism and political involvement of Liberation Theology was quite justified. With it comes the *new* People of God Church,' (*Supra* at Martin, p 485).

Eisenhower moved in his chair, looking directly at Quinn, "The idea behind Communism, Humanism, Modernism, Liberation Theology is that man is celebrated as a god – and God is thrown out or substantially diminished so as to be on equal level of man. What they all do in the end is remove God to open the way for Satan's control over man. What Arrupe said to Secretary General U Thant and the General Assembly of the United Nations, 'We (Jesuits) are pledged to work with right-minded men of all creeds and races for a more truly human society, justice and peace, a sense of family and of joint effort among the nations…' Martin, in his book, *Jesuits,* commented, 'Surely, a magnificent expression of secular humanism,'" (*Supra* at Martin, p 397).

"Sir, if I may interrupt, I'm sure that you read Dostoyevsky's last book, *The Brothers Karamazov*, in the chapter 'The Grand Inquisitor' he gives an insight on the Jesuits. I remember reading the conversation between the Inquisitor and the Prisoner, impliedly Jesus, who never speaks. The Inquisitor refers to Satan as the 'dread Spirit,' with an initial cap indicating that it's a proper noun, the name of Satan," (Dostoyevsky, *The Brothers Karamazov*, Signet, New American Library, NY, 1957, p 227). Ivan tells his brother, Alyosha, that he has written a poem in prose and tells him of the poem. The poem is called The Grand Inquisitor and it takes place in the 16th century, in which Jesus is a silent character. Humanity still awaits Jesus' promised return, but now with greater faith, since fifteen centuries have passed that man has ceased to see signs from Heaven. The story is set in Spain, in Seville, in the most terrible time of the Inquisition, when fires were lighted every day 'to the glory of God,' and 'in the splendid act of faith the wicked heretics were burnt.' He, Jesus, came down to the 'hot pavement' of the southern town in which on the day before almost a hundred heretics had, 'for the greater glory of God,' been burned by the Cardinal, the Grand Inquisitor, in a magnificent 'act of faith.'…He (Jesus) came softly… everyone recognized Him,' (p 229). When the Cardinal, now dressed in a coarse monk's cassock, sees that He raised a girl from the dead, who Jesus had done as noted in Luke 8:54, the

Cardinal/Inquisitor has Him arrested. 'So completely are the people cowed into submission and trembling obedience to him, the cardinal, that the crowd immediately makes way for the guards,' (p 230). The guards take Him to the ancient palace of the Holy Inquisition. The day passes into night, and in the pitch darkness of the prison cell, the iron door of the cell is suddenly opened and the Grand Inquisitor, the Cardinal wearing the monk's cassock, comes in carrying a light; he is alone. 'He stands in silence…At last he goes up slowly, sets the light on the table and speaks. 'Is it Thou? Thou?'…*Why, then, art Thou come to hinder us*?...I know not who Thou art and care not to know…But tomorrow I shall condemn Thee and burn Thee at the stake as the worst of heretics. And the very people who have today kissed Thy feet, tomorrow at the faintest sign from me will rush to heap up the embers of Thy fire,'" (p 230).

"The Inquisitor tells the Prisoner: 'that He hasn't the right to add anything to what He has said of old. One may say it is the most fundamental feature of Roman Catholicism…all has been given by Thee to the Pope, they say. And all, therefore, is still in the Pope's hands, and *there is no need for Thee to come now at all. Thou must not meddle for the time, at least.*' That's how they speak and write too – the Jesuits, at any rate,' Ivan tells Alyosha, 'I have read it myself in the works of their theologians….Hast Thou the right to reveal to us one of the mysteries of that world from which Thou hast come?'

Ivan tells Alyosha: 'my old man (Inquisitor) asks Him (Jesus), and answers the question for Him. 'No, Thou has not; that Thou mayest not add to what has been said of old, and mayest not take from men the freedom which Thou didst exalt when Thou was on earth. Whatsover Thou revealest anew will encroach on men's freedom of faith; for it will be manifest as a miracle, and the freedom of their faith was dearer to Thee than anything else in those days fifteen hundred years ago. Didst Thou not often say then: 'I will make you free'? But now Thou has seen these 'free' men,' Ivan explains to Alyosha, 'the old man (Inquisitor) adds suddenly, with a pensive smile. 'Yes, we've paid dearly for it,' he goes on, looking sternly at Him, 'but at last we (the Jesuits) have completed that work in Thy (Jesus') name. For fifteen centuries we have been wrestling with Thy freedom, but now it is ended and over for good. Dost Thou not believe that it's over for good?...But let me tell Thee that now, today, people are more persuaded than ever that they have perfect freedom, yet they have brought their freedom to us (Jesuits) and laid it humbly at our feet. But that has been our doing. Was this what Thou didst? Was this Thy freedom?' (p 231)

That freedom is mocked, 'No science will give them bread so long as they remain free. In the end they will lay their freedom at our feet, and say to us (Jesuits): 'Make us your slaves, but feed us.' They will understand at last, that freedom and bread enough for all are inconceivable together. Never, never will they be able to have both together! They will be convinced, too, that they can never be free, for they are weak, vicious, worthless and rebellious. Thou didst promise them the bread of Heaven, but, I repeat again, can it compare with earthly bread in the eyes of the weak, ever sinful and ignoble race of man? And if for the sake of the bread of Heaven thousands and tens of thousands shall follow Thee, what is to become of the millions and tens of thousands of millions of creatures who will not have the strength to forego the earthly bread for the sake of the heavenly?...we (Jesuits) care for the weak too. They are sinful and rebellious, but in the end they too will become obedient. They will marvel at us and look on us (Jesuits) as gods, because we are ready to endure the freedom which they have found so dreadful and to rule over them – so awful it will seem to them to be free. But we shall tell them that we are Thy (Jesus') servants and rule them in Thy name. *We (Jesuits) shall deceive them again, for we will not let Thee (Jesus) come to us again. That deception will be our suffering, for we shall be forced to lie,'* (p 234).

'But man seeks to worship what is established beyond dispute, so that all men would agree at once to worship it....what is essential is that all may be *together* in it. This craving for *community* of worship is the chief misery of every man individually and of all humanity from the beginning of time....They have set up gods and challenged one another: 'Put away your gods and come and worship ours, or we will kill you and your gods!' And so it will be to the end of the world...But Thou (Jesus) didst reject...(that which would have) made all men bow down to Thee alone – the banner of earthly bread. And Thou hast rejected it for the sake of freedom and the bread of Heaven....' (p 234).

'Didst Thou forget that man prefers peace, and even death, to freedom of choice in the knowledge of good and evil? Nothing is more seductive for man than his freedom of conscience, but nothing is a greater cause of suffering....Thou didst choose what was utterly beyond the strength of men, acting as though Thou didst not love them at all – Thou who didst come to give Thy (your) life for them! Instead of taking possession of men's freedom, Thou didst increase it, and burdened the spiritual kingdom of mankind with its sufferings forever. Thou didst desire man's free love, that he should follow Thee freely, enticed and taken captive by Thee. In place of the rigid ancient law (Pharisaism/Judaism), man must hereafter with free heart decide for himself what is good and what is evil, having only Thy image before him as his guide,' (p 235).

'There are three powers, three powers alone, able to conquer and to hold captive forever the conscience of these impotent rebels for their happiness – those forces are miracle, mystery and authority. Thou hast rejected all three and hast set the example for doing so....And man cannot bear to be without the miraculous, he will create new miracles of his own for himself, and will worship deeds of sorcery and witchcraft, though he might be a hundred times over a rebel, heretic and infidel....Thou didst not come down (from the Cross), for again Thou wouldst not enslave man by a miracle, and didst crave faith given freely, not based on miracles,' (p 235-6).

The Inquisitor tells Jesus, 'We have corrected Thy work and have founded it upon miracle, mystery and authority. And men rejoiced that they were again led like sheep, and that terrible gift (freedom of choice) was, at last, lifted from their hearts,' (p 237).

'And who will believe you about freedom?...That's not the idea of it in the (Russian) Orthodox Church...That's Rome, and not even the whole of Rome, it's false – those are the worst Catholics, the Inquisitors, the Jesuits!...We know the Jesuits....They are simply the Romish army for the earthly sovereignty of the world in the future, with the Pontiff of Rome for Emperor... that's their ideal, but there's no sort of mystery about it....something like a universal serfdom with them as masters – that's all they (Jesuits) stand for,' (p. 240).

The brother, Ivan, who had written the poem assures his brother, Alyosha, that he is not a Mason nor about to join 'the Jesuits, to join the men who are correcting' God's work, (p. 242).

Alyosha replies, 'Your Inquisitor does not believe in God, that's his secret!' (p 241)."

Eisenhower had listened quietly, "That was one of my favorite books. It's prophetic that such an outstanding writer came from Russia, his sentiments are more meaningful because he did know Russia so well. It's almost as though his book was foretelling of the coming of Lenin's Bolshevik Revolution, October 1917; foretelling of the visitation from the Lady of Fatima. Foretelling of Vatican II."

Eisenhower continued, "The Jesuits took over the administration of the Spanish Inquisition; the Franciscans had brought the Inquisition to the New World, to America. 'Napoleon tried to abolish it in France, and then in Spain and other western and central European countries in 1808, but failed. It had been established by Papal Bull in 1478 and lasted 3.5 centuries. Just 62 years after the Inquisition had begun, the Jesuits were formed, in 1540. The public displays of punishment were instruments of social control,' (Perez, J., *The Spanish Inquisition: A History*, 2006; Waterstones.com) It was after Napoleon's defeat that it was resurrected, but during Napoleon's reign the people had had a taste of freedom from it and it finally ended 19 years later, in 1834.

Although the Popes and Jesuits did that – tortured people to force conversion to Catholicism, the Lady of Fatima, 1917, gave the world the Third Secret of apostasy in the Church hierarchy. One has to wonder, what was going on in the Jesuit mind? How could they have gone from one extreme to another? How did they get from the Inquisition, Dostoyevsky's account of the Inquisitor telling Jesus to go away, we're handing it, to enthroning Satan on the Throne of Peter? Or was Alyosha correct, the Inquisitor did not believe in God; did any of the Jesuits ever believe in God? Had they always been for Satan from their inception?"

Eisenhower frowned, "I remember that passage: 'They will marvel at us (Jesuits) and look on us as gods, because we are ready to endure the freedom which they have found so dreadful.' Had the Jesuits believed that they had taken on the suffering of freedom; did they actually believe that Jesus giving mankind the freedom of choice between good and evil to be a show that Jesus did not love mankind? Had the Jesuits found that they could not handle that burden of freedom? Did the Jesuits think that mankind and their Order of the Society of Jesus should turn over that freedom to Satan, that it would cause less suffering? Was Dostoyevsky prophesying the failure of the Jesuits' ability to handle that burden of freedom of conscience? Was Dostoyevsky prophesying when he wrote: *We (Jesuits) shall deceive them again, for we will not let Thee (Jesus) come to us again. That deception will be our suffering, for we shall be forced to lie.*' Was that the prophecy Vatican II?"

Eisenhower was pensive, "'For we will not let Thee, Jesus, come to us again – it's the same thing that Adam Weishaupt had said, in 1776, about the Illuminati, 'We will infiltrate the Vatican and once inside we will never come out.' Or had Dostoyevsky read that about the Illuminati and applied it to the Jesuits? Did he connect the two as having the same mission? Dostoyevsky had lived somewhere around 100 years after Weishaupt."

Quinn replied, "The question today, in the promotion of an un-American culture of dependence on government handouts, have Americans become willing to turn over their freedom of life, liberty, and the pursuit of happiness because they prefer to be taken care of by the Jesuits, by Satan – and that that enslavement of them is preferable to Jesus' freedom to choose good over evil? Is it easier to sit down and wait for the earthly bread to be handed to them by the United Nations, rather than living free and in faith of Jesus' promise of Heavenly bread?"

"Well," Eisenhower replied, "we'll see how the American people respond. Certainly, there is a percentage who will stand up immediately and fight for freedom – they have already chosen the heavenly bread. But not all will. Not all did during the First American Revolution, it was only a small percentage, 3-10% of the colonials who fought. The others did nothing, but gained from the independence. I'm sure something of that nature will occur, again."

"But, Sir, wouldn't you say that this Revolution will be different – we now know what is going on. It's not a matter of freeing oneself and family from the tax burden of a King George, sitting on another continent. We now know that Satan walks the earth; that Satan sits on the Throne of Peter; we know that we must fight to save our eternal souls from Satan. This, today, is a different fight! And our enemy lives among us! He's not a continent away. Our enemy controls our military! At least, for now."

"I agree, son, but some people will not hear the Word; they are absolutely oblivious as to what is going on in this country. Some will, indeed, choose Satan, but the minority will respond to the call to muster. They will fight for Jesus. They will fight for their souls and the souls of their children.

And as to the Jesuits and their questionable evolution away from their original mission, we ended up with Arrupe's successor, Jesuit General Peter-Hans Kolvenbach, who appointed Michael Amaladoss, SJ, as his assistant. And what Amaladoss said certainly can be construed as representative of the Jesuit General and the Society. Amaladoss stated, 'The Church may be called on to die…this is true of all religions,' (*Supra* at Martin, p 484). This statement clarifies that the Jesuits' mission today is to bring about the destruction of the Roman Catholic Church. The greatest trait of a Jesuit is his patience. But they are planning and working toward killing the Church of Jesus. Satan has surely captured their souls. Since then, Kolvenbach resigned, and we now have Alonso Negrete, a Spaniard, who spent most of his career in the Far East."

Eisenhower bent forward, resting his arms on this thighs, "In this war between the Society of Jesus, the Jesuits, and the Vatican, 'each has organizations of manpower and equipment, and each has a grip on the levers of immense worldly power. Both perform on a passionless and universal plane with motives that do not permit the vulnerability of human feelings. And both assume time is on their side,' (*Supra* at Martin, p 37).

The 'real issue in the war is always the practical authority and the spiritual purpose of the Church. These Church traditions would be rejected and replaced by whatever authority and materialistic mission might be in vogue,' (*Supra* at Martin, p 24). This is modernism. And it leads to man becoming godlike, therefore, without the need of God. It relies on scientific discovery – the God particle that they claim eliminates all evidence of God's hand in Creation.

In an interview with an Italian journalist-writer that appears in his book, *The Ratzinger Report,* 1985, Ratzinger, who is now Pope Benedict XVI, stated, 'Since Vatican II, and because of a false interpretation of its documents, there is not one area of Church belief and morality that has not been corrupted,' (*Supra* at Martin, p 485). And this was the point of Communist Pope John XXIII calling together the Second Vatican Council, so the Jesuits and the Zionist Jews could bring about this destruction of the Church, with a little help from their friends – the KGB, the Illuminati, and the Masons. And it's quite likely that these were the secular groups that participated in the Enthronement of Satan.

And one cannot talk of Vatican II and not consider the influence of Karl Rahner, a German Jesuit expert for Vatican II Council. His theology was the basis of much of the content of the Council's teaching. 'Since 1965, Karl Rahner, leader of the wolf pack of Catholic theologians have lacerated and shredded the flanks and the very substance of Catholicism,' (*Supra* at Martin, p. 22). Rahner taught theology at a prestigious Jesuit university. He taught several generations how to cannibalize their own faith with logic, skepticism, and disobedience. Rahner was devoted to the antipapal and anti-Catholic point of view,' (*Supra* at Martin, p 25), and openly criticized the papacy and Roman authority."

Eisenhower sat up straight in his seat, "I feel as though I should interrupt this discussion of the Jesuits to bring the necessary history to understand how the Jesuits came about. What was going on in Europe that saw the need of them."

"Absolutely, Sir," Quinn responded.

"To quickly define the social politics that we're talking about as separately defined, but elements of each are instituted collectively and come out of the Renaissance, allegedly the period of Enlightenment. But to understand the Dark Ages, the Middle Ages, and the Renaissance, we must begin with the Roman Empire, which had its 'beginning as the Roman Republic in 509 B.C. And in 63 B.C., Roman troops occupied Palestine/Judea, and Jerusalem fell to the Romans. In 40 B.C. Herod the Great was appointed as King of Judea by the Roman Senate. But it will take three years, however, before he and the Roman Empire conquer Jerusalem and place him on the throne. Of course, you've heard of Antony and Cleopatra, who both committed suicide in 30 B.C. Then with Roman Emperor Augustus, the Republic became the Roman Empire, 24 B.C.' (www.biblestudy.org/roman-empire/rise-and-fall-of-roman-empire-map.html).

'To gain the favor of the Jews, Herod proposed to rebuild the Second Temple, which had stood almost 500 years and was in need of repair. Work began in 20 B.C.; the main building was completed in ten years, but the erection of the outer courts and the embellishment of the whole were carried on during the entire period of Jesus' life on earth (John 2:20). The temple was completed in A.D. 65. The Roman legions took the city of Jerusalem by storm…(Titus') soldiers set fire to the temple. The destruction of the Second Temple began on the 9th of Ab (Hebrew month), the very same day the destruction of Jerusalem's First Temple began in 585 B.C. The temple's demise was completed on Ab 10 in Hebrew year (civil) 3831, which corresponds to Sunday, August 5, A.D. 70,' (www.biblestudy.org/biblepic/picture-of-second-temple-in-jerusalem.html).

Now, just prior to the completion of the refurbishing of the Second Temple/Herod's Temple, Roman Emperor Nero began the Roman Empire's first persecution of Christians, in A.D. 64. Some 30 years or so after the death and resurrection of Jesus. By A.D. 117, the Roman Empire reached its largest extent under Emperor Trajan. And between A.D. 284-305, the last and most vicious persecution of Christians by the empire occurred during the reign of Diocletian. And then came Constantine I, or Constantine the Great, who legalized Christianity with his Edict of Milan in A.D. 313, which ends Rome's persecution of Christians. And in A.D. 330, Constantine makes Byzantium the capital of the Roman Empire, moving the capital out of Rome. The last Roman Emperor who will rule over the whole Empire is Theodosius I, in A.D. 379-395. And in A.D. 380, Theodosius made Christianity the official state religion of the Roman Empire. After his death, his two sons ruled, one over the Eastern, or Byzantine Empire, with the other ruling over the Western Roman Empire,

A.D. 395. In A.D. 410 the city of Rome was sacked by Alaric, King of the German Visigoths. Some consider this the fall of the Western Roman Empire. In A.D. 476, the Western Roman Empire collapses as Emperor Romulus Augustus is forced to abdicate by Germanic General Odoacer; others see this event as the fall of the Western Roman Empire. Then in A.D. 800, Pope Leo III crowned Charlemagne, Charles I, as the first Emperor of the newly established Holy Roman Empire. In A.D. 1453, the Eastern Roman (Byzantine) Empire ends with the death of Roman Constantine XI and the capture of Constantinople by the Ottoman Turks. (*Supra* at www.biblestudy.org/roman-empire)

As to the 'Holy Roman Empire, it was not holy, not Roman, and not an Empire, and existed from December 25, 800 to August 6, 1806. It was a peculiar political institution whose name came in to use around A.D. 1254. It was holy in that the pope tried to assert religious control in Europe; (remember the Inquisition ran from 1478 to 1834.) It was Roman in that it tried to revive the political authority of the Roman Empire in the west as a countermeasure to the Byzantine Empire in the East, (which still existed until 1453). Under the Holy Roman Empire, there was no central government, no unity of language, no common system of law, no sense of common loyalty among the many states within it. Over the centuries, boundaries shifted and shrank drastically,' (www.britannica.com/ EBchecked/topic/269851/Holy-Roman-Empire/10194/Additional-Reading). The Holy Roman Empire began with 'Pope Leo III crowning Charlemagne I as the Emperor; it ended when Emperor Francis II abdicated in 1806, as the last Holy Roman Emperor,' **Error! Hyperlink reference not valid.**TimeLineCharlemagne.html.

These years of the Dark Ages, A.D. 410 to A.D. 1410; Muhammad, A.D. 570 to A.D. 632, founded Islam and changed the complexion of the Middle East; Muslims capture Jerusalem in A.D. 638; the Church of the Holy Sepulchre (A.D. 335 to A.D. 1009), the site of Christ's crucifixion, burial, and resurrection, was destroyed by Hakim, the Muslim Fatimid Caliph (Head) of Egypt in A.D. 1009; Holy Roman Empire, A.D. 800 and A.D. 1806; Satan was released from the bottomless pit about A.D. 1030; A.D. 1054 Schism, the Catholic Church breaks in two, Roman and Eastern Orthodox; Pope Urban II called for the First Crusade to help fight against the Muslims, A.D. 1095; Order of St. John (the Hospitallers) starts in A.D. 1113; Order of the Knights Templar begins in A.D. 1120; the Medieval Inquisition, against groups that threatened the Catholic Church authority, A.D. 1184-1230; the Fourth Crusade, A.D. 1202-1204, is seduced by the Venetians – 'The Venetians agree to furnish the ships to take the Crusaders across the Mediterranean if they first seize Zara on the eastern coast of the Adriatic [Zara was a Christian city, ('its king was a crusader,' http://www.umich.edu/~marcons/Crusades/timeline/ detailedtimeline.html)] – Zara was a naval and commercial rival of Venice. In spite of the pope's protests, the crusaders besieged and captured the city of Zara. Then the Venetians persuaded the Crusaders to turn their arms against Constantinople (the largest and wealthiest European city during the Middle Ages; it was all Christian, and the chief bulwark (principle defense) of Europe against the Arab and Turk/Muslims), before the crusaders attacked Egypt, the center of the Muslim power. No 'infidels' could have treated in worse fashion this home of ancient civilization. The Crusaders burned down a great part of Constantinople, slaughtered the inhabitants, wantonly destroyed monuments, statues, paintings, and manuscripts – the accumulation of a thousand years (that Satan was in the bottomless pit). Much of the movable wealth the crusaders carried away. Never, declared an eye-witness of the scene, had there been such plunder since the world began' (www.middleages.org.uk/the-fourth-crusade.htm); 'The Children's Crusade, A.D. 1212, a French boy of 12 years set out to rescue the Holy Sepulchre – some declared that it was inspired by the Holy *Spirit*…others …confident that the whole thing was the work of the Devil – 30,000 French children…sailed from (Marseilles)…were betrayed, and sold as slaves in Alexandria and other Mohammedan slave markets. In Germany…50,000 crossed the Alps into Italy…2-3000 sailed away into oblivion…many (of the 50,000) were sold into slavery, A.D. 1212' (http://www.middle-ages.org.uk/the-childrens-crusade.htm); badly weakened by the Fourth Crusade, Constantinople fell easily to the Muslim Ottomans, A.D. 1453; the Spanish Inquisition – to convert Jews, Muslims, and Illuminatus to Christianity, A.D. 1478 to A.D. 1834; the Roman Inquisition, against any who deviated from Catholicism, atheist and heretics, A.D. 1542-1860; the European Witch Hunts, A.D. 1480-1750; the establishment of social societies of Freemasonry, as opposed to ancient stone masons, began in England in 1717; the American Revolution, aided by France, begins in 1776; and the French Revolution, A.D. 1787 to 1799, all of these events folded into each other throughout Europe. Chaos reigned. 'And when the thousand years shall be finished, Satan shall be loosed out of his prison, and shall go forth (A.D. 1030), and seduce the nations….' Rev. 20:7.

And note that the quarrel over rank has continued throughout the history of mankind.

One of these elements that directly impact us is the Freemasons. The Freemasons were stone masons who had been 'emancipated according to the medieval practice of restrictions and control of *local guilds* (unions) in order that they might be able to travel and render services, wherever any great building was in process of construction,' (www.newadvent.org/ cathen/09771a.htm).

'Speculative Masonry began with the foundation of the Grand Lodge of England, June 24, 1717, with three degrees: apprentice, fellow, master; at this time old lodges had almost ceased to exist. The NEW lodges began as convivial (social) societies, and the characteristic Masonic spirit developed but slowly. This spirit, finally, as exhibited in the new constitutions was a contradiction to that which (drove)…the earlier (stone-building) Masons. These facts prove that modern Masonry is NOT….a revival of the older system, but rather that it is a new order of no greater antiquity than the first quarter of the eighteenth century. This is noted in two English editions (the 1723 and 1738) of Anderson's Freemason 'Constitutions.'

In the text of the 1738 Constitution: 'I. Concerning God and Religion. A Mason is obliged by his Tenure to observe the moral law as true Noahide (sons of Noah, the first name of Freemasons)…for they all agree in the three great articles of Noah, enough to preserve the cement of the lodge….The Mason is called a 'true Noahide,' i.e., an adherent of the pre-Christian and pre-Moses system of undivided mankind.'

Maimonides, a very influential Medieval Jewish philosopher, A.D. 1135 – A.D. 1204, was a Jewish Rabbi and physician. He had written numerous works. One was the *Mishnah Torah*, in which he wrote that the precise observance of the Seven Noahide Laws by a non-Jew Gentile makes that Gentile a Righteous Person who, therefore, would share in the World to Come – the new, eternal world of the future. The Seven Noahide Laws, a Jewish moral code, known as the seven commandments of the Sons of Noah, that the Jewish Rabbi offered to the Gentiles. (Clanton, R., www.auburn.edu/~allenkc/chrnoach1.html) The Seven Noahide Laws were created and written by Rabbi Maimonides.

The U.S. Congress, 'after dismissing the House of Representatives, after being told voting was over, those who stayed behind passed a Joint House and Senate Resolution, which was signed by the President of 1991, and became Public Law 102-14, and is called the 'Education Day, U.S.A.' 'These rules make the belief in Jesus Christ a crime punishable by decapitation by guillotine!...The American people are bound by a set of monstrous rules, called Noahide laws,' (U.S. Congressman Bill Dannemeyer, 1979-1992, www.takebackourrights.org /docs/Christians-full%20page.html).

In the 'Oral Torah…recorded in the (Babylonian) *Talmud* (Sanhedrin folio 56b), it is explained that all these seven laws given are coded within the verse Gen. 2:16…'Of every tree of the garden you may surely eat.'…The revealed *Torah* is G-d's (sic) 'Tree of Eternal Life,' and from that time on, Gentiles can obtain a share in the future World to Come (*the culmination of the Messianic era*) if they choose to observe their Seven Commandments as their part in the Written and Oral *Torah* which G-d (sic) gave through Moses. (Noahide Laws Sources; http://noahide.org/article.asp?Level=395&Parent =90)

The World to Come is defined as: 'a time. Judaism divides existence between this World and the World to Come. We live in the current World, which will undergo a complete cessation. After its death, there will only be quiet and desolation; the World as we know it will cease to exist. All things will no longer be alive; all souls will be brought to the Realm of Souls, a temporary place for the purpose of the naranchai (a conglomerate of the spiritual elements of a human) to be recharged. After this current World lies dormant in desolation for 1000 years, the World to

Come will be resurrected; souls will be reunited with their bodies. Even the physical will have a much more elevated, holier nature to it, as it was before the sin of the Tree of Knowledge. The body and soul of man will be fully integrated, and as one, will be holy. The Messianic Era is separate from the World to Come (its time lies at the end of this current World, and just before the desolation of this World). In the Messianic Era, disease will disappear entirely, pain will be eradicated, women will give birth easily without pain, and *all the curses Adam and Eve received for their sin will be nullified.* The main function of the Messianic Era is spiritual growth. We will no longer be subject to the rule of oppressors, no war, and no crime anywhere on earth. All sin will disappear completely. This Messianic Era has yet to take place, but it will be during this Era of this current World that the Messiah will be our first king, teaching the world how to attain those things of curing disease, getting rid of pain, and world peace. The Messiah will die after a long happy life. His son will reign and then die; the grandson will be king until this Messianic Era ends. Then the 1000 years of desolation begins, with the World to Come to follow. These are the two Worlds of Judaism. (www.beingjewish.com/soul/future.html)

And for the non-Jew Gentile to share in the World to Come, they must strictly live the Seven Noahide Laws offered by the Jews. 'This obligation, to teach all the peoples of the earth about the Laws of Noah, is incumbent upon every (Jewish) individual in every era.' (*Mishnah Torah*, Law of Kings 8:10 – which Maimonides wrote during the Middle Ages.)"

Eisenhower stretched his back, somewhat restless with the story, he continued, "The number one of the Seven Noahide Laws – is the prohibition of idolatry. Judaism does not believe in Jesus Christ, therefore, to worship Jesus and His Holy Ghost, violates the first of the Seven Noahide laws. It's a matter of language-interpretation debate whether Maimonides wrote that to break these laws one should face the death penalty. It's alleged that the death penalty is taken out of context from the *Talmud*. But with the current evidence, the death penalty is a fact."

Eisenhower picked up the Bible and turned to Genesis, "Now, the *Talmud* also claims that the two commandments given to Noah, Gen. 9:1-10, which state: 'Increase and multiply, and fill the earth…every thing that moveth and liveth shall be meat for you…saving that flesh with blood you shall not eat (understood generally to mean – no cannibalism or eating the flesh of a live animal)…Whosoever shall shed man's blood, his blood shall be shed: for man was made to the image of God…Behold I will establish my covenant with you (Noah), and with *your seed* after you…And with every living soul that is with you, as well in all birds as in cattle and beasts of the earth, that are come forth out of the ark, and in all the beasts of the earth.'"

Eisenhower lay down the Bible on the conference table and tapped on the page from which he had just read. He looked at Quinn, "You'll note that God is talking with Noah and states that He is going to establish a covenant with Noah and his seed. Seed is singular, but there were three young men on the Ark with Noah and all their wives. If all three young men were Noah's sons, why doesn't it read 'your seeds'? As in - with each of your sons. But stating only, 'with your seed,' implies a lineage through one living child; Noah was very old at the time and never did have other children. One must also consider that God goes on to itemize the other souls on the Ark with whom He will make a covenant. God addresses the others as being other than Noah's seed, 'and with every living soul that is with you.' This is because God was addressing Sem as the only seed of Noah, separate and apart from Ham and Japheth. God covenants with Ham and Japheth as well – never to bring a flood on the earth, again, and requires that Ham and Japheth are not to cannibalize or murder, either. There were only two laws. And for Maimonides to read some sort of a code into these verses to come up with Seven Noahide Laws is plainly absurd. And within the *Talmud*, each of those Seven Noahide Laws have a subset of laws. It's all a smoke screen. These collective Noahide laws require non-Jews to live by Pharisaic/Judaic laws created by Ezra the Edomite, but those adherents are separately classified as Noahides – non-Jews. They are attempting to bring the world under one religion, the worship of Satan. And it's all about hiding all mankind within one lineage – a lie! Satan's deceit! They continue to bury the events of the Garden of Eden; bury the fact that Cain was the son of Satan and Eve; bury the fact that Black Ham and Yellow Japheth could not have been fathered by Noah, who was White. It's physiologically impossible! All mankind is not of God!

It is absolutely physically impossible for Noah and his one wife to produce three different races of people – three sons with three different Y-chromosomes. It's all a lie!

What we have here is that the Masons established a new organization with a Constitution requiring that Masons agree with the Rabbis that all non-Jews should abide by the Noahide Laws that were created by Rabbi Maimonides – and all of this took place during the Middle Ages. Maimonides was born, A.D. 1135, about 100 years after Satan was let out of the bottomless pit, A.D. 1030.

But there is more. Did you note the reference in the Jewish idea of the Messianic Era at the end of this current World – its reference to the Tree of Knowledge, as in the Garden of Eden where Satan seduced Eve to 'touch,' to have sexual intercourse, under the Tree of Knowledge! And in the Messianic Era the curses placed on Adam and Eve – they will be wiped away in the Messianic Era. Who is going to wipe away those curses that God imposed? Only God can do that – not some king. Sounds like a seduction of Satan that he will teach the world how to attain those things of curing disease, getting rid of pain, and world peace, getting rid of the curses placed on Adam and Eve. And that utopia of the Messianic Era will come about – just as soon as all mankind repents – and then the king will appear. And repentance can only occur when Christians stop worshipping Jesus!"

Quinn interrupted, "That sounds as though this Messianic King will be the Antichrist – one who will deny Jesus and His Holy Ghost. What did John say, 'Who is a liar, but he who denieth that Jesus is the Christ? This is Antichrist, who denieth the Father, and the Son,' (1 John 2:22).

Eisenhower replied, "The repenting necessary to bring on the Messianic Era requires getting rid of Jesus from every institution, every Church, every prayer, every holiday, from every school! It's the number one of the Seven Noahide Laws for Gentiles; those who believe in Jesus are considered to be worshiping idols. And we now have law that gives our government the right to kill all Christians, Pub. Law 102-14."

"And I agree with your statement, Quinn, especially for the fact that Maimonides classified Islam as a Noahide religion," Eisenhower remarked. "Islam does not believe in Jesus or His Holy Ghost. One has to wonder if the Spanish Inquisition was wrong – or another way to look at it, the Jews and Muslims and Illuminatus are getting back at the Christians for that Inquisition. But, in any event, history is not far behind us; the quarrel of rank is close at hand."

Quinn frowned, "So, this is why we're looking at the United Nations and the U.S. Government cracking down on Christians – repent of the belief and worship of Jesus! The U.S. Military prohibits military chaplains from using Jesus in prayers or Mass – and last year they forbade the use of the name Jesus during Military funerals! 'Houston National Cemetery, three veterans organization are to take the Dept. of Veteran Affairs to court over claims that they have censored prayers and demanded that words be submitted in advance for government approval.'" (Stevens, J., www.dailymail.co.uk/news/article-2010015/veterans-BANNED-saying-God-Jesus-military-funerals.html?ito=feeds-newsxml.)

Quinn's voice hardened, "The U.S. Navy policy requires non-sectarian prayers outside of worship services. A military jury convicted a Navy chaplain of a misdemeanor for disobeying his commanding officer by wearing his uniform while delivering a prayer 'in Jesus' name.' (www.wnd.com/2006/ 09/37913/)

Even in the hospital that you died in, Sir, Walter Reed Military Hospital," Quinn added, "Chief of Staff C. W. Callahan instituted a policy that prevented family members of wounded military soldiers from bringing in Bibles and other religious materials to loved ones. Rep. Steve King of Iowa got the policy overturned; he said, 'It means that a priest (could not)…bring in the Eucharist, couldn't offer the Last Rites…." (www.theblaze.com/stories/ walter-reed-medical-center-bans-bibles-religious-materials-then-overturns-bizarre-policy/)

Quinn surmised, "They're at work all over the country, trying to get rid of Jesus, so they can bring out the Antichrist to be king. For their 'Messianic Era.' That's the bottom line!"

Eisenhower interjected, "Albert Pike is considered one of the great geniuses of Freemasonry, and in his book, *Morals and Dogma*, published in 1871, p 213, Pike states, 'Every Masonic Lodge is a temple of religion; and its teachings are instruction of religion.' On p 104 of his book, he writes: 'Masonry is a Pagan Mystery religion: Masonry, like all the Religions, all the Mysteries…conceals its secrets from all except the Adepts and Sages, or the elect, and uses false explanations and misinterpretations of its symbols to mislead those who deserve only to be mislead (sic)….Truth is not for those who are unworthy or unable to receive it, or would pervert it.' On p 321, 'Lucifer, the Light-bearer! Strange and mysterious name given to the spirit of darkness! Lucifer, the Son of the Morning! Is it he who bears the Light…? Doubt it not!'

In Anton LaVey's book, *The Satanic Rituals: Companion to The Satanic Bible,* p 21, 'Satanic ritual is a blend of Gnostic, Cabalistic, Hermetic, and Masonic elements….' And in the Introduction of the Masonic Bible, it says: 'Man is immortal.'" (http://www.cuttingedge.org/ce1046.html)

Eisenhower frowned, "It would seem that they are saying that man is either an idiot or a god?"

"Well as far as the Jewish teaching about the World to Come, man will be 'holy,' Quinn replied, "but only those who follow Judaism."

Eisenhower explained, "That would be the Zionist Jews, Islamist, Masons, and the Christians who give up Jesus, whose souls will go to the Realm of Souls during the 1000 years of desolation. It sounds more like they will be joining Satan in the pit after Jesus returns. And as to the French Revolution, it was driven by Freemasons,' (www.newadvent.org/cathen/ 09771a .htm), '1787 – 1799, and it *resulted in the Jewish population of France being granted full citizenship*, on September 27, 1790,' (http://faculty.unlv.edu/gbrown/hist462/resources/ chrono.htm).

'The French Revolution is an important factor in all of this sabotage by Satan and his descendants. It began with a financial crisis. (Just as they have brought about today's global financial crises.) Among other things, what the Revolution accomplished, on October 5, 1793, the French Republic calendar was adopted that was devoid of all Catholic religious associations and was used officially until January 1, 1806,' (*Ibid.*).

During the French Revolution, on November 10, 1793, 'the Festival of Reason was celebrated in Notre Dame, replacing Catholic symbolism with the secular principles of knowledge, reason, and political liberty. All Catholic churches in Paris would be closed a short time later,'" (*Ibid.*). It was a purposeful desecration of God's temple that was dedicated to His Mother."

Eisenhower continued, "The Festival of Reason was celebrated at the suggestion of Pierre Gaspard Chaumette, who favored the French Republic and the fall of the monarchy, King Louis XVI. During the Festival they placed the wife of printer Antoine Francois Momoro, Sophie, on the high altar of Notre Dame. Notre Dame, meaning 'Our Lady,' was built as a Catholic Cathedral between 1163-1345. Momoro openly wrote of his opposition of the constitutional monarchy and the Roman Catholic Church.

The Festival of Reason was a worship of the goddess of reason, or wisdom – as in King Solomon worshipping Astarthe, the pagan goddess, which led to the first diaspora of the Israelites and God's affliction of the seed of King David that we continue to endure today.

'On November 9-10, 1799, Napoleon staged his military coup d'etat. He became the First Consul of *The Consulate*,' (*Ibid.*).

Napoleonic Wars occurred between A.D. 1800 and A.D. 1815. Napoleon declared France as a hereditary Empire and crowned himself the Emperor, on May 28, 1804. Napoleon 'left durable institutions, an administrative system of the prefects (high officials), Napoleonic Code of Law that was the main influence in the 1800s civil codes of most countries of continental Europe and Latin America. He also left a judicial system, Banque de France and the country's financial organization, the centralized university, and military academies. He signed a concordat, agreement, with the papacy, in 1801, which defined the status of the Roman Catholic Church in France and ended the breach caused by the Church reforms during the French Revolution. This also gave him the right to nominate bishops, bishoprics, as parishes were redistributed, and it allowed the erection of seminaries. Napoleon believed that the people needed a religion, and that religious peace had to be restored to France. He was well-educated and well-read, and known as an enlightened man of the 18th century. To revive France's expansion overseas he intended to occupy Louisiana, which had been ceded to France by Spain in 1800. He changed the history of France and the world,' (www.britannica.com/EBchecked /topic/402943/Napoleon-I). And, yes, he got rid of the Inquisition and feudalism. But on TV documentaries, they claim "some people think" that Napoleon was the Antichrist of his day; but they never tell you who the "some people" are. This is a deliberate distortion of history. He was far from the Anti-Christ.

The Napoleonic Wars also resulted in a 20-year treaty, the Treaty of Chaumont, March 1814, among Austria, Russia, Prussia/Germany, and Great Britain, which bound them together as allies against Napoleon,' (*Ibid.*). He was finally defeated by Great Britain's Duke of Wellington, at the Battle of Waterloo, June 1815, and put on the Island of St. Helen, where some think that he was poisoned."

Quinn had taken in all of Eisenhower's words, but what nagged him was the outcome of it all. Finally, he said, "Sir, according to the Jewish philosophy about the lifting of the Adam and Eve curses during the Messianic Era. There's one more thing to consider, General. The curses are written in Gen. 3:14-15; I read it last night. God condemned Satan to crawl on his belly and eat earth. That would be made void; Satan would stand upright. The enmity between Satan's seed and Eve's seed would be made void. No longer would Satan's descendants 'lie in wait for' the heel of Eve's descendants. No longer would Eve's descendants crush the head of Satan's descendants."

Quinn looked in to Eisenhower's eyes, "This thing. This curse. Between Eve's descendants and Satan's descendants – it will end, be nullified. How, Sir? How will it be nullified? If not by God. And the Jewish philosophy doesn't say that God will end it, but that the Messianic king will end it. How? How can a human king end a supernatural curse?"

Eisenhower nodded his head, "They have to kill the descendants of Adam and Eve, so that they can no longer 'crush the head' of Satan's descendants. They have to kill all the Whites. Any Christian who does not follow the Seven Noahide Laws – in other words, those who do not follow the religion of Judaism – will be murdered. They are planning to murder all who believe in Jesus Christ. That's the real purpose of the FEMA concentration camps. They are actually extermination camps. The curse will be over because the descendants of Adam and Eve will be dead, that is, unless they worship Satan. And then the world will die and enter 1000 years of desolation, but the Jewish philosophy of the Messianic Era makes it clear that only those who follow Judaism, Islam, and the Seven Noahide/Judaic religion – satanic worship – will be resurrected."

"It seems to me, Sir," Quinn replied, "That this Jewish philosophy comes from the Christian New Testament, but with a twist – that evil will be resurrected instead of sent to hell. I can't help think how Satan countered God's command to Eve, when Satan deceived her, 'No, you shall not die the death,' if she touched the Tree of Knowledge of Good and Evil, Gen. 3:4. She would not die the death, if she had intercourse with Satan. The Jewish philosophical term, Realm of Souls, where all the Jews, Muslims, and Noahides go to after the desolation of this current World – sounds more like another name for the pool of fire and brimstone. Rev. 19:7-15, states: 'And when the thousand years shall be finished, Satan shall be loosed out of his prison (the bottomless pit, let loose 100 years before the birth of Maimonides), and shall go forth, and seduce the nations, which are over the four quarters of the earth, Gog and Magog (Yoon Won-Shik-moon and his UN Troops), and shall gather them together to battle, the number of whom is as the sand of the sea. And they came upon the breadth of the earth, and encompassed the camp of the saints (the United States), and the beloved city. And there came down fire from God out of heaven, and devoured them (UN Troops); and the devil, who seduced them, was cast into the pool of fire and brimstone, where both the beast and the false prophet shall be tormented day and night for ever and ever. And I saw a great white throne, and one sitting upon it, from whose face the earth and heaven fled away (as the Messianic Era ends in desolation of the current World), and there was no place found for them (except the Realm of Souls, the pool of fire). And I saw the dead…and another book was opened, which is the book of life; and the dead were judged by those things which were written in the books, according to their works….And hell and death were cast into the pool of fire. This is the second death. And whosoever was not found written in the book of life, was cast into the pool of fire.'

And, Sir, in Rev. 21:1, it tells of that Jewish philosophical World to Come, 'And I saw a new heaven and a new earth. For the first heaven and the first earth was gone, and the sea is now no more.'

Whoever came up with that Jewish philosophy of the Messianic Era, its king who will end the curses of Adam and Eve, and of the coming of the World to Come – they took it all from the Christian New Testament written by Jesus' Apostle, John, 64 years after Jesus ascended into Heaven."

"I agree, son," Eisenhower replied.

"And this business of a Messianic Era, the three kings, the Messiahs who are going to teach how to free the world of disease, eradicate pain, and make childbirth easy. When will the first king show up?" Quinn asked.

"Oh," Eisenhower replied, "But they already have."

Quinn sat up straight in response, "They've reigned already?"

"You've heard of the UN World Health Organization, WHO. It was established in 1948 through the United Nations. Its Directors have worked on vaccines against disease, the Avian Flu, SARS; they have educated undeveloped countries regarding child delivery techniques. These teachings of the Director of WHO fulfills the Jewish philosophy of the Messianic Era king. And, as to pain, we have over the counter drugs, to morphine, to a number of methods to rid us of pain. These things listed that the Messiah king would teach the world – have flowed through the WHO out to the world. Look at the *position* of the Director, instead of the seven individuals who have held that position, since it is the power of the position that brings these cures to the world. Most diseases are now curable, or under control, at least to enough of an extent to satisfy the Jewish philosophy of the Messianic Era, and remember, these teachings do not stop people from dying, but have extended the average life span. I think it's safe to say that we are currently living under the last Messianic King, the Directorship of the World Health Organization. The Director will assist the Secretary General of the UN on the vaccines that will be administered to the Christians held in the FEMA camps. It is during the last WHO Director, Messianic King, that this World will end – the Jewish philosophy doesn't say that the King will bring it about himself. It doesn't say who will bring it about, it only says that the end will come after their kingship comes into the world."

"But it said his son, and his son, and his son."

"That only denotes lineage of the position. It denotes the continuing of the office of King – Director. Let's look at it this way – what else could be taught that we don't already know? How much would those few cures that we do need add to what we have now? Is there a cure from a disease that would delineate the Director from another individual, to show that the other individual is greater than the Director, and therefore, the Director of WHO is not the Messianic King? What else could a

Messianic King give us, if he does not already exist in the world?"

"I see what you're saying," Quinn frowned. He tried to think of some dramatic increase to what the world already has that could cause the world to point to a king and say that he was the Messiah of the Jewish philosophy. Because he could not, he thought that it proved that we are indeed in the end times. We even have the ability to create organs for transplant, to create nerves to heal paraplegics, we have plastic lens to cure the blindness of cataracts. We have medical technology that is beyond what the Messianic philosophy promises. All that is needed to complete their list is ridding the world of the Adam and Eve curses.

Eisenhower noted, "They've already established a new Sanhedrin and Court for Bnei Noah. They have developed an expertise in Noahide law. The Sanhedrin will respond to the legal questions of all the Beni Noah, *and will recognize all organizations that have accepted the Sanhedrin as their highest halachic (Jewish law) authority*. The Sanhedrin recognizes the subcourt, the *Beis Din* for Benei Noach (Sons of Noah), as the main officiating court in matters pertaining to Benei Noah. (http://thesanhedrin.org/en/index/php?title=Hachrazah _5767_ Cheshvon_ 16a).

Eisenhower looked at Quinn, "All systems are in place. They even have the National Defense Authorization Act of Fiscal Year *2012*, Title X, Subtitle D – Detainee Matters, Sec. 1031 (a): Congress affirms that *the authority of the President* to use all necessary...force *...(of) the Armed Forces of the United States* to detain ...(b)(2) ...*any person who has committed a belligerent act*...(c) The Disposition of a person…*may include* the following: (1) *Detention*...without trial *until the end of the hostilities*...(c)(4) *Transfer to* the custody of...any...foreign country, or any... *foreign* entity...." Effective as of January 1, 2012.

They legally have the right to transfer American citizens for trial in a Noahide Court, *Beis Din*. These Beis Din courts exist in the United States, and lawyers are trained to represent clients before these courts." Eisenhower paused for a moment.

Quinn sat dumbfounded, but he couldn't help equate their plans with the Inquisition trials.

"Let me try to make an analogy," Eisenhower continued. "While the U.S. Congress established the Federal Reserve to print our money without making an amendment to the U.S. Constitution, at any point in time, the U.S. Congress under the same reasoning can establish, with the power of Art. III, Sec. 1, 'inferior Courts as the Congress may *from time to time* ordain and establish.' The number and types of our courts already established does not limit the current Congress for establishing more types and numbers of courts. The Constitution only established the U.S. Supreme Court, all other courts are left to Congress to establish. And if the Congress establishes the Beis Din court, which is assisted by the newly re-established Sanhedrin in Tiberius, then the Beis Din court can try people for worshipping Jesus. The situation is the same as the Federal Reserve

Act, and the 16th Amendment, whose passage is arguably fraudulent, but it allows Congress the power to lay and collect taxes on *incomes – only*. Yet the U.S. Supreme Court decided that the tax mandated in the healthcare law is allowable under the 16th Amendment. It's not. The healthcare law is taxing behavior, not income. Income doesn't enter the picture at all – the behavior of not buying healthcare causes an American citizen to be taxed! Payable to the Internal Revenue Service. It's a false legal decision, and they know that. The three branches of our government have completely thrown out the Constitution; and their laws and legal decisions are mangled to bring about whatever evil act they want to commit and to cover their asses. How can you detain an American citizen without a trial? How can you transfer an American citizen to a foreign entity?! Yet, that's what the National Defense Authorization Act of Fiscal Year 2012 stipulates that they can do!

And to cover their asses, they throw in a paragraph stating that nothing 'in this section shall be construed to affect (as in influence) existing law…relating to the detention of United States citizens.' Who are they kidding? If you want to get nitty gritty, the use of the word 'affect' only means to influence existing law; that clause is saying that there is no protection against this law overriding the rights of citizens. There is distinctly missing the correct word – 'effect' which means result; 'an effect is that which is produced by the action of an agent' (American Heritage Dictionary, 2nd College ed., Houghton, Boston, 1976, p 439). The agent in this case being the law. In other words, this law will not protect American citizens from losing their rights to a speedy trial, attorney, habeas corpus arraignment, charges stipulated and sentence rendered, Miranda warning of the right to remain silent! By using the word 'affect' they are only stipulating that the National Defense Authorization Act will not influence other laws already existing regarding the detention of U.S. citizens. And it won't influence other existing laws – BUT it will *overturn* all existing laws!

This National Defense Authorization law is unconstitutional just as the Federal Reserve Act is unconstitutional because the U.S. Constitution Art. I, Sec. 8, cl. 5, states that the power lies with the U.S. Congress 'to coin Money, regulate the Value thereof.' But with the Federal Reserve Act of 1913, Congress turned their power over to a handful of private, mostly foreign owners of the Federal Reserve. And the unsolvable national debt stems from the interest that American citizens are charged - that they would not have to pay, if Congress did their Constitutional duty to coin and regulate the value of our money! Congress is specifically restricted by the U.S. Constitution, Art. V, 'The Congress…shall propose Amendments to this Constitution… (and said Amendments) shall be valid to all Intents and Purposes, as Part of this Constitution, *when ratified by the Legislatures of three fourths of the several States*.' The Congress never put the Federal Reserve Act through this process. Therefore, the Federal Reserve Act of 1913 is unconstitutional. Congress ignored their oath to uphold the Constitution. The Federal Reserve Act of 1913 is an act of treason by our Congress! Yet the Federal Reserve continues to charge Americans interest on the money they tell our Treasury to print.

The healthcare law, as a tax-revenue-raising law was unconstitutionally issued from the Senate, per Art. I, Sec. 7, cl. 1 of the Constitution, but the U.S. Supreme Court overlooked the Constitution in making its decision that the healthcare law is constitutional. They don't care about the constitutionality of these laws, they put a law in to the system and enforce that fraudulent law; the cries from citizens to uphold the Constitution be damned! They do this with all our laws. We can only expect that they will continue this treason.

As to the First Amendment freedom of religion, it can be argued that worshipping Jesus is a threat to national security."

Quinn cried, "They're planning to indoctrinate the minds of our children! Against Jesus!"

Eisenhower paused, suddenly feeling a bit melancholy, wishing he was president with the knowledge he now held. He looked at Quinn and gave him a fleeting smile; then he looked down at his hands with their vagueness of ghostly dimension that reminded him that his life had ended.

He cleared his throat and continued, "Under Capitalism, which we used to have in the United States – it is the only system that allows the 'American Dream' – that if you work hard enough, are smart enough, take the risk of losing your house or what assets you may have mortgaged – you can achieve great success regardless of where you started from. It's an economic system where the means of production and distribution are privately or corporately owned and development is proportionate to accumulation and reinvestment of profits gained in a free market. This is what is hanging on by a thread against Jewish, Muslim, and Jesuit assault against the U.S. This is the system that has allowed a person in the poor class to rise through hard work, perseverance, risk-taking, and intelligence up to the rich class. Where every penny earned is then spent on an asset that brings in dollars, which invested in the next asset, earns millions of dollars. These entrepreneurs are the ones that employ 85% of Americans. Their hard work gave the majority of the country jobs and an income that allowed all citizens to live independently from government handouts. Capitalism is the system that gives Man true dignity – by doing all he can to take care of his family, and therefore, makes the family a strong independent unit in society, free to choose whether or not to worship Jesus.

On the other hand, Socialism and Communism strip man of his dignity, so much so that his will, his back is broken. This is the specific reason that they are instituting it here in the United States – to break the back of the middle class, so they will not rise up in revolution."

"I understand, Sir," Quinn replied. "We need to get back to our independent, capitalist roots. The individualism of hard-work ethic that provides freedom from feudalism, freedom from the government deciding whether or not we'll get medical care for our babies and our parents – those who the government has determined are not useful for the common good, therefore, expendable." Quinn shook his head, "What a mess we're in. Americans have to realize that they have to stop this now, before it's too late."

Eisenhower nodded, "In Matt. 24:14, it tells us when God's punishment of the Israelites will end: 'And this gospel of the kingdom, shall be preached in the whole world, for a testimony to all nations, and then shall the consummation come.' The consummation is the fulfillment of God's promise to Solomon to punish the 'seed of David, but yet not for ever' (3 Kings 11:39) – this will be the end of the time of the Gentiles; the end of the non-Israelites' control over the Israelites. The end times means: the end of the Zionists Jewish and Muslims control over the Israelites.

It will come when all is known of the quarrel of rank, of the bloodlines of the Zionists and Muslims and the Christians. Remember, the elite control education – the last thing they want is for the true Israelites to know who they are. The end will come when the whole world knows that Satan sits on the Throne of Peter and knows who put him there. The end will come when all Americans know that their Congresses and their Presidents have enslaved them to those of the bloodline of Satan. Their method has always been deceit – of who the Zionists really are. Such as the deceit that Israel is America's allied. When, in fact, Israel uses America as its bitch!"

Quinn looked at Eisenhower, "The Zionist Jews greatly fear that if the upright realize that they are descended from Adam, the Zionists, the wicked, will lose power over them. That is, until the Zionists hand control of the earth over to Satan. It has been Satan's wish to control the earth since the Garden of Eden. It's best to think that we are all from Adam, one man, and that we all share his genes. It's best for the upright that way, or the Zionist Jews will kill the upright the way they killed Jesus. But the Talmudic instruction to keep silent is actually a threat to their wicked bloodline: don't turn to Jesus or we'll get you, too!"

The thought flashed into Quinn's mind, "The USS Liberty. Its attack by the Zionist Jews was to keep the world from finding out that Israel had committed war crimes. The Liberty was an American ship full of the upright – at that time, it was the greatest technological naval intelligence ship on the seas, steaming in international waters of the Mediterranean Sea, on June 8, 1967, during the Arab-Israeli 6th Day War. The U.S. had taken a neutral stance in the 6th Day War. And just after Zionist Israeli Defense Forces had won a battle against the Egyptians, and having no place to house the several hundreds of captives, the Israelis shot the surrendered, unarmed Egyptian soldiers; Israeli generals sent out missions to kill fleeing Egyptian soldiers. It was then that the Zionist Israelis realized that the intelligence-gathering equipment on the Liberty had documented their acts of mass murder. For the repetition of gunfire in a slaughter sounds quite differently from the irregular back and forth gunfire of battle. The Liberty had the evidence of Israeli war atrocity that would be revealed to the world. A war atrocity that was not too different than the Holocaust that the Israelites had suffered; the Zionists had left Germany before the war began. No longer could they seek the pity of the world for being a victim of unforgivable, ungodly hate. Now, the world would see the blood on their hands from an ungodly killing, as Cain had murdered his defenseless, unsuspecting brother, Abel. So, they set out to commit a greater war atrocity – the murder of their unarmed American ally who had rescued their Israelite shield from concentration camps, who had supported their statehood, who gave them billions of dollars in aid every year. They sent out Israeli jets, bombers, torpedo boats, to wipe away the evidence of their Zionist ungodliness. They attacked the USS Liberty that they could see was flying the American flag, that they could see had no offensive armament, and for two hours they hit the Liberty with napalm, rockets, cannon, bombs, and strafing of an undefended allied ship. They saw the U.S. sailors without weapons; they saw the U.S. sailors climbing into life rafts to escape – and aimed their guns at them. They saw those U.S. sailors, as they shot and killed them, less they should escape and tell the world of their Zionist war atrocity. The Zionist Israelis saw the U.S. sailors running to hide on deck, running as their napalm flames burned them alive. The death that they inflicted was through the greatest of pain. Between 1:57pm-4pm, in the broad daylight of clear skies, they murdered 34 Israelite/Christian Americans and wounded 174 of them – whose tax dollars had provided Israel with weapons that were now unmercifully turned against them. President Lyndon Baines Johnson concealed and altered evidence of the attack. The U.S. Zionist-controlled Congress refused to investigate. The survivors had been prohibited for 40 years from talking about the attack, or face imprisonment. President Lyndon Baines Johnson, at the height of the attack, told all US Naval ships, jets, to turn back and not go to the defensive aid and rescue of the Liberty. It's been rumored that Johnson was in a tirade - 'I want to see that ship [USS Liberty] on the bottom of the ocean!'"

Quinn remembered that Johnson had been a member of the Foreign Affairs Private Council. The Council that has been charged, since 1921, with carrying out the plan for the New World Order - with its members installed in every American institution: military, academia, corporate, finance, education, media, and medicine. Placement on the U.S. Supreme Court and other high office is not based on merit, but on the membership and connection to the Foreign Affairs Private Council.

Quinn realized now, the why of the intentional attack on the USS Liberty, "Had the intelligence gathered by the USS Liberty of the Zionist Israeli Defense Forces' slaughter of Egyptian POWs, the Zionist Jews, their State of Israel, would be exposed for who they are, ruthless murderers and descendants of Satan.

The Zionist Jews would no longer be able to make an international plea for pity, for compassion, for being helplessly surrounded by their enemies. If the world had the evidence collected by the USS Liberty, of the grand-scale slaughter of unarmed Egyptian soldiers that the Israelis committed, the deceit of the Zionist Jews would forever fail. They would lose the military protection and money of the superpower Christian nation of the United States."

Quinn had read that the way the Zionist Israelis work is that they poke, poke, poke the eye of their neighbors to get the neighbors to fire back, then the Israelis launch an outright slaughter. Then, they yell: We have the right to defend ourselves!!! Defense Minister General Moshe Dayan revealed this strategy in taking the Golan Heights. The Israelis wanted that agricultural farmland; they sent a tractor into the demilitarized zone, moving ever closer, until the Syrians shot their rifles. It gave the Israelis the excuse to use heavy artillery and then send in the Israeli Air Force to bomb the Syrians. (Interview with Rami Tal, Associated Press reports, May 11, 1997.)

"But the USS Liberty was not shooting at the Israelis; the ship had no weapons of war; the ship belonged to their ally; it was sailing in international water; it was broad daylight; the Zionist Israelis can't yell that they were defending themselves. Oh, sorry, it was a mistake, they claimed. Quinn thought, then they must be blind! Or incompetent idiots! Or liars! And the U.S. Congress and LBJ allowed American sailors to be murdered and then helped the Israeli Government cover up and deceive the world about what the Israelis did – to the unarmed Egyptian soldiers and the sitting duck of a ship that was unarmed, and filled with allied, non-combatant, innocent American sailors. The web of Satan's deceit casts a wide net. This is blatant treason against their own countrymen and against the U.S. Military!"

Eisenhower replied, "At the Battle of Trenton, Washington captured 913 Hessian mercenary soldiers in a one-hour fight – causing him to take the prisoners back across the Delaware into Pennsylvania and shelter. He didn't slaughter them! And he hadn't sworn to any Geneva Convention! That's the difference between the upright and the wicked, Quinn."

Quinn responded, "But it's not just the Israeli Defense Forces - we see their monolithic ruthless conspiracy includes our government. The U.S. Congress aided and abetted the deceit of the attack on the USS Liberty. President Lyndon Baines Johnson aided and abetted in that deceit, also, therefore, both Congress and LBJ are guilty of treason in conspiring with a foreign military to murder American sailors and destroy a U.S. Naval ship. The U.S. Constitution, Art. III, Sec. 3, cl. 1: Treason against the United States, shall consist (of)...*adhering to their Enemies, giving them Aid and Comfort*."

Suddenly, it hit Quinn, "'adhering to their Enemies'! The American people – in revolting against the U.S. Government – are not adhering to their Enemies! They are fighting the enemies of our country – our leaders! The American people are the country – we cannot be our enemy – but the leaders in our government are the enemy – enemy to the legal document that binds the American people in to a nation! It finally hit me, General, – Americans cannot be arrested for trying to overthrow the U.S. Government – it's our country! It's our Constitution – our Revolution is to protect our Constitution from its enemy – the thugs in Washington! Our Second Revolution will not be like the French Revolution – for after the fight, our Constitution will, once again, govern our country!"

Quinn turned to Eisenhower, "Hide the quarrel over the rank - that was the idea of the Pharisees, alias Rabbis, that the Judaic Zionist Jews of today continue to hide within their *Talmud.* But their actions - attacking an American Naval ship - and convincing the U.S. Government - to help them cover up their murder of American sailors - it's their winning that quarrel over rank. The Zionist Jews use our own government against us - to continue their deceit of being a small, helpless country just trying to survive. What bull!"

Quinn shook his head slowly from side to side, "It sounds as though they are quite confident in winning that final quarrel over rank." Quinn paused a moment, and added, "But I think that the majority of Adam's descendants don't know that there is a hidden quarrel going on. I don't think White Americans even realize that they are descended from Adam, Abraham, or Jacob/Israel. Americans have had a past of racial tension - between Whites and Blacks, but I don't think they ever looked at the Zionist and thought of them as a separate race from White America - yet, in fact, they are. And their race is descended from Satan."

Quinn sat forward in his chair, "Sir, the Universal Jewish Encyclopedia states that the '*Babylonian Talmud* – derived from Babylonian thought and Chanaanite religious practices.' We know that Chanaanites were descendants of Ham who was Black, and that they worshipped Ba'al – not the God of Abraham. There is also a controversial statement made by a Rabbi, which blatantly exposes the Zionists as a race separate from the White race. Likely, the controversy stems from the exposure that the Zionists are not ready to accept. Yet the statement makes perfect historical sense."

Quinn searched the computer on the conference table, "Here it is, Sir: *Rabbi* Emmanuel Rabbinovich's Speech to Emergency Council of European Rabbis_in Budapest, Hungary, January 12, 1952, and received with acclaim,' (http://rense.com/general45/full.htm).
The Rabbi said, 'We will openly reveal our identity with the races of Asia or Africa. I can state with assurance that the last generation of *White Children* is now being born. Our Control Commissions will, in the interests of peace and wiping out inter-racial tensions, forbid the Whites to mate with White. The White Woman must cohabit with members of the Dark races, the White Man with Black Women. Thus, the White race will disappear, for mixing the Dark with the White means the end of the White Man, and our most dangerous enemy will become only a memory. We shall embark upon an era of ten thousand years of peace and plenty, the

Pax Judiaca, and *OUR RACE will rule undisputed over the world.* Our superior intelligence will enable us to retain mastery over a world of Dark Peoples....There will be no more religions. Not only would the existence of a priest class remain a constant danger to our rule, *but belief in an afterlife would give spiritual strength to irreconcilable elements in many countries, and enable them to resist us.* We will, however, retain the rituals and customs of *Judaism* as the mark of *our hereditary ruling caste*, strengthening our racial laws so that no Jew will be allowed to marry outside OUR RACE, nor will any stranger be accepted by us.'"

Quinn turned to Eisenhower, "The majority of Americans look at the country as being controlled by incompetent, corrupt Democrats and Republicans, and some are aware that there is of some sort of push into a New World Order. But they only view a NWO as a strategy that would make the rich richer. I think the thought has always been that America will stop the NWO at the polling booths. They see 'Take back our country' as a political slogan. What Americans don't understand is that Satan's children literally exist and have literally conquered them. Most Americans still do not understand that through the Federal Reserve Act foreign Zionist Jews *conquered* the United States of America. It's nothing less than a conquering! President Lyndon Baines Johnson's signing the Civil Rights Act was really about allowing the increased number of Pharisaic/Zionist Jewish immigration, which had been previously limited. What most Americans don't understand - their endgame is your soul. It has nothing to do with the rich getting richer. That's only their secondary reward. That's Satan's reward to them for capturing Israelite souls."

Quinn looked at Eisenhower, "I think another way that the Pharisaic/Judaic wicked look at themselves: We are descended from an evil one - so we are allowed, we have the right! To do these things to you. We are better, our father was an angel - your father was made of 'the slime of the earth'; we are more intelligent than the ones descended from the upright one - therefore, the wicked ones should control the upright ones - for their own national security! Yeah, that sounds good! National security from the boogeyman. But they failed to tell Americans that they are the boogeyman. And their plan for a New World Order won't come about unless every Christian turns against Jesus, or every Christian is dead!"

Eisenhower replied, "I'll add to Rabbi Rabbinovich's statement. Goldwin Smith, a Jewish Professor of Modern History at Oxford University, in 1981, said: "We (Zionist) Jews regard our *race* as superior to all humanity. And look forward not to our ultimate union with other races, but our final triumph over them."
(http://meetchristians.com/new/tr_fr_view_thread.php?TID =122219)

With a frown, Eisenhower said, "They have done that through the Federal Reserve and through Vatican II, through our schools at every level, through our military, through countless unlawful legislation."

Quinn sighed, "Their own Talmudic argument shows that they realize Satan impregnated Eve and that they are descended from Satan and that they want to keep it quiet. Their own deceit shows that there is CHOICE! The 'wicked should not *say*' that means that they could say: 'We are descendants of a wicked one…hence we are not to be blamed....'"

He continued, "While Satan gave his genetic material to Cain, only God can create a soul. Satan was an angel created by God; God gave Satan a soul; God gave Satan free will. There is free will, and Satan chose to do evil – but his only power is seduction, deceit, which he uses to destroy good souls. We must be vigilant against Satan lying in wait, to trip the heal of those descendants of Eve, Gen. 3:15."

It suddenly occurred to Quinn, as he thought again of the verse: 'I will put enmities between thee (Satan) and the woman, and (between) thy (Satan) seed and her (Eve) seed' – Eve is the mother of all mankind, Satan is the father of those descendant of Cain, Ham, and Japheth – but Eve is their mother; not just the mother of those children she had with Adam. That would explain the fighting between the Jews and Muslims, the threat that the Rabbis impose on the Zionists, and the threat that the Imams impose on the Muslims. It explains the Sunnis Muslims and the Shite Muslims fighting each other.

"In the Old Testament, and known to the Pharisees - there is the Book of Josue, which common opinion holds that Josue wrote himself, therefore, it was written before the time of the Pharisees, therefore, they knew of it. In Josue 24:1-16, 'And Josue gathered together all the tribes of Israel...and they stood in the sight of the Lord...And he spoke thus to the people: *Thus saith the Lord the God of Israel*:..But if it seem evil to you to serve the Lord, *you have your choice*: choose this day that which pleaseth you, *whom you would rather serve*, whether the gods (Cain/Satan) which your fathers served in Mesopotamia (Cain's city of Eridu and Babylon)…but as for me and my house we will serve the Lord....And the people answered, and said: God forbid we should leave the Lord, and serve strange gods.'"

Quinn sat back in his chair, remembering that Maggie told him that this revolution is the only war for which she would sacrifice her children in battle. This is what she meant whether she realized it he didn't know. This war will be for the fight of our souls - those who fight for the Father, against Satan, will be choosing to follow Jesus, who had died an excruciating death for the eternal salvation of the souls who choose to follow Jesus. The Roman soldiers whipped him with leather lashes that had metal points. Through excruciating pain, He offered us salvation; we owe Him big time! Through excruciating pain – He showed us what Satan had to offer us. Quinn realized that Maggie is ready to make the same sacrifice that Abraham was willing to do for the Father - sacrifice his *only* son, Gen. 22:2. God the Father, in love with those who love Him, sacrificed his *only* Son to save our souls. The Father is not asking of us more than what He had done for us. Quinn thought how badly it must have broken His heart to see His *only* Son suffer such tortures. Moloch never did that for those who gave - transferred - their children to him.

Quinn also wondered, did Jesus come at that time because the Law of Moses had been thrown aside? The Pharisees had made His Temple a place of evil moneychangers - His upsetting their tables was His destruction of the Second Temple - the Roman Legions were just the demolition crew. Jesus told his disciples, Matt. 10:5-6, 'Go ye not into the way of the Gentiles...But go ye rather to the lost sheep of the house of Israel.' Quinn realized that it is in the house of Israel that the satanic Pharisees had taken control of the Israelites and forced them to live by their new Pharisaic religion.

"This is when the Pharisees' captivity of the Israelites was broken, destroyed by the Roman Legions - who killed or scattered the Israelites," Quinn mumbled to himself. "The Pharisees emerged under a new name, Rabbis, but had no independent foot hole until the State of Israel was established after WWII. But even still, the rabbis' greatest influence came at the time of Vatican II - when the Zionist and Jesuits Enthroned Satan into the Catholic Church and Jesus and the Holy Ghost were taken away!"

Quinn thought of Maggie's upset in their discussion of Vatican II's destruction of the Catholic Church. She had said that Vatican II eliminated the priest's prayer after the giving of the Eucharist - the Quod ore sumpsimus. But Vatican II restored it under pressure. The prayer: "What has passed our lips as food, O Lord, may we possess in purity of heart, that what is given to us in time, be our healing for eternity."

But the Vatican never restored what Vatican II took away: the Corpus Tuum and the Placeat tibi. During the most holy part of the Mass, where the priest held up the Eucharist over his head and prayed: "May your Body, O Lord, which I have received, and your Blood, which I have drunk, cleave to mine inmost parts: and grant that no stain of sin may remain in me, whom pure and holy mysteries have refreshed: who lives and reigns, world without end. Amen."

The Placeat tibi the priest used to pray after communion, after the Eucharist the priest had given to a kneeling communicant, after making the sign of the cross - now both of those homages are gone, too. The Placeat tibi that Vatican II removed: "May the lowly homage of my service be pleasing to Thee, O most holy *Trinity*: and do Thou grant that the sacrifice, which I, all unworthy, have offered up in the sight of Thy majesty, may be acceptable to Thee, and, because of Thy loving kindness, may avail to atone to Thee for myself and for all those for whom I have offered it up. Through Christ our Lord. Amen.' This prayer was never restored."

Quinn immediately thought of the contrast of the prophecy of Malachias 1:7-14, where he speaks God's words to the Pharisees: "To you, O priests, that despise My name...You offer polluted bread upon My altar...In that you say: The table of the Lord is contemptible...Cursed is the deceitful man...making a vow offereth in sacrifice that which is feeble to the Lord: for I am a great King...."

In Quinn's opinion, the taking away of the priest's prayer – seemed to Quinn was the Pharisee coming out in Rabbi Heschel - the

Jewish negotiator within Vatican II. In Quinn's opinion, Rabbi Heschel was attempting to destroy the Catholic Church. In Quinn's opinion, Rabbi Heschel was attempting to prevent Adam's descendants from entering the Kingdom of God. In Quinn's opinion, Rabbi Heschel won that quarrel over rank.

Vatican II also removed the Leonine prayers at the end of the Mass, one of these prayers asked Michael the Archangel to protect the Catholic Church. Also removed was the reading of the Last Gospel.

Quinn thought of his research the night before - how he had concluded that Michael had defeated Satan, locked him into the bottomless pit, and that Satan was now loose for a short time. In Quinn's opinion, Rabbi Heschel, who intervened in Vatican II in negotiating changes to the liturgy, along with the Jesuits, are stopping Christians, the Israelites, from calling on Michael the Archangel to protect them from Satan. Why else would a prayer to Michael the Archangel, who had defeated Satan before, be eliminated from the Mass – Michael is the protector of the Catholic Church! Eight days after Pope Paul VI was elected, they Enthroned Satan on the Throne of Peter – and then Vatican II was reconvened in to session – and then they removed the one prayer that would protect the Church from Satan.

And this is why we will now fight the Battle of Armageddon - yes, yes, Quinn thought. The Pharisees were losing their quarrel over rank with Jesus, John 12:19, so they had him killed. Jesus came to free the Israelites from the grip of the Pharisees; he also came to save our souls; but even more importantly – He came to confront Satan. All of mankind and all of creation sat on the precipice of hell. All of that allowed for Satan to be put in the bottomless pit for 1000 years, and be released to seduce the nations, which he has done. And now, we're in the end times. The end of God's affliction of the seed of David – the affliction of the true Israelites.

The more Quinn thought about it, the more he felt he was right. The Pharisees had held the Israelites captive for over 400 years. I think there is more to Jesus coming when He did. Jesus came to confront Satan – they call it the temptation in the desert. But it was no temptation. It was a confrontation. Jesus had come to put Satan into the bottomless pit with the help of Michael the Archangel – to keep the end times on schedule.

Quinn smiled quietly, wait till He gets his hands on the Zionist Jews and Muslims of today! Suddenly, a chill ran over Quinn's body, for somewhere from the ethereal sphere, he heard, he felt, the deep, angry voice of God. He sat up quickly, shaking his head as if to shake off the awareness of God's voice, so fearful was he of God's anger.

Eisenhower leaned forward and rested his arms on the conference table, "You see, Quinn, it's not actually a fight between lineages, it's a fight between those who believe in the Father, Son, and Holy Ghost, and those who are loyal to Satan. ***That's the fight!*** This is the reason for a true revolution to take place - the people against their Rabbis, Imams - and Popes - because all of them are taking their souls to hell with them."

Quinn nodded in understanding. "I think this is what Jesus was referring to when He said to His disciples, in Matt. 16:11, 'Beware...*of the doctrine of the Pharisees....*'

"And here is such a doctrine of the Pharisees," Eisenhower said as he clicked onto the *Talmud,* to Book 10, Vol. II, Part II, 'His will is the supreme rule of our being. Do His will as thy own, submit thy will to His will. *Be bold as a leopard, light as an eagle, swift as a roe (Eurasian deer), and strong as a lion, to do the will of thy Father, who is in heaven.*'"

Immediately, the *Talmud's* words, leopard, eagle, lion jumped out at Quinn after spending the previous night reading the words as they described the second beast in Revelations. The beast, he thought, that represented the United Nations. Rev. 13:1, "And I saw a beast coming *up out of the sea*...(2) And the beast, which I saw, was like to a leopard, and his feet were as the feet of a bear, and his mouth as the mouth of a lion.' Quinn had equated the U.S./eagle, UK/lion, Russia/bear, China/leopard, and France/roe; those were the countries that established the UN Charter.

Quinn thought to himself, between this *Talmud* verse and *Douay Rheims* verse - at least four of the countries are connected to each other and accounted for in symbolism. The *Talmud* is instructing – set up the United Nations. The Bible is warning of its existence. This Rev. 13:1 describes the second beast, the United Nations, who will do the will of the first beast, Satan. Eisenhower had heard Quinn's previous thought, "And yes, Quinn, that Talmudic verse does reflect the countries who wrote up the United Nations Charter, as does Revelations. Hence, the United Nations is the focal point, as well as the leaders who wrote up its Charter.

But we have a problem – they have controlled our culture for decades, morally bringing us to the edge of hell. Our bloodline will not protect us.

In Romans 9:6, Apostle Paul wrote, 'For all are not Israelites that are of Israel...Neither are all they that are the seed of Abraham, children: but in Isaac shall thy *seed be called*...That is to say, not they that are the children of the flesh, are the children of God; but they, that are the children of the promise, are accounted for the seed...And it shall be, in the place where it was said unto them, You are not my people; there they shall be called the sons of the living God.'

That means that even though they are not of the true Israelite bloodline, if they choose the Father, Jesus, and His Holy Ghost, they shall be called the sons of the God of Abraham. And it also means, those of the Israelite bloodline must choose Jesus to be saved. Their bloodline alone does not save them."

Eisenhower closed the Bible, "Both the Zionist Jews and the Muslims have maintained their following through violence. And through violence the Pharisees/Kenites demanded the crucifixion of our Messiah, our Christ."

Eisenhower was determined, "We cannot let the Zionist Jews take our Messiah from us, again. Not again! But they are still seducing us

Christian Americans to sin to keep us from the salvation of Jesus. Abortion is the same as transferring our children to the idol Moloch, but before the babe is born. The new healthcare mandates that Christians violate their faith by forcing them to provide women with birth control coverage, which includes abortion – but Muslims are exempt from participating in insurance, while Christians are financially penalized if they don't buy coverage, which in the end, pays for those abortions. Hence, the law encourages only Christians abort their children. Even if they don't, the law mandates that Christians go against their faith! Thus, condemning their souls to hell!

The Jewish media brought us fornication as everyday life. That was accomplished by glamourizing the 1960s activist groups such as the Students for a Democratic Society, the Woman's Movement, the Sexual and Drug Revolutions. The purpose of those movements - at the time of the Second Vatican Council - was to bring American Christians in to greater sin.

President Lyndon Baines Johnson advocated the use of birth control, and the U.S. Supreme Court established in *Baird* the right of unmarried people to possess contraception. Betty Freakman wrote a book read throughout America's college campuses, encouraging young women to participate in and enjoy sex - without marriage. It changed societal behavior in America, away from traditional Christian values. While those movements quieted, their offshoots still exist on campuses today – many are organized by Muslim college students.

Today, state governments have picked up the destruction of the bodies and souls of America's children – the Mayor of NYC, Grebmoolstein, has mandated sexual education of grade-school and high school children - over the wishes of parents. It's an attack on the young minds not ready for any public discussion of sex - it's a mental rape of these grade-school children. It's a psychological invasion of intimate private space in the mind - opening it to public lust. The media does its duty, owned by the Zionists, air TV programs showing teen sexual promiscuity. Zionists have changed the laws and the culture to create another Sodom and Gomorrah here in the United States. It's a preparation for satanic promiscuity that will ultimately lead to no marriages, with a world of only fornicators. They have no intent to educate - their intent is to strip the psychological barrier of privacy from around every individual and insert in the child's subconscious mind that the government has a right to be in that private space - that's the actual intent of Mayor Grebmoolstein - prepare the minds of the children - so that the government can impose the sins of Satan - to bring the child's soul in to sin. Grebmoolstein is giving the souls of America's children to Satan!

And to the parents, the Mayor is saying - we are taking control of your children - whether you like it or not. Today, the Mayor has ordered hospitals to lock up baby formula next to controlled substances – thereby, over the long term, changing the mindset of nurses to view formula as harmful and the Mayor imposing on a new mother a psychological shame for requesting formula for her newborn! The shame is intentional. The Mayor will take control of children by using the weapon of political correctness – until society bullies every new mother in to submission, which could then easily change state laws mandating breast feeding. But breast feeding is not the actual intent of the Mayor of NYC – it's the mindset of society that he wants to change. Just as Communist China takes children out of their homes because the government of China has determined that the child will become an Olympian, even if the child and parents don't want it. Parents' response – we don't completely own our child – she belongs to the state. That Communist mindset is coming to America!

Mayor Grebmoolstein's sister is a Commissioner for the NYC Commission for the United Nations. She acts as a liaison between the Mayor's office and the United Nations."

Eisenhower stopped, then added, "Another way they are taking control of the minds of our children – setting them up to accept Communism – is through academics, taking Jesus out of historical citation. In the early 1990s, for the first time in nearly 2000 years of history, college professors began to require their students use BCE to signify Before the Common Era and CE for the Common Era, changing the meaning of the C from Christ to Common, as though Christ had never existed. The division of historical events is still measured before and after the birth of Christ – but only a curious child's
question would get an explanation. It had always been BC, Before Christ, and A.D., Anno Domini - the year of our Lord, meaning Jesus Christ. They cannot rewrite 2000 years of historical events and documents - so they blur the past indicators by adding the E for era after BC - so that our children never connect BC to Jesus Christ. To them, BC will be understood as Before the Common Era; A.D. is now written: Common Era. The schools mandate this change. And the continual sacrifice is taken away in yet another way. Satan's net is very encompassing."

Quinn nodded, "Yes, I noticed that. And I taught my kids what they were up to. To counter their assaults, I inform my children on their every evil manipulation. Go ahead, I told them, write BCE to pass the course, but outside the classroom, use B.C. and A.D., and educate everyone you know."

He then turned to the *Talmud* on the computer screen, "That satanic web – that idea of every area of life is being invaded to change society to worship Satan – that instruction comes from the *Talmud's* Book 10, Vol. II, Part II, Ch. II, it reads: 'Consider three things…remember that there is above thee an *all-seeing eye*, an all-hearing ear, and a record of all thy actions.' And again, 'Consider three things…remember *whence thou comest, whither thou goest*, and before whom thou wilt have to render account for thy doings.'"

Quinn thought to himself – they came from Satan and they will go into hell with him. But the language of the verse sparked Quinn's memory – of the dialogue between Jesus and the Pharisees, John 8:14-24, Jesus said, 'I am the light of the world: he that followeth me, walketh not in darkness, but shall have the light of life.' The Pharisees therefore said to him: 'Thou givest testimony of thyself: thy testimony is not true.' Jesus answered, and said to them: '*Although I give testimony of myself, my testimony is true: for I know whence I came, and whither I go: but you know not whence I come, or whither I go…And in your law it is written, that the testimony of two men is true. I am one that give testimony of myself: and the Father that sent me giveth testimony of me.' They said therefore to him: 'Where is thy Father?' Jesus answered: 'Neither me do you know, nor my Father: if you did know me, perhaps you would know my Father also…Whither I go, you cannot come…You are from beneath, I am from above. You are of this world, I am not of this world.* Therefore I said to you, that you shall die in your sins. For if you believe not that I am he, you shall die in your sin.'

Quinn's mind was flooded with thoughts about Jesus' words – 'In *your* law it is written, that the testimony of two men is true.' It suddenly hit him – is this yet another reason that Jesus called Himself the Son, instead of God the Father – so that the law would be satisfied – that the testimony of the Son and the Father would be deemed the testimony of two men, therefore, true. Jesus had hinted at His being the Father, 'if you did know me, perhaps you would know my Father also,' but He did not outwardly declare it.

"I still think," Quinn mumbled, "if He told everyone that He was the God of Abraham, God of Creation - everyone would have dropped dead with fear. I know I would have. I mean, think of it!"

Quinn reasoned the two passages – the *Talmud's* 'remember whence thou comest, whither thou goest' pertained to this earthly life. Jesus' words – 'Whither I go, you cannot come' separated the earthly from the Heavenly – the immediate from the eternal. 'You are from beneath,' meaning earth, at the least, as opposed to Jesus being 'from above,' meaning Heaven. 'You (Pharisees) are of this world,' of fleeting, earthly riches, which is all that Satan could possibly promise through his teaching of deceit.

Those earthly riches were instituted by the Pharisee Chief Priest, Annas, head of Talmudic law, who had set up money-changing in the outer court of the Second Temple. He and his son-in-law, the High Priest Caiphas, 'were profiteering' from the moneychangers, (www.graspinggod.com /jesus-and-the- moneychangers.html). In the outer court of the temple, Gentiles would come from out-of-town, and to get into the outer court, the Gentiles had to pay a temple tax, which could only be paid in the temple currency per the Oral Law of the *Talmud*, not yet written down. Annas interpreted that Oral Talmudic Law as instituting a temple tax and interpreted that the tax must be paid in temple currency. Therefore, their foreign currency had to be changed to temple currency – with a charge of interest for exchanging the currency.

Quinn thought for a moment – isn't this what the Federal Reserve is doing to us today, for us to use our own money?

It was Annas who set up and Caiphas who maintained the financial monopoly, 'taking advantage of those whose religious sentiment led them to worship the Lord,' (*Ibid.*).

Gentiles were forbidden to go from the outer court into the temple, and 'were killed by the Jewish guards' when they tried (*Ibid.*). Therefore, the worship by Gentiles was confined to the space of the outer court. Annas and Caiphas allowed merchants to set up shops inside this court. 'But the merchants were desecrating the court and ruining the spiritual atmosphere of this holy place,' (*Ibid.*) because cattle and sheep, as well as doves, were brought into the court for sale to those who wanted to sacrifice the animals. The animals cried in hunger and messed the floor of the court – the noise and repugnant and disgusting smell of animal urine and feces added to the chaos of merchants, the money-changers, and the Gentiles exchanging their currency, certainly made a mockery of the worship of God. This disease-ridden environment was created by and was the practice of the head leaders of the *Talmud.* Thus, their Talmudic verse – know from where you came and where you go – was restricted to earthly riches the Pharisees gained by profiteering from others who wanted to worship the God of Abraham – regardless of the filth the Pharisee Chief Priests had instituted to block or diminish that worship.

Jesus promised eternal, Heavenly riches and preached that the 'Kingdom of God is within you,' (Luke 17:21). Quinn reasoned, after reading of the mockery that the Pharisees and the Vatican II Jesuits had made of institutionalized religion – Jesus was teaching – don't look to these institutions for God – have a personal relationship, within yourself – talk to God. This is what Jesus meant.

Quinn thought, too, of President Franklin Roosevelt putting the *Talmud's* 'seeing eye' on the dollar bill, the symbol of the New Age of Horus, the symbol of satanic worship, also known as the New Age religion. Certainly, the seeing eye on the dollar bill connected the Talmudic promise of earthly riches to the Federal Reserve and its owners.

And Quinn remembered his research of the previous night, in Gen. 16:8, Agar, the mother if Ismael, being asked by an angel of the Lord, "He said to her: 'Agar, handmaid of Sarai, whence comest thou? and whither goest thou?' This angel of the Lord who spoke to Agar/Hagar was not from the God of Abraham, for the God of Abraham was not Agar's god, her god was the goddess Wadjet, Eye of Ra, the image of a cobra – a serpent. The Eye of Horus/Satan was an ancient Egyptian symbol of the descendants Mesram, son of Ham, who first settled Egypt. 'Of all the nations of antiquity, none was so infamous for idolatry, as Egypt…the worship of the serpent was in her early history...There is scarcely an Egyptian deity which is not occasionally symbolized by the serpent….The great consideration in which the symbolical serpent was held by the

Egyptians…(and this is the reason for his appearance in Egyptian hieroglyphics). The serpent was deemed symbolical of the divine wisdom, power, and creative energy; of immortality and regeneration….the genius who governed all things, and was symbolized by the serpent.' (http://www.sacred-texts.com/etc/wos/wos05.htm). Earth, Water, Air, and Fire were all symbolized by some posture of the serpent. The divine wisdom is what Satan had granted Solomon. The Egyptian assertion that the serpent was the genius who governed all things – was Satan's desire from the time that God gave that power to Adam. In Egypt, through his bloodline, Satan had won in the quarrel over rank. The worship of Satan was born and bred into Agar/Hagar, the mother of Ismael, long before the Pharaoh gave her to Sarai/Sarah, Abraham's wife. The gift was an infiltration of satanic evil into the house of one of God's chosen. The angel of the Lord that spoke to Agar was the same angel that Eve spoke of when Cain was born.

Agar never forgot her Egyptian bloodline or home, for she 'took a wife for (Ismael) out of the land of Egypt,' (Gen. 21:21). For had she accepted the God of Abraham, she would not have gone back to Egypt, brought an Egyptian wife to Ismael, unless she and Ismael worshipped the Egyptian goddess Eye of Ra, a serpent, regardless of the jealousy of Abraham's wife, Sarah. Through King Solomon and one of his Edomite/Egyptian wives, descended Ezra. In reading the *Babylonian Talmud*, which Ezra had created, the worship of Satan continued throughout the ages from Agar, Ismael, and through Solomon and his Edomite wives, down through Ezra, through the Pharisees and their *Talmud* – just as it continues to today – through Islam, Judaism and Vatican II.

It seemed obvious to Quinn that the *Talmud* would make such a similar statement as the angel that Quinn had concluded was Satan talking to Agar, the Egyptian servant from the House of the Pharaoh. The Eye of Ra was the god intended to protect the Pharaoh. Quinn wondered if the sin that the *Talmud* was speaking of was the sin of leaving Satan to follow the God of Abraham, Jesus. Was this Talmudic passage a threat to its followers? 'Remember...before whom thou wilt have to render account for thy doings' - an evil entity, Satan. This threat must be taken seriously just as the warning to anyone who killed Cain, that they 'shall be punished sevenfold. And the Lord set a mark upon Cain, that whosoever found him should not kill him,' (Gen. 4:15). God was warning that Satan would punish the murderer of his only son – sevenfold.

It suddenly hit Quinn and he had wondered why he didn't make the connection last night. The Pharisees were Kenites, of the House of Rechab, of Ham - Ham was Black! He remembered also reading in John 8:15, when Jesus was talking to the Pharisees: "Jesus answered, and said to them: *You judge according to the flesh*...." The Pharisees were Black! This verse is saying that Jesus was telling the Pharisees that they judge according to bloodline; that they were against Jesus because he was White from Adam and Eve, and they were Black from Satan and Eve. The Black Pharisees governed, judged, and punished the White Israelites who had returned to Jerusalem from Babylonian captivity. Jesus knew he came from God the Father, who was White. The Pharisees only knew their own father, who was Black. Satan is Black!

In the Dead Sea Scrolls on Genesis 4:1:

> And Adam knew his wife Eve, who was pregnant by Sammael [Satan], and she conceived and bare Cain, and he was like the heavenly beings, and not like the earthly beings, and she said, I have gotten a man from the angel of the Lord."

At the time Eve made this statement, the only beings that she knew was Adam and Satan; both had impregnated her in the Garden of Eden, heaven. The earthly beings - Adam and Eve - were White! The heavenly being, Satan, was Black.

Quinn turned to Eisenhower, "Sir? The city of Eridu! Archaeologically speaking, Eridu, located in the southern part of Mesopotamia, is the oldest city of the world; it was built by Cain. There are archeological records that estimate Eridu dates back to 5200-4500 BC; that is close to the time of Adam and Eve in the Garden, and later in Haran. Haran is outside the Garden of Eden in southern Turkey, which is considered the northern part of Mesopotamia.

The descendants of Eridu claimed that their civilization was brought by their god or his advisor. The name for advisor is Abgallu - it translates: Ab = water; gal = big; lu = man. The advisor was: water big man. Or, the man of the big water. One could consider that Cain, having been sent out of Haran by God, went east of the Garden of Eden, came down the Tigris River, stopping to gather food, got on the parallel-flowing Euphrates River and came down to the area of Sumer. Cain was intellectually superior to the Neanderthals he found in the Eridu area and they worshipped Cain as their god. After all, God put a mark on Cain, Gen. 4:14-15, to keep the Neanderthals from killing him. They had to think he was a god or god's advisor.

He and the Neanderthals built the city of Eridu.

I've read that the first people of Eridu migrated from northern Mesopotamia to southern Mesopotamia, and brought with them the Sumarran culture. The Sumerians were the children and grandchildren of Adam and Eve; they carried a Semitic Y-chromosome. The Sumerians migrated from Haran to Eridu.

"I'll continue that analysis for you, Quinn," Eisenhower replied, "In Sumer-Dingu language their word for god was: Enki, which meant governor of moral behavior on earth - ruler of earth, vegetation, animal and man. The Sumerians are considered to be of unknown origins. That's because all evidence of them has been intentionally destroyed - just as today's college professors have prohibited the use of "BC/Before Christ and the A.D./Year of Our Lord."

The word for divine leader is En, considered Son of Anu. Anu means 'creator.' This is where the word Annanuki comes from. This refers to God, the Garden of Eden, and His creating Adam and Eve. Those Sumerian kings claimed lineage to Adam and Eve, divine leaders who were created by God. Adam was the Son of Anu."

"As in many 'creators' noted in the *Talmud*?" Quinn asked.

"Exactly! It is known that Cain's people worshipped him as a god. It would appear that when Cain went down and built Eridu - he established himself as the ruler over the earth, the people, creatures, and vegetation - the power that Cain's father had coveted in the Garden. The power that God had given to Adam. But the Sumerian kings followed Cain down to Sumer and made a separate claim of being from a line of divine leaders. The quarrel of rank! Today, the media shows documentaries that assert that Annanuki are extraterrestrials who engineered our DNA centuries ago. In fact, there were no extraterrestrials – there were Sumerians, descendants of Adam and Eve, and Cain and his Neanderthal wives, who were superior to the Neanderthals. But with this hypothesis of extraterrestrials presented as a fact, the Jewish media are trying from every angle to dismiss the idea of separate bloodlines."

Eisenhower leaned toward Quinn, "This war that we are about to face will be quite difficult because of one thing."

"What's that?" Quinn was curious.

"Regardless of bloodline," Eisenhower explained, "regardless of our past sins, Zionist Jews, Muslims, Atheist, and Christians, can all have everlasting peace, everlasting salvation - they all can choose Jesus and be resurrected up into Heaven with the Holy Father, *but only* if they ask Jesus to be their Lord and Savior and repent their sins. Matt. 18:3, Jesus said to his disciples, 'Amen I say to you, unless you be converted, and become as little children, you shall not enter into the kingdom of heaven.' Matt. 12:31, Jesus said to the Pharisees, who had blasphemed the Holy Ghost, 'Therefore I say to you: Every sin and blasphemy shall be forgiven men, but the blasphemy of the Spirit shall not be forgiven. (32) And whosoever shall speak a word against the Son of man, it shall be forgiven him: *but he that shall speak against the Holy Ghost, it shall not be forgiven him, neither in this world, nor in the world to come.'*

Vatican II, the Zionists and Jesuits who took the Holy Ghost out of all the prayers committed this blasphemy. This fight between good and evil has continued throughout the ages of mankind. People need to realize that it is occurring all around us, today!"

The difficulty is how will we know, if they wait until they are on the battlefield. In Acts, 2:21, 'And it shall come to pass, that whosoever shall call upon the name of the Lord, shall be saved.' And how will we know if their words are true or if it's another deceit?"

Quinn replied, "If they wait until on the battlefield, as far as I'm concerned, it's too late to save their lives, but not too late to save their souls."

"I agree," Eisenhower said.

Quinn thought of the Prophet Joel in telling of the end times - the 'terrible day of the Lord.' Joel 3:10-17, in which God instructs: *'Cut your ploughshares into swords, and your spades into spears*. Let the weak say: I am strong...and *come, all ye nations, from round about, and gather yourselves together: there will the Lord cause all thy strong ones to fall down*...Let them arise, and let the names come into the valley of Josaphat: for there I will sit to judge all nations round about...Nations, nations in the valley of destruction: *for the day of the Lord is near in the valley of destruction*...The sun and the moon are darkened, and the stars have withdrawn their shining...And the Lord shall roar out of Sion, and utter his voice from Jerusalem: and the heavens and the earth shall be moved, and the Lord shall be the hope of his people, and the strength of the children of Israel...And you shall know that I am the Lord your God, dwelling in Sion my holy mountain: and Jerusalem shall be holy *and strangers shall pass through it no more*.'

Quinn had understood these verses to mean that God was calling all Americans to revolt - as with the American Revolutionaries, who had picked up their pitchfolks to fight. Americans should convert all that is in their households that can be converted to a weapon - so they must do - to fight Satan's army.

Quinn thought it was just as Jesus had told his disciples, go preach in the house of Israel - to the lost children of the God of Abraham - the Christians in America, the children of the God of Abraham; they are now lost - and have sinned against the Law of Moses. Just as the Pharisees had corrupted the Israelites they dragged back to Jerusalem as a cover for their Pharisaism - so God will come into America where His children are. For the Zionists have corrupted their Christian culture and seduced them in to sin. The tribulation that we are allowing the Zionist and Muslims to inflict upon us is not of God. We turned away from God; Americans were seduced and have been following, or at least, allowing Satan's children to seduce them. If Americans did not stop them, then they chose to be with the Zionists and their father, Satan. From this Americans must repent. Now, is the time for Americans to choose, as Jesus said, 'He that is not with me, is against me; and he that gathereth not with me, scattereth,' Luke 11:23.

He recalled, Leviticus 20:1-5, "And the Lord spoke to Moses, saying: Thus shalt thou say to the children of Israel: If any man of the children of Israel...give of his seed (children) to the *idol Moloch*, dying let him die: the people of the land shall stone him...And if the people of the land neglecting, and as it were little regarding my commandment, let alone the man that hath given of his seed to Moloch, and will not kill him: I will set my face against that man, and his kindred, and will cut off both him and all that consented with him, to commit fornication with Moloch, out of the midst of their people."

Quinn said to Eisenhower, "If we allow the Mayor of NYC, or the federal government, or the United Nations to take control of our children, to turn them over to Satan - then God will set His face against that man and all that consented with him - every American citizen!"

'For the *day of the Lord is near in the valley* of destruction' Quinn understood to mean the United Nations and its building - a valley sits on a lowland between ranges of mountains - the tall buildings of New York City were the mountains, and along the valley bottom flowed the East River, right next to the UN building.

Quinn remembered the image of watching American Christians jumping out of the Twin Towers to their death rather than burn in the hot flames of burning jet fuel. The Zionist Jews and Muslims had colluded in attacking the buildings with planes/missiles. The Zionists planned and the Muslims flew the planes and took the credit. The Zionists and Muslims had made New York City the valley of destruction. The Zionist who rented the Twin Towers didn't come into the building on his regularly scheduled time that day. And that day he told the Fire Department to 'pull' building number 7 that he owned – the one in which the Zionist's tenants were: CIA, U.S. Secret Service, IRS Regional Council, Security and Exchange Commission, Mayor's Office of Emergency Management, American Express International, and Standard Chartered Bank. How could this combination of tenants not have a sufficient fire sprinkler system to put out the fire from the embers that fell on it. And where was the security that these tenants must have had that didn't put out the small fires, but, instead, allowed it to burn all day. That same Zionist who had just weeks before rented the Twin Towers, insured them against terrorist attack, and received $4 billion in insurance payout on each building – remember from where you came and where you are going – to gain earthly riches promised by Satan!

But what really heightened Quinn's suspicions was the fact that most of the members of the 9/11 Commission were members of the Foreign Affairs Private Council. He knew for sure everything they reported was a lie, a deceit to bring about the FAPC's founding goal – destroying the power of the United States. The next step was to declare war – but not against Saudi Arabia from where most of the Muslim hijackers were from, but against Afghanistan for the poppy fields and Iraq for the scroll that some say taught the conjuring up of demons – for the scroll that suddenly disappeared from Iraq's national museum, right after the US Military had taken the city of Baghdad. And for another scroll that was buried in a mountainside and was whisked away by US Military helicopters in a secret, quick-strike mission; the scroll said to show the way to open the pit, to let out the evil demons from the underworld. The taking was to enhance the Black Projects conducted by the US Government. The wars achieved FAPC's goal to get Americans in to debt by multiple trillions of dollars to break the economy of America, and bring Americans to their knees. The Zionist attack provided the excuse to pass the Patriot Act and the Homeland Security Act that put the President on the throne of a dictator with the ability to spy on individual Americans that may revolt as they realized their country is being turned in to a Communist dictatorship and they had lost every right granted under the Constitution. The attack on the Twin Towers led to today, where spy drones fly over American soil, photographing when an American leaves his house and records where he goes and who he interacts with – as in knowing from whence he came and whither he goes, and who he is accounting to – as Talmudic verse threatens. Yet nothing is done to shut down Muslim paramilitary training camps, 35 at last count, from Springfield, Massachusetts to Malibu, California – they still operate unimpeded. It was the Zionist Jews, the owners of the Federal Reserve, putting the ring of slavery into the upper lip of the American citizens.

"There's one other thing that I want you to read, Quinn." Eisenhower pulled the laptop computer toward him and typed in *Douay Rheims* online Bible. "Daniel the Prophet had been captured when the Babylonians destroyed Jerusalem and Solomon's Temple, taking all who were in the Kingdom of Judah into Babylon, including non-Israelites. Jesus, Himself, referred to Daniel as a prophet, Matt. 24:15, and that Daniel's prophecy of the coming of the 'anointed,' which Jesus fulfilled, Dan 9:24. In Dan. 9:22, Gabriel tells Daniel of the coming of Jesus Christ. Daniel said: 'And he [Gabriel] instructed me...(24) *Seventy weeks* are shortened upon thy people...that transgression may be finished...and *everlasting justice may be brought*; and vision and *prophecy may be fulfilled*; and the *saint of saints may be anointed*.'"

Eisenhower turned to Quinn, but Quinn interrupted, "The 'saint of saints may be anointed' - that's Jesus Christ. The First Wave of Israelites were 48 years in Babylonian captivity, from Nebuchadnezzar's capture in 586 BC, until Cyrus the Great conquered Babylon and freed the Jews to rebuild their Second Temple. The Israelites came in three waves of freedom, beginning in 538 BC. The first wave of Israelites, in captivity for 48 years, built the Second Temple, between 538 BC and 517 BC and dedicated in 516 BC. The Second Wave of return, 457 BC, came the Israelites, *led* by Ezra, spent 70 years in captivity. The Third Wave return, in 444 BC; these people spent 142 years in captivity; they came back and rebuilt the walls.

Quinn thought for a moment, then said, "Daniel's prophecy is pointing to Ezra taking the Israelites back to Jerusalem – after 70 years (70 weeks in Daniel's prophecy) in Babylonian captivity. It's pointing to Ezra. Ezra needed to take the Israelites back to Jerusalem in order to establish his dictatorship and new religion under the stolen identity and heritage of the Israelites - away from all others - hence the name Pharisees - which means separatists.. The holy city of David, Jerusalem, where the Ark of the Covenant had been kept, became the city of Ezra and Pharisaism. This second, Ezra captivity had to occur when it did, so that Jesus could bring everlasting justice to the Israelites and all who believed in Him."

Ezra got back all the gold of Jerusalem that King Nebuchadazzar had taken from the Israelites, plus gold from the treasury of the Persian Kings Cyrus, Darius, and Artaxeres, and a promise of whatever else they needed. And the gold was to be delivered to 'the chief of the priests [Ezra], and of the Levites, and the heads of the families of Israel in Jerusalem, into the treasure of the house of the Lord.' 1 Esdras/Ezra 8:29.

But Nehemias, their governor, admonished the noble and magistrates, who had been appointed by Ezra. Ezra was given this power as a result of threatening the three Persian kings with the wrath of their Israelite God. When Nehemias came back to Jerusalem to build the walls, with the Third Wave of Israelites, he found what Ezra had established. Ezra had the power of a dictator, 2 Esdras 5:1, "Now there was a great cry of the people, and of their wives against their brethren the Jews...." The Jews were ready to sell all their land and vineyards, or borrow money from Ezra's treasury in order to buy food, during a famine. They bemoaned the idea that they had financially put their children in to bondage, unable to redeem them. Nehemias rebuked Ezra-appointed nobles and magistrates: 2 Esdras 5:7, 'Do you all charge your brothers' interest?' Charging interest on money loaned to one's brother was forbidden in the Law of Moses (Lev. 25:36-37; Deut. 23:19), which Ezra threw out when he established his own law of the *Talmud.*

And you can see in 2 Esdras 8:6-13, 'Esdras (*Ezra)*...the priest and scribe...the chiefs of the families of all the people, the priests, *and the Levites were gathered together to Esdras (Ezra)...that he should* interpret *to them the words of the law.'*

This is where Ezra began the figurative interpretation - beginning his new religion - Pharisaism!"

Eisenhower nodded, "Let's go back in time to when Solomon was dying, people argue that it was in 957 BC, others 931 BC, but I only mention this to give you some point of reference."

"Got it," Quinn replied.

"All right. Going to the deceit that led to the breakup of the united Kingdom of Israel. Background: God told the children of Israel, 3 Kings 11:2: You shall not go in unto them (marry the daughters of) 'Pharao...Moab... Edom...Sidon....'

The verse continues to warn that such wives would turn their husbands' hearts to worship their gods. But Solomon married these women, the Egyptian and Edomite - he had 700 wives and 300 concubines; most for political connections. And, in his old age, he did turn to worship Astarthe and Moloch idols, building temples to them, in which children were sacrificed (3 Kings 11:5-7). So God told Solomon, (3 Kings 11:11), 'Because thou has done this, and hast *not kept my covenant*...I will divide and...(tear apart your)...kingdom, and will give it to...(your) servant....I will rend it out of the hand of thy (Solomon's) son.' But God said that he would give (3 Kings 11:13) *one tribe* to...(Rohoboam) for the sake of David my servant, *and Jerusalem which I have chosen.*'"

Eisenhower looked up from the Bible, "Remember this - God

gave Solomon's son *one* tribe. We expect that son to be Rohoboam, but is it? Or is that son actually to be born in the distant future, as a son of the House of Solomon?

After the Exodus, Josue succeeded Moses in leading the Israelites - the twelve tribes, each tribe fathered by a son of Jacob/Israel. Josue gave the Tribe of Benjamin land that included Jerusalem and bordered the north of Judah. Later in history, David was the first the King of Judah, Saul was the king of the other tribes of Israelites. After Saul and his sons died in battle, David became the first king of the united Kingdom of Israel. King David later conquered the Jebusites, descendants of Canaan, who had previously refused to give up control of Jerusalem. David made Jerusalem the capital of the united Kingdom of Israel. When the tribes split after David's grandson, Rohoboam, became king, the Tribe of Benjamin remained loyal to the House of David and joined the Tribe of Judah, and the two tribes became the Kingdom of Judah, sometime around 930 BC. So, the actual son of Solomon, Rohoboam, had two tribes over which he ruled as king. This does not fit with 3 Kings 11:13.

Then came the conquest over the Ten Northern Tribes by the Assyrians, 721 BC. There had always been two tribes left, until attacked by the Babylonians, descendants of Nemrod, the son of Ham, descendant of Satan (Gen. 10:6-10). All the people living in the Kingdom of Judah were considered Jews by the Babylonians who captured them in 586 BC, although not all were Israelites of the Tribes of Benjamin or the Tribe of Judah. Others in their ranks were the descendants of Satan. But upon the release of the Israelites and the descendants of Satan from Babylonian captivity, collectively, they were all forevermore called Jews. Thus, God's people and Satan's people were lumped together into one people. The remnants left of the Tribes of Benjamin and Judah and descendants of Satan, are therefore, considered only *one* tribe that returned to Jerusalem with Ezra. As God had said in 3 Kings 11:13, 'Neither will I take away the whole kingdom, but I will give *one tribe* to thy son for the sake of David my servant, *and Jerusalem which I have chosen*.' God had chosen Jerusalem, the City of David, for the crucifixion of Jesus."

Eisenhower sketched out on paper, "Let's make the assumption that the Garden of Eden was approximately 5400 years ago; Noah and his son, Sem, and Ham and Japheth lived about 5200 years ago; that Abraham and his son, Isaac, and Ismael lived some 5000 years ago; that King David and his son, Solomon, lived 3000 years ago; and we know that Ezra was alive in 457 BC, or 2469 years ago. This is our approximate timeframe.

If we begin about 5000 years ago, to the time of Isaac, the son of Abraham, Isaac told his son, Jacob/Israel – the father of the Israelites, 'Take not a wife of the stock of Chanaan' (Gen. 28:1). Chanaan was the brother of Mesram (father of the Egyptians), both Chanaan and Mesram were the sons of Ham who was Black, (Gen.10:6). Therefore, Egyptians were of the same Black stock as Chanaan. But Esau, twin brother of Jacob/Israel, both of White Adam stock, Esau 'went to Ismael, and took to wife...the daughter of Ismael....' (Gen. 28:9). Ismael was the son of Agar, the Egyptian (Gen. 16:1). And Agar 'took a wife for (Ismael) out of the land of Egypt,' (Gen. 21:21). Hence, Esau married into the Egyptian stock of Satan, and through this marriage Esau fathered the mixed race of Edomites, who were of White Adam and Black Egyptian stock. Centuries later, White King Solomon married a Black Edomite woman; through that marriage descended Ezra, 600 years later. The Edomites were *in* the Kingdom of Judah when the Babylonians attacked and brought them back to Babylon. The Black Edomites, along with the Tribe of Benjamin who had joined the Tribe of Judah, King David's tribe and the bloodline of Jesus, were all taken together into Babylonian captivity. The Babylonians called all of them Jews. Ezra, the Black Edomite, was a distant Israelite through the bloodline of Solomon, David, and Jacob/Israel. But on his mother's side, Ezra was from the Edomite/Egyptian stock of Satan. Ezra, rose to power in Babylon, captured the Israelites and dragged them back to Jerusalem under penalty of death, and forced them to follow his Ezra-created *Talmud*, which approved of worshipping the idol, Moloch, (*Talmud*, Book 8, Ch. VII, Mishna VIII: "Said R [Rabbi] Abiu: Our Mishna is *in accordance with him who says* that Molech is not an idol *at all.").* Therefore, Ezra was that son, as in a descendant of Solomon and one of his Edomite wives, that God had promised Solomon to whom He would give *one tribe* (3 Kings 11:13). Ezra, half Israelite and half Edomite/Egyptian, was both of good and of evil who God used to punish the seed of David: 'I will for this afflict the seed of David, *but yet not for ever.'* (3 Kings 11:39."

We can see in 1 Esdras/Ezra 6:7-12, allegedly written by Ezra, the proof of his dictatorship and his threat against the Persian kings, to call upon the God of Abraham to punish them, if they did not give him the power that he desired. Cyrus the Great decreed: 'And let that temple of God be built by the governor of the Jews, and by their ancients...*to wit*, that the king's chest, that is, of the tribute that is paid out of the country beyond the river, the charges be diligently given to those men, lest the work be hindered...And *I have made a decree: That if any whosoever, shall alter this commandment, a beam be taken from his house, and set up, and he be nailed upon it, and his house be confiscated*....And may the God, that hath caused his name to dwell there, destroy all kingdoms, and the people that shall put out their hand to resist, and to destroy the house of God, that is in Jerusalem. *I Darius have made the decree, which I will have diligently complied with.*'

In 1 Esdras/Ezra 7:20, 'And this is the copy of the letter of the edict, which King Artaxerxes gave to Esdras the priest, the scribe instructed in the words and commandments of the Lord, and his ceremonies to Israel....It is decreed by me, that all they of the people of Israel, and of the priests and of the Levites in my realm, that are minded to go into Jerusalem, should go with thee...And to carry the silver and gold, which the king and his counselors have freely offered to the God of Israel, whose tabernacle is in Jerusalem...And all the silver and gold that *thou shalt find in all the province of Babylon*, and that the people is willing to offer, and that the priests shall offer of their own accord to the house of their God, which is in Jerusalem...Take freely, and buy diligently with this money, calves, rams, lambs, with the sacrifices and libations of them, and offer them upon the altar of the temple of your God, that is in Jerusalem...*And whatsoever more there shall be need of for the house of thy God, how much soever thou shalt have occasion to spend, it shall be given out of the treasury, and the king's exchequer, and by me (King Artaxerxes)*...I Artaxerxes the king have ordered and decreed to all the keepers of the public chest, that are beyond the river; that *whatsoever Esdras the priest, the scribe of the law of the God of heaven, shall require of you, you give it without delay*...All that belongeth to the rites of the God of heaven, let it be given diligently in the house of the God of heaven: *lest his wrath should be enkindled against the realm of the king, and of his sons*...*We give you (Esdras/Ezra)* also to understand concerning all the priests, and the Levites, and the singers, and the porters, and the Nathinites, and ministers of the house of this God, that you have *no authority to impose toll or tribute, or custom upon them*...And *thou Esdras (Ezra)* according to the wisdom of thy God, which is in thy (Ezra's) hand, *appoint judges and magistrates, that may judge all the people, that is beyond the river, that is, for them who know the law of thy God, yea and the ignorant teach ye freely*...*And whosoever will not do the law of thy God, and the law of the king diligently, judgment shall be executed upon him, either unto death, or unto banishment, or to the confiscation of goods, or at least to prison.'*

Eisenhower explained, "These two decrees from two Persian kings, who had conquered the Babylonians, shows Ezra's use of the power of the God of Abraham to bring about Ezra's power - that of a dictator! The Israelites were compelled to learn the *Talmud*, under penalty of death! While the Israelites were freed by these kings, the Israelites were not allowed to go elsewhere, but only to return with Ezra."

Eisenhower paused a moment, and then continued, "Jerusalem is where the Israelites were being held captive by the Ezra-founded Pharisees, at the time of Jesus. Jerusalem was the battlefield! Jesus came; His blood was spilled on the battlefield; His life was sacrificed for the remission of sins for many. *This holy City of David is where the turning point of mankind occurs.* Jesus *only* came to Jerusalem because this is where the overt battle for souls would begin. The battle between Jesus and the descendants of Satan, the Pharisees, and Satan himself openly begins here. This is where and when Jesus confronted Satan. This is when Michael the Archangel put Satan into the pit. The 1000-year imprisonment had to begin when it did, at the time of Jesus – so Satan's release for a little time would occur, now – in our day. Satan literally walks the earth, today!

Okay? Are you with me, still?"

"Yes, sir," Quinn nodded.

"Now," Eisenhower continued, although King Rohoboam and the Kingdom of Judah worshipped idols (3 Kings 14:22), his later successor, Asa, being like King David, took away the idols, including his mother's and destroyed the grove in which she worshipped, but Asa did not take away the idols in the high places (3 Kings 15:11-14) of the elite. And continuous idol worshipping in the Kingdom of Judah finally led to their Babylonian captivity.

In Babylonian captivity and after their return to Jerusalem, is when the theft of the identity, theft of the heritage of the Israelites occurs. By Ezra and his Pharisees. Ezra was a lawyer, a politician, with the ability to control, manipulate, and lead people - the skills needed for the task at hand. God brought the remnants of the Tribe of Judah and Benjamin in to a single tribe, as a separate country, apart from any another country - to plant the seed of Christianity. God ended the captivity to establish the Jews as a separate country – a separate battlefield.

But, still, God is hurt and angry with the Israelites, who followed Ezra's Pharisees in worshipping idols: 'from the days of your fathers you have departed from my ordinances, and have not kept them: Return to Me, and I will return to you, saith the Lord of hosts... (the Pharisees') words have been unsufferable to me, saith the Lord...(But) they that feared (respected) the Lord spoke every one with his neighbour: and the Lord gave ear, and heard it...(therefore) they shall be My special possession, saith the Lord of hosts, in the day that I do judgment...I will spare them...' (Malachias 3:7-17).

"I think I understand, sir," Quinn said, "We know that Ezra was evil, for it was Ezra who oversaw the priests and their offering of 'polluted bread upon (God's) altar.' It was Ezra who is considered the father of Judaism and its *Talmud.* The Israelites, who knew him in Babylon, did not want to follow Ezra to Jerusalem, they only did so because King Artaxeres was going to take their property in Babylon, put them in prison, or kill them. Those were the only options the Israelites had.

We also know that Ezra brought the people of Israel back to Jerusalem in 457 BC, and that the prophet Malachias flourished in 400 BC. That it was Malachias who wrote the Prophecy of Malachias in 400 BC., because why would Ezra write a prophecy in which God is slamming him. Upbraiding Ezra."

"That's right, Quinn," Eisenhower replied. "And here in the prophecy of Malachias 1:7, God said, 'To you, O *priests, that despise my name...If you offer the blind for sacrifice, is it not evil? and if you offer the lame (animal sacrifice) and the sick, is it not evil? offer it to thy (YOUR) prince*, if he will be pleased with it, or if he will regard thy face, *saith the Lord of hosts...I have no pleasure in you, saith the Lord of hosts: and I will not receive a gift of your hand.'*

Malachias 1:4, God said, 'But if *Edom (Edomites)* shall say: We are destroyed, but we will *return and build up what hath been destroyed*: thus said the Lord of hosts: They shall build up, and I will throw down:

and they shall be called the borders of wickedness, and the people with whom the Lord is angry for ever.' This prophecy is talking specifically of Ezra, the Edomite, 600 years descended from Solomon and his Edomite wife, as 'son' of Solomon. It was Ezra who wrangled the return of the Israelites to 'build up what hath been destroyed.'

God speaks of Edom, and the father of Edom was Esau, Jacob/Israel's twin brother who gave up his birthright and turned against God and married, among others, an Egyptian woman, and worshipped the gods of his wives, Satan. It is from Esau's lineage that come the Edomites, who lived in Judah with the Israelites - both were captured by the Babylonians and the Babylonians called both, the Israelites and the Edomites - the Jews of Judah. It was from the Edomites that Ezra came and, in Babylon, stole the identity of the Israelites and captured them to take them *back to Jerusalem to rebuild Solomon's Temple* - the Second Temple. But in A.D. 70, after the crucifixion of Jesus, God, as He promised in Malachias 1:4, used the Romans to destroy Ezra-the-Edomite-controlled Second Temple, which was built up by the lineage of the people who God is angry for ever. The borders of wickedness - means the twin brother of Jacob/Israel - Esau's lineage were border - were almost like the Israelites, but were wicked!"

Quinn listened intently to Eisenhower, "In Malachias Ch. 2:4-5, 'And you (Pharisee priests) shall know that *I sent you this commandment*, that my *covenant might be with Levi, saith the Lord of hosts...My covenant was with him (Aaron) of life and peace*: and I gave him fear: and he feared (respected) Me, and he (Aaron)...turned many away from iniquity....But you (Pharisees) have departed out of the way, and have caused many to stumble at the law: *you have made void the covenant of Levi* (the *priesthood*), saith the Lord of hosts...Remember the law of Moses my servant, which I commanded him in Horeb for all Israel...*Behold I will send you Elias the prophet, before the coming of the great and dreadful day of the Lord.*'"

Eisenhower closed the book and tapped on it, "This is the only sign we can count to signal the end of times - the coming of Elias, which was told to us by the God of Abraham and Jesus, His Son."

Eisenhower and Quinn looked at each other for a moment, finally Eisenhower said, "I know. We won't be able to tell if Elias is the Antichrist. People are saying that the Antichrist will come and the world will love him that he is going to bring peace to the world, solve all the problems. And then he's going to turn on the world."

Quinn concluded, "But if it's Elias, and people say - don't follow Elias, don't believe him - he's the Antichrist. This will be the final deceit Satan plays on the world."

Quinn sighed, "What do we do, sir?"

Eisenhower paused, "Well, son, we need God to speak to our souls, our hearts, our guts. We need to pray. And one thing that I've noticed in life - you can see the light of God in a person's eyes. God's light always shows in a person's eyes. But also in Revelations, it says that God will send two witnesses, and that was President Kennedy and me. Now, all we are waiting for, before Jesus returns, is Elias.

Quinn replied, "So, this Israeli treaty, the 3.5 years tribulations when the Antichrist breaks the treaty is all a smoke screen - they want us to sit tight and do nothing - while they turn up the heat in boiling the frog - while the frog thinks he's okay until he sees the sign - the frog is actually getting cooked to the point that he won't be able to fight them."

"Exactly!" Eisenhower cried. That's exactly right, Quinn. Satan is deceiving us into complacency, we have the time - until the Third Temple is built in Jerusalem - when in fact, it will never be built, again. Jerusalem has served God's purpose, for His beloved servant, King David, and for His most beloved Son, Jesus. God doesn't want His Temple built in Jerusalem because it will not be His temple, but Satan's.

Let me show you one more thing, I think that it will explain what I'm talking about. The Zionists Jews living in Jerusalem today follow and continue to teach the following law from the *Talmud*."

Eisenhower went to the *Babylonian Talmud,* Sanhedrin, Folio 55b, "'A maiden aged three years and one day may be acquired in marriage by coition.'"

Quinn read it and looked over to Eisenhower in shock. Eisenhower clicked on Babylonian Talmud, Kethuboth, Folio 11b, "'When a grown up man has intercourse with a little girl it is nothing, for when the girl is less than this (three years old), it is as if one puts the finger into the eye, tears come to the eye...[(fn 7)] again and again but eyesight returns, so does virginity come back to the little girl under three years.'"

Eisenhower brought up the Qur'an verse 65:4, showing that the Qur'an permits grown men to marry and have sexual intercourse with pre-pubescent girls. "This indicates Islam copied the traditions of the Pharisees - Judaism."

Quinn felt sick to his stomach, as if he might vomit. Eisenhower saw his grimaced face and patted him on the shoulder, "There is nothing in the Law of Moses that allows a grown man to have sexual intercourse with a little girl. And for the Zionist Rabbis to teach this Talmudic lesson shows that they, with Ezra as their founder, created a new religion. Judaism is not the religion of the God of Abraham or Moses. These are very evil people Quinn, but we're going to help God end their reign. We're going to end the time of the Gentiles - the time of the non-Israelite Zionists and Muslims!

But there is also the Catholic Church to consider. The Russian Communist Bolshevik Revolution, in 1917, led by Lenin, wanted to destroy the church, but the Masons convinced the Communists that the Catholic Church was too valuable as an organized body, to outright destroy. The best strategy, the Masons convinced the Communists, was to co-opt the Church – use it as a cover – while the Communists bring their ideology into the church, which could then dictate that ideology to all

Catholics through Canon Law. And while the Masons could use the Catholic Church to bring about their one-world religion. Since Communists are atheists, one could argue that the Communists were duped because the Masons do worship an entity that they considered to be a god, Satan. The end game of the Masons is that one day they will be in a position to force the world to worship Satan, even to the surprise of the Communists.

It was during the Renaissance that the Catholic Church was very corrupt, selling indulgences for salvation and Bishopric offices that brought about the Reformation with people like Martin Luther. This was when Protestantism arose. And at that time, Catholic Bishops and priests had become political, ruling like kings. They cared less for the spiritual reason for the Church's existence. This opened a void that the Masons filled. Masonry had broken away from their vocation of building Cathedrals. This is the time period that the Masons began to worship Satan, aka, Lucifer – the bearer of Light and Knowledge. And on May 1, 1776, Adam Weishaupt established the Illuminati. 'Weishaupt received a doctorate of law from the Jesuit-controlled University of Ingolstadt;…(he) joined the Freemasons of Munich to see how they operated and then created the Illuminati' (http://one-evil.org/people/people_18c_ weishaupt.htm). It was Weishaupt who said, 'We will infiltrate that place (Vatican) and once inside we will never come out. We will bore from within."

Eisenhower paused, "The idea of illumination, enlightenment – of knowledge stems from the Tree of Knowledge in the Garden of Eden, where Satan convinced Eve to touch the Tree – to have intercourse with him. He impregnated her with his son, Cain. And evil was born into the world. The true enlightenment is – evil has lived among us from the beginning – and true evil continues to live among us today, 2012."

Eisenhower looked down and then continued, "Communism had its roots in Russian tradition. You see, son, the Russians acquired from the Byzantine Empire not only the Eastern Orthodox faith, but also careful theoretical defense of absolute and undivided power. When the Romanovs cast off the oversight of the nobility within a generation of taking power, they tightened the grip of power even further. Czar Peter the Great, 1696, possessed absolute and unlimited power. He swept away all traces of local self-government and he replaced it with his hand-picked men, who sat on an administrative council (Carlton Hayes, *A Political and Social History of Modern Europe*).

Czar Peter the Great deprived the Patriarch of Moscow from controlling ecclesiastical organizations and vested all powers of the Church government in a body, called the Holy Synod. Its members were bishops, but whose chief was a layman, and all were personally chosen by the tsar himself. No appointment to ecclesiastical office, no sermon preached, no book published, unless approved by the Holy Synod. In the Western Roman Empire, the Catholic Church maintained some degree of independence from secular rulers. But in Byzantium, the Orthodox Church was a bureau of the Central Government. The Byzantines transmitted their religion and tradition to the Russians, including utter dependence of the Church upon the state. (http://econfaculty.gmu.edu/bcaplan/museum/czar2.htm).

This Russian authoritarian tradition strongly influenced the Russian Marxists, and through them, much of the world socialist movement.

Quinn quickly interjected, "Czar Peter sweeping away local self-government is the same thing that President Tsaeb's White House Rural Council, with all his hand-picked cabinet members, is doing by going out to farmers and ranchers – to tell them how to use their land; and to increase their taxes."

"Exactly!" Eisenhower replied, "But also with the U.S. instituting the United Nations Agenda 21, whose agents have taken over state and county governments, instituting UN regulations, to implement their scheme of land-taking from private Americans. It's the same thing that the Russian czars did – which easily translated under Lenin's Communist dictatorship, as the government having the right of absolute power over every aspect of the lives of citizens. Much as Ezra did to the Israelites."

"Last night, I read some of Karl Marx's Manifesto of the Communist Party, where Marx said 'This talk about free selling and buying (of property by the Middle Class)...have no meaning when opposed to the Communistic abolition of buying and selling of the bourgeois (the Middle Class)...and (elimination) of the bourgeoisie itself.' Marx and Communism are completely against the Middle Class owning their own property."

Eisenhower continued, "And Lenin was the first to actually institute Communism. Under the Czars, Russia had a system of feudalism, a serfdom society. Lenin took that Russian tradition of absolute power from Tsar Nickolas II and used it himself against the Russian people. 'The Russian Marxist movement had preceded Vladimir Ilich Lenin by two decades. But it was Lenin who split off a militant faction from the rest of the Russian Social Democratic Labor Party and forged it into a potent weapon for totalitarian revolution' (http://econfaculty,gmu.edu/ bcaplan/ museum/history.htm).

It was Lenin who murdered Tsar Nickolas, his family, and even his dog, although Nickolas had abdicated the throne months before. It's a difference of ideology – as the dictionary defines ideology: the body of ideas reflecting the social needs and aspirations of an individual, group, class, or culture. The question lies, who has the power to inflict his ideas on the culture. The Czar or Lenin? Alexander Solzhenitsyn wrote in, *The Gulag Archipelago*, 'Ideology is what gives evildoing its long-sought justification and gives the evildoer the necessary steadfastness and determination...Thanks to ideology , the twentieth century was fated to experience evildoing on a scale calculated in the millions.'

"You see, son, the mistake people make today is that they think there is no evil – maybe a crazy person here or there, a thug who steals pocketbooks, drug cartels, or a CEO who absconds with corporate billions, or a political party with left or right leanings. They have no clue that there is actual evil that lives among us – such as those who have taken control – have co-opted the Catholic Church. They are connected to the United Nations, which has co-opted the United States, especially its military. As U.S. Secretary of Defense Leon Panetta said in a Senate hearing: 'The U.S. would seek international (United Nations) permission for Syria action (by U.S. Military Forces)...we would then come to Congress and inform you...and whether we would want approval from Congress.'

And yes, Karl Marx was for the Proletariat Class, the poor who worked, but could not afford to buy a house. Our Congress forced those sentiments on our banks – demanding that mortgages be given to the poor they all knew could not afford to pay a mortgage, especially at a variable rate that the Federal Reserve controlled on a date certain to bring about foreclosures. They gave mortgages without any money down in some cases; they created the housing bubble and then burst that bubble, which led to the depression we're now in. It all led to giving greater power to the Secretary of the Treasury, so he could point to a small business owner – and claim that in the determination of the Secretary – that business is harmful to the American economy – and we are going to take your assets and close you down!"

The Dodd-Frank Act of 2010 gives the Secretary of the Treasury the power to shut down businesses. 'Geithner said the first non-bank financial companies deemed systemically risky will be named this year, and the department (of Treasury) will release more plans for an overhaul of housing finance,' (www.bloomberg.com/news/2012-02-02/geithner-says-systematically-risky-firms-to-be-named-in-2012-2-.html). This is historic in that the Dept. of Treasury now has the power to buy a controlling interest, yet not pay 51%, in any financial company.

Marx denounced both personal freedom and property rights as manifestations of what he called 'bourgeois freedom,' freedom of the property-owning Middle Class. Marx found fault with the doctrine of the rights of man because, Marx said:

> None of the supposed rights of man, therefore, go beyond the egoistic man, Man as he is, as a member of civil society; that is, an individual separated from the community, withdrawn into himself, wholly preoccupied with his private interest and acting in accordance with *his private caprice*...Thus man was not liberated from religion; he received religious liberty. He was not liberated from property; he received the liberty to own property. He was not liberated from the egoism of business; he received the liberty to engage in business. (*Ibid.*)

With the Dodd-Frank Act of 2010, one could say that an American has received the liberty to engage in business, or be shut down on the say of one man, Secretary of the Treasury.

This is the same as the United Nations' Land Policy – no one would be allowed to privately own land.

This is clearly counter to the U.S. Declaration of Independence that 'all men are…endowed by their Creator with certain inalienable rights….' Such as the right to be free from the United Nations dictating that U.S. citizens be put into human settlements, and free from being redistributed over the national territory, at the prompting of the United Nations. And the UN's land policy is counter to the U.S. Constitution, 'We the People of the United States…(to) secure the Blessings of Liberty to ourselves and our Posterity (Children) do ordain and establish this Constitution for the United States of America.'

That Constitution is the boiled down concepts that have been carried down though the civilizations of Jerusalem, Athens, Rome, and London, according to Russell Kirk, in his book *Roots of American Order*, 1974. Kirk suggests that the United States of America is thousands of years old when you consider the ideology of liberty, its emphasis on individualism in work ethic and accountability. While the concept of Communism is actually the oldest form of government, used in the primitive civilization, when there were very small groups of people that populated the world, living in commune-style quarters. This was the only way people could physically survive nature. As the world population grew and weapons and tools improved, they likely faced the same problems as in the U.S. counterculture-revolution communes of the 1960s – where jealousies arose due to the women being up for grabs by any man of the commune, upon his demand for sex with the woman of his choosing. And where all money was dumped into the community piggy bank and spent on the needs of the group, regardless of whether every member donated to the bank.

But Christianity is the true reason for what makes America what we are. The genius of Christianity, specifically Christianity's idea of individualism, as in St. Thomas Aquinas' uniqueness of soul, as opposed to Plato's unity of soul. Aquinas' logic leads to the notion – that one is responsible for his individual behavior. As with the Ten Commandments – Thou – as in You – shalt not have strange gods before me. *Thou* shalt not kill. *Thou* shalt not commit adultery. *Thou* shalt not steal. The Commandments are not addressing the collective society, but each individual of the society, and when you have each member of society standing strong, the whole cannot be destroyed. Thus, the only way to conquer the United States is to eat away at the Christian foundation, pull it up by its roots – one Commandment after another. This is why they sue towns to get them to remove the Ten Commandments from courthouses. If they could, they'd tear down the U.S. Supreme Court building – on the eastern pediment of the building is a sculpture Moses, sitting front and center, holding two tablets containing the Ten Commandments. Underneath is carved: 'Justice the Guardian of Liberty'.

Kirk, in *Roots of American Order*, quotes Orestes Brownson, the 19th century American thinker, who wrote that every nation has a task given it by Providence to realize; for the American Republic that destiny was to reconcile liberty with law. (Randy, 8/5/2011; www.goodreads.com/book/show/1128046.Roots_Of_American_Order)

Unfortunately, the laws of the United Nations Charter, Agenda 21, UNESCO, UN Children's Rights cannot be reconciled with American freedom. The Homeland Security Act, the Patriot Act, the Tsaebcare Healthcare law – cannot be reconciled with American freedom. The effects of the 1960s counterculture revolution continue to have a destructive impact on Christian values and the Ten Commandments, since today, the divorce rate is up to 80% and drug use is more widespread. Christian values are thrown aside when the Mayor of NYC demands to teach grade-school children sex education before they even have a thought about sex; and condoms are handed out to high school students; and in some states, teenagers can request abortion without parental knowledge or consent. Our destiny to reconcile liberty with law is being skewed by evil forces.

Kirk argued that 'the framers of the Constitution took it for granted that a moral order, founded upon religious beliefs, supports and parallels the political order,' (*Ibid.*) Defined as such, one need only remove the moral order, or remove the religion upon which those beliefs rest, then one may chip away at the Constitution as being irrelevant to political order. And that was the purpose of the 1960s counterculture revolution – destroy the moral order. That counterculture revolution still exists today through political correctness to destroy the practice of the Christian religion, by such methods as prohibiting benediction at public events and school graduation, prohibiting military chaplains from saying Jesus in public prayer while in uniform, taking crosses off public lands, prohibiting Merry Christmas speech or Christmas pageants in schools, on the outcry of one unidentified person – for political correctness does not allow that even one person might be offended – even though that person may be working for Satan.

Schools send home flyers that show that the school will celebrate: Jewish Hanukkah for one week, Dec. 8-16; African Kwanzaa for one week, Dec. 26-31; and Winter Holiday, Dec. 25th, but nothing is said of Christmas. The satanic bloodlines of Zionist Jews and Blacks are openly celebrated, but the bloodline of Sem is banned. The Zionists abide the Seven Noahide Laws that are not the Ten Commandments; and Kwanzaa abides Seven Principles that include the celebration of unity, collective work and responsibility, and cooperative economics in honoring the values of ancient African cultures – who were descended from Ham, who was descended from Satan.

Thus, Christianity and western ideology that once separated the individual from the state – no longer function, therefore, the state takes control of the individual.

'In Ravi Zacharias' 1996 book, *Deliver Us From Evil*, he writes of the Founding Fathers and the precepts with which they wanted to govern, could only have been possible within a biblical framework. Only within this context, where law finds its ultimate origin in a God who loves us, can law move beyond external compulsion (legal restrictions on behavior) and work in the hearts of men (and their free choice to do good). For law to truly bind a people together, there must be an inner desire to keep the law because it is good. Otherwise laws become little more than a random set of rules, and have to be multiplied endlessly. And liberty, if it also has no objective point of reference, moves from being a freedom to do what you ought, to license to do whatever you want,' (*Ibid.* at Randy).

Doing whatever one wants to do runs counter to the Ten Commandments – such as Nike's T-Shirt slogan: 'Just Do It,' and Dave Dudley's song, 'If It Feels Good Do It.'

As Congress continues to pass unconstitutional laws, the UN's Land Policy, UN Agenda 21, will increasing impose their laws, their usurpation over the US Constitution to the destruction of Americans' ability to pursue the personal buying and selling of land as they see fit – as is the blessing of liberty. Americans signed on to the Constitution of the United States to govern this Republic, a federalist system – Americans did not agree to be governed by the United Nations or Agenda 21!

Karl Marx's solution to human emancipation was Communism, but it is actually defending tyranny and oppression. His argument is a re-packaging of despotism to please modern sensibilities, a feat of intellectual marketing, propaganda. (*Supra at econfaculty.gmu.*)

Quinn interjected, "Here in the U.S., prior to the 1960 decade and Vatican II, we had a culture called, 'Mom and apple pie,' which described a life-style of our Christian nation – a respect for motherhood and going to Mass. Most Americans went to confession on Saturdays, and fasted from midnight until Sunday morning before receiving Communion. After Mass families had Sunday dinner with family. With the hippy counter-culture movement of the 1960s, brought about by pop singers like The Beatles, their music, evolved with Hollywood celebrities involved with voodoo, communes of shared women on demand and shared financial resources, Anton LeVey, in 1966, establishing the Church of Satan, and the American Christian culture was forever changed. The movement to destroy moral order was also helped by the CIA bringing LSD and marijuana onto college campuses that later spread through the use by professionals. During the 60s, the divorce rate in the country rose to 50%, as the drug and sexual revolutions coincided with the feminist movement with its demand for abortion as a right of all women. President Lyndon B. Johnson pushed for ready use of birth control pills by all women.

The counterculture revolution brought with it a deliberative destruction of the Christian moral code of behavior that was the norm in the United States of America.

In his book, *Between Two Ages*, Zbigniew Brzezinski wrote, 'Escape from Reason. In its extreme form, this mood - dramatized by the student riots in California, at Columbia University, throughout France, in West Berlin, in London, Rome, Belgrade, Warsaw, Tokyo, and much more lethally at the University of Mexico (where scores of students were killed in the fall of 1968)…(this mood) has elevated action for action's sake into a moral principle. 'Action is the only reality; not only reality but morality as well' proclaimed Abbie Hoffman, the leader of the American Yippies.'

'Probably the best known anti-war (Vietnam War) dissident was Abbie Hoffman. On January 1, 1968, Hoffman and Jerry Rubin started the Youth International Party, or Yippies. This was not an organized political force but rather a common term used to describe those who participated in Hoffman and Rubin's pranks (such as throwing dollar bills onto the floor of the New York Stock Exchange),' (Abbie Hoffman, 5/11/2000. http://www.trincoll. edu/classes/hist300/newpage2.htm).

Quinn continued, "In October of 1967, Abbie organized the "exorcism of the Pentagon" in which he and demonstrators from the Peace march in Washington, D.C. surrounded the Pentagon and tried to levitate by mental force. The attention pranks like these gained in the national media convinced Hoffman that the peace message would only get out by getting as much publicity as possible. (*Ibid.*)

In the Chicago Seven trial, Abbie Hoffman testified. (http://www.law.umkc.edu/faculty/projects/ftrials/Chicago7/ Hoffman.html).

At trial, Hoffman testified, "We circulated leaflets that said:

"Join us in Chicago in August for an international festival of youth, music, and theater. Rise up and abandon the creeping meatball! Come all you rebels, youth spirits, rock minstrels, truth-seekers, peacock-freaks, poets, barricade-jumpers, dancers, lovers and artists!

It is summer. It is the last week in August, and the NATIONAL DEATH PARTY meets to bless Lyndon Johnson. We are there! There are 50,000 of us dancing in the streets, throbbing with amplifiers and harmony. We are making love in the parks. We are reading, singing, laughing, printing newspapers, groping, and making a mock convention, and celebrating the birth of FREE AMERICA in our own time.

Everything will be free. Bring blankets, tents, draft-cards, body-paint, Mr. Leary's Cow, food to share, music, eager skin, and happiness. The threats of LBJ, Mayor Daley, and J. Edgar Freako will not stop us. We are coming! We are coming from all over the world!

We demand the Politics of Ecstasy! We are the delicate spores of the new fierceness that will change America. We will create our own reality, we are Free America! And we will not accept the false theater of the Death Convention.

We will be in Chicago. Begin preparations now! Chicago is yours! Do it!'

Do it!' was a slogan like 'Yippie.' We (Hoffman et al) use that a lot and it meant that each person that came should take on the responsibility for being his own leader-that we should, in fact, <u>have a leaderless society</u>."

Quinn added, "Hoffman was a real piece of work. Wasn't he?"

"Yes, he was," Eisenhower replied, adding, "While all this drew America's attention, Vatican II was held and the Catholic Church was eclipsed by the Communists when Pope John XXIII was 'elected.' John XXIII was the pope of 1960, who was supposed to reveal the Third Secret of Our Lady of Fatima. The Blessed Mother had appeared to three children in Portugal, the last appearance on October 13, 1917 – just 12 days prior to Lenin's Bolshevik Communist Revolution, October 25, 1917. But John XXIII had refused to reveal the Secret.

Vatican II took away of the continual sacrifice by changing the Catholic Mass, taking out reverence of Jesus' sacrifice: no more sign of the cross when the priest gives the Eucharist - no more saying 'the body of Christ' - Thus, there is no association of Jesus dying on the cross to the Eucharist. Thus, the giving of the Eucharist becomes nothing more than a community meal."

Quinn paused a moment, "When you think about it - since Second Vatican Council, in 1965, took away the continual sacrifice – Satan was Enthroned on the Throne of Peter, therefore, I think we can say that Satan was in the Church throughout that Council's sessions. I think, the Blessed Mother's appearance at Fatima was a warning of these things in 1960, before they occurred.

The Vatican withheld that warning from us, but of course, Satan was calling the shots. He captured many souls during the 60s decade, as a result. And Christianity has been under attack since - and they are tightening the screws on that: Happy Holidays, Winter Festival, Holiday Tree, have replaced Merry Christmas and Christmas Tree, especially in the schools. Songs taught to pre-kindergarten and first graders took out the name Jesus, replacing His name with Tsaeb's name. The U.S. Military, in the summer of 2011, prohibited using the name of Jesus and God in prayers during veterans' funerals; they took out all the crosses from chapels and put them in a storage shed. Military Chaplains were forbidden to use the name of Jesus when praying with soldiers or in their sermons.

Jesus keeps getting pushed away. And how many Christians left the Church after they took the continual sacrifice away? The apostasy started at the top - with Popes John XXIII, Paul VI, and John Paul II and their connection to the United Nations - their establishing the Council, with Paul VI re-establishing the Council after Pope John XXIII's death and signing off on the Church reformation. They handed Jesus' Church to Satan. They did away with the notion that the Catholic Church is the one and only true Church, founded by Jesus; that the Bible is without error; and they did away with the continual sacrifice in the Roman liturgy. It paved the way for liberal churchmen to make additional, radical changes contrary to Canon Law and tradition, 'in the spirit of Vatican II.' Most of all, there has been a tremendous decline in men going into the priesthood, women into the convent, and tremendous erosion of Catholic Church attendance.

It was all told to Lucia by the Blessed Mother. There was a priest who had read the Third Secret, who said that there are scores of high-ranking clergy, bishops, cardinals working in the Vatican and Rome, who belong to Satan - they are his servants. That there are servants of Satan working outside the Church in various organizations - their aim is to destroy Catholicism, the faith, doctrine, and practice of the Roman Catholic Church, but keep the facade - make it a front – because the 'appearance will be a stabilizing factor in human affairs.'"

Quinn related what his research the night before had turned up about the Catholic Church, "The most strategic outcome of Vatican II, is the change that they instituted in its Constitution – and which counters the Creed of faith: that the Church is the one, holy, Catholic, and apostolic Church – they have added to the Church's Constitution: 'Nevertheless, many elements of *sanctification and of truth are found outside* its visible confines.'

They also changed: Chapter II of the Church Constitution to now read: 'On the People of God, *the Council instructs that God wills* the salvation of entire groups of people, *instead of individuals*...participation in the Church...constitutes the defining characteristic of the *new* People of God' (Lumen Gentium, 9).

Vatican II Council instructs that '*All human beings are called to belong to the Church*...the Church knows that she is joined in many ways to the baptized, who are honored by the name of Christ, but who do not however profess the Catholic faith...or have not preserved...communion under the successor of Peter....' (Lumen Gentium, 16).

In this, the Council names the Jews and Muslims. But in Matt. 22:14, Jesus speaking with the Pharisees, Jesus said: 'For *many are called*, but few are chosen.' *Many are called* – NOT *All* are called! The Church Constitution's Lumen Gentium is wrong – and explicitly counter to what Jesus had said – given to us by an eye witness of the teachings of Jesus!

Vatican II Council changed the liturgy in the same manner, Matt. 26:28, Jesus said to his disciples: 'For this is my blood of the new testament, which shall be *shed for many* unto remission of sins.' Now, the new Vatican II Mass states that the blood of Jesus was shed *for all*! This is clearly wrong! Both in fact and in essence. This is absolute heresy!"

It occurred to Quinn that Vatican II had created a new religion. He remembered as a child that the tabernacle was before the worshippers, at the center of the altar and that when entering the church his family would bless themselves with holy water held at the door of the church, and a worshipper would make the sign of the cross and genuflect in recognition that the body of Christ was in the tabernacle on the altar. There was a railing that extended to the sides of the altar with a gate in its center - and no worshipper was allowed to go beyond that railing and enter the sacred space of the altar. Priests wore finely embroidered vestments. Communion vessels were made of gold or silver. Bells were rung in the preparation of the Eucharist, calling for worshippers to note the sacred and pray. And to receive communion one had to go to a priest for confession and receive absolution, and do penance; then fast from mid-night the night before; then worshippers knelt along the railing and waited for only the priest to give them communion, and only on the tongue of the worshipper, and only after the priest had made the sign of the cross and the worshipper replied by making the sign of the cross themselves and saying, Amen. The worshipper had learned in First Holy Communion instruction, at the age of 6, that they were never to chew the body of Christ, but to allow it to melt and then swallow the Eucharist. They were instructed to return to their pew and pray and not talk. The only music was a Gregorian Chant. Traditional prayers represented the sacredness of the Roman Latin Mass.

After Vatican II, gone is the communion railing; communion is now received after standing in line; no one is allowed to genuflect; Holy Communion is given by a non-priest who did not make the sign of the cross; and the worshipper receives the Holy Eucharist in their hand; fasting is shortened to minutes before receiving the Eucharist; music is popular or jazz style – as was used in the Yippie counterculture movement; priests wear vestments with craft patches of a chalice or other abstract design; people turn to each other and shake hands in community socializing gesture."

Quinn mumbled to himself - Vatican II did, indeed, create a new religion! Every bit as much as Ezra had created with Judaism.

Eisenhower replied, "The French philosopher, Jean Borella, wrote a book called *Lacharite profanee*, in which he asserts that post-Vatican II Council - as in the Spirit of Vatican II - 'intends to annihilate all forms that establish a distinction between the sacred and the profane.' Borella argues that there are three stages of degradation of the Christian soul. In the first stage, grace and faith are received as a gift by Christians. The state of grace is buttressed for Christians by both a supernatural religious order and a natural religious order - which are tensions and oppositions. The supernatural tensions are: Creator/creature, sacred/profane, sacred place/secular places, sacred vestments/secular vestments, etc.

The natural religious order tensions are: man/woman, parents/ children, upright persons/indecent persons, master/disciple, etc. Borella states that these distinctions are what Vatican II Council has tried to destroy - blurring the distinctions. Borella offers the example of a historic moment at the Vatican II Council meeting when a specially prepared schema concerning upholding the rights of the Church and the defense of sacred tradition was put forward for a vote, but the vote was suspended by Cardinal Lienart for further discussion in accord with wishes of the Vatican II 'reform' block (those who wanted to change the Church). Borella argues, an 'advanced' clergy 'pursues its own intellectual and cultural modernization...striving to transform the celebrations of the

Eucharist into the congregation's celebration of itself,'" (Prof. Emeritus Howard Kainz, Marquette Univ., www.thecatholicthing .org/columns/2011/the-spirit-of-vatican-ii.html).

"It sounds as though the Spirit of Vatican II has succeeded in instituting the congregation celebrating themselves," Quinn replied. "It goes back to Humanism and the celebration of Man as a god. So, just who is this Spirit of the Vatican II Council?"

"Well, let me first say," Eisenhower replied, "that Cardinal Ratzinger, now Pope Gregory XVI, once criticized self-constructed liturgies (by individual Bishops around the world) are analogous to the Hebrew worship of the Golden Calf." (*Ibid*)

Eisenhower adjusted himself in his chair, pushing the computer away from him, "'The Spirit of Vatican II has no precise definition, but references to this spirit are connected to liberalism,' such as the Novus Ordo liturgy/Mass. The receipt of communion by hand - completely and intentionally destroys the sacredness of the Eucharist! That was precisely their mission, as Borella stated, the 'intentional annihilation of the distinction of the sacred and profane.'" (*Ibid*) They want the profaned to be seen as sacred so that people will accept Satan as being on the same status as God, by lowering the status of God down to Satan.

Quinn offered, "And a lot of these churches took out the Holy Water from the fonts, replacing them with sand, during Lent. Too many complained, so the Vatican stated that the water should not be removed during Lent. Holy Water is used to baptized infants as Christians; for exorcisms, to send demons fleeing. Holy Water is a sacramental tool to remit venial sins. Blessing oneself with Holy Water and saying the prayer: 'By this Holy Water and by Your Precious Blood, wash away all my sins, O Lord,' (www.catholic homeandgarden.com /Holy%20Water.pdf). Holy Water is a powerful tool against Satan! But, then, their aim is to take away our weapons of fighting Satan."

"It doesn't stop there, Quinn," Eisenhower said, "'Some priests have denied older communicants, who remember the kneeling rails, so they kneel on the floor in the communion line. Those are the priests who have the 'Spirit' of Vatican II. Some Bishops interpret kneeling as "dissent" and "disobedience." I think the Church authority that approved the taking away of the kneeling rails was the Congregation for Divine Worship and the Discipline of the Sacrament, and they held that communicants must obey this Church rule to stand, when they know of the rule. If they know and knell anyway, its disobedience. It is also against Church rule for the communicant to genuflect before receiving communion; the post-Vatican II custom is to bow one's head. All this, even though John Paul II held in GIRM 162.3, that communicants should not be denied Holy Communion because they kneel. It all stems from liturgists, who believe that kneeling is alien to modern culture and is an unsuitable posture for the modern "democratic" man, even when worshipping. Liturgists argue that standing to receive communion is the "Resurrection posture." This standing posture was codified in the new, revised GIRM promulgated by Pope John Paul II' (GIRM 162.3) (http://sacredheartbfl.org/Parish_Life /Fr_Dans_Corner/ reform.htm). But these decisions of denial by Bishops come from Vatican II's instituting collegiality - where Bishops have as much authority as the Pope, to deny the kneeling communicant. And collegiality, this sharing of papal power destroys that power, giving by default, greater power to the Black Pope, the Jesuit General. It also makes porous the integrity of the Church that will lead to its implosion.

Eisenhower sighed, "This is what I want you to note: these unnamed liturgists decide on their own that kneeling was an unsuitable posture. Who was complaining that they had to kneel when receiving communion? How is the modern "democratic" man too good to kneel? Where do they come up with this pat conclusion without statistical information to support their argument - they make their statement and that's it - everyone is to change, or else! And the whole system needs to change. Why? To save the pride of the modern man - he's too proud to kneel? Isn't that one of the big seven deadly sins? Pride!"

Quinn nodded in understanding of Eisenhower's point.

Eisenhower continued, "This is what Borella was talking about - blurring the distinctions between sacred/profane, Creator/creature. It's about taking away God, replacing His position of honor with the modern man."

Quinn snide, "This is what results when Vatican II Council allowed 2000 non-Catholic religious to observe their discussion - it wasn't ecumenism, it was an interfaith dialogue - whereby Catholicism ended up getting thrown away. And isn't that standing position, a man who does not kneel before his God, called Humanism?"

"Well, I'll answer your question in a moment," Eisenhower responded, "But what worries me more than any other evidence, that is greater than any other sacrilege - is the changing of every Catholic catechism and every liturgy to institute the Holy Spirit - and the removal of - the absolute exclusion of the Holy Ghost, the third person of the Trinity! This is most dangerous, Quinn, most dangerous!"

Eisenhower cleared his throat, "In Luke 4:1, the Spirit, who leads Jesus into the desert to tempt Him, I my opinion, is Satan. The whole purpose of the meeting of Jesus and Satan was the temptation of Jesus to give up His power to Satan; that way Jesus wouldn't have to be crucified and He would get the souls of Satan's children, besides the souls of the Israelites. And Satan would become the ruler of all Creation. This meeting was the biggest of powwows, a meeting of the greatest power players, the highest of rollers - coming together in the desert - man to man sort of thing, and no other support staff. To call it a temptation minimizes the gravity of the meeting. This specific meeting was *the* apex of creation; the precipice of mankind's fate. It was a question of how much God loves His people versus how much Satan wanted control over Creation. The stakes were everything in existence.

Luke 4:1 specifically states that Jesus was 'full with the Holy Ghost...and was led by the Spirit into the desert.' Luke uses two different names within the same sentence - both are capitalized as proper nouns, as names. Here, Spirit is not an adjective; is not talking of the essence of God. I think Luke is telling us that these are two separate entities - the Holy Ghost and the Spirit. Satan is an angel - a spirit!!! If Vatican II Council took away the continual sacrifice of Jesus and His new testament – by taking away 'for the sins of many' - changing it to 'the sins of all,' Vatican II took away the words of Jesus and inserted their own words. They got rid of the Second Person of the Trinity, Jesus. And, if Vatican II took away the Holy Ghost in every prayer and in the liturgy and replaced it with the Holy Spirit - they are doing the same thing, taking away the Third Person of the Trinity. I think this is proof that Satan took over the Catholic Church, during Vatican II. And don't forget Pope Paul VI's statement that '*From some fissure the smoke of Satan has entered the temple of God...*' I think this is what he was talking about."

Eisenhower looked at Quinn, "And, again, the Spirit is initial caps, therefore, it's a proper noun, a name. And throughout the Bible, the proper name, Lord, is initial caps, but when the use of the pronoun 'my' refers to God, it is always in the lower case - not My. Therefore, in Luke 4:1, if Spirit was referring to God - to the Holy Ghost, it would have been written 'spirit,' in the lower case, because it would have been a pronoun, or an adjective that describes the essence of God. This lower case of pronouns is the style that all Biblical writing uses. The initial capitalization of Heaven, or My, as it pertains to God, is the modern English style of writing. Hence, Spirit as written in Luke 4:1, is a name, and it is not referring to the Holy Ghost – not two different names – within the same sentence?!"

Eisenhower frowned, "You see, son, the only time the Holy Spirit is named in the Old Testament is in the Book of Wisdom, and it was 'written in the person of Solomon and contains his sentiments' (Douay Rheims Holy Bible, Book of Wisdom, p. 696). At the time of its writing, the New Testament would not be written for another thousand years. And remember, 'Solomon worshipped Astarthe' (3 Kings 11:5), she was the Canaanite goddess of wisdom and sister of Baal. I want to read to you these verses of the Book of Wisdom that are Solomon's sentiments. There are two chapters and verses, in which Solomon's sentiments refer to the Holy Spirit. And, again, Solomon conjured up demons!"

Eisenhower opened the Bible and turned to Wisdom 1:5, 'For the Holy *Spirit of discipline* will flee from the deceitful, and will withdraw himself from thoughts that are without understanding, and he shall not abide when iniquity cometh in.'" Eisenhower looked up at Quinn, "Who is the Holy Spirit of discipline?"

"I don't know, I never heard of the Holy Ghost as a disciplinarian," Quinn responded. "And I never heard of the Holy Ghost fleeing from anyone. I have read that demons flee during an exorcism, when they hear the name, Jesus Christ. If Solomon worshipped the devil, evil spirits, and called up demons, this verse as his sentiment we should read in opposition to what we understand to be good. The 'Spirit of discipline' could be Satan, since Satan is the keeper of hell, in which sinners are disciplined.

To 'flee from the deceitful' is relative; what is deceitful to Satan is truth to God the Father.

To 'withdraw himself from thoughts that are without understanding' is also relative; Satan does not understand love, kindness, charity, or prayer to God to obtain these virtues. Satan would flee from that prayer. And the Holy Ghost will not flee from the insane who do not have cognitive reasoning, nor flee from one who is confused; the Holy Ghost understands the frailty of the human mind, and would stay to protect those who are without understanding.

To 'not abide when iniquity cometh in' is, again, relative to the reading of this verse of devil-worshipping-Solomon's sentiments. What is iniquity? It is wickedness, it is sinfulness, it is a grossly immoral act. Solomon's worship of Astarte required the death sacrifice of the firstborn infants and sexual rituals (www.themystica.com/mythical-folk/articles/astarte.html). The killing of babies and group/public sexual rituals Solomon did not view as wicked, did not view as iniquity. Solomon's view of iniquity is upside down to our definition of iniquity. Thus, this portion of the verse must be read that when goodness comes in the Holy Spirit will flee!"

"I completely agree with your analysis, Quinn," Eisenhower responded. "And that's my point. That's my concern with Vatican II taking out the Holy Ghost from the liturgy and all prayers and inserting the Holy Spirit. Have they brought Satan into the Church? Are Catholics worshipping Satan unknowingly?"

Eisenhower turned the pages of the Bible, "Now, here in Solomon's prayer, asking for wisdom, as I read it, I'm going to insert what I think the proper noun could be after the pronoun. Okay? This is from the Book of Wisdom 9:17, this is Solomon's prayer: 'And who shall know thy (Satan's) thought, except thou (Astarte) give wisdom, and send thy (Satan's) Holy Spirit from above.'

Eisenhower turned to Quinn, "At this time in history, it's safe to assume that Satan is still in Heaven, above, albeit looking like a serpent. If wisdom is Astarte, Solomon's goddess, is the Holy Spirit her brother, Satan? 'Coinage portrayed Astarte as the heavenly dove of wisdom... (Walker, 1983, p 253-254, www.themystica.com/mythical-folk/articles/astarte.html).

Then there is Wisdom 10:1-5. Now, Quinn, I want you to listen as I read, with the idea that Solomon is talking about Astarte. I'll read it inserting what I think is the appropriate proper noun. See if this makes sense to you. Remember, this is written in the person of Solomon; this verse is the sentiment of Solomon, and was written around 930 B.C."

"Yes, sir," Quinn replied.

Wisdom 10:1-5: 'She (Astarte) preserved him (Satan), that was first formed by God the father of the world, when he (Satan) was created alone...And she brought him (Satan) out of his sin (seducing Eve), and gave him (Satan) power to govern all things...But when the unjust (Cain) went away from her (Astarte) in his anger, he (Cain) perished by the fury wherewith he (Cain) murdered his brother (Abel)...*For whose cause (Satan's)*, when water destroyed the earth, wisdom (Astarte) healed it again, directing the course of the just (Satan) by contemptible wood (the Ark)...Moreover when the nations (Ham and Japheth) had conspired together *to consent* to wickedness (follow their father, Satan), she knew the just (Satan), and preserved him (Satan) without blame to God (Astarte's adversary), and kept him (Satan) strong against the compassion for his (King David's) son (Solomon).'

So, are these verses talking about Satan, or Adam, and/or of Cain? Who are they talking about ?" Eisenhower asked. "Only Cain killed his brother out of anger. Certainly, when water destroyed the earth, the verse is talking about the Great Flood. But it goes on to call the ark 'contemptible wood.' Noah received directions on how to build the ark from God. Why would Solomon's sentiment be that the ark was made of contemptible wood? The wood was selected by God, Gen. 6:14, 'Make thee an ark of timber planks.' Or even worse, what if Solomon was referring to the Ark of the Covenant being made of contemptible wood! Yet, 'make that which the Lord hath commanded…The ark (of the Covenant)...' (Exodus 35:1-12), which was made of 'setim wood' (Exodus 37:1) just as the tabernacle had been made of 'setim wood,' (Ex. 36:31-33).

Consider, Satan was created alone, after God created the Heavens, but before God created the earth and all the creatures on it, then, Gen. 1:26, God said, '*Let us* make man to our image and likeness.' Who is the 'us' that God is talking to? I think he was talking to the angels, of whom Satan, at that time, was the most beautiful! It was not the creatures of the earth that he had just created, because God is going to make mankind in '*our* image,' Gen. 1:26. It was then that, Gen. 1:27, 'God created man to his own image.' And after all this creation, in the Garden of Eden, Gen. 2:7, God 'formed man of the slime of the earth....' God said, Gen. 2:18, 'It is not good for man to be alone: *let us* make him (Adam) a help like unto himself.' Satan and the rest of the angels were with God in the Garden of Eden. Adam and Eve were the *last* of God's creations - Adam was not alone in the world! But it's likely that Satan was, having been created first. This is what is meant in: Wisdom 10:1-5: 'She (Astarte) preserved him (Satan), that was first formed by God the father of the world, when he (Satan) was *created alone*.'"

Eisenhower adjusted himself in his chair, "Solomon had fully turned against God (3 Kings 11:9). So, let's look, again, at the portion of Wisdom 10:5, 'Moreover when the nations had conspired together to consent to wickedness, she knew the just, and preserved him without blame to God, and kept him strong against the compassion for his son.' The nations here are the Tribes of Israel.

Let's substitute Solomon as the 'just' - because Astarte saw Solomon as 'just' since he had sacrificed children to her. Astarte 'preserved Solomon without blame to God' - is this saying that she didn't blame God because she understood God's anger when Solomon stopped worshipping Him and turned to her? 'And kept him strong against the compassion for his son.' Is this verse, Wisdom 10:5, saying that Astarte kept Solomon strong by God's compassion for David! Solomon did remain king over the united Kingdom of Israel. Solomon, personally, was 'preserved' only because he was the son of David.

'Compassion for his son' is referring to: 3 Kings 11:5-13, 'But Solomon worshipped Astarthe...The Lord therefore said to Solomon: Because thou has done this...I will divide and rend thy kingdom... nevertheless in thy days I will not do it, for David thy father's sake....' This is the only time in the Bible that God does not go against someone specifically because of the compassion God feels for the person's father. Therefore, Wisdom 10:5 could only refer to Solomon.

The Book of Wisdom, Solomon's sentiments, give all credit to Astarte for his salvation against the wrath of God, Wisdom 10:5, 'Kept him strong against the compassion for his son.'

"And, by the way, the Old Testament, Ecclesiasticus 1:9, says that God created wisdom in the Holy Ghost. The name, Holy Ghost, is not specific to the New Testament only."

Eisenhower took a deep breath, "What I'm trying to say is that Solomon, a known devil worshipper, is the only one in the Old Testament to refer to the Holy Spirit, as a noun, a name! And not as in the essence or nature of God, as in Kings, Judges, Exodus, where they referred to the spirit of God - which is clearly the essence of God – a descriptive adjective, not a noun, as in a name! The Books of Exodus written by Moses and Judges written by the prophet Samuel were known to Solomon; King David would have seen to it. Why in Solomon's prayer for wisdom did he not refer to the spirit of God as those other Old Testament books referred to God's essence?

Ecclesiasticus came 700 years after Solomon's time; 200 years after Ezra's time, and 'written 200 years before Christ…and directed by 'the spirit of God.' (Douay-Rheims Version, *Holy Bible*, p 713, 1609). It is the only time that the Holy Ghost is named in the Old Testament books. It differentiates Solomon calling upon the Holy 'Spirit.'

"Sir," Quinn interrupted, "I read the book, *Windswept House*, by Malachi Martin, a former Jesuit. *Windswept* is a fictional novel, but I think that it upholds your suspicion. Martin tells a story that he later said was true, but that he could only present the truth as fiction. The story is that Lucifer was enthroned within the Roman Catholic Citadel, on June 29, 1963, the feast day of Saints Peter and Paul. A requirement of this enthronement was that a pope named Paul had to be elected, to signal the Availing Time of the Prince. So, just eight days after Pope Paul VI had been elected on June 21, 1963, they enthroned Satan – on June 29, 1963. The intent was that 'every element of the Celebration of the Calvary Sacrifice,' the crucifixion of Jesus, 'must be turned on its head by the other and opposite Celebration,' (p 7). 'The sacred must be profaned. The profaned must be adored.' Jesus must be replaced by the supreme and bloody violation of the dignity of the Nameless One. Guilt must be accepted as innocence. Pain must give joy. Grace, repentance, pardon must all be drowned in an orgy of opposites.' It must be the perfect 'enactment of sacrilege, the ultimate ritual of treachery,' (p 7). It must be performed by the 'Prince's trusted Guardian in Rome...*The immediate aim of every Ceremonial, he knew, is to venerate "the abomination of desolation,*" (p 8). Now the further aim 'must be to oppose the Nameless Weakling in His stronghold...to secure the Ascent of the Prince in the Citadel as an irresistible force...to make full possession of the Keys entrusted to the Keeper (Pope) by the Weakling (Jesus),' (p 8). And the Guardian's list of names – the Participants in the Roman Chapel – turned out to be men of the highest caliber, High-ranking churchmen, and laymen of substance,' (p 9).

The Concelebration, which would put Satan on the throne of Peter, was held both in St. Paul's Chapel in the Vatican, Rome, and in a chapel in South Carolina, known as the Mother Chapel of the United States. It was in this Mother Chapel that the Bishop was well versed in satanic ritual. They would need someone who understood the 'contradictory principles upon which all worship of the Archangel is structured.' It was this particular Bishop whose 'desire to encompass the ultimate strategy in that battle - the end of the Roman Catholic Church as the papal institution it had been since the Nameless Weakling had founded it,' (p 8).

They needed two chapels in simultaneous celebration because the security of the Vatican buildings would detect the noise, of chanting and of screams of their drugged victims, a little girl who they laid upon an altar with a train of bishops, cardinals, monsignors, each taking their turn in raping her, which in such a small body, was excruciatingly painful. To her little puppy, they cut out its sexual organs in a manner that would inflict the greatest pain on the puppy and to the little girl, who was unable to move from the drugs, to protect her puppy.

The men involved had been 'selected, co-opted, trained and promoted in the Roman Phalanx over the decades, while others represented the new generation dedicated to carrying the Prince's (Satan's) agenda forward for the next several decades.' They 'all understood the need to remain undetected; for the Rule says, "THE GUARANTEE OF OUR TOMORROW IS TODAY'S PERSUASION THAT WE DO NOT EXIST," (p 9). Participants, men and women, 'had made their mark in corporate, government, and social life.' A young child was for the

'Violation-of-Innocence.' The point of the ceremony was for the Prince (of Darkness, Satan) at long last 'Consummate his Most Ancient Revenge upon the Weakling', Jesus, (p 9-10).

'Darkness of will would become so profound that it would obscure even the official objective of the...(Vatican's) existence: the *perpetual adoration of the Nameless One (Satan)*,' (p 10).

The Bishop of the Mother Chapel, in South Carolina, United States, was exceedingly excited by his conducting the Concelebration that he said, 'This will be the capstone of my career. The capstone Event of the 20th century!'

After preparations were made, the celebration began. In the Vatican, the Roman Phalanx entered St. Paul's Chapel. 'Some of these were of the most illustrious men currently to be found in the collegium, hierarchy, and bureaucracy of the Roman Catholic Church. Among them, too, secular' men, (p 10).

Part of the implements of the ceremony, at the east side of the South Carolina Chapel, was a Crescent Moon and a Five-Pointed Star with Goat-Points raised upward,'" (p 11).

Quinn noted that the Crescent Moon is a symbol of Islam, the Five-Pointed Star is a pentagram, used in satanic rituals. He told Eisenhower, "in the peak of the celebration, the two groups prayed: 'The Triple Crown of Peter According to the adamantine will of Lucifer So that You reign here. So that there One…Mighty Congregation Of Man and Woman, Of animal and plant….' Then they all agreed that whoever among them might become Pope that they would 'transform the ancient Enmity (Satan, Gen. 3:15) into Friendship, Tolerance and Assimilation as these are applied to the models of birth, education, work, finance, commerce, industry, learning, culture, living and giving life, dying and dealing death. So shall the *New Age of Man* be modeled,' (p 19). Then each of the Cardinals, Bishops, and monsignors agreed to the oath to - 'intentionally and deliberately desecrate the Sacrament of Holy Orders,' (p 19). Then each of them 'solemnly swore that his administration of office would be bent to fulfill the aims of the Universal Church of Man,' (p 20). Then each of them swore to *'transfer Lordship and Possession of his soul from the Ancient Enemy (Jesus), the Supreme Weakling, to the All-Powerful Hands of our Lord Lucifer,'* (p 20). Then each of them pricked his left thumb with a golden pin and pressed a 'blood print beside their name on the Bill of Authorization,' (p 20)."

Quinn looked at Eisenhower, "Sir. I think that your concern for the appearance that they removed the Holy Ghost, the Third Person of the Trinity - and replaced it with the Holy Spirit, or, as we know him, Satan - is true. Not only that, it was Pope Paul VI, who wrote a letter to his successor, informing him of the Concelebration and enthronement of Satan on the seat of Peter. This is why his successor, John Paul I, was assassinated - he knew that the Cardinals, Bishops, and monsignors of the Vatican and of the Mother Chapel in South Carolina - had given Satan the

Church of Jesus Christ! When Pope Paul VI died, the Cardinal Camerlengo, the Pope's Secretary of State, had overlooked the papal-sealed letter to Paul's successor, because of all his duties during the vacancy of Peter's chair. This Secretary of State Camerlengo, along with his associates both in the Vatican and their secular boosters, had made a compact - the goal of the Concelebration - 'to do their part in effecting at last the desired and fundamental transformation in Church and papacy,' (pp 21-22). They needed a complaisant successor to Peter's chair. The Cardinal Camerlengo was inside the Conclave overseeing the election of that proper man. But he neglected Pope Paul VI's papers; and the one letter, which would expose the Concelebration of the enthronement of Satan, had been left in a 'special pigeonholed in the Cardinal's desk,' (p 22). And the Conclave voted for the one man who was totally unsuitable for the plans laid by the Camerlengo and his associates to transform the Catholic Church, (p 22).

As a result, John Paul I, had opened the sealed letter left by Paul VI. He knew what they had done. It was a smoke-screen to suggest that John Paul I was to investigate the Vatican bank malfeasance, and therefore, the reason why someone might have poisoned him - it became an accepted rumor. It kept eyes from searching further, for another reason for John Paul I's murder. Remember their Rule says, "THE GUARANTEE OF OUR TOMORROW IS TODAY'S PERSUASION THAT *WE DO NOT EXIST.* The bad guys were accounted for. So everyone thought.

But this John Paul I had also visited with Sister Lucia, the last living child of the vision of the Lady of Fatima. Lucia had told John Paul I of the Third Secret, which the 'pope of 1960' had refused to disclose against the wishes of Heaven, asking that this particular pope reveal it. Pope John Paul XXIII was that 'pope of 1960.' Part of the Third Secret was the mandate of the Blessed Virgin Mary to consecrate Russia to her, (p 5), or there would be grave worldwide consequences. Russia had become communist on October 25, 1917 with Lenin and his Bolshevik Revolution, right in the middle of WWI. Later, China, Cuba, North Korea would fall to communism."

Quinn continued his analysis, "The Virgin Mary appear six times to the children of Fatima, May 13, 1917 was the first time, October 13, 1917 was the last time – just 12 days prior to Russia's fall to communism. The Third Secret of Fatima was to be revealed by the pope of 1960, John XXIII, a communist and Freemason.

John XXIII oversaw the preparations, the setup of the abomination in the Temple – of the Concelebration, the enthronement of Satan. They couldn't have setup the complexity of the event in just eight days. By the time Paul VI was elected, everything had already been planned – they were just waiting for a pope named Paul to be elected and then they could activate their plans.

Remember Jesus telling His Apostles of the end times, the end of the punishment of the seed of David – the consummation, it will come when:

> 'When therefore you shall see the *abomination of desolation*, which was spoken of by Daniel the prophet, *standing in the holy place*: he that readeth let him understand.' Matt. 24:15.

This is talking about the enthronement of Satan on the Throne of Peter – it occurred on June 29, 1963. Satan is the abomination of desolation!

> And the prophet Daniel spoke of the end times: 'And from the time when the continual sacrifice shall be taken away, and the *abomination unto desolation shall be set up*, there shall be a thousand two hundred ninety days.' Dan. 12:11.

Pope John XXIII, less than 100 days in to his pontificate, on January 25, 1959, announced the convocation of the Second Vatican Council. This was tantamount to the announcement that they would be taking away of the continual sacrifice – Jesus, which was the result of Vatican II.

Between December 16, 1959 and June 29, 1963 – there are one thousand two hundred and ninety days – as noted in Daniel's prophecy, Dan. 12:11. What happened on December 16, 1959? The only thing that happened in the Vatican was that Pope John XXIII sent a letter to the Archbishop of Turin, Maurilio Cardinal Fossati, about the preparations for the celebration of the first centennial death of St. Joseph Cafasso of Turin. (www.vatican.va/holy_father/john_xxiii/ letters /1959/) Cardinal Fossati had the responsibility of guarding the Shroud of Turin in the Chapel of the Cathedral of Turin. The Shroud is still there to this day.

What do you make of that, sir?" Quinn asked.

"It would seem to me that if we apply Daniel's prophecy describing the 'continual sacrifice' and if this letter that Pope John wrote is the only thing that occurred at the Vatican on December 16, 1959 – then I think we can conclude that we are being directed to look at Cardinal Fossati. He attended Vatican II, but it doesn't appear that he played any major role in it. The one outstanding note about Fossati is his responsibility to care for the Shroud. And what is on the Shroud but the image of a crucified man – Jesus was crucified - the 'continual sacrifice' is Jesus. The Shroud has been scientifically tested and found to be authentic. But it isn't even necessary that it is Jesus' burial cloth – it is of a crucified man. That alone indicates that Jesus is the 'continual sacrifice.'"

"Sir, I read about the blood stains on the Shroud that they indicate that two Roman soldiers beat Jesus at the same time – He was never given a chance to take a breath between lashes. Sir, do you know what they used on Christ?"

"Unfortunately, I do. Jesus was given the third level of punishment called verberation, which was associated with crucifixions; it was the most severe degree of beating. The whips were used as a form of torture; the Flagrum whip was for intense torture. The Flagrum was made

with numerous leather lashes with metal points on the ends – two of these whips were used on Jesus. While one soldier reared his arm back to take a swing, the other soldier was striking the back of Jesus. When he pulled back his arm, the other soldier came down immediately – in other words – it was a constant clawing away of His skin. This verberation level of whipping continued till the brink of death."
(http://c.o.a.t.tripod.com/index_files/page0002.htm)

Eisenhower swallowed hard, "The crown of thorns had to be carefully crafted because the thorns of the qundaul bush had spikes one inch to one and one half inches long. The maker of the crown had to take painstaking effort to protect himself. When they placed it on Jesus' head, the one inch spikes pierced his entire scalp. He was half dead by the time they brought Him back to Pilate – to the people. The people took no pity on him and cried again for his crucifixion, instigated by the Kenites, the descendants of Satan."

Quinn and Eisenhower looked at each other quietly. Each had known war, each had killed in battle; both realized that the crucifixion of Jesus was not of this earth. Each recognized the evil that existed then, now walks the earth. It was the level of evil that both would have to face in the coming revolution.

Finally, Quinn said, "As to Daniel's prophecy, it would not fit the timeline of Vatican II, which was announced on January 25, 1959 by John XXIII, and convened by him, on October 11, 1962. John died on June 3, 1963 and Paul was elected on June 21, 1963, Satan was enthroned June 29, 1963. The other thought to consider – why did Pope Paul VI select his pontificate name – Paul? Was it to accommodate the satanic rule that a pope had to have the name Paul before Satan could be enthroned?

Daniel's prophecy indicates two events: the question is, are they – the letter that was sent to the keeper of the Shroud on which Jesus' image is contained, which would tell us that the continual sacrifice is Jesus, and is the second event the enthronement of Satan on the Throne of Peter – the criteria of the prophecy is that there is 1290 days between these two events – and the prophecy is, indeed, fulfilled by only these two events.

Eisenhower interjected, "Keep in mind that Daniel was of the royal blood of the kings of Juda, King David. Daniel had been taken into Babylonian captivity, so his prophecy comes more than 400 years before the birth of Jesus. Relative to our time, his prophecy references an event of 2000 years ago, Jesus' crucifixion, and the event of June 29, 1963 – when Satan literally took over the Catholic Church – just prior to Pope Paul VI reconvening Vatican II, on September 29, 1963. Exactly three months after Satan was enthroned, Vatican II destroyed the Catholic Church.

And it was through Vatican II changes that they took Jesus away – out of the Catholic Church – His own Church! And Satan, today, remains standing in the holy place."

Eisenhower continued, "As to Pope John XXIII initially calling for Vatican II, it's obvious why he did. He was a known communist according to FBI reports. 'In 1948, when Pius XII was threatening any prelate who supported communism, Roncalli/John XXIII, then serving as the Vatican's first permanent observer at the United Nations, established ties with Palmi Togliatti and other members of the Italian Communist Party…Togliatti informed Soviet officials that Roncalli would be the 'ideal man' to establish a 'working compromise' between the Church and communism, (U.S. Dept. of State confidential biography, 'John XXIII,' issued date: no date, declassified February 15, 1974, see Manhattan, Murder in the Vatican, pp 29-30; www.thepopeinred.com).

'At the instigation of U.S. Secretary of State, John Foster Dulles, CIA Director Allen Dulles, Cardinal Francis Spellman of the Archdiocese of New York met with Pius XII to 'leak' confidential information and to ask for Roncalli's (Pope John XXIII) removal from the Vatican…Pius XII complied by elevating Roncalli to the College of Cardinals and transferring him to the Patriarchate of Venice…at the age of 72, (it was thought) he'd spend his remaining years in 'pastoral work,' (U.S. Dept. of State Confidential Biography, 'John XXIII,' *Ibid.*)

'At the close of WWII, Roncalli was sent to Paris where he became close friends of French President Vincent Auriol and Maurice Thorez, the leader of the French Communists, and Edouard Herriot, leader of the Radical Party. Thorez sent a letter to the Kremlin, stating that Roncalli was an ideal prelate and said to Soviet officials, 'Roncalli understood Marxism like a Marxist, and if the Communist Party had not been sponsoring a program of militant atheism, Roncalli might have been the best 'Christian comrade' in the Roman Catholic Church' (U.S. Dept. of State secret dispatch, 'John XXIII,' issue date: November 20, 1958; *Ibid.)*

'Cardinal Siri (according to FBI sources) had obtained the necessary votes and was elected Pope Gregory XVII, on October 26, 1958, during the Conclave' (U.S. Dept. of state secret dispatch, 'Cardinal Siri,' April 10, 1961, declassified February 28, 1994; www.theimmaculateheart.com/gregoryxvii. htm)

The election of a pope was declared on Vatican radio and heard by millions listening in Italy and the rest of Europe; the Palatine and Swiss Guard were ordered to report to St. Peter's Basilica for the announcement of the name of the Holy Father; more than 200,000 Catholics in St. Peter's Square saw the white smoke and had gathered under the window waiting to receive the blessing of the new pope, but he did not appear. Monsignor Santaro, Secretary of the Conclave of Cardinals informed the press that the smoke had been white and that a new pope had been elected. On four ballots, Cardinal Giuseppe Siri of Genoa, Italy, had been elected the supreme pontiff, according to FBI sources.'" (www.thepopeinred.com/ 1988.htm).

Eisenhower cleared his throat, "Now this is where Roncalli's French communist connection comes in to play: the French Cardinals annulled the voting results. They claimed that Siri's election would cause widespread riots and the assassination of several prominent bishops behind the Iron Curtain. (U.S. Dept. of State secret file, 'Cardinal Siri, issue date: April 10, 1961, declassified: February 28, 1994; (www.thepopeinred.com)

'Behind the locked doors of the Conclave, they threatened Siri after his election and prevented him from taking the papal chair (*Portugal Daily News* article, documenting Roncalli's membership as a freemason, November 21, 2002). The Masonic '4th Republic' of France, in 1953, announced that Roncalli had been initiated into the Order of Rosicrucians while serving as the Vatican's Charge d'Affairs in Paris during 1935. 'In 1994 Portuguese Newspaper 'O Dia' and Correio deDomingo published the Fatima International's (a historic review organization)...press release that claimed Cardinal Angelo Roncalli...was a Freemason.' www.opusdeialert.com/ roncalliamason.htm

It was then, after they threatened Siri, that Roncalli was elected as Pope John XXIII, on October 28, 1958. His first act was to elevate Archbishop Giovanni Battista Montini (later, Pope Paul VI), Roncalli's fellow 'progressive.' Next, Roncalli/John XXIII, appointed an additional 23 Cardinals to ward off any attempt by the old guard to regain control of the Vatican; many of these Roncalli Cardinals were well-known for their leftist, socialist sentiments (Manhattan, *Murder in the Vatican*, p 37; Richard P. McBrien, *Lives of the Popes*, Harper, San Francisco, 1997, pp 371-72)

Cardinal Siri, Pope Gregory XVII, was the actual 'pope of 1960,' but the French Communist Cardinals and Pope John XXIII stole it from him. Pope Gregory XVII spent the next 30 years of his life under house arrest in a convent, watched daily.

Now, consider the vision of Our Lady of LaSalette to Melanie Calvat, in 1846, a fully approved Church Apparition, in which Our Lady revealed: 'Rome will lose the faith and become the seat of the Antichrist...The Church will be eclipsed....' (www.thepopeinred.com).

In 1878, Fr. Gaudentius Rossi's comment was published in *The Christian Trumpet*: 'Many powerful and influential persons in Europe are at present agreed and determined to use all their efforts to elect an anti-pope...to have a man who will favor their impious (unholy) designs against the Catholic religion...(and) are engaged in preparing the way to the approaching advent of an anti-pope.'"

Eisenhower reminded, "Our Blessed Mother appeared to Melanie Calvat in 1846 to tell that the Church would be eclipsed, and She appeared to the children of Fatima in 1917 to reiterate that message."

Quinn nodded quietly.

Eisenhower, resting his elbows on the conference table, his hands folded together below his chin, he leaned forward, "Before John XXIII was elected – the world knew that there was a Third Secret to be read by the Pope of 1960, per the children's statement that it was the wish of the Lady of Fatima. Therefore, they knew that the Pope of 1960 had to be an anti-pope. They put away the rightful pope and elected Pope John XXIII, now the illegitimate Pope of 1960. John read the Secret, on 'August 17, 1959.

Sister Lucia, the oldest of the children before whom the Blessed Mother appeared, held that the Blessed Mother said the secret would be more clear in 1960 (www. fatima.org/crusader/crthird/sfrpg05). But 'John XXIII decided…not to reveal the third part of the 'secret,' (www.vatican.va/roman_curia/ congregations/cfaith/documents/rc_con_ cfaith_ doc_20000626_message-fatima_en.html).

John XXIII had read the Secret with his 'confessor' and had it read to Cardinal Ottaviani, Prefect of the Holy Office, before he decided not to reveal it to the world.

'On February 8, 1960, a Vatican press release stated: 'The Third Secret would not be revealed,' and continued on to cast the most ignominious suspicion upon the credibility of Sister Lucia and upon the whole of the Fatima Message. This did immense harm to the Fatima cause, which had resulted in many conversions and the consecration of Italy to the Immaculate Heart of Mary. Sister Lucia replied…'God Himself Who had been disregarded, Who had been ridiculed in front of the world,' (www.fatima.org/crusader/crthird/sfrpg05)."

Quinn replied, "One might argue that as Pope John XXIII disobeyed Our Lady in 1960, it opened the way for the Jesuit General False Prophet, the Black Pope, to lead the Concelebration of the enthronement of Satan in 1963 onto the Throne of Peter, in Rome – and this allowed the Antichrist then to move into the United Nations onto the Secretary General's seat – by possessing each of the Secretaries General. Thus, the trinity of evil was installed to where they hold their positions, today."

"One could argue that, and rightfully so," Eisenhower replied. "Not only that, looking at what Vatican II did to the Catholic Church, Satan expects to forever hold his position on the Throne of Peter, giving his orders to the UN Secretary General, as to how Satan wants the world to be controlled. You can see their removal of defenses against evil in the changes that Vatican II made to exorcism!" Eisenhower said.

"The result of Vatican II, which opened with Pope John XXIII, and reconvened under Pope Paul VI, Vatican II got rid of the Rite of Exorcism given to infants prior to the Sacrament of Baptism, as a consequence of original sin. It's the out-breathing of the demon by the infant…(and) the inbreathing of the Holy Ghost by ministers, to symbolize the infusion of sanctifying grace by the sacrament.

And there is the exorcism of a possessed person. Vatican II, without consulting exorcist priests, dropped 12 of 21 directives to the exorcist while performing an exorcism, which had been followed for 385 years by exorcists. They essentially left the exorcist without a weapon against the demons. No longer are exorcists allowed or taught to: #4 asks the demoniac…what he feels…so (that the exorcising priest) can learn which words greatly disturb the demons, so as then to bear down on them and repeat them all the more. #5, the priest should stay alert for tricks; #6 demons hide…the exorcist should not stop until he sees signs of liberation; #8 Some demons point out an act of witchcraft…(to cause possession)…and a way to undo (the possession)…be careful not to have recourse to sorcerers, fortune-tellers…on this account; #9 sometimes the devil grants…relief and permits (a possessed person) to receive the Holy Eucharist…countless devices and tricks of the devil to deceive man, which the exorcist should beware; #13 Also relics of Saints…safely and properly fastened and covered, may be reverently applied to the chest or head of the possessed.'"

Eisenhower paused, "Have you noticed that Vatican II also removed all the statues of saints inside the churches? This is why!"

He continued with the directives that Vatican II dropped: #14 Exorcists should not engage in a great deal of talking or ask unnecessary or curious questions…But he should command the unclean spirit to be silent, except to answer his questions. Nor should he believe the demon if he pretends to be the soul of some saint or deceased person or good angel; #15 necessary questions…concern the number and names of the possessing spirits, the time and reason they entered; #16 The exorcist should read and carry out the exorcism with strength, authority, great faith, humility and fervor; #17 The exorcist priest should observe…which words the demons tremble more and then…repeat these words more often…he should continue for two, three, or four hours; #19 If he is exorcising a woman, he should always have persons of integrity with him…close relatives… the exorcist should be careful not to…occasion of an evil thought to himself or the others; #20 While he is exorcising, he should use the words of Scripture…(not) someone else's. He should command the demon to tell him if he is held in that body because of some magic, or sorcerer's signs or devices. If the possessed person has consumed things…he should vomit them up. If they are elsewhere outside the body, he (demon) should reveal where they are, and once found, they are to be burned. The possessed person should also be advised to make known all his temptations to the exorcist.'" (Fr. X, Summer of 2002, 'the New Rite of Exorcism, The Influence of the Evil One, LMM Magazine, www.latinmassmagazine.com/articles/articles_2002_SU_Father_X.html)

"And that's not all that Vatican II took away from the Rite of Exorcism, they took away the Athanasian Creed, which is used during exorcism. The reason is found in the Creed's first lines: 'Whosoever will be saved, before all things it is necessary that he hold the Catholic Faith…and the Catholic Faith is this, that we worship one God in Trinity…For there is one Person of the Father, another of the Son, and another of the Holy Ghost….' Vatican II did away with Catholicism, the Church of Jesus, and did away with the Holy Ghost, hence, they had to get rid of the Athanasian Creed." (*Ibid.*)

And Vatican II of Pope John XXIII and Pope Paul VI also got rid of the prayer to Michael the Archangel, the protector of the Catholic Church: 'St. Michael the Archangel, defend us in battle, be our protection against the malice and snares of the devil. May God rebuke him we humbly pray; and do thou, O Prince of the Heavenly host, by the power of

God, thrust into hell Satan and all evil spirits who wander through the world for the ruin of souls. Amen.'

Vatican II stripped from the Catholic Church and Catholics all defenses against Satan!

As to the Third Secret that John XXIII kept from the world. 'Paul VI read the contents (of the Third Secret)…on 27 March 1965…deciding not to reveal the text….John Paul II…asked for…the third part…on 13 May 1981' (www.vatican.va/roman, *Supra*). While John Paul II revealed the secret, there is much controversy as to whether it is the real secret.

The Mother of Jesus was putting the Third Secret before the pope who was setting up that abomination – and he refused to reveal the secret. By his refusal to reveal the Third Secret, Pope John XXIII revealed himself to be the Antichrist of the 1846 vision. Upon his death, Pope Paul VI became the Antichrist, upon the enthronement of Satan on the Throne of Peter, the UN Secretary General became the Antichrist.

Eisenhower pulled up the Vatican website, to Pope Paul VI's speech before the United Nations and Secretary General Thant, on October 4, 1965. "There's no English version of this speech."

"Well, Sir, I might be able to help you out. It's been many years since I studied French, but let's give it a try," Quinn said as he began to read Pope Paul VI's speech:

'Ce que vous proclamez ici, ce sont les droits et devoirs fondamentaux de l'homme, sa dignite, sa liberte, et avant tout la liberte religieuse. Nous sentons que vous etes les interpretes de ce qu'il y a de plus haut dans la sagesse humaine, Nous dirions presque: son caractere sacre.' (www.vatican.va/holy_father/paul _vi/speeches/1965/documents/hf_p-vi_spe_19651004_united-nations_fr.html)

Quinn frowned, "I think it's says, 'What you proclaim here, at the United Nations, are the rights and the basic duties of Man, his dignity, his freedom, and above all his religious freedom. We feel that you are the interpreters of what he has of higher human wisdom, we might say, almost sacred character.'"

"The 'we' in the syntax is the 'royal we'; it really means - I, as in the Pope thinks, the Pope feels, etc." Eisenhower added.

"So," Quinn offered, "The Pope is saying that it is up to the United Nations, the Secretary General, to determine what rights mankind will have; what duties will be placed upon mankind; what amount of dignity will be allowed mankind; how much freedom mankind will be allowed; and what religious freedoms mankind will be allowed. Pope Paul VI is leaving the interpretation of mankind's wisdom to the Secretary General and General Assembly of United Nations; that they are the interpreters of whether mankind has a sacred character – or, if the Secretary General determines that mankind has no wisdom, the United Nations must instruct man on his every activity.

Sir," Quinn asked, "do you mind if I look up one of Pope Paul's other speeches to try and put these of his words in to perspective?"

"Go right ahead, son," Eisenhower replied.

Quinn quickly found Pope Paul VI's speech of March 26, 1967, entitled "Populorum Progressio." (http://www.vatican.va/holy_father/paul_vi/encyclicals/documents/hf_p-vi_enc_26031967_populorum_en . html)

Quinn quickly scrolled through the speech, looking for something to jump out at him. He found a paragraph with the heading: 'Issues and Principles.'

"Sir, if I may read these few lines to you."

Eisenhower nodded, "Go ahead."

Quinn read Pope Paul VI's statement: "And the recent Vatican II Council reiterated this truth: 'God intended the earth and everything in it for the use of all human beings and peoples. Thus, under the leadership of justice and in the company of charity, *created goods* should flow fairly *to all*.'" (Vatican II document: Church in the World of Today, no. 69: AAS58 (1966), 1090 [cf. TPS XI, 306]

Quinn paused a moment, "As I recall, God said, 'Let (man) have dominion (control) over the fishes of the sea, and the fowls of the air, and the beasts, and the whole earth, and every creeping creature that moveth upon the earth,' (Gen. 1:26).

God did not say, let the Secretary General of the UN control them. Up until the United Nations was formed and has taken from man God's gift to man, a man who went out and caught a fish – it was his to eat, his to sell, just as most of the Apostles were commercial fishermen. Just as shepherds guarded their own flock and sold the wool and meat for their own livelihood. Just as cattlemen, here in the U.S., have done so since the first settlers came, and sold the meat to butchers and the leather to craftsmen – who created shoes, belts, and the like, for their personal profit. The Vatican supports the United Nations in taking all those lands, animals, and created goods away from man – and giving dominion over it all to Satan, administered by the Antichrist, the Secretary General of the U.N."

"Sir," Quinn said, "I don't see anything in God's words that says one person creating a good must give it to all – I see nothing of Communism in God's words."

Eisenhower nodded.

"Paul VI's speech continues," Quinn said, "'All other rights, whatever they may be, including the *rights of property* and *free trade*, are to be subordinated to this principle... *Redirecting these rights* back to their original purpose must be regarded as an important and urgent *social duty*.'"

Quinn sighed heavily. "Sir, it seems that Paul VI was agreeing with the UN's Land policy and its Agenda 21 – which is that no one should own private property - and that it is a social duty to turn over all ownership of property to the United Nations!

This goes to the United States presidents taking 29% of the land mass of the continental U.S. from private owners and states.

This also goes to Satan wanting control over the earth and all things on it," Quinn added. "There's another paragraph of this speech that I would like to read to you, sir."

Eisenhower nodded, again.

"'The Use of Private Property,' Pope Paul VI, said, 'As St. Ambrose put it: 'You are not making a gift of what is yours to the poor man, but you are giving back to him what is his. You have been appropriating things that are *meant to be for the common use* of everyone. The earth belongs to everyone, not to the rich,'" (*DeNabute*, c 12, n 53: PL 14.747, cf J.R. Palanque, *St. Ambroise et l'empire roman*, Paris: de Boccard (1933) 336 ff.).

They conjure a story of empathy for the poor man, villainizing the rich man – but they aren't taking from the rich man and giving to the poor man – they are taking from the rich man and giving control of these lands and goods, these God-given rights, to the Secretary General, to the Antichrist to administer for Satan! They don't give a damn about the poor man, he's a tool to insight pity and outrage, to win support of their theft!"

"That's absolutely, correct," Eisenhower responded.

Quinn continued, "Now, Paul VI said, in his own words, 'These words (of St. Ambrose) indicate that *the right to private property is not absolute and unconditional*. No one may appropriate surplus goods solely for his own private use when others lack the bare necessities of life. In short, as the Fathers of the Church (Jesuits) and other eminent theologians (descendants of Satan) tell us, *the right of private property may never be exercised to the detriment of the common good.*'"

Eisenhower asked, "And who determines what is the 'detriment of the common good'? That goes back to Pope Paul VI's speech to the United Nations, he's giving them the power to determine what is considered for the common good – what should be taken from the rich man, as Paul VI said, *'What you proclaim here, at the United Nations, are the rights and the basic duties of Man*, his dignity, his freedom, and above all *his religious freedom*. We feel that you are the interpreters of what he has of higher human wisdom, we might say, almost sacred character.'"

"I noted, Sir, that the first paragraph of this Populorum Progressio speech states: 'The progressive development of peoples...With an even clearer awareness, since the *Second Vatican Council*, of the demands imposed by Christ's Gospel in this area....'"

Quinn did a quick 'find' to search for the name of Jesus; His name had never been used in this speech. Quinn looked at Eisenhower, but paused a moment before he spoke.

"What's on your mind, son?" Eisenhower asked.

"Vatican II Council removed Jesus, and with the latest proof, they removed the Holy Ghost and replaced His name with the Holy Spirit - which was used in the Old Testament by ONLY Solomon, who worshipped idols and conjured up demons." Quinn sighed, "The word 'Christ' is a noun that means the anointed, the messiah. Sir, before I say what I think about this, allow me to read a few more lines from Pope Paul VI's Populorum Progressio speech. 'A National Duty 48. The duty of promoting human solidarity also falls upon the shoulders of nations:'

Paul VI quotes Vatican II Council: 'It is a very important duty of the advanced nations to help the developing nations...' (Vatican II document: Church in the World of Today, no. 86: AAS 58 (1966) 1109 [cf TPS XI, 319]

Then Paul says: 'While it is proper that a nation be the first to enjoy the God-given fruits of its own labor, *no nation may dare to hoard its riches for its own use alone*. Each and every *nation must produce more and better goods and products, so that...it may contribute to the common development of the human race.*'

Then in paragraph 'One Standard for All 61...In order that international trade be human and moral, social justice requires that it restore to the participants a certain equality of opportunity....'

And in the paragraph entitled, 'The Obstacles of Nationalism 62...Haughty pride in one's own nation disunites nations and poses obstacles to their true welfare....'

Sir, that statement seems to be pointing directly at the United States - how proud are Americans of their country! Although our President Tsaeb has gone around the world trashing our country. It would seem that this progressive/communist movement of the Vatican II Council and our own Presidents have the same mission - destroy America, take its wealth, the goods Americans make, and give it to the United Nations - and punish Americans for our love of our country."

Quinn moved on to another paragraph in the speech: "'Justice and Peace 5...We sought to fulfill the wishes of the (Vatican II) Council...to add another commission...in this way they can further the progress of poorer nations and international *social justice*... (for) the development of all mankind.'

Then there is paragraph 'A New Humanism Needed 20...even more necessary still is the deep thought and reflection of wise men in search of a new humanism....'

Quinn paused, sighed heavily, well aware of the gravity of his remarks, "I mean to say, Sir, Pope Paul VI even has a paragraph in his speech entitled, 'Common Good,' which is the quintessential Communist bottom line - everything must be for the common good of man. That is, for the workers, not the elite who are above all that commonality, not the elite who control the workers, not the elite of the United Nations who control the means of production, who control the laws of the United States! They will continue to live as kings. This is all directed at destroying the American middle class. And a pope calling for a new humanism – which elevates Man over God – that's just incredulous!

In this Common Good paragraph, Paul VI states: '24. If certain landed estates impede the general prosperity because they are extensive, unused or poorly used, or because they bring hardship to peoples (nations) or are detrimental to the interests of the country, *the common good sometimes demands their expropriation.* Vatican II affirms this emphatically. At the same time it (Vatican II) teaches that *income thus derived is not for man's capricious use, and that the exclusive pursuit of personal gain is prohibited*. Consequently, it is *not permissible* for citizens who have garnered sizeable income from the resources and activities of their own nation to deposit a large portion of their income in foreign countries for the sake of their own private gain alone....' (Vatican II document: Church in the World, no. 71: AAS 58 (1966), 1093 [cf. TPS XI, 308].

This language, 'income thus derived is not for man's *capricious* use...' comes directly from Karl Marx' argument in his *On the Jewish Question.* Marx said: man 'acting in accordance with his *private caprice*...he was not liberated from property; he received the liberty to own property. He was not liberated from the egoism (the ethical belief that self-interest is the just and proper motive for all human conduct) of business; he received the liberty to engage in business.' (econfaculty.gmu.edu *Supra*)

Pope Paul VI's speech echoes Karl Marx, and they both sound like a propaganda ad for President Tsaeb's Executive Order 13575, forming the White House Rural Council:

"Strong, *sustainable* rural communities are essential to winning the future and ensuring American competitiveness in the years ahead. *These communities supply our food, fiber, and energy, safeguard our natural resources, and are essential in the development of science and innovation.* Though rural communities face numerous challenges, they also *present* enormous *economic potential*. The Federal Government has an important role to play in order to *expand access to the capital necessary for economic growth, promote innovation*, improve access to healthcare and education, and *expand outdoor recreational activities on public lands*."

Tsaeb sent out to the rural communities a representative from each of his 26 presidential cabinet secretaries – going out to farms and ranches - to determine if they are too big, whether portions are unused - and especially poorly used – they went out looking for natural resources located on private land – they went out to determine – by those who have never planted a vegetable or raised a cow in their lives – whether Tsaeb should take those lands from Americans.

It's a dog and pony show - they are out there to take that land. The Internal Revenue service is out on the farms and ranches, too - to make sure a successful American rancher is paying his 'common good' fair share of his income. It goes to all the presidents taking land from private owners and states – so far, 650 MILLION ACRES, or 29% of the continental United States has been taken and now belongs to the federal government, which has handed it over to the United Nations. And they recently announced plans to take more land.

As Paul VI stated - 'it is not permissible for citizens' to 'garner sizeable incomes from the resources' that they privately own, privately break their backs working on! Who the hell is he to say that it is NOT PERMISSIBLE!!!! But then, President Tsaeb, by sending out his entire cabinet to these farms and ranches - looking to expropriate – to steal, land and natural resources from the American middle class, Tsaeb is carrying out Paul VI's mandate – but it's also the United Nations' mandate!!!

And now, President Tsaeb has military drones flying spy missions over farms and ranchers with the EPA sending the farmers warnings to follow EPA's unconstitutional regulations. The EPA and Tsaeb are breaking the 4th Amendment: 'the right of the people to be secure in their persons, houses, papers, and effects, against unreasonable searches and seizures…and no warrants shall issue, but upon probable cause' to search!"

Eisenhower interjected, "It's called Liberation Theology, communism; it began with Pope Paul VI; it's Christianized Marxism that the Jesuits first carried out in South America."

Quinn's voice lowered in anger, "What President Tsaeb is doing with his White House Rural Council, Lenin did in Russia after he and his Red Army of Bolsheviks took control of Russia. Lenin set down quotas for the peasants, still living under feudalism, demanding the peasants to give all their crops to the state. Vladimir Lenin organized the Bolsheviks and brought about the Bolshevik Revolution on October 25, 1917 - Communism. It was Lenin who ordered the murder of Tsar Nickolas II and his entire family, including the dog, after Nickolas had already abdicated the Russian throne in February of 1917."

"Did you note the dates that you just quoted, Quinn?" Eisenhower asked, "Our Lady of Fatima appeared on October 13, 1917, her sixth appearance since May 13, 1917, requesting that the Pope consecrate Russia to her Immaculate Heart. And 12 days later, Lenin brought Communism to Russia, on October 25, 1917. After the Bolshevik Revolution, it was determined that there were two obstacles, the United States and the Roman Catholic Church.

Pope Paul VI's successor, Pope John Paul I, told Sister Lucia, who witnessed the Lady of Fatima, that he was going to carry out the consecration of Russia. John Paul I's assurance that he would consecrate Russia to the Blessed Mother – and his knowing that Satan had been enthroned – were the reasons that he was assassinated."

Quinn adjusted his seat, "Sir, last night in my research, I read an article by Joseph deSainte-Marie, O.C.D. (www.fatima.org/consecrussia/reflections.asp). In his footnote 5, he spoke of the demand for the consecration of Russia, Lucia writes: 'In the course of different communications, Our Lord has not ceased to insist on that request, promising recently, if Your Holiness deigns to make the consecration of the world to the Immaculate Heart of Mary, with special mention of Russia...to shorten the days of tribulation.'" (From Sister Lucia's letter to Pius XII, December 2, 1940).

deSainte-Marie wrote that 'There are two requests clearly distinct, and the one peculiar to Sister Lucia's mission is the request for the consecration of Russia.' In other words, not the consecration of the world."

deSainte-Marie also stated in footnote 6: that 'Lucia wrote to Fr. Goncalvese, May 4, 1943: 'The Holy Father's act was incomplete, as a response, that is, to the demands of the Blessed Virgin of Fatima. In a letter to Fr. Aparicio, March 2, 1943, Sister Lucia wrote: 'The consecration of that country (Russia) was not made in the terms demanded by Our Lady.'

deSainte-Marie then stated in footnote 7: 'The 1942 consecration became collegial in 1954...Encyclical Ad Coeli Reginam, ordered all the bishops to renew (the 1942 Act) with him on May 31 (1954). But it was still a question of the consecration of the world, even if Russia was mentioned in veiled terms. In 1954 it was 'the peoples of Russia' that the Holy Father consecrated to the Blessed Virgin (not the country; not its government), but by an act with which the bishops could not be associate. So, that the demands of Our Lady of Fatima have still not been met.' Then on 'May 13, 1982, Pope John Paul II performed the Act of Consecration of the world - and essentially the same world consecration was done again on March 25, 1984. Yet, neither one fulfilled the Lady of Fatima's request.'

By this time, Sir, one must conclude that the Vatican does not want to stop communism from spreading around the world; the Vatican is explicitly, repeatedly, disobeying the Blessed Mother of God! How can they be called the followers of Jesus Christ!?"

Eisenhower frowned, "It doesn't appear that they are."

"It also goes to the message of the Lady of Fatima," Eisenhower added. "Lucia said it contained Apocalyptic contents. A Pope was also killed in the vision - John Paul I, the pope of 33 days. They wanted Russia to be communist - without God. Lucia had said that Rev. 8 to 13 showed the vision. Rev. 9:2, the bottomless pit is opened. Rev. 9:11, Satan is let out of the bottomless pit."

Quinn asked, "Weren't there several people who read the actual letter, not the fraudulent one issued by the Vatican - and they all indicated essentially the same thing - that the Vatican becomes the throne of the Antichrist. That there would be a great apostasy, starting at the top, where Cardinals will go against Cardinals, Bishops against Bishops. That sounds like collegiality that was established with Vatican II, which is the opposite of what Jesus had stated to Peter: Matt. 16:18 - 'upon this rock I will build my church.' This collegiality is how Satan will fracture the Church from within - create fissures in the Church of Jesus Christ. Priests who venerate Blessed Mary will be scorned and opposed within the Church. The Church will be full of those who accept compromises and the demon will press many priests and consecrated, sacred souls to leave the service of the Lord."

Quinn paused a moment, "I remember hearing a radio broadcast once where callers called to speak to a priest who had read the Third

Secret. He said he couldn't talk about it, but he affirmed a caller's question that a Jesuit priest had told him that the Third Secret stated that the last Pope will be under the control of Satan. The priest also affirmed that one Cardinal had said that their Christian lives and faith will face dangerous threats that will impact the world. That coincides with John Paul II saying that Christians will have to give up their lives for Christ."

Quinn said thoughtfully, "When you think about it - Second Vatican Council in 1965 took away the continual sacrifice, Jesus. It gives proof to the Concelebration that Malachi Martin's book, *Windswept House*, describes in that allegedly fictional story. I think Martin was reporting a true event; he had been in the Vatican at the time; he was in close association to Cardinal Augustin Bea, who basically organized the Second Vatican Council. Martin had access to rumors and to the Cardinals and Bishops involved in that Concelebration. Martin was aware of their Vatican II plan to implement Satan's control, slowly. At first, only removing the altar rails and saying the Mass in the vernacular, then with probably the most important prayers removed.

Throughout the 1960s morality took a turn away from the traditional culture of our Christian nation - we had the Sexual and Drug Revolutions, the Feminist Movement, and we had the UN Nuclear Non-Proliferation Treaty - all happening during the 1960 decade - the beginning of which the Blessed Mother wanted us to be warned, by the 'Pope of 1960.' The Catholic Church would become the seat of power for Satan."

Eisenhower listened intently, knowing that Quinn had to get it all off his chest. Finally, he said, "They replaced the Holy Ghost with the holy spirit. In the spirit of Vatican II, they say. And they actually mean it; every step they take to destroy the sacredness of the Church the Bishops say the change is within the spirit of Vatican II, they mean as Satan has dictated!"

Quinn sat quietly thinking a moment, then said, "Oh. Yes. I started to say – along with that priest on the radio, the one who had read the Third Secret, that he affirmed that a Cardinal had said that Christians' lives and faith will face dangerous threats that will impact the world. Well, I remember reading that Pope John Paul II had said that the Rosary is the answer to this evil, when talking about the content of the Third Secret of the Lady of Fatima. He said, 'put everything into the hands of the Mother of God - pray the Rosary. And allegedly he said, 'be prepared to undergo great trials *in the not-to-distant future, trials that will require us to be ready to give up even our lives, and a total gift of self to Christ and for Christ.*' He said it is possible to alleviate this end times tribulation; we can't stop it - this is the only way that the Church can be renewed.

But if he said that, why did he write in his *Redemptor Hominis* that 'we are speaking of every man, because...with each man Christ has united Himself forever.' These two statements do not mesh with each other. In the first, John Paul II is warning us that evil has infiltrated the Catholic Church. That we should be ready to fight it, to the point of giving up 'even our lives'! That's an incredible statement by a sitting pope. Yet his words in *Redemptor*, 'with each man Christ has united Himself forever' - in 'every man' is counter to what Jesus had said. 'For this is my blood of the new testament, which shall be shed for many unto remission of sins' (Matt. 26:28) - not for all, not for every man! Whose side is Pope John Paul II on?"

Allegedly, John Paul II had said, 'How many times, indeed, has the renewal of the Church been effected in blood? This time, again, it will not be otherwise. We must be strong, we must prepare ourselves, we must entrust ourselves to Christ and to His Holy Mother, and we must be attentive to the prayer of the Rosary.' And when he said that this cannot be stopped - it goes to what Jesus told his disciples about the end, Matt. 24:6 'And you shall hear of wars and rumors of wars. See that ye be not troubled. *For these things must come to pass, but the end is not yet.*'

It seems that God the Father is outraged with the popes and cardinals and bishops - and us Christians. And the Mother of Jesus - being a mother - has interceded to help repair our relationship with God – and will ask for our pardon of our culture that took a bad turn, beginning in the 1960s and has lasted to today. And maybe we Christians gave in too easily to the sin; maybe we should have confronted the Vatican back in 1965, instead of just walking away from the Church – it was OUR Church, after all. Maybe we should confront today's pope and tell him to get rid of Satan – why can't we do that?" Quinn looked at Eisenhower for permission.

"The permission isn't mine to give, Quinn," Eisenhower replied. The two sat without speaking; without looking at each other.

It suddenly occurred to Quinn, "General, if Satan is in control of the Catholic Church - the Church of Jesus - and Vatican II took away the continual sacrifice - who are Catholics worshipping?"

"They are worshipping Satan - it's his Church, isn't it? At least, for now," Eisenhower replied.

"So, this might be a sign of the end times," Quinn said, "Satan is in control of the Catholic Church, Jesus' Church - Jesus is coming back to defend His church. 'The gates of hell shall not prevail against it,' Matt. 16:18. Vatican II was the first skirmish in the Battle of Armageddon."

Quinn thought for a moment, "This revolution of ours is going to be a very delicate matter. I would, at this point, do small operations – car accidents of known leaders; medical 'errors'; private plane crashes. I would eliminate as many as I could with that strategy, before they realized that a revolution was going on."

"You're absolutely right, Quinn, and that's our strategy – at least for now," Eisenhower replied.

Quinn sat back in his chair and asked, "Where do people get the idea that before the end times a peace treaty signed by Israel will be broken?"

"They claim a peace treaty is indicated in Dan. 9:26-27, but they misinterpret or are deceived in to thinking that an Israeli peace treaty is implied.

Dan. 9:26-27, states: 'And after sixty-two weeks Christ shall be slain: and the people that shall deny him shall not be his. And a people with their leader that shall come, shall destroy the city and the sanctuary: and the end thereof shall be waste, and after the end of the war the appointed desolation. And He shall confirm the covenant with many, in one week: and in the half of the week the victim and the sacrifice shall fail: and there shall be in the temple the abomination of desolation: and the desolation shall continue even to the consummation, and to the end."

These two verses of Daniel's prophecy are an agreement between Jesus and His followers. The verses mean:

Christ preached for 62 weeks; he was arrested and killed;

'The people that shall deny Him' – were the Pharisees – they are not of Jesus' lineage – they are Edomites.

'A people with their leader shall come' – they were General Titus and the Roman Legions who destroyed the Second Temple sanctuary and the city of Jerusalem in A.D. 70, 40 years after the Pharisees killed Jesus.

'The appointed desolation' refers to Malachias 1:4, when God said that he would throw down what Edom/Edomites said they shall build up – and refers to Ezra, the Edomite, convincing Cyrus the Great to let the Israelites rebuild Jerusalem, 538 BC. Thus, God sent the Roman Legions, who then destroyed everything that the Edomite, Ezra, said he wanted rebuilt. All was completely destroyed, and the Israelites left Jerusalem.

Jesus confirmed the covenant 'with many,' Matt. 26:28 – during the Last Supper, on Thursday, at sundown.

'In one *week*,' beginning on Sunday, the first day of Passover *week* – Jesus 'confirmed the covenant 'with many,' as cited in numerous scriptural passages, depicting the mutual acceptance of the covenant/agreement by both Jesus and His followers:

> John 12:1, 'Jesus therefore, *six days* before the pasch (Passover), came to Bethania, where Lazarus had been dead, whom Jesus raised to life.';
>
> John 12:11, 'Because many of the Jews, by reason of him (Lazarus), went away, and believed in Jesus.';
>
> John 12:12-13, 'And on the *next* day, a great multitude that was come to the festival day…Took branches of palm trees, and went forth to meet him….';
>
> John 12:19, 'The Pharisees therefore said among themselves: Do you see that we prevail nothing? Behold, the whole world is gone after him.';
>
> John 12:20, 'Now there were certain Gentiles among them, who came up to adore on the festival day.';
>
> John 12:26, Jesus said, 'If any man minister to me, let him follow me; and where I am, there also shall my minister be. If any man minister to me, him will my Father honour.' (This is

an element of the covenant/agreement that warrants that if you follow Jesus your soul will spend eternity in Heaven);

John 12:27, 'Father, save me from this hour. But for this cause I came unto this hour.' (This is an element of the covenant/ agreement that Jesus would fulfill: Jesus would die for our sins);

John 15:17, Jesus said, 'These things I command you, that you love one another.' (This is the element of the covenant that worshippers must fulfill);

Matt 22:37-38, Jesus said, '*Thou* shalt love the Lord thy God with thy whole heart, and with thy whole soul, and with thy whole mind. This is the greatest and the first commandment.' (This is the key element of the covenant/agreement – if an individual (Thou) fails to fulfill this specific element of the agreement – the agreement is broken);

John 12:28, Jesus said, 'Father, glorify *thy* name. A voice therefore came from heaven…';

John 12:29, 'The multitude therefore that stood and heard, said that it thundered.';

John 12:30-32, 'Jesus answered, and said: This voice (from Heaven) came not because of me, but for <u>your sakes</u>. Now is the judgment of the world: now shall the prince of this world be cast out. And I, if I be lifted up from the earth, will draw all things to myself.' (This voice element of the covenant/agreement was the assurance/ warrantee of the Father; the element of 'Now is the judgment of the world' is the guarantee that Jesus/Michael the Archangel would remove Satan; 'Now shall the prince (of darkness) of this world be cast out' is the guarantee that Jesus will put Satan into the bottomless pit; 'And I, if I be lifted up from the earth' is an element of the covenant/agreement that is a teaching, a proviso, that one must be individually responsible for his actions and that no one should *assume* that they will be taken up to Heaven, ie, those of the bloodline of Adam and Eve.);

Matt. 28:19-20, Jesus said to His disciples, 'Going therefore, teach ye all nations; baptizing them in the name of the Father, and of the Son, and of the Holy *Ghost*. Teaching them to observe all things whatsoever I have commanded you: and behold I am with you all days, even to the consummation of the world.' (This element of the covenant/agreement promises leadership to the followers of Jesus, a customer service, to teach them the commandments of God, and warns that any member of that leadership who does not obey: 'baptizing them in the name of the Father, and of the Son, and of the Holy *Ghost'* – will be reckoned with at the end of the affliction of the seed of David);

John 12:35-36, 'Jesus therefore said to them (His followers): Yet a little while, the light is among you. Walk whilst you have the light, that the darkness overtake you not. And he that walketh in darkness, knoweth not whither he goeth. Whilst you have the light, *believe in the light, that you may be the children of light*.' (This is an element of the covenant/agreement that stipulates that an individual follower must believe in Jesus to enter into Heaven, and thus, bloodline is irrelevant.);

John 18:39-40, Pilate said to the Chief Priest Caiphas, the Pharisees and Jews, 'But you have a custom that I should release one unto you at the *pasch* (on Passover): will you, therefore, that I release unto you the king of the Jews? They cried they all again, saying: Not this man, but Barabbas....'

Daniel's prophecy stated: 'And in the half of the week the victim and the sacrifice shall fail' – The use of 'victim' and 'sacrifice' denotes blood-letting, as when sacrificing a lamb, which is mandated as a reminder of God bringing the Israelites out of Egypt. Thus, the lamb sacrifice indicates Passover, which is in mid-week of Passover week, or in 'the half of the week.' Jesus was crucified on Passover – 'in the half of the week' – and failed, as in, He died. Resurrecting on Sunday makes Thursday the relative midpoint of the week, as opposed to the beginning or end of the week. In Daniel's prophecy, Passover falling on mid-week indicates the year that Jesus was crucified – and the year that Jesus locked Satan into the bottomless pit.

According to U.S. Naval Observatory Astronomical Applications Department, Passover began on Thursday, April 6, A.D. 30, at 6PM, and ended on Friday, April 7, A.D. 30, at 6PM. (http://judaismvschristianity .com/Passover_dates.htm). The U.S. Naval Observatory chart indicates that the only other Thursday/Friday Passover was in A.D. 27. That would be too early for Jesus to die, since he was baptized in the 15th year of Roman Emperor Tiberias Caesar's reign, Luke 3:1:22, which ran from August 19, A.D. 28 to August 18, A.D. 29. After His baptism Jesus began His ministry. And according to Dan 9:26, 'And after sixty-two weeks Christ shall be slain...' Therefore, Jesus preached for one year, two months, and two weeks. That means that He was baptized on or about January 15, A.D. 29, which is in the 15th year of Tiberias Caesar. April 7, A.D. 30 was also the day that 'Passover and the Sabbath coincided,' (Jim Bishop, *The Day Christ Died*, p 237 fn).

On Thursday, at 6PM, Passover supper, or the Last Supper, was eaten by Jesus and His Apostles.

At 3AM on Friday, April 7, A.D. 30, Jesus was arrested – tried by Annas, then Caiphas, and then Pilate. He was whipped simultaneously by two Roman soldiers using metal-pointed Flagrum whips. A Roman soldier pressed onto Jesus' head a crown made of qundaul bush twigs with 1 ½ inch thorn spikes. The soldiers dressed Jesus in a breech clout, since Pilate allowed the Jewish custom of covering (*Ibid.*) the condemned. Barely able to hold Himself upright, a soldier placed a 30-pound timber on his shoulder. 'This was the 'crosspiece'; the upright part of the cross was always left standing at the place of execution and was used many times,'

(*Ibid.* at p 300) Followed by two thieves who had not been scourged, Jesus staggered as he followed the Roman soldier leading the small procession out of the City of David to 'Golgotha,' which means skull-like; Calvary is a Greek translation,' (*Ibid.* at p 301 fn). The road from the arch of the prison grounds, to Golgotha 'was almost exactly 1000 paces, about 3000 feet,' (*Ibid.* at 301). The road, Via Dolorosa, was 'hardly more than twelve feet wide, up a slight incline, then sharply down into the valley below. It was lined with houses and shops. Crowds argued loudly for guilt or innocence as the parade moved by. The legionaries moved the crowds back, and the soldier who led on the horse shouted continuously for the people to make way for the soldiers of Rome,' (*Ibid.* at 302). So weakened by the pain from the scourging of metal points that ripped His flesh from His back and the thorns continuing to tear his scalp from his skull, rivulets of blood flowing down his head, Jesus fell under the weight of the crosspiece timber pressing heavily on His shoulder. Simon of Cyrene, a farmer, was ordered to carry the timber; Jesus continued to stagger up the 'formidable hill leading to the Gennath Gate' and out of the City of David. (*Ibid.*) As the procession passed the society of charitable women who cried in seeing Jesus in such pain, Jesus struggled say to them, 'Daughters of Jerusalem, weep not over me; but weep for yourselves, and for your children. For behold, the days shall come, wherein they will say: 'Blessed are the barren, and the wombs that have not borne, and the paps that have not given suck,' (Luke 23:28-29). Jesus was speaking of the Roman Legions destroying the Second Temple and the City of David, Jerusalem, 40 years later.

Many sons have died for the noble cause of fighting for their country, and fortunately, mothers are told when it is all over and her son is out of pain and at rest. But the Blessed Mother saw and heard the nails being driven into Her Son's feet and wrists. She heard His cries of excruciating pain. Outnumbered and out-powered by the Roman soldiers, she could not stop them.

"The Phoenicians were the first to devise crucifixion. They had tried death by spear, by boiling in oil, impalement, stoning, strangulation, drowning, burning – and all had been found to be too quick. They wanted a means of punishing criminals slowly and inexorably, so man devised the cross. It was almost ideal, because in its original form it was as slow as it was painful (men often lived two and more days in the burning sun).... A secondary consideration was nudity. This added to the shame of the evildoer and, at the same time, made him helpless before the thousands of insects of the air, while the carrion birds and the small animals held back until the crucified was dead. The Romans adopted the cross as a means of deterring crime... When the revolt of Spartacus was suppressed, six thousand men were crucified in a single day...later they abandoned spikes and ropes and drove nails through wrists and feet and found that, unless the victim was a tower of strength, he would expire within a few hours,' (*Ibid.* at Jim Bishop, p 308).

John 19:30, 'Jesus therefore, when he had taken the vinegar, said: *It is consummated.* And bowing his head, he gave up the *ghost*.'

Jesus died on Passover as it immediately preceded the Sabbath, which is a Friday, Luke 23:53-54: 'And taking him down, he wrapped him in fine linen, and laid him in a sepulchre… And it was the day of the Parasceve, and the sabbath drew on...'

Parasceve was the preparation of three meals before 6PM on Friday, at which time the Sabbath began.

Jesus was crucified at noon, on Friday, on April 7, A.D. 30, and died at 3PM. He was laid in the tomb on Friday before 6PM. From Friday at 6PM to Saturday at 6PM is one Hebrew day. Saturday at 6PM to Sunday at 6PM is a second Hebrew Day. Sunday at 6PM to Monday at 6PM is the third Hebrew day. Sunday between 6PM to midnight is the morning of the third Hebrew Day. Thus, on April 9, A.D. 30, Jesus was resurrected from the dead. John 20:1, 'And on the *first* day of the week (Sunday), Mary Magdalene cometh early, when it was yet *dark*, unto the sepulchre; and she saw the stone taken away from the sepulchre.' Thus, approximately, sometime between the hours of 10PM and midnight, on Sunday morning, April 9, A.D. 30, Jesus was resurrected from the dead. Luke 9:22, Jesus had said, 'The Son of man must suffer many things, and be rejected by the ancients and chief priests and scribes, and be killed, and the *third* day rise again.' Sunday, approximately 10PM-12PM, April 9, A.D. 30 – was the dark morning of the third *Hebrew* day.

Daniel's prophecy then refers to the enthronement of Satan – 'there shall be in the temple the abomination of desolation' – The word abomination in Daniel's time meant a false god, one that left desolation of the soul in his wake.

'And the desolation shall continue even to the consummation, and to the end,' which means that Satan will remain on the Throne of Peter to the completion of God's punishment of the seed of David – when Jesus returns. Rev. 20:9-10: 'And there came down fire from God out of heaven, and devoured them; and the devil, who seduced them, was cast into the pool of fire and brimstone, where both the beast And the false prophet shall be tormented day and night for ever and ever.'

In other words, Quinn, there is nothing in Dan. 9:26-27 that indicates that any treaty is to be signed by Israel – that's just not going to happen. In the meantime, thinking that they will have time to live foolishly until they hear that a treaty is about to be signed by Israel, people won't repent of their sins, won't prepare their souls for judgment by Jesus; they will be caught by surprise. Perhaps, end up being cast into the pool of fire and brimstone."

Having no further questions, Quinn nodded, "Thank you, sir, I really enjoyed our discussion. It helped me to put it all together."

"Ok, Quinn," Eisenhower said as the two men stood up. "We won't be meeting here at the Pentagon, again. We meet in a different place each time, to keep the evil 11th dimensional spirits from finding us. And we don't put out a collective telepathic call; we call one to the other individual general and soldier, and we use code. You'll learn that as part of your training."

"Yes, sir," Quinn said.

Eisenhower paused a moment, looked down at the floor, "Son. There's just one more thing that you should know – about me. I don't want you to hear it from someone else and wonder why I didn't tell you, now."

Quinn's stomach fell. He had already decided to follow Eisenhower's orders, he didn't want to hear something now that would cause him to doubt his decision – what he and the country was about to take on was far too important to question any aspect of the mission.

"Sir," Quinn said.

"It's about December 16, 1959 and Pope John XXIII's letter to the Archbishop of Turin, the letter that points to the one place on earth that houses the image of Jesus Christ – on the Shroud – which has been in Turin since 1578 – except for the ten years it was hidden in the Abbey of Montevergine by the Benedictine monks, to keep Hitler from getting his hands on it. It was returned specifically to Archbishop Fossati in 1946."

Eisenhower sighed, "Pope John XXIII's letter to Fossati was sent on December 16, 1959. That was ten days after I had visited John XXIII at the Vatican. I was the only U.S. President that had met with John. It was December 6, 1959. My mission was to try to convince John XXIII not to go through with the convening of Vatican II. I told him of the FBI reports that had exposed his Communism and membership in the Freemasons."

Quinn was rigid on his feet, bracing himself for what he had expected to hear that he had already questioned the night before. Was Eisenhower one of God's witnesses?

Quinn quickly recalled Revelations, the Apocalypse 11:7-9: "And when they shall have finished their testimony, the beast, that (had) ascendeth (rose) out of the abyss, shall make war against them, and shall overcome them, and kill them...and their bodies shall lie in the streets of the great city...and they of the tribes, and peoples, and tongues, and nations, shall see their bodies for three days and a half: and they shall not suffer their bodies to be laid in sepulchres."

Quinn realized that Eisenhower and Kennedy had each lain in state for three days and the world saw them there. Satellite coverage of the funeral provided citizens and leaders in Japan and in the Soviet Union – Nikita Khrushchev, Kennedy's enemy – view the funeral procession, as well as 23 other countries.

Eisenhower continued, "I was a witness, a prophet, for God through my speech – the one they refer to now as my Military-Industrial Complex speech. Kennedy was a witness for God through his Monolithic speech – about the secret conspiracy that is a ruthless enemy of the United States. His speech was more than a warning about Communism – it was about Satan taking over the world – about the Jesuits, who are working for

Satan, creating a New World Order – the New Age - that will be handed over to Satan. And one day, soon, Satan and his Antichrist, U.N. Secretary General Yoon Won-Shik; and his False Prophet – Alonso Negrete, the Black Pope, General Secretary of the Jesuits will soon announce themselves to all mankind, as the Trinity of Evil."

"It IS you!" Quinn cried. "You had lain in state at the Washington National Cathedral, then at the U.S. Capitol from March 29, 30, and on the 31st they had your funeral services, and on April 2nd, you were buried in Abilene, Kansas. Your son, Doud, lies between you and your wife, Mamie in the 'Place of Meditation.' Your grave is not a sepulchre, not a tomb! You fit the Rev. 11:7-8 description of a witness who will warn the people.

"Quinn was excited with the clarity of it all, "Kennedy – he was murdered by them – he laid in repose in the East Room of the White House, November 23, 1963, then in the U.S. Capitol November 24, 1963, and his funeral was on November 25, 1963. (Rev. 11:8) He was buried in Arlington National Cemetery – only the second president ever to be buried there. He has no tomb, no sepulchre, either! One million people lined the funeral route; government leaders and members of royal families saw his dead body carried to its grave. Even the Pope sent representatives. There were nations from around the world that viewed the funerals of both you and Kennedy – it's all stated in Rev. 11:9. And every American watched it on television.

Your deaths signify that the 'second woe is past,' (Rev. 11:14)."

Quinn stopped, "But what about the earthquake of Rev. 11:13, and about the 'tenth part of the city fell'? What about that?"

"In this case, the earthquake means the shaking of the world by political means. It was a big step in destroying our country. The tenth of the city fell – it refers to what happened after Kennedy was assassinated – Lyndon Baines Johnson became President. One of his signature issues of his administration was the Civil Rights Act. No one realizes that it's primary, hidden goal was that it increased the quota of Israeli Jewish immigrations allowed to immigrate into the United States – along with other acts that led to the New World Order. LBJ was their man!

They had tried to kill me in office – first with causing my heart attack; it almost killed me. It caused an aneurysm that later gave me a stroke. So, if I had died in office, they would have had Nixon step in to the Presidency. And what did Nixon accomplish after he succeeded Johnson? He dramatically increased financial aid to Israel. Nixon established diplomatic relations that opened the way for China's imminent superpower status. Congressional legislation followed that destroyed a tenth part of the American middle class, with jobs being sent to China. Cities across the United States were devastated when factories and plants closed. The physical destruction was as bad as if an earthquake had struck.

With Nixon establishing that U.S./China relationship he was able to bring about détente with the Soviet Union, after a 21-year estrangement.

Nixon then went to Moscow in May 1972 and signed the nuclear arms limitation treaty (SALT 1) with Soviet Communist Leonid Brezhnev. That treaty allowed USSR reconnaissance satellites to fly over the United States. What else did they spy on? That opened the way for Tsaeb to sign an arms treaty with Russia, in 2010 – which cuts a third of our nuclear weapons stockpile. Tsaeb is establishing a nuclear strategy that is a radical change in direction from all other presidents. Tsaeb is implementing a U.S. strategy for the coming new age. For the first time in U.S. history, Tsaeb explicitly told our enemies that as President, he will not use nuclear weapons against nonnuclear nations who actually attack the U.S. with biological or chemical weapons, or a cyber-attack that brings our country to its knees!"

Eisenhower asked, "Do you see that they have a patient, long-term strategy and everything leads to the next act that will bring about the New World Order that will be controlled by Satan? To do that they first have to destroy the United States and the Roman Catholic Church. Well, the Jesuits have destroyed the Church. Now, they are bearing down on the United States. We are the last stronghold against the New World Order."

"Yes, sir!" Quinn replied.

"President Tercart gave the Panamanians our Panama Canal – that we bought and we built up as our greatest military strategic asset; it's now controlled by China; President Jeffers gave China the antiballistic missile guidance chip; the Jesuit controlled Federal Reserve is destroying our dollar and our economy; and during all these years, you have the numerous U.S. Congresses sending American middle class jobs out of the country. And under Tsaeb's healthcare, banks are no longer allowed to give college students tuition loans – the government will decide who goes to college by issuing student loans – and it won't be White Christians – those descendants of Adam and Eve! They'll be the ones whose taxes will pay for the descendants of Ham and Japheth to go to college. And the one thing a student should take from a college education – is how to analyze. How to think! But even worst that anything else, Tsaeb's healthcare mandates that Christians sin against the Commandment of God, Thou shalt not kill, by forcing Christians to pay for women to have abortions."

Eisenhower paused a moment, picked up the Bible and turned to Leviticus 20:1-5:

'And the Lord spoke to Moses, saying: Thus shalt thou say to the children of Israel: If any man of the children of Israel…give of his seed to the idol Moloch, dying let him die: the people of the land shall stone him. And I will set my face against him…because he hath given of his seed to Moloch…and profaned my holy name. *And if the people of the land* neglecting…my commandment, let alone the man that hath given of his seed to Moloch, and will not kill him: *I will set my face against that man and his kindred, and will cut off both him and* *all that consented with him*, to commit fornication with Moloch, out of the midst of their people.'

Eisenhower closed the book, took off his reading glasses and turned to Quinn, this is what Tsaeb is forcing Americans to do, their payment for his healthcare is a payment for abortion – abortion is an early sacrifice of one's child to Moloch – Satan! Every American who consents to Tsaeb's healthcare is literally giving their soul to Satan! And God will turn His face from those Americans who do nothing to stop Tsaebcare.

"They're intentionally destroying us and our country!" Quinn whispered.

"That's correct, son," Eisenhower replied, "through every one of our institutions, including our military that has kept us safe from attack – when they get through with the United States, it'll be a Third World country, full of ignorant citizens who can't think their way out of a paper bag, and absolutely defenseless against the Antichrist U.N. Secretary General Yoon Won-Shik and his UN Troops. You could reason that it doesn't matter if we are in the end times, we have to stop this destruction of our country.

Their strategy is a slow moving, inch-by-inch steam roller over the middle class. Franklin Roosevelt signed the Social Security Act that was supposed to be voluntary, a tax on one percent of income, which would be kept in a Trust Fund. Then Lyndon Johnson and the Democratic Senate and House transferred the money into the General Fund, so that Congress could spend it. The Democrats eliminated tax deduction of Social Security payments. Al Gore had the deciding vote to tax Social Security Annuities. Timmy Tercart was the president who started giving immigrants Social Security payments, when they never paid a dime into the system. Social Security went from 1% tax on our income to 85% of our income, and Congress is claiming that the program is going to crash, so they have to cut payouts to Americans who paid into the system all their working lives. They have us coming and going.

But it's all driven by the Jesuits. They worked with the Soviet Union in financing and arming the Nicaragua Revolution – Jesuits even fought in the revolution – it was the testing ground for implementing Communism, Modernism, also known as the New World Order. It was the Soviet Union's aim to dominate Nicaragua for its geological location – between the North and South American continents, giving a staging platform for ready access into the United States. It's located with ready access to both the Pacific and Atlantic Oceans. How Nicaragua fell, so would all the Central American countries – and finally, the Jesuits would rid the hemisphere, the world, of Roman Catholicism. The Junta, officers who held state power after the revolution, relied so heavily on the Jesuits that they did everything to support the Jesuit's 'People's Church.' The Junta sent out Gestapo-squads out to beat anyone who spoke out against the Jesuits holding government posts.

The questions come to mind – why has the United States government allowed more than 35 Muslim paramilitary training camps inside the United States mainland? How are the Jesuits helping them?"

Eisenhower smiled, "I'll give you a hint. In Tsaeb's speech in

Cairo, Egypt, while promising the Muslims that he would provide increased number of diversity and religious visas from Islamic-terror-sponsoring nations – increase in student exchange, increased investments in U.S. Muslim communities, expand scholarships and internships for Muslims; telling of a new fund to support technological development in Muslim-majority countries and to help transfer ideas to the marketplace – let's stop here a moment – Tsaeb is talking about his America Invents Act, which will allow the easy theft of Americans' inventions. Especially, since Tsaeb ordered the Director of NASA to give Muslims jobs; it gives them ready access to our space engineering inventions.

Now, let me continue Tsaeb's statement in that speech to the Muslims of Cairo – 'All these things must be done…Americans are ready to join…Muslim communities around the world to help <u>OUR</u> PEOPLE pursue a better life.' The man gives a laundry list of what he is going to take from Americans to give Muslim-majority countries, and then ends the paragraph with 'to help OUR people.'"

Eisenhower looked Quinn in the eye, "I think the man just showed his hand – he's a Muslim! That's why, besides the Jesuit backing, Tsaeb is supportive of the Muslim paramilitary training camps inside our borders. That's why he punishes our Border Patrol officers, if they arrest illegal aliens. Hezbollah, Hamas, and Al Qaeda have been arrested crossing our borders – Tsaeb wants them to be able to pass easily into the Muslim paramilitary camps. That's why he's also increasing the Federal Civilian Police Force 'to be as well- equipped as the U.S. Military' – to take down Americans who protest these Muslim training camps – and his dictatorship."

"I think that there is more than enough evidence that Tsaeb is a traitor – leaking military secret operations – the leaks help the Muslim countries. But, sir, I do have one last question, just exactly what do they mean by the New Age, as it applies to the Jesuits and the U.S. Government, and the United Nations? I remember back in the sixties, I believe it was 1969 that the 5th Dimension singing group came out with the musical *Hair*'s rendition of Age of Aquarius. If I remember the words correctly: 'When the moon is in the 7th House and Jupiter aligns with Mars, then peace will guide the planet and love will steer the stars.'

I'm beginning to think that what is going on through the Jesuits worldwide and the secular European powers are about to bring on the alleged enlightenment of the Illuminati with that sunshine of that song! And the name of the group – the 5th Dimension – tied with that song? I see a hand behind the scenes. I found in my research last night two things: We're leaving the Age of Pisces and entering the Age of Aquarius. And the 5th dimension in physics is a level of existence that they think brings Eisenstein's theory of space-time in to a relationship with the timeless and eternal. So that in the 5th dimension, space allows the movement of consciousness at the level of greater awareness – to see the unity of life and matter from a higher plane of reality. On that higher level of existence, we have a better view of what is reality. This all goes to the drugs used in the hippy/yippie movement of the sixties – the striving for greater awareness of reality through drugs. For me, all I cared about in the sixties is what I could hold in my hand and what my eyes could see. But then, I was young and foolish." Quinn smiled.

Quinn thought for a moment, "I remember reading Nietzsche's *God is Dead.* He argued against Judeo-Christian morals. That a person should be who they are, not constrained by master and slave morals. That the nobility that held power established what were good morals for their benefit, and the peasants twisted those master-moral virtues to appear evil for their benefit. In his *Revaluation of All Values*, he argued that mankind has entered a downward spiral toward complete decadence. That modern man was decaying on the inside through his 'advanced' morality."

"It would seem that Nietzsche is exposing the results of the Jesuit intervention in worldwide culture," Eisenhower offered. "The peasants twisting the virtues of morality is what gave Lenin his Bolshevik Revolution. But then, Tsar Nickolas II was no saint as a leader, either. Some man will always rise to take control, and if he has an army following him, he will always be successful. The majority of people only want to live in peace, able to feed their children, go on vacation, and enjoy the gifts of God. But the common man must realize that he cannot afford that luxury. He can no longer sit on the side lines; he must choose sides. There will always be those with a satanic-like drive to control the common man. That is, until the end times when God will put an end to all that evil."

"I think you're correct, sir. Most Americans could care less what the government is doing, as long as it stays out of their house and their daily functioning with their families. But now the government has changed exponentially in an aggressively intrusive way."

"Now, as to your question about the Age of Pisces versus the Age of Aquarius, and of course, you realize that we're not talking about birth signs, but astrological constellation ages."

"Yes, sir, I realize that," Quinn said.

Eisenhower sat back down and opened the laptop computer on the conference table. "I love this Internet; I can find anything I want within seconds! You know, Quinn, that the Internet, the worldwide web is the idea of Joseph C.R. Licklider, an American, who was educated in America! This is the kind of technology that Tsaeb's America Invents Act will allow to be stolen from Americans in the future. Fortunately, the U.S. Defense Department hired Licklider back in 1962, when the U.S. Constitution and its patent law had not yet been thrown out.

On this website," Eisenhower pointed at the screen, "it talks about the differences between the Age of Pisces and the Age of Aquarius. Let me interject here that each of the 12 astrological ages of constellations spans an approximate 2150 years, in which the Earth's rotational axis is wobbling in to a different location, into a different age. The wobbling is called processional movement. It completes this axial rotation across some

26,000 years altogether. All right?"

"Got it," Quinn said.

"To the website. It claims that 'in no other age of human history had faith…risen to the large scale as it has in this (current) Age of Pisces…it has been the meteoric rise of one religion, Christianity…One of the symbols of Christianity is the fish…"

Quinn interrupted, "The sons of thunder!"

Eisenhower looked at Quinn, "That's right. Mark 1:16-20, Jesus called Simon, Andrew, and the sons of thunder: James and John, 'Come after me, and I will make you to become fishers of men.'

Eisenhower turned back to the website:

'The age of Pisces can be described as the age of revelation versus reason, then the Aquarius age will be the age of collective integrity versus individual dignity. In the Piscean Age we looked to have our minds and souls revealed to us, either through our imaginations or interpretations of Divinity…We're already at the dawn of the Aquarius age…modernity has crept into almost every nook and cranny of human life everywhere…(commercial marketing) ads…constantly compel us to evaluate our social standing and our connections to others…we are never quite good enough as we are…and if we are not connected together (through cable, television, cellphones, Internet, electricity, gas)…we cease to exist…(this leads to the) future… struggle for individual dignity and expression versus…majesty of collective's network…peace will be based on conformity…government will watch your every move…(commercial) marketing will put us into groups *without* individuality…and individual destines.'" (http://return2thesource.wordpress.com/2012/01/25/the-darker-side-of-the-age-of-aquarius-2/)

"There seems to be a relationship between this technological, commercial grouping of people and the Jesuit corralling the people, for Satan's control through this perspective of modernism. For this Age of Aquarius.

Eisenhower frowned, "As to the Jesuits, listen, Quinn, the other thing that you need to know is that, as President, John Kennedy made a trip to see Pope Paul VI, on July 2, 1963, just three days after the enthronement of Satan. Kennedy met with Pope Paul personally, to give him the message that the FBI had reported to Kennedy about the enthronement, and to ask the Pope to reverse the enthronement. But the Pope refused, saying he couldn't. At the time of the meeting, Paul had no other response; he was taken aback by the FBI's knowledge of the events of June 29, 1963. Obviously, there was a U.S. spy in the Vatican. The Jesuits aren't the only ones who know how to infiltrate!

What Pope Paul did was respond in a letter to Kennedy: 'with candor your (Kennedy's) words recall the higher moral principles of truth, of justice and of liberty. We find a spontaneous harmony with that which Our Venerable Predecessor, Pope John XXIII, said in his last Encyclical Letter, '*Pacem in Terris*,' when he presented anew to the world the

Church's constant teaching on the dignity of the individual human person, a dignity which the Almighty Creator bestowed in creating man to His own image and likeness....'" (Collection: Papers of JFK, Presidential Papers, President's Office Files; Series Name: Special Correspondence; Contributor: Cushing, Cardinal Richard J., 1895-1970, Paul VI, Pope, 1897-1978, Digital Identifier: JFKPOF-032-001; www/jfklibrary.org/Asset-viewer/Archives/JFKPOF-032-001.aspx)

It was never certain what the Pope meant, whether he was dealing with a system, a Jesuit system, that he had no power to control, or whether there were spies all around him, keeping him from reversing the enthronement. It was not something he was going to attempt, and that's the bottom line. That alleged 'dignity of the individual human' is an allusion to Renaissance humanism; modernism, where man is on equal footing with God because science has come up with the Big Bang theory – whereby the universe created itself. This attempt to define Church teachings in the light of modern revolutions and science and philosophy – ends up putting that dignity of man in a standing position when receiving the Holy Eucharist. That dignity of the democratic modern man is that he is too self-valued to kneel before his Creator. Science today is working toward ousting God from all creation – Darwin's theory was one such attempt – man came from an evolved amoeba – hence, there never was any Garden of Eden. We're all from the same parent – there are no good and evil bloodlines. But always remember their satanic rule: 'THE GUARANTEE OF OUR TOMORROW IS TODAY'S PERSUASION THAT WE DO NOT EXIST.'

"It seems to me, sir, that the only thing that's going to stop all this is armed revolution."

Eisenhower paused, then asked Quinn, "Have you seen the Youtubes showing the millions of blue coffins they already have in the FEMA camps?"

Quinn mumbled, "Yes. I've seen them."

He looked at Quinn for a moment and then asked, "Have you ever read of Mordechai Nisan Kiyunim, he's been cited in the Official Publication of the World Zionist Organization, August 1984, pp 151-156, as saying, "If gentiles refuse to live a life of inferiority, then this signals their rebellion and the unavoidable necessity of Jewish warfare against their very presence,' (http://meetchristians.com/new/tr_fr_view_thread.php?TID=122219).

And as you know, Jews erroneously, intentionally mislead, by referring to anyone who is not a Zionist as a Gentile. The Zionists are the Gentiles. They are very organized worldwide in their goal to take control of the world and hand it to their father, Satan. Right now, they have waged a covert war with the Muslims over who will take control of American law – Noahide Law or the laws of the Qur'an. But either one will give the United States to Satan. It's a silent fight between brothers to be the favorite of their father.

Quinn moaned quietly, as a chill ran down his spine. He thought of his children and of Maggie; all of them are Christians. How would he be able to protect them all; how could he fight in this revolution and protect them? He decided to consider those thoughts when he got home. But now he wanted to learn as much as possible of what had been going on to bring us to where the world is today. Somehow, in his childhood and in his young adulthood, he never considered the events of the past as having any impact on today's world. All of those events he left behind in his history classes and he now lived in the real world. He laughed a snide admonishment of himself. We all think that we live in the real world of today, enlightened by science, mocking those of the past who lived without air conditioning, TV, and cell phones. He had always felt superior to those of the past because of the technology that science brought to today's world. What he had come to realize was that today we live in another type of Dark Age; a total oblivion as to what Satan and his descendants were preparing for the world, for Christians. Satan had deceived us, yet again.

Eisenhower continued, painfully so for Quinn, "The United Nations has made a decision to accept the applications for Consultative Status of non-governmental organizations (NGO); one of them is the Institute of Noahide Code,' (www.un.org/en/ecosoc/docs/2011/dec%202011.228 .pdf). This means that the United Nations is going to, at least, consider instituting the Noahide Laws throughout the world.

And there is movement towards getting the United Nations to consider them. 'A conference advocating for the acceptance and adherence to the Noahide Laws was held on December 22, 2010. Mr. Joop Theunissen Deputy Chief of the NGO branch of the United Nations Economic and Social Council <u>signed a proclamation pledging to keep the Laws of Noah</u>. *Their observance is <u>required</u>, so that the vision of the United Nations – to have a settled and civilized world*, in which economic justice and *righteousness* will prevail.... Following the conference the participants...agreed to support these ideas of 'Unity and Youth' to help bring *world peace with the Laws of Noah*,' (http://noahide.org/article.asp? Level= 596&Parent=88).

Quinn sighed heavily, looked at Eisenhower, "Sir, how in God's name did we get to this point?"

Eisenhower frowned, nodded, "I understand, son. I understand how you feel." He thought for a moment and then began, "The elements that we face today actually began in the 3rd century with Plotinus, A.D. 205-270, who founded Neo-Platonism. They affect us today because Neo-Platonism was resurrected in the early Italian Renaissance; it is very similar to Arius' theory; Arianism denied the divinity of Jesus, which led to the schism of the Catholic Church in 1054, just 20 years after Satan was let out of the bottomless pit; and Neo-Platonism gave a basis to the Christian Humanist of the Renaissance – the dignity of man – which today has been essentially instituted through the Jesuits into Vatican II documents and Church constitution. Neo-Platonism eventually led to the Age of Enlightenment of the 18th century, while traditional churches still supported and defended the kings of Europe, Enlightenment subsequently led to America's Declaration of Independence and the instituting of the notion of equality, freedom of speech and press. But eventually, it will all lead to getting rid of God and put Satan in control of the earth. I realize that seems a long stretch, but bear with me as I attempt to explain the connections.

Let me first say this, Plotinus was a pagan, which only means that he was not Christian and not Jewish. And Muhammad had not yet created Islam. You can see this in the *Ennead, On the Life of Plotinus and the Arrangement of his Work*, #23. This was written by his student, Porphyry, and was translated by Stephen MacKenna, 2004, www.sacred.texts.com/cla/plotenn/ enn001.htm. In it, Porphyry writes that Plotinus, upon his death, 'entered the celestial circle where…Minos and Rhadamanthus and Aeacus, the sons of God, are enthroned as judges of souls…as welcoming him (Plotinus) to their consort to which are bidden spirits pleasing to the Gods – Plato, Pythagoras, and all the people of the Choir of Immortal Love, there…made happy by the Gods.'

Porphyry gets this notion of Minos, Rhadamanthus, and Aeacus and their being judges of the dead from Homer's *Odyssey*, Book 4.560ff, *Prophecy delivered to Menelaus*, www.perseus.tufts.edu/ cgi-bin/ptext?lookup=Hom %2e+Od%2e+4%2e561%2d569. The Odyssey is a Greek mythological epic poem, written by Homer in the 8th century BC. And Porphyry also gets the idea from Plato's use in *Gorgias*, line 524A, before 348 BC, and Virgil's use in his *Aeneid*, 44 BC. Thus, Porphyry places Plotinus, as well as himself, in the company of the great classics. Rhadamanthus was one of three judges of the dead, judging the souls of easterners, Asiatics, who were virtuous – together the righteous Asiatics and Rhadamanthus dwelled in the Elysian Fields of the Underworld of Hades. Aeacus was a judge of the dead souls of westerners; Minos cast the deciding vote, according to Plato."

"In other words," Quinn interrupted, "Porphyry claims that Plotinus, a real human being, entered a Greek myth – that his soul went to Hades! Additionally, that Hades was a good place!"

"Yes. And this is problematic to conflate reality and mythology. Where is the line of demarcation? Is there a difference, in the minds of Plotinus and Porphyry, between reality and myth? Did Plotinus base his Neo-Platonism on mythology?"

Eisenhower continued as he gestured, "But let's move on. It's necessary to briefly examine Neo-Platonism, which held that the source of all things is the One – everything emerges from the One. Hmmm, it just occurred to me – I've always assumed that Plotinus was referring the One to God, as in the God of Abraham, but that's not necessarily so. He could be talking about Haides the King of the Underworld, the god of death and the dead, ruler over all the other gods of Hades. Is Plotinus actually saying that the One is Satan? Anyway, Plotinus asserts that from the One there emerges Mind or Intellect, in which eternal ideas (like Beauty, Justice, etc.) are found. Both the One and Mind are eternal, unchanging, outside of time. Next there emerges Soul, and in this appears the experience of time. From the Soul emerges matter, the material world, which is farthest from the One. At the level of Soul, we find not only time but also space and matter, material bodies, birth and death,' (www.wku.edu/~jan.garrett /arius.htm).

Quinn interrupted, again, "Immediately, I have a problem with this theory – from the Soul comes matter! That the Soul is inside of time! Sir, as I understand time – from what the Bible, Gen. 1:5, says, 'there was evening and morning one day.' says time began after the universe was created – that the rotation of the earth on its axis brings about day and then night – this day and night is time. It would be intuitively incorrect to say that the Soul was created after the universe was created – created inside time.

Eisenhower agreed, "But there is a difference between Biblical time dependent on the earth's rotation on its axis and philosophical time having to do with space and time. I don't want to bother with time. Keep in mind that philosophy is a presentation of puzzles, or a maze, if you will. The greater the maze a philosopher can create while contemplating his navel, the greater he is considered. If answers result, they are non-provable. And to our exercise philosophical time is irrelevant, for the moment, at least. Let's just say philosophical time distinguishes between eternal rather than non-eternal beings.

But there is a disconnect between the Neo-Platonic model of the Soul and Plato's model of the Soul, even though Plotinus allegedly used Plato as a guide for Plotinus' philosophy. This disconnect is everything. It is the basis, if you don't consider Philo of Alexandria, the Jewish philosopher who lived during the time of Jesus, it is the beginning of the problems we face today, which I'll explain later.

Now, Plotinus based his logic of the One, the Mind, and Soul on a presumption that he created, which opposes Plato and is false. Plotinus asserted that the One is outside of time, that is, he existed before time began, thus before the universe was created. And Plotinus assigns the Soul as being created after the universe was created, therefore, the Soul was create inside time. This is wrong! For me, it makes no logical sense. The Soul is an eternal entity, cannot be destroyed, as the universe, the earth, can be destroyed – look at the stars, supernovas, they are created and die – they are made of matter and don't live in the spiritual world as we do," Eisenhower gestured toward the spirits sitting around the conference room table. Even you," Eisenhower pointed at Quinn, you are alive, your living body is made of matter, but here is your soul. Our bodies have died, but we continue to exist as souls. Your soul will go back to your living body – your body relates to Biblical time, it sleeps at night and works in day, but your soul does not.

"The Soul never dies and only God, the God of Abraham, can create a soul, thus it is eternal. Yet Plotinus states that the Soul was created inside time, therefore, non-eternal. Time begins, as you pointed out, with the rotation of the earth, and that rotation creates a time for us on earth, but not in the universe. The universe does not have a day and night as we do on earth. That is, except relative to our seeing the creation and death of stars according to our time here on earth. And relative to how long it takes for that vision of activity to reach us here on earth after passing through the distance of space. Plotinus argued that Soul was created at the same time that planets and galaxies were created, making them non-eternal. But time in other galaxies, on other planets do have a time that is or could be different than ours – depending on the speed of rotation of those planets being either faster or slower than the rotation of earth, and whether they have a solar system. And what about distant stars without a solar system like ours – those stars have a beginning and an end, yet their timeframe of existence is not measured by any nearby sun. The point is that time is relevant to location - space. Beyond that, however, Plotinus placing the Soul inside time, implies that the Soul does die, has an end just as the stars have an end, eventually. But we know through evidence of our existence that Soul must have been created outside of time, as an eternal being. Plato's description of the Soul being eternal relates to the entire universe, and that is correct.

Eisenhower lean back in his chair, gestured with his hands, "You see, Plato had it right when he argued that God 'did not make the Soul *after* the body of the Universe.' Time is relative – to us, but God is relative to all existence, our bodies are not. For God, time does not exist, at least, not the way we think of time. God gave us time to order the chaos. Plotinus is creating chaos. Okay?"

Quinn nodded quietly.

"Plato argued, 'for when He put them, the Soul and the Universe, together He would never have all owed that the elder, Soul, should be ruled by the younger Universe …*Whereas He made the soul in* origin*…prior to and older than the body (the Universe)*, to be the ruler and mistress, of whom the body, the Universe, was to be the subject,' (*Plato*, The Collected Dialogues, Hamilton, E. et al, ed., Bollinger Series LXXI, Princeton, 1987, *Timaeus*, 34b8-c6.)

"That makes sense to me," Quinn replied. "But Plotinus is saying the opposite. As I understand Plato, the Soul being eternal was made in origin – in the beginning – before God set out to create the universe, earth, and man."

"Exactly, and when you think about it – these pseudo intellectuals, such as Plotinus, think that everything begins in the Mind, that is to say, that God existed and then He created the Mind, the Mind is eternal, outside of time, and the Mind created the Soul inside time, suggesting that the Soul is less and non-eternal, that the Soul participates in time and created Matter, earth, space, etc. They use the word emanate as in – the Soul flows out – falls out of the Mind, but regardless of saying create or emanate – they still have it wrong – the Soul is primary, original, eternal. God is Soul and Intellect; God created the universe and our individual souls. This is a very significant difference to Plotinus' philosophy.

Plotinus says that the activity of Soul creates individual souls. Plotinus assigns a task to the Soul – that the Soul must think creatively about the Forms of the Mind, which are eternal, such as Beauty, Justice, Evil, Goodness, Virtue, etc., etc. – Plotinus takes from Plato his idea of the eternal Forms. The eternal Form, say that of a chair – is anything that supports a person's bottom as their body is bent at the knees and hips. That's why they can call both a stool and a throne – a chair, appearance makes no difference. In other words, in its eternal Form, a thing must possess certain traits or function to give it a unique Form. Good has different traits than Evil, their traits cannot intermingle in identifying one separate from the other. Okay?"

"Got it," Quinn said.

Okay, so Plotinus argues that the task of the Soul is to think about these eternal Forms creatively, and when it does the result is that the Soul creates numerous individual souls. The Soul becomes divided outside of itself, through action, which is contemplation, *Ennead* III.8.4. 'This division of the Soul is the Cosmos – the creative act of the Soul is also referred to as Nature. When the individual soul reflects upon Nature as its own act – this individual soul is capable of attaining insight into the essence of the Mind. But when the Soul views Nature as something outside of its own creation – evil and suffering ensue. For you see, Plotinus argues that the One does not act to produce a cosmos (universe) or a spiritual order, but simply generates from itself, a power which is the Mind/Intellect, and it's up to the Mind to contemplate ordered thoughts that produce the Being of eternal Forms. Plotinus holds that the Mind, therefore, is the sole First Principle of life,' (www.iep.utm.edu/neoplato/).

In other words, without the Mind there would be nothing, no life. Plotinus states that 'the One subsists by thinking itself as itself,' (*Ibid.*) – and the One does nothing else except generate from Itself the Mind/Intellect. The One, therefore, generates the Mind and goes back into Itself, oblivious to what the Mind and the Soul later created."

"It would seem to me," Quinn responded, "and I will assume here that Plotinus is talking about God, that Plotinus assigning God to spend His time thinking of only Himself, separates God from mankind. And Plotinus also divides God, when he claims that God generated from Himself a power that is the Mind. Then leaves it up to the Mind to only think of the eternal Forms of things that only the Mind decides will exist. In other words, God does not decide what exists – only the Mind does. And that it is up to the Soul to bring those eternal Forms in to existence. The Soul is the production manager of an assembly line in a factory – working from the blueprints that the Mind designed. Plotinus has created a model of God as three separate entities, though the Mind and the Soul are less than the One – they came into being from the One generating the Mind. And since Plotinus' Mind is eternal – he implies that the Mind is as divine as the One. But the Soul, created inside time – is not divine, not eternal. Why does he make this argument?"

Eisenhower smiled, "Very good, Quinn. The Why of it all. Well, his guide was Plato, but that doesn't answer the Why of any type of philosophy that makes this all so complicated. It seems to me that these philosophers try to elevate themselves to an elite status by inventing – which is what they are doing – inventing a very complicated functioning model – like a chess game with the pieces restricted by rules assigned by the game's inventor, Plotinus.

For me, I look at it this way. God existed – having so much power, He created the angels, buddies that He can hang out with, so to speak. He created the universe to look at, the way an artist creates a masterpiece – because He can, and because it's nice to look at. Everything was pleasing to Him, but God was lonely. And just as a man and woman decide to have a second or third child to bring fullness to their family, God created mankind. He created mankind to have someone to love – and for them to love Him. I think God is very much involved in our lives, Quinn, – and is not spending His time contemplating Himself. That is just absurd – to even consider that, one must be a narcissist always thinking of themselves, therefore, God being better than I, surely He thinks only of Himself – because they would. They are projecting their personality onto God."

"And beyond that," Quinn added, "The idea that contemplates Himself – thus not involved in our lives, separating mankind from God, opens the way to evil. If mankind feels helpless in the world, and we all suffer simply because we are attached to bodies that every day move towards death – we look for an omnipotent being to take care of us. If God is viewed as not involved with our suffering, our fear, then where else can we turn – but to Satan? Mankind must realize that God is involved, but the seed of David is still being punished for Solomon and the Israelites' worship of Satan."

"That punishment stated in the Bible has been washed aside, a seduction of Satan through the work of Plotinus, for one." Eisenhower straightened in his chair. "So, that was Plotinus in the 3rd century. I'll touch upon his student Porphyry, A.D. 234-305, in a minute; he's the one that organized Plotinus' essays in the *Ennead.* But right now, let's talk about Arius, who lived in Egypt, in A.D. 256-336. So, Arius was 14 years old when Plotinus died, but 49 when Porphyry died. It is arguable that Arius read the *Ennead*, the compilation of Plotinus' work, because Arius' philosophy is quite similar to Plotinus'. By the way, Plotinus was born in Egypt, but, according to Porphyry, refused to tell of his genealogy or have his image painted or sculpted.

Arius, was a Black Libyan Christian priest living in Egypt, and came up with the idea that Jesus was not divine. This creates great turmoil 'within Christianity for a century,' (www.bookrags. com/research/arius-and-arianism-eoph/).

But in the beginning of the century, the 4th century Christians – such as those who attended the First Council of Nicaea, in A.D. 325, which was convened by Roman Emperor Constantine I, who had legalized Christianity in the Roman Empire, tried to resolve Arius' assertion.

'The 4th century Christian intellectuals wanted a systematic understanding of the meaning of their faith – they turned to the current Greek philosophy, and, at the time, the most influential was Neo-Platonism, this is Plotinus' philosophy. 'Many Christian theologians of the 4th century tried to understand the relationship between God, Jesus Christ, and the Holy…(Ghost) on the same model. The Christian theologians' understanding of God the Father is modeled heavily on the Neo-Platonic One. Jesus Christ is assigned the same relative position as the Intellect (Mind) in Neo-Platonism. Jesus is generated from God the Father. Jesus is caused, brought into existence, by God the Father, but God the Father is uncaused; He always existed. But all this causation takes place in eternity, outside of time. The Neo-Platonic model would dictate that Jesus Christ, though divine, (but brought into existence by the Father, He, therefore) would be a lesser god than God the Father,'" (*Ibid.*).

Eisenhower looked at Quinn, "This is where all the trouble began, you might say – this is what the Zionists and the Muslims take for their argument. Jesus, as a subordinate god, makes the worship of Jesus, idolatry. This is the argument that our U.S. Congress has put before the American people with the Education Day USA legislation, imposing the Noahide Laws on people, which they are about to enforce. Plotinus' and Arius' notion that Jesus, in their philosophy, is demoted to a lesser god. Prior to Plotinus was the philosopher Origen, A.D. 185-254, who described Jesus as Word, and ascribed a lesser and derivative nature to Jesus. And before Origen, in 20 BC to A.D. 40, was Philo of Alexandria, a Jewish philosopher – in the day that Jesus was with us. All of these philosophers held a view of a hierarchical nature between God and Jesus. 'Philo asserted that Jesus was a mediator between the transcendent (above human) reality and the material world, as well as noting biblical accounts of the Son's obedience to the Father. By contrast, Arius denied any communication or participation of essence between the Father and the Son.', (*Ibid.*)."

What Plotinus argued was the absolute opposite of what Plato had asserted. Plato is saying that God made the Soul – outside of time, therefore, eternal. Plotinus argued that the Soul emerges from the Mind, notably inside time. That's blatantly illogical. Plotinus argued that the One is uncaused, no one made Him. Plotinus then postulates, as in – to ASSUME the truth...with NO PROOF as a basis of an argument – that the Mind was made by the One, and that Soul was created/emerges from the Mind, and then that Matter is created/emerges from Soul. This is a ludicrous argument – these 4th century Christian intellectuals buying in to this argument cannot be considered intellectuals. They bought in to a fad – the latest fad that would titillate their egos as learned men and separate them out as intellectuals from the peasants – we do this kind of thing today. It's hubris. Mankind always wants to point to someone and think – I'm better than he, and they are disgusting, therefore, my shit doesn't smell and theirs does. It's a way to keep oneself feeling safe, creating a buffer zone between them and the mob mentality of bullying and bashing of the weakest – that permeates society, every society.

And I believe that every other argument ever made about the Soul – is that it is immortal, therefore, eternal! I mean, Sir," Quinn sighed, "I could go on and on quoting other works of Plato, quoting the Bible, quoting other philosophers – to prove the point that the Soul has always been consider immortal, therefore, eternal, therefore outside of time. Sure, there are those who believe that when we die – that's the end of us, but then they don't believe that a Soul exists in the first place. So, let's leave them out of the argument."

Suddenly Quinn laughed, "Look at us! Here we are – in full expression of our Souls – Sir, your body died, but your soul lives on! That is a clear separation between the eternal Soul and the non-eternal material world of our bodies."

Eisenhower smiled and nodded, yes, the Soul is eternal, therefore, it must have been created outside of time – for time has no impact on it, cannot diminish it, cannot kill it."

"I'd like to know who the hell this Plotinus character is – and especially those 4th century Christian, alleged, intellectuals – were they like today's Jesuits who have taken control of the Catholic Church – like the Jesuits who wrote Jesus and the Holy Ghost out of the Mass, out of the Catholic prayers?" Quinn asked.

Eisenhower frowned, "I have to interject a note here. There are several things to consider – who is good; who is bad; who is noble, but has been corrupted? You see, son, Satan's end goal is to show the world that God is weak – that he, Satan, would be a better god. Once that is achieved Satan will then capture all our souls; he will then have dominion over the earth and all those living upon the earth. That is straight from Genesis and Satan's jealousy of Adam – and Adam's lineage. Satan uses seduction, a powerful tactic, to cause a good soul to be an unintended carrier to convince others to do evil. This carrier is a host, just like a person being a carrier of a virus, for the host is critical to evil. The host hides the message of evil, while unknowing spreading that evil. There are many tools, souls, that Satan uses of which we must be aware, for there is devious artistry in them. A good soul is used like a knife to surgically cut an intricate design of evil. When Satan is able to use an institution, or a good soul in achieving his goal to humiliate and corrupt everything God has made, Satan sees that as delicious. The fundamental nature of God's adversary is flawed because he, Satan, doesn't realize that he is going to fail. But along the way, when he is able to take the institution of the priesthood and corrupt it with priests sexually abusing children – it's not his end goal, it's just a delicious appetizer, for it undermines everything that is God's.

So, the use of philosophy as a way to frame religion, Christianity, has a significant consequence. Anytime you hand over to another the foundation of your faith and conditions of your worship – Satan takes over. Every individual must think for themselves – what and who God is. This is what Jesus meant, Luke 17:21, 'Neither shall they say: Behold here, or behold there. For lo, the kingdom of God is within you.' Ask the question: Who are the philosophers to 'assign' Jesus Christ to the position of the Mind, and assert Jesus is a lesser god? How are those philosophers better suited to define your belief in Jesus – than you are?

I would like to give philosophy a definition, but 'philosophical issues and reflections are notorious for their inconclusiveness – it is virtually impossible to give one universally accepted definition of philosophy. Philosophy pursues questions rather than answers. It questions given answers. A philosopher is someone who can make a riddle out of any answer. Also, philosophy changes historically both in respect to its content and its character. The nature of philosophy is better determined by making reference to its attitude, source, and objective. The source of philosophic questioning is the sense of wonder, a childlike wonder of just about everything. Philosophy starts with bewilderment, astonishment, amazement about the world, life, and ourselves. Philosophy reveals the illusion of knowledge where none in reality exists. Philosophy constantly remains on the level of conceptual analysis, critical examination, new ideas, and so time and again fails to produce definitive 'positive results. Philosophy studies the questions that are in principle not answerable. Questions such as, 'Does God exist?' resist definite answers by their very nature,'"(Zunjic, www.uri.edu/personal/szunjic/philos/whystudy .htm).

Eisenhower continued, "'Philosophy reveals the illusion of knowledge where none in reality exists'! (*Ibid.*) And Christianity looking for a systematic understanding of the meaning of their faith borrowed from Greek philosophy, as Garrett (*Supra*) stated, was wrong. Yet, it is arguable, that Constantine I, in legalizing Christianity, was a noble soul that Satan used – in evil artistry to effect a delicious appetizer that washed away the words of Jesus – the kingdom of God is within you. Constantine's error was in looking to those who can only offer an illusion of knowledge to determine the meaning of faith – for this hands your faith over to evil manipulation.

Eisenhower pensively rubbed his chin, "There is religion and its conceptual articulation (theology), that is, religion's expression by clear language, 'both are grounded on a revealed truth. Religious beliefs cannot be proven by strict demonstration. The certainty of these beliefs is based on personal acceptance of religious tradition and authority. The common aim of both religion and theology is to strengthen our convictions and to give us an overarching sense of life and the universe. By contrast, philosophy is a critical activity – its aim is not to uphold any set of beliefs but rather to undermine everything that tends to get instilled in the mind. Philosophy often challenges faith and dogmatic tenets (beliefs proclaimed as true), offering instead only doubt and uncertainty. At best, philosophy is innocent but useless trifling, hair-splitting distinctions, and controversies on matters concerning which knowledge is impossible and with its protracted questioning only complicates our life and disturbs the peace of our mind.'" (*Ibid.*)

"I understand what you are saying, Sir," Quinn responded.

Eisenhower nodded, "Now, you have Niccolo Machiavelli, 1469-1527, an Italian philosopher during the Renaissance who rejected the views of Aristotle and Thomas Aquinas as unrealistic. Machiavelli asserted that the ideal sovereign (king/president) is not the embodiment of the moral virtues; rather the sovereign does whatever is successful and necessary, rather than what is morally praiseworthy. And with Rene Descartes (1596-1650) – remember his assertion – 'I think, therefore, I am.' Descartes is considered the father of modern philosophy."

Quinn nodded.

"Descartes asserted that many philosophical doctrines were meaningless and false. He proposed to begin philosophy from scratch. He tried to determine what he knows for certain. Through this process, Descartes realized that some of the ideas he had could not have come from his own mind, but only from God; he proved that God exists. What is significant about his findings is that he concluded that God would prohibit his being deceived about everything."

Eisenhower paused a moment, "So, when you ask who were these philosophers, Plotinus, Porphyry, Philo – it doesn't actually matter in view of what their message was and how did it corrupted or humiliated God, humiliated His Son. Plotinus, Arius, Philo may well have been good souls, intending to do good, or they may been evil with a clear intent to cause a schism in the Church, as Arius' notion that denied the divinity of Jesus. Our job today is to look at the philosophy that had such a great impact on religion, society, and decide for ourselves – does it make any sense?"

Eisenhower sat up straight in his chair, "Let's put the whole thing in perspective, which isn't easy – in the 4th century, the Council of Nicea in A.D. 325, which attempted to reach an orthodox consensus and unify Christendom as the official religion of the Roman Empire. There was the struggle between Christianity and Paganism.

Plotinus had lived in the 3rd century, A.D. 205-270; he was a mystic as well as a philosopher who used Plato as his guide – whose Neoplatonic movement was motivated by the desire of Plotinus to revive the pagan philosophical tradition, as stated by George Henry Lewes, in his book, *A Biographical History of Philosophy,* Routledge & Sons, 1892, p 294. 'as Plotinus had endeavored to revive the religious spirit of paganism.'

Then there was Plotinus' student, Porphyry – Porphyry applied

'Neoplatonic doctrines to traditional pagan religion and myths,' (Emilsson, Eyjolfur, *Porphyry*, The Stanford Encyclopedia of Philosophy (Summer 2011 Edition), Edward n. Zalta (ed.).

And Porphyry is portrayed by Bidez in, *La vie de Porphre*, 1913, 'as someone prone to religion and superstition. Porphyry also commented on the *Chaldean Oracles*, a pagan religious text of the 2nd century A.D. that later Neo-Platonists took for a divine revelation. Porphyry's interpretation of religious matters opened the way for later developments and the subsequent tradition of pagan Neo-Platonism.' (*Ibid.*).

Porphyry edited Plotinus' essays, and organized them into the *Enneads.* Porphyry wrote *Against the Christians*, 'which was an educated man's studied attack on Christian theology. He attacked Christians' intelligence, integrity, and morals to undermine the new, up-start religion, Christianity,' (R. Joseph Hoffman, www.scribd.com/doc/40065026/Porphyry-s-Against-the-Christians-TheLiterary-Remains).

Eisenhower sat back in his chair, "Then you had Marsilio Ficino, 1433-1492, and Pico della Mirandola, 1463-1494, who rediscovered, translate, the original texts of Platonism. Ficino brought the pagan philosophy, Neo-Platonism, of Plotinus and Porphyry to the early Italian Renaissance. These were the 'brilliant Italian thinkers,' (www.iep.utm.edu/ neoplato/) that you asked about.

Marsilio Ficino, 'Christianity,' he said, 'must rest on philosophic grounds' – this is the fellow who introduced Platonic philosophy to Europe. Ficino followed the thought that began with the Egyptians and advanced until Plato takes up the mysteries of religion and cast them in a form that made it possible for the neo-Platonist to set them forth clearly,' (www.newadvent.org/cathen/06067b.htm). Remember that the Egyptians descended from Ham, a descendant of Satan.

The question to ask this brilliant intellectual, Ficino – why – must Christianity rest on philosophic grounds when Jesus told us in His Own words – the 'Kingdom of God is within you,' Luke 17:21. And since philosophy is a critical activity that undermines and challenges faith, why ground Christian faith on something that will destroy it? Ficino, as a philosopher who can make a riddle out of any answer, elevates himself intimidatingly above the peasants who have not studied philosophy. His words demand that attention be given to what he says, rather than what Jesus said. Why should Christianity be grounded on a puzzle that was created by a riddle master? The lofty study of philosophy, study of riddle-making, opposes what Jesus told us: 'unless you…become as little children, you shall not enter into the kingdom of heaven,' (Matt. 18:3). Children love purely, without riddles, without the arrogance of the riddle masters.

This is the intersection of leaders opposing citizens, the intersection of Popes opposing the faithful – the intersection of Satan's deceit and individualism. Here, is where mankind surrendered its survival of body and soul to those few who will take them to hell.

And as to Pico della Mirandola, another neo-Platonist philosopher of the Renaissance, he's famous for his Oration on the Dignity of Man, called the 'Manifesto of the Renaissance.' It was a public discourse given in 1486 by Pico, all about the attributes of human capacity and human perspective. Pico taught that humans had an amazing capacity for achievement. This speech was a key text of the Renaissance Humanism. Pico was 'the first Christian scholar to use Kabbalistic (Jewish) doctrine in support of Christian theology; he was going to publicly speak in defense of 900 theses (propositions) drawn from Greek, Hebrew, Arabic, and Latin writers, but Pope Innocent VIII prohibited the discourse; Pico spent time in prison for his attempt.

Pope Innocent VIII, 1484-1492, is another major player in the chaos of the time. It could be argued that he did more to hurt the Catholic Church and mankind, especially woman, than any other human that walked the face of the earth, besides Satan himself."

Quinn sat up straight in his chair, preparing for the worst.

Eisenhower leaned forward, "What this individual did started with his buying his election as pope. His opponent within the Conclave sought revenge by stripping the Vatican treasury. Innocent VIII," Eisenhower spurt out air in disgust, shaking his head, "How ironic the name he chose for himself. Well, he decided to institute programs to bring money into the Vatican. He created 'offices that he sold, sold indulgences (release from punishment due for sin), increased tariffs set on nobility for their investitures by the Catholic Church; he patronized the slave trade of Spain and Portugal, receiving a share of the profits. Then he came up with somewhat of an ingenious idea – to create a witchcraft scare. He issued a Papal Bull, Summis desiderantes, December 5, 1484, that would take severe measures against magicians and witches in Germany, thus, making the population fearful that they were overrun with witchcraft. He issued a number of Papal Bulls that strengthened the power of the Inquisition and found new ways of burning people – Papal Bull Summis desiderantes affectibus (1484), reinforcing the standing Church law, allowing marriage annulment and seizure of assets of any person (almost exclusively women) found a heretic. He targeted rich and ancient families and stole all their wealth under the pretext of heresy, particularly noble women of wealth. Then this piece of," Eisenhower took a deep breath and held it for a moment, trying to calm himself. "'Pope Innocent VIII commissioned two Dominican monks heavily involved in both satanic practice and ritual murder, Henrich Kramer and James Sprenger, to write Malleus Maleficrum (The Witches Hammer) – one of the most unholy and bloodthirsty books in human history. You see, he needed a manuscript to spread fear and panic concerning the devil worship and witchcraft. He had it copied and sent out to all the Bishops to promote the fear of witches among the congregation. Then he issued another Papal Bull – the unbelief in witchcraft as heresy and women are more likely to become witches 'because the female sex is more concerned with things of the flesh than men.' When Moorish Granada, Spain fell in war, in celebration, he distributed over 100 of the finest Moorish slaves among the Curia (Vatican administration) and to his friends as gifts! At the time of his death, the Vatican was overrun with more than 100 illegitimate children with cost of maintaining his women – he never married, but had 16 illegitimate children which caused a financial crisis. (http://one-evil.org/people /people_15c_ Innocent_VIII.htm).

The witch hunts that he began lasted 300 years. It took women 400 years to get over the trauma – for the punishment was always made on a public platform. On one occasion they stripped the women from the waste up, lashed them with whips, then one woman's breast was cut off and shoved into her mouth. Women stopped all socializing too fearful of even talking to other women less someone would accuse them, by association, of being a witch. It was a time of the 'pricker' – without credentials sometimes a man would walk into a village and point to any woman that he wanted to exam, of course, in the presents of another village woman. Sometimes the other woman would do the examining, sometimes the pricker would examine – every inch of the woman's body – looking for signs that indicated that she was a witch, such as a mold. The pricker, usually working for the pope, would use an instrument that was rigged to give a false positive reading that the woman was a witch. No one could stop the pricker, no one."

Quinn replied, "I read that Malleus Maleficrum – the obvious is that it was written by sociopaths who hated women and everything about them. It's also obvious that the hatred came from their lust of women that they could never charm. By becoming a pricker for the pope – they were able to paw the body of any and every woman they desired. The woman's father, brother, or husband could not stop the pervert – or they would be burned alive as a witch, also. As you said, Sir, the intersection between the Popes and the faithful – Satan and individualism – thinking for ourselves – that these witch hunts were of evil origin and must be stopped and then stopping it. But they didn't stop until Napoleon stopped it.

Okay," Quinn sighed, "What we had going on in the 4th and 5th centuries is the spread of pagan Neo-Platonism, taken up by Christian humanists, and a pope that was obviously the Antichrist of his day.

Quinn was enraged, there seemed to be no stopping him, so Eisenhower sat back and listened.

"No one gives thought to the idea that when Jesus was with us, trying to communicate who He was – introducing Himself as: 'I am the Son of,' was essential the language of the time in identifying oneself to the community. Being the son of a man, being a member of that man's family, told the community everything – so they could immediately accept or reject a stranger. Just as some people had proclaimed, He is the son of David – the last righteous king of the Israelites. It told of lineage. And lineage was the most important issue for the people of the time.

The Bible identifies people by saying – he is the 'son of,' as in,

'John the Apostle…was the son of Zebedee…the Beloved Disciple of Christ, and stood by at his crucifixion…,'" (Douay Rheims, NT, p 103).

Another way to look at it – if Jesus went up to people and said, 'I am God' – here's a miracle to prove it, and He snaps His fingers and the moon comes within 100 feet of earth without crashing, without tidal surge; He snaps His fingers again and the whole earth trembles with deafening noise – people would fall over dead from absolute fear. Remember Exodus 20:19, and the people said to Moses: "Speak thou to us, and we will hear: let *not* the Lord speak to us, lest we die." To say that 'I am the Son of God,' while people might tremble, the 'son' is never seen as being as powerful or as deadly as the father. Think of a Don, father of a mafia family, if you will. You tick him off and you're dead where you stand. Tick off the son, and the son needs to get permission from the Don before he can take you out; the son must show the father respect! Meanwhile, you have recourse to the Don. Okay, let's assume that Jesus told everyone that He is the Son, instead of 'I am God,' to prevent such debilitating fear. He could then concentrate on His message, that is, – John 13:34, 'A new commandment *I* give unto you: That you love one another, as I have loved you, that you also love one another.'

Quinn paused for a moment, "Ok, and let's look at the Gospel of John for a minute. The Book of John identifies Jesus. St. Jerome relates, that when John was earnestly requested by the brethren to write the Gospel, John answered he would do it, if, by ordering a common fast they would all put up their prayers together to the Almighty God; which being ended, replenished with the clearest and fullest revelation coming from Heaven, he burst forth into that preface, '*In the beginning was the Word*, and the Word was with God, and *the Word was God*…That was the true light, which enlighteneth every man that cometh into this world. *He was in the world, and the world was made by him*, and the world knew him not…And *the Word was made flesh, and dwelt among us*,' (*Ibid.* at NT, p 103, John 1:1-14, Douay Rheims)

So, as to these 17th century Christian theologians – allegedly intellectuals, how is it that they didn't know John 14:7-15? Or did they intentionally ignore it?

Sir, Jesus talked to His Apostles after the Last Supper – John was at the Supper; John is a first person witness to these words of Jesus, and quoted Jesus in an ancient document. Therefore, Fed.R.Evid. Rule 803(16) 'Hearsay Exceptions; Availability of Declarant Immaterial. The following (evidence) are not excluded by the hearsay rule: Statements in ancient documents…a document in existence 20 years or more the authenticity of which is established.'

The Holy Bible, in which the Book of John gives his eye-witness account of the statements made by Jesus at the Last Supper, is considered an ancient document, admissible in a court of law.

And Fed.R.Evid. Rule 803(18) 'Learned Treaties…statements contained in published treatises… on a subject of history…established as a reliable authority by…expert testimony…the statements may be read into evidence….'"

Eisenhower said, "I agree, son," as he picked up the Bible, turned to John 14:7-15, and read the words that Jesus spoke to the Apostle Philip: 'If you had known me, you would *without doubt* have known my Father also: and from henceforth you shall know him, and you have seen him.' Philip saith to him: Lord, shew us the Father, and it is enough for us. Jesus saith to him: *Have I been so long a time with you; and have you not known me? Philip, he that seeth me seeth the Father also.* How sayest thou, Shew us the Father? Do you not believe, that I am in the Father, and the Father in me? The words that I speak to you, I speak not of myself. But the Father who abideth in me, he doth the works. Believe you not that I am in the Father, and the Father in me?...If you love me, keep my commandments.'

Quinn replied, "Jesus is telling Philip that He and the Father are One and inseparable. Jesus is in the Father and the Father is in Jesus – because they are the SAME person! I think that the Father came onto earth in the form of a young man; why not He's God! As the Son, people could relate to Him. Yes, if God walked up to me and said, I am God, I'd drop dead of a heart attack! As a Son, I'd relate Him to my own son, or I would relate to Him because I am a son, or if my age, I'd think of Him as a brother – it would be much less intimidating."

Quinn thought for a moment, "Sir, would it be correct to follow that logic – that God is normally in the form of the Holy Ghost, a spirit?"

"That's right, Quinn. God the Father, God the Son, God the Holy Ghost – are different names for the same Being. They are not divided Beings, but God shows Himself in these different shapes so that humans can relate. As humans – we are able to understand God the Father, as a Creator, as one who issues discipline. As a Son, we can relate as a brother, talk intimately with Him – the way one brother would tell his brother of an act he committed, but would never tell anyone else in the world. As the Holy Ghost – well, that's the true form of God. Something that as a human, we can only assume what He must be like, but not necessarily able to relate enough to have an intimate relationship with Him – which is what God wants – for us individually to have an intimate, working, loving relationship with God. This is how the Kingdom of God is within you, individually! If you love someone, you want them to love you – you have to put yourself on a level that they are able to relate to – so they will look at you, listen to you tell them that you love them. But for now, the true form of God is not something that we need to know."

Eisenhower put down the Bible on the conference table and then said, "At some point along the way, there came the Arian Controversy, Arius was a Christian presbyter who 'insisted that Jesus Christ was substantially distinct from, though of like or similar substance with God the Father. This view was later called Unitarianism. And the Arian position continued to be influential with the Eastern Mediterranean Church while the Western branches of the Church lean toward Athanasius' position – that Jesus and God the Father were of the same substance. This theological controversy thoroughly mixed in with the politics of the Roman Empire. Roman Emperor Constantine I convened the Council of Nicaea (A.D. 325), for the purpose of development of a statement of faith that could unify the Christian Church – Athanasius's view was adopted; Arius' view was rejected. Constans, one of Constantine's sons and heir, supported the Nicene Creed and Athanasius view that Jesus and God the Father were of the same substance. In about…(A.D. 350), Constans was murdered; his brother became sole ruler of the Empire and worked to eliminate the Nicene (Creed) theology. A third theological position emerged, that of Aetius, who held that Jesus Christ was not of the same substance as God the Father and was not even of like substance. By…(A.D. 383), the official Church had accepted the view of Athanasius (that Jesus and God the Father are of the same substance) and expanded the doctrine to that of the Trinity,' (to include the Holy Ghost), (*Supra at Garrett.*).

'When the Arian Unitarian position was revived in England thirteen centuries later, in the 17th century, the view is very different. Arian Unitarianism was allied with a devotion to freedom of speech with an emphasis on tolerance and limiting the province of faith to matters that cannot be resolved by reason alone. This John Locke take on Arianism influenced many of the founders of the American Republic,' (*Ibid.*). I'll say more about Arius in a minute.

The issues we face today stem from the period of the Renaissance, which arose as a result of the collapse of Roman civilization, in A.D. 410. The Renaissance is interpreted as the Italian Renaissance that ran between the 13th century to the 16th century and the Northern European Renaissance that ran between the 15th century to the 16th century, which 'rapidly declined with events of the Reformation. Within the Northern Renaissance, the Christian Humanist group wanted to reform the Catholic Church, but their efforts prepared the way for many Catholics becoming Protestants. The Christian Humanists took up the Medieval Church's constant argument that an Apostolic standard laid down in the early Church was and remained the Christian ideal – it was simple and vibrant. This Apostolic timeframe began with the 1st century and ran to the 5th century Christian writers, including the New Testament. The Italian Humanists, with whom religion played a less significant role, rejected the Christian authors as the classics; they focused on the works of the 1st century BC to 1st century A.D. and later added the great works of the Greeks. During the Northern Renaissance, the intellectual climate made it possible for an upsurge of the mystic movement. The individuals of the mystic movement held that inner piety and lifestyle led to the ability of an individual to communicate directly with God through contemplation. The inwardness of religious experience helped create an atmosphere conducive to communicating with God. But this eliminated the need for priestly middlemen performing formal religious rituals and services,' (www.student/unl.edu/cis/ hist100w05/online _course/unit3/Isn09-tp03.html).

Italian Humanists with hostile intent, imposed the term Middle Ages. Humanists asserted that 1000 years of darkness and ignorance separated them from the ancient Greek and Roman world – they made that claim to highlight their own Humanist work and ideals. In other words, the Humanists invented the term Middle Ages to distinguish themselves from the Dark Ages, brought about by the fall of Rome and the Roman Empire. While it is argued that the Roman Empire fell either in A.D. 410 or in A.D. 476 – it was in 1453 that the Roman Empire was snuffed out completely.

But the general consensus is that the sack of Rome, in A.D. 410, by Alaric the German Visigoth, had enormous impact on the political structure and social climate of the Western World. 'The Germanic tribes that forcibly migrated into southern and western Europe in the 5th century were converted to Christianity – but retained many of their German customs – their changes in forms of social organization that they introduced rendered centralized government and cultural unity impossible. The Roman Empire had retained the Greek culture of science and the arts. The Roman Empire's system of efficient, agriculture, extensive road networks, water-supply system, and shipping routes – all decayed substantially under the Germanic tribes that did not have the Roman centralized government, or the Greek artistic and scholarly endeavors.' This was the period of the Dark Ages.

What we are experiencing today comes out of the world that arose, as the ancient world ceased to exist. For Christians, it could be argued that it was a good thing that the Roman Empire fell. Christians suffered in the Roman world of 'Diocletian, the Roman Emperor from A.D. 284-305, who persecuted the Catholic Church. He had won the last triumph that Rome ever held – it was over Persia/Iran. He thought that the Roman Empire was too large, too unwieldy for one head. He divided his power, granting inferior title of Caesar to two generals, Galerius and Constantius, in A.D. 292. Diocletian kept Thrace, Egypt, and Asia. General Maximian was given Italy and Africa. General Galerius was stationed on the Danube; Constantius was given Gaul, Spain, and Britain, but supreme power remained with Diocletian. None of them resided in Rome, thus preparing for the downfall of the City of Rome. Diocletian held power for 21 years and then retired. He is associated with the last and most terrible of all the ten persecutions of the early Church. Yet Christians enjoyed peace and prosperity during his reign. But General Galerius convinced Diocletian to become persecutor of Christians,' (www.newadvent.org/cathen/05007b.htm).

Both Galerius and Maximian at the Council held at Nicomedia in A.D. 301 resolved to suppress Christianity throughout the Roman Empire. An edict was issued to 'tear down the churches to the foundations and to destroy the Sacred Scriptures by fire and those who were in honourable stations should be degraded if they persevered in their adherence to Christianity' (Eusebius, op. cit., VIII, ii). Three additional edicts, issued in A.D. 303-304, marked successive states in the severity of the persecution: Bishops, presbyters, and deacons should be imprisoned; they should be tortured and compelled by every means to sacrifice; the third edict: the laity and clergy were included in first and second edicts. Eusebius and the Acts of the Martyrs tell of the massacre of the whole population of a town because they declared themselves Christians (Eusebius, loc. Cit., xi, xii; Lactant., 'Div. Instit.,' V, xi). After Diocletian abdicated as Emperor on May 1, 305, Galerius and Maximian continued the persecutions for another seven years afterwards,' (*Ibid.*).

But as I said, I would talk about Arius at greater length for he was an important figure in this conflict that we face today," Eisenhower continued, "He lived, A.D. 250-336, a Black Libyan, therefore, descended from Ham, and a Christian priest in Alexandria, Egypt. He came up with his own theological interpretation known as Arianism. He taught that the relationship of the Trinity person, Jesus the Son, was subordinate to the Father. It denied the Divinity of Jesus Christ. That denial is called Unitarianism. It is the ultimate scope of Arian opposition to what Christians have always believed. Arianism teaches that Jesus is the Son as a second, or inferior God, since God Himself is made out of nothing and existed before the world of the ages. God alone was without beginning, un-originate; the Son was originated, therefore, not consubstantial with the Father, not equal in dignity or co-eternal. This is where Arius almost seems to have copied Plotinus' philosophy. Roman Emperor Constantine I saw Arius' rebellion against the Christian Church as heresy; so, Constantine called together the First Council in Nicaea, in A.D. 325, in which the Council came up with the oath of faith called the Nicene Creed that all Catholics were to recite. (www.newadvent.org/cathen/01707c.htm)

Alaric the German Visigoth and the Germans were descendants of the Assyrians, cousins of the Israelites, since both were descendants of Sem (Gen. 10:22), therefore, they shared the same Y-chromosome as Sem. Sem was White and the first-born and genetically the only son of Noah (Gen. 10:1), and Noah was descended from Adam (Gen. 5:1-3), and since Abraham was descended from Noah (Gen. 10:1-26), and King David was descended from Abraham, and Jesus was descended from King David (Matt. 1-25), therefore, Jesus was descended from Adam and Eve. The largest ethnic group in the United States is German; they are descendants of Adam and Eve. Adam and Eve were created by God (Gen. 2:7-22). The German's were created by God.

After the Assyrians conquered and took the Ten Northern Tribes of Israelites, in 721 B.C., back north (4 Kings 17:6), they both later migrated up into Europe. The Romans called the Assyrian and Israelites the Germans, meaning 'war men'; the Germans called themselves Deutsch. (www.originofnations.org/Great_German_Nation/germany/history_of_germany.htm)

The 'ancient Assyrians were the greatest war-making power in all history,' (Dr. Hoeh, Herman, *Plain Truth Germany in Prophecy*, Jan. 1963).

The Assyrians and Israelites migrated from the Caucasus and the countries around the Black and Caspian Seas, around A.D. 100-200.

For 1000 years, December 25, 800 to August 6, 1806, the Germans ruled Europe as the Holy Roman Empire, and saw themselves as the true bearers of the Christian Reich/Kingdom. They were entrusted with a world mission to be the protectors of Christianity.

No other political structure arose in Europe to provide stability. The Roman Catholic church was the only force capable of providing a basis for social unity. Society attempting to structure itself politically on a spiritual basis ended with the rise of artistic, commercial, and other activities anchored firmly in the secular world in the period just prior to the Renaissance. After the dissolution of the Roman Empire – Europe arose as one large church-state known as Christendom with two distinct groups – the ecclesiastical/church hierarchy and the secular/political leaders. Supreme authority was wielded by the pope in the ecclesiastical hierarchy and by the emperor in the secular. The two groups fought, and Pope Gregory VII won. The 13th century (A.D. 1200s) was the height of the medieval, Middle Ages. Many kinds of social units proliferated – guilds/freemasons, associations, civil councils, monastic chapters. The crucial legal concept of representation developed – political assembly whose members had full power to make decisions binding upon the communities. The breakup of feudal structures, strengthening of city-states in Italy and emergence of national monarchies in Spain, France, and England – and cultural developments such as secular education – culminated in the Renaissance and its look back to classical learning for inspiration,' (www.britannica.com/EBchecked/topic/ 380873/Middle-Ages).

The political structure of 'Feudalism was in Europe, Russia, Japan, and China. It was a Medieval contractual relationship among the upper class – whereby the lord granted land taken from those of the conquered and gave to his men in return for military service. It was a political system, but it also maintained social order. It was a localization of political and economic power in the hands of lords and their vassals and by the exercise of that power from the base of castles, each lord dominated the district in which the castle was situated. This formed a pyramidal form of hierarchy. A division of governmental power spreading downward over various castle-dominated districts, reached down to the lesser nobles. Manorialism is the social and economic relationship between peasants and their lords. In Germanic Europe, the pyramid ended at a level below the king or emperor, at the level of the great princes. In England, feudalism was imposed by the Normans (William the Conqueror). In France the kings used their positions and were feudal sovereigns. In both England and France, the kings were at the top of the pyramid. Although not all portions of Europe were feudalized,' (www.mesacc.edu/dept /d10/asb/anthro 2003/glues/feudalism.html). Under feudalism, ownership of all land was vested in the king; serfs held the land through contract; worked the manor. Serfs received protection in return for personal services and for dues. But with the Black Plague and the death of millions that cut across all classes, the end of feudalism began. 'With the increase use of money, instead of land, as a medium of exchange, the increase of serfs living as free men, and the formation of the nation-states with monarchies interested in reducing the power of the feudal lords – Feudalism ended,' (www.allpaintings.org/v/Northern+Renaissance/).

During the Renaissance of the 13th century, 'Thomas Aquinas recovered Aristotelian logic. The logical procedures so carefully laid out by the ancient Greek philosopher Aristotle were used to defend the dogmas of Christianity. In the 14th and 15th century there emerged in Italy and France a group of thinkers known as the 'humanists.' Back then, they were practicing Catholics, not as in today's political debate where they are seen as anti-religious. In those earlier centuries, humanist argued that to worship God involved admiration of his creation, in particular the crown of His creation – humanity. By celebrating the human race and its capacities they argued they were worshipping God more than the priests who harped on original sin and called on people to confess and humble themselves before the Almighty. Some humanists claimed that humans were like God, created not only in his image, but with a share of his creative power. The architect, musician, and scholar, by exercising their intellectual powers, were fulfilling divine purposes,' (http://public.wsu.edu/~brians/hum_303/enlightenment.html).

'This celebration of human capacity, though it was mixed in the Renaissance with elements of gloom and superstition (witchcraft trials flourished in this period)...The goal of Renaissance humanists was to recapture some of the pride, breadth of spirit, and creativity of the ancient Greek and Romans, to replicate their successes and go beyond them....By cleaning and sharpening the tools of antiquity, the Europeans thought they could reshape their own time,' (*Ibid.* at wsu.edu/~brians).

And there was Michael de Montaigne, A.D. 1533-1592, who was among the most learned humanists of the 16th century Renaissance. He was a French Roman Catholic, and considered the father of modern skepticism. While he was a humanist, he thought that humans were not able to attain true certainty. Thus, he depended only on his own judgment.

'Michel de Montaigne…asked…in his Essays: 'What do I know?'…he meant that we have no right to impose on others dogmas which rest on cultural habit rather than absolute truth….he argued that morals may be to some degree relative…This shift toward cultural relativism…continue(d) to have profound effect on European thought to the present day…it is one of the hallmarks of the Enlightenment…the Enlightenment thinkers used the examples of other cultures to gain the freedom to reshape not only their philosophies, but their societies. It was becoming clear that…there were many possible ways of being human,' (*Ibid.* at wsu.edu/~brians).

Probably the most threatening to the Church was Montaigne's question, 'If we cannot be certain that our values are God-given, then we have no right to impose them by force on others. Inquisitors, popes, and kings alike had no business enforcing adherence to particular religious or philosophical beliefs,'" (*Ibid.* at wsu.edu/~brians).

"This goes back to Dostoyevsky's Grand Inquisitor," Quinn replied, "to the Jewish philosophy, to Maimonides' imposition of his Seven Noahide Laws and their subset of laws that Maimonides had created. It goes to today and the Education Day USA law that our Congress imposed upon American citizens to follow the Noahide Laws. Who were the Popes of those numerous Inquisitions to force Catholicism on the Jews and Muslims? Who are the Jews and Muslims to force their religion of Noahide Laws and Shariah Laws on Christians? They are all participating in that quarrel over rank. And none of it was what Jesus left us – as Dostoyevsky's Ivan character points out – Jesus left us with freedom of conscious to choose to do good or to do evil – and we cannot turn over that freedom to the Jesuits or the Jews or the Muslims."

Quinn continued, but his anger broke through, as it seeped in to his words, "This Education Day USA law is our Congress acting as those Inquisition Popes, going against our Declaration of Independence, our Constitution! General, I don't want to impose my Christianity on Jews or Muslims, and I don't want them to impose their religion on us Christians. I don't want the Vatican to think they own me, either. I want to be left alone! Whether you call God, Father, Jesus, or the Holy Ghost, God wants us to look at Him and choose Him through faith and love, and reject Satan. But that choice is strictly ours – regardless of any Inquisition, regardless of Education Day USA law, or FEMA camps. It doesn't seem to me that if Jesus was against the teachings of the Pharisees, the traditions of men, and called them, 'You serpents, generation of vipers, how will you flee from the judgment of hell?' (Matt. 23:33) – and those Pharisees are today's Zionist Rabbis, teaching the same traditions of men – I doubt that Jesus would approve of Vatican II, and what the Jesuits have done to His Church, either. For our Congress to legislate through the Education Day law that Christians are to be forced to obey the Jewish Maimonides-created Seven Noahide Laws - which are the same as the *Talmud* taught by the Pharisees during Jesus' time – then they are all doomed to receive the judgment of hell!"

Quinn was restless in his chair, "Jesus told his disciple, Thomas, who had doubt that Jesus had resurrected from the dead, Jesus said to him, "put in thy finger hither, and see my hands; and bring hither thy hand, and put it into my side; and be not faithless, but believing,' (John 20:27). What other proof does one need that Jesus is God. I mean, if God is omnipotent, then why can't He appear as a young man; why can't change in to a figure of a Son, though His natural state is the Holy Ghost. After all, He's God –

these kinds of abilities are what make Him God – unlike man. I don't like these institutionalized religions, I think they are about power – they help Satan gain power over mankind and the earth – that's what it's all about. I just want to be left alone – who the hell do these people think they are telling me who I can and who I cannot to believe in – who the hell are they!? God doesn't even force me to believe in Him – who is any man to force me?"

"Well, don't be so ready to jump in to humanism, Quinn. This new form of scientific certainty makes the assumption that 'the good scientist…is willing to test all assumptions,' and 'radical doubt was necessary for this new sort of certainty,' and 'knowledge depends on evidence and reason.' ((*Ibid.* at wsu.edu/~brians). That is agreeable, but during the Renaissance the Church objected to Galileo's (1632) argument in support of the Copernican notion that the earth rotates the sun. In reality, today's scientists assert the Big Bang Theory without evidence, and contrary to their own scientific quantum mechanics findings. In other words, we cannot depend on every scientist to be truthful. Scientist, as well as the hierarchy of the Church, can both be seduced by Satan."

"Let's continue our discussion," Eisenhower prompted, "Now, the Age of Enlightenment must be looked at with what was going on around these intellectual thinkers. While their ideas were discussed, Europe was plagued with fanaticism. 'The 17th century was torn by witch-hunts and wars of religion…Protestants and Catholics denounced each other as followers of Satan…people could be imprisoned for not attending any (Church). All publications…were subject to prior censorship by both church and state…Slavery was widely practiced…The despotism (absolute power) of monarchs exercis(ed) far greater powers than any medieval king…and scripture (was) quoted to show that revolution was detested by God (just as the former leader of the House of Congress told pastors to preach that the faithful's duty is to obey their government)…There had been plenty of intolerance and dogma to go around in the Middle Ages, but the emergence of *the modern state made its tyranny much more efficient and powerful*.' (*Ibid.* at wsu.edu/~brians).

But out of the chaos came capitalism. 'During the late Middle Ages, peasants had begun to move from rural estates (of feudalism) to the towns in search of increased freedom and prosperity. As trade and communication improved during the Renaissance, the ordinary town-dweller began to realize that things need not always go on as they had for centuries…It was not only contact with alien cultural patterns which influenced Europeans, it was the wealth brought back from Asia and the Americas which catapulted (launched) a new class of merchants in to prominence, partially displacing the old aristocracy whose power had been rooted in the ownership of land (and labor contracts with peasants). These merchants had their own ideas about the sort of world they wanted to inhabit, and they became major agents of change, in the arts, in government, and in the economy,' (*Ibid.* at wsu.edu/~brians). This new-found freedom would change the world, enough of the masses were let out of the corral, you might say," Eisenhower smiled and then continued.

"'Individualism had been chiefly emphasized in the Renaissance by artists…(very importantly) it became a core value (of social culture). The ability of individual effort to transform the world became a European dogma, lasting to this day. But the chief obstacles to the reshaping of Europe by the merchant class...were the…absolutist kings and dogmatic churches…the general trend is clear: *individualism, freedom and change replaced community, authority, and tradition as core European values*. Religion survived, but weakened and often transformed almost beyond recognition; the monarch was to dwindle over the course of the hundred years beginning in the mid-18th century to a pale shadow of its former self. This is the background of the 18th-century Enlightenment. Europeans were changing, but Europe's institutions were not keeping pace with that change. The Church insisted that it was the only source of truth…Most important, the middle classes…were painfully aware that they were paying taxes to support a fabulously expensive aristocracy which contributed nothing of value to society…and those useless aristocrats were unwilling to share power with those who actually managed and…created the national wealth.'" (*Ibid.* at wsu.edu/~brians).

Quinn replied, "This is what Americans are facing, again, today. Our elite government officials have taxed us back in to slavery, and with every law they pass they have stripped our rights of freedom from their oppression. They are trying to put us back into that corral of feudalism, peasantry. Our government has ignored our Constitution that had its foundation in the Enlightenment. And Tsaeb, through his Executive Order of July 6, 2012, has taken control of the Internet, our greatest weapon against their tyranny. Foolishly, for them, Americans know that the day they shut down the Internet – it is the signal for every American to literally take up their guns – for they have begun the final battle against our freedom. The day that the Internet is shut down every American will fight – covertly. Americans know they must stay out of the streets; they know that they must shoot from behind every tree – and every tree in America will become the Tree of Knowledge of Good and Evil. And today we know enough to choose good. We will not be seduced by Satan, again."

Eisenhower nodded, "Yes, Americans have seen enough movies like *Red Dawn* to know that they must fight covertly. But remember, Eve had just been created; she had no idea who Satan was, but we know – we've seen his capacity for evil, we've seen what he has accomplished with seduction – like that of the Venetians seducing Crusading Christians to destroy other Christians, destroy a 1000 years of manuscripts, paintings, and all the rest – we've seen his seduction too many times throughout the history of mankind. And don't think that Satan will not seduce Americans to fight other Americans – don't think Satan will not reward those who slaughter the followers of Jesus with the loot of their deaths and, in the end, reward them with eternal damnation. Don't think that Satan will not send his evil bloodline to destroy the Library of Congress, just as he had done to destroy the Great Library of Alexandria."

Eisenhower sat back in his chair, folding his arms across his chest, "There is a great lesson to be learned from Montaigne – depend only on our own judgment, not that of the elite rulers of this world. I think what Dostoyevsky was telling us, too, is that these rulers are our masters only because we allow them to be – we now have seen that we cannot depend on them – we cannot turn over our freedom to them. This is what our Founding Fathers saw as well.

Chapter 9

Some of the astral projecting soldiers chosen by the Generals to serve under Quinn were retired veterans of Operation Freedom; others were retired Special Ops and Special Forces commanders, and military jet pilots. Still others were currently serving in Iraq and Afghanistan; some serving in South Korea and Germany. In those theatres, their bodies left behind were being guarded in jails or hospitals, protected while their souls reported for duty. But the other astral projecting leaders were private citizens, engineers, computer experts, chemists, cops, state troopers, biologists, nuclear physicists, and war strategist hobbyist. All of them had been ordered to select a trusted family member or friend to pray over their bodies while their souls trained in the 11th dimensional powers.

Eisenhower had left after his meeting with Quinn and the astral projecting leaders. Will Booker explained to them, "The Pentagon is a good place for us to meet because it's difficult for telepathic powers of evil spirits to penetrate this building. There's an electromagnetic barrier lining the walls that continuously vibrates signals to cause a white noise effect so that listening devices can't penetrate into the room. But as the General told you, we will not meet here again; never the same place twice; and never on a rotational basis that has any manor of predictability.

I'm going to ask that the living soldiers who are here through astral projection join up with an 11th dimensional soldier. We don't want you getting lost or getting captured by the evil 11th dimensional spirits. For us to communicate more efficiently, the evil 11th dimensional spirits will be called the Jesuit Society or JSs. We are the good guys of the 11th dimension and we'll be called Quinn's Regiment, or QRs."

When Booker finished, he announced, "Gentlemen, we are headed for the Montana Territory and the field on which they fought the Battle of the Little Bighorn. We have made contact with the Sioux spirits who fought on that battlefield and at Wounded Knee Creek, South Dakota. Those spirits continue to dance the Ghost Dance there and have agreed to fight with us. They will provide camouflage for us against detection by the evil 11th dimension spirits while we train."

Within minutes the legion of QR spirits penetrated the walls of the Pentagon. Two by two the QRs flew in formation with the astral projecting spirits on the right side to make way for the silver thread that connected back to their living bodies. After leaving the Pentagon, they did a loop around the White House, the Lincoln Memorial, and then the Capitol. Finally, soaring high above the treetops, over the cities, over the Appalachian Highlands, across the Mississippi, over the plains and farmlands of the mid-section of the country they flew, heading for southeastern Montana.

As they grew closer to the battlefield of the Little Bighorn, drums could be heard, loud and foreboding. Their incessant beat raced the heart and stirred the emotions of the QRs. The dreaded sound announced the war to come. Their fearless taunting permeated the cosmos. A threat made real, as it announced to the stars and planets that the Indians were unhappy with the White man's constraints. In a continuous, never-ending rhythm the drums intended to taunt the minds of the guilty – God would be returning.

The landscape of the wide river valley of Little Bighorn River was embraced by the Wolf Mountains on one side and the Bluffs on the other where Custer rushed his company of Cavalry to their destiny with death at the hands of Chief Sitting Bull. Quinn looked at Booker without speaking, and then back at the wide valley. On the hill of the Battle of the Little Bighorn, Quinn saw a circle of Indians dancing, chanting the words: 'the whole world is coming, a cleansing is coming.' During their lives they had danced and chanted until they dropped from exhaustion. The War Department had banned the religious dance, declaring it was a war dance that scared the White settlers.

Now that the Indians were ghosts, Quinn wondered if they ever stopped beating the drums and dancing the Ghost Dance. The dance had been revealed to a Shaman in a vision, during an eclipse, with a message that a time would return for the Indian people when they would, once again, be free and happy as they had been before the White man came and took their lands, their guns, their food, and leaving them unable to defend against the arbitrary will of those who controlled the United States of America.

In 1599, the Acoma Pueblo Indians of New Mexico greeted Spaniard Don Juan de Onate with friendship, but he declared himself 'the master of domain.' When the Acomas fought back, the Spaniards lost 20 men while killing 800 Acomas. For the final measure of control, Onate ordered a foot cut off every male 25 years and over and males between 12 and 24 years were sentenced to 20 years of hard labor. After 80 years of forced labor and destruction of the Acoma's way of life, they rebelled and drove the Spanish south.

In the long tradition of North and South American Indians, scalping the enemy was further endorsed by the English in 1689 when the English declared war on all Eastern Indians and offered a bounty on their scalps. The English provided sharp knives for this purpose. Again, in 1755 the General Court of the Province of Massachusetts offered a bounty for scalp: 40 pounds for every male, 20 pounds for every female and child under 12 years of age. During the War of 1812, the English offered the Chippewa a bounty for scalps of the English enemy. And along the way, the French paid the Indians a bounty for scalps of the French enemy.

Quinn wondered if the U.S. government treaties with the Indians that kept the nomadic Indians from walking off the confines of the reservations meant the striking of the foot of Eve's seed by Satan's seed. Even though American Indians were descendants of yellow Japheth, Eve was their mother, also, through Cain. That would mean that among the descendants of Satan – there would be enmity.

The treaties confined the nomadic Indians either north of the Black Hills in Dakota Territory, or south in Oklahoma; both locations the White man found undesirable. The Indians' entire way of life was destroyed in the poverty and isolation of the reservation. It began when the federal government used the land west of the Mississippi as one big reservation, calling it Indian Country, and moved eastern tribes there, under treaty guarantees.

With the 1834 Indian Intercourse Act, the White man was prohibited from entering Indian country without a license. But with wagon trains going to Oregon, California miners seeking western gold fields, and the Robber Barons planning the transcontinental railroad the Indian Country was an obstacle that needed to be eliminated. In 1851, the federal government declared a new policy of 'concentration.' The concentration policy assigned limited boundaries, reservations, to each tribe for 'as long as waters run and the grass shall grow.' The Indians wanted access to hunting the buffalo as was their custom, but the White settlers intruded into Indian reservations and demanded the government protect them. Gold miners touched off warfare among the Cheyenne and Arapaho.

When the two tribes asked for peace, the Colorado militia led by Col. John Chivington attacked the sleeping group, ordering his men to kill and scalp the 'big and little.' Chief Black Kettle raised an American flag, then a white flag, but Chivington ignored the peace signs. Chivington's men continued to club, stab, and scalp the Indians. As a result, the federal government moved the tribes to other locations, to make way for the gold rush miners' access to the land promised 'forever' to the Indians. The miners then started against the powerful Sioux and began the Sioux War of 1865-67 that flared more intensely when the federal government made known the plans to connect the mining towns by building the Bozeman Trail through the heart of the Sioux hunting grounds. After the Sioux massacred Capt. Fetterman and his 82 soldiers, the White man declared Indians to be savages and unfit for civilization. But construction of the Bozeman Trail was halted.

In 1875, fighting began with the Black Hills Gold Rush. The Sioux nations gathered to stop the miners entering into their hunting grounds. The Sioux were led by Chiefs Rain-in-the-face, Crazy Horse, and the Shaman Chief Sitting Bull. It was there, at the Little Bighorn that Lt. Col. George Armstrong Custer rushed to surround what he thought to be a small band of Indians, and instead found the largest gathering of Native Americans ever assembled in the United States, 2500 Sioux warriors. The White man was so outraged that the Sioux had defeated the reckless Custer that within months the U.S. Calvary surrounded and conquered the Sioux nations.

In 1889, the ‘Great Sioux Reservation’ was cut in two and reduced by about one half by a treaty cession. The ceded lands were thrown open to settlement by proclamation in the next spring, and were at once occupied by the Whites. Payment for the lands was delayed, the annuity goods failed to arrive until the winter was nearly over, the crops had failed through attendance of the Indians at the treaty councils in the preceding spring, epidemic diseases were raging in the camps, and Congress cut down the beef ration by over four million pounds on the ground of the stipulated money payment, which, however, had not arrived. (www.newadvent.org/cathen/14017a.htm)

By 1890, the Teton Sioux of South Dakota were starving and restless, and turned to the Ghost Dance. The promise of the Ghost Dance vision of a Paiute messiah, Wovoka, was that the Whites would vanish and Indians would reunite, and a new earth would come upon the old. Dancing the Ghost Dance was intended to hasten the fulfillment of the prophecy. But after the Calvary banned the Ghost Dance, touching off violence and killing Sitting Bull, frightened Indians escaped and joined his brother, Chief Big Foot. The remnants of Custer's 7th Calvary pursued and took them to the army camp at Wounded Knee Creek in South Dakota. The unanswered question of who started the violence at Wounded Knee ends decisively with the Calvary's new machine guns, which had been trained on the encampment before the violence broke out. The machine guns began firing a shell a second, killing 250 unarmed men, women, and children of the Sioux nation.

What happened to the American Indians did not occur in isolation, Quinn thought to himself. There was a planned cause and effect that was to result in the greater wealth of a few and the slaughter of the American Indians – the planned murder of those who had been taught about and believed in Jesus Christ. In 1909, 10,000 of 25,000 Sioux were officially reported as Christian, converted by missionaries.

Quinn thought, the essence of political struggle is a cosmic battle between God and Satan for the soul of man. The struggle is between the international financial elite dedicated to Satan, led by the Illuminati, and against the remnants of humanity that still uphold God's Commandments.

Back in the 1890s, government at all levels granted manufacturers the money, land, and other resources that came mostly from Indian Country. President Lincoln and congress granted millions of acres of public domain land that the government took from the Indians that they slaughtered or starved on reservations. Between 1850 and 1871, during the internment of Indians in concentration camps called reservations - that were moved when the White man found gold on the reservation – Lincoln and Congress gave 170 million acres of land to 80 railroads.

In 1862, during the Civil War, Lincoln signed into law the *Pacific Railway Act, giving outright the largest holdings of land, gold, oil, coal, gas, and real estate, which were taken from the Indians, and Lincoln gave to corporations.* The Pacific Railway Act authorized the Union Pacific and Central Pacific to construct railroad and telegraph lines across the country. *The Northern Pacific Railroad was granted 39 million acres.* The Civil War stripped from the South the power to compete for or dispute rail line locations. In 1862, Lincoln also signed The Homestead Act that granted

160 acres of land to individual American settlers.

The corrupt congress, in granting these millions and millions of acres of free land to a dozen corporations, set up a scenario of overbuilding of the railroad. Track lines paralleled each other; Robber Baron, Jay Gould, built a line only to force a rival line to buy it at inflated prices. Gould and other Barons bought and sold rail lines, watered their corporate stock and milked their assets. Competition between lines became so pressurized it brought about handshake deals that were never honored, offerings of unsustainable carrier rates, the consolidation and buying up of rivals at a reckless pace that was financially disastrous, ending in bankruptcy for a quarter of the railroad corporations.

Quinn knew that it had been well documented that members of groups such as the Triple Commission, Foreign Affairs Private Council, and the Billerbuggers control the largest corporations and banks, and, in kind, control the major industries as energy, transportation, telecommunications, entertainment, the pharmaceuticals, minerals, and agriculture. Many grew their wealth on the government handouts of the 1800s.

When the railroad corporations went bankrupt, J. Pierpont Morgan rescued them and Morgan walked away with control over the railroad industry. Did Morgan create the chaos to bring about his control of the entire industry? Did Morgan bring about the banking crises of 1907? They say timing is everything and Morgan was efficient and orderly in his approach to business. The man known as the king of the Robber Barons had great sway over the federal government.

After the Indians were taken off their land, the next logical step was to set up the stripping of the federal government of its gold. First, in 1900, the gold standard act was signed into law. The next step was to create a crisis in the stock market. Done! But how and who was powerful enough to control the stock market, J. Pierpont Morgan, who was backed by the Rothschilds of Germany. All one needed to do is call in the immediate payment of the notes loaned to buy stock; who floated that lending; who called in full payment? Morgan was wealthy enough to loan money to the federal government. The stocks were sold to pay off the called-loans. As the price of the stocks dropped, banks who made loans to buy the stock lost money. Bank depositors demanded their money and a run on the banks occurred all across the country, bankrupting many banks. It all started when one man attempted to buy up all the copper stock. His idea was to short sell the stock. A rumor began the run on the Knickerbocker Trust Co.; the bank was wiped out; unemployment rose; food prices soared; J. Pierpont Morgan convinced other Robber Barons to infuse money into the banks and restore confidence. Much like today, in 2011, with the planned mortgage fraud being carried out, there's an increase in unemployment, food prices are soaring, price of gold skyrocketing, and the dollar plummeting. The elite are on schedule.

Quinn had read that Morgan was the American liaison for Nathan

Rothschild's interest in creating the Federal Reserve System. Morgan worked with the Knickerbocker family patriarch in setting up the banking cartel.

J.P. Morgan was four generations removed from a founder of Sale University. J.P. Morgan's father, Julius Morgan, an American financier was a covet agent for the British branch of the Rothschild family. This status allowed Morgan to sell U.S. gold bonds in Europe during 1895-1896.

William Jackson established a chapter of the Illuminati, in 1832, at Sale University called the 'Craniums and Erects.' President G.W. Schirf, his father and Senator Sean Merry are members.

Quinn found that a group of Erectsman stole the skull of Goyathlay, from its grave for the Erectsmen to use in their worshiping rituals in the cave, at Sale University. This occult satanic group instigates and establishes conflicts and then controls both adversaries to further their goals. Their target is the Christians of the world, the descendants of Adam, and they will spread plague, create wars, use mind control chemicals to bring about their endgame of forced worship of Satan, or death.

Slaughtering the American Indian or incarcerating them in internment camps, reservations, was one step in controlling the west, its natural resources, gold and silver, its food supply, and thereby controlling the economy of the United States. Those days were a practice run for what the Robber Barons plan to do today.

But before the Craniums and Erectsmen there was the Illuminati - with the same goal. European aristocracy and Jewish moneylenders, who had been called Pharisees during the time of Christ, joined through marriage, money, and satanic worship. The Illuminati was the idea of Govenor Shields back in 1770, who hired a 22-year old boy, the son of a Rabbi/Pharisee, raised as a Catholic. Shields wanted the cream of European elite brought into a secret cult with the aim of destroying Western Civilization, where Adam and Eve's descendants prospered. Shields used bribes of money and sex to control men in high places; and if exposure did not threaten them, Shields was not adverse to murder.

The boy, Weishaupt, wrote: "The great strength of our Order lies in its concealment, let it never appear, in any place in its own name, but always covered by another name, and another occupation. None is fitter than the three lower degrees of Freemasonry; the public is accustomed to it, expects little from it, and therefore takes little notice of it."

"Weishaupt wrote: 'One must speak sometimes in one way, sometimes in another so that our real purpose should remain impenetrable to our inferiors.' The real purpose is to turn the world over to Satan's control, therefore, deceit is their primary method of engagement.

The elite Jewish families of Germany contributed financial backing and personal leadership, to aid in the spread of the Order.

The U.S. Congress, whether duped, bribed, or threatened, formed the National Monetary Commission after the 1907 banking crisis. And in

1910, Senator Nelson W. Aldrich of Rhode Island brought together bankers and economists in conference of Jekyll Island. The purpose was to reconstruct the American banking system that they had caused to end in crisis. Included in the conference were J.P. Morgan & Co. partner Henry P. Deedee, National City Bank President Frank A. Vanderlip and Kuhn, Loeb, and Co. partner Paul M. Warburg. Their fear of being found out before they could institute the Federal Reserve System that each would privately own caused them to refer to each other only by first names. A consultant to the group, Benjamin Strong, Jr., was selected to be the first president of the Federal Reserve Bank of New York.

Using foreign central banks' propaganda, pressure on Woodrow Wilson by his financial backers, Wilson signed the Federal Reserve Act of 1913 on December 23, 1913, after slippery passage through a skeleton-crew of Congress, and while America was rushing around buying last-minute Christmas presents.

The 16th Amendment to the U.S. Constitution was instituted, arguably without ratification, in 1913, to provide congressional ability to enslave Americans' by taking their income tax money to pay the private Robber Barons in the Federal Reserve con game. "The Congress shall have power to lay and collect taxes on incomes, from whatever source derived, without apportionment among the several States, and without regard to any census or enumeration." In twenty years, the U.S. Government would be bankrupt and in 98 years, the national debt would exceed $16 Trillion dollars, largely due to the interest charged by the private Federal Reserve owners. The U.S. Constitution, Art. 1, Sec. 8, cl. 5, provides that only the U.S. Congress has the power "To coin Money, regulate the Value thereof...." No Constitutional Amendment has been passed to give that power to a private group of people. An Act of Congress, the Federal Reserve Act of 1913, is illegal on its face. Therefore, America does not owe payment on the national debt.

To effectuate an Amendment to the Constitution, Art. V of the Constitution governs the process: "When ratified by three fourths of the several states...." This is a seven-year process, passing through the legislatures of each state for an up or down vote, without any modification to the text written by the federal Congress. Hence, the 16th Amendment to the Constitution is illegal because it was never ratified.

The Federal Reserve Act of 1913 established an illegal paper cartel and gave to mostly foreign private owners the U.S. central banking system. Those owners are: The Rothschilds of London and Berlin; Lazard Brothers of Paris; Israel Moses Seif of Italy; Kuhn, Loeb of Germany, Warburg & Co. of Germany; and the Lehman Brothers, Goldman, Sachs and the Rockefeller families of New York.

The Federal Reserve System, these private families, order the U.S. Treasury to print money for those families to loan back to the U.S. Government at 6% interest on every dollar, to hold the transactions on their computers. They then loan against that 6% income to anyone they wish, including foreign adversaries of the U.S., but since its establishment in 1913, the Federal Reserve has prohibited anyone, including Presidents and Congress from auditing their books. The 16th Amendment personal income tax was shuttled through to pay the interest on the loan to the U.S. Government. The Federal Reserve Act required the government to pay these private families in gold bullion, which the government ran out of in 1933.

President John F. Kennedy was against the Federal Reserve Central Banking system.

> (U.S. Presidential) Executive Order 11110
> Amendment of Executive Order no. 10289 as amended, relating to the performance of certain functions affecting the department of the treasury. By virtue of the authority vested in me by section 301 of title 3 of the United States Code, it is ordered as follows:
> SECTION 1. Executive Order No. 10289 of September 19, 1951, as amended, is hereby further amended - (a) By adding at the end of paragraph 1 thereof the following subparagraph (j): "(j) The authority vested in the President by paragraph (b) of section 43 of the Act of May 12, 1933, as amended (31 U.S.C. 821 (b)), to issue silver certificates against any silver bullion, silver, or standard silver dollars in the Treasury not then held for redemption of any outstanding silver certificates, to prescribe the denominations of such silver certificates, and to coin standard silver dollars and subsidiary silver currency for their redemption," and (b) By revoking subparagraphs (b) and (c) of paragraph 2 thereof.
> SECTION 2. The amendment made by this Order shall not affect any act done, or any right accruing or accrued or any suit or proceeding had or commenced in any civil or criminal cause *prior* to the date of this Order but all such liabilities shall continue and may be enforced as if said amendments had not been made.

JOHN F. KENNEDY THE WHITE HOUSE, June 4, 1963"

Executive Order 11110 is still valid. According to Title 3, United States Code, Section 301 dated January 26, 1998.

President Kennedy was assassinated on November 22, 1963 (five months after signing this Executive Order). And immediately after his assassination, the United States Silver Certificates that he had issued through his Order, $4.2 billion backed by silver, were taken out of circulation by President Lyndon B. Johnson, a member of the Foreign Affairs Private Council. The Federal Reserve Notes, backed by nothing, continue to serve as the illegal currency of the U.S. and the world reserve system.

But the story cannot be told without mentioning the Gold Standard. At the end of WWII, Franklin Roosevelt and Winston Churchill came up with the idea of an International Monetary Fund. Their representatives, along with 40+ country representatives, met at Mount Washington Hotel, in Bretton Woods, New Hampshire. As a result of that conference, the treaty called: *Articles of Agreement* was signed in December 27, 1945, that included the establishment of the International Monetary Fund, the World Bank, and GATT (General Agreement on Tariffs and Trade). Washington, DC, was selected as the permanent headquarters site. Their job is to oversee exchange rates, give financial and technical advice to its members, and *to address global economic problems*. The 187 member nations had to deposit gold for their subscription fee. The cover story, purpose: Foster *global* monetary cooperation; secure financial stability; facilitate international trade; promote high employment; promote *sustainable* economic growth; *reduce poverty* around the world - per the IMF website. The bold, italicized words are the buzz words of the New World Order.

Key to all this: Members must agree to maintain their exchange rates based on the U.S. dollar, with the U.S. promising to keep the value of the U.S. dollar based on gold. Member countries, such as China, Germany, Russia, Poland, Australia, Ukraine, Chile, France, Japan, and Arab countries, have recently met secretly, without the United States, pursuant to discussion of refusing to accept the U.S. dollar as the world reserve currency. If foreign oil is not purchased by U.S. dollars, and the U.S. has to exchange dollars for another currency to purchase foreign oil, everything becomes more expensive. In the U.S., there will be massive inflation; no bank loans. Foreign countries will stop accepting the dollar for goods and services, and exchange for other currency will produce a lower return against the dollar. China warned the U.S. not to pass the Healthcare litigation because it would significantly harm the U.S. economy.

Tsaeb and the U.S. Congress threw away $800 billion on the Stimulus Package that went to Tsaeb's campaign backers, to the ACORN group, and to fund the Healthcare Death Panel. This spending was the deliberative, intentional attempt to cause the national debt to skyrocket. As a result of this and other out-of-control massive spending by Tsaeb, Standard & Poors lowered the U.S. triple A credit rating, and as a result of the drop in credit rating, foreign countries are quietly selling off their investment holdings of U.S. dollars. The executives of Standard & Poors lowered the credit rating of Greece, which resulted in riots in the streets. The President of Standard & Poors, who lowered the credit rating of the United States, is an Indian and a member of the Foreign Affairs Private Council. His replacement comes from Citibank, which is connected to the Rockefeller family.

When a country, the world, is on the gold standard, the country cannot print currency above the amount of gold in their treasury. This standard stabilizes inflation, keeping it low. This restricts the Federal Reserve economic 'stabilizing policies.' The Feds cannot print money, charge interest on what they print, therefore, they cannot flood the world, the U.S., with a large supply of money - and cause inflation. Inflation is caused when supply of money goes up and demand for money goes down, and when the supply of goods goes down while the demand for goods goes up. When the supply of money is up, people will exchange the currency for hard gold - this is key. The treasury eventually runs out of gold.

Roosevelt and Churchill sucked into their web - originally 40 something countries; today there are 187 members, able to take out national loans from the International Monetary Fund through the World Bank - repayable in gold. As of August 2009, the IMF had $83 billion worth of gold, the third largest official holder of gold in the world.

The contrived banking crisis of 1907 provided the excuse for pushing through the Federal Reserve Act of 1913. The stock market crash of 1929 was used as an excuse to bring about the Great Depression. But it was Franklin Roosevelt's New Deal and his other social programs that prolonged the Great Depression seven years longer, and impacted international trade, leading to economic crisis in foreign countries.

FDR's executive order that confiscated the private money, gold coins, from the American people, redeeming at $20.67/ounce; while foreigners were still able to redeem U.S. dollars for gold from the U.S. Treasury - and FDR sold foreigners gold for $35./ounce. That price continued until 1971. Basically, FDR stole the money from Americans and made a profit on its resale. The redemption of U.S. dollars for gold by foreigners continued until 1971 when Nixon took the country off the gold standard.

FDR's New Deal and the confiscation of privately owned gold did not remedy the high unemployment, which was 15%. After his 1935 Fair Labor Standards Act, unemployment jumped to 20%. The country went in to a recession within a depression. His New Deal policy blocked recovery by artificially inflating prices and wages. He allowed 19 industries to collude without fear of being prosecuted by antitrust laws; wages were increased beyond market forces. Consumers could not afford to pay for goods or services. FDR's policies of run-away spending, government regulations, and gross devaluation of the dollar prolonged the Great Depression to 15 years.

And today's president Tsaeb and Congress are repeating FDR's policies. The Federal Reserve is following their past model by increasing the printing of U.S. dollars, keeping interest rates artificially low, which the Feds know devalues the dollar. Tsaeb, Congress, and the Federal Reserve are committing treason with their war against the United States economy. Their motive is to destroy the independence of the country and make it interdependent on other nations. As a consequence of these factors, the IMF is calling for a global currency and a global bank - a global Federal Reserve System to administer the "Bancor" currency. The IMF, the UN, and the U.S. Government are working to bring about a global currency controlled by a global bank - and the Antichrist. The bottom line of every act is religious, not economics.

The Jesuits worked to bring about WWII, and as Churchill said: "You must understand that this war (WWII) is not against Hitler or National Socialism, *but against the strength of the German people, which is to be smashed once and for all*, regardless whether it is in the hands of Hitler or a Jesuit priest."

The largest ethnic group in the United States is German, descendants of the Assyrians; the second largest is Irish, descendants of King David and cousins of the Germans. This is the purpose of putting 23 million Americans out of a job or in jobs less than they qualify for and putting 43 million on food stamps. Under Tsaeb, household income has dropped by $4000. In four years Tsaeb added $5.4 trillion to the national debt with outrageous spending practices. This is why Tsaeb refuses to allow American oil drillers to drill in U.S. territory, to create a shortage of gasoline and drive up prices. That is, besides making America dependent on its enemies to sell oil to them; and besides making the U.S. military prohibitively expensive – requiring cutbacks to national defense. To break the backs of the American Middle Class, but more importantly – break the minds of Americans, so they think of themselves as helpless dependents on the U.S. government and other countries. Individualism is viewed as bad, selfish, and frightening. “In-this-together society” is the new moral standard; also known as Communism. The weapon of Political Correctness will be used in Tsaeb’s class warfare to silent dissenters of Communism. Those who believe in individualism and achievement through competition will be demonized. It is psychological warfare to turn Americans in to obsequious slaves of the New World Order. The New World Order will be touted as the solution to the problems that they, the evil, caused in the first place.

In 1785, it was revealed that the goals of the Illuminati were the abolition of patriotism, marriage, morality, family, governance through laws, all religion – specifically Christianity, and the institution of government-controlled education of children. These stated goals are the same as Marxism and Communism. And the same as the New World Order, Freemasonry, Club of Rome, Trilateral Commission, and the Round Table.

These secret groups with their satanic endgame have infiltrated every aspect of American life for more than 100 years. And for their own profit, brought on the Civil War, stripping southern planters of their political power. As a result, their northeast, rival manufacturers had few legal or social barriers. With a hands off approach, the corrupt Congress of the early 1900s did not regulate industrial activity.

Remembering all these things he had read, Quinn objected to the Robber Barons obtaining their great wealth through bribing the U.S.

Congress and murdering those who got in their way. Quinn knew that they put a hit out on Kennedy for his executive order. They stopped at nothing. They intermarried for the purpose of merging wealth with wealth and maintaining their evil bloodline, but the bloodlines are not content with just their incredible wealth. They have an agenda to force all of mankind to worship Satan as they do. It is, indeed, a war between good and evil. They specifically researched how many newspapers they would need to own to control the minds of the American citizens.

But even before that, the telegraph lines that the Robber Barons owned played up the notion that the Indians were savages, specifically to cultivated fear in the White man. The Homestead Act of 1862 created an approach-avoidance tension among easterners and their demand that the U.S. Government do something with the Indians to clear their way to settle on free land. As a result of such propaganda, it gave the excuse to make the Indian reservations smaller, allowing Congress to pass the Pacific Railway Act that gave the gold, silver, and other minerals to the Robber Barons to mine and lands on which to build their railroad lines. It gave tremendous wealth to a handful of individuals – for free! It gave these families the wealth, therefore, the power, to institute the New World Order, today.

The Ghost Dance of the Indians was a clash of religions. The White man had a religious belief that the United States had a manifest destiny to prosper, a God-given right to expand from the Atlantic to the Pacific, and even into the Indian reservations if the settlers and miners so desired. This belief held that whatever it took to achieve that destiny was allowable since invasion into Indian Territory was necessary to enhance the country's economic, political, and social controls.

Indian reservations made the Indians wards of the state. They promised them food, but didn't provide it, causing the death of many Indians. In 1492, there were more than five million Indians in the U.S. In 1800, during the time of treaty, there were 600,000 Indians, but by 1900, only 250,000 had survived the broken promises of the treaty. To destroy the Indian civilization, the U.S. government provided free ammunition to the hunters to kill the mainstay of Indian life, the buffalo. In the end, under the Presidency of Ulysses S. Grant, who vetoed a bill that would have protected the buffalo, Grant promoted the slaughter of 60 million buffalo. By the time President Cleveland signed the bill, the buffalo in the southern plains was extinct, with only 500 buffalo still existing in the northern plains. While the Indians used every part of the buffalo for food, clothing, shelter, tools, and utensils, and buffalo waste burned as fuel, the White man shot buffalo from trains, taking only the tongues and hides. But more importantly, the White man intentionally decimated the buffalo to decimate the Indians. The connection between the Indians and buffalo was a spiritual blessing of survival. The satanic nature of killing off the buffalo was an attempt to also kill the soul of the Indian.

At Wounded Knee, Chief Big Foot was ordered to surrender all weapons of his warriors. He agreed. But as the Calvary set up cannon above the encamped Sioux and soldiers ordered the warriors to place their guns in a heap; the Indians became nervous. And the soldiers feared them and refused to believe that they had surrendered all their guns and went searching their teepees. The Indians became more nervous. To calm them, Yellow Bird began to dance the Ghost Dance, a dance to return their freedoms to them; it was a dance of hope and peace. When Yellow Bird told the Indians to wear their shirts of the Ghost Dance, the soldiers fired the machine gun upon the Indians. The massacre of more than 250 Indians ensued. The soldiers shot women and children trying to run away. It was Adam's descendants murdering Satan's descendants – yet both were Christians.

At the Battle of the Little Bighorn, General George Armstrong Custer ordered Reno to take his company and charge the village of Indians encamped along the Little Bighorn River in the wide floor of the river valley between the Wolf Mountains and the Bluffs. Reno's soldiers killed women and children along with the warriors before they were met with a barrier of warriors and were forced to turn around. At first, getting off their horses and shooting back until they could retreat among the trees; some soldiers soon remounted and rode their horses and followed the others up into the Bluffs for safety. When the Indians became aware that Custer had headed north along the Bluffs, the Indians made chase through the wide-open valley. Custer had split his battalion, making them more vulnerable against the twenty five hundred Sioux warriors from the village that he had sent Reno to attack. The folly of Custer was in not reading his scouts' report of the numbers of Indians that they would face when attacking the Sioux village. An arrogant Custer faced the insult that folly garners. He and his men were slaughtered. An arrogant man served an arrogant government, June 25, 1876.

Will Booker and the astral projecting spirits and the ghost soldiers of wars past approached the Sioux and Cheyenne spirit warriors of the Little Bighorn. The QRs hovered off to the side, as the Indian spirits chanted and danced the Ghost Dance. They danced above the ground, some wearing ceremonial buffalo-horned headdresses. The privilege had been won by deed. Other Sioux warrior spirits wore single eagle feathers tucked into a leather ban around the head, with braids wrapped in animal fur hanging down onto their chests. In a wider circle higher above the dancers, the elder chiefs overlooked the ceremony. Quinn was struck by the ghostly essence of the elder chiefs with their long white hair flowing freely. Standing next to the elders were thick-furred, sharp-eyed wolves, self-assured and strong.

The power drums echoed off the rising moon and filled the evening air with a unity of soul that caressed Quinn's vaporous face. He had never imagined the existence of life in such a way. As he watched the Sioux spirits dancing, he thought of God creating the universe. He thought of the Douay-Rheims Bible verses of Genesis, of the bloodline of Satan and Eve, and the evil of the Robber Barons that he was convinced were the modern descendants of Satan's Japheth bloodline. He wondered about the Indian bloodline and weather it matter. And he thought of the war that was to come to America and Christians fighting for their souls. He looked down at his body, its vague apparition, and realized the truth. Only the God of Abraham could have brought all this about, he was sure of it. He longed for Maggie to be there with him, to feel the presence of God in the universe as he had never felt Him before, to hear the power drums that caressed his soul, as he wanted to caress her.

As Booker, Quinn, and the other QRs hovered close by, the circle of warriors dancing the Ghost Dance opened their circle wider and wider, allowing the QRs to land inside their circle of protection. Will Booker explained to the QRs that the JSs knew of the Ghost Dancers and have heard their chants; they won't look for us here; we'll blend in with the chanting. The cosmic chanting is an expected sound in the universe.

As the sun was setting behind the Wolf Mountains, Quinn looked at the broad expanse of brown prairie grass, its small blue flowers, the lack of trees and edible vegetation and felt immensely vulnerable. The only way to have won a battle under these conditions was to greatly outnumber the enemy, but even then a leader would be risking high casualties. There was nothing in the environment behind which to take cover. Custer was a goddamned fool, Quinn thought. He set up his soldiers to be murdered by his profound lack of discipline and attention to strategic planning -- knowing the numbers of your enemy.

Booker was standing next to Quinn. "I agree," Booker said.

Quinn turned to him, "What?"

"I know what you're thinking," Booker answered, and then kind of chuckled, "And I mean that. I'm reading your mind."

"Hmmm. I'm going to have to watch what I think," Quinn replied.

"Well, I think I might be able to answer your question of the Indians carrying the Y-chromosome of Adam."

"You heard that!" Quinn exclaimed.

"Yes. You have to be careful around 11th dimensionals, Quinn. "But I just want to tell you that the American Indians are the descendants of Japheth, just as the Mexicans and the Asians. But what is important is that many were converted to Christianity by missionaries. But before that – all their tribes were taught the Law of Moses by the Essenes. There is physical proof – in the Holy Stones of Ohio and the Los Lunas Decalogue of New Mexico. These artifacts were discovered in 1860. Of course, there are some who don't believe, but scholars have placed them to be earlier than 1000 years old. Look for the squared Hebrew alphabet used on the stones. The name of Moses is written on the Decalogue, with the abridged version of the Ten Commandments. The New Mexico, Los Lunas Stone is a boulder with its inscription dated to be 500-2000 years old, written in Old Hebrew that was used by the Lost Tribes of Israel. It has an inscription referring to 'brought you out of Egypt.' That stone also has an abridged version of the Ten Commandments.

There is a connection with these stones to the Essenes sect of Jews of Qumran, who scholars think wrote the Dead Sea Scrolls. The Pharisee and Sadducee Jews of the Temple and city and their bastardizing the Law of Moses outraged the Essenes. The Pharisees wrote the *Talmud*, Jewish religious law used by Zionist Jews, today. The Law of Moses is treated as our U.S. Constitution, spoken of grandly when the occasion calls for it, but not followed. The Essenes were a monastic group who lived near the Dead Sea, in Israel, in desert isolation around the time of Jesus. They abandoned Qumran at the time of Roman incursion in A.D. 68, two years before the destruction of the Second Temple in Jerusalem, in A.D. 70. The Essene monks had apocalyptic visions that included the overthrow of the 'wicked priest' of Jerusalem and the evil people and, in the dawn of the Messianic Age, they recognized their Essene community as the true Israel."

"Are you telling me that the Native American Indians carry the Y-chromosome of Adam?"

"No. They carry the Y-chromosome of Japheth. When the Romans took control of Jerusalem in A.D. 68, the Essenes realized that they had to leave; they had to survive to spread the word of God. They split up to be sure that some part of them would survive. They buried their work, their Scrolls, in pottery jars in the desert around the Dead Sea. Then some sailed along the coast of the Mediterranean, up the Spanish coast to Ireland, over to Greenland and down to eastern Canada and the United States. Others walked northeast up through Russia and, after building boats they crossed over the Bering Straits, hugging the Aleutian islands, and sailed down to the west coast of the United States. Each group came across the Native Americans and taught them the Law of Moses.

And, yes, most of the Robber Barons are descendants of Japheth."

"My God!" Quinn mumbled. He shook his head, "It difficult to get my head around all this. J. Pierpont Morgan is a descendant of Satan! Sitting Bull and his brother Big Foot, both murdered by the Calvary, carried Japheth's Y-chromosome!"

"That's right, Quinn."

Quinn was still a bit dazed when Booker stepped forward, "Gentlemen, there is another reason why I brought you to this location. What you are all thinking could only be achieved by you actually seeing this battlefield. The absolute stupidity of Custer to attack when he had no knowledge of the numbers of the enemy."

Booker moved about the center of the circle, looking at the faces of the QRs listening to him. There is a book called The Art of War, by Sun Tzu, written in 500 BC. Tzu was a Chinese general, and his main focus was contrary to Custer's. Many of Custer's men hated him; he drove them without mercy while he hunted, while he deserted to visit his wife. Custer was a general who lived outside military discipline and law. General Tzu, on the other hand, believed that a military commander stood for the virtues of wisdom, sincerity, benevolence, courage, and strictness. Tzu recognized earth as comprising distances, great and small, danger and security, open ground and narrow passes, the chances of life and death. Tzu, I can wager, would never have fought on this battlefield. But the most important of Tzu's principles is that moral law causes people to be in complete accord with their ruler, so they will follow him regardless of their lives and undismayed by any danger. And, from my perspective, you must first show your soldiers that you, too, live by those principles. Here, on the Battlefield of the Little Bighorn, Custer proved Tzu correct. *Tzu claimed that the opportunity of defeating the enemy is provided by the enemy himself.* Custer provided that opportunity to Sitting Bull and Crazy Horse."

Booker took a step forward, "Gentlemen. Our training will focus first on preventing our giving the enemy the opportunity of defeating us. The easiest way to do that is through telepathy. Right now, I'm speaking to you through my mouth. But for the next hour, I'm only going to speak to you through telepathy through my mind. Please take a seat on the grass.

"We're going to take the easiest route in teaching this. Close your eyes; let your body relax. Listen to the drums; don't try to shut them out. Hear them, feel them, be one with them. Listen to my voice; get a fix on me talking to you while the drums play in the background. I'm going to send you a telepathic message. Focus on me; I am among the drums, beating rhythmically. Listen for me.

Quinn quieted himself and listened to the drums' rhythm, feeling the deep foreboding beat. Their message reached out to the universe to warn the evil with a piercing dread: God's kingdom come; Thy will be done; Your judgment comes; Your judgment comes.

Quinn's mind drifted off to thoughts of Jesus Christ; His crucifixion at the hands of the Kenites, descendants of Satan's son Cain, and to the Shroud of Turin that showed the stains of one who suffered at the hands of sadists. Thought upon thought passed as he drifted deeper into his mind. His only awareness were the cosmic drums and his thoughts of Christ. The grass of the plains fell from beneath him as he began to float above the ground, he floated deeper within his mind so that the drums seemed further out in the distant universe. Till finally the only awareness he had was his mind, his thoughts speaking to him. And there in the space of his mind was another voice answering his thoughts, a soothing voice speaking to him. You have been chosen, all of you, because of your love for Jesus Christ. You are to be his legion of angels against the evil. Quinn answered, let God's will be done.

Will Booker continued to speak telepathically to the spirits of Quinn's Regiment. "We will fight the Pharisees, the Sadducees, and scribes, and their Judaism of Zionist Jews of today. They are of Satan's bloodline. We will fight the Muslims, the other bloodline of Satan. You will be outnumbered by the world, but you will be victorious; trust in God."

Will Booker recited the Word: John 12:10-19, 'But the chief priests thought to kill Lazarus also...Because many of the Jews, by reason of him, went away, and believed in Jesus... when Jesus resurrected Lazarus, the 'Pharisees therefore said among themselves: Do you see that we prevail nothing? behold, the whole world is gone after him.'

Booker explained to the QRs, these Words have brought you here. Pharisaism is today's Judaism, and these Zionist Jews are the enemies of the God of Abraham. You are God's army. God knows your hearts; you are Quinn's 11th Regiment!

When Booker stopped his telepathic message, the drums played louder and louder, their warning stretching out still further into the Universe, as if to affirm Bookers thoughts. So too, were the Sioux Indians of God's army. And now soon to come would be the fulfillment of the vision of Paiute Shaman, Wovoka, when dust would cover the ground and a new world would begin.

Chapter 10

It was within the rhythm of the universe and of the echoing drum beat, like a shooting star flaming across the night sky, he came. As he approached, Will Booker stepped out of the circle of the 11th Regiment, and the apparition of the sky stepped onto the earth. He was an ancient man that glowed in the white robes of holiness. His white hair and long beard was that of a wise man who had busied himself with thoughts of life and the observation of the battle between good and evil. He looked at Booker and nodded a silent greeting. Then he turned to Quinn, holding out his hand, "So, you are Quinn."

Quinn was startled that such a being would know his name. After a moment, he began to stand, but Elias motioned for him to remain seated. Elias walked around inside the circle of the 11th Regiment; he looked at each man's face to size up the man. He smiled, "I see you have questions. I am the Prophet Elias; I'm here to answer them for you."

He turned to Quinn, "Let's begin with the leader."

"Ah. Well, I guess I'd like to know, why? Why is there a battle between good and evil?

Elias smiled; his deep voice was strong, "Of course. The Why of it all. It is simple." His arms opened wide in the expectation of the obvious, "This is about covetousness! Satan was jealous of Adam because God give Adam control over the earth, Gen. 2:19. God had created Satan first, His most beautiful angel, therefore, Satan thought that the power over the earth should be his. This is about pride! Satan decided to take that power by seducing Eve and impose his own bloodline amidst God's bloodline. This is about revenge! Satan's plan was that in time his children would turn over the world to him. So, this is about theft and worshipping false gods! Through Eve, Satan fathered Cain who was a fraternal twin of Adam's son, Abel. This is about adultery! Later, through Noah's wife, Satan created the bloodlines of Ham and Japheth, the Black and Yellow races, known as the elite, the Gentiles, to defeat the White race of Adam and Eve, Gen. 3:15. This is about honoring thy father and thy mother. About bearing false witness! Jesus' lineage goes back through Sem to Adam and Eve, who were created by God, Luke 3:23-38. This is about murder!"

Elias turned to the man on Quinn's right, "Harry. What is your question?"

Harry's eyes opened wide with fluster, "Ah." He looked at Quinn and then at Booker standing across the other side of the circle. He looked back at the holy man. "Ah…ah…well. I wonder how do the evil carry out their plan?"

Elias took a step to the side, looking down at the grass, "Now that is a little more complicated. To hand the earth over to Satan, the Gentiles have used their positions of power to control every facet of the lives of the Israelites."

Elias paused, then turning back to Harry, "The Gentiles have instituted their indoctrination of children through school curriculum enforced by the Dept. of Education following the dictates of UN Agenda 21. Ever increasingly, the educational system dummies down student knowledge. Communist teachers manipulate or punish independent, critical thinking of students. The media is required by Agenda 21 to aid and abet this educational system by indoctrinating and distracting minds and destroying the Israelite/Christian culture of honoring Father and Mother and the Ten Commandments. TV commercials invade the minds of intimate space that strip away emotional boundaries so that satanists can invade. Indoctrination is achieved by school curriculums omitting historical events and hiding the knowledge from children of their lineage being of Sem, Ham, or Japheth. This is done so that all children, later as adults, believe the propaganda that they are all God's children, when they are not. As all God's children, the next step is to claim that their God is Satan, not the God of Abraham. Through such ignorance, through such indoctrination, the Gentiles will eventually make everyone dependent on government handouts, and thus enslave them. Indoctrinating the mind of children prepares them for acceptance of the satanic world about to be openly instituted.

I'm sure you read Plato's Republic, haven't you, Harry?"

"Well, no sir. I have not." Harry was embarrassed.

"Plato warned of childhood indoctrination. Plato said: "Picture men dwelling in a sort of subterranean cavern (*a Cave*)...Conceive them as having their legs and necks *fettered from childhood*, so that they remain in the same spot, able to look forward only, and prevented by the fetters from turning their heads....(514.1-b)...such prisoners would deem reality to be nothing else than the shadows of the artificial objects (515.c)...When one was freed (by the Internet) from his fetters...*what do you suppose would be his answer if someone told him that what he had seen before was all a cheat and an illusion, but that now, being nearer to reality and turned toward more real things, he saw more truly?* And if also one should point out to him each of the passing objects and constrain him by questions to say what it is, *do you not think that he would be at a loss and that he would regard what he formerly saw as more real than the things now pointed out to him?"*

Elias smiled at Harry, "You'll find that at 515.c.5-d.5, Republic, Book VII.

"Yes, sir. Thank you sir," Harry replied.

"But the Gentiles have not stopped there," Elias continued, "They need the right people to control the laws and institute legislation that sets up the day that the Gentiles can hand over to their father, Satan, open control and legally sentence to death those who continue to believe in Jesus Christ. They came up with U.S. Public Law 102-14 (H.J. Res. 104): March 20, 1991, called Education Day, USA Proclamation," Elias closed his eyes and recited:

"Whereas the justified preoccupation with these crises must not let the citizens of this (U.S.A.) Nation lose sight of their responsibility to transmit these (Seven Noahide Laws) ethical values from our distinguished past to the generations of the future." Elias cleared his throat, "They take aim at the Christian children of America."

Elias slowly walked within the circle of the 11th Regiment, "You see, Maimonides wrote the Seven Noahide Laws to offer the non-Jew. In his *Mishnah/Talmud*, Chapter 10, concerning Jesus Christ, Maimonides wrote: 'It is a (religious duty) *to eradicate Jewish traitors*…and to cause them to descend to the pit of destruction, since they cause difficulty to the Jews and sway the people away from God, as did Jesus of Nazareth and his students... May the name of the wicked (Jesus) rot.' (http://watch.pair.com/law.html) Punishment for worshipping Jesus Christ is decapitation under the Seven Noahide Laws of Maimonides."

Elias sighed heavily. "But the Gentiles also need to control the Presidency. They need the President to sign in to law such legislation to allow them to carry out their plan to further enslave the Israelites so that they are too weak to rebel. One of God's witnesses, John Kennedy stated in his Speech at Columbia University, on November 13, 1963, "The high *office of the Presidency* of the United States of America has been used to *foment a plot to destroy America's freedom*, and before I leave office, I must inform the citizens of their plight!' But sadly, ten days later they assassinated President Kennedy."

Elias walked back and forth within the circle of Quinn's Regiment as a professor instructing, "You see, once you have the Congress and the Presidency under Gentile control they can do almost anything. At least, they think they can. He looked up at Quinn, frowning, "World War I was contrived to bring about an international treaty that would create the League of Nations. But it did not convince the American people to enter a world collective of nations and, thus, Senators could not vote for the League of Nations – and get re-elected. And they had to hold on to those seats of power. The thing is, 'President Wilson was asking for not only a major change in the international system itself, but for no less (than a) major change in the way the United States would conduct its own international business in partnership with other nations,' David M. Kennedy, the historian said that. Yes, it was David who said that."

"So," Elias continued, "they had to try a different approach to bring about the League of Nations. The Gentiles came up with an event that would guaranty the outrage of the Israelites, such that they would support a treaty. They arranged the bombing of Pearl Harbor. And the assurance of outrage came from the filming of the attack on Pearl Harbor." Elias stopped his pacing and looked at Quinn, "This is the same reason they filmed the bombing of the World Trade Towers on 9/11/2001 that showed Israelites jumping from the burning buildings, which was then repeatedly aired on TV again and again."

Elias paced, "The Gentiles demonstrated what evil could do.

They involved the Israelites in a second generation of world war. In WWI fathers died, in WWII their sons died. By then, the Israelites accepted a treaty that they were promised would assure peace and national security. The Gentiles wasted no time. No time at all. World War II ended with the surrender of Germany and Italy on May 7, 1945. The U.S. Senate ratified the United Nations Treaty on July 28, 1945. President Harry S. Truman signed the United Nations Treaty as the Supreme Law of the land on August 8, 1945."

Elias stopped, his voice lowered, "But in actuality, the United Nations is not for the purpose of world peace and security. No. No. The United Nations is the vehicle through which Satan controls the earth."

The brow of his glowing face knitted, "The United Nations is the seat of power of the Antichrist!"

"Indeed, the worshippers of Satan wrote the United Nations Charter to establish the throne of the Antichrist. It began with President Franklin Delano Roosevelt; he came up with the name change – no longer called the League of Nations – to deceive that it was not the treaty that Americans had rejected, but a new idea altogether. He coined the name, United Nations. But it would do the same work of the League.

He was joined by England's Prime Minister, Winston Churchill and later by USSR Socialist Russia, France, and China's dictator. These are the five permanent members. Together, they gave power to the Antichrist, specifically in 'Chapter VII: Article 42. ...the *Security Council*...may take such action by air, sea, or land forces of Members of the United Nations as may be necessary to maintain or restore international peace and security...Article 43. All Members of the United Nations, in order to contribute...undertake to *make available to the Security Council, on its call...armed forces, assistance, and facilities, including rights of passage (into a Member's country (the U.S.))*...Article 48. The action required to *carry out the decisions of the Security Council...shall be taken* by all Members of the United Nations *or by some of them, as the Security Council may determine*. Article 49. The Members of the United Nations shall join in affording mutual assistance in carrying out the measures *decided upon by the Security Council*.'"
(www.un.org/en/documents/charter/chapter7.shtml)

Elias continued, his heart heavy with sadness ignited his anger, his voice raised. The power drums and the Ghost Dancers joined his anger. Together their voices and drums thundered about the place of the Massacre of Greasy Grass. Off the Bluffs and Wolf Mountains their voices rumbled. Elias cried, "The evil of these people knows no end! They attacked the World Trade Center to incite outrage of the Israelites in order to bring about the Patriot Act, the Department of Homeland Security, and FEMA concentration camps – to spy on the Israelites."

Elias lifted his arms to the heavens, "They murdered 3000 Israelites in order to raise the national debt and destroy the United States economy and the value of the dollar. They will bring the followers of

Christ into complete financial captivity under Satan, so they may not be able to buy or sell without the mark of the beast!"

The power drums beat faster, louder, filling the cosmos with the warning of God's revenge. "They will bring the United States under the servitude of the United Nations – under the rule of Satan!"

The drums beat with the fury of Elias' voice, "The United States is the largest Christian nation. The Gentiles must deliver her to Satan! They will put the enemy into the U.S. Military and destroy it from within! Then they will murder all who believe in Jesus Christ!"

Quinn and his Regiment sat on the brown prairie grass, transfixed by God's prophet. Quinn couldn't help wonder, if this is a prophet's anger, what would God's anger against the Gentiles be like? He thought of his Special Ops buddies who were murdered to prevent them from exposing the evil of the Gentiles and hoped that God's revenge against them would be complete.

Elias dropped his arms to his side and hung his head and listened to the drums as they quieted their anger.

Finally, he turned to the QRs waiting for his words. "Harry, my son."

Harry sat up straight, "Yes, sir."

"Your question of how they carry out Satan's mission is very complicated, and I will tell you more, later. But it also leads to the question – Who?"

Harry still hadn't gotten used to speaking to such a holy man; it was all too unreal, this other dimension of existence. He wondered, where had it been all his life? How is it that he was never told of it; had anyone else known of it? That is, anyone who was alive.

Elias continued as he began to pace, again. "Deceit! That is their method. Deceit in every realm. Noah's Ark was another main deception that they continue today, saying that we are all from God; we are all brothers. Deception, my son."

Harry mumbled, "Yes, sir."

"Let me give you an answer that you might understand more clearly. The Y-Chromosome," Elias said. In the background of his words, the power drums played softly, as if biding their time to thunder under the stars of the universe.

"The first mankind were the Neanderthals. These are the people who left 150,000-year-old relics littered about the world. Cain ran in to them when he reached Eridu. They thought he was a god and he used their strength to build the first city of the world. But I digress in my story." Elias smiled at the QRs.

"Let me move immediately to my point," Elias said.

"Very concisely," Elias gestured with one hand, "Sem was White, Ham was Black, and Japheth was Yellow. It is a biological impossibility for three separate races to come from the same father and mother who were White. The Y-chromosome, which determines, at least gender, is handed down from father to son throughout all generations essentially unchanged. Dominant genes are black skin and black eyes. It takes two recessive genes to produce a redheaded child with ruddy-white skin. The presumptive *cover* theory taught is that as mankind walked out of Africa a Negroid and entered colder climates, evolution of the skin and coloring of eyes occurred over hundreds of thousands of years."

Elias chuckled sarcastically, "This is a calculated lie. A scientific impossibility. This teaching is the politically-correct weapon being used to silence reasoning and force acceptance of mangled scientific facts. *Crucially - this illogical claim that three races came from the same man and woman hides the fact that Satan's seeds live among us, today."*

Elias moved quietly about the circle of QRs. "The truth is that Noah's ark landed, after the Great Flood, on Mount Ararat in Turkey. From the western plateau of Turkey, Sem, Ham, and Japheth proceeded out to father today's people of the world 5600 years ago. Sem was descended from Adam and Eve; Ham and Japheth were descended from Satan - as was Cain.

The lineage of Adam down to Noah and through his son, Sem, down through the ages is: Abraham to Jacob, later to King David, and finally to Jesus Christ. (Luke 3:23-38) They had ruddy white skin, red or blonde hair, blue, green, or grey eyes; and King David was estimated to be 6'7" tall. These are the characteristics of the true Adam and Eve/Hebrew /Israelite bloodline. (Gen. 10:22-11:27; 1 Kings 17:42, and Matt. 1:1-16)"

Elias stopped, his hands held out in supplication, "You all know of the male Y-chromosome, don't you?" He smiled as he looked to one QR's face to another. "You, Jeffrey, my son. What do you know of the Y-chromosome?"

Jeffrey was excited, as if the only child in the class that knew the answer to the teacher's question. His face lit up as he recited the answer, "'A *male has a Y-chromosome essentially identical to that of his father, and his father's father, and his father's father's father, and so on* <u>*back indefinitely through all ancestral generations*</u> *on the Y-chromosome line.'* I read that in National Genealogy. Soc. Quart. 2000, Vol. 88, No. 2, pp 122-143)" (Roderick, Thomas H., Ph.D., *Y Chromosome DNA and the Y-Line,* Center for Human Genetics, Genetics & Genealogy; http://genealogy.about.com/library/authors/ ucroderick1e.htm."

"I also, sir, read that the 'single nucleotide polymorphism (SNP) DYS199 in the Y-chromosome is found in all five Native American populations and Asian populations (Native Siberian populations, Siberian Eskimos, and Asian Chukchi), <u>*but not in African, Australoid, or Caucasian populations*</u>. These studies show that all Native American populations are related to Asian populations.' I read that in a book by Lell G.T. Brown, MD. et al., SpringerLink, 1997, *Y-chromosome Polymorphisms in Native American and Siberian Populations: Identification of Native American Y-chromosome Haplotypes, Human Genetics*, Vol. 100, Numbers 5-6, 536-543; www.godandscience.org/cults/sld033.html."

Elias smiled broadly, "I love an enthusiastic student! So, Jeffrey, what else do you know about genetics?"

"Sir. I know that '*Neither* the NRY haplogroup composition of the majority of Ashkenazi Jews *nor* microsatellite haplotype composition of the R1a1 haplogroup within Ashkenazi Levites is consistent with a major Khazar or other European origin.'" Jeffrey sat proudly and announced, "I read that in a book written by Goldstein, David B. Goldstein. His book is called, *Jacob's Legacy: A Genetic View of Jewish History,* Yale Univ. Press, 2008. Goldstein, Duke Univ. Dept. of Molecular Genetics and Microbiology."

"Excellent," Elias said, "You should advise Harry on how enlightening reading can be."

"William," Elias walked over to the large man sitting in the QR circle, "what deductions can you make from Jeffrey's reading?"

"Sir. I would determine, sir, that the Khazars have always been misidentified as Ashkenazi Jews, such as the Rothschilds, but they are not. Khazars do not share the Y-chromosome of the Ashkenazi Jews, nor the Native American Indians, nor Asians, nor Africans. Therefore, sir, I would determine that the Khazars did not come from Japheth or Ham. Therefore, the Khazars had to have descended from Sem."

"And your determinations would be correct, William. The Khazars are descended from Noah's son, Sem. Khazars are genetic Semites. Japheth's Yellow race Y-chromosome descended to both his son Magog and grandson Ashkenaz, Gen 10:2-3. Ham fathered the Black race. Gentlemen, the Israelites as well as the German Assyrians are the White race, as were Adam and Eve."

"Now, Quinn," Elias pointed, "back to your question of why. It is a battle between good and evil, between the descendants of Adam and the descendants of Satan. Evil uses seduction to capture the souls of the good. Such was the case of King Solomon."

Elias began to walk in a circle inside the circle of the QRs sitting on the prairie grass. "Ohh, it was indeed an evil seduction. It was a seduction whose consequences are meted out to all of you, today. A seduction that vibrates unto the end of times."

Elias stopped, "This is why we are here. Here at the battlefield of the Massacre of Greasy Grass, the Battle of the Little Bighorn. Custer was an Israelite, and he was seduced by Satan – as Satan whispered in his ear to nudge his arrogance and attack the Sioux and Cheyenne when he didn't know the number of his enemy. So to, did Satan whisper in Solomon's ear – build the idols for your foreign wives to worship before – it will not harm you. Just as he had whispered to Eve, you will not die the death. And so Solomon built the idols of Astarthe the goddess of the Sidonians and Moloch the idol of the Ammonites. Solomon also built a temple to Chamos, to worship Ham, Satan's son, the idol of Moab, on the hill next to Jerusalem, 3 Kings 11:5-7."

Elias continued the story of evil, "Then late in Solomon's reign, the wives that he was told not to marry finally seduced him – they were Egyptian wives of the seed of Satan through Ham's son, Mesram. Solomon had built a temple to Moloch, who requires child sacrifices – requires the roasting of infants on the idol's arms. And following their King, the Israelites worshipped these idols of Solomon. Solomon also conjured up demons. Finally, God told Solomon '***Because thou has done this,'*** He would divide the kingdom of Israel - not in Solomon's time - but in his son's time, 3 Kings 11:11-12."

Elias looked into the eyes of each of the QRs as the power drums began to play louder, rumbling against the Bluffs and Wolf Mountains. "Remember this," Elias' voice raised, "This is the true reason that the Israelites have suffered – because they, too, worshipped Astarthe and Moloch, along with Solomon, 3 Kings 11:38-39 – and their suffering from the time of Solomon, down through their descendants, the Israelites will continue to suffer until the end times. This is what we await – the end of that affliction."

Elias walked over to Quinn, "When your Regiment goes to the Dome of the Rock, you will find evidence there of the worship of Astarthe, a pole. You are to destroy it!"

Elias lowered his voice and the drums played softer and the night grew darker, "God had been very close to King David, the 6'7" man built for war, and had made him the only king of the United Kingdom of Israel, the Twelve Tribes of Israelites – those stiff-necked people of Irish, Scottish, English, Norwegians, Swedish, Danish, Scandinavians, Finish, Polish, Ukrainians, Russians, and Khazars. For David's sake, God would give to Solomon's son, the reign over – one tribe – the remnants of the Tribe of Benjamin, who owned Jerusalem, and the Tribe of Juda – the Kingdom of Judah, the place of birth of both King David and Jesus, 3 Kings 11:32."

Elias turned his face to the side, looking at the QRs as he walked before them, "And God would give the Ten Northern Tribes of Israelites to Solomon's servant, Jeroboam, to reign over."

Elias took a few more steps and stopped; his eyes looking down at the prairie grass at his feet, "So, God made a covenant with Jeroboam - if you will obey My Ten Commandments and My principles, as David had, I will give you the Ten the Northern Kingdom of Israel."

Elias lifted up his arms, "But evil had its way." He dropped his hands and looked at Quinn, his voice lowered, "Satan seduced Jeroboam. Satan whispered in his ear, 'You shall lose your power to Rohoboam, Solomon's son, if the Israelites go up to Solomon's Temple to worship the God of Abraham.' So, Jeroboam made two golden calves and told the Ten Tribes of Israelites to worship them instead of going to Jerusalem. Jeroboam told them that the golden calves had delivered them from Egypt. And, sadly, the Northern Tribes of Israelites bought into this absurdity. And this ridiculous worship of golden calves 'became an occasion of sin.' Jeroboam also made priests of men who were not of the Tribe of Levi.

And this was directly against the everlasting ordinance that God had made with Aaron, 3 Kings 12:28-32." Elias paused a moment, then said, "The Israelites obeyed their King and disobeyed their God! And for this, hell would be visited upon them!"

Elias sighed, his head bowed, he looked sideways at the QRs, "The Israelites raised the wrath of God against themselves. God said, 'Therefore I will give your women to strangers, your fields to others for an inheritance: because from the least even to the greatest all follow covetousness: from the prophet even to the priest all deal deceitfully...For behold I will send among you serpents, basilisks, against which there is no charm: and they shall bite you, saith the Lord. *My sorrow is above sorrow, My heart mourneth within Me...*why then have they provoked Me to wrath with their idols, and strange vanities?' Jeremias 8:10-19."

Elias paced back and forth a moment. When he stopped, his voice was ominous, "And so God's wrath came upon the Ten Tribes of Israelites, in 721 B.C. The ancient Assyrians – 'the greatest war-making power in all history,' cousins of the Israelites, and known in the 21st century as the Germans, attacked the Israelites. These ancient, most powerful warriors, swept out of the north, captured the Northern Kingdom of Israel, and took the Ten Tribes into captivity up north. 'From there the Israelites became lost to history...They determined to go to a country 'where never man dwelt,' that they might be free from all contaminating influences. That country could only be found in the north." (Church of Jesus Christ of Latter-Day Saints; www.institute.lds .org/manuals/old-testament-institute-student-manual-2/ot-in2-04-2kg-D.asp)

But the only thing that got lost in history was the description of their physical traits, traits of white and ruddy flesh, red hair and blue eyes – which were assigned to the Irish, Scottish, English, and Vikings. The white skinned blondes were called Norwegians and Danes. The Israelites could not be hidden, so their description was stolen. The description of Israelite traits that emerged from history was that they had dark skin and eyes with hooked noses, and short stature. But this is the description of the Edomites. Deceit of Satan!

Today, the largest ethnic group in the United States is German – once called the Assyrians, the greatest war-making power in all history.

The second largest group in the U.S. is Irish – one of the Twelve Tribes of Israelites in 21st century America. Why are these facts significant? It means that Satan's focus is on the United States. Winston Churchill exposed Satan's end game. Churchill was a satanist who said: 'You must understand that this war (WWII) is <u>not</u> against Hitler or National Socialism, <u>but against the strength of the German *people*</u>, which is to be <u>smashed once and for all</u>, regardless whether it is in the hands of Hitler or a Jesuit priest.' Harry, you can find that written by Emrys Hughes, *Winston Churchill, His Career in War and Peace*, p 145; Winston Churchill, Illuminati-London Bombing In Perspective, by Henry Makow, PhD, 7-24-5; http://rense.com/ general67/curch.htm."

Elias stopped in front of Quinn. He held out his vaporous hand and pointed at Quinn, "You Quinn, you know of the Prophet Ezechiel. You read of him in your research, did you not?"

Quinn nodded, "Yes, sir. I did."

"And what did you find, Quinn?" Elias asked. "Please tell your Regiment."

"Ezechiel prophesied during Babylonian captivity of God's restoration of Israel – 'for God's holy name sake,' Ez. 36:22. This was because in the Tribe of Judah was God's royal line. God had told the Prophet Samuel to go to 'Isai the Bethlehemite: I have provided me a king among his sons.' When David was brought before Samuel, God told Samuel, 'Arise, and anoint him, for this is he.' Samuel anointed David with Holy Oil, 1 Kings 16:1-13. Centuries later, Jesus came through God's royal line, from the House of David, the Tribe of Judah, Matt. 1:1-16."

Elias smiled, "It is good that you know this, Quinn, for you will marry into God's royal line."

"Maggie?"

"Of course, Quinn. Maggie is of God's royal bloodline." Elias turned from Quinn, looking at the other QRs, "What else did you find about Ezechiel's prophecy, Quinn?"

"That God had said, 'Because you,' that is the Israelites, 'have borne the shame of the Gentiles' – God identified the Gentiles. They are the Babylonians who were descendants of Black Ham, Gen. 10:10. And God said: 'And I will bring *men upon you*, My people Israel, and they shall possess thee for *their* inheritance,' meaning that the Gentiles would possess the Israelites, and that the Israelites '*shall no more henceforth be without them*,' Ez. 36:6-12."

"Excellent, Quinn. Excellent," Elias said. "God forewarned of the theft of Israelites' heritage - by Ezra the Edomite, the man that God brought upon the Israelites, who dragged them back from Babylonian captivity to Jerusalem - to inhabit the cities. And, today, the men God brought upon the Israelites are the Ashkenazi Zionist Israelis, the descendants of Japheth, son of Satan – to possess the Israelites as their inheritance."

Elias slowly turned, looking at each of the faces of the QRs, "You have all heard of the Federal Reserve Act of 1913 – it is God's promise of men will own the Israelites as their inheritance."

Elias frowned and pointed at the QRs, "This is your affliction, for you are the seed of David!"

Suddenly, Elias felt pity of the descendants of Adam, for these men of Quinn's Regiment had all their lives followed Jesus Christ. He decided, instead, to soothe their fears. "Jesus told his disciples that Jerusalem shall be trodden down by the Gentiles, the non-Israelites '*till the* times *of the* nations *be fulfilled*,' Luke 21:24. The Edomite Jews and the Muslims are those Gentiles that have trodden down Jerusalem. You will face them on your mission to the Dome of the Rock. The time of the nations will be fulfilled at the end time – when God ends the affliction of the seed of David."

Elias stood in the center of the circle of QRs, held his hands up to the heavens and cried out, "Time, and times, and a half time! Dan. 7:25-28." Elias suddenly laughed, "how often has man tried to understand the meaning of those words. Assigning 1 and 1x, and .5 to the expression – foolish men!"

"Quinn!?" Elias laughed.

"Are you having a good time here tonight?" Elias cried out.

"Ah. Yes, sir. I am."

"Did you have a good time at your children's wedding? You have two children – two weddings – two times a good time."

"Yes. Sir." Quinn said hesitantly.

"Time! It's not a year! Time and times and half time is not a mysterious number of years placed in a formula!" Elias laughed.

"Time and times and a half time – are events! Events of suffering that the Israelites must endure by the men that control them! Daniel prophesied that the Antichrist shall crush the saints and the Israelites will be delivered in to the hands of the Antichrist 'until a time and times, and half a time.' 'Hitherto is the end of the word.'"

Elias looked at the QRs sitting on the battlefield of the Little Bighorn, watching his every move, listening to his every word. "The Antichrist has crushed the saints, those martyred for the love of Jesus the Christ. The seed of David has been delivered to the Antichrist – for centuries – for a time and times and a half time of historical events. Of wars and famines and massacres and diseases. Until the end of the word. The end of God's word, His promise to afflict, but not yet for ever.

You seed of David," Elias' voice whispered in the softness of the drums, "the end of your affliction is at hand. You are the Sons of *man* of Ezechiel's prophecy. The *man* is Adam! The first man that God made. Cain is the creature that Satan fathered.

But, first, you must overcome Gog and Magog – the sons of Japheth, son of Satan, who fathered the Asians, Mexicans, the Central and South Americans, the Native American Indians, and the Edomite Zionist Israelis. For these are the people who are 'over the four quarters of the earth,' who Satan has seduced. These make up the army of Gog – the army of the world – the army of the United Nations.

The Antichrist will gather them together to battle against you, you sons of David, so many as to equal the sand of the sea, Rev. 20:1-7. Satan has seduced Gog, a man who is of the land of Magog. Gog is an Asian. He is the chief prince of Mosoch and Thubal. Gog is the Antichrist that you will war against!"

Elias walked slowly, along the front line of Quinn's Regiment, "I tell ye, you sons of David, set thy face against Gog – against the Secretary General of the United Nations of the world, Yoon Won-Shik, for he is the man from the east. The Secretary General of the United Nations is the

Antichrist! So says the Prophet Ezechiel, 38:2-39:8."

Elias pointed to the eastern heavens and cried out, "The Land of Magog is Korea! And the Prince of Mosoch is South Korea! The Prince of Thubal is North Korea! Tonight, under the stars of the great universe, I tell you, again, of Ezechiel's prophesy: The Lord has said – 'Behold! I come against thee, O Gog! And against your army! I come against the Persians, and Ethiopians, and Libyans, and Gomer'– the Ashkenaz Zionist Israelis!

'Prepare and make thyself ready, and all thy multitude that is assembled about thee, and be thou commander over them.'"

Elias looked at Quinn, "Son! You understand that Gog – the Antichrist is the Secretary General of the UN, Yoon Won-Shik?"

"Yes, sir. I understand," Quinn replied.

Elias looked at Harry, "Son! You understand that Gog shall be visited, after many days: *at the end of years*?"

"Yes, sir. I understand," said Harry, "The UN is 67 years old, which are only minutes measured against the 6000 years of mankind's existence to now, and now is the end of 3000 years of the affliction of the seed of David."

Elias smiled at Harry and then walked on to William. "And you, William. Do you understand that 'Gog shalt come to the land that is returned from the sword.'"

"Yes, sir," William said. "The Antichrist came from Korea and was enthroned in the UN in 2007. Yoon Won-Shik took his seat when some Americans were returning from war in Afghanistan and Iraq."

Elias walked several steps, stopping in front of Jeffrey, "Jeffrey, do you understand 'and is gathered out of many nations, to the mountains of Israel which have been continually waste:'"

"I think it means the Israelites who have been gathered, who came from many countries of the world to the mountains – to the skyscrapers of New York City through Elis Island where legal immigrants came to the U.S. 'Continually waste' means that the old buildings of NYC are continually torn down for new buildings to be built."

Elias smiled and moved on to the next QR, "And you are Donald?"

"Yes, sir."

"Donald, do you understand, 'but it has been brought forth out of the nations, and they shall all of them dwell securely in it.'

"I understand it to mean that the United States was brought forth out of the nations to be the strongest, richest nation of the world. And the Americans. That is, the Israelites dwell securely in it because a World War has never been fought on its soil."

"Very good, Donald." Elias walked on to another QR sitting on the prairie grass. "And you, Scott, do you understand 'And Gog shall go up and come like a storm, and like a cloud to cover the land.'

"I see that as Gog, the Antichrist, the UN Secretary General, will go up and come like a storm – that is, he's going to attack the U.S. with so many soldiers as to appear like a cloud."

"Excellent, my son," Elias praised. "And you, Frank, do you understand 'Gog and your army. Projects shall enter into thy heart and Gog shall conceive a mischievous design.'

"The way I see it, sir, is that the Antichrist and his UN Troops will institute the project of taking the guns from Americans. They are looking to collect data from states that require us to register our guns. The UN wants to know the names and addresses of American gun owners; the number of their guns and the types of guns they own. Somehow that information is supposed to make the world peaceful. But the mischievous design – is that they only want to make sure they collect each gun. They want to know how well the Israelites are armed before they go to war with them."

Elias turned and walked to the center of the circle of QRs and preached. "And Gog, the Antichrist, the UN Secretary General will say: 'I will go up to the land which is without a wall' – you know that Zionist Israel has walls, but the United States – the home of the Israelites has no walls. And Ezechiel prophesized that the Antichrist said: 'I will come to them that are at rest, and dwell securely: all these dwell without a wall, they have no bars nor gates' – this is the United States of America – of the Israelites who dwell securely inside their country.

And Gog, the Antichrist said: 'to take spoils, and lay hold on the prey, to lay thy hand upon them that had been wasted, and afterwards re-stored, and upon the people that is gathered together out of the nations, which has *begun* to possess and to dwell in the midst of the earth.'

The prey are the Israelites, Americans, that had been wasted – killed and held captive in ancient times, by the Assyrians, Babylonians, Romans; and in modern times, by the Japanese, Germans, and Vietnamese. And today, by the Federal Reserve. And they were re-stored here in the United States where they came out of the nations of the world. And since 2007, the Antichrist, the UN Secretary General has begun to possess the Israelites with his UN Agenda 21 and land-takings for UN Biospheres, and through cap and trade taxes. They have built underground military labs and bunkers in which they will dwell when the great war will take place."

Elias moved about slowly, his voice soft amid the power drums that distracted the evil spirits with their never-ending reminder that God's wrath will one day come upon them.

"'Therefore, thou son of man, prophesy and say to Gog: Thus saith the Lord God: shalt thou not know, in that day, when my people of Israel shall dwell securely?'

And thou shalt come out of thy place from the northern parts, thou and many people with thee, all of them riding upon horses, a great company and a mighty army.

And thou shalt come upon My people of Israel like a cloud, to cover the earth. Thou shalt be in the latter days, and I will bring thee upon

My land: that the nations may know Me, when I shall be sanctified in thee, O Gog, before their eyes.

In that day of the coming of Gog upon the land of Israel saith the Lord God, that *My indignation shall come up in my* wrath.

In that day - there shall be a great commotion upon the land of Israel.

And I will judge Gog with pestilence, and with blood, and with violent rain, and vast hailstones: I will rain fire and brimstone upon Gog and upon Gog's army and upon the many nations that are with Gog.

And I will make My holy name known in the midst of My people Israel and My holy name shall be profaned no more: and the Gentiles shall know that I am the Lord, the Holy One of Israel.'"

Elias paused a moment, and as the power drums beat louder, Elias' deep voice bellowed to the heavens, "'*Behold it cometh, and it is done, saith the Lord God:* this is the day whereof I have spoken!' Ezechiel 38:2-22; 39:8."

Chapter 11

It was close to 9pm in the evening when Maggie first noticed Quinn's body flinch, as if being jolted by a small electrical charge. She quickly sat upright, as dread passed through her own body. She grabbed the bottle of Holy Water sitting on the nightstand and sprinkled Quinn's body. And in quick succession, she took up the cross on her Rosaries that she had been praying and laid it on his chest. Booker's words flashed through her mind. The words that she was to recite in case a spirit tried to possess Quinn's body. But as she started to recite them, Quinn opened his eyes and smiled at her. "What a ride, Maggie! What a ride!"

In relief, Maggie relaxed her body and sighed, "For you maybe!" Then she smiled, "Booker told me you were meeting with the ghost of Eisenhower. What was he like? What did he say?"

Quinn sat up, shaking his head in disbelief, looking around the room to see that he was really home and wondering if he had actually been to Montana. It all seemed like an incredible dream. "Maggie!" Quinn cried, as he reached out and took her by the shoulders, "It was unbelievable, so…so… miraculous! Eisenhower is such a great man. And then I went to Montana. I saw the Sioux warrior ghosts! Maggie, I wished that you had been with me. What an incredible experience." Quinn began to tell Maggie of the telepathic and telekinesis training with the QRs.

"Stop right there, just for a moment. I need to use the lady's room – right now!" Maggie said, as she rushed to the bathroom, "I was too afraid to leave your body."

Quinn stood up, and stretched his body as if making sure his soul was securely in control of it. "Let's get something to eat!" he cried out to Maggie.

Both had too much to tell each other to spend time cooking or driving to a restaurant. They couldn't put off telling each other what they had learned since dinner at Maggie's the night before. They ordered pizza to be delivered.

After they finished eating and Quinn had told Maggie all of what Booker had confirmed of Maggie's research on the Y-chromosome of Satan, and Maggie had told Quinn what she had read in *The Art of War*, they took up the topic of J. Pierpont Morgan, the king of the Robber Barons. There was no end to what they wanted to discuss.

But just as Maggie began to talk about the Knickerbocker Trust and the contrived 1907 stock market scandal, she couldn't hold back a yawn that only made Quinn yawn in return. Seeing the other looking half asleep, they laughed softly. "Quinn, we're so ridiculous. What good are we, if we don't take care of ourselves? We've been awake for what? 36 hours? I'm too tired to count. We need to sleep. I have to go home."

As Maggie stood up to leave, Quinn got up, "You never got any sleep last night and today you've been on guard duty all day. You can't drive. You'll fall asleep at the wheel."

"But..."

"No buts," Quinn admonished. "I have a guest bedroom. You can use that. I'll get you a pair of my pajamas."

"Okay. How can I resist warm cozy pj's?"

"There's no reason to."

The next morning, Maggie awoke to noises in the kitchen and the smell of bacon and coffee wafting up the stairs, calling her to the kitchen. She quickly got out of bed and went into the bathroom, showered and dressed. She was famished. But more than that, she couldn't wait to see Quinn.

"Good morning!" she called to Quinn as she entered the large kitchen. "How are you this sunny morning?"

"Hey, Maggie! Good morning. Have a seat at the island counter and I'll get your breakfast."

Maggie sat down on one of the high stools placed around the island. The wide seats were made of soft, leathered-covered cushions with a wide rim of leathered cushion across the back and on the short arms. "Oh, these are very comfortable; sometimes kitchen stools are flimsy."

"Can't have flimsy around here with the friends I have coming and going," Quinn responded, as he took plates and cups from a cabinet.

"You have a very nice house, Quinn. It's very big. How many rooms do you have?"

"There are three bedrooms, two baths; off the dining room I have an office. It's big for someone living alone, but I've owned it many years and it's familiar, comfortable. And there's room for when the kids come to visit. I did a little renovation here and there. I like to work with my hands."

"Did you renovate the kitchen by yourself?"

"With a little help from my friends who know more about it than I do. One of my friends installed the granite counter. He has his own business. Two other friends helped me install the cabinets and the new appliances. We watch a lot of This Old House," Quinn laughed.

"You've all done an excellent job. And the bathroom is beautiful, too." After a pause, Maggie added, "I like to work in the garden, myself," Maggie replied.

Pouring Maggie's coffee, Quinn confessed, "I hate yard work!"

Quinn served bacon and scrambled eggs to Maggie and sat down across from her. "Do you realize, Maggie, how much we have in common? That is, except for yard work," Quinn smiled.

"Yes. I've noticed that. We both have a great deal of passion for our country. We both like to shoot guns!" Maggie smiled in return.

"Yes, we do!" Quinn said, "But we also suffered a bad ending to our marriages."

"How long ago did your wife die?" Maggie asked.

"A little over five years ago. She was sick a long time, too," Quinn added. "She fought breast cancer for about 12 years. It was hard on the kids. My son got married a few months before she died so she could be there. My daughter married three years ago. They've both started their own families, now." Quinn ate quietly for a moment and then asked, "How long have you been alone?"

"I've been divorced 29 years. I was granted an annulment by the Catholic Church. But I don't go to Church anymore. Not since I realized that with Vatican II, the New World Order is controlling it.

"They're getting rid of Jesus in His own church," Quinn said. "Satan's deceit. Can we rely on the priest anymore?"

"I wonder if we ever could," Maggie explained, "as a Catholic, even before Vatican II, I was taught by priests that the priests were intercessors for Jesus and that we should not read the Bible, but go through the priest to seek God's Word. I was actually taught that I could not pray directly to Jesus, only a priest could do that for me."

Maggie took a sip of coffee, then laughed, "One day, when a priest sneezed in front of me, I said, 'God Bless you,' and the priest responded, 'You don't have the authority to do that.'

Maggie laughed louder, "So, I said to the priest, 'Oh, forgive me, I take it back. May God not bless you!'

Quinn smiled broadly.

Maggie continued, "I remember when I was going through a period where I had lost everything, my marriage, my house, my health, and my job. Yet, with all that, I had three small children to care for on my own. It was so bad that I cried to Jesus and I told Him that I was sorry, but I needed to speak to Him. I had no strength to go on alone. I told Him that I know that the priests taught me that I could not, but I needed to speak to Him. I begged Jesus to forgive me for talking, for praying directly to Him, I didn't mean to be disrespectful, but I needed Him so badly. I didn't think that I would survive, otherwise.

Catholics were told that we wouldn't understand the scripture; it's only allegory, anyway. It's not a true history, only moral stories. But if you read scripture, there's a lot there that teaches us about the Word of Jesus and who His enemies are. You get a sense of Jesus, His manner of speech; He becomes familiar to you; you become one with Him; He's not just your God, He's your best friend. You learn how He answered the Pharisees when they tried to entrap Him. You begin to realize that the Bible is factual, and not at all allegory. The Bible teaches us that Satan exists. But in light of Vatican II, should we trust the priests to teach us of Satan's existence and his deceitful ways? Are we idiots that we cannot understand the Word of Christ? Is the history of Exodus a myth; are the Ten Commandments a myth? Are the Dead Sea Scrolls a myth? If so, are all institutionalized religions using faith to make money off people? It's one way or the other."

Maggie took a bite of English muffin and a sip of coffee, and then continued, "It is common knowledge that the Jesuit Black Pope controls the Church from the shadows and is planning to take the throne of

Solomon - Solomon who worshipped the Egyptian pagan idols of his wives. It's common knowledge that the Jesuits lead the Illuminati; that Satan uses deceitful methods; that the priests raped children and the Pope attempted to maintain the Church's policy of secrecy of those molestations; so, how can people rely on what a novus ordo seclorum priest tells them? The New World Order controls all the Christian Churches through their tax status, not just the Catholic Church. And when Jane Celosini was Speaker of the House, she told, and maybe even threatened a change in tax status, if pastors did not preach Romans 13 to Christians that it is their religious duty to obey her Communist government policies, a government that is taking us to the worship of Satan!"

"Was it Cardinal Law who talked about the Pope's policy of secrecy?"

"Yes, Cardinal Law visited Pope John Paul II, about the boy from Boston. That boy was the first of many that followed, in suing the Church for their part in allowing pervert priests to molest altar boys. Everyone knows that the local Bishops were told of priests molesting altar boys and that the Bishops moved those priests to other parishes without warning to the new parishioners. Cardinal Law returned from Rome and said that John Paul II decided to continue the policy of not reporting the molestation to the police, of not defrocking those pervert priests, of not warning anyone in the next parish! But the people of Boston said, Oh, no, you're not! Cardinal Law and the Pope, and all those Bishops involved, should have been indicted and prosecuted for aiding and abetting after the fact of one molestation and before the fact when they reassigned the pervert, who continued to commit the rape of children! People were looking for the prosecution of Cardinal Law, so they transferred him out of Boston, immediately. They later hid him in the Vatican."

Maggie's voice raised in anger. "Who's worse, the pervert who committed the atrocity or the man with power to stop it, but instead covered it up? If that isn't Satan at work, I don't know what is!"

"Not a good situation," Quinn responded. "I'd hate to be anyone of them when they stand before Jesus. Though it doesn't seem that they believe in God! If they do, how can they destroy the lives of children and not stop the practice of shuffling the perverts. These guys didn't stop; they were repeatedly caught and moved to another parish. Where were the Bishops' outrage!"

"I don't think Christians understand what has been going on; they don't see the big picture. But they will in the end times. You can't tell me that good Cardinals or a good Pope would say that policy of secrecy was a valid idea. If you wanted to destroy the Catholic Church, or destroy the religion of Christians, how better to do it than to allow sexual perverts the ability to repeatedly commit the most heinous of crimes, the rape of children! How many people turned away from the Church as a result of those perverted priests? My guess is that setting loose those demons inside the Church was strategically planned by Satan and his bloodline, to empty the Church of Jesus Christ in their push for the New World Order."

"Are you one who turned away from the Church, Maggie?"

"The last time I was at Mass and watched the altar boy carry the book up to the priest to read, all I could think about was how those altar boys were so small, so young, and suddenly the room began swaying, the altar started to swirl. My blood pressure must have shot up. It wouldn't stop. I had to go outside. I haven't been back." Maggie held her coffee cup up to her lips and mumbled, "They took my Church from me. I didn't leave. They took it from me."

Quinn said, "But Jesus said to Peter, in Matt. 16:18, 'That thou art Peter; and upon this rock I will build my church, and the gates of hell shall not prevail against it.'"

"It would seem," Maggie replied, "that for the moment, Satan has gained a foothold. Perhaps that is why Jesus will be returning soon. To close the gates of hell that have been rendered ajar."

"It would seem so," Quinn said. He paused for a while, then asked, "Where do you go to celebrate Christ?"

"I have no where to go. I mean, I pray, but I don't have the body of Christ, the Eucharist. The hymns. At Mass, my heart used to swell with the love of God whenever I listened to the Mass, remembering His sacrifice for us. The reading of scriptures written by the Apostles were a history lesson connecting me to Jesus Christ. I heard Him speaking to me when I listened to the scripture reading. It taught me of the Apostles' devotion to Jesus and what was expected of me as a Christian. I connected emotionally with the Apostles in our love for God. And I connected with the congregation when we heard those scriptures together, at the same time. Sometimes, I talked about the scripture with people I met for the first time at Mass. I came away from Mass with a sense of reaffirmation and direction; a sense of togetherness with God and His community. It's different than reading the Bible on my own.

During Communion, the priest is no longer *allowed* to make the sign of the cross before giving the Eucharist. The priest says 'Corpus Christ' – to me, that's a town in Texas because the rest of the Mass is in the language of the community, whether English or Spanish; Latin is no longer used – unless you can find another Church and at a specified time – as though its taboo. They took out the sign of the cross during the prayer of Doxology, 'Through Him, with Him, and in Him in the unity of the Holy Spirit, all honor and glory is yours, Almighty Father, for ever and ever.' It's the prayer of the Trinity."

Quinn responded, "The International version is: For from him and through him and to him are all things. To him be the glory forever! Amen."

"Where is the Holy Ghost? Where's the Almighty Father? Where is Jesus? This is what I'm talking about - they have disrespected them! And I won't be part of that."

Maggie paused, then continued, "The last Gospel of the Mass has been omitted. They no longer say the Leonine prayers: They no longer pray to Michael the Archangel the Protector of Christ's Church! The one who defeated Satan! They no longer pray the Hail Mary, Hail Holy Queen, Oh God, or the Most Sacred Heart of Jesus!

What's wrong with these people?! Those prayers signify a holy family - the Father, the Holy Ghost, the Son, the Mother, and the Protector – Michael, the Commander of God's Legions of Angels. And Pope John XXIII, Pope Paul VI, and the Second Vatican Council took all that from me."

"They won't prevail, Maggie. One day, after the war, you'll have that back."

"You know, Quinn. When you think about the war that is coming. Of the end of times that is to come. You wonder."

"About what?" Quinn asked softly.

Maggie looked at Quinn's eyes, kind and warm. "I wonder," Maggie sighed. "I wonder about death. About the life hereafter. About our corporal bodies that we won't have in death. That is to say, there won't be marriage after death." Maggie sighed heavily this time. It was difficult for her to speak of such things especially being alone with Quinn in his house. Somehow it seemed a dangerous topic in the setting of Quinn's home; his bedroom nearby.

Finally, "Have you thought of sex? I mean. About having sex before you might die in the war. This will be the last we will possess our bodies. The last we can touch and feel each other's warmth. Each other's caress. It's very difficult."

"What is difficult?" Quinn asked in almost a whisper.

"We could die soon. I've tried to live a Christian life all these years. But I want to be with you before we die."

Quinn listened quietly.

"I question, how can I sin, or ask you to sin, when I know it will hurt God? I love Him. And what is love if not to control desire when that desire will hurt the beloved? Especially when I know that it's what Satan wants me to do, to hurt God and lose my soul to him. But I look at you and I want you like I've never wanted another man. You say we have so much in common - well, when I look at you, I see me. All my life, without realizing it until I met you, I've wanted a man who is my mirror image. You are that man, Quinn. You are my male counterpart." Maggie stopped and took a sip her coffee, more to give Quinn a chance to think about what she was saying than to quench her thirst. Quinn waited quietly for her to continue.

"You are my male counterpart because you love God as much as I do. God is the foundation of our principles. You overcame many similar hardships in life; hardship you had no control over that could have destroyed you. But you prevailed because you knew God loved you and would always be there for you, just as I did. You're smart; you're an independent thinker. And regardless of what you've been through;

regardless of your broken heart, you are kind. And I know that you don't want me for sexual pleasure of the body, but for becoming one in our love for each other. You want me to love you just the way you are, an average guy. And I want that, too. I'm just an average girl." Maggie's eyes filled with tears and she paused for a long time. Quinn remained silent.

"Quinn, I want with all my heart and mind to make love to you," she took a deep breath and looked up to the ceiling for a moment. Then she looked deeply into Quinn's warm brown eyes, "But I can't make love to you. And I know that this may be our last chance to feel our bodies embrace, but I can't sin. I don't want either of us to lose our souls to Satan."

"We could marry, Maggie," Quinn said.

"But do we know each other well enough to consider marriage?" Maggie replied.

"As you said, we share the same love of God, the same principles, and those are the elements that every marriage needs. The things that ruin a marriage are financial problems, but I'm comfortable in my retirement; this house is paid off. We like to do the same things." Quinn smiled, "And if you snore, I can always sleep in one of the empty bedrooms."

Maggie laughed. "I don't think that I snore. And if you do, I don't think that it would keep me awake. Actually, I think it would make me feel safe hearing you close by me."

Maggie grew quiet. After a moment, "You know Quinn. It's very, and I do mean very difficult not to jump on your bones."

Quinn smiled, "And I yours, Maggie. So, what do you say," Quinn reached his hand across the counter, taking hold of Maggie's hand, "Maggie, will you marry me?"

Maggie looked into Quinn's eyes and smiled, "Yes. I will, Quinn."

Chapter 12

The 11th dimensional generals were about to meet deep inside Colorado's Cheyenne Mountain military defense facility that once housed the North American Aerospace Defense Command, NORAD. The generals chose the control-center room because it was in warming-stage abandonment and it had giant viewing screens on which to plot the attack. The ghosts of U.S. Army Generals Washington, Lee, Grant, Sherman, Patton, McArthur, Bradley, Air Force General LeMay, and Fleet Admiral Nimitz would be the strategists for the Second American Revolution that eventually would bring about the worldwide end-times.

The apparition of General George S. Patton, 3rd Army Commander of U.S. Forces, WWII European Theatre, permeated the wall and became a solid form. His shiny field helmet carried four stars, and his tailored, brown field jacket held numerous medals, including two Silver Stars, a Purple Heart, two Distinguished Service Crosses, and three Distinguished Service Medals. He wore khaki riding breeches, and at his hips hung an ivory-grip Colt .45 and Smith & Wesson .357 magnum, his 'killing gun.' Brown Calvary boots came up to his knees. A riding crop in his hand, he tapped it pensively against the palm of his other hand. The war room was not unfamiliar to the General, since he had visited many times in the past to watch operations. Back then, the multiple computers arrayed on u-shaped desks that faced the viewing screens across the upper front wall seemed like a strange weapon of war. But he had watched and learned their importance and their capabilities.

As he walked in and around the desks, he was torn by the love of going in to battle again and his heart weighing heavily for the soldiers who died fighting for the freedom of Europe, and thus, the United States. It all seemed for naught. He thought back to the Blood and Guts speeches he gave, telling his soldiers how he 'pitied those poor bastards' that they'd be going up against. Looking around, he wished he could say it to all Americans, because they would be the soldiers, every man, woman, and child of them – fighting for the very life of America, as well as their own.

He wanted to tell the whole country what he had said to his soldiers, "We're not just going to shoot the bastards; we're going to cut out their living guts and use them to grease the treads of our tanks. We're going to murder those lousy Hun bastards. The Nazis are the enemy. Wade into them. Spill their blood; shoot them in the belly. We're going to kick the hell out of him all the time and we're going to go through him like crap through a goose." On the face of it, it was a gory image, but just as a football coach revved up his players, the General revved up his soldiers to do what was necessary to win a war, and in war people died – it's kill or be killed. War was going to come to the American people, whether they wanted it or not, for the enemy was at the door about to take over the United States of America.

Patton was troubled because he understood that Americans were deeply hated by their enemies, and he knew that they didn't comprehend the magnitude of that hatred or its consequences.

Today, America's enemies are the Muslims, Zionist Jews, Russia, China, and the Jesuits, and he wanted to tell all Americans to kick the hell out of all of them. Go through like crap through a goose every Hezbollah, Hamas, and al Qaeda that had invaded the U.S.! That had set up their paramilitary camps across America and were now only waiting for the order to go out into the towns and slaughter every American that they encountered. At the same time, he did, indeed, pity America's enemies, for nothing bonded Americans together better than the love of their country. The only problem Patton foresaw was warning Americans before the Muslim terrorists attacked, first.

Fighting for America was in Patton's blood; his ancestors had fought in the Revolution, the Mexican War, and on the side of the Confederacy during the Civil War. He had prepared himself for war at West Point and the Army War College, and competed in the military Olympics with sword fencing, shooting, horseback riding, swimming, and cross country running. In France, he organized the American tank school and trained the first 500 American tankers. At the battle of Meuse-Argonne Operation, he led the tank charge, using pigeons and a group of runners to communicate with the other tanks on the field. The German tanks had radio communications between each other. It was Patton's lead tank that busted through the locked gates of the Buchenwald concentration camp. He was the first leader to force the German citizens of the neighboring town to face what they had allowed to happen inside Buchenwald, man's inhumanity to man, for which they were responsible. The order had become the standard used by other generals.

"I can't say that I'm surprised to find you are here first, George!" Bradley said sarcastically, as his apparition appeared in the control center. His field helmet displayed his 5-star General's rank, but his brown waist jacket and long pants with shorter boots were regulation Army uniform.

"Brad, are you mocking me, you son-of-a-bitch!" Patton laughed.

Bradley confessed. "No, George. I was just thinking that I have never had a real chance to tell you how impressed I was at the speed you covered Normandy. No one but you could drive a tank division 40 miles a day. Your 3rd Army liberated and conquered 81,522 sq. miles; 600 miles across France, Belgium, Luxembourg, Germany, Austria, and Czechoslovakia. George, I think you were the greatest field commander of WWII, and maybe in history. One victory after another. You were incredible! The only thing that stopped you was FDR and Churchill. If Roosevelt hadn't redirected your gas supplies to Montgomery in the north, you would have taken Berlin. Everyone knows that, George."

"Brad, those sons-of-bitches gave Berlin to the Russians to take. But worse yet, it was the way they did it. I'm telling you, Brad, there'll be no cutting off gasoline and ammo supplies to Americans the way FDR did to our boys in Metz, France. It breaks my heart that American boys were attacked all night long, outnumbered by the Germans. Unable to escape because they had run out of gasoline! When our boys ran out of ammo, they fought hand-to-hand combat." Patton sighed, "My God, I wish I had been with them." Patton walked passed Bradley in quiet contemplation, then whispered, "Jesus Christ! Hand-to-hand combat! Against all odds of winning! How much braver can a soldier be?"

Patton walked up to the giant viewing screens mounted on the walls, thinking quietly, then asked Bradley, "How can a Commander in Chief sacrifice his soldiers for a foreign country's victory? FDR took away their ammo and the gasoline that would have allowed their retreat. And he did it just to keep our division from taking Berlin! FDR is singularly responsible for the slaughter of our boys in Metz. That's the kind of dirty politics that no one ever talks about. Sacrifice of our brave fighting soldiers to give the Russians the glory of taking Berlin."

"The scuttlebutt is that FDR is serving eternity in hell," Bradley tried to comfort.

"Jesus assigned him to the right post," Patton replied, adding in reverie, "My wish is that Dante was right that the lowest depth of hell is reserved for those who betrayed their benefactors. Those American boys were Roosevelt's benefactors!" Patton cried.

"Gentlemen," Washington greeted as his apparition manifested itself into the room. His white skin had a rosy complexion not unlike the many paintings of the first Lieutenant General of the Continental Army.

Bradley and Patton snapped to attention, "General Washington!" Bradley replied, "Sir, it's good to see you, again."

"Indeed. Sir!" Patton greeted.

Patton was 6'2" and Washington was 6'3" and both stood as if their backs were made of steel rods for they had the awareness of being a role model for their troops. Their images alone commanded attention and respect, but the sternness of their faces created a greater depth of admiration for their individual character and loyalty to their troops and country. That sternness was a result of the responsibility they had taken on during life and now, again, in death.

Washington took off his military tricorn, black felt Continental infantry hat and placed it on a console desk. His dark blue coat with buff-colored trim and pewter buttons touched his upper thigh as he walked. His white shirt exposed ruffles at the collar and wrists of the dark blue coat. A buff-colored waistcoat covered the waistline of the white wool breeches. His white hair was tied at the nap of his neck.

He walked over to Patton. "As I entered the mountain, I heard what you were saying about FDR as Commander in Chief. That kind of politics is treasonous. Our problem was with the Continental Congress having no power to raise money to support the Revolution because we were not yet free from King George; politics that caused the death of soldiers just the same, however. Not all our men had uniforms; and old, torn uniforms could not be replaced. In Trenton, my men suffered greatly with frostbite of hands and feet. In fact, some of our men were barefoot except for the wool scarfs that they wrapped around their feet. After we crossed the Delaware River, we had to march through that terrible snowstorm, but the storm also allowed us to get close enough to the Hessians without being seen."

Washington turned and took a few steps away from Patton and Bradley, "When my men complained that the snow had gotten into their rifles, I told them to use their bayonets." Washington looked back at Patton, "Sometimes, I regret having taken such a hard line, but the Battle of Trenton was important; we needed that victory. And it did bring more volunteers into the Continental Army. So, perhaps their suffering, their courage was worth it in the end. It was their sacrifice that gave us our country."

Before Patton or Bradley could respond, General Lee's apparition materialized. He removed his Confederate uniform hat, "Good evening, Gentlemen." He nodded to Patton and Bradley before walking over to Washington to shake his hand. "General Washington, I have always admired your ability to keep your men fighting against great odds at the Battle of Trenton."

"Thank you, Lee. But I think it was their love of freedom and their dream of independence that drove them forward during such brutal adversity."

In life, Lee's wife had been the granddaughter of Washington's wife, Martha. Lee thought Washington to be a great man and even in death, Lee was awe struck by his presence.

Lee nodded to Washington, "As you say sir, freedom from King George was a great motivator."

Just then, General Grant's apparition manifested itself. "Generals!" The bearded man greeted. Although he had been president following the Civil War, Grant's apparition appeared in his Civil War Union uniform that showed the scars of battle. He walked over to Washington, "Sir. I await your orders."

Washington nodded to the much shorter man and then replied, "We will be listening to a military commander of later experience, General McArthur; he will be with us, presently."

"Yes, Sir," Grant replied and then turned, "General Lee, I am in hopes that we can put aside our last encounter. We need to join forces in this war, for the good of the country. After all, General, we did fight together during the earlier Mexican War."

"Sir. I do not recall your face from the Mexican War," Lee said, "But I know you, of course. It was after Lincoln appointed you that the tide changed in the Civil War and you and Sherman enforced your plan against the Confederacy."

"The Mexican War was, for many of us," Grant replied, "our initiation after West Point. But as to the Civil War, it is likely that we generals knew each other too well – had been taught the same tactics and counter-tactics – to fight against each other."

"I often wondered when President Lincoln would send in a general for the Union Army that was a stranger to me," Lee responded.

"Knowing how your enemy thinks is of great benefit," General William Tecumseh Sherman interjected, as his ghost emerged through the wall of the control center. His red hair and beard portrayed a much younger man in contrast to the white hair of Lee, Washington, and Patton. "General Washington," Sherman came to attention, "My respects, Sir."

Washington nodded, "At ease, General."

Sherman then turned to Lee, "Today, we are able to invisibly penetrate our enemy's war room. But our greatest advantage is a Union fighting together against the enemy that has invaded that Union. For surely, the foreign invaders, the United Nations, plan to take the whole continent. It will force the 26 states that are taking steps to secede to come together to save our country from foreign threat."

Sherman's mere presence caused Lee's great temper to flare inside him. Just at the sight of him reminded Lee of Sherman's March to the Sea. Lee's life-long, practiced struggle to control that temper kept it in check, for the moment, at least. "I expect that we will correct the injuries of the past."

Washington offered, "When this is all over, the first thing we must do is to re-write the Constitution to give the citizens a direct forum to recall their Senators and Congressmen when corruption has captured their mortal souls. And no agency of the Executive Branch shall be able to create and institute law; the EPA must go! We must also institute an amendment prohibiting all corporations and unions from contributing to political campaigns. We cannot let another Tsaeb foreigner be certified by only the Speaker of the House. Certification must be nailed to the door of every town hall and approved by every state. We will end Tsaeb's method of bundling of campaign donations that cannot be checked. That bundling of contributions was a cover for foreign contributors, especially the large contributions of Saudi Arabia."

Lee added, "We must take the power away from Congress to regulate commerce. Their absolute tyranny comes through the zealous misuse of that constitutional power. A simple Amendment must be made that provides that all commerce must flow freely between the States and no State or Federal law may obstruct it. That was the original intent of the Commerce Clause – to make sure that commerce flows, and nothing more. Congress must also be subject to every law they pass. The States will vote on the benefits and wage increases that the Federal Congress shall receive. And the States must be given the power to try members of Congress. Congress must face imprisonment for passing any law that is counter to the Constitution. Any law that gives away Congressional power, such as the Federal Reserve Act, will mean the penalty of imprisonment of the Congress who voted for such law. Furthermore, the power Congress gave the Presidency to make laws through Executive Orders and Proclamations is one such abomination. No law can consume or subsume a treaty, such as the Clear Water Act attaching the United States to the Law of the Sea Treaty – done without the Constitutional requisite of Senate approval. Tsaeb's healthcare bill that allows him to appoint commissioned officers to the Ready Reserve Corp is strictly forbidden by Art. I, Section 8, cl. 16 of the Constitution. That authority was given to the States. That is the power of a dictator! That was never the intent of the Founding Fathers!"

Just then the apparition of General Stonewall Jackson appeared, and after first showing his respect to Washington, he immediately continued on with the discussion at hand. His stern face showed his anger, "Lincoln's Emancipation Proclamation was a farce; a political maneuver. The south had already formed its own country, its own government; all we needed was for England and France to recognize us as a separate country. But as soon as Lincoln had the victory at the Battle of Antietam, he issued that Proclamation to keep England and France from doing just that! Sherman, if we have another ultimatum as the one that Lincoln issued to the south - 100 days to come back into the Union, and if we did, we could keep our slaves - this Revolution will be for naught.

Did Lincoln think we were fools? We might have kept our slaves, our economy, for a few years, but we knew he'd take them from us eventually. The damnable Emancipation Proclamation never addressed the North's prohibition to keep their slaves; there was no question that they could, but the south could not!? Why do you think South Carolina seceded before Lincoln's inauguration? They knew Lincoln was going to free our slaves. Lincoln didn't give a damn about slavery; his only concern was to hold on to the Union. And whatever political maneuvering he had to go through to accomplish that, he did, including his Proclamation that did not free the northern slaves! How could we have been a Union if the northern states, Maryland, Missouri, Delaware, and Kentucky could keep their slaves? Even in D.C. These were states that would have remained slave states. All of them had thousands of slaves each; how could the south have competed against the northern economy with those uneven odds? You had one man with the power of a dictator controlling the South and screwing the southern economy to the wall!"

Jackson's voice raised in anger, "There will be no more Proclamations or Executive Orders from the Office of the Presidency after this Revolution!"

Lee looked at Sherman, "I expect that General Jackson will be as much of a stonewall in these feelings as he was at the Battle of Manassas."

It was an intentional slap in the face, a reminder that Jackson had won that battle, capturing 11,000 Union soldiers, in the first major land battle of the war.

"I expect, General Sherman, that we will not have a repeat of your March to the Sea and your ravaging and looting a 60-mile swath in your pathway. The destruction of our railroads and the Sherman neckties you left in its wake reeked great suffering upon the southern people."

Sherman's blue eyes flared in temper, "General Lee, how can you make that charge when you did the same in attempting to break the East-West supply line of the Union Army!'

Lee began to lose his great temper, "Confederate soldiers didn't burn the private property of the northerners! We paid the people for the food we took; your men did not, Sir! The north was flourishing during the war; barns were bursting with food. You took all the food the southerners had and left them hungry!" Lee accused, as he took a step toward Sherman. "Your teenage army, General Sherman, left Columbia a wasteland!"

"It was a hard war!" Sherman defended, as he moved toward Lee. "The worst that I could make it, the faster it would end. But I didn't order the burning of Columbia, sir! My troops took that upon themselves. They got carried away and burned more of Atlanta than I had ordered." Sherman's anger focused and his voice grew louder, "But my troops had a loyalty and a toughness not seen since the time of Julius Caesar!"

Lee charged, moving closer to Sherman, "Your total war tactic was only to humiliate and break the heart of the South!"

The two men were now almost nose to nose, "And that's why the South resents you the most!"

Lee's faithful commander, Stonewall Jackson, moved in behind Lee. Grant took notice and moved in behind his close friend, Sherman. At that very moment, the ghost of Sam Houston materialized. "Gentlemen!" he looked at Lee and Stonewall, "I warned the south. When everyone was ramping up for war, I told you, think about what you are contemplating. After the expenditure of hundreds of millions of treasure and hundreds of thousands of lives are lost, you might gain southern independence, but I doubt it." Houston moved his large frame slowly around the four men in standoff position, "I told you that the North was determined to maintain this Union. They are not a fiery, impulsive people like yourselves for they live in colder climates, but when they begin to move in a given direction they move with the steady perseverance and all-consuming power of a mighty avalanche."

Houston stopped with Sherman on his left, Lee on his right, "Gentlemen, need I say it again, if the destruction of this Union be its fate, I wish the ruins be the monument of my grave. If we do not move away from the past and fight the Muslims and the Zionist Jews and their leader, Satan, my monument will be at the gates of hell."

"Generals!" Patton cried out, stepping toward the five men, looking at all the ghosts that were in the room. "Jesus Christ! Not a peacemaker among us!" Patton laughed.

The four men didn't move, not even Grant took notice of Patton to show his aversion to his profanity. As in life, Grant continued in death his principle to never retreat, just as he had refused to do in the Forest of the Wilderness, after Lee had attacked Grant's army and inflicted great losses.

Patton cajoled, trying to break the standoff, "Stonewall, here, is as bloodthirsty for battle as I am!" He turned back to Stonewall, "You knew my uncle, Waller Patton; he died of wounds from Pickett's Charge at Gettysburg. You knew my grandfather George S.; he was killed at the Battle of Opequon – both fought for the Confederacy. But today, we are here to save the Union."

The men remained unmoved from their threatening positions. In desperation, Patton turned toward Washington, "Sir, please."

The three-quarter length jacket of Washington's Continental Army uniform flowed like a judge's robe, as he walked toward the men poised for fight. The white ruffle of his shirt protruding below the jacket's sleeve fell upon the gray wool of Lee's Confederate uniform as Washington's hand took hold of Lee's shoulder. His other hand took hold of the dark blue wool of Sherman's Union uniform. The three men seemed related by the uniqueness of their tall stature, and except for Patton and Houston, it could have easily shut out the others from what became their private discussion. If anyone could make the Generals listen, it was Washington.

"Gentlemen, instead of fighting the Civil War all over again, let's learn from it. You were all teachers. Lee you were once Superintendent of West Point; Sherman you were Superintendent of Louisiana State Military Academy." Washington turned toward Stonewall, "Stonewall, you were a professor of artillery. Even Patton, here, organized the American tank school in Bourg, France, and trained the first 500 American tank fighting soldiers. Grant, you wanted to teach math. All of you graduated from West Point. The Civil War has many things to teach us; it was the first modern war, the first time the telegraph was used in war, the first time that the railroad was used to move troops. The south used land mines for the first time. The war that we are about to engage in will also offer us military firsts. We need to focus on those firsts. All of you are Americans and great patriots, and now your country needs you to work together.

Gentlemen, the Continental Army fought to institute the most unique government ever known to mankind, a popular government for and by the people that allows its citizens' to take action in self-determination, to seek their own prosperity. The founding framework came out of previous civilizations, from Athens, Rome, London – they were the research for our experiment. And we have learned of the changes needed to keep our enemies from ever again conquering us from within We know now how to prevent the need for a third armed revolution – which is now our only recourse to save our country.

There is not an American in this country that will allow us to be taken. There is no army in the world who can take down our Union, only ourselves. But if we leaders do not put the past behind us and join together, what cohesive force will hold Americans together, to lead them? For when the time comes, Americans will be screaming from the hilltops, from the valleys, for the blood of the enemy! If chaos reigns in that fever-pitch outrage, we will soon face the world on our doorsteps, because if we show a lack of leadership, foreign countries will attack individually, on their own – forget the United Nations. Gentlemen, we must show a united front to Americans and the world."

The men looked at Washington, and as if answering their father, Lee and Sherman replied in unison, "Yes, Sir!"

Whether their anger subsided in self-control, or whether it was put off for expression on another day, it didn't matter. The sons had to obey their father out of respect and because he was right, division brought weakness and the tempting smell of victory to foreign countries in the possibility of destroying both the North and the South. The sons obeyed his order. Lee looked at Sherman and held out his hand; Sherman shook Lee's hand in friendship.

At that moment, Fleet Admiral Chester Nimitz materialized in the control room. Nimitz had replaced Kimmel at Pearl Harbor shortly after the Japanese had bombed the battleships. FDR had used Kimmel as a scapegoat. Before the time of the attack, FDR had ordered the battleships to be docked in a row while the aircraft carriers had been ordered to sea without their task force escorts. FDR had issued a direct order to Kimmel and General Short, Commander of the Army Forces in Hawaii: "the U.S. desires that Japan commit the first overt act." Kimmel and Short obeyed the Commander in Chief of the Army and Navy of the United States, regardless of what else they thought.

After the attack on Pearl Harbor and the Island of Oahu, and in a pre-emptive political strike to silence the Congressional voices that were demanding a Congressional investigation be made of the surprise attack on Pearl Harbor, FDR handpicked U.S. Supreme Court Justice Owen Roberts to lead a presidential investigation commission. But the Roberts' Commission asked no questions of the cryptographers or radio operators; no Navy documents had been reviewed because Rear Admiral Leigh Noyes, Naval Director of Communications, had re-classified all pre-Pearl Harbor Japanese military and diplomatic intercepts and directives as Top Secret just four days after the attack and only days before FDR appointed the presidential commission. That Top Secret classification prohibited even Congress from reviewing official records. And FDR did not order Rear Admiral Leigh Noyes to rescind his Top Secret classifications that would disclose that FDR aided and abetted an attack by the enemy of the United States of America.

Noyes, instead, took it a step further and placed the revealing documents into Navy vaults with the order that they not see the light of day for 54 years. Noyes further ordered that all notes or anything in writing be destroyed. But all notes, written by military personnel, on military property, are the property of the U.S. Government and can only be destroyed by an act of Congress. All cryptographers kept personal files of classified documents, therefore, Fleet Admiral Ernest King, who oversaw the censorship, threatened cryptographers and radio operators that they were to say nothing of the messages they decoded, now or after retirement, or they would face imprisonment and loss of Navy benefits if they did. Only portions of the vaulted documents were released under the Freedom of Information Act, but they disclosed that the U.S. Navy had decoded the Japanese messages. And, one day, would disclose that President Franklin D. Roosevelt knew that the Japanese were going to bomb Pearl Harbor – and when they would attack.

The Japanese top admiral had gone on Japanese naval airwaves to speak to the Japanese fleet; the intelligence was passed directly to the White House, to FDR, that said Japan planned to attack Pearl Harbor in the first part of December. Ambassador Joseph Grew had learned from his contacts that Japan had planned a carrier attack on Pearl; the Japanese carrier force was discovered by Station CAST on Corregidor. In January 1941, Ambassador Grew warned the White House. On April 22, 1941, Chief radioman Leroy Lankford gave the first details; the carrier force command was centered aboard HIJMS Akagi. Lankford told the White House, word for word, what the Japanese commander was telling his fleet. To pass this intel on to the White House, U.S. Navy monitoring stations relayed the message from Dutch Harbor, to Territory of Alaska, to Samoa, to Hawaii, to Corregidor, and to two San Francisco stations the every move of Japanese Vice Admiral Nagumo and the carrier Akagi. Nagumo had violated every Japanese security code. Lt. John M. Lietwiler, U.S. commanding officer of Station CAST on Corregidor, sent a message to FDR: we have decoded and translated Japanese Naval operations code.

On October 9, 1941, FDR receives a briefing on the status of atomic bomb research; FDR asked if a bomb can be built. On November 5, 1941, Nagumo issues radio orders, making it clear that the Japanese will attack the U.S. and the English and Dutch colonies in the pacific, in the first part of December. On November 9, 1941, FDR is told that a nuclear bomb is feasible. By mid-November, Navy cryptographers and radio operators tell FDR that Pearl is the target and the method of attack is a carrier raid. On December 2, 1941, Nagumo's message: attack will commence on December 8, 1941. On December 7, 1941, Pearl Harbor is attacked – almost one year after FDR knew of the planned attack.

On January 19, 1942, FDR approves building a nuclear bomb. December 28, 1942, FDR approves producing nuclear weapons. July 17, 1944, the plutonium gun bomb, "Thin Man," is abandoned. February 4-11, 1945, FDR, Churchill, and Stalin meet at Yalta. April 12, 1945, FDR dies in the arms of his mistress. July 26, 1945, Potsdam Proclamation; Japan rejects surrender plan. On August 6, 1945, a U.S. B-29 bomber, the Enola Gay, named by the pilot after his mother, drops a nuclear bomb on Hiroshima. August 8, 1945, Russia invades Manchuria, Japan. On August 9, 1945, the U.S. drops a nuclear bomb on Nagasaki. On August 14, 1945, Japan surrenders.

FDR withheld all pre-Pearl Harbor attack decoded and diplomatic intel from Kimmel and Short, and after FDR's Roberts Commission Report assigned blame of Kimmel and Short, FDR charged the two with dereliction of duty. Admiral James Richardson condemned the findings, stating that "It is the most unfair, unjust, and deceptively dishonest document (13,000 page Roberts Commission Report) ever printed by the Government Printing Office. I cannot conceive of honorable men serving on the commission without greatest regret and deepest feeling of shame."

In his 1955 book, *Admiral Kimmel's Story*, Husband Kimmel wrote:

> The Navy Department thus engaged in a course of Conduct which definitely gave me the impression that Intelligence from important intercepted Japanese messages ["Magic"] was being furnished to me. Under these circumstances a failure to send me important information of this character was not merely a withholding of intelligence. It amounted to an affirmative misrepresentation…Yet, in fact, the most vital information from the intercepted Japanese messages was withheld from me. This failure not only deprived me of essential facts. It misled me. I was not supplied with any information of the intercepted messages showing that the Japanese government had divided Pearl Harbor into five areas and was seeking minute berthing information as to the berthing of ships of the fleet in those areas, which was vitally significant. (http://www.ihr.org/jhr/v16/v16n6p35_Weir.html)

There was no doubt, FDR knew ahead of time of the attack to be inflicted upon Pearl Harbor, and intentionally withheld warning and allowed it to happen, which resulted in the irretrievable sinking of the USS Arizona, and severe damage to the Utah, Oklahoma, Cassin, Downes, Shaw, and Oglala. There were 2897 Americans killed, 879 wounded, and 26 missing. On Oahu, severe damage was done to the Army's hangars with 188 aircraft destroyed.

The reason FDR wanted Japan to commit the first overt act, which was intentionally and extensively caught on film just as the 9/11 attack on the World Trade Towers, was because FDR secretly wanted to go to war. The American people wanted nothing to do with war, whether in Europe or in the Pacific; the nation wanted isolationism. FDR lied by telling the American people that he was an isolationist, also. To get the American people to consent to his declaring war on Japan, FDR needed the American people to be outraged – therefore, film crews were at the ready to capture that instigation of outrage – the filming of the Japanese murdering their sons and daughters by drowning in sinking ships, burned alive, and blown to smithereens.

And FDR wanted the battleships sunk, just as Lyndon Baines Johnson wanted the Israelis to sink the USS Liberty. FDR thought battleships were outdated for WWII, so he ordered them docked in a row at Pearl, when he knew precisely when the Japanese were going to attack, and against the wishes of Kimmel who wanted them at sea. FDR wanted his war to be fought with aircraft carriers; those ships he ordered to sea, out of harm's way, before the attack.

After the Japanese inflicted severe damage to the U.S. Pacific Fleet, FDR declared war on Japan and Germany; three days later, Germany and Italy declared war on the U.S., as part of the tri-pack agreement the two countries had with Japan.

Before the war, the Japanese Navy had been half again as large as the U.S. Navy, and the disparity grew even larger in favor of the Japanese after Pearl Harbor. Before the war, the Japanese had 15 aircraft carriers all stationed in the Pacific; the U.S. had five aircraft carriers stationed in the Pacific and four stationed in the Atlantic. After the war, the Japanese had two carriers left, and the U.S. had 100 aircraft carriers and escort carriers, built by the American people during the war. Parts for carriers and aircraft were manufactured in converted U.S. appliance and auto factories, while shipyards assembled on a 24/7 schedule. U.S. factories today are fewer because congressional laws benefit manufacturing in foreign countries such as Mexico and China, albeit their producing far inferior appliances and autos. And defense system parts are being manufactured by foreign countries – one of whom withheld delivery of those parts because they didn't like U.S. foreign policy. The Defense Department had to hunt around the U.S. for a small business tool and die maker to manufacture the parts. Hence, Tsaeb's war against small businesses with his healthcare mandate of small businesses to provide expensive insurance, and running small business out of business.

The U.S. Congress and its President have intentionally taken from Americans their ability to turn on a dime the manufacturing of its defense system as they were able to do following the declaration of U.S. entry in to WWII.

Prior to the declaration of war and because of Americans' demand for isolationism, FDR could only assist England through the Lend Lease agreement to loan them 50 destroyers, for which England gave the U.S. use of their naval bases around the world for 99 years. When the Germans sunk two U.S. ships, nothing was made of it, for the sake of FDR, Churchill, and Hitler. Hitler did not want to antagonize the U.S. and had issued orders to the German Navy to stay clear of U.S. vessels. But, in any event, no case could be made that the Germans knew they were U.S. ships. It was better for all sides to ignore the incident, for now, since FDR and Churchill had other methods to bring Americans into the war; both awaited the attack on Pearl Harbor. Churchill knew that once the Americans declared war on Germany that England would win. Prior to the U.S.' entry in to the war, England was losing all the battles with Germany, except for the Battle of Britain, but England won only because of the undisclosed help from the U.S. Without the U.S., the Germans would have invaded England. The only way supplies were getting into England was by U.S. supply ships.

Both Churchill and Roosevelt wanted the Japanese to attack Pearl Harbor to manipulate the will of the American people. FDR's plan to present the films of the attack on Pearl to the American people was an intentional tactic to cultivate and deepen the heartbreak and humiliation of the American people. He could then declare war in both the Pacific and European Theatres with their strong support and urging. After the attack on Pearl Harbor, FDR's main concern was public opinion of the attack; did his plan work? He needed Americans to be sufficiently outraged to support his declaration of war against Japan. Sacrificing Kimmel and Short was necessary to redirect the American people's attention away from FDR and insulate him from the charge of poor leadership in keeping America safe. It kept FDR from being recognized as the traitor that he was; as the murderer of all the Americans who died at Pearl Harbor. It gave the American people someone to blame for their heartbreak and their humiliation before the world while FDR was seen as the leader responding to American outcry for justice and to assuage their national pride. The filming of the attack incited their rage by showing sailors struggling to survive a sinking ship, and being told that more than 1100 did not make it out. It gave FDR the ability to manipulate and provoke Americans to let go of their strong stance on isolationism and back FDR's secret desire to destroy Japan. Japan's intent was to neutralize the U.S. Pacific Fleet and protect the Japanese advance into Malaya and Dutch East Indies.

The Japanese had been a country living in isolationism until July 8, 1853 when Commodore Perry sailed into Tokyo Bay, leading four black steaming ships with guns. The Japanese thought the ships "giant dragons puffing smoke." Perry was able to convince the Japanese to sign a treaty on March 31, 1854, allowing American ships to buy supplies to replenish coal, water, and other necessary provisions for the U.S. commercial whaling fleet, to allow American ships the use of ports in Shimoda and Hakodate for U.S. trading markets, and for Japan to help American ships and persons shipwrecked off the Japanese coast. In the 87 years between the isolated Japanese people seeing Perry's four black ships and the bombing of Pearl Harbor, the Japanese had built a navy that was second only to England's world's largest fleet. At the time of the attack on Pearl Harbor, the U.S. naval fleet was the third largest.

Japan became dangerous because of their feudal system under an Emperor and their ownership of the world's second largest naval fleet. As a small country without natural resources, Japan first conquered Manchuria in 1931, a single country at the time, and then further advanced into Asia, kicking out the Germans, Dutch, and English from their Asian colonies. Japan needed rubber and coal and, consequently, advanced on southeast Asia and Pacific Islands to obtain those resources. FDR banned all U.S. exports of scrap iron, steel, and oil into Japan. Japan lost 90% of its oil supply, which crippled its economy and military. The Japanese were convinced that if they destroyed the U.S. Pacific fleet based at Pearl Harbor, it would lead to cracks in the fabric of American society and threaten America's stability. The Japanese saw themselves as a superior people to the Americans.

The Battle of Tsushima, fought in the Tsushima Strait, May 27-28, 1905, between the Japanese and Russian navies off the northwest coast of Japan, in which Japan destroyed the Russian fleet, emboldened Japanese arrogance. It also gave focus to the big fleet battle theory used in future naval battles in creating the same conditions. The Tsushima Islands were a barrier to the coastal assault of Kublai Khan, in 1281, when he led his Mongols in ravaging the islands on their way to take Japan, until a Kamikaze, a divine wind, typhoon, stopped the Mongols. Kamikaze pilots of WWII were a divine wind created by the Japanese Emperor. The big fleet battle theory was the focus of Yamamoto in the Battle of Midway, and Halsey's focus in the Battle of Leyte Gulf. But Yamamoto's plan in attacking Pearl Harbor entailed 353 Japanese Zero fighters, bombers, and torpedo planes, and utilized the new and overwhelming ability of air power to devastate big gun ships. The big fleet battle theory had been translated in terms of big air battle theory, with the Japanese planes being superior to U.S. aircraft.

Japanese Admiral Isoroku Yamamoto, who was ordered to plan the attack on Pearl Harbor, had warned his arrogant superiors, do not wage war against the U.S.; you are out of your league. After hearing of the success of his plan on Pearl with a relative small loss of Japanese planes and pilots, Yamamoto responded, "I fear all we have done is awaken a sleeping giant and filled him with a terrible resolve." FDR in holding back the intel on the planned attack so that the Japanese could kill as many American sailors and soldiers to the greatest extent possible, filming that carnage, and in showing it to the American people, FDR ensured that the sleeping giant would be awoken and filled will a terrible resolve.

When American cryptographers and radio operators intercepted a message that Yamamoto, the architect of the Pearl Harbor attack, would be flying from one Japanese held island to another Japanese held island, at a specific time certain, the U.S. sent out 12, P38 Lightning long-range fighters with the mission to kill Yamamoto. The Americans not only shot down Yamamoto's plane, but they also shot down the dozen transport planes and eight Japanese Zero fighter escort planes, over a chain of small islands in the Pacific. Mathematics gave American navigators and determined fighter pilots that almost impossible victory. Yet today's American schools have lowered their standards of teaching to the lowest able student in the classroom, so as not to offend those less capable of learning. The target of the Political Correct weapon encompasses all American citizens. Michael Alison Chandler of The Washington Post, wrote on September 9, 2011, that SAT scores have dropped to their lowest point in four decades.

The giant's terrible resolve was also demonstrated in the American-made guns and ammo, highly prized in the world, then and now, as one Japanese captain observed after American pilots strafed their island bunker, picking up a 50 cal. shell casing, said, "Look how this shell is exquisitely made! We will never win against the Americans." At the time,

Japanese 50 cal. shell casings were made of papier mache. Today, President Tsaeb ships all spent brass casings to China.

If the war in the Pacific taught nothing else, it taught that the indoctrination of undying loyalty to the Japanese Emperor, instilled in the Japanese under their feudal system, the Samarai Warrior Code, which led to the Kamikaze pilots' suicide mission by 18-20 year old, unmarried men, also caused Japanese POWs to view their American captives as their masters. The awoken sleeping giant, now filled with a terrible resolve by the Japanese and its own president, was displayed by Ken Cowan leading a 16-man crew on the USS Gillespie Destroyer off Okinawa, in shooting down three Kamikaze planes. The last coming straight for them at 200 miles per hour, as the 16-man crew stood fast with not one man leaving his post, while one man pulled the trigger and the others fed the ammo, with the shouts of "Keep feeding the ammo!" At 400 yards away, the Kamikaze piloted plane was shot out of the sky. The Japanese were ordered to commit suicide to maintain their serfdom; the Americans volunteered their lives for freedom. As Yamamoto said to his superiors, I have lived among them; you think Americans are only interested in their cars and appliances and this is a mistake. Americans are a very proud and just people. President FDR knew this, also, and used it against them. President George Schirf used it against Americans after the 9/11 attack, as well. Today, the United Nations Convention of the Rights of Children requires that U.S. schools teach American children that they have a duty – not to their own country, but to the world – and that they are citizens of the world. That their rights come not from their country, America, but from the United Nations.

> "United Nations Convention on the Rights of the Child, Article 17: States Parties (the U.S.)...shall ensure that the child has access to information and material from a diversity of national and international (unspecified and unknown) sources, especially those aimed at...spiritual and moral...Article 29: Parents may send their children to private schools, however all such schools must support the principles contained in the UN Charter…Special Rapporteur's (special agents) will investigate within countries and will report findings to the United Nations Commission on Human Rights."

The Nazi Germans and the Japanese had no better ally in fighting America than President Franklin Delano Roosevelt, a 32nd degree Freemason and a member of the Order of Nobles and Mystics, which was founded by the descendants of Muhammad. It was FDR who put the "seeing eye" on the dollar, a symbol of the eye of the great architect, Satan.

Nimitz had been the Commander of the Submarine Division 20 for two years; he was promoted to Admiral and took over for Kimmel at Pearl Harbor; on December 19, 1944, he later became Fleet Admiral; on September 2, 1945, he was a U.S. Signatory to the surrender of Japan aboard the USS Missouri. In December 1945, he became Chief of Naval Operations. After the war, later in his life, Nimitz was Special Assistant to the Secretary of the Navy and goodwill ambassador for the United Nations to explain to the public the major issues confronting the United Nations. It wasn't until after his death that Nimitz found, to his horror, how he had been duped and used by a treasonous president and was told of the satanic control over the United Nations. He now wanted in with the war against the foreign invader that had conquered the Office of the Presidency.

The sleeves of Nimitz' dark blue naval uniform carried the gold braid of Fleet Admiral, his chest carried the medals, including the one he received for saving a drowning sailor he dove into the sea to rescue. More than anything, he wanted to right the wrong he had spoken about the righteousness of United Nations. His slender figure and handsome classic face and white hair made him look as though he'd been chosen for the part by a casting director. But as a graduate of Annapolis, graduating with distinction especially in math, the title of Commander of U.S. Naval Forces in the Pacific was deserved. With confidence he greeted the Generals, and walking over to General Washington, he saluted.

Washington returned the respect, "I'm most pleased to have you in this war, Admiral. As I have said before, it follows that as certain as that night succeeds the day, that without a decisive naval force we can do nothing definitive, and with it, everything honorable and glorious."

"Yes, Sir," Nimitz agreed. "General, I have on a card on my desk three questions I always ask myself. Is the proposed operation likely to succeed? Looking around this control room and knowing who else will be joining us, my answer is: we will succeed. What might be the consequences of failure? As we well know, failure gives Satan control over the world and our souls. This cannot happen. And the third question: is it in the realm of practicability in terms of materiel and supplies? I think with the spirit army of veterans and with the help of living American patriots working with us, we will gather the weapons and supplies needed to conduct this war."

"General Washington, Sir." Curtis LeMay said, as his ghost materialized in to the control room.

Washington turned and received LeMay's salute. "If I may interject, Sir, while we have spirit soldiers, there are evil spirit soldiers that we will face; perhaps these evil spirits were given some demonic power by Satan. The lesson of history, the Pyrrhic victory, achieved by King Pyrrhus of Epirus in defeating the Romans at Heraclea in 280 BC and Asculum in 279 BC, I think is pertinent today. The Pyrrhic victory teaches that expending such resources of man and machine that leaves the victor with irreplaceable casualties will, in the end, cause the loss of the war. The Romans could replace the soldiers they lost, but King Pyrrhus could not. It was the same in the South during the Civil War."

LeMay turned to Lee, "You faced the same conditions in the Civil War. You were scraping the bottom of the barrel to come up with troops, while the North was only waging war at half tilt, with plenty of men to induct into the Union Army. Unless we come up with a weapon that can destroy evil spirits, we cannot assume victory. We need to be able to annihilate energy. We need a new weapon."

Curtis LeMay was to the Air Force what Patton had been to the Army. His men fondly referred to LeMay as Old Iron Pants, and sometimes Bombs Away. Like Sherman and Grant, LeMay could often be found chomping on a cigar. His square face with eyes that observed without moving his head, and his large frame immediately signaled that he just as soon kill you as to look at you. He was one of the best pilots of WWII, and the first to receive aerial navigation training and became the best navigator. He thought President John Kennedy was a coward, and Eisenhower indecisive. LeMay had wanted to bomb North Vietnam "back to the Stone Age." He did not fear using nuclear weapons, but thought delivery should be by manned missions rather than missiles, to bring precision upon the target. He created the flying box formation that became the standard in flying. He was the first to drop incendiary bombs, using hundreds of planes flying at low altitude, at night, over the cities of Japan. As a member of the Joint Chiefs of Staff during the Cuban Missile crisis, he advised Kennedy to send Navy and SAC fighter planes to surround Cuba and, if need be, "fry it!" When the standoff between Russia and the U.S. was peacefully resolved, he said it was "the greatest defeat in our history." He proposed a "Sunday Punch," a surprise nuclear strike, on the Soviet Union. Some called him the most dangerous of all generals.

Six months before Pearl Harbor the Army had established the Army Air Forces, June 20, 1941. LeMay spent his career working toward separation of the Air Force into its own independent force. In 1948, he was made Commander of the Strategic Air Command, SAC, and turned it into an efficient modern, all-jet force. He implemented tests of 24-hour bomber and tanker alerts, and by rotation, kept some bombers in the air at all times. He demanded very high standards of his aircrews, and established the vast aerial refueling system. He developed the strategic ballistic missile force, strict command and control system, and established an unprecedented readiness capability that the world has ever known. At a moment's notice, the U.S. was ready to execute an all-out nuclear attack. In his personal life, he was an avid HAM radio operator and established the single side band, SSB, and installed it on SAC bombers.

He and Sherman were of like minds. LeMay stated, "You have to kill people and when you've killed enough, they'll stop fighting."

Looking at Nimitz, LeMay argued, "Removing Fletcher as Commander of the Saratoga was wrong. Pyrrhic victory! The Japanese had a superior navy to ours; Fletcher was right when he took the Saratoga and its task force out of harm's way at the Battle of Guadalcanal. Fletcher knew carrier warfare; the Japs had sunk the Yorktown under his command. With only four carriers left, in the Pacific, they were the only defense against the Japs advancing across the Pacific and attacking the continental

U.S. While it would have been a logistic nightmare for the Japanese to attack our continent, their arrogance also decided their attack on Pearl. You used Fletcher's experience to lead every carrier we had, the Saratoga, the Wasp, and the Enterprise back to the South Pacific. The Hornet was still at Pearl undergoing repairs. Of all the carrier commanders, he had the experience to understand the need to protect the Saratoga.

Washington interjected, "Gentlemen, this is not the time to re-fight the wars of the past; we need to join together."

"Excuse me, sir," Nimitz replied, "but I would like to respond to General LeMay's charge that I was wrong in removing Vice Admiral Fletcher. I think it might put things to rest, Sir."

"With permission," Washington replied.

Nimitz turned to the larger LeMay dressed in his General's blue Air Force uniform, "First, I agree about your statement of Pyrrhic victory, we learned that in our bombardment of Iwo Jima. The battle for Iwo Jima, or Sulfur Island, lasted 36 days, the Marines called its Mt. Suribachi, Meatgrinder Hill." Nimitz smiled with melancholy at the memory, "One of the youngest Medal of Honor recipients was Marine Sgt. Darrell Cole, he was 14 years of age when he enlisted; he was 17 when he was killed on Iwo Jima. The missile destroyer, USS Cole, was named after him. Al Qaeda bombed that destroyer on October 12, 2000." Nimitz turned and took a few steps away from LeMay and then turned back, "The Battle of Iwo Jima was the largest combat employment of Marines in history. One out of three Marines were either wounded or killed trying to take Iwo Jima. During the first three days of that battle, six battleships and five destroyers bombarded that island. None of that bombardment, including 6000 tons of shells and bombs before noon on the day of the landing, made a dent."

Nimitz paced the floor, again, and then turned back to LeMay, "It was the Japanese General Kuribayashi, defending Iwo Jima, who put that Pyrrhic victory tactic to work against U.S. forces. He was told to hold the island even though we would eventually take it, but he made it costly and with little reward for us. As soon as he arrived on Iwo Jima, Kuribayashi kept four of the 80 aircraft then based on the island and sent off the rest, along with the civilians. He constructed only token numbers of pillboxes even though his superiors ordered him to put in a full line of them along the beach, but he knew we'd take them out, and we did take out the few he had constructed. We also destroyed the four planes and the few buildings located on the surface of the island, but we couldn't touch the underground bunkers. He provided for ventilation against the heavy sulfur fumes present in those sulfur mines. He planned an elastic defense through those tunnels from one underground cave to another, with entrances and exits. The defense was only to wear down the U.S. invasion, use up our ammo. And once we got on the island, we used incendiary weapons when the Japs refused to come out of the caves; we suffocated or burned them alive." Nimitz began to pace again, "But as to Fletcher, he was commanding the Saratoga task force, Noyes - you know the one who re-classified pre-Pearl

Harbor Japanese decoded messages..."

"Yeah, I know that bastard, go ahead," LeMay responded, as he took out a cigar and lit it up.

"Noyes commanded the Wasp, Kinkaid commanded the Enterprise. They rendezvoused with the Saratoga and planned to meet Turner's amphibious invasion fleet, the largest amphibious landing force tried in history. Turner's plan to take Guadalcanal was on the line. The Saratoga, Wasp, and Enterprise met up with Turner's force at the Fiji Islands on July 26th. Turner's invading Marines hit Guadalcanal, and by August 7th, the Japanese fighters arrived and tried to destroy Turner's fleet. Fletcher was concerned and thought his top priority was to protect the American carriers; the only other carrier left was the Hornet. And as you mentioned, it was parked at Pearl for repairs, so Fletcher took the Saratoga and its task force away from Guadalcanal. Turner was pissed at Fletcher, and, as was his usual manner, Turner never hesitated in strongly expressing his opinions. Admiral Ernest King wanted Fletcher's hide. You know King, at the time, he was the Fleet Admiral, he was the one who gagged all the cryptographers and radio operators and threatened them with imprisonment, if they told anyone that FDR knew of the invasion as early as a year previous to the attack. There was nothing that I could do to protect Fletcher. I agree that caution was needed to keep what we had left of our fleet. But you understand the politics of the brass; I was out ranked and defenseless against them."

LeMay agreed, "There won't be that kind of treason going on during this war!"

General Douglas McArthur's ghost materialized at that moment. "General Washington," he said, then turning to the other generals, "Gentlemen."

McArthur's tall lanky body with sloping shoulders did not radiate the same imposing physical threat of Washington, Patton or LeMay broader frames, but his air of confidence gave pause to a mind that could outwit most, and therein it was noted, his danger lie. Though these generals were of different generations and wars they held common traits, and master of horse riding was one of them. Washington was an avid foxhunter, Patton was a Cavalryman, Grant had a unique gift that today would classify him as the horse whisperer. He also broke the riding record at West Point, and as for McArthur, he could ride and shoot before he could read and write. Another commonality between Patton and McArthur was in their approach to domestic threats.

When Patton was training troops at Ft. Benning, Georgia, and his men would go on a weekend pass and visit Phoenix City, Alabama, across the river, they were frequently beaten, robbed, and even murdered by organized crime mobsters. Patton personally drove a tank through the strip of bars and brothels, destroying them all. At Ft. Riley, Kansas, during a fight in a honky-tonk town called Junction City, thugs took capture of and threatened to kill one of Patton's Black soldiers. Patton ordered his

Calvary to mount, and taking a borrowed cannon, he and his men moved against the area of Junction City. Patton threatened to level the area unless his man was turned over. The Black soldier was immediately released.

Amidst the Great Depression, thousands of ragged WWI veterans, along with the wives and children, gathered in Washington, DC, to petition Congress to make early payment of their war bonuses. All were camped in the squalor of a shantytown nearby. Not unlike Patton's response to rescue his soldier taken by local thugs, McArthur set upon the veterans with tanks, four troops of Calvary with drawn sabers, and a column of steel-helmeted infantry with fixed bayonets. McArthur saw the group as a communist revolt.

In the spirit world of the 11th dimension, both Patton and McArthur had conferred during the illegal protest march of one million illegal Mexicans, marching in the cities across America and Washington, DC, demanding immediate citizenship. The May 1, 2006 march, May 1st being Communist May Day, broadcasted on TV throughout the day, gave notice to all Americans the identity and face of their enemies who had invaded their country and now were blatantly and illegally, demanding their jobs, their wealth, and their freedoms. At the 11th dimension meeting, Patton and McArthur decided to wait until the revolution that they now came together to strategize, instead of bringing out the Calvary, drawn sabers, tanks, and cannon against the invaders. Wait until the time is right, they concluded. Another of their commonalities was that they hated Communism with a passion. McArthur said of Communism that it is a cancer "eating deeper into the body politic." McArthur had said to Patton during the 11th dimension meeting, "It had been my duty in life to defeat Communism and only God and those Washington politicians could stop me. And I knew God's position on Communism, so it was only the Washington politicians that concerned me."

McArthur's father had received a Medal of Honor during in the Civil War for his exploits at Missionary Ridge. Grant and Sherman immediately translated the honor onto the son. McArthur had been the Supreme Allied Command of Southwest Pacific and later became the youngest Chief of Staff of the Army in the previous 50 years. For 25 years, he held the highest scholastic average at West Point, in engineering. Along with Eisenhower, and later Bradley, McArthur was a five-star general, and at that level, a general is not allowed to retire, hence McArthur's speech in Congress, "Old soldiers never die, they just fade away."

McArthur saw the need to take and protect the Philippines as the best staging area for the final assault against the Japanese home islands. The Japanese were heading down to capture the Philippines, New Guina, New Zealand, and Australia. Their final goal was the Battle of the Coral Sea where the Japanese would cut the shipping supply lines between the U.S. and Australia. For five hours, the Japanese pounded the Bataan Peninsula, the island fortress of Corregidor. FDR needed McArthur's genius, and fearing his capture, ordered McArthur to go to Australia. After he left, the Japanese took the Philippines. McArthur felt a strong moral responsibility to free all the Philippine Islands from the brutal Japanese and promised them, "I shall return." And he did, two years later.

In 1950, McArthur was appointed Commander of the UN forces in Korea, launching a brilliant counter attack at Inchon and routing North Korean armies. He led the forces to the border between North Korea and China. But the Chinese intervened, and with a massive Chinese army, sent McArthur and the UN forces in to retreat. McArthur publicly called for an expansion of the war to include China; instead, Truman relieved McArthur from his command. McArthur went into a barn-storming mode across the country, exposing Truman for selling out Asia to Communism. As President, Eisenhower had asked McArthur his advice on ending the Korean Police Action. McArthur suggested a peace conference, and if not successful, use the nuclear bomb to destroy military concentrations and installations in North Korea and sow their fields with radioactive materials; bomb China, and land Chinese National troops inside Manchuria to overthrow the Communist government of China. Eisenhower never sought his advice again.

In the control room deep inside the Cheyenne Mountain military facility, Washington walked over and stood before the large viewing screens on the walls, "Gentlemen," he addressed the generals and admiral who were now talking in small groups. Hearing Washington's voice immediately silenced their discussions, as they turned their attention to the first General of the country. "I express my gratefulness to you all for taking on another war for the sake of our great country. I ask that you give allegiance to the Supreme Commander of this war, Douglas McArthur. I have entrusted in McArthur to presently determine the strategy because of his military adventures and successes displayed as Supreme Commander of all Allied Forces in the Pacific Theatre during WWII."

Washington took hold of the lapels of his coat, his left thumb covering a pewter button, the white ruffles of his shirt sleeves lay against his chest, "As John Guthner said, 'Never in history had there been a commander so economical in the expenditure of his men's blood.' For every allied soldier killed, McArthur killed ten Japanese. FDR recognized McArthur's strategic genius and except for ordering McArthur to leave the Philippines and go to Australia, he had left McArthur on his own to fight the war in the Pacific. Gentlemen, I present you with your Supreme Commander, General McArthur."

The generals and admiral offered a short applaud, as McArthur walked over to Washington and shook his hand, "Thank you, Sir, for your trust in me. I will not let you down."

Washington instructed the generals, "Please be seated at the desks."

"Then let's get started." McArthur replied. Taking out his corncob pipe, he began to pack it with tobacco. In return, Grant and Sherman lit up their cigars and leaned back in their chairs to listen to McArthur. LeMay continued to chomp on his cigar, flicking the ashes on the floor next to his chair. All took seats at the desks facing the large viewing screens mounted on the wall.

"If someone would turn on the screens. General Jackson, you'll find an independent generator over there in the corner just behind your chair. It was installed to serve this room only. No one on the outside will know we are using it."

As the screens blinked on, they displayed a world map grid. McArthur walked over to the control panel and selected the button to show only the United States and its borders.

"Gentlemen," McArthur began, "The enemy has tied the United States into a Gordian knot, invading our country in layers from within, in every facet of our lives, from education, healthcare, food supply, economy, financial system, manufacturing, media, culture, laws, taxes, attacks against Christianity, to giving visas to Muslims, etc., etc. A major front is at each of our borders where they have allowed Hezbollah, Hamas, Al Qaeda, Iranians, and Russians come across the southern border." McArthur pressed buttons on the console to light up arrows, indicating invasion across the southern border. "Still another front, the Muslim training camps. The Hezbollah, Hamas, and Al Qaeda, et al. go directly to these training camps once they cross our border."

McArthur pressed buttons on the console to light up the sites of the Muslim camps. He picked up a pointer and touched upon each light as he named the city and state. "One in Jessup and another in Commerce, Georgia; Marion, Alabama; York, South Carolina. The others are located in Hancock and another in Deposit, New York," McArthur continued, "The one in Holy Islamville, South Carolina is huge and extremely active. The others are located in Houston, Texas; Coldwater, Michigan; Buena Vista, Colorado; Oak Hill, California; Onalaska, Washington; and Red House, Virginia, that one alone has 120 acres. The one in Trout Creek Pass, Colorado is over 100 acres. One is located in Philadelphia, Pennsylvania, another in Springfield, Massachusetts, one in Hyattsville, Maryland, one in Bethany, West Virginia; Meherrin, Virginia; Dover, Tennessee, and one in Mecca Circle, Wayne County, Georgia. As you can see, they are concentrated along the east coast and southern states. Islamberg, New York, is the headquarters. Sheikh Mubarak al-Gilani is the leader of the terrorist group called the Muslims for America and he's set up the training camps. He is seen as a direct descendant of Muhammad. That means he carries the Y-chromosome of Satan. He recruits from colleges and over the Internet. The camps are anywhere from 25 acres to 300 acres. In one investigation, at first appearance, it seemed as though the camp was empty, but out of a small shed attached to a house-type structure, emerged 50 plus men. This indicates that there is an underground facility, likely hiding munitions. And from the surrounding woods inside the camp came a few hundred men. They are trained in setting off explosives, scaling mountains, murdering guards, kidnapping, and various other paramilitary tactics. It is known that they have weapons of mass destruction. Gentlemen," McArthur set down the pointer, "They have quietly invaded our country to set off hundreds of attacks across the country in the most populated areas, all at one time, once they are given the signal."

McArthur turned to the generals, took a drag from his pipe, and then continued, "It's been reported this week that the ATF command has issued orders for their men to stand down on stopping AK-47s, M-16s, fully automatic guns, grenade launches, and ammo from being shipped from the U.S. down to Mexican cartels. The order came from either Tsaeb or his Attorney General, the only two with the power to do this. They've both denied it. The guns are going to the MS-13 gang members, as well as the Russians, Hezbollah, Hamas, and Iranian troops inside Mexico, along with the Mexican Military. Gentlemen, we can presume that these forces are heavily armed, and working with them are the drug cartel armies, who want ready access across the border. The Mexican Military has been for decades escorting the drug gangs in retrieving their million-dollar drops from safe houses 100 miles inside the U.S.

It has also been reported that one of their elites, Egroeg Rooss, has been buying up U.S. ammo manufacturing companies. The UN has tried for decades to take guns away from Americans. Congress has been telling them that they cannot issue a direct law because of the Second Amendment and Americans won't allow them to get away with it. The UN argued that a .38 pistol would satisfy the Second Amendment, but Congress still said no. So the UN requires registration of the type of gun and the name and address of gun owners. States that already require gun registration are turning over their databases to the UN. Other States will soon be required to register guns and do background checks in order to eliminate as many Americans as possible from owning a gun. The 2010 census takers input names and addresses into a GPS system, and from there they mapped a grid that matched gun owners to the locations, so it will allow the UN troops to go directly to only the doors of the gun owners – or just blow up the entire block. The Department of Homeland Security has put up spy drones, and of course, they have those GPS locations of the gun owners – and can watch them going to and from militia meetings. The militia can be rounded up quietly without Martial Law being declared, which would wake the sleeping giant – America. The National Defense Authorization Act of 2012 gives Tsaeb the power to detain the militias, or as they call them, belligerents – that is, every American citizen who opposes their conquering of America. Tsaeb can order the military to arrest without charges, without trial – anyone Tsaeb wants. This is similar to the legislated power given to Hitler.

In the meantime, the UN is trying an alternative tactic – take control of ammo. If they can't disarm Americans one way, they'll try another. The Dept. of Homeland Security and U.S. Immigration and Customs Enforcement, in 2012, contracted to buy 450 million rounds of

.40 caliber ammo over the next five-year period, and in Tsaeb's first year they bought 200 million hollow points. (www.theblaze.com/stories/why-is-homeland-security-buying-450-million-rounds-of-) These purchases not only drive up the price of ammo, they are arming Tsaeb's army.

Tsaeb has shipped all the spent brass casings to China's military. The feds now require American manufacturers to smash casings that they have already purchased, and have followed up with visits to manufacturers to smash the casing themselves. The smashed brass is unusable to American manufacturers for reloading and selling the new bullet for a cheaper price. Tsaeb voted to ban most rifle ammo used in hunting and sport shooting; he endorsed a complete ban on handgun ownership. When in the Illinois Senate, Tsaeb endorsed a bill to increase by 500% the federal taxes on guns and ammo to make them unaffordable. Fortunately, the bill failed. But their mission remains: Get guns out of the hands of Americans so Americans can be controlled. With over a trillion rounds of ammo already owned by private Americans, it's not likely that the elite will ever succeed. And Rooss buying up the US ammo manufacturers now is a little late in the game. But he'll likely make the cost of ammo prohibitive for the average American citizen, or he just won't sell ammo to Americans.

And while he was working on that, Tsaeb's healthcare bill, Patient Protection Affordable Care Act, Section 5210, establishes a Ready Reserve Corps by amending Section 203 of the Public Health Service Act. This Sec. 203(a)(1) says the Ready Reserve is for service in time of national emergency. In other words, for riots or revolution. Section 203(a)(2) All commissioned officers shall be citizens of the United States. There's no civil-service law requiring an exam to test candidates, no law will restrict their pay. Section 203(a)(3) Tsaeb gets to appoint the commissioned officers for the Ready Reserve Corps, and commissioned officers of the Regular Corps shall be appointed by the President with the advice and consent of the Senate. But in the next Section 203(b) the Ready Reserve Corps officers shall be deemed to be commissioned officers of the Regular Corps officers.

After serving one year in the U.S. Military, a foreigner will be given U.S. citizenship; 55,000 foreigners have joined the U.S. Military to gain citizenship. (www.armybase.us/ 2010/01/foreigners-in-u-s-military-get-fast-track-to-citizenship/)

In other words, using these laws, a foreign Muslim may serve one year in the U.S. Military, be given U.S. citizenship, and then Tsaeb can appoint the Muslim as a commissioned officer in the Ready Reserve Corps, and then the Muslim will be considered a commissioned officer in the Regular Corps. Then put on duty to break Americans who are revolting.

This is the maneuvering around law so that individually a law looks clean, but it interconnects with another law that allows for the invasion and ultimate takeover of our U.S. Military. John McCormack of The Weekly Standard, on January 5, 2012, wrote that our President is giving pink slips to 100,000 active duty personnel. This amounts to a 10-

15% decline in Army and Marine Corps numbers over the next decade. (www.weeklystandard.com /blog/616064.html)

Tsaeb's Patient Protection Affordable Care Act, further amends the Public Health Service Act, under Section 203(2)(B) and (C) The Ready Reserve Corps shall be available and ready for calls to active duty during national emergencies, and be available for backfilling critical positions left vacant during deployment of active duty Commissioned Corps members.

This is the most critical section, this 203(2)(C) – to be available for backfilling – for those on active duty. This would apply, also, to the vacancies left by the 100,000 active duty American personnel being fired by the President – in 2012. This point in time of getting Americans out of the military is timely in giving the Palestinian-Hamas the time to migrate into the U.S., join the military for one year, be given U.S. citizenship, be chosen by Tsaeb to be commissioned officers in the Ready Reserve Corps and emerge as Regular Corps officers, and be put on active duty on the streets of America – fully armed with U.S. weapons – all paid for by the American taxpayer.

The pink slips to American military-men in 2012 coincides with President Tsaeb signing a Presidential Determination No. 2009-15 of January 27, 2009, giving $20.3 million from the U.S. Emergency Refugee and Migration Assistance Fund – money for housing and food for Muslim Palestinian 'refugees' from Gaza. The Determination was published in the Federal Register, Vol. 74, No. 22, February 4, 2009, Presidential Documents. This act allowed hundreds of thousands of Palestinian-Hamas refugees to move into the United States.

In several easy strokes, the President gets rid of Americans serving in the Army and Marines and substitutes them with foreign Muslims, who were given citizenship after one year of military service. In quiet rotation – the U.S. Military is replaced by foreigners – Muslims will control our military weapons, and America is conquered without Muslims firing a shot. Again, all paid for by the American taxpayer.

This new Muslim Army goes hand in hand with the Dept. of Homeland Security's power to move entire populations into FEMA camps and to perform biomedical experiments on any and all Americans.

Gentlemen, this is a very dangerous situation on several fronts. It gives these people license to move people into FEMA camps and give them hot shots, at the least. Under the Homeland Security Act, they also have the legal right to perform medical experiments on Americans that they pick up, at their discretion, just as Hitler's known sadist, Dr. Mengele did during WWII. And it puts American women into FEMA camps under Muslim control and gives them hidden access to use American women as sex slaves, as the Japanese used Korean women for the Japanese troops during WWII.

MacArthur paused for a moment, "The UN peacekeeping missions have repeatedly resulted in rape of women and children. Child prostitution thrives wherever blue berets decamp – even in UN compounds. In Mozambique in 1992, UN soldiers recruited girls aged 12 to 18 years into prostitution. (http://whatreallyhappened.com/RANCHO/POLITICS/UN/peace.html)

MacArthur paced a few minutes, quietly thinking, "Tsaeb has put together his own Muslim, foreign army answerable to only Tsaeb and in control of our military weapons – and with the legal authority to medically torture and imprison any American citizen, group, or town. This has been accomplished through Executive Orders of Tsaeb and past presidents and laws passed by Congresses, each adding to the destruction of America. All of this has brought us to where we are today – conquered from within."

MacArthur paused a moment to let his words sink in, and then he reiterated them, "The bottom line – foreign Muslims control U.S. Military weapons – and no one is the wiser."

LeMay threw his cigar down on the floor and smashed it with the heel of his shoe, grinding it in to shreds.

Patton groaned, "We need to get that son-of-a-bitch! We need to get all of them!"

The hackles of Stonewall's neck were raised with a bloodthirst for battle, as he turned toward the corner of the room and recited every curse word he had ever heard in his life, except for taking the Lord's name in vain.

Sherman's usual penchant for incessant talking was dumbfounded by the ability of the President of the U.S. to commit such blatant treason with no one in the government able or willing to stop his treason. The man of vision and intensity had already begun a genius plan of attack. But now, Sherman thought quietly, he would impose the glorious side of war, the absolute destruction of the enemy, the U.S. Government.

Grant looked over at his military partner and knew he was scheming in his head to specifically get Tsaeb and the congressmen and women who voted on the healthcare legislation. In Grant's mind, his plan included the members of government who were part of the continuity of government, for they would hold the power that the world would listen to – should the first wave of satanic politicians be dethroned. If the members of the continuity of government, the COG traitors, were not destroyed, there would be no end to the cycle of Communist takeover. The excuse of protection from foreign terrorist attack was a lie; the COG was only to assure that any revolution by the American people would be quickly shut down with one satanic leader after another, an endless stream of demons taking control of the power of government, the military, and the killing of Americans who dared to fight for Christ.

"Gentlemen," McArthur called out, "I understand your outrage, but we have numerous types of armies to confront, not just the United Nations troops already inside America, but: union members, illegal aliens and drug gangs, socialist and communist Americans, besides the Muslims and Zionist Jews, and besides Tsaeb's army. All of these groups will send out their members into the streets to insight chaos, and unfortunately, a million or more Americans will respond to them. Both sides of that first wave will be slaughtered. Martial Law, which is their aim, will then be declared and all constitutional rights will be officially gone. But after this initial action, the war will not be fought in the streets with rocks thrown at the White House or the Capitol. This will be a covert war.

They have waited to show their plans to take down America until after they had developed all the technology necessary to control Americans. We need to teach the American people how to block their technology. Americans need to wrap their cellphones completely in aluminum foil to block any kind of GPS signals that the government can pick up. Putting GPS locators in cars, making it mandatory, again with the excuse to find people who have had auto accidents, was in fact, so the government could track their car's movement. These devices need to be removed from cars. The American people must be taught how to and think about moving about without detection."

"To your point, General," Patton stood up, "there is technology out there that citizens can buy, at least for now, that is a weather tracker with night vision. It gives wind direction for long-range shooting, used for integrated targeting. It's excellent for night and early morning shooting. With a software capability, it allows for wireless transmission of a wealth of data to a laptop for analysis."

McArthur paced the floor, "What the government is coming up with next is mobile radar detectors, telling Americans it's for their own safety, the big governmental lie, so that people are x-rayed coming and going from shopping malls to detect who are carrying guns. The government is accomplishing two things, surveying how many Americans actually carry guns when they are out and about; and, secondly, the more radiation they can shoot at Americans the sicklier they'll become and less able to fight UN troops when they send them down the streets. They'll also deform fetuses inside wombs of women who are out shopping. Their aim is to cause miscarriages, or establish cause for necessary abortions, and to damage women's wombs; it becomes imposed radiation birth control. The radiation also sterilizes the men. They're already doing this radiation detection to people walking down the street, or shooting radar beams at truck drivers as they pass by. These radiation beams are done by a man holding a gun, which has no measure of time of exposure to the radiation. If the man doesn't like the person's looks, he can hold the radiation beam on them longer and cause them cancer and long-suffering death. They are irradiating people for being in the wrong place at the wrong time. Think of a microwave oven loose on the streets and stores - without Americans even knowing about it."

General Washington stood up, "We had never imagined such abuse of the Constitution or technology. We never conceived of such horrendous attacks against our fellow countrymen." Washington shook his head and tapped his fist against his chest, "Mother of God, please help us against such of Satan's demons who hold control of the United States."

McArthur made his way over to Washington, resting a comforting hand on Washington's shoulder, "Sir, you pray for all of us. We need the American people to know that they must move with stealth, join in small groups of those they trust, communicate with other groups they know. They must be constant in their small attacks. They must keep the enemy on defense at all times. They must also kill their neighbor who is a Communist, who will expose them to the authorities. We, the spirit generals must fight with them, communicate with them a plan of battle."

"Forgive me, McArthur," Washington cried, "I was momentarily taken aback. The destruction of our country has been planned with such genius, such complete devastation, it is overwhelming. Please continue." Washington went back to his seat and took a deep breath.

McArthur continued, "We cannot allow them the ability to track Americans. At the local town and county levels, they cannot know where we'll spring up next. Americans must be on the offensive. Every American must either observe and report to the militias or join a militia. And in every town and county, Americans must keep track of the coming and going of all types of vehicles, military and rental trucks and vans. Note Mexican gangs, foreigners, and any kind of unusual movements and report them to the militias.

Those living around the Muslim training camps must do this; when they hear gun shots; when they see vehicles moving men; keep a written schedule of everything they see coming in and out of those camps. At all times, Americans must know how many Muslims are inside the camps. If all Americans did this, they will be fighting the local battle that will end in winning the war. Destroying the legs, the foundation of the enemy at the local level will prevent the enemy from mobilizing against the country at large."

McArthur took his pipe out of his shirt pocket and packed it with tobacco. As he held a match to it, he drew the flame inside the pipe with small breathes then puffed out the smoke. The generals watched quietly, anxious for him to continue.

"We have the legions of dead soldiers from all the American wars fought in the past, and they will be led by either a living soldier in an astral projection state, or by leaders who are also dead. We have made contact with the American militia groups throughout the country. They have agreed to follow our orders.

First, we've assigned them to stop the local and state governments that have been corrupted and infiltrated by the United Nations through Agenda 21 Sustainable Development. We've taught them how to follow the local leaders by hacking into their computers, especially their online banking. We trained them on what information to look for and how to determine if something has been written in code.

Quinn's Regiment is still in specialized training; his unit is a combination of spirit soldiers and astral projecting soldiers, and they've been sent on a practice exercise to get them used to working together. As a practice operation, they followed local judges, cops and state troopers. What we found in some places such as Massachusetts, the State troopers barracks is cleaned by illegal aliens. We sent out orders to reconnoiter these places for bombs or biowarfare weapons that the illegal aliens might have left behind. The spirits have gone inside meetings; followed judges, cops, and troopers home and have identified the corrupt. Then they gave the information to the local militias to deal with them when the time comes. We didn't bother shadowing the politicians; they're all corrupt; we know that and the militia will take care of them, later. They know where they live and their hours of coming and going, for when the time comes to kill them. The militia also made one-on-one contact with the cops and state troopers who are patriots. So, we've identified our local army as the cops and troopers coming under the command of the militia groups. These militia men and women have trained in firearms, combat fighting, and the disarming of bombs. They have searched out every nook and cranny in their locality looking for places to launch special ops stealth attacks and regrouping. They have begun to attack corrupt local politicians and cops through the guise of an auto accident, sudden heart attack, or massive stroke. We also have patriot doctors and nurses working in hospitals - giving hot shots and insulin to non-diabetics, to Muslims, Zionist Jews, and illegal aliens. Those medical units of patriots are small; Muslims have in great numbers infiltrated the medical profession on a grand scale and have murdered many Christian patients already. The hospitals have been a battlefield that have killed many. The best way to take care of these enemies is to let them think that America is still sleeping." McArthur paused a moment.

"The longer we can keep our attack under the radar the better."

He walked over to the map of the United States, "Now, the larger elements. We have to think in layers, such as town, city, state, and federal fronts as well as to standard battlefields north, south, east, or west. We're dealing with an army that has taken over positions of power, the two Muslims on the Homeland Security advisory board, for instance.

Basically, what the enemy has done is by-pass a military invasion, as I just noted earlier, and, by running for political office with the winners appointing the enemy in to positions such as the Attorney General. It's a symbiotic relationship maneuver. Of course, the voting machines have been corrupted; they program them to pick their man or woman as the winner.

As to Congress, it's a Sodom and Gomorrha in D.C. We'll just infect them all with biowarfare viruses if they get to the underground bunkers before we get them. All we need to do is infect one of them with a deadly disease and then let them all run together into their bunker. The bunkers will serve as a petri dish and, finally, their tombs."

As he quietly paced back and forth, McArthur was pensive. Finally, he continued, "We cannot let anyone escape and come back at us another day. In this war there will be no prisoners, only dead enemies.

Unfortunately, that means a million or more dead government people and another multiple-million foreigners. We have the manpower, guns, and ammo to get that job done. And we must realize that the enemy is in every socio-economic layer. From the ACORN, SEIU, AFL-CIO, and all the teachers unions who have been indoctrinating America's youth to accept Communism, to the Sean MacSham, Glover Money level of multi-millionaire, to Pickles, Willy and Missy Shakes, Egroeg Rooss, Jose Fatig, Terp Dochmar at the multi-billionaire level, to the owners of the Federal Reserve - multi-trillionaire level. Then there are the thug organizers working now in the Middle East, Joe Dirt and his wife, Beatrice Horned. Dirt led the Weatherman, a Communist group who bombed the NYC Police Headquarters in 1970, the Capitol Building in 1971, and the Pentagon in 1972. There are the union leaders, Dick Tripet of the AFL-CIO, Amos Fragil of SEIU, and Shad Kather, founder of ACORN.

All of these levels must be approached at the same time, but through different methods. We've had spirits tailing them from a distance, since each of these people has one evil spirit at their side at all times. Against these individuals, where they are so surrounded by their own security, we'll use the spirits to get to them to strangle or poison them. It will appear as if they are having an anxiety attack. Suddenly, each will feel a spirit's hands wrap around their throat squeezing their esophagus shut, until they suffocate. Where there is a living spy among them, he or she can poison the coffee, liquor, or the food, whatever the situation calls for.

The problem we face with the trillionaires, those who own the Federal Reserve, is that they have a small army of evil spirits surrounding them, who are able to call up more evil spirits within minutes. I'll talk more about that problem later, we have a problem that is about to explode momentarily, which could begin the revolution before we're ready. Before there is leadership to guide the living Americans."

McArthur paced the floor in front of a desk, his head bowed in contemplative pose, "There is a group of Americans, they are not militia, not terrorist," McArthur paused, "They have good, patriotic spirits. They are mothers who are angry about what the government, the Congress and the pharmaceuticals have been doing to their families, to their children - increasing the number of vaccines that inject 84% higher mercury levels than are regarded as safe. Congress' mandate has given their children Autism, birth defects, holes in their hearts - it's a method of population control. Many of these babies will die. Their husbands have been disenfranchised during the Schirf regime and now with Tsaeb's full-blown Communist takeover; they've been without jobs for several years without hope of getting another. They are between 40 and 50 year olds. Their husbands have joined local militias. They have military training and are training the others. The wives have gathered in secret and have collected themselves from across the country to the hills of North Carolina for training exercises. What they are planning is an all-out assault on the

White House. They see the women more able to get close enough to the White House to invade it. Specifically, they have enough in their numbers and have made contact with two Culper spies located inside the White House, who will be working with them to set up the assault. The spy stationed in the kitchen will close off the escape route for the President. At that time, they will storm the White House."

"Sir, if I may ask a question," Patton said.

"Patton," McArthur recognized.

"How can a mob of great enough numbers even get close to the White House without security knowing? They have snipers positioned on the roof of the White House and buildings next door. Anyone could call the D.C. police and have reinforcements within minutes."

"Yes, you're right. But these people have thought of all these contingencies. Some mothers are possessed by scientists and military tacticians, for them this is playtime. Others have fathers who fought in Vietnam, giving them some pointers. While the husbands and wives go fight in their separate theaters of war, the grandparents are taking care of the children.

They have people working for a local cable provider as installers with the clearance and paperwork to go under the streets allegedly to do repairs. They also have several FBI, two CIA, three in the NSA, and one Secret Service agent that will assist in their plan. These are Culper spies; General Washington can answer specific questions about the Culper spies, later. But that spy network that he set up during the Revolutionary War has continued on throughout the history of the country. They will use the courier system to deliver messages. The couriers are Culper spies that are possessed with good spirits. Only the Culper spy will know the other spy, and only the spirit will know what the message is, and if the Culper spy is captured, even under torture he won't reveal the message because he won't know it. It is a tremendous sacrifice for the living Culper spy.

They're going to utilize the Vietnam War strategy of the Wild Weasels, F4 Phantom planes. One of the fathers was a pilot in Vietnam. There had been a great number of planes shot down, so they had to come up with a way to jam the North Vietnamese radar. They came up with a pod that sends out bursts of very energized microwaves, emitted by powerful generators carried on the planes. They would turn the bursts of microwaves on and off as they flew along, so the plane could not be found. In the On position, the Vietcong could locate their position by back-tracking the signal after it jammed their radar. In the Off position they could not, and the plane, the Wild Weasel, had moved from the detected location. First you see it and now you don't. The possessed Americans are planning to use generators carried in a dozen vans that will send out bursts of microwaves as they continuously drive the van around the city of D.C., that is, around the White House, the Capitol Building, and the Supreme Court. This will jam the cell phones and wireless Internet technology used in Blackberries and iPods. No one in the city will be able to send out messages for help or receive warnings. The way the technology works is that sound waves coming at each other cancel each other out; it cancels out all radar, microwaves, and radio waves. The authorities can't use triangulation to detect where the energized microwave bursts are being emitted from because the bursts will be turned On and Off while the van is moving. When their radar comes on, the van won't be located at that site. And they will use so many vans zig zagging throughout the city that they won't be able to single out even a few. It'll appear like white noise in the general atmosphere of the city.

Inside the White House, the Secret Service spy will loop all electrical security by recycling it so the alarms won't be triggered. The windows and curtains in the White House have coded into their fabric a material that is impervious to radar, so once inside the White House, the numbers of the mob or what they are doing can't be detected from outside. The most key position of all the Culper spies is the switchboard operator, and another in the White House kitchen, with another one in the Capitol Building. The cable men working underground will cut the cable, so there won't be any TV broadcasting, and they'll also cut landline telephone service, except through to the Culper spy telephone operator, who will inform callers that all lines are busy. The NSA Culper spies who control the Echelon Project, which is a bank of computers that listen into phone calls, will redirect all wireless communications; basically scrambling all phone calls in and out of the city. They also plan on using Culper spies as couriers to hand deliver messages to each member of the Cabinet and the members of Congress who are part of the unconstitutional Continuity of Government plan, to tell them that there is an emergency secret meeting at the White House at a time certain. This way they bring them all into the White House so they are killed during the invasion.

As to the cover for the invading mob, they have applied for and have received a permit to assemble in Lafayette Park, across from the White House. The permit was granted to Agnes Whiffle of Arkansas for the Granny Quilt Crafters of America, protesting the price of cotton. They specifically chose an innocuous cause to avoid attention. Some women will color their hair gray to make them look older; some have padded their clothing to make them look fatter. From the edge of Lafayette Park, they will look like elderly grandmothers. Their weapons will be disguised inside the quilts they will carry, including Tasers that they will use on the White House gate guards; while they are down the women will handcuff the guards. They made contact with the Capitol Police Culper spies and ten of them will allow the alleged protesters access to the street and gates of the White House once they begin to mosey on over. Somewhat of an innocent flooding over from Lafayette Park, as they chat about quilting and family heirlooms. This will occur exactly at the time the Cabinet members will be arriving. They have look outs everywhere to synchronize all the movement around the city. The Culper spy in the White House kitchen will put exceptionally strong sleeping pills in the coffee of the snipers before they go on roof duty. They'll be out for 24 hours.

The buses used to bring in the Granny Quilt Crafters of America protesters will drive around the city until they receive notice and then turn to block the city's intersections and then abandon the buses. Taking with them the keys, of course.

They have also organized parties, neighborhood block and college campus parties. There are three college universities strategically located near the White House. The students will be given free beer to come to live-concert parties. But once the parties get going, spirits will possess the living and spread the throng of students and neighborhood parties out closer to the White House and Capitol - spreading the chaos enough to block streets. Between the buses and the hundreds of people blocking streets, nothing will move in or out of the city.

There will be enough dismantling of security, enough numbers in their mob of 'grandmothers.' Each has pledged their lives. If twenty get shot down, the others will continue to overtake the invasion of the White House. We're looking at brave Americans who have had enough with our country being invaded, taken over by the Communists, and our economy intentionally destroyed. And they are hooked up with good spirits who were veterans, scientists, and military tacticians in life. Once inside the White House, they plan to kill everyone they see. They will take no prisoners. None. You don't mess with a mother's child."

"Excuse me, Sir, who the hell came up with this plan?" Sherman asked.

McArthur smiled, "A woman with a vision. I mean a psychic vision."

"A psychic vision?" Sherman asked.

"This is a patriotic group that originally met on various other patriotic websites. After reading their posted comments, one began to contact another off the website and this type of contact multiplied exponentially, until they had formed their own private group. They created their own code of communication. It bloomed from there, each one individually questioning a new recruit and then bringing them into the newly-formed group. They now have seven hundred in their group. One of their members is a woman with extreme psychic ability. She even communicated telepathically with several aliens on a UFO. It was she that had a vision of a mob inside the White House."

"What is she? A reincarnated Irish Celtic warrior?" Patton laughed.

McArthur smiled, "She is Irish. She is an Amazon. She does have red hair. She is beautiful." McArthur paused a moment in reflection. "It might be interesting, before I tell you of the Irish American woman's vision, to consider what Yeats wrote of Ireland, and perhaps," McArthur nodded toward Patton, "perhaps she is a descendant of an ancient warrior woman or mystic."

McArthur continued, "Yeats wrote of Ireland that 'blame is on

Ireland because of the blood shed for her, because of the love of her by her countrymen.' Is that love of Ireland, which Yeats wrote about, any different than the passionate love Americans have for America? And remember, the second highest population in America is of Irish descent. The American heart is the United States of America. So too, is America our spiritual vessel of love for Jesus. If we lose our land, we lose our souls, and we lose our God. The love Americans have for America is a passionate love of her. There is a fear that her death is their abandonment. That they will never see Christ. And that they could not endure that loneliness. There is fear of their loss of freedom, for surely, it will be gone without a successful revolution. Revolution and the blood that will soak her fields is the only thing that will cleanse her of Satan."

Sherman and Grant looked at each other and nodded recognition of the truth. LeMay called out to McArthur, "When? That's all I want is a day and time!"

"I'll second that question," Patton cried.

The other generals and admiral mumbled remarks to each other like crazed dogs waiting to be released from their chains so they could charge at the one bone in the center of the floor. Each dog barking his ferocity to be greater than the next. Each more capable of tearing Satan in to bloody shreds upon which the others could feast.

McArthur took a drag on his long-stemmed pipe then smiled as he related the Irish American woman's vision. "The mob had killed everyone in the White House. As the mob made their way from room to room, checking ten times ten in every closet and under every desk where survivors might hide, and though finding them dead, as they passed the bodies, each member of the mob stabbed the bodies repeatedly. Each had to drive his knife into the body to find yet another organ to mince. They cut off ears, fingers, and scalps as trophies. It was a gruesome vision. And in the end, the psychic saw a group of men dragging the President inside the Oval Office of the White House, strip him of his clothes, but before killing him, they slammed him down on top of the presidential desk and ripped off his cock and balls, then gutted him, and while he was still alive they hung him by the neck from a light fixture."

"It doesn't sound as though this is the work of good spirits?" General Lee replied.

"That's where the whole vision becomes strange," McArthur agreed. "After the mob of Americans had invaded with the help of good spirits inside the White House, after they had killed everyone, the mob couldn't get to the President because he was locked inside the Oval Office with his Secret Service people. The Culper spies had blocked their escape route tunnel, so security got Tsaeb back into the Oval Office. It turns out that those Secret Service and Farkin Muslims that provide Tsaeb with security were possessed by evil spirits that manifested themselves once inside the locked Oval Office. Tsaeb had served Satan's purpose and was no longer of any use to them. The evil spirits blocked the mob from entering the Oval Office. It was the evil spirits who castrated the President, gutted him, and then hung him. The woman reported the vision to the group and warned of the evil spirits taking over the attack on the White House.

In her vision, she saw absolute terror on the face of the President as these evil spirits grabbed hold of his body. He was completely surrounded with their hands tearing at his clothes, ripping them off his body, slicing his face and body with their long claws and hooked nails. She heard his screams while their claws tore off his cock and balls. After he was hung she heard even louder screams from the President as she saw demons come up out of the ground and take his body and soul down to hell. He was dead but still screaming; his body still felt the pain."

"Jesus Christ," Patton cried. "That's one hell of a way to deal with that son-of-a-bitch! So, if these people, the Granny Quilt Crafters of America, have already planned this attack, should we leave them alone and just supplement that invasion? Or do we stop them?"

"This is what I've been thinking about," McArthur responded. "I think we need to contact them and organize our attack on the other fronts to synchronize with theirs. In other words, we can launch our plan against Congress and the Supreme Court at the same time. But we need to get the union leaders and the Federal Reserve, also. That means we need to move up our attack by a month. Can we be ready by then? We need to communicate with the good spirits without letting the evil spirits know what we're doing and that's the difficulty we face. If we help with the attack, it's going to alert the evil spirits and the whole invasion of the White House could fail.

But if that woman with the vision is right, and Tsaeb's Secret Service turn into evil spirits, as Satan's army comes to claim Tsaeb's soul – what then? We know that Tsaeb has had two evil spirits following him since birth. After they take Tsaeb down to hell, will the legions of evil spirits come back into the White House and prevent the mob from leaving? The bottom line, we need a weapon to disintegrate the evil spirits."

"When is this Internet group planning their invasion?" Grant asked.

"Six months from now. In six months, we need to invent and build at least 5000 disintegrating weapons. Or we have to stop the attack on the White House."

"Maybe it would be better to stop them. I don't know that we can get these weapons made in six months," Patton offered. "We can't utilize the military complex to manufacture these weapons. They're the enemy! For 5000 of these weapons, we can't go to a small local tool and dye shop, either. We'll need a manufacturing plant to get these built. How do we do that without notice?"

"This is the other problem. I sent a couple of spirits out to talk to the floor supervisor of a plant in Massachusetts. They manufacture titanium implants, knees and hips."

"Isn't Massachusetts lost to the Communists? How can you get a floor supervisor to re-tool the plant for manufacturing of the weapon?" LeMay asked.

"The people of Massachusetts voted Ted Kennedy into office out of sympathy for the assassinations of his brothers, John and Robert. It was an unspoken promise, taking care of the family of a native son who died in service of his country. Otherwise, they hated Teddy; he became a traitor. That Chappaquiddick set up scared the shit out of him. They had underwater scuba divers helping to rescue him, while they murdered her. That's how they got him to vote and lobby other Senators to side with the Zionist Jews. You saw how they murdered John, Jr. and his wife and sister-in-law; he was going to expose those who killed JFK.

McArthur took a drag on his corncob pipe as he took a few steps, his eyes looked down at the floor, his left hand rested on his hip, he continued, "But getting back to the contact at the implant factory. The floor supervisor said that the employees are with us."

As he paced the floor several more steps, he turned toward the generals, "The floor supervisor said he can fire those who he thinks will rat on us, there are plenty of patriotic Americans to fill their positions. And he can get the necessary department heads on his side to fudge the numbers of orders shipped and material ordered. The factory is still using the Just-In-Time model of manufacturing that the Japanese came up with. Excellent way to get shut down when your material for manufacturing comes only from one country and it's under internal strife. But we can use all that, now, to screw with the paperwork. Claim there was a shortage of titanium shipped to the factory. Etc., etc."

He took another drag on his pipe, then, "Titanium would be very good to use in designing a non-magnetic gun."

"Excuse me," LeMay said, "At some point, the public will know what happened in Washington. But this war must be fought through stealth attacks by small numbers. A continuous, Special-Ops-type of assault from different directions. It needs to be continuous to keep them off guard. But that won't be feasible when the country, the world, hears what happened in D.C. The Joint Chiefs will take over; Martial Law will be declared. The American people have been waiting for Martial Law to be declared under the last two regimes. They have already decided that they will not obey Martial Law. Once the Joint Chiefs try to move troops into towns, the American people will attack them. That will result in the UN taking over and releasing their troops now on U.S. bases."

"I agree," McArthur answered. "After the attack on the White House, there will be several people claiming power over the country, and whoever that might be will immediately declare Martial Law. And I agree that the American people will not tolerate any kind of Martial Law; they will either carry on as they have in the past, coming and going at will, or they will take to the streets to kill illegal aliens and Muslims. And vice versa. And if the federal Congress is not killed, Americans will march on the Capitol Building, but by the time they get there, the congressmen and women would have escaped through the underground tunnels that come out on the other side of the Treasury building. We'll have an absolute mess with people roaming the streets across America looking for food, killing neighbors for it, and killing politicians and UN troops. It's going to be a blood bath. Especially when the SM-31 gangs, drug lords, illegal aliens gathered in hostile takeover of neighborhoods across the country. This chaos is almost impossible to control through any military action, that is, without bombing the entire neighborhood.

This is why there has to be a pro-active assault on the SM-31 gangs and illegal aliens; anyone who looks like a Muslim or Mexican will be killed on sight where they stand. You can count on college students carrying weapons; the Muslim college students are carrying and are waiting for the signal to kill the Christian and Jewish students they dorm with, go to class with. There will be battles fought all over the country.

It's also likely that those in power behind the scenes will allow all this chaos in order to whittle down the numbers before they call the Chinese military down from Canada. It's a hell of a chessboard that has been set up. It's a Gordian knot, as I said earlier. They have Americans surrounded from within and from without. With Communists and Satan's descendants holding all military power. Generals Oliver McPhil and Darren Zeus are both members of the Foreign Affairs Private Council. John M. House, the Secretary of Defense is also a member of the Foreign Affairs Private Council. I'd like to know how many Christians these traitors sent in harm’s way over in Iraq and Afghanistan. We need to get our military back home, but these military leaders will keep them out of America until after the expected revolution is put down. That is, unless the military bring themselves home. We need these forces back in America, by spring."

The treason kept mounting up in all areas of government and overwhelmed the generals and admiral who had fought with such passion to keep America free.

Patton cried out, "Does this shit ever end!?"

McArthur tapped his extinguished pipe on the palm of his hand to clear the ashes left inside, then tucked the pipe into his shirt pocket and continued, "Let's finish with what forces we have to face."

As he spoke, he pointed to the states that housed the Muslim training camps, ACORN groups, Muslim college student and social associations, illegal aliens, and union leaders and their henchmen. What might be expected is that teachers may lead high school students that they have indoctrinated to follow the UN Communist doctrine - to fight against their parents and other patriots. That's the other urgency to have this revolution now, before these kids get into college and into the business world and impose the New World Order on all Americans. They are almost a lost generation. Lost to Satan.

Now, the all-spirit armies will attack these groups. Unfortunately, even American high-schoolers who were indoctrinated. All the Muslim training camps and soldiers will be completely destroyed. What is of some concern is that Tsaeb and Jeffers signed papers allowing the grandson of the founder of the Muslim Brotherhood into our country. He had been banned, but thanks to Tsaeb, he now comes and goes at will. He's been coordinating the Muslim training camps with the Muslim college student and social groups here in America with the Farkin Muslims who have been protecting Tsaeb along with the Secret Service. As Tsaeb said in his campaign, he wanted a Federal Civilian Police Force as well equipped as our U.S. Military. Why? Tsaeb and the grandson of founder of the Muslim Brotherhood have been working on pulling these groups together as a Muslim war unit inside America; Tsaeb's personal army. Tsaeb gave the Muslim Brotherhood $1.5 billion without Congressional approval.

The Muslim Brotherhood has worked across the Middle East, stirring up revolt. Tsaeb has supported the uprisings, to give the Muslim Brotherhood a foothold in each country to bring about the Islamic Caliphate before it becomes the Middle East Union. They didn't originate it, but are moving in on that revolt, trying to end up as the leaders of the newly formed governments of those countries. They began in Tunisia, then Egypt, and are working in Libya, Yemen, Jordan, Algeria, Sudan, Syria, Pakistan, Turkey, and Iran. There is a plan to take the Middle East and turn it all into Sharia law; kill all the Christians; take control of Israel, specifically Jerusalem; and, of course, kill all the Zionist Jews. This is the world caliphate that the Muslims are working for. When that gets hot and heavy, and before the U.S. government goes to Israel's aid, the Muslim war unit, Tsaeb's personal Muslim army, will attack from inside America. Now, we can see why Tsaeb gave the Israelis 187 F22 Raptors; he expects the Muslims to take them when they conquer Israel and then use them against the United States."

Looking at the floor, McArthur made a pensive hesitation, resting his hands on his hips. Finally, he looked up at the generals and admiral, "We don't care about the Zionist Jews; they aren't the descendants of the Israelites; they are the modern-day Pharisees. Jesus condemned the Pharisees; John the Baptist called them vipers. The Zionist Jews are one head of the Illuminati. They do not live by the Law of Moses, but by Satanic law that the Pharisees wrote, the *Talmud.* No, gentlemen, and we don't care if the other head of the Illuminati, the Muslims, take down their competitors in world domination. Both are our enemies. The Muslims and Jews vie for Satan's favorable blessing. We only care about those F22 Raptors. We must take back our technology from the hands of our enemies. This won't be a stealth venture, not in capturing all 187 jets. This is going to be an overt attack against Israel. An important mission in this war will be to precisely time our taking the jets before the Muslims take Israel, but close enough to the conquering of Israel to make it look as though the Muslims took the jets as part of their attack on Israel. We need the Gulf Wars pilot spirits to fly these planes out of Israel - all in one day!

Everything must occur on one day - the invasion on the White House and the Capitol; those on the list to fill the positions of Continuity of Government; the taking down of the leaders of the cartels, the union leaders, local Muslim and Zionist leaders, the Federal Reserve leaders, UN leaders, and so on. In each of these groups, the leaders' second, third, and fourth in line to take over must also be taken. Everything must be attacked on the same day - a shock and awe. And the American military must bring themselves back home at least by the day after. They can't come before; it will set the Muslims, Zionists, and the UN troops into action before we can get to them."

McArthur stopped and turned to the generals, "There is a puzzle, a question as to the fighting ability of the Muslims. What the U.S. Military forces have found in fighting in Afghanistan and Iraq is that the Muslims are lazy, smoke pot, and are lack-lustered soldiers. They have absolutely no self-discipline. It takes a great deal of prodding from the U.S. soldiers to get them to do anything. Maybe it's from too many generations living in a state of war; living under dictators, so that now there's nothing left to their will to fight. But can we translate that to state for sure that they will fight poorly inside America? Not all of them are as bloodthirsty as those depicted on cable TV. And it doesn't take bravery to surround one captive with 20 Muslims to cut off the captive's head. That's a sure sign of cowardice. At the same time, in the U.S., they see themselves as living inside a Christian stronghold; killing Americans, they think, will be a turkey shoot. And, at last, they get to kill those they hate with a passion. But, still, I think that it's safe to say, Muslims will not fight as fiercely as Americans. Americans will be fighting for their freedom that they see as being taken by a foreign invader; they will fight to their dying breath."

McArthur continued, "Another front is the United Nations. Under its Charter, the UN has the legal authority to invade the United States as soon as they see any kind of revolution taking place in America. In fact, they may invade for any 'breach of the peace.' That's the way Roosevelt structured the UN's power, but after he died - in his mistress' bed, the Charter was signed by Harry Truman. President Harry S. Truman was Worshipful Master of Grandview Lodge, Missouri, Grand Master of Masons of Missouri, Sovereign Grand Inspector General, 33 degree, Honorary Member of Supreme Council, Honorary Grand Master of International Supreme Council Order of DeMolay, awarded 50th golden anniversary of Freemasonry."

Chapter 13

With a quiet gasp, McArthur stopped speaking. All his senses immediately focused on the sound that had suddenly infiltrated the control room. It was soft and melodic, barely distinguishable, at first. The generals heard it, too, and looked around the room. They knew a spiritual being was about to permeate the walls; an entity that they had not expected. As the sound gently streamed into the room, they stood up in anticipation. Finally, they felt the words, ever so gently, caress their souls. It was as if they were overhearing an angel singing in prayer to God, "Oh Lord, my God, when I in awesome wonder, consider all the worlds Thy hands hath made, I see the stars, I hear the rollin' thunder."

Off in the distance, thunder rumbled across the skies above the Cheyenne Mountain and echoed down into its caverns. The generals listened in silence, as the sound of the celestial voice sang, "I found throughout the universe displayed. When Christ shall come and take me home, what joy shall fill my heart. Then I shall bow in humble adoration and there proclaim, my God, how great Thou Art."

Slowly, the image of a tall woman began to materialize inside the control room. Her voice now clear and sweet, "Then sings my soul, my Savior God, to Thee, how great Thou art, how great Thou art."

The generals remained standing, in silence, mesmerized by the tall, red-haired woman. An ancient tribal crown of gold and silver sat atop the thick copper waves of hair that hung down her back to her waist. Her voice strong and soothing, greeted the generals, "Gentlemen. Felicitations ta ye, all. I am Queen Macha Mong Ruadh, ruler of all Ireland in my lifetime, 377 ta 331 BC. Gentlemen, I have come ta fight with ye."

Washington choked out a slight gasp. "Ahh. Madam. Your Highness. When I crossed the Delaware there was a woman strong such as yourself that aided in rowing and then in combat, but I think we fight a different war today."

"I understand ya warnin'. But if ye lose this war the consequences will be worse for American women than the price that Celtic women paid when Ireland adopted Roman law. St. Patrick brought the Roman law with Christianity and forever changed our Celtic traditions of women. Takin' from 'em all their rights of ownin' property. A right only given back of late. I think I understand better than any of ye what 'tis at stake in today's revolution. 'Tis one thing that Roman and Greek cultures destroyed the power of the Celtic woman, but today, the Muslims' Shariah law will castrate women; a much greater consequence of defeat."

Macha of the Red Hair, she had been called, walked among the generals. Her long white dress danced off her heals as she walked. The sheerness of its fabric lay softly on her large breasts and round hips, displaying her ability to give life. Her broad shoulders and strong arms, muscled thighs showed her ability to take life away. Her skin was white with a soft, natural rosy glow on her cheeks. Her sparkling blue eyes looked deeply in to the eyes of each general as she walked passed, capturing their hearts one by one. Her body was straight with confidence and resolve. She feared no man, knowing she could fight any one of the generals, rendering them helpless in quick fashion.

"I am here," she told them, "ta fight the Muslims. I'll not go back in ta the night without defeatin' 'em."

McArthur slowly walked over to the woman, not without trepidation, for his observation was that a woman in battle could be far more vicious than any man. He had read the claim proffered that no troops could take down a Celtic man, should he call upon his wife to assist him. "Queen Macha," he finally uttered, "I, ah, don't think, ah, it would be feasible...."

Macha intercepted with a tone of determination, "I will go in ta battle against the Muslims, with or without ye! The Celtic warrior women are ready for this war."

"But," Patton stepped forward, "Queen Macha. I think it would be best if... ah, if...."

LeMay interrupted, "What he's trying to tell you is that you need to stand down."

Queen Macha walked up to LeMay, "Need I show ye my ability? I am ready, and that 'tis ya last warnin'."

"I was just trying to explain," LeMay countered, taken aback by a woman warrior dominator facing him in equal stature without fear. He had remembered studying her victorious battles.

"Let me explain, ta ye. Ta all of ye generals," Macha said. "Da ye know what they will do ta the American women they allow ta live? 'Tis aside from gang rapin' 'em. Da ye know what they do ta 95% of their own Egyptian women? In 1995, they passed a law bannin' any law that prohibits the castration of Muslim girls. The Muslims intend to bring that same law to America."

Macha walked over to Patton and looked at him with piercing blue eyes. Then on to McArthur. Then she turned to the others, "'Tis Shariah and Sunni Islamic law. 'Tis not in the Qur'an; 'tis Muslim culture and tradition; Sunna Code of Behavior. We are well beyond talk of wearin' a burqu. 'Tis the Shariah law that await the American women; the cutting off of a girl's clitoris, sewing shut her vagina, to be cut open by her husband before he fucks her. This is what American women will endure, if ye lose this war."

"Jesus Christ!" Stonewall cried out.

"Ah, General Sherman, on ye March ta the Sea, ye chose ta turn the other way, not ta be involved when it came ta ya men's sexual pleasure. Ye gave ya men freedom ta seek out prostitutes in New Orleans. General McArthur, Admiral Nimitz, ye both worked with the U.S. government and local police ta allow prostitution at Pearl Harbor. 'Tis ta say, gentlemen, the Muslims understand, as did ye, as did the U.S. Military, that men want access ta women. The castration of wee Muslim girls, the cuttin' and sewin' shut of Muslim wives' vaginas are the control that Islam' Sunna Code of Behavior promises their armies, their men who blindly follow the Qur'an and the Code. But this Islamic practice is Satanic!

All of ye have used women ta keep ye armies followin' ye. It goes ta the primal fear that all men experienced going through puberty; the overwhelmin' fear that there won't be a woman available ta fuck."

Macha turned away, her head bowed as she thought; her heart was heavy with sadness for the little girls of Islam. But the sadness steeled her resolve to kill the Muslim men who will do this to the American women, if America loses this war. Her personal interest to save the American girls and women came from the Irish being the second largest ethnic population in America, after the Germans. These women were her descendants and she had followed them overtime, watching over them throughout the centuries.

Finally, she continued, "No human bein' wants ta be used as a jacks, as with prostitution, but the Muslims' Sunna Code of Behavior crosses the line of demonic pleasure."

Macha walked along the map of the world projected now on the control room viewing screen, "Interestin'," she said, then turned to the generals, "Did ye know that the Muslims of the world have never contributed anythin' ta mankind. Muslims have only brought in ta this world the forced conversion ta Islam at the point of a sword. The ancient people of the Persian Empire were too impatient ta study or invent, but always ready ta steal and appropriate from the Babylonians, who themselves copied the inventions and crafts of the Assyrians, the descendants of Sem, Noah's only son. Taday's Germans."

Macha paused a moment, "Generals. What we are facin' started thousands of years ago, only now comin' ta a head. We are about ta face Satan, himself. Besides the corruption of Eve in the Garden of Eden, there are three important events that put civilization on the road of evil - the corruption of King David, the enslavement of Jews by Ezra and his Talmud, and the burnin' of the Great Library of Alexandria. Satan 'twas behind all. These singular events gave us the world we have today. It will end in the Second American Revolution and the return of Jesus Christ to battle Satan."

She turned to the generals, a yellow glow encircled her body as she continued to speak, "Exodus occurred in 1436 BC. During their wanderin' in the desert, Moses wrote the Torah, the Pentateuch - one of those books 'twas Deuteronomy. God told Moses ta write a warnin' in Deuteronomy - that the book would be a witness against the Israelites. Some 450 years afterwards, King David became the first king of the 12 tribes of Israelites, 986 BC."

Macha took a few steps, quiet at first, and then posed a hypothesis, "Let's look at historical events from a different perspective. She picked up Sherman's Bible, "May I?" Sherman nodded assent. And Macha began to read:

1 Kings 16:1-13, 'And the Lord (God) said ta Samuel: How long wilt thou mourn for Saul, whom I have rejected from reigning over Israel? fill thy horn with oil, and come, that I may send thee ta Isai the Bethlehemite: *for I have provided me a king among his sons....* Isai therefore brought his seven sons before Samuel: and Samuel said ta Isai: The Lord hath not chosen any one of these. And Samuel said ta Isai: Are here all thy sons? He answered: There remaineth yet a young one, who keepeth the sheep. And Samuel said ta Isai: Send, and fetch him....He sent therefore and brought him. Now he was ruddy [redhead] and beautiful ta behold, and of a comely face. And the Lord said: Arise, and anoint him, for this 'tis he. Then Samuel took the horn of oil, and anointed him in the midst of his brethren: and the spirit of the Lord came upon David from that day forward....' 2 Kings 5:2-4 'and the Lord said ta thee: Thou shalt feed my people Israel, and thou shalt be prince over Israel. The ancients also of Israel came ta the king (of Judah) to Hebron, and king David made a league with them in Hebron before the Lord: and they anointed David ta be king over Israel. David was thirty years old when he began ta reign, and he reigned forty years....' 2 Kings 6:12-18 'So David went, and brought away the ark of God...into the city of David with joy. And there were with David seven choirs, and calves for victims. And when they that carried the ark of the Lord had gone six paces, he sacrificed an ox and a ram: And David danced with all his might before the Lord: and David was girded with a linen ephod. And David and all the house of Israel brought the ark of the covenant of the Lord with joyful shoutin', and with sound of trumpet....And when he had made an end of offering holocausts and peace offerings, he (David) blessed the people in the name of the Lord of hosts.' 2 Kings 7:8-15 'And now thus shalt thou (Nathan the prophet) speak to my servant David: Thus saith the Lord of hosts: I took thee out of the pastures from followin' the sheep ta be ruler over my people Israel.... 'And when thy (David's) days shall be fulfilled, and thou shalt sleep with thy fathers, I will raise up thy seed (Solomon) after thee, which shall proceed out of thy bowels, and I will establish his kingdom. He (Solomon) shall build a house ta my name, and I will establish the throne of his kingdom for ever. I will be ta him a father, and he shall be ta me a son: and if he commit any iniquity, I will correct him with the rod of men, and with the stripes of the children of men. But my mercy I will not take away from him, as I took it from Saul, whom I removed from before my face.' 3 Kings 2:10-12 'So David slept with his fathers, and 'twas buried in the city of David....And Solomon sat upon the throne of his father David, and his kingdom was strengthened exceedingly.' 3 Kings 11:33-39 'Because he (Solomon) hath forsaken me, and hath adored Astarthe the goddess of the Sidonians, and Chamos the god of Moab, and Moloch the god of the children of Ammon: and hath not walked in my ways, ta do justice before me, and ta keep my precepts, and judgments as did David his father. Yet I will not take away all the kingdom out of his hand, but I will make him prince all the days of his life, for David my servant's sake, whom I chose,

who kept my commandments and my precepts. But I will take away the kingdom out of his son's hand and will give thee ten tribes. And ta his son I will give *one* tribe, that there may remain a lamp for my servant David before me always in Jerusalem the city which I have chosen, that my name might be there... *And I will for this (Solomon's idolatry) afflict the seed of David, but yet not for ever.*' 3 Kings 12:20 'And it came ta pass when all Israel heard that Jeroboam 'twas come again, that they gathered an assembly, and sent and called him, and made him king over all Israel, and there was none that followed the house of David but the tribe of Juda only.'"

Macha put down the Bible, "King David had a long-time close advisor, Ahithophel, who 'twas known for his wisdom. He also had a general, Urias, in his army. The granddaughter of Ahithophel and the wife of Urias - 'twas Bethsabee. There 'twas no reason that a woman of such relationship would have been introduced ta David; her grandfather 'twas David's friend and would never have thought to present her as a possible wife to David. In her grandfather's mind, she 'twas a child. But Bethsabee would have known of David - likely from the time she had been a girl. Stories were told ta her by her family, and later by her husband, Urias. Stories of David's magnificent military ability and courage. Bethsabee felt a romantic, one-sided love affair that began in her girlhood. One that no one knew about. Now, as a woman, ta meet David, she could only set a stunnin' trap - he had ta immediately view her as a woman, not as a granddaughter, not as a wife, but a woman equal ta the level of his manhood. This 'twas pure primal attraction between a man and a woman. Bethsabee struck with surprise, an intimate display ta cause an explosion of David's lust for the perfect sexual object. She took a bath within his view. She intentionally and sensuously caressed her large breasts by dryin' 'em with a towel, provokin' his desire ta do the same. Her breasts responded in gleeful movement, as she leaned ta dry the place his cock lusted ta penetrate. The foreplay 'twas her's alone. 'Twas a seduction! He 'twas a king; a king can have whatever he wants! But she had the excuse that she 'twas his general's wife and granddaughter of his closest advisor. David would have left her alone had she protested. No servants responded ta her screamin' in protest because there 'twas no protest. No one knew that they had been intimate until she realized that she had become pregnant durin' their moment together. Her pregnancy and Urias refusin' ta be with her 'twas the only way that the Nation of Israel found out about Bethsabee's and David's adultery.

Bethsabee's trap had ta be stunnin' ta make him want her enough ta commit adultery. He 'twas a priestly king and only his promise ta his God kept him from takin' this sensuous woman. But then, in his lust for her, he had already committed adultery. Why not actually hold her, penetrate her? He 'twas a conqueror; he needed ta conquer her. And she knew it.

Now, let's view her strategic attack. In their first encounter, it 'twas not David takin' Bethsabee after a chance encounter of viewin' her naked body. Bethsabee seduced David, by takin' a bath in a space that she knew could be seen by David. I proffer ta ye, that the bath 'twas only an excuse for her ta display her naked body before David! Let the man see her voluptuous curves, ta entice him ta hunt her, so she can capture him! An innocent approach ta a priestly king 'twas the only way ta seduce such a man. A woman knows this." Macha smiled a knowing smile.

"Why else 'twas she there at that time and place, naked, takin' a bath in the open? She certainly could see that there 'twas a balcony above her open terrace; she certainly knew that it 'twas the balcony of King David. The whole of the Nation of Israel knew where their beloved King lived! 'Twas it the first time she bathed in open view of anyone walkin' on the balcony above her bathtub? Had anyone seen her bathtub permanently located out in the open, would they not have questioned her modesty? How would a normal husband respond ta this arrangement? Or did Bethsabee order her servant ta place a bath in the right location, only for that day? She 'twas married ta a general who had told her, perhaps complained about, King David would be at home on this particular day, while he had ta go inta battle. Biblical evidence 'tis that David did not know her and asked who she 'twas. Did she order her servant ta come back and help her out of the bath when they saw David 'twas risin' from his nap? What 'tis more seductive than watchin' an innocent woman dry her body after bathin'? A woman who knows her prey 'tis watchin' her? Had she, at previous times, seen David look out from his balcony? 'Tis it not usual ta look out from a balcony? Had it been a routine for her ta bath in the open, David would have seen her before that day. Generals! This 'twas the first time she bathed under the open view of King David's balcony for the sole purpose of seducin' King David! She knew David 'twas up there; she knew that her husband would not be comin' home that night and for the next couple of months.

'Bethsabee the daughter of Eliam,' 2 Kings 11:3. 'Eliam the son of Achitophel the Gelonite.' 2 Kings 23:34. 'Achitophel the Gilonite...from his city Gilo,' 2 Kings 15:12. Gilo was a city that Josue gave ta the Tribe of Judah, Josue 14:1; 15:12, 13, 20, 21, 51.

Therefore, Bethsabee was an Israelite of the Tribe of Judah, but wedded ta a Hittite, 'Urias' (2 Kings 11:3). Up ta this time, David had been faithful ta God's commandments, until Bethsabee seduced David inta the sin of adultery. And later, murder. Her husband, Urias, 'twas the descendant of Cush, the eldest son of the Black-skinned Ham, father of the Ethiopians and Sudanese, descendants of Satan. Did Urias know of Bethsabee's secret love of David - before he married her? Did Urias deliberately build up in the mind of Bethsabee how powerful and magnificent a man King David 'twas, so that Bethsabee would desire David ta the point of seducin' him? Did Urias let it slip that David would be at home on that day, while he, her husband, would be leavin' for the battlefield? Did Urias tell Bethsabee that David napped on the rooftop in the afternoon? Did Urias sexually excite Bethsabee before leavin' for battle that mornin' - but withhold consummation of his foreplay just before ecstasy, leavin' her cravin'? Then as he walked out their door, did Urias say one more time what a great man David 'twas, remindin' her of her romantic day dreams of bein' David's lover?

Or did Bethsabee act on her own because she just wanted the power of David's Kingship? She grew up around the secondary power of her grandfather, the wise advisor of King David. She had married a general, but David 'twas the greatest prize of power. And when their son, Solomon, became king and she wanted ta speak ta him, she 'twas treated as a queen: 3 Kings 2:19, 'Then Bethsabee came ta king Solomon...and a throne 'twas set for the king's mother, and she sat on his right hand.'

King David's corruption began with the sin of adultery with Bethsabee, but only after David saw her naked body, as she allegedly innocently bathed out in the open. David could not let Bethsabee go, so he had ta bring about the death of Urias, ta free Bethsabee from her marriage. 'Twas the murder of Urias that made David incapable of buildin' the Temple of God. This 'twas God's punishment for His priestly king. Satan's seduction of Bethsabee brought about the seduction of David, and David's carnal lust for her brought about the murder of Urias. Satan's purpose of seducin' these people 'twas ta delay the buildin' of a Temple in which ta rest the Ark of the Covenant, and in which the Israelites could worship God.

Adam and Eve were God's chosen people and the true Israelites are their descendants. Satan delayed the buildin' of the first proper Temple in the history of God's chosen people that 'twas built ta honor and worship God, Satan's adversary. Satan's later seduction of Solomon caused the loss of the Ark of the Covenant and the tablets upon which God wrote His Laws. The tablets are physical proof of God's existence. Physical proof that God wants us ta love Him and each other."

Macha opened the worn Sherman Bible and held it out, "Here, in 2 Kings 11:2, ye will find that written evidence.

Macha continued to explain to the generals, "Urias was a Hittite, carryin' the Y-chromosome of Satan. He refused ta sleep with Bethsabee 'by the welfare of thy soul I will not do this thing,' 2 Kings 11:11. By the welfare of the soul of David? 'Twas ta despoil the soul of David! If Urias would not sleep with Bethsabee, David's impregnation of her would be known by all the Nation of Israel. By Urias sleepin' on the couch with the servants, Urias made public that the impregnation of his wife could not be by him, since he had previously been away in battle. Urias, the seed of Satan, by his behavior, 'tis tellin' the Nation of Israel that their priestly King David had sinned against the Commandment of their God, 'thy shalt not commit adultery.' 'Tis exactly why David wanted Urias ta sleep with his wife, ta prevent the Nation from knowin' of David's sin, for how could he ask the Nation ta abide God's law, if he, their king, did not?"

Macha turned, "But what about Urias' disobedience of a direct order from his king? Urias had a devious plan. He 'twas a soldier. Ta Urias, death in battle 'twas inevitable. But destroyin' King David's reputation as a priestly king had greater reward. Urias 'twas a soldier for Satan, with orders ta wound Satan's adversary. Indeed, Urias 'twas able ta stab the God of Abraham in His heart. And it also gave Urias immortality. Because of his act of disobedience - his name 'tis remembered today, 3000 years later."

Macha continued to hold the Bible, "There ye have it in writin', generals, that David put Urias in mortal danger ta cause his death. Thou shalt not murder! In seducin' David ta murder him, Urias led David's soul ta mortal sin. Why else would Urias not follow the commandment of his king and sleep with his beautiful wife? How would it have been for the welfare of David's soul for Urias not ta sleep with his own, beautiful, wife? For the welfare of - 'tis ta be for the benefit of; ta protect and help. Urias did not protect David's soul; he exposed David's sin of adultery and tempted David in ta murderin' him. 'Tis the evil that Bethsabee and Urias, brought on the House of David," Macha argued. "That eventually led ta the destruction of the Nation of Israel and the scatterin' of God's chosen people through the union of David and Bethsabee - because of the sin committed by their son, Solomon, who had been seduced by his Egyptian wives ta worship Satan. The common denominator - seduction. The same seduction Satan used on Eve in the Garden of Paradise, ta bring Cain, Satan's son, inta the world."

Macha lowered her voice, "Moses 'twas used by God ta gather the Tribes of Israelites and lead 'em out of Egypt, ta deliver 'em from Satanic enslavement by the Egyptians, as God had said he would. "But I will judge the nation which they shall serve, and after this they shall come out with great substance." [Gen. 15:14]

And David 'twas used by God ta take the land of Chanaan by war, 1 Chronicles (Paralipomenon) 14:17; the land that God had promised ta Abraham for his descendants. For the first time, under David's kingship, there 'twas a Nation of Israelites, descendants of Adam and Eve. God had told Moses ta write Deuteronomy ta warn the Israelites before committin' their great sin of worshippin' false idols; ta warn the Israelites of Solomon's waste of their nation."

Macha raised the Bible while she spoke, "David's most grievous sin, allowin' himself ta be seduced. Bethsabee's seduction of David that later brought Solomon inta the world. 'Twas Solomon who handed the Nation of Israelites ta Satan. Bethsabee stole the throne of David for her son, Solomon, durin' a time of David's old-age infirmity, from David's older son and rightful heir, Adonias, 3 Kings 11:1.

Macha explained, "2 Kings 1:24 Adonias was politically campaignin' among the local leaders of the Nation of Israelites ta accept him as their king, but before they could make up their minds ta support the rightful heir ta the throne, Nathan, the prophet, seduced Bethsabee. Now, 'twas the time ta deceive David in ta thinkin' that he had promised his throne ta Solomon. Nathan sent her in ta David, and Nathan would be another voice in support of her lie. Nathan spoke a very clever and artful lie by announcin' that Adonias had already been declared king by others, knowin' 'twould injure David's royal pride. 'Tis an intentional provocation against David's authority as king ta be the proper one ta declare the successor ta his throne. Nathan only implies that David had previously told him that 'twas ta be someone other than Adonias. David's short-term memory 'tis from Bethsabee, who only a minute before 'refreshed' his memory that he had promised the throne ta Solomon. In his badly failin' health and poor memory, David's mind 'twas outflanked by Nathan and Bethsabee, and thus, he must believe the two of 'em or admit his frailty of mind. For he also can't remember why he thought Adonias should not be king, but on his mind 'tis the affliction of his pride that 'twas others and not him who declared Adonias 'twas king. If he goes along with the deceit, he can recover his pride and assert his power as king for one last time and die a man and not the helpless shell his age and health caused him ta be. And what if they are right, David might have thought; what if at one time he thought 'twas wise, why else would he have promised the throne ta Solomon?"

Macha held the Bible ta her breast while she spoke, "Solomon 'twas a usurper ta the throne. He ended up worshippin' Satan. He conjured up demons. He built idols for his Egyptian wives ta sacrifice infants ta Moloch; Solomon's Egyptian wives were descendants of Satan."

Macha explained the method of worshipping Moloch, "'twas Solomon who built the idol of Moloch, god of the sons of Ammon, in which the descendants of Satan would set a fire inside the idol and then place a cryin' infant babe on the arms of the idol and watch the babe burn ta death. For Satan requires a blood sacrifice. God does not – 'tis the lesson of Abraham and Isaac."

Macha's body suddenly convulsed with the image such evil brought to her mind, but more than her revulsion of burning infants was the greater need to tell the American people of the depth of evil that they should expect in the coming war against Satan's descendants. Just as Satan had infiltrated the ancient House of David, Satan had infiltrated the Office of the Presidency of the United States by way of Tsaeb, the foreign Muslim usurper. Tsaeb had voted repeatedly, prior to his presidency, in the Illinois Senate to allow infanticide of babies who survived abortions. And Tsaeb was now the President. If they could murder babes, and if they could roast helpless infants, then there would be no limit to what Satan's descendants, now in the United States, would stop at in the war that was to come to Americans. The generals listening to Macha deep inside the Cheyenne Mountain control room bowed their heads in sorrow at the idea of the evil that had conquered America that they had fought so hard to defeat.

After a moment, Macha asked, "What 'tis the difference between roastin' an infant on the arms of a stone idol and an abortion where they rip off the arms and legs of the infant while inside 'tis mother's belly, or murder them outright if they survive that abortion? Women have been seduced inta thinkin' that 'tis all right ta abort their babe given ta them only by God. Satan does not care if you roast an infant, rip off its arms and legs, or murder an infant; he takes the blood sacrifice as a worship of him just the same! Satan does not care if the woman 'tis aware that she 'tis sacrificin' ta Satan; 'tis enough for Satan that she knows that she's killin' God's gift ta her!"

She paused another moment and then, "Then there 'tis the second event in history that brings us ta the world we have ta face." She walked slowly around the control room, as she collected her thoughts.

"God continued His affliction of the seed of David, His punishment of the Israelites' sin of worshippin' idols even after Solomon. And, thus, He allowed Ezra ta enslave and uproot them while they were establishin' a life in Babylonian captivity. In Babylonia, the Israelites had remembered their sin against God and went back ta worshipping Him and obeying His laws of the Torah. They had prosperous lives, livin' in the lush fertile valley. They did not want ta return ta Jerusalem and start all over. But their past sin 'twas the most grievous, worshippin' idols as their King Solomon had done. 3 Kings 11:33-39 'Because he (Solomon) hath forsaken me, and hath adored Astarthe...and Moloch… *And* I will for *this afflict the seed of David....*' Among others, God used Ezra ta carry out His punishment of His people. God allowed Ezra ta see the opportunity ta use the cover of the Israelites' identity ta establish the religion of Satan - Pharisaism, ta enslave the Israelites under threat of death by the Persian kings of Babylon, if the Israelites refused ta return ta Jerusalem with Ezra. The Israelites were specifically threatened with death, if they did not learn and obey the Talmud! 'Tis known as Judaism, today.

But remember, generals, the last of that passage, the Israelites will be 'afflicted': '*but yet not for ever*.' 'Tis been since 930 BC when Solomon died - 2942 years ago! The Israelites have suffered for almost 3000 years. Are we comin' ta the end of that punishment? Does the phrase the 'end times' refer ta the endin' of that punishment? Will Jesus come ta battle Satan ta end that punishment that God has allowed Satan ta wreak over His chosen people? Only Jesus can stop Satan.

Jesus gave us two warnin's, Matt. 24:9, 'Then shall they deliver you up to be afflicted, and shall put you ta death: and you shall be hated by all nations for my name's sake.'

The other warnin' 'tis in Matt. 24:14, 'And this gospel of the kingdom, shall be preached in the whole world, for a testimony to all nations, and then shall the consummation come.' The Internet allows the preaching of the gospel to the whole world. The Internet 'tis the greatest evidence that we are in the end times – the consummation – the fulfillment of God's promise to afflict the seed of David.

But I'm getting' ahead of myself. There 'tis the issue of the burnin' of the Great Library of Alexandria. 'Tis a lesson of history that we must be mindful of taday, for we have the Library of Congress, in

Washington, DC, that 'tis equal ta or greater than the ancient Library. Satan and his evil spirits will target it as he did in Alexandria. Satan brings darkness inta the world – that includes destroyin' the knowledge that Satan exists. In the Library of Congress are books that expose him, and teach the works of great minds that give mankind a better quality of life. Books that teach of Jesus' love and our redemption.

Macha was thoughtful for a moment. The generals waited quietly, and then she spoke, "'Twas St. Patrick who brought Christianity ta Ireland and instilled a sense of literacy, the love of books in ta Celtic tradition, bringin' with him the books of the Temple of Serapis, the daughter library of the Library of Alexandria. 'Twas the Irish monks and scribes who translated from Greek and Latin the great books of Serapis saved from destruction by the Egyptian Coptic Christian Pope Theophilus of Alexandria 'Twas Ireland who preserved civilization durin' the Dark Ages. 'Twas the next Pope, the Patriarch of Alexandria, Cyril, who burned the Library of Alexandria."

McArthur countered, "There are others who were blamed for the burning of the Library. Julius Caesar was blamed when in 48 BC he pursued Pompey into Egypt and was intercepted by the Egyptian fleet at Alexandria. Caesar ordered the ships in the harbor to be set afire. It is alleged that the fire spread and destroyed the fleet, but also burned down part of the city. Caesar wrote himself of starting the fire in the harbor."

Macha countered, "Caesar only wrote of settin' fire ta the ships in the harbor! Caesar 'twas hated by his enemies, remember 'et tu, Brute' when the Senators stabbed Julius Caesar ta death? His enemies blamed him for the atrocity of burnin' such a center of knowledge, of burnin' almost 700,000 works written by the world's greatest philosophers, scientists, historians, mathematicians, astronomers, and poets brought in from around the ancient world ta Alexandria by Ptolemy II. Every ship that came inta the harbor at Alexandria 'twas searched by armed guards, lookin' for scrolls and books. They took 'em, copied 'em, keepin' the original for the Library, and returned the copy ta the owner. Ptolemy II invited, housed, and financially supported the great minds of the world, who came ta Alexandria ta write, research, and ta translate the works brought by Alexander the Great from the countries he conquered.

But where 'tis ya proof that Caesar actually caused the destruction of the Library when he 'twas targetin' the Egyptian fleet in the harbor? There 'twas a storage buildin', containin' no more than 40,000 ta 70,000 books that were in harm's way of the burnin' fleet. 'Tis said that they were the translated copies scheduled ta be returned to their owners. The number 'twas insignificant. There 'tis no proof ta the contrary. And the fire that Caesar set 'twas on the other side of the city from the Great Library. The entire city of Alexandria would have had ta have burned, first. There 'tis no evidence of that. And why, after Caesar's death, would Mark Antony give Cleopatra 200,000 scrolls, if she did not have a library ta put them in?"

Macha walked up to McArthur, slowly circling him while she challenged the philosopher's knowledge of events. "After the death of Alexander the Great, his empire 'twas divided by his generals. His general, Ptolemy, got Egypt and began the steps towards Alexander's dream of a great library in Alexandria. Ptolemy knew Aristotle and convinced him to leave his works to the Library; and under Ptolemy II, Aristotle's private library in his school, the Lyceum, 'twas brought ta the Library of Alexandria. The last of the Ptolemy Pharaohs, Cleopatra VII, 'twas protected in her affair with Caesar, and after Caesar 'twas assassinated by the Senate, she had an affair with Mark Antony. But the succeeding Western Christian Roman Emperor viewed Mark Antony's adultery with Cleopatra as an abomination and conquered the country of his mistress. When she died the Library was still standin' in 30 BC.

The great Library of Alexandria contained so many documents that they sent the overflow ta a daughter library, set up in the Pagan Temple of Serapis. It stood until A.D. 392. The Roman Emperor, Theodosius I, A.D. 379-395, made Roman Catholic Christianity the official religion of the Roman Empire, A.D. 380, which included Alexandria, Egypt. Theodosius granted permission ta Theophilus, Patriarch of Alexandria from A.D. 385 ta 412, ta raze the pagan Temple of Serapis, the sister library, and build a Christian Church on its ruins. In A.D. 392, Theophilus led an alleged 'Christian' mob in destroyin' the Temple of Serapis, the Serapeum." (www.newworldencyclopedia.org /entry/Theodosius_1?oldid=811502)

Three years after the death of Alexandrian Pope Theophilus, in A.D. 412, and after his buildin' of the Christian Church on the ruins of the Temple of Serapis, the Library of Alexandria continued. Theon is said ta be the last member of the Library, but 'twas his daughter, Hypatia, a female Greek philosopher, mathematician, and astronomer, who 'twas considered the last Head Librarian. This proves that the Library of Alexandria existed in A.D. 415. For 'twas in A.D. 415 that the allegedly Coptic 'monks' murdered Hypatia. Hypatia 'twas not Jewish and not Christian, therefore, considered pagan by the standards of the 5th century.

McArthur counted, again, "Some say that to convert the Temple of Serapis into a Church, Christians destroyed the overflow documents."

"And they'd be wrong," Macha answered. She approached McArthur, ready for his intellectual challenge.

She argued, "Antoninus had prophesied that the Temple of Serpis, at the Serapeum, the sister library of the Library of Alexandria - would be destroyed. (Penelope, *Supra*) 'Tis likely he made sure Hypatia knew of his prophecy. Antoninus was an older contemporary of Hypatia, and as well as she, a Neoplatonist and pagan. Antoninus had his own school near Alexandria, at Canopus, Egypt. He 'twas known ta have ability ta see inta the future, and he had seen that after his death that all the pagan temples would be destroyed. The Temple Serapis in Alexandria, he said, would pass into formless darkness and be transformed. Antoninus died in A.D.

390; the Serapis 'twas destroyed in A.D. 391. Eunaplus describes that 'when Patriarch Theophilus presided over the abominable ones...and though they could not allege even a rumour of war ta justify them, they demolished the Temple of Serapis...their military tactics ensured that the thief would escape detection...these men boasted that they overcame the gods....They imported monks, as they called them...(who) led the lives of swine, and openly did...unspeakable crimes...For in those days every man who wore a black robe...possessed the power of a tyrant.' (*Eunaplus, Lives of the Philosophers and Sophists,* Translated by Wilmer Cave Wright; www.tertullian.org/fathers/eunaphus_02_text.htm)

'Twas no Christian civilians who destroyed and looted the Temple of Serapis, they were Theophilus' mercenaries! His thugs!

But Hypatia had responded ta Antoninus' warnin' by secretin' out the works stored at the Serapis, ta St. Patrick, A.D. 387-461. When St. Patrick went ta Ireland ta do missionary work, there were no cities, so he established monasteries in northern, central, and eastern Ireland that became centers for both trade and knowledge. Monks and scholars were fleein' inta Ireland and Patrick put them ta work translatin' and teachin' those Irishmen that he had converted the Latin and Greek languages. Because the Irish did not censor the pagan influences within their culture or in books comin' in from the Continent - and those works smuggled in by Paulus Orosius, a monk and historian, A.D. 385-420, from the Temple of Serapis - the Irish monks translated those works - while the rest of the world was livin' through the Dark Ages. (*How the Irish Saved Civilization*, by Thomas Cahill; www.livingarts originals.com/Irish-saint-patrick.html)

Remember, Hypatia's father taught her about all the religions of the world. She knew of Solomon's worship of demons; she knew of Judaism and its *Talmud* - of the Jewish philosopher Philo of Alexandria and his corruption of Heraclitus theory of *Logos*, which Philo corrupted ta hide the proof of God's existence. She knew Pope Celestine 'twas weak against the aggressive, power-hungry Cyril, who carried the Y-chromosome of Satan, and who was plannin' ta take control of the Christian Churches of the world. She knew that there were no cities in Ireland at the time, therefore, none of the religious conflict occurrin' at the time, as in the large city of Alexandria. She knew that St. Patrick had been sent ta Ireland ta do missionary work among the Irish. She knew Patrick was a scholar, establishin' Irish grammar. She knew that Patrick and the Irish did not censor the pagan influences - as did Paulus Orosius, the monk and historian, also know. What better place in the world ta send the documents than ta the quiet monasteries that Patrick 'twas establishin' in Ireland - away from the power struggle going on within the Christian Church between the Popes of Rome, Constantinople, and Alexandria.

The people of Alexandria adored Hypatia; they would have helped her and Paulus Orosius. As a historian, Orosius cherished the works of great minds, as did Hypatia and Patrick. The three worked secretly together ta save the documents housed in the Temple of Serapis -

after bein' given the warnin' of the known psychic, Antoninus, that the Temple 'twas goin' ta be destroyed. Hypatia loved Plato's work and would have been sure ta smuggle his works out of Alexandria.

The Greco-Roman culture 'twas heavily invested in scholarly work, 'twould have been against everythin' the Roman Emperor Theodosius I believed in for him ta destroy the books. When Rome conquered the Greek Empire, it continued on with Greek culture of philosophy and learnin', it did not destroy it; it embraced Greek knowledge."

MacArthur interrupted, "'The Roman Emperor Constantine I 'legitimized Christianity as a protected religion of the Roman Empire. Though he converted to Christianity he continued to pay attention to other deities, and this is seen in his poems and other dedications.'" (Holland Lee Hendrix, Pres. and Faculty, Union Theological Seminary, Frontline, www.pbs.org/wgbh/pages/frontline/shows/religion/why/legitimization .html)

As he spoke, MacArthur walked toward the viewing screen hanging on the wall of their meeting room under Cheyenne Mountain, "'In a life or death battle for control over the greatest empire ever known on Earth until that time, in October A.D. 312, Constantine I faced off with the tyrannical Maxentius. In facing superior forces, instead of praying to idols that don't help, Constantine turned to his father's monotheistic god. He prayed for help. And in front of Constantine and his whole army, a cross was emblazoned across the sky with the words: 'In this sign you will win.' Constantine's question, who was his father's god, was answered that night in his dream: 'It was the Christ of God.'" (Ken Curtis, Ph.D.; www.christianity. com/Church History/11629643/) Constantine and his army wore a cross on their uniforms and defeated Maxentius; Constantine became the Roman Emperor. As a result, Constantine ended the persecutions of Christians in the Roman Empire. But he had one foot in Christianity and one foot in paganism."

Patton stood up and added, "It was after Constantine when Theodosius I, the last Emperor of both the Western and Eastern Roman Empire, who tried to unify the Western and Eastern Christians under the Nicene orthodoxy, in A.D. 381." Patton turned to Macha, "And I agree with your implication, there is a difference between Theodosius wanting to destroy the pagans' blood sacrifices in the temples throughout the empire. Theodosius likely saw that the destructions of the temples would lead to pagans being converted to Christianity. But to destroy the works of the great Greek minds of mathematics, astronomy, philosophy, physics, was against the established culture of the Roman Empire. Indeed, Queen Macha, that is a matter of a different nature."

General Stonewall added, "Theodosius banned pagan blood sacrifices throughout the Roman Empire. For Jesus, the Son of God, taught that His Father only asked for self-sacrifice and to love Him."

"That's right, Stonewall," Patton offered, "The lesson of Abraham and Isaac is that God does not require a blood sacrifice. Yet, the Zionist/Pharisaic Jews of Israel are now learning how to sacrifice animals when the Third Temple is built. The Zionists know that a blood sacrifice is required by Satan - such as abortions. But then those Zionist Jews of Israel are not the descendants of the Israelites. But it matters not," Patton grunted, as his arm gestured a dismissal, "the Third Temple will never be built." He walked back to his chair and sat down.

Sherman added, "After Christ's death on the cross, Matt 27:51 'And behold the veil of the temple was rent in two from the top even to the bottom, and the earth quaked, and the rocks were rent.' This implies that the veil that secluded the part of the temple that only the Pharisees could enter had been torn away to expose the evil of the Pharisees! This is most significant, since this precise place, its precise design was mandated by God. Exodus 26:31-33 'Thou shalt make also a veil of violet and purple, and scarlet...And thou shalt hang it up...And the veils shall be hanged...and within it thou shalt put the ark of the testimony, and the sanctuary, and the holy of holies shall be divided with it.'

With the crucifixion of Jesus, followed by the tearing of the veil of the temple, it's God destroying and abandoning Jerusalem. He had held up the City of David for the sake of the coming of Jesus, but now that Jesus had been resurrected, and God knowing that the Zionist would return today, God is not there. God is in the United States. It is here that the majority of His chosen people reside."

"Precisely right, Generals," Macha responded. "What followed in history 'twas somewhat as significant to mankind. Hypatia 'twas murdered and the great Library of Alexandria 'twas burned down. Pope Cyril of Alexandria 'twas behind both atrocities. Yet, Cyril later 'became one of the first Black Saints in Christianity.' (Fr. Cyprian Davis, O.S.B., The National Black Catholic Congress; www.nbccongress.org/features/in-the-beginning.asp) Note that Cyril 'twas Egyptian and Black, therefore, a descendant of Ham. Cyril carried the Y-chromosome of Satan. And Satan wanted the Dark Ages to fall upon mankind, and Cyril gave that ta Satan.

Cyril's parabalanoi - his army of thugs - viciously murdered Hypatia, burned the Library of Alexandria, and then Cyril attacked the popular Nestorius, the Pope of Constantinople, on Nestorius' view of the two natures of Jesus and got Nestorius deposed as Pope. Cyril 'twas a busy little devil. And he taught his disciple and successor, Diosorus, all his ways. Cyril set things in motion and Diosorus would strike the final blow."

Macha walked around the control room under Cheyenne Mountain, looking at the Generals, "'Twas after the murder of Hypatia and the burnin' of the great Library of Alexandria and after the death of Cyril that Diosorus became Pope of Alexandria. He went ta the Council of Chalcedon, A.D. 451, convened by the new Pope of Rome, Leo I, and the Byzantine Emperor, in Constantinople, Turkey, ta settle the dispute between the Egyptian Christians and the Roman Christians over the nature of Jesus. The Council came up with the Chalcedonian Creed that asserted the two natures of Jesus, one divine nature and one human nature. Which 'twas Nestorius' definition of the natures of Jesus, and for which he 'twas deposed. But Diosorus continued with Cyril's teachin's that held that there 'tis only one nature of Jesus, which 'tis divine and human that are united together and that they did not separate even when He 'twas on the cross. Diosorus rejected the Council's finding of two natures of Jesus.

Why 'tis this conflict significant? Enough ta divide the church; ta get the Pope of Constantinople removed? ‘Tis significant because ‘tis another of Satan’s deceits, just as he deceived Eve in the Garden of Eden – you will have the knowledge of God. Satan’s henchmen pose this question of the nature of Jesus – ta lead man ta think that they can understand the Divine. To lead man to think that he has the wisdom of a god. It speaks ta the ego of mankind, his pride, and Satan’s use of man’s pride to trip him up. ‘Tis Satan’s oldest trick. The question itself ‘tis a red herring meant ta divide people. And indeed it did; it weakened the Christian faith; it caused many ta turn ta Islam, the worship of Satan; it resulted in the death of millions. Mankind’s challenge ‘tis ta balance logic and feeling. And faith ‘tis a type of feelin’. Faith ‘tis love. Faith says, I cannot use logic ta determine the nature of Jesus; no one ‘tis capable of understanding the nature of Jesus. Faith leads us ta realize that we must respect the boundary between God and man.

Macha sighed, “Diosorus cried that the Roman Catholic Church fought for power, by upholding that Jesus had two natures. But who 'twas really fightin' for the power? Diosorus demanded that, he, as the Pope of Alexandria, 'twas considered the ONLY Pope in the first centuries. Diosorus claimed that the Pope of Rome and the Pope of Constantinople were considered Bishops. Diosorus stated that they were equal ta him, but a Pope 'twas considered as an older brother ta the Bishops. Expectedly, the older brother bosses his younger siblin's. Diosorus settled the dispute by separatin' the Egyptian Christian sect from the Roman Church followin' the Council of Chalcedon. Pope Leo I of Rome gained support from the other Bishops and the Emperor, and Diosorus was excommunicated from the Roman Catholic Church. (www.newworldencyclopedia.org/entry/ Ecumenical_Council?oldid= 820470; and www.newworldencyclopedia. org/entry/Pope_Diosorus_1_of_Alexandria?oldid=932778)

"What you're leading up to," General Lee said, "Is that Cyril fought to oust Nestorius, the Pope of Constantinople, only because Nestorius was one of the most powerful men in the Roman Empire. It was Nestorius that could usurp Cyril's plan to control all the Christian Churches. And Nestorius was going after the heretics and would soon come to the heresy of Cyril's claim of the single nature of Jesus. So, Cyril got the jump on Nestorius and claimed, first, that Nestorius was the heretic, so that Nestorius subsequent claims against Cyril would only be viewed as responsively defensive - illegitimate. At that time, Cyril had the Pope of Rome, Celestine, wrapped around his finger - getting Celestine to give him the Commission to investigate for and report to Celestine on Nestorius' heresies alleged by Cyril. Celestine even gave Cyril the order to deliver to Nestorius his sentence of being kicked out of his powerful seat as Pope of Constantinople and his excommunication. (New Advent, Catholic Encyclopedia, http://712 educators)

"Tis proof of Cyril's sadistic character trait as a descendant of Satan!" Macha added, "And after Cyril's success in gettin' Nestorius deposed, and against the weak Celestine - Cyril assumed that he 'twas now the most powerful - that he 'twas the Pope over all the other Christian Bishops. And this 'tis what he taught his successor, Diosorus. 'Tis Satan takin' control of the Church of Jesus."

Macha walked pensively toward the world map showing on the viewing screen of the control room. "With the monasteries set up and runnin' and translation of the Greek works continuin' after the death of St. Patrick, we have the Irish preservin' civilization durin' the Dark Ages of Europe, A.D. 476-1000, that followed the murder of Hypatia and the burnin' of the Library of Alexandria. Historian Paulus Orosius wrote in his *The Apology of Paulus Orosius* that 'in some of the temples there remain up ta the present time book chests, which we ourselves have seen, and that, as we are told, these were *emptied by <u>our</u> own men in <u>our own day</u>* when these temples were plundered.' (The Apology of Paulus Orosius (1936) Translated by Irving Woodworth Raymond; http://penelope. uchicago.edu/~grout/encyclopedia_romana/ greece/paganism/ serapeum.html)

'In our own day,'" Macha emphasized, "that 'tis, when Hypatia received word of Antoninus' psychic vision and they secreted out the books and sent them on ta Ireland before Theophilus could destroy the Temple of Serapis. The books and scrolls of Serapis were secreted away durin' the constant religious upheaval in Alexandria between the Jews objectin' ta the new Coptic Christianity. The Coptics and the Pharisaic Jews created a bloodbath in Alexandria - the warrin' between Satan's children."

Macha began to tell of the brutality of the Black Cyril, Pope of Alexandria, the carrier of the Y-chromosome of Satan through his lineage from Ham.

"In Alexandria, A.D. 415, Orestes, the city Prefect of Alexandria, the governor, a Greek who 'twas baptized a Roman Christian by the Archbishop of Constantinople, disputed with Cyril because Orestes refused Cyril's encroachment on Orestes' civil administration. Cyril wanted control over the Christian Churches and the government of Alexandria, Egypt. Cyril brought in other 'monks' - his parabalanoi mercenaries - from outside of Alexandria ta fight with him in a violent response ta Orestes' independence. The monks attacked Orestes in the street; the monk, Hierax, hit Orestes with a rock, and 'twas arrested. The Jews of Alexandria pressured Orestes ta kill Hierax, in retaliation.

Now, there were true monks who worked with Hypatia in the Library. Hypatia was adored by the true monks and the citizenry of

Alexandria. Cyril was a monk prior ta becomin' Pope of Alexandria. "Tis known that Cyril's parabalanoi thugs, estimated ta be 500 men dressed as monks, attacked Hypatia. The Pharisaic Jews of Alexandria wanted ta do away with the Christians. But the Jews also wanted ta do away with the true monks workin' in the Library with Hypatia because they were translatin' the history of the Jewish Pharisees and their *Talmud*, exposin' their lineage of Satan. The Mishnah part of the *Talmud* was written by A.D. 220, and the Gemara part of the *Talmud* was finished by A.D. 500. Hypatia had read the Greek translation of the Torah - she knew that the *Talmud* was a different religion altogether. All these dynamics were comin' together. Cyril wanted power over Alexandria. Cyril wanted the Jews out. The Jews wanted the Christians out. Both the Jews and Cyril knew that Hypatia's knowledge could expose their connections to Satan. Both wanted her dead. 'Twas good for the Jews ta blame 'monks' and 'Christians' for cuttin' up Hypatia's body with shells - ta prove the new Christianity was evil. 'Twas good for Cyril ta say 'twas the Christians, too - but his reason 'twas ta prove that he had a loyal, violent followin' - the message in that 'twas: don't mess with Cyril! Cyril, as a child of Satan, wanted ta give the Church of Jesus an evil image. And Cyril didn't want anyone ta know he paid parabalanoi mercenary thugs ta murder Hypatia. And then Cyril used these mercenaries ta oust the Jews - and plunder the gold from their synagogues and homes - but that 'twas seen as Christians fightin' Jews - not mercenaries fightin' Jews. So, for everyone's convenience, the blame goes on ta the Christians and the true monks of Alexandria who murdered Hypatia - the very people who adored her.

The Eastern Churches and later the Roman Church saw Hypatia's murder as reason to anoint Cyril as a saint - for he got rid of paganism, killin' Hypatia. But you don't get rid of paganism by the death of one person - you burn up their pagan Greek works - collected in the Library of Alexandria. But that 'tis too big an atrocity for the Roman Church ta openly applaud or ta be put on SAINT Cyril, even though all the evidence points ta his burnin' the Library. Instead, they pointed ta everyone in multiple directions - ta Julius Caesar, the Caliph Umar, and to the numerous Christian-Jewish riots. That way, the truth will never be known. And Cyril can have his sainthood."

Stonewall walked around the control room, summarizing Macha's words. "So, Orestes succumbed to the demands of the Jews and ordered the public torture and killing of Hierax the alleged Coptic monk. Then the Jews lured more Coptics into the street at night by yelling that the Coptic Church was on fire. Coptics rushed out and the mob of waiting Jews killed many of them. Then Cyril led his parabalanoi in retaliation against the Jews and Pagans. The Coptics blamed the Greek Pagan Hypatia for influencing Orestes to stand fast against Cyril's encroachment of power in to civil matters, since she influenced people from all around the empire who came to listen to her, and she taught many who later held positions in government and Church hierarchy. So, the parabalanoi, dressed as monks, murdered her. Those parabalanoi were of Egyptian blood, and carried the Y-chromosome of Satan."

Macha walked toward Stonewall, adding, "'Twas known of Hypatia ta be a Greek beauty, virtuous, and a brilliant woman by even her adversaries. She 'twas a wise, noble philosopher, lovin' things of the mind. She would explain the difficult points of Plato and Aristotle ta any who stopped her in the street. Not so of Cyril, the Coptic Patriarchate of Alexandria. No one asked Cyril about his writin's. His writin's were not in the Library of Alexandria!

The 4th century historian, Socrates, wrote that no other people in the world other than the Egyptians brought about chaos and violence as quickly for any reason whatsoever, leavin' a trail of bloodshed in their wake. Socrates also wrote that Cyril wanted ta politically control Orestes. As a result of the night that the Jews yelled that the Coptic Church was on fire and the Jews massacred many Coptics, Cyril led a mob of Coptics against the Jews, lootin' their synagogues. And after Cyril had the Jews expelled from Alexandria, their possessions were stolen by the parabalanoi as their added reward.

While Cyril blamed Hypatia for influencin' Orestes ta stand fast against Cyril's control, this 'twas no reason to murder her, especially as savagely as they did. Especially, since there was no proof of her influence. But the historians write of the parabalanoi, attacking Hypatia, that they: 'dragged her from her carriage inta a Coptic Church, stripped her naked, and battered her ta death with roofin' titles, and while she 'twas still twitchin' they beat her eyes out,' so wrote Deakin, 'orgastically tore her body limb from limb, took her mangled remains out from the church and burned them.' (*Hypatia of Alexandria*, Michael A.B. Deakin)

This is the satanic titillation received in destroyin' life.

Mangasarian wrote that 'a few historians even inferred that the monks had asked her ta kiss the cross, ta become Coptic and join the nunnery, or they'd kill her.'" (*The Death of the Classical World*, Mangasar Mugurditch Mangasarian)

Macha felt disgust for the children of Satan.

"Be that, as it may," Macha quieted herself for a moment, "Mangasarian wrote that these Coptic monks, 'under the leadership of Cyril's right-hand man, Peter the Reader, shamefully stripped her naked, and there, close ta the altar and the cross, scraped her quiverin' flesh from her bones with oyster shells.'

Thereafter, Orestes succumbed and became a *Coptic* Christian, which ended the religious riots in the streets of Alexandria, as Satan's henchman took control. Cyril was sainted for destroyin' idolatry and destroyin' Hypatia, and 'tis viewed today as the Father of the Coptic Church of Egypt. It should read: The Antichrist of the Satanic Church of Egypt. As a result of one of Satan's Antichrist's murder of Hypatia, all the philosophers fled from Alexandria. The satanic mystics shut down philosophy, science, mathematics, and invention. And the world fell inta the Dark Ages.

The Egyptian Coptics were descendants from Cain through Ham and his second son, Mesram, which name in Hebrew means 'land of Egypt,' where Mesram went and populated. The very name Coptic means from Egypt and the word Egypt 'tis derived from 'ta cover, ta veil.' Ta veil the offsprin' of Satan!"

Macha walked toward MacArthur, "Remember, general, Hypatia was a mathematician and astronomer. And I told ye about how Hypatia would explain the difficult points of Plato and Aristotle ta any who stopped her in the street. Other than injurin' the pride of Cyril, why else 'tis that significant? Well, I'll tell ye the real reason for murderin' Hypatia and burnin' down the Library of Alexandria."

She turned to face the generals seated in front of the viewing screen on the wall of the control room under Cheyenne Mountain. "The story leads us - the world - ta what we're about ta face, today."

Macha continued, "Plato wrote *Cratylus*, in which Plato had Socrates sayin' that the 'opinion of Heraclitus, that all things flow and nothin' stands; with them the pushin' principle...'twas that cause and rulin' power of all things...' (*Cratylus* at 401, d). In *Cratylus*, Socrates states: 'Heraclitus 'tis supposed ta say that all things are in motion and nothin' at rest; he compares them ta the stream of a river, and says that ya cannot go inta the same water twice.' (*Ibid.* at 402, 6)

How 'tis Heraclitus significant ta Plato? Plato's 'family 'twas an ancient one with political connections in high places.' (*See*, *Plato*, ed. Hamilton et al., Introduction xiii, Bollingen Series LXXI, Princeton, 1987.) Plato 'twas from the elite, and he 'twas the elite of the ancient world.

Hypatia, the last Head Librarian of the Library of Alexandria, 'twas known ta be brilliant, known ta be a scholar of Plato, therefore, she read *Cratylus* and knew of Heraclitus and his notion that the first principle of life is flux. She knew the physics of the idea; she 'twas a mathematician and an astronomer.

So what? ya might ask. Well, give a look ta Heraclitus' first principle of life that everythin' 'tis in flux. And by the by, Heraclitus 'twas of the Greek city of Ephesus, 582-496 BC, on the western coast of Turkey, near the Garden of Eden, near where Noah's Ark landed after the Great Flood.

Heraclitus' philosophy 'twas picked up by the Stoics. They held that Heraclitus 'twas the inspiration of their own conception of divine fire, identifyin' this divine fire with the *Logos* that Heraclitus specifies as the world's explanation principle. (www.trincoll.edu/dept/phil/philo/phils /heraclitus.html) In other words, the Stoics believed that the major part of their philosophy was based on the ideas of Heraclitus.

Stoicism was an Athens, Greece, Hellenistic philosophy that spread as a result of the conquests of the Greek, Alexander the Great. The Library of Alexandria, in Egypt, surely held the works of the Greek Heraclitus. The world's knowledge was housed in that Library.

But only the elites of the countries that Alexander the Great had conquered knew of the Hellenistic philosophy and culture that was brought into their countries. The ordinary citizen knew nothing of Heraclitus and his theory. 'Tis significant.

Heraclitus' theory was that all things in nature are in a constant state of flux, and are connected by logical structure and pattern; this theory Heraclitus called *Logos.*

But then there was the Jewish philosopher and Pharisee, *Philo* of Alexandria, 30 BC to A.D. 40, who was a representative of the Jews in complainin' ta the Roman Emperor of the abuse Jews suffered at the hands of the Christian Coptics. *Philo* claimed Moses taught all the Greek philosophers.

Philo merged Pharisaism/Judaism with the Greek Hellenistic culture of Alexandria, and interpreted Heraclitus' *Logos* as the essence associated with divine wisdom. In Judaism 'tis interpreted as God's medium for communicatin' with the human race. 'Tis an intentional misdirection of meanin'. 'Twas a lie!

[Approximations: Heraclitus lived between 582 B.C. and 496 BC; Ezra dragged the remnant Israelites back to Jerusalem in 457 B.C.; Plato lived between 428 B.C. and 348 B.C.; Aristotle, who taught Alexander the Great, lived between 384 B.C. and 322 B.C.; *Philo* lived between 30 B.C. and A.D. 40; Jesus lived between 3 B.C. and A.D. 30; Apostle Matthew wrote his Gospel six years after Jesus' Ascension, A.D. 36, in Hebrew or Syro-Chaldaic spoken by Jews in Palestine at that time, translated into Greek in the time of the Apostles; Apostle Mark wrote his Gospel ten years after Jesus' Ascension, A.D. 40, in Greek; Apostle Luke wrote his Gospel 24 years after Jesus' Ascension, A.D. 54, in Greek; Apostle John wrote his Gospel 63 years after Jesus' Ascension, A.D. 93, in Greek.

The Romans destroyed Jerusalem and the Second Temple in A.D. 70. It was the final desolation of the last two tribes of Israelites that had been brought back from Babylonian captivity against their will by Rabbi Ezra (Esdras), who had enslaved the remnants of Israelites under Pharisaism/Judaism; the philosopher/seer Antoninus died in A.D. 390; the Temple of Serapis was destroyed in A.D. 391; Hypatia lived between A.D. 370 and A.D. 415. Cyril became Pope of Alexandria in A.D. 412.]

'Philo 'twas a Jewish aristocrat and leader of the large Jewish community of Alexandria...and spent time in Jerusalem where he had intimate connections with the royal house of Judea. *Philo's* brother, Alexander, was the chief tax collector in Jerusalem, and one of the richest men in the east...His wealth financed the silver and gold sheathin' which adorned the doors of the Second Temple (Josephus, *War* 5.205). Alexander also loaned a fortune ta Herod Agrippa I (*Antiquities* 18)...*Philo* wrote extensive defenses on the Jewish Pharisaic religion and commentaries on contemporary politics. He offers commentary on all the major characters of the Pentateuch...but...not a word about Jesus,

Christianity, nor any of the works in the New Testament...Accordin' ta *Philo*, the Greek philosophers had 'borrowed from Moses' and had received their insights from the God of the Jews...(*Philo* said:) 'all one had ta discern 'twas the hidden meanin' of words....'" (*Jesus Never Existed*, Kenneth Humphreys; www.jesusneverexisted.com/philo.html)

Whether you call it the Hebrew/Semitic-language-of-Noah's-first-son-Sem the Pentateuch or the Torah, or the Old Testament - the Hebrew Bible 'twas not translated in ta the Koine Greek language, which 'twas called the Septuagint, until sometime between 250 B.C.-100 B.C. (Matthew K. Clifton; http://the7ones.com/ 2010/02/15/origin-of-the-septuagint-what-do-we-really-know/) - almost one hundred years after the death of Plato, and more than 70 years after the death of Aristotle. And there 'tis no indication that Socrates, Plato, or Aristotle could read Hebrew. Philo's claim that the Greek philosophers borrowed from Moses 'twas an impossibility. There 'tis no proof that the Hebrew Bible was translated before 250 B.C.

'Twas Ptolemy II who sponsored the Alexandrian Jews ta translate the Torah/Pentateuch. Therefore, Hypatia had this copy of the Greek translation of the Torah, this Septuagint, available ta her in the Library of Alexandria. 'Tis known that her father taught her the religions of the world - that means that Hypatia read the Torah. 'St. Jerome translated the Septuagint in ta Latin, A.D. 387-390; the New Testament about A.D. 383 - at the request of the Pope, and therefore, this Latin Vulgate translation is the Roman Church's authoritative version of the Hebrew Bible.'" (S. Angus; www.bible-researcher.com/vulgate1.html)

"Well, why would *Philo* write about Jesus or his apostles?" Patton asked, "Jesus exposed the Pharisees - that they were descendants of Satan!" Patton looked around the control room at the other Generals and then back to Macha, "The bastard was a descendant of Satan! Do you really think that *Philo* would give publicity to the Son of God - his father's enemy! His writing of Jesus would have given historical record by the opposition - that Jesus existed and was the Son of God! In not writing anything of Jesus, you've got Humphreys today claiming that Jesus never existed. And asserting that because *Philo* never wrote of Jesus this is proof that Jesus never existed! This is what they are trying to do all over the country - take Jesus out of the American culture!"

Macha nodded at Patton, "'Tis exactly right, General. Exactly right." Macha turned and took a few steps, "Plato's account of Creation, written in *Timaeus*, 'influenced men for centuries up ta and in ta the Middles Ages, 'tis a statement of scientific truth combined with mythical truth in which great spiritual truths could be found. Plato suggests that 'tis better ta use one's mind on the questions of creation than ta pass them by indolently without tryin' ta think about them.' (*Plato, Timaeus, The Collected Dialogues*, ed. Hamilton *et al.*, Bollingen Series LXXI, Princeton, 1987.)

'Tis what Hypatia read - Plato advisin' her ta spend time thinkin' about creation. In *Timaeus*, Plato says that 'Time ever 'tis, never has been, nor will be, it can be described as past or future only figuratively. Time 'tis a movin' image of eternity.'" (*Ibid.* at p 1151)

Macha pressed buttons on the console that controlled the large viewing screen on the wall of the control room deep beneath Cheyenne Mountain, and suddenly, there was a live view of the stars, constellations, and the outer heaven. As she and the Generals looked at the heaven, Macha recited Vaughan: "'I saw Eternity the other night, Like a great Ring of pure and endless light, All calm, as it was bright: And round beneath it, Time in hours, days, years, Driven by the spheres Like a vast shadow moved.'" (*Ibid.* at p 1151)

MacArthur replied by quoting from *Timaeus*: "'Time and the heaven came into being at the same instant, having been created together, so that, if ever there was to be a dissolution of them, they might be dissolved together. It was framed after the pattern of the eternal nature...for the pattern exists from eternity, and the created heaven has been and is and will be in all time. Such was the mind and thought of God in the creation of time.'" (*Timaeus* at 38.b.5)

MacArthur continued, "Plato's notion of the eternal Form. As with the eternal Form of a chair - that which supports the bottom of the human body when the knees and hips are bent. Language and imagination construct the copy of the eternal Form of the chair - making it into a kitchen chair, an office chair on wheels, an upholstered chair - they all look differently and have different names, but they all perform the same task of supporting the bottom of the body when the knees and hips are in a bent position. In *Timaeus*, Plato must refer to the eternal universe and its copy. As the Creator, the eternal Form of the universe is in God's Intellect. The reality of the universe only exists in the mind of God. What we see are only the expressions of that reality. So, when we look out to the heaven," MacArthur sighed, "we're looking at the expression of the mind of God."

"In *Timaeus*," Macha added, "Plato wrote a dialogue among Socrates, Critias, Hermocrates, and Timaeus, in which Timaeus 'tis explainin' his notion of creation. Timaeus states: 'I am askin' a question which has ta be asked at the beginnin' of an inquiry about anythin' – *'twas the world...always in existence and without beginnin'*, *or created, and had it a beginnin'? Created, I reply*...havin' a body, and therefore sensible, and all sensible things...are in a *process of creation* and created. Now that which is created must...be created by a cause....If the world be indeed fair and the artificer good, 'tis manifest that we must have looked ta that which is eternal...then look ta the created pattern...And havin' been created in this way, the world has been framed in the likeness of that which is apprehended by reason and mind and is unchangeable, and must therefore of necessity, if 'tis admitted, be a copy of something...' (*Ibid.* at 28.b.4-29b) Plato 'tis clearly writin' that the world, the universe, 'twas created by God. The world had a beginnin' only because of the creation by God. The eternal Form argument presented by Plato in *Timaeus* is Plato's conclusion that everythin' that 'tis visible and invisible ta us humans 'twas first conceived in the mind of God - and that His ideas are primary and what He created 'tis a copy of what 'tis in His mind."

Macha continued to recite from *Timaeus*, "'Wherefore also God in the beginnin' of creation made the body of the universe ta consist of fire and earth.' (*Ibid.* at 31.b.7)

Plato wrote: 'Wherefore also findin' the *whole visible sphere not at rest...out of disorder he brought order*...the creator, reflectin'... intelligence could not be present in anythin' which 'twas devoid of soul. For which reason, *when he was framin' the universe, he put intelligence in soul*, and soul in body, that he might be the creator of a work which 'twas by nature fairest and best...*we may say that the world came inta bein' -- a livin' creature truly endowed with soul and intelligence by the providence of God*....' (*Ibid.* at 30.4. – c)

Plato 'tis not sayin' that the universe existed prior ta God! Plato 'tis sayin' that as God created one thing and then the next - He, then, put a Soul inta the universe - ta make His creation complete - and that without the Soul - there 'twas chaos of the bodies that He had created. Plato 'tis claimin' that without a Soul - there 'tis chaos. There must be the One with its parts of Intellect and Soul - for there ta be completeness of creation.

But what *Philo*, the Pharisee of Alexandria, argued 'tis that there 'twas life and God happened along and put it all inta order. That's a lie! 'Tis deceitful! 'Tis from Satan! The dictionary's definition of chaos: 'The disordered state *of unformed matter* and infinite space supposed *by some religious cosmological views to have existed prior to the ordered universe*.'

But there 'twas no disorder, no confusion! The chaos that Plato speaks of - occurred between the time that God created the physical bodies of the universe and God joinin' the universe with the Soul that He created, first!

He could not join a Soul ta the universe until after He had created the universe. Just as when God created Adam: Gen. 2:7: 'And the Lord God formed man of the slime of the Earth: and breathed inta his face the breath of life, and *man became a livin' soul*.' So, too, God created the universe and with its creation created time and inta it all He breathed a livin' soul.

Ye cannot pour milk inta a glass before you make the glass! There 'tis no suit until the tailor sews the pieces together, but before he sews the pieces together, the tailor has ta lay the pattern, cut out the individual pieces before he can sew them together.

But *Philo* the Pharisee 'tis sayin' that the universe existed before God came along and sewed the bodies of the universe together, bringin' order ta the chaos. And that creation of the universe took place outside of time. When, in fact, God created the universe and time simultaneously! Not the universe and then time."

MacArthur interrupted, "Plato is saying that God's Intellect designed the pieces so that time was part of, an element of, its being, and then He sewed the universe and time to the Soul that He had previously created. In *Timaeus*, Plato wrote: 'For there were no days and nights and months and years before the heaven was created, *but when he constructed the heaven he created them also*. They are all parts of time, and *the past* and future are created species of time, *which we unconsciously but wrongly transfer to eternal being*, for we say that it 'was,' or 'is,' or 'will be,' but the truth is that *'is' alone is properly attributed to it*, and that '*was*' and 'will be' are *only to be spoken of becoming in time, for they are motions*, but *that which is immovably the same forever cannot become older or younger by time, nor can it (the universe) be said that it came into being in the past*, or has come into being now, or will come into being in the future, nor is it subject at all to any of those states which affect moving and sensible things and of which generation is the cause. These are the forms of time, which imitates eternity and revolves according to a law of number.' (*Supra* at 37.e - 38.9)

And Hypatia understood this! Hypatia understood that *Philo's* butchering of Plato was self-serving - the first attempt to lead civilians to think that God did not create matter, the universe - the first attempt at the Big Bang theory!"

"Indeed, General!" Macha replied, "*Philo* can argue that the Greek philosophers got their ideas from the God of Moses, but Philo did NOT get his own idea of creation from the God of Moses, but from Satan! And Hypatia knew this, also!"

Macha took a few steps in pensive thoughtfulness, "In *Philo's* exposition of the world - it has no beginnin' and no end, *'Philo* places the creative activity and the act of Creation outside time. *Philo* rejected Greek philosophy that did not harmonize with Jewish Talmudic tradition, but used parts of Greek philosophy for defendin' and justifyin' the Jewish *Pharisaic religious truths*.' *Philo* interpreted the Old Testament allegorically, claimin' that the allegorical interpretation 'tis the real one and only the initiated could comprehend.' (www.jewishencyclopedia.com /view.jsp?artid=281&letter=P.)

'Philo appropriated Platonic philosophy,' (Harold W. Attridue, Professor, Yale Divinity School; www.pbs.org/wgbh/pages/frontline/ shows/religion/portrait/hellenisticculture.html.) - and then he manipulated Plato's philosophy, as well as manipulated the Law of Moses - ta fit the religion of the Pharisees' *Talmud* - Judaism.

'Runia concludes, the importance of *Philo's* contribution ta Patristic (fathers of the early Christian Church and their writin's) thought lies above all in his (*Philo's*) role as a mediator between the biblical and the philosophical tradition.' (Allen Kerkeslager, U. of Penn., reviewing David T. Runia, *Philo in Early Christian Literature: A Survey*, Fortress Press, Minn., 1993; Bryn Mawr Classical Review 95.03.16; http:// bmcr.brynmawr.edu/1995/95.03.16.html)

Philo tried ta give credibility ta the relatively new Pharisaic religion of the *Talmud*, by usin' part of the honored Greek philosophers' ideas ta justify Pharisaism. But, if *Philo* 'tis correct in sayin' that the Greek philosophers got their ideas from the God of Moses - why did he reject parts of those ideas? And if the Greek philosophers got their ideas from the God of Moses - why were most of those Greek ideas outside of *Pharisaic truths*? If the Greek philosophers got their ideas from the God of Moses; and *Philo* rejected most and used only parts of Greek philosophy; *Philo* rejected most of the God of Moses! Pharisaism rejected the God of Moses! And Hypatia knew this!

Plato writes Timaeus' statement: 'Wherefore also *God in the beginnin' of creation made the body of the universe ta consist of fire and Earth. But two things cannot be rightly put together without a third*; there must be some *bond of union* between them. And the fairest bond 'tis that which makes the most complete fusion of itself and the things which it combines, and proportion 'tis best adapted ta effect such a union....God placed water and air in the mean between fire and Earth, and made them ta have the same proportion so far as 'twas possible...*thus he bound and put together a visible and tangible heaven*. And for these reasons...the *body of the world was created...havin' been reconciled ta itself, 'twas indissoluble by the hand of any other than the framer....* (*Ibid.* at 31.b.7 - 32.c.5)

Philo rejects this part of Greek philosophy. *Philo* rejects: that God 'in the beginnin' of creation created the body of the universe, and therewith created time. *Philo* rejects: time 'twas created contemporaneously with the universe. *Philo* rejects: that the creation of the Sun, Earth, Moon, and their rotatin' motions - their movements, created time. *Philo* places the creative activity and the act of Creation outside time - *Philo* the Pharisee said: 'it has no beginnin' and no end.' This is the Big Bang theory that they are pushin' today - *ta eliminate God havin' a hand in creation.* But creation and time did, in fact, accordin' ta Plato, have a beginnin', and 'tis end comes when God ends it: 'twas 'indissoluble by the hand of any other than the framer.' Plato is sayin' that God can end the planets, and thus, time. *Philo* rejects this idea of Plato: 'it has no ...end.' *Philo*, the Pharisee, is rejectin' the supremacy of God! Just as the Big Bang theory today rejects the supremacy of God!

Indeed, *Philo* 'twas the first ta assert the Big Bang theory that the universe created itself and then God came along and ordered it, since 'Before *Philo*, the Pharisee, there 'twas no explicit theory of creation ex nihilo (creation out of nothin') ever postulated in Jewish or Greek tradition.' [http://www.iep.utm.edu/ philo; by Marian Hillar] *Philo* was the first ta present the Big Bang theory - which is: Nothin' at all existed - and like magic - the universe appeared - Bang! Without stimulus. 'Tis the deceit of evil!

The model of creation asserted by *Philo*, the Pharisee, 'tis: '*the direct agent of creation 'tis not God himself, but Logos.'* *Philo* believes that the Logos 'tis 'the man of God.' (Conf. 41) or the shadow of God that was used as an instrument and a pattern of all creation (LA 3-96). *The Logos converted unqualified, unshaped pre-existent matter, which Philo describes as 'destitute of arrangement, of quality, of animation, of distinctive character and full of disorder and confusion,'* (Op. 22) into four primordial elements: (Philo states in LA 1.329): For 'tis out of that essence that God created everythin', without indeed touchin' it himself, *for it 'twas not lawful (according ta Pharisaic law) for the all-wise and all-blessed God ta touch materials which were all misshapen and confused,* but he created by the agency of his incorporeal powers, of which the proper name is Ideas, which he so exerted that every genus received its proper form.'" (http://www.iep.utm.edu/philo; by Marian Hillar)

Macha smiled, "I think that the slime of the earth can be considered misshapen and confused material, but yet, Genesis 4:7, which in the Torah, says: 'And the Lord God *formed* man of the slime of the earth: and breathed into his face the breath of life, and man became a living soul.' To form 'tis ta handle the slime and ta shape it inta the man, Adam. The act shows God's love of man. But *Philo* takes that away from mankind. He takes it away from God!"

Macha cleared her throat, "Philo does not say whose law he 'tis referrin' ta that does not allow God ta touch pre-existent and disordered matter. 'Twould seem that 'tis a 'Pharisaic interpretation' that only the 'initiated' Pharisees would know of and chose ta teach the captivated Israelites. And *Philo* referrin' ta Logos - as 'the man of God' or 'the shadow of God' used as an 'instrument and a pattern of all creation' - 'tis deceivin' - for it minimizes God while it also makes everythin' god-like; it sets up the argument that there 'tis no evil. Therefore, evil 'tis disguised as god-like, and man 'tis uninformed until evil has captured his soul.

Philo the Pharisee rejected: Torah, Genesis 1:1: 'In the beginnin' God created heaven, and earth (3) And God said: Be light made. And light was made. (5) And he (God) called the light Day, and the darkness Night; and there was evenin' and mornin' one day.' 'Tis the Law of Moses that Philo rejected! Yet, from 6PM of one day to 6PM of the next day is one Hebrew day.

Why 'tis this important ta us today? It has to do with the discovery of subquantum kinetics, the true physics.

In the Greek language, logos means: reason. Heraclitus used the word logos ta name his theory of the first principle - the basis of life: everythin' 'tis in flux. Ta have life, there must be movement, fluidity of matter. In that theory of movement of matter, comes the realization that life 'tis being continually created and continually dying. God set this fluidity of matter inta motion when He created the universe. But *Philo* rejects this and misdirects civilians by usin' the word logos ta name the shadow of God who ordered the pre-existent universe - that has no beginnin' and no end, and therefore 'tis static. And *Philo's* assertion 'twas picked up by both Christianity and Islam. But when LaViolette 'twas telepathically givin' this principle that everythin' 'tis in flux, LaViolette used this message ta develop subquantum kinetics - the true physics.

Plato states, 'I will not now speak of the first principle or principles of all things...*because 'tis difficult ta set forth my opinion accordin' ta the method of discussion* which we are at present employin' (*Timaeus*, 48.c.2). Plato also writes Timaeus' statement: 'And now I will endeavor ta show you the disposition and generation of them by an unaccustomed argument *which I am compelled ta use. But I believe that you will be able ta follow me, for your education has made you familiar with the methods of science*.' (*Ibid.* at 53.b.8-11)

Timaeus 'twas talkin' ta Socrates - who demoted the importance of institutional knowledge, ie., math or science. Socrates thought knowledge was a matter of recollection - questionin' brought about the recollection already in-born. Timaeus 'twas also talkin' ta Critias, who was an associate of Socrates and Plato's great uncle - and a leadin' member of the Thirty Tyrants, a pro-Spartan oligarchy installed in Athens that reduced the rights of Athenians, limitin' the number of citizens who could vote or carry a weapon, or receive a jury trial. Critias was a traitor ta Greece. He 'twas not a man of science.

The other person Timaeus was talkin' ta in this book by Plato - was Hermocrates - an advisor ta a Spartan general; he was a general of Syracuse, Sicily - but so bad as a general that he was dismissed; became an admiral and so bad at that that he 'twas banned from Sicily. 'Tis safe ta say that Hermocrates 'twas not a man of math or science.

Timaeus, himself, 'twas a Greek Pythagorean philosopher. So, when Plato wrote that 'I believe that you will be able ta follow me, for your education has made you familiar with the methods of science' - he 'twas not referrin' ta the characters in the book - but ta those who would come later ta read this work, who were educated. Plato writes Timaeus as sayin' that he 'tis 'compelled to use' an unaccustomed argument - did he mean, use a code! 'Twas Plato tellin' future readers ta use their education ta figure out that code?

This language followed Timaeus talkin' about the 'winnowin' machine - the receptacle - that 'presented a strange variety of appearances, and bein' full of powers which were neither similar nor equally balanced, 'twas never in any part in a state of equipoise, but swayin' unevenly hither and thither, was shaken by them, and by its motion again shook them, and the elements when moved were separated and carried continually, some one way, some another. As, when grain 'tis shaken and winnowed by fans and other instruments used in the threshin' of corn...In this manner, the four kinds or elements were then shaken by the receivin' vessel (receptacle), which, movin' like a winnowin' machine, scattered far away from one another the elements most unlike, and forces the most similar elements inta close contact. Wherefore the various elements had distinct places also before they were arranged so as ta form the universe.'" (*Ibid.* at 52.d.6-53.7)

Macha looked at the generals, "'Tis talkin' about the formation of a wormhole - never in a state of equipose, but swayin' unevenly, and full of powers. Plato 'tis callin' upon the educated ta figure out his coded language.

Plato wrote: 'What nature are we ta attribute ta this *new kind of being*? We reply that 'tis the receptacle, and in a manner the nurse, of all generation. I have spoken the truth, but I must express myself in clearer language, and this will be an arduous task for many reasons...*But the forms which enter inta and go out of her are the likenesses of eternal realities modeled after their patterns in a wonderful and mysterious manner*...(*Ibid.* at 49.4; 50.c.3) 'Wherefore the mother and receptacle of all created and visible and in any way sensible things *'tis not ta be termed Earth or air or fire or water, or any of their compounds*, or any of the elements from which these are derived, but *'tis an invisible and formless being which receives all things and in some mysterious way partakes of the intelligible, and is most incomprehensible*.' (*Ibid.* at 51.4-b.2) Does a nurse not help us pass through our illnesses? Is the nurse the wormhole, passin' a body through ta another place in the universe? Why else does Plato call it a nurse?

'Every man may be said ta share in true opinion, but mind is the attribute of the gods and of very few men. Wherefore also we must acknowledge that *one kind of being (the receptacle)* is the form which 'tis always the same, uncreated and indestructible, never receivin' anythin' inta itself from without, nor itself goin' out ta any other, but *invisible and imperceptible by any sense*, and of which the contemplation 'tis granted ta intelligence only. Any there 'tis another nature of the same name with it, and like ta it, perceived by sense, created, *always in motion, becomin' in place and again vanishin' out of place*, which is apprehended by opinion jointly with sense. And there is *a third nature (of the receptacle),* which *'tis space and is eternal*, and admits not of destruction and provides a home for all created things and is apprehended, when all sense 'tis absent, by a kind of spurious reason, and 'tis hardly real -- which we, beholdin' as in a dream, say of all existence that it must of necessity be in some place and occupy a space, but that what 'tis neither in heaven nor in Earth has no existence...we have only this dreamlike sense, and we are unable ta cast off sleep and determine the truth about them...*it exists ever as the fleetin' shadow of some other, must be inferred ta be in another (that is, in space), graspin' existence in some way or other, or it could not be at all*. But true and exact reason, vindicatin' the nature of true bein', maintains that while two things (that is, the image and space) are different they cannot exist one of them in the other and so be one and also two at the same time.'" (*Ibid.* at 51.e.6-52.c.9)

Macha declared, "Plato 'tis describin' the wormhole! And Hypatia knew this! She was an astronomer and mathematician, an expert of Plato's writin's, and educated in all the religions of the world. And as Head Librarian of the Library of Alexandria, she had unlimited access ta all the great writings of the world. Access ta Aristotle's claim that somethin' cannot be created from nothin' - antithetical ta *Philo's* later Big Bang theory. Hypatia had access ta Aristotle's claim that the heavenly bodies were made of a fifth element, aether; access to Aristarchus (310-230 B.C.) who 'twas the first ta mathematically prove that the Earth revolved around the Sun."

(Snow, T.P., *The Dynamic Universe*, West, St. Paul, 1991, p. 46, 56)

Plato writes in *Timaeus*, '*Whereas he (God) made the soul in origin and excellence prior to and older than the body, to be the ruler and mistress, of whom the body was to be the subject.*' (*Timaeus* at 34.b.9) Here, Plato 'tis statin' that God created the soul, first, before there were the elements ta form in ta a universe. And then, God created the elements that make up the body of the universe, so He could bring them together as the body of the universe.

By assertin' the Big Bang theory, *Philo* also eliminates Plato's claim that the universe has a soul. 'Tis Plato's notion that the Soul permeates the universe - he says that the Soul 'tis older than the universe. *Philo* implies with this Big Bang theory that the universe has no soul or that, if the universe does have a soul, that it created its own soul when in burst inta existence.

Plato wrote in *Timaeus*, *'Now when the creator had framed the soul accordin' ta his will, he formed within her the corporeal universe, and brought the two together and united them center to center. The soul, interfused everywhere from the center ta the circumference of heaven,* of which also she is the external envelopment, *herself turnin' in herself, began a divin' beginnin' of never-ceasin' and rational life endurin' throughout all time.*' (*Ibid.* at 36.d.8 – 37) Plato 'tis sayin' that the Soul of the universe 'tis female, which would indicate that the universe's Soul is separate from God's - for Plato refers ta God as 'he.' And Plato 'tis sayin' that the universe's life began with God and that God set inta motion a universe that perpetuates itself.

Plato writes: 'And the contraction caused by the compression thrusts the small particles inta the interstices of the larger [*Ibid.* at 58.b.7]...the elements are borne up and down and hither and thither toward their own places, for the change in the size of each changes its position in space. And these causes generate an inequality which 'tis always maintained, and *'tis continually creatin'* a perpetual motion of the elements in all time.'" (*Ibid.* at 58c-5)

MacArthur lit up his pipe, took a drag, as he listened pensively to Macha. Finally, asking, "Are you attributing Plato's description to LaViolette's Mother Star in the center of the Galaxy that continually creates other stars and galaxies, or to what the New World Order people claim is a Black Hole?"

"Well," Macha smiled, "Let's continue ta look at Plato's clues. And one 'tis a brainteaser. If nothin' else speaks of a code in Plato's *Timaeus,* this verse might convince you:

> 'First then, in my judgment, we must make a distinction and ask, What 'tis that which always 'tis and has no

becomin', and what 'tis that which 'tis always becomin' and never 'tis? That which 'tis apprehended by intelligence and reason 'tis always in the same state, but that which 'tis conceived by opinion with the help of sensation and without reason 'tis always in a process of becomin' and perishin' and never really 'tis.' (*Ibid* at 27.d.4)

'Tis Plato talkin' about a wormhole? Wormholes that form and then disappear? They cannot be apprehended through intelligence - measureable, visible, are never in the same state - 'tis only our opinion that we know of them.

Sherman turned to Macha, "If I understand you correctly, you are saying that Hypatia, being an astronomer and mathematician - knowing the works of Plato, *Timaeus* specifically, and knowing of Heraclitus' idea that everything is in flux - that she put all the pieces of the puzzle together - Sagittarius' arrow and Scorpio's tail both pointing to the center of the universe - our Milky Way Galaxy - that she was able to deduce that the Mother Star, as LaViolette calls it, located in the center of the Galaxy is the soul of the universe - where God created the universe - and that everything being in flux - the universe was created in the beginning by God, and then the universe has from there, the Mother Star, has continually created itself ever larger. As it converses with itself, self-sufficient and needing no additional hand of God. Is that correct?"

"Yes, General. That's what I'm proposin' - and that Cyril of Alexandria had Hypatia murdered because of this knowledge. It wasn't her popularity that he was jealous of, but her popularity 'tis what he feared - she had contact with so many people that listened ta her every word - that she could teach this proof of God's existence. Teach that evil existed! Cyril came ta power in A.D. 412, and by A.D. 415, the year he saw for himself her popularity - learned that she wasn't cooped up in the Great Library doin' research and teachin' a few scholars - he then had her murdered.

For you see, Generals," Macha continued, "'the Great Library of Alexandria, next ta the Mouseion or Museum, 'twas only open ta the royal family, scientists, and researchers. The 'daughter library' at the Serapeum/Serapis Pagan Temple, 'twas the one opened ta the public - and it carried only the copies of *some* of the works housed in the Great Library." (The Great Library of Alexandria, by Heather Phillips, Assistant Branch Librarian, U.S. Courts Library; http://unllib.unl.edu//LPP/ phillips.htm)

Some of the works of the Great Library were never seen by the public - such as the proof of God's existence. The only portion of Heraclitus' work that survived were 100 sentences; mostly repeated in other philosophers' work, includin' Plato. Obviously, Heraclitus' work burned in the Great Library. The next time we see Heraclitus' theory that - the first principle of life that everythin' 'tis in flux - 'twas after the telepathic message given ta Dr. Paul LaViolette, who from that message developed the subquantum kinetics - a whole new physics. 'Twas truly a telepathic message from an angel of God - for LaViolette had not heard of Heraclitus until years after he developed subquantum kinetics. This new physics supports the theory that God exists. No one else knew of this physics until LaViolette published his research, which 'tis used by the United States Government in Black Projects, *after* they read LaViolette's 1985 paper and subsequent books. With it the government has been able ta develop vehicles that travel faster than the speed of light - superluminal flight - 1570 years after the murder of Hypatia! Cyril of Alexandria destroyed that knowledge when he burned down the Library of Alexandria."

Macha casually walked around the room, passing Sherman, passing MacArthur, stopping next to the chair of Patton. She rested her hand on Patton's shoulder, "Hypatia was educated by her father, Theon, but also at the school of Neoplatonism, founded by Plotinus, who lived A.D. 204/5 to 270. Plotinus 'twas the most influential philosopher of antiquity after Plato and Aristotle. Plotinus held that Plato needed ta be *interpreted*, and as a result, Plotinus became the principle source for understandin' Plato by Christianity, Islam and Judaism in their formative periods. Their theological traditions looked ta ancient Greek philosophies for the language and arguments with which ta articulate their religious visions. Platonism expressed the philosophy that seemed closest ta their own theologies. (Gerson, Lloyd, "Plotinus," The Stanford Encyclopedia of Philosophy (Fall 2008 Edition), Edward N. Zalta (ed.), URL=http://plato.stanford.edu/archives/fall2008/entries/plotinus)

MacArthur interrupted, "Plotinus said that metaphysics consisted of three principles: 'The One (Good), Intellect, and Soul. The One is the first principle of all things; it is self-caused and cause of being for everything else in the universe. The first derivation from the One is Intellect - whatever properties things have, they have owing to there being Forms, the eternal and immutable; unchanging entities that account for or explain the possibility of intelligible prediction. Plato wrote in *Timaeus* that the Form of Intelligible Animal was eternally contemplated by an Intellect called 'the Demiurge.' Or the Creator. This contemplation Plotinus interpreted as cognitive identity, since if the Demiurge was contemplating something outside of itself, what would be inside of itself would be only an image or representation of eternal reality - and so, it would not actually know what it contemplates, as that is in itself. 'Cognitive identity' then means that when Intellect is thinking, it is thinking itself. The role of Intellect is to account for the real distinctness of the numerous kinds of Forms, virtually united in the One.'" (*Ibid,* Gerson)

Basically," MacArthur offered, "Plotinus is saying that God is made up of Himself, His Intelligence, and His Soul. And that all that exists are first in the mind of God, the Creator - the One - and His intellectual contemplation is of existence and is expressed by way of the

Eternal Form - eternal because the Forms are always held in the mind of God. But also because they have properties that are unchangeable, because once changed they become something other than the eternal Form of something. One property of the eternal Form of the human is that it bends at its joints. And the human's use of the eternal Form of a table - is that the table accommodates the human's bent joints - upon which he can rest his elbows, to eat from, bend his head over to read a book that is sitting on the table, or write a letter on the table, or build something on the table. Regardless of how the table may be otherwise designed, painted with flowers or made of plastic, wood, or steel - to be a copy of the eternal Form of a table, it must first accommodate the human's bent joints as the human sits at the table. And this is separate from a bench, at which the human body stands next to when working. A second property of a table is that it must have a flat surface upon which an object may rest, above the ground. To be a copy of the eternal Form of a table, this accommodation of the human body or object can never change."

Patton stood, "I'd like to get in on this argument; Doug, you're not the only one who studied Plotinus."

"The floor is yours, George," MacArthur responded, as he waved his pipe-clenched hand in broad gesture.

Patton took a few steps toward MacArthur and began, "The third principle is the Soul. Plotinus stated that 'the Soul is NOT the first activity of life, for the activity of Intellect is the highest activity of life. Plotinus associates life with desire. But in the highest life, the life of Intellect, where we find the highest form of desire, that desire is eternally satisfied by contemplation of the One through the entire array of Forms that are internal to it. Soul is the principle of desire for objects that are external to the agent of desire. Everything with a Soul...acts to satisfy its desire. This desire requires it to seek things that are external to it - such as food.'" [*Ibid,* Gerson]

Patton looked around at the Generals and Macha, "In *Timaeus,* Plato is implying that everything in nature is parallel - the shadow form of the human is parallel to God, both have the One, the Intellect, and the Soul. In *Timaeus,* the Soul of God - is controlled by his Intellect. While God is living, and life is associated with desire - God's desire is satisfied by thinking of all the eternal, unchanging Forms that He holds inside his mind. The claim is that God is in continual contemplation of Himself. It can be argued that Plotinus is saying that God is completely tied up in thinking of Himself, his creation, and thinking of all the multitude of different eternal Forms only He holds in his mind - which also include the Forms of emotion, joy, laughter, anger, guilt – they each have an eternal Form held in God's mind." Patton chuckled, "That's how I know when you're ticked off, Doug, because every human has in him, a copy of that eternal Form of anger. Therefore, I see in you what I feel in me."

MacArthur smiled, took a drag from his pipe, then motioned, "Continue on, George."

"For us individual humans, we shadows of the eternal Form of human, desire is: I'm hungry, I desire food, or I want a woman. But the Intellect asks - is the food safe to eat or has it gone bad; has it been poisoned? Is the woman willing or must I charm her; if not, do I rape her? Desire for objects that are external to the human involves the Soul, the principle of desire. A Soul acts to satisfy its desire. And in that drive to satisfy, our Soul sometimes sins, depending on what our Intellect reasons and allows. The Intellect asks, are there others more in need of the food? And raping the woman is in the realm of the lowest level of sin - when her desire is to be left alone, unharmed, my desire crushes her desire by physical violence.

Hypatia's desire was to ride in her carriage to the Library; Cyril's desire was to cut the skin off her bones. If Cyril's Intellect told his Soul that cutting the skin off Hypatia was permissible and a reasonable thing to do, then two of his principles, Intellect and Soul, approved of such an act and because his Intellect and his Soul are off shoots to his One and joined to his One - it makes him, metaphysically, entirely evil. The three principles make him Cyril of Alexandria, the man. These three principles working internally in him are given expression by his external activity - his murder of Hypatia and his burning down of the Library of Alexandria. All to keep the proof of God's existence from the people of the world. To submerge the world into the Dark Ages."

Macha added, "As LaViolette said in his book, *Earth Under Fire*, at p 3, "In the course of even one...(dark age), much of the technical advancement of the previous cycle of civilization could be lost...a technically advanced body of knowledge probably would not survive for very many generations."

"May I just inject a note here," General Washington asked, "This is why President Timmy Tercart, a member of the Foreign Affairs Private Council, instituted the cabinet position of Secretary of Education - and why there are teachers' unions - it is all to dumb down the education of teachers and American children - so they will never be able to understand LaViolette's new physics - will never understand the fight that continues between God and Satan for the soul of humankind. The purpose of the United Nations-Agenda 21-controlled U.S. Dept. of Education is to put America into a long-sustained Dark Age - and teaching that there is only one adjective in the English language, and that word is: 'amazing.' But more than that, everyone using the same adjective denotes a oneness of mind - the oneness of a controlled mind."

Washington paused. He moved about stiffly, straightening his waistcoat as he stood; then said, "Once in history, came a man - Alexander the Great - with the dream of preserving the world's knowledge in one place, where the world, its scholars, researchers, and teachers could access the works of the great minds of the world that came before - this one man had a dream of enlightenment, and it was ended by one man - of darkness - the descendant of Ham, a carrier of the Y-chromosome of Satan - Pope

Cyril of Alexandria. Ham's other descendant today occupies the Office of the Presidency of the United States, Tsaeb. And by one act after another, Ham's descendant is destroying the largest Christian nation of the world - the United States of America."

Patton responded, "I think all of us here, General Washington, agree with your words." Patton looked at the floor as he began to pace, then added, "There is another element in all this discussion - the Soul. Yes, there can be sin pursuant to the Soul's drive to satisfy its desire. But there is another aspect controlled by the Soul. Lloyd Gerson writes of Plotinus' interpretation of Plato, noting that the 'the internal activity of the Soul includes a plethora of psychical activities of all...living things.'" [*Ibid,* Gerson]

Patton thought for a moment, "Psychical pertaining to the mind, as in extrasensory perception or mental telepathy - the ability abides in the Soul. A Soul that is good will receive telepathic messages from God, His Soul - the Holy Ghost - to help mankind - as the message LaViolette received that led him to develop the physics of subquantum kinetics that supports the existence of God. And that telepathic ability of the Soul - is working among and between Americans. Telepathically, Americans are exchanging the message that the only way to release America from being destroyed by traitorous government leaders and foreign entities - is armed revolution. *Covert* armed revolution!"

Stonewall interjected, "There is the eternal Form of Evil. And evil has taken control of America. And the Soul of humans can discern evil, hence Satan's need to deceive at all times; always just one step ahead of being seen. We need to look at Plotinus and his interpretation of Plato's words, that: 'matter is to be identified with evil and privation of all Form or intelligibility.'" (*Ibid.* Gerson) "If matter, without intelligence or order - is, therefore, without an eternal Form - it is not of God, and thus, it is evil. 'The fact that matter is in principle deprived of all intelligibility and is still ultimately dependent on the One is an important clue as to how the causality of the latter operates.'" (*Ibid.* Gerson) What is being said by this language," Stonewall offered, "'is an important clue' as to how God operates. Is Plotinus trying to tell us something - about a clue?

Plotinus asks and answers: 'If matter or evil is ultimately caused by the One (God), then is not the One, as the Good, the cause of evil? Yes! He is (Plotinus answers). If anything besides the One is going to exist, then there must be a conclusion of the process of production from the One.' (*Ibid.* Gerson) If evil exists, then God ends the creation process. God created the shadow heavens, the universe, man, and woman. Then God created evil to be triggered within the previously-created angel named, Satan - and that evil was triggered by God giving Adam power over the Earth, and Satan uses woman, Eve, to steal that power from Adam. Mankind recreates itself through the Soul satisfying its desire. The universe recreates itself through its Soul's desire. Plato, Heraclitus, are not just proving that God exists, but that evil in the form of Satan exists!

'The beginning of evil is the act of separation from the One by Intellect, an act which the One itself ultimately causes.' (*Ibid.* Gerson) This is Plotinus telling us that Plato knew that only God could create evil and cause the evil to separate from Him. That Plato is saying that God created Satan and caused Satan to separate from God. As a student of Plotinus' school, Hypatia knew that Satan exists. It means that Satan caused Cyril to murder Hypatia and burn the Library! It means that God wants us to struggle against Satan and the cycles of dark ages that humankind has endured. The End of Days - brought on by the coming Superwave will knock humankind back to the Stone Age - except for the elite, who have prepared for only themselves underground bunkers."

Patton continued, "'The end of the process of production from the One defines a limit, like the end of a river going out from its sources. Beyond the limit is matter, or evil. According to Plotinus, matter is the condition for the possibility of there being images of Forms in the sensible world. From this perspective, matter is identified with receptacle or space in Plato's *Timaeus* and the phenomenal properties in the receptacle prior to the imposition of order by the Demiurge.' (*Ibid.* Gerson) Going out from the river - was referring to the evil Cain going down the river from the Garden of Eden!

If Plato is saying that matter is outside of God, that matter is evil - Plato is encoding *Timaeus* with a warning that there exists evil outside of God. Cain was procreated by Satan and Eve, not as Adam and Eve were created by God."

"Excuse me," General Sherman intruded. "There is one thing in all of this that I would like to make clear. Stonewall, you quoted Plotinus, Plato, as saying that - 'prior to the imposition of order by the Demiurge', the Craftsman, God. If there are eternal Forms - held only in the mind of God, the Creator, before He created the shadows of those Forms, we humans, for instance, how could chaos exist prior to God bringing order to that chaos? If anger, laughter, matter, all have eternal Forms - that is to say, all of these things were in the mind of God - then chaos also has an eternal Form - and thus chaos existed first in the mind of God - prior to God creating the shadow of chaos. In other words, there was no prior chaos to be ordered - *after* God came along! I disagree with Plato, and as a Neoplatonist - defined as one whose philosophy is based on Plato, but *different* enough to be called a Neo-Platonist - which Hypatia was, I think she also disagreed with that point of Plato. For Plato to say that chaos existed prior to God is to throw out, is to destroy, his own argument of the eternal Forms. And as brilliant as she was, I think Hypatia realized that the chaos that Plato refers to - did not exist prior to God. Yet, this is exactly what Philo the Pharisaic Jew was teaching - that chaos existed prior to God's existence.

And this business of the end of the process of production from the One, that is to say, the end of God creating everything - the end of that process defines a limit. And that beyond the limit is matter, or evil. And

Plato presenting - that matter is the condition for the possibility of there being images of Forms. It would seem to me that Hypatia, being educated in Plotinus' school, using this reasoning, that she deduced - that beyond Plato's Earth, Sun, and our solar system's planets, that matter did extend beyond these planets. On a clear night, the heavens are filled with stars - she was an astronomer - she looked up and saw these stars - she at least questioned that the limit is unseeable - and I suggest that she applied that theory - that matter is a condition of the possibility of images of Forms - to the fact that God created the eternal Form of matter beyond what she saw. And possibly she thought that matter created itself, after God began the process of creating everything else.

The difference between Plato and Hypatia - Plato was an armchair philosopher who did no experiments, while Hypatia was both an astronomer and an mathematician who went outside, who did empirical research. Plato 'had no notion of trying an experiment and is hardly capable of observing the curiosities of nature which are 'tumbling out at his feet.' (*Supra* at Benjamin Jowett) Plato wrote down the dialogues Socrates had with his students; scholars conflate Plato and Socrates, assigning Plato's written words as to be from either Socrates or Plato. So was it Socrates or Plato who is often found arguing that knowledge is NOT empirical? That knowledge comes from divine insight and recollection of that insight.

Plato is talking of two different things, or he is confused himself - either everything has an eternal Form - and everything was created by God - or this thing about matter, non-intelligible, therefore not created by God. Plato is confused - or he is indicating a conflict in his reasoning - and that by doing so, Plato is telling us to look further in to this issue about matter.

Beyond that, Plato is saying that 'if one should separate himself from God, the Good, he does become evil - as with Cyril of Alexandria. But Plato says that matter is deprived of all intelligibility - that it is non-intelligible because it has no Form. To be consistent in his argument of eternal Forms - Plato must admit that matter does have an eternal Form, whatever shape that it might take. Hypatia looked for matter's eternal Form. She looked for the center of the universe - the mother receptacle. And that's what made her dangerous to Cyril! Hypatia would have proof that Satan existed, and eventually would find that Cyril was a descendant of that evil bloodline!"

Macha answered, "You would be correct, General Sherman. Plato contradicts his own logic. So, we have to ask, can we interpret that that confusion is a result of an encoded message in *Timaeus*? In *Timaeus*, Plato writes: 'To know or tell the origin of the other divinities is beyond us, and we must accept the traditions of the men of old time who affirm themselves to be the offspring of the gods -- that is what they say -- and they must surely have known their own ancestors...they declare that they are speaking of what took place in their own family, we must conform to custom and believe them....according to them, the genealogy of these gods is to be received and set forth.'" (*Timaeus* at 40.d.6-14)

Macha continued, "Plato was referrin' to the migration of Cain after God sent him out of Harran, after he murdered Abel. Cain went down the Tigris River and brought with him the Sumarran culture established by Adam and Eve in Harran - northern Mesopotamia. When Cain, a Black man, established his own community in Eridu - they called themselves black-headed, or Sumerians. They claimed that their civilization was brought by their god or his advisor - that is to say, it came from Cain, the son of Satan and Eve and raised by Adam and Eve. What Cain knew of civilization came from Adam."

MacArthur sighed as he stood up, "Plato is correct in pointing to the genealogy of these alleged gods. I cannot help thinking that Hypatia noted this clue - Plato was telling Hypatia to look at who these gods were! Plato wrote that there were visible gods 'as well as those other gods who are of a more retiring nature...the creator of the universe addressed them in these words. Gods, children of gods, who are my works and of whom I am the...father, my creations are indissoluble (spirits), if so I will. All that is bound may be undone, but only an evil being would wish to undo that which is harmonious and happy.' (*Ibid.* at 41.3-b.2) Hence, only evil would bring about a dark age."

Sherman cleared his throat, "But what I found as a clue in *Timaeus* was when Plato wrote: '*And now listen to my instructions. <u>Three tribes of mortal beings remain to be created</u>* -- without them the universe will be incomplete...'" (*Ibid.* at 41.b.6)

Sherman continued, "I expect that you all understand this, as I do, to refer to the three sons of Noah: Sem, Ham, and Japheth - these sons are the fathers of the three tribes needed to make the universe complete! This is definitely referring to Noah's sons, since Plato wrote: 'if they were created by me and received life at my hands, they would be on an equality with the gods. In order then that they may be mortal...do ye, according to your natures, betake yourselves to the formation of animals, imitating the power which was shown by me in creating you. The part of them worthy of the name immortal, which is called divine...of that divine part I will myself sow the seed (giving of their souls), *and having made a beginning (Adam and Eve), I will hand the work over to you (mankind)*. And do ye then interweave the mortal with the immortal...beget living creatures, and give them food and make them to grow, and receive them again in death.' (*Ibid.* at 41.c.2-d.3)

Plato is referring to lineage - beget living creatures - from Adam down to Noah and his three sons - the three tribes that fathered the world after the Great Flood!"

Sherman paused as he took a step towards the viewing screen on the wall; he then turned to Macha. "Plato wrote, 'And having made it (the mixture containing the remains of the four elements, God) divided the whole mixture into souls equal in number to the stars and assigned each soul to a star...according to which their first birth would be one and the same for all....'" (*Ibid.* at 41.d.8-e.3)

Sherman straightened his body and turned toward the generals, "Plato describes the laws God gave that they were to conquer love mingled with pleasure and pain - also fear and anger, and if they did they lived well during their appointed time, they would return to their native star that had been assigned to them at their birth." Sherman walked slowly as he continued, "Plato goes on to say, 'The creator sowed some of them (mankind) in the Earth, and some in the moon, and some in the *other instruments of time*.'" (*Ibid.* at 42.d.2)

MacArthur interrupted, "At first glance, it seems that Plato is talking of the in placement of the soul into the body - encased in a mortal body - that this movement of its course that it takes is its growth and that it eventually calms down and makes the individual a rational being. But in a second review, the question arises -- is Plato talking about a wormhole? More precisely, is Plato describing traveling through a wormhole?"

"Correct," Sherman responded, "Plato writes of the very great and mighty movement of the soul completely stopped the revolution of the soul by their *opposing current* and so disturbed the nature - that the three double intervals 'between 1, 2, 4, 8 and the three triple intervals between 1, 3, 9, 27, together with the mean terms and connecting links which are expressed by the ratios of 3:2 and 4:3 and of 9:8 - and that 'these, although they cannot be wholly undone except by him (God) who united them, *were twisted by them in all sorts of ways,* and the circles were broken and disordered in every possible manner, so that when they moved *they were tumbling* to pieces and moved irrationally, at one time in a reverse direction, and then again obliquely, and then upside down...and when (man) is in such a position, both he and the spectator fancy that the right of either is his left, and the left right...If...*the revolutions of the soul come in contact with some external thing, either of the class of the same or of the other, they speak of the same or the other* in a manner the very opposite of the truth, and they become false and foolish, and there is no course or revolution in them which has a guiding or directing power.'" (*Ibid.* at 43.c.6-44.6)

Sherman asserted, "I think that Plato is telling of a man passing through a wormhole -- to the other side of the universe where up is down and down is up, and therefore, seems false and foolish to the life here on Earth. The mathematical sequences of double, triple intervals, and ratios - make no sense to describe the journey of a soul's encasement into a body, but they could have a bearing on mathematically solving - how a wormhole acts. Three double intervals between 1,2,4,8 could be put into a formula along with the three triple intervals 1,3,9,27 with the ratios of 3:2 and 4:3 and 9:8. Is it some sort of algorithm to show the way to where the wormhole is, or how it operates?

Don't leave out Plato's statement that after God had 'sown them', these men in the Earth, some in the moon, *and some in the other instruments of time* - these other instruments of time being the wormhole....'" (*Ibid.* at 42.d.3-e.3)

Sherman continued, "The question is why - why does this one element - matter - have no eternal Form? What is Plato indicating; certainly he saw the conflict in his reasoning. Does his argument indicate a clue - look to matter - look to the ether, space. I can imagine that he's pointing to matter - it is through this matter that the wormhole exists.

Gerson writes of Plotinus' interpretation: 'Matter is only evil in other than a purely metaphysical sense when it becomes an impediment to return to the One.' Perhaps, that is the key: 'matter is only evil when it becomes an impediment to return to the One.'

Gerson wrote: Matter 'is evil when considered as a goal or end that is a polar opposite to the Good. To deny the necessity of evil is to deny the necessity of the Good. Matter is only evil for entities that can consider it as a goal of desire.'" (*Supra,* Gerson)

The sin of the Soul is to desire the limitless - to desire the evil," MacArthur added.

"To desire to be God himself, you mean," Sherman interrupted. "Isn't that what Satan desired, to be god of the Earth and all that inhabited it. Cain was known as the god of the Earth and all the animals and man. He was carrying out the desire of his father, Satan."

"I agree," Macha answered. "Looking at the description of what appears to be a wormhole, Plato shows us a world upside down as we know it – is he telling us that this is what evil is doing to us, turning us upside down – good is evil and evil is good, or is Plato going back to the idea of flux; we see one world, but it continually changes.

Heraclitus's first principle of life that everythin' is in flux, along with many other philosophers whose works were housed in the Library of Alexandria, support the premises of subquantum kinetics. The first physicist ta develop subquantum kinetics is Dr. Paul LaViolette. LaViolette was given, by telepathic means - the information: 'the basis of existence is flux.' He was given Heraclitus' first principle of life, although LaViolette didn't hear of Heraclitus until years after he developed subquantum kinetics. But after LaViolette received that telepathic message, he realized that if you have flux ya can have structure. But if ya start with structure, things are static. The real essence 'tis the ether, which is in constant flux, but 'tis non-material. This led ta LaViolette's development of subquantum kinetics. But 'tis totally contrary ta the subquantum mechanics that they teach in the universities.

Subquantum kinetics explains the reality of other dimensions and all the forces of conventional physics. Quantum structures 'tis the explicit manifestation; it emerges, evolves, from the implicit order of subquantum kinetics. Creation is tied ta the level of gravity potential of subquantum kinetics. But 'tis in the subquantum kinetics level that leads ta the continuous creation of matter - it doesn't happen all at once. The Big Bang theory of creation is false.

LaViolette said that the ancients had subquantum kinetics physics

- that means that Hypatia knew of this physics - and with this technology, 'tis possible ta do superluminal space travel - flying faster than the speed of light. The hieroglyphics that showed figures wearing a space-travel suit that today's astronauts wear - but they weren't figures of aliens, but our ancestors! The open system means that creation starts when there is a chemical-like feeding it; it ends when 'tis no longer fed, and energy can come ta an end. The concentration of the material composing the ether are the energy potential fields that form the basis of all matter and energy in our universe. The ether, or space beyond the Earth's atmosphere - the heavens, is the material upon which electromagnetic waves travel. Energy, called tired light, and matter can dematerialize ta a homogeneous state. When the ether flux slows down, tied ta a lowering of the gravity potential, matter can reappear and photons can gain energy, the so-called Pioneer effect. This vast flux is in the unseen level of subquantum kinetics.

LaViolette states that the mechanical universe cannot arise spontaneously - as in the Big Bang theory. There, in the Big Bang theory, creation of the mechanical universe requires the miraculous occurrence of a precursor, an initial impulse *supposedly* arising out of a state of non-existence. But without the hand of God. 'Tis irrational that something would happen out of nowhere without a stimulus; it goes against all their other laws of physics. Subquantum kinetics says, instead, that the creation of matter and energy is an orderly process that stems from a pre-existing subquantum continuum. 'Tis a set of well-ordered reaction processes occurrin' at the subquantum level. Heraclitus' theory: all things in nature are connected by logical structure and pattern. Heraclitus' work was in the Library of Alexandria, along with the other process philosophies that support subquantum kinetics.

LaViolette has said that subquantum kinetics leads ta a view of God that he is not separate from the Creation. He is the Creation as it evolves. LaViolette said that he does not use the word Creation ta just refer ta the material universe creation, but also to the levels that we have no direct knowledge of. The Creation is unfathomably immense and beyond our understandin', and hence God 'tis All that 'Tis.

(Dr. Paul LaViolette, International Journal of General Systems, 1985; www.etheric.com/LaVioletteBooks/ether.html; www.youtube.com/watch?v=8dy-0-aDV3g for Superwave Project Camelot interviews Dr. Paul LaViolette. Two of LaViolette's books: Genesis of the Cosmos and Subquantum Kinetics: The Alchemy of Creation)

Heraclitus's first principle of life that everything 'tis in flux - 'twas the cause of the fire at the Library of Alexandria. Heraclitus' theory was describin' the same kinetic physics that was long ago encoded in symbol in the Hellenistic-influenced Egyptian Dendera Zodiac of 50 BC and the European Gypsy Tarot card arcana. Someone encoded the technology to save it. After thousands of years of being buried, it 'twas telepathically given ta astrophysicists LaViolette. LaViolette 'tis a maverick physicist who received the telepathic message that the basis of everythin' is flux.

This telepathic message and LaViolette's subsequent development of subquantum kinetics 'tis the only way modern mankind would have known of the physics that proves God created the universe.

LaViolette states: 'What universities teach 'tis that energy 'tis conserved, the first law of thermodynamics, and 'tis wrong; and they know 'tis wrong. Yet they continue ta teach it in all the universities. They don't teach subquantum kinetics in the universities, and once filled with garbage, 'tis difficult for physicists ta change ta the truth. But! The Black Projects of the U.S. Government use the subquantum kinetics technology taken from LaViolette. And the U.S. Government 'tis keepin' the technology a secret. "Kinetics 'tis used in Black Projects, but whose controllin' the Black Projects? Some people suggest that they aren't from Earth."' (Project Camelot, *Supra*)

The truth 'tis - with subquantum kinetics, light loses energy, in the voids between galaxies, and leaves the physical universe. For a ghost ta appear or disappear depends on change in gravity potential. When gravity is lighter, the ghost dematerializes; when gravity is made heavier, the ghost reappears. The continuous, open system of subquantum kinetics alchemical feeds and if the feeding stops, waves disappear - and the physical universe would dematerialize. This 'tis the constant hand of God, creatin' matter. 'Tis proof of God's presence 'tis with us forever.

Astrology goes back to Sumerians, 4000 BC, who settled in Mesopotamia. The horoscope Zodiac system was developed in Babylonia, circa 500 BC. It had only the conjunctions and the horoscope itself. Greek philosophy - added the 'houses.'

Only Hipparchus, Claudius Ptolemy, Theon of Alexandria (Hypatia's father), and Proclus were aware of the precession of the equinoxes, and Proclus didn't believe in it. Precession revealed the existence of the astrological zodiac so the failure to understand it could lead to it being lost again. Theon and Proclus also recorded the alternative theory of 'trepidation,' later common among the Arabs and Indians: (trepidation being) the cardinal points oscillated over an arc of 16 degrees. Although the background of astrology 'tis Babylonian Mesopotamian with its sporadic horoscope omens, the *concept of continuous influences* belong ta the world of Greek philosophy. Modern realists reject interpretive rise of the houses, going back to the Babylonian model for the most part. (www.skyscript.co.uk/sidereal.html)

Hypatia was taught by her father, Theon of Alexandria, at an early age all that he knew of mathematics, astronomy, astrology, and the world religions. (Ginny Adair, www.agnesscott.edu/Iriddle/women/hypatia.htm) - what he knew she knew, and some say that she was more brilliant than Theon. Theon, A.D. 335-405, edited and arranged Claudius Ptolemy's *Handy Tables*, A.D. 90-168, which were intended for practical computations of solar, lunar, and planetary positions more rapidly than the tables of Ptolemy's *Almagest.* (www.ibiblio.org/ expo/vatican.exhibit/ exhibit/d-mathematics/Ptolemy_geo.html)

Claudius Ptolemy describes the construction of the zodiac in *Almagest,* A.D. 150. Ptolemy converted Hipparchus' planetary locations to ecliptic coordinates and then shifted the values to account for precession over intervening centuries. (www.brittanica.com/EBchecked/topic/16707/Almagest)

Precession of the equinoxes - is the slow westward shift of the equinoctial points along the plane of the ecliptic - a slow angular wobble that the Earth maintains as it rotates on its axis. (www.youtube.com/watch?v=VsD2Nku6Zqo)

Hipparchus, 129 BC, developed the theory of solar motion and discovered precession, which was available to Ptolemy via the Library of Alexandria. (http://farside.ph.utexas.edu/syntaxis/Almagest/node3.html)

But who encoded the subquantum kinetics inta the Egyptian Dendera Zodiac? Alexander the Great brought astrology to Egypt, circa 330 BC. Derek and Julia Parker, Parker's Encyclopedia of Astrology, 1990, state that under the Greeks, and in particular Ptolemy in his book, *Tetrabiblos*, the planets, Houses, and signs of the zodiac were rationalized and their function set down. An image of the zodiac by Ptolemy has a crucifixion cross and Jesus Christ driving a chariot with four white horses in the center; in the next ring 12 naked female figures that represent the hours; in an outer ring 12 clothed apostles that represent 12 months; and out from that a ring of the 12 zodiac signs. Under the image: 'Zodiac and months from Tetrabiblos of Ptolemaios Manuscript from 8th center A.D. Geographia of Ptolemy; Rome, Biblioteca Apostolica Vaticana from Bibliotheque Helios in the center, identified as the Christ by the cross....' (http://historyhuntersinternational.org/2010/05/15/the-ptolemaic-zodiac-from-where-the-sun-shines/)

In his book, *Sphaera*, Franz Boll states that the work (of the zodiacs) is a mixture of two cultures....The expectation of the coming of the Messiah at the conclusion of the Galactic Cycle of Pisces, and the beginnin' of Aries 'twas a universal phenomenon configured by the universal science of cosmology (not astrology)....Boll admits that the Dendera zodiac is an amalgamation of some of the most ancient and most modern images of that time, p. 163...Ancient astronomers (showed) that the center of our Milky Way Galaxy is in Sagittarius, near the arrow point of the archer, the star named Sagittarius 'A'. Modern science also locates the black hole at the center of the galaxy....The image of Circular Zodiac of Dendera is achieved through the principles of sacred geometry...the most dynamic image of the heavens ever created.' (http://quakerstar.org/dendera.htm)

Astrophysicist LaViolette states that modern scientists calling the center of our Milky Way Galaxy a Black Hole are wrong. LaViolette calls the center, the alleged Black Hole, a Mother Star that produces matter - it ejects star clusters seen as a halo of the galaxy. Every galaxy is creating matter. The creation rate 'tis highest at Mother Star, as it creates and cools off, cyclically. The zodiac sign, Sagittarius, 'tis arrow 'tis pointin' ta this

Mother Star of creation. Scorpio's tail 'tis also pointin' ta the center of the Mother Star, the center of our galaxy. (Project Camelot, *Supra*) 'Tis from the center of this Mother Star that 'tis coming the Superwave ta strike Earth."

Macha read the words of Jesus from the Bible, Matt. 24:36, "'But of that day and hour no one knoweth, not the angels of heaven, but the Father alone.' Only the Father, for only the Father created the Mother Star, and thus, knows when the Superwave will hit Earth and all in the universe.

In *The Temple of Man*, Chapter 7, Schwaller deLubicz states that the 'figures are the primary, secret writings...the figures...must be interpreted.' (Quakerstar, *Supra*) These figures of Sagittarius and Scorpio are pointin' ta the creation of God. Look ta this creation for the end times. 'Tis from here it will come. 'Tis from here that the Superwave will originate - finally spreading across the universe - ta our solar system - burnin' every microchip, burnin' all electronics - defense systems - puttin' the world back to the dark ages. The Zodiac is encoded with this information.

The Circular Zodiac of Dendera should be looked upon as a multifaceted chronometer of cosmic cycles...it serves as our most important artifact of an instrument of scientific record, (p. 138 *The Dawn of Astronomy,* Lockyer) (Quakerstar, *Supra*)

The subquantum kinetics developed by LaViolette also explains the spiral galaxy, the center of our Milky Way, that has started its outburst cycle - it has periodic, cyclical outbursts. This subquantum kinetics (SQK) is based on alchemical changes. SQK also explains the Superwave - cosmic wave electrons, gamma waves, x-rays, light and radio waves and gravity waves - the whole spectrum, traveling at the speed of light. These Superwaves occur cyclically, small and large - the large either at the beginnin' or at the end of an ice age on Earth. One large Superwave occurred 26,000 years ago; a small one 5300 years ago just prior to the Mayan calendar. We are due for one. We are in a danger period; we're on the fringe of a galactic volcano; a very active volcano; we should expect an explosion shortly; comin' from our galactic center.

The Galactic Superwave will wipe out every communication, roast satellites, fry electronic circuits, cars with chips won't work, the chips will be fried. At the forefront of the Superwave will be a dense shock front of cosmic rays and the electromagnetic pulse associated with the wave will act like a high altitude nuke explosion. Telephones made of fiber optics might survive, LaViolette stated. The forefront could last only minutes, preceded by a gravity wave causin' earthquakes all over the Earth, not just in one place. This will be the first warnin' - things shakin', caused by the Superwave - all of it travelin' at the speed of light.

The Superwave caused the Great Flood, LaViolette said. An ice sheet covered most of the Earth, but when the Superwave hit the protective sheet that surrounds our solar system, it pushed the protective sheet into the Sun, turnin' it reddish. There is dust that orbits the Sun normally - the

Superwave pushin' the protective sheet against the Solar winds, causes the dust to hit the Sun, which then burns up the dust in massive super corona ejections that melted the ice sheet around the Earth. This Superwave triggered conditions for the Sun becomin' more active.

And the cosmic dust around the Earth can create a warmin' effect because the wave can scatter light that normally go out into space, causin' that light ta come back onta the Earth in sort of an interplanetary hot house effect. And this would have melted the ice sheet on Earth.

The Earth and the Moon were engulfed in corona ejection and caused particles on the Moon to melt. The Mars space rover found glazed rocks on the surface of Mars, which was also hit by the Superwave. This is why so many ancient cultures all over the Earth speak of a Great Flood - it was caused by a Superwave. There are inland flood deposits caused by freshwater that point to this theory. There are not saltwater deposits inland; pole shiftin' would have caused the oceans to slosh around, but there is no evidence of that theory. Today, we don't have an ice sheet. LaViolette states that we are in the eye of the hurricane; we can't see the Superwave coming at us; but it will come without warnin'. Just as the Book of Matthew states.

In his interview with Project Camelot, LaViolette was told of another witness, Jake Simpson, who worked in Black Projects said that the U.S. Government sent out a superluminal craft outside our solar system - on that flight, they picked up a wave headin' toward Earth - they calculated that the Superwave will hit sometime between now, 2011 and 2017. LaViolette stated that this is the problem with Black Projects; they are completely isolated from the rest of the world; discoverin' things as if they found them themselves for the first time, while those who have been doin' a lot of work are kept out of the loop. But his books are circulated through the Black Project scientists.

LaViolette described that *when our solar system is hit by a Superwave, the Sun will become reddish and the Moon will be blotted out. It will come without warning, traveling at the speed of light.* (Project Camelot, *Supra*)

Macha picked up the Bible and read: Matt. 24:27, 29-30, where Jesus said: 'For as lightnin' cometh out of the east, and appeareth even into the west: so shall also the comin' of the Son of man be....And immediately after the tribulation of those days, *the sun shall be darkened and the moon shall not give her light*, and the *stars shall fall from heaven*, and the powers of heaven shall be moved: And then shall appear the sign of the Son of man in heaven: and then shall all tribes of the Earth mourn: and they shall see the Son of man comin' in the clouds of heaven with much power and majesty.'"

When she finished reading, Macha put down the Bible and took a few steps passed the large viewing screen on the wall.

"Generals," she said quietly, "When the Superwave hits, every airplane or helicopter flyin' will fall from the skies - around the world -

when the planes' engines electrical systems and microchips are fried. Every defense missile, every fightin' jet, every tank, transport vehicle, and every aircraft carrier and submarine will have their electronics burned out. Every car usin' microchips ta control brakin' will continue on until they collide with other cars. The electronically-controlled pneumatic brakes on trains will be fried and trains won't stop until collision or fly off their tracks. Every elevator will fall inside the shafts of the tallest buildin's. Every person who takes the microchip mark of the beast will be burned. And every computer handlin' - bankin' transactions, mortgages and credit cards balances, medical records, the stock market, social security checks, defense systems will all be destroyed. Missiles could be launched inadvertently, LaViolette said. All security systems will be rendered useless - open to pillagin' and plunderin'. All electrical power will be gone - people will die on operatin' tables, lightin' and instruments will be fried. People, ranch and farm animals caught outside likely will not survive the x-rays and gamma wave pulse that will be part of the Superwave. If people don't have paperwork set aside that they can grab quickly, they won't be able to prove who they are, or of what country they are a citizen. All wealth will be wiped out; safes dependin' on microchips or an electrical system will be forever locked. Multiple-millions of people will die around the world, and mankind will be back in the Stone Age of equality where only the strong survive. Animals that supply our food will be gone.

We are goin' inta the Second American Revolution, and durin' that revolution the Earth will be hit by the Superwave now on 'tis way toward Earth, as we speak."

There was quiet in the control room underneath the Cheyenne Mountain as Macha and the Generals contemplated the world in chaos and the death of multiple millions of people and animals. Just then General Stonewall stood up, his Bible in his hand, and he turned to Matt. 24:21-22, and he read the words of Jesus aloud: "For there shall be then great tribulation, such as hath not been from the beginning of the world until now, neither shall be. And unless those days had been shortened, no flesh should be saved: but for the sake of the elect those days shall be shortened."

Macha nodded, "Thank you Stonewall, we need to be reminded of Christ's words." She paused a moment, "In Ptolemy's zodiac - Christ and His crucifixion cross are in its center - this shows the Mother Star in the center of our Milky Way Galaxy - the creator of the continual creation of matter and energy - who is God. The circular design of Ptolemy's zodiac shows that from the center - the Superwave will explode from the center of our Galaxy and spread out in a 360 degree direction, passing through the entire universe.

Hypatia knew of this SQK physics, she knew of Jesus' warnin' of the Superwave - her father taught her all the world's religions. Hypatia's works were obliterated and the contents of the Library of Alexandria were destroyed soon after Hypatia's death. Not a single scroll remains; a small fraction of copies of the books survive, preserved in other libraries. (Carl Sagan's book, *Cosmos*, 1980; www.alexpetrov.com)

All this knowledge of the Superwave was burned in the Library of Alexandria, all of Heraclitus' work of the first principle of life - life is always in flux. Always changin'. In *Timaeus*, Plato wrote: 'I will not now speak of the first principle...for this reason --- because it is difficult to set forth my opinion accordin' ta the method of discussion which we are at present employin'. Because the discussion was a code. Plato said, 'Do not imagine...that I should be right in undertakin' so great and difficult a task. Rememberin' what I said at first about probability, I will do my best ta give as probable an explanation as any other...I call upon God and beg him ta be our savior out of a strange and unwonted inquiry, and ta brin' us ta the haven of probability.'" (*Ibid.* at 48.c.2-e) 'Twas after this that Plato wrote of the receptacle - the Mother Star - the center of the Milky Way Galaxy.

With Hypatia's murder came the Dark Ages and her murderer, Cyril of Alexandria - the Patriarch or Pope of Alexandria, was sainted. Cyril had brought in his monks who literally tore apart the body of Hypatia. No records show who Cyril's father was, only that his mother was Greek and that Cyril was born in Egypt. He was Black, therefore, his father must have been Egyptian. Cyril hated Hypatia; Hypatia was the last Head Librarian of the Library of Alexandria. Hypatia 'twas murdered, on her way home from the Library, in A.D. 415. All the philosophers fled Alexandria upon hearing of Hypatia's murder. The citizenry did not access the Library, only the world's elite, and now they were gone. Caliph Umar's general conquered Alexandria in A.D. 641; 226 years after Hypatia's murder, therefore, there was no Library when the Muslims entered the city.

While the Library at Alexandria housed the knowledge of the world, the knowledge was not given or taught to the average person - only to the elite of the world. Therefore, the Library had no impact on the citizens of Egypt. The U.S. Black Projects has technology only seen in science fiction novels - superluminal flight/faster than the speed of light. But they keep it a secret. The Black Projects have the technology for free energy, free communications, but they keep it to themselves. Why are the elite building underground bunkers - to save themselves from the coming Second American Revolution, or to hide from the Superwave they know will soon be hittin' Earth. Or perhaps, both. Did the 2.3 trillion dollars missin' from the Pentagon's budget go inta the Black Projects superluminal crafts and/or the underground bunkers for the elite?

Are the UFOs that are now so plentiful comin' from the U.S. Government and not from outer space aliens? Is the U.S. Government plannin' the attack that Rudolph Messinger spoke of in his speech ta the Leachburg group in 1991: "Fear of the unknown or of an overwhelmingly powerful enemy *is how we will get them* to willingly relinquish all their individual rights. *We need Americans to cooperate in giving up their rights. Otherwise, we'll have an uncontrollable revolution on our hands*."

The point of all this - the children of Satan have controlled the proof that God exists. And the proof that evil, Satan, exists. Cyril of Alexandria murdered Hypatia and burned the Library of Alexandria ta keep the secret. And today, 'tis kept a secret by the U.S. Government - and the Vatican, the Rabbis, and the Imams.

Dr. Pete Peterson, Project Camelot interviews, said that the Vatican library has 'stuff that 'tis contrary ta beliefs' that the Pope 'keeps from the public' that Peterson opines 'tis 'remnants from the Library of Alexandria.' (www.youtube.com/watch?v=ooSRh7V68uk)

'Tis the Vatican, the Black Pope, keepin' from the public the proof that God created the universe? Are they hidin' it so today's scientists can present ta the world the foolish notion of the Big Bang theory, which counters all their sub-theories of physics? The Big Bang theory claims that the universe was created WITHOUT God's hand!

But why 'tis this history a warnin' ta Americans of today? 'Tis two-fold. The 'powers that be' are keepin' free energy and communication, and the speed of light travel from Americans - the American' taxpayer dollars paid for the government's development of the research stolen from Tesla and LaViolette, but Americans do not benefit from it. Americans still have ta pay for electricity and gasoline and heatin' and coolin' - when it could be free ta 'em. The elite throughout the ages have controlled this technology.

The fire in the Library of Alexandria will be duplicated, in a "legal" sense - with the destruction of individuals' ownin' their inventions. Up until September 16, 2011, the way of filin' of a patent was protected by the U.S. Constitution, Art. I, Sec. 8, cl. 8, Congress shall: 'secur(e) for limited times ta authors and inventors the exclusive right ta their respective writin's and discoveries' - 'tis known as the inventors' 'right of first ta file.' Under the Patent Law of 2007 that they renamed as the America Invents Act of 2011 that Tsaeb signed on September 16, 2011, ANYONE who files the patent application FIRST owns the invention - NOT the inventor. Before September 16th, on the back side of a Filin' Receipt received from the U.S. Patent and Trademark Office 'tis a notice ta inventors: Beware the theft of your invention by China and Mexico! After September 16th, a notice should go out ta every American - all your inventions can be easily stolen by everyone! LaViolette should be very careful of computer hackers!

Generals, the distinquishin' asset that puts the United States of America above all other countries - 'tis its technology. Now, if patent attorneys, or corporate or foreign computer hackers, or staff in the Patent Office - ANYONE who gets their hands on the patent application and files it under their name - they own the patent - and the billions of dollars it will create in the marketplace. Not ta mention denyin' the United States from usin' the technology for their national security, their weapons systems, medical biowarfare, and medical cures.

This America Invents Act of 2011 'tis up there with the atrocity of the burnin' of the Library of Alexandria. We have President Tsaeb, a

Muslim, committin' an atrocity of equal destruction against the United States. The United States will become a country of slaves ta the world of Satan's children, not just the families of the Rothschilds, or Soros, or Rockefellers, but the whole world of satanic seed! That 'tis, unless we stop them.

'Twas a dark day when the seed of Satan took control of Alexandria. And the days of America grow darker, still, livin' under the Muslim-conquered satanic government. Jesus warned of the end times when He told his apostles, sayin' that 'For there shall be great tribulation, such as hath not been from the beginnin' of the world until now, neither shall be.' Matt 24:21. Think back for a moment what has happened just in the recent history: the Great Depression; the nuclear bombin' of Hiroshima and Nagasaki; Hitler's extermination and concentration camps; WWI; WWII, Pearl Harbor; Korean Police Action; Vietnam; the Gulf Wars; the bombin' of the World Trade towers; the wars of Afghanistan and Iraq. None of that will compare ta what Americans and the world 'tis about ta face - the purest evil of Satan! Rev. 12:17, 'And the dragon was angry against the woman (Eve): and went ta make war with the rest of her seed, who keep the commandments of God, and have the testimony of Jesus Christ.' Right now, the Muslim Brotherhood is crucifying Coptic Christians in Alexandria, Egypt.

'Twas Cyril who brought Satan inta the Egyptian Coptic Christian Church, as Solomon had brought Satan in ta the House of David. As the Jesuits brought Satan inta the Vatican. But Satan had always been in the Zionists *Talmud*, and consequently, its duplicate religion, Islam."

Macha stopped for a moment, looked around the control room deep beneath Cheyenne Mountain.

"In Alexandria, 'twas the battle of the serpent's children, the Japheth/Pharisaic/Rabbinic Jews and Black/Egyptian Coptics. They were the same Pharisaic Jews that Jesus accused, John 8:44, "Ye are of ye father the devil, and the desires of ye father ye will do. He was a murderer from the beginnin', and stood not in the truth; because truth 'tis not in him. When he speaketh a lie, he speaketh of his own: for he 'tis a liar, and the father thereof.' Jesus was talkin' about Cain, the father of the Pharisees."

Macha began to tell of Pope Cyril of Alexandria, "He had been a monk for nine years when he succeeded his uncle Theophilus as the Patriarch/Pope of Alexandria, in A.D. 412. He had five missions: get rid of the Jews; get rid of Hypatia the pagan; destroy the Library of Alexandria and the knowledge housed in there that proved that God exists, and therefore, that proved Satan exists; de-throne Pope Nestorius of Constantinople; create a schism between the Roman and Eastern Churches. And he was successful in all his missions.

'In late A.D. 414 to early A.D. 415, years of tension between the Jews of Alexandria and the Gentiles reached a climax beginnin' with a series of riots and finally an assault was made by the Jews against the Christians in the city. That next day, Cyril demanded all Jews be removed from the city. Cyril himself led an army of Christians against the Jews, plunderin' and destroyin' the synagogues....' (http://persweb. wabash.edu/facstaff/royaltyr/AncientCities/web/rel%20372%20project /JEWS.htm]

Mission one accomplished.

'Hypatia is thought to have collaborated with her father, Theon, on both the *Almagest* of Ptolemy and the *Elements* by Euclid. She herself wrote the astronomical cannon (probably Book III) of the *Almagest* that established a geocentric model of the universe. She would have occasion ta meet with the magistrates of the city, no doubt offensive ta her enemies. One of her students, Synesius of Cyrene wrote of Hypatia that she 'legitimately resides over the mysteries of philosophy.' Synesius wrote to Hypatia: may you 'always have power, and long may you have it and make a good use of that power.'

Patriarch Theophilus, Pope of Alexandria, destroyed the Serapeum in A.D. 391 - the temple being used as the sister library of the Library of Alexandria - but those books had been secreted out because Hypatia had been told of a prophecy that the Serapeum 'twas ta be destroyed.

Theophilus destroyed the Serapeum - because it 'twas an actual pagan temple, servin' as an annex ta the Library of Alexandria. Theophilus didn't destroy the Library because 'twas not a temple, thus he had no excuse, no order, nor permission from the Roman Emperor Theodosius I, who had ordered the pagan temples ta be destroyed all over the Empire, includin' the pagan Temple of Serapeum.

When Cyril succeeded his uncle, Theophilus, as patriarch, he needed his own political triumph over paganism. In Hypatia, he found it. After her murder, wrote John Nikiu, LXXXIV 101-103, all the people surrounded the patriarch Cyril and named him the new Theophilus,' for he had destroyed the last remains of idolatry in the city.' (http://penelope.uchicago.edu/~grout/encyclopedia_romana/greece/paganism/Hypatia.html)

But all of that was a cover for the real reason Cyril murdered Hypatia. It 'twas her knowledge that God and Satan existed; her knowledge of creation; her knowledge of the wormhole that Plato wrote about in *Timaeus.*

The *Suda*, a 10th century Byzantine encyclopedia...describes Hypatia...the whole city rightly loved her and worshipped her in a remarkable way, but the rulers...envied her...when Cyril was passing her house...saw a great crowd...and told Hypatia was about to greet them...Cyril was so struck with envy that he immediately began plotting her murder and the most heinous murder at that...a throng of merciless and ferocious men...attacked her. (http://penelope.uchicago.edu/~grout/ encyclopedia_romana/greece/paganism/hypatia.html.)

'Twas not the Christians of Alexandria who murdered Hypatia, it 'twas Cyril's army of monks - the parabalanoi - his strongmen who murdered Hypatia. (*Secret History of the Witches,* by Max Dashu; www.suppressedhistories.net/secrethistory/hypatia.html)

The Christians loved Hypatia, and Hypatia was the last Head Librarian of the Library of Alexandria, they loved her works, which were housed in the Great Library. They would not have destroyed the Library.

'Twas Cyril who led his mob to destroy the Library of Alexandria - ta destroy all the work of the Greek pagans. In particular, Heraclitus' and Hypatia's work. Missions 2 and 3 accomplished.

But this is why the Egyptian Dendera Zodiac was encoded with the secret proof that God existed, and perhaps it was Hypatia who encoded it. The Tarot 11 arcana cards serve as a key to unlockin' the code of the Zodiac - revealin' the proof of the existence of God and Satan. Antoninus had prophesied that the Temple of Serpis, the Serapeum, the sister library of the Library of Alexandria - would be destroyed. (Penelope, *Supra*) 'Tis likely he made sure that his contemporary, Hypatia, knew of his prophecy. It 'twas equally important that the existence of Satan be kept a secret, too. If ye don't know an enemy 'tis out ta take your soul - you have no defense ta prevent the takin'.

Cyril also started the schism between the Roman and the Eastern Christian Churches. 'Twas a battle for control over the world's Christians. 'Bishop Nestorius of Constantinople and Bishop Cyril of Alexandria battled over the terminology of the nature of Jesus Christ, Christology. Nestorius was a powerful speaker; 'twas recommended ta Emperor Theodosius II, who appointed him as Bishop of Constantinople. He suddenly became one of the most powerful men in the Roman Empire. He used his power ta vehemently attack heresy. Cyril became his most outspoken opponent' - an indirect method of becoming powerful himself. 'The Roman Pope called the Council of Ephesus in A.D. 431 ta settle the dispute between the two Popes, and found for Cyril's version of Christology. Nestorius was dethroned and returned ta his monastery, later exiled. (www.publications.villanova .edu/concept/2005/Nestorius_ and_Cyril.htm, by Ben Green)

Mission 4 accomplished.

Finally, Emperor Theodosius II got involved. But Nestorius' inadequacy ta make a convincin' case for his orthodoxy...that gave his opponents (Cyril) - cause and opportunity ta depose Nestorius.' Nestorius representin' one sect and Cyril representin' another sect caused the two sects ta separate.' (Ben Green, *Ibid.*)

Mission 5 accomplished.

'In 1951, in his encyclical...Pope Pius XII (wrote)...'let those who are involved in the *errors* of Nestorius... penetrate with clearer insight inta the mystery of Christ and at last accept this definition (of the natures of Christ) in its completeness....The Decree on Ecumenism of Vatican II detailed a specific commitment ta reunification with the Eastern Churches...recognizin' 'unity in difference' in theology. In 1971, Pope Paul VI and His Holiness Mar Ignatius Iacob III, signed *The Common*

Declaration. The (previous) division of the Churches 'twas recognized as a serious obstacle ta *world mission.*' (Walter Kasper, *Current Problems in Ecumenical Theology,* Pontifical Council for Promoting Christian Unity, I) (Ben Green, *Ibid.*)

Over terminology of several words – an argument that man has no ability to consider – Cyril was able ta separate Christians from each other for 1540 years, or more than 15 centuries, from A.D. 431 ta 1971. But now that they are ready to openly institute the New World Order controlled by Satan enthroned on the Throne of Peter, the two sects are brought together."

Macha stood quietly, looking into the eyes of each of the generals and admiral waiting for her next words, "After Satan was released from the pit, 1000 years after the death of Jesus, in A.D. 1030 – twenty-four years later came the *Great* Schism of the East and West Churches, A.D. 1054.

Generals. Twenty-four years after Theodosius proclaimed Christianity as the official religion of the entire Roman Empire, A.D. 391, Cyril burned down the Library of Alexandria, A.D. 415, and brought the world inta the Dark Ages – the Dark Age of not knowing the proof of God's and Satan's existence.

Theodosius died in A.D. 395; after his death the Roman Empire was divided inta Western and Eastern empires; the Goths sacked Rome on August 24, 410. The collapse of civil administrations left the Church of Roman, the Bishops, in charge of administration of the cities. The Goths moved inta Rome, and fewer and fewer people could speak both Latin and Greek, fracturing communications between the Western and Eastern Churches. Both language and cultural bonds between the churches disappeared. The churches then developed different rites and viewpoint of doctrine.

Cyril 'twas the Antichrist of his day - yet 'tis celebrated as a saint by both Roman Catholics and Eastern Orthodox Churches."

Macha paused, letting her words sink in. "Jesus returned ta destroy the Second Temple, signified by his turnin' over the tables of the moneychangers. He came to release the last of the Israelites from the bondage of Ezra's Talmudic enslavement and to save the souls of many. Jesus gave Michael the Archangel the order to put Satan inta the pit for the first time ta get him out of the way of Christ's mission. Satan 'twas released for his promised short time, in A.D. 1030. Instead of repentin', Satan attacked Christ's church. In his Homily of Pope Paul VI, the Ninth Anniversary of the Coronation of His Holiness, June 29, 1972: Referrin' ta the situation of the Church after Vatican II, Pope Paul VI confessed: '*from some fissure the smoke of Satan has entered the temple of God.*' Jesus Christ said that 'the gates of hell shall not prevail against' His church. [Matt. 16:18] If there 'tis smoke, there 'tis fire, and Jesus will return before Satan completes his world mission: to control all the creatures of the Earth – the power that God gave ta Adam, and Satan's mission to judge the livin' and the dead, the power that God gave to Jesus."

Intermission

The Declaration of Independence
Thomas Jefferson, July 4, 1776

Following the advice and form of the Declaration - *That whenever any Form of Government becomes destructive...it is the Right of the People to alter or to abolish it, and to institute new Government, - it is their right, it is their DUTY, to throw off such Government, and to provide new Guards for their future security. - To prove this, let Facts be submitted to a candid world.*

LIST OF GRIEVANCES

1. The taking of 650 million acres of land from private citizens of America, with more takings to come. Or 29% of the United States land - given to Yoon Won-Shik, Secy. General of the United Nations.
2. The Federal Reserve Act of 1913, which bankrupted the U.S. in 20 years; still being managed today. U.S. Constitution, Art. I, Sec. 8, cl. 5: "Congress shall have the power to coin Money, regulate the Value thereof..." Art. V, "The Congress, whenever two thirds of both Houses shall deem it necessary, shall propose Amendments to this Constitution...shall be valid to all Intents and Purposes, as Part of this Constitution, when ratified by the Legislatures of three fourths of the several States..." No amendment was made to the Constitution to transfer power to coin and regulate the value of money, from Congress to the Federal Reserve owners: : Lazard Brothers, Israel Moses Sief, Kuhn, Loeb & Co.; Warburg & Co.; Lehman Bros.; Goldman, Sacks, and the Rockefeller family.
3. The 16th Amendment, which was never ratified as required by the U.S. Constitution Art. V, and illegally instituted taxes on income, 1913.
4. The Internal Revenue Service, an illegal collection agency for the private owners of the Federal Reserve. U.S. Constitution, Art. I, Sec. 8, cl. 1: "The Congress shall have Power to lay and **collect** Taxes." Congress did not process an amendment to the Constitution giving its power to collect Taxes to the Internal Revenue Service, which collects taxes for the Federal Reserve.
5. Allowing Israelis to bomb the USS Liberty cruising in international waters without investigation or repercussions, and for silencing all witnesses for 40 years under threat of imprisonment.
6. Refusal to drill on the world's largest oil reserves, the United States, strategic to national security, requiring U.S. to be dependent on Muslim countries that hate the U.S. Instead, releasing military *emergency* reserves of gasoline for consumer consumption.
7. As a result of 9/11, the establishment of U.S. Northern Command (CINC-NORTHCOM), for watching Americans inside the continental

United States. Defense Secretary Danny Rummysfield called it "the most sweeping set of changes since the unified command system was set up in 1946." As a result of 9/11, establishment of the Patriot Act and Homeland Security Act.

8. President George W. Schirf's Patriot Act used for invasion of privacy; to spy on every American without a search warrant and use collected intel against a citizen in a court of law.

9. President George W. Schirf's Executive Order 13235, of Nov. 16, 2001, in which President Schirf..."**declared a national emergency** that requires the use of the Armed Forces of the United States, by Proclamation 7463 of September 14, 2001 [50 U.S.C. 1621 note], because of the terrorist attacks on the World Trade Center and the Pentagon...***To provide additional authority to the Department of Defense to respond to that threat***...**I hereby order that the emergency CONSTRUCTION authority at 10 U.S.C. 2808 is invoked...at the discretion of the Secretary of Defense...."**

A Halliburton subsidiary, KBR, received a $385 million contract from the Department of Homeland Security to provide **'temporary *detention* and processing capabilities'**...The **contract** -- calls **for preparing** for **'an emergency influx of immigrants, *or* to support the *rapid development* of *new programs'*** in the event of ***other emergencies***."

10. President George W. Schirf's Homeland Security Act of 2002:

The Director of Homeland Security (DHS) took control of all FEMA responsibility, such as the building of FEMA detention-concentration camps across the country.

11. President Tsaeb cut by 60% the funding of training and arming of U.S. commercial pilots, to defend against terrorists attempting to take control of passenger airplanes.

12. President Tsaeb said on July 15, 2011: “In addition to the $400 billion that we’ve already cut from defense spending, we’re willing to look for hundreds of billions more.”

Over the last two years (2010 and 2011), President Tsaeb has cut $800 billion from Defense.

13. President Tsaeb signed the Budget Control Act of 2011, on August 2, 2011, which included Tsaeb’s idea of sequestration.

- the law mandates sequestration (the removal of) funds that run over the discretionary spending caps set by the law for each of the next ten years (www.ssa.gov/legislation/legis_ bulletin_080211.html)

- Sequestration/removal of $500 billion in defense spending, negatively effecting the training of US military, updating of military defense systems, and the buying of Naval ships.

- Sequestration cuts will have significant and negative consequences for US national security.

President Tsaeb requires all US Military to ‘go green’ changing to fuel that costs $27 per gallon.

14. President Tsaeb ***added*** Israel to the terrorist list as a state sponsor of terrorism.

15. President Tsaeb and the United Nations ***delisted*** from a list of terrorists, Muslim Brotherhood financier, Youssef Nada, Egyptian-born global terrorist.

a. "Youssef Nada is the man in whose house the infamous Muslim Brotherhood blueprint for Islamic infiltration known as The Project was found in 2001. The Project is a Muslim manifesto roadmap for infiltrating and defeating the West. (www.theblaz.com/stories/white-house-visitor-may-have-ties-to-the-project-a-muslim-roadmap-for-infiltrating-the-west/)

b. Hisham Yahya **Altalib** is an Iraqi-born Muslim identified by the FBI as Muslim Brotherhood operative, who was the first full-time Director of Leadership Training Dept. of Muslim Students Assn. of U.S. and Canada, a long time Muslim Brotherhood front group whose explicit goal is to "conquer" America through Islamic propagandizing. (Michelle Malkin, 9/26/2012; http://amarillo.com/opinion/opinion-columnist/2012-09-26/malkin-white -house-hosts-muslim)

c. On March 30, **Altalib visited the White House**...Four days later, White House officials welcomed a foreign delegation of the radical Sharia-enforcing Muslim Brotherhood from Egypt. (*Ibid.*)

d. Altalib founding member of SAAR Foundation and the International Institute of Islamic thought. FBI and Customs officials think SAAR/SAFA laundered money for a plethora of violent Muslim terrorist groups, from Hamas and Hezbollah to al-Qaeda and the Palestinian Islamic Jihad. (*Ibid.*)

16. **President Tsaeb gave to the Muslim Brotherhood, $1.5 billion of U.S. taxpayer money** - ***without the consent of the U.S. Congress***, on **March 22, 2012**.

June 30, 2012, Mohammed Morsi, of the Muslim Brotherhood was sworn in as President of Egypt. December 2012, Morsi signed the Islamist Constitution of Egypt.

Google Translation of Egyptian Secular News Media, on **August 16, 2012**, reporting: "Confirmed correspondent Sky News Arabic in Cairo that the demonstrators belonging to the Muslim Brotherhood **CRUCIFIED** opponents of Egyptian President Mohammed Morsi naked on the trees in front of the palace presidential, while torturing others." (http://www.godlikeproductions.com/forum1/message1966353/pg1)

"Muslim Brotherhood terrorized secular media...people were being CRUCIFIED.

Attacks are part of Muslim Brotherhood campaign to intimidate and censor Egypt's Secular media exposing the group's Islamist agenda...One such channel was shut down by Egyptian President Morsi. Al Azhar, Egypt's most authoritative Islamic institution, has just issued a fatwa calling for more violence and oppression, saying that 'fighting participants in anti-Muslim Brotherhood demonstrations planned for 24

August 2012 is a religious obligation.'"
(http://www.algemeiner.com/2012/08/16/muslim-brotherhood- crucifies-opponents-attacks-secular-media/)

"An escalation in an ongoing siege against Egypt's oldest indigenous religious community (Coptic Christians). The White House admitted the bombing targeted Christian worshippers. The administration left unmentioned the (Christian) church that the jihadists burned that day in the city of Maiduguri. State Dept. did condemn attacks by gunmen on Iraqi Christians…mentioned the…bombing at the Our Lady of Salvation Catholic Church in Baghdad that killed 58. Public approval of the U.S. in most Muslim-majority countries has reset to the extremely low level it was before…became president, and in some cases is even lower." (Washington Times Editorial, 1/4/2011, http://www.washington times.com/news/2011/jan/4/when-muslims-kill-christians)

<u>Dearborn, Michigan</u>, Muslim Festival: young children and teenagers yell obscenities and **stone Christians** wearing T-shirts displaying the name of Jesus. Police do not stop the children from stoning Christians, but warn Christians to get out that their signs are enraging the Muslims. (Pat Dollard, 9/28/2012, video of stoning; http://patdollard.com/ 2012/09/cops-to-nswer-in-court-for-stoning-of-christians-by-raging-muslims-in-michigan)

<u>President Tsaeb spoke before</u> UN, 9/21/2011: "The future MUST NOT belong to those who slander the prophet of Islam." Diana West stated: "I can't think of another instance in which an American president has publicly uttered such a rank betrayal of American principles." (Diana West, 9/28/2012; www.dianawest.net/Home/tabid/36/EntryId/2252/The-Anti-Blasphemy-Anti-First-Amendment-President.aspx; Cindy Simpson, 9/29/2012; www.americanthinker.com/blog /2012/09read_this_while_you_can .html?utm_medium =twitter&utm_source=twitterfeed)

- **The Muslim Brotherhood is on the U.S. terrorist list.**

- **FBI** veteran, John Guandolo, who worked on cases after 9/11, stated that the **prominent Islamic organizations in the United States are <u>all</u> controlled by the Muslim Brotherhood.**

Every major Muslim organization in America is a front group for the Brotherhood, which has raised millions for Hamas, al-Qaeda, and other terrorist groups.

The U.S. Justice Dept. has identified no fewer than 61 Muslim Brotherhood figures and entities operating within the United States, i.e.:

1) Council on American-Islamic Relations (CAIR), the largest Muslim-rights group in the U.S. and is based in Washington, D.C.

2) Islamic Society of North America (ISNA)

3) North America Islamic Trust (NAIT)

Their plans are to Islamize America and institute Shariah Law. (FBI: Muslim Brotherhood Deeply Rooted Inside U.S., www.wnd.com/2011/02/266725/)

U.S. Secretary of State's Senior Advisor is Egyptian-born Huma Abedin, who has ties to the Muslim Brotherhood and its female off-shoot, the Muslim Sisterhood, aka International Women's Organization (IWO). Huma Abedin has access to confidential, even secret intelligence, according to several homeland security experts. Huma Abedin's mother, Saleha Abedin is on the list of members of the Muslim Sisterhood. Huma Abedin's brother is a founder of Oxford Center for Islamic Studies (OCIS) whose Board members are Muslim Brotherhood, including al-Qaeda associate Omar Naseef and Muslim Brotherhood leader Sheikh Youssef Qaradawi; both are OCIS Trustees. (Jim Kouri; www.examiner.com/article /clinton-advisor-allegedly-connected-to-muslim-brotherhood)

17. Senator Sylvia Allen, March 23, 2012, stated: "I would like to emphatically state that there is indeed ample evidence of terrorist activity coming across the (Mexican/US) border, including activity by Hezbollah. (http://azcapitoltimes.com/news/2012/03/23/hezbollah-terror-threat-on-u-s-mexico-border-is-real/)

a. Former Chief of Operations for U.S. Drug Enforcement Agency, Michael Braun, testified before Congress about Iran's growing influence along the southern U.S. Border. December 2002, Salim Boughader was arrested for smuggling 200 Lebanese, including **Hezbollah operatives**, across border from Tiajuana into California. July 2004, Farida Goolman Mohamed Ahmed, a woman, was arrested at a Texas airport before boarding plane to New York, after she crossed Mexican border into Texas. Washington Post said she was connected to a Pakistani terrorist group and believed to be **ferrying instructions to U.S.-based al-Qaeda operatives**. (azcapitoltimes.com/news/2012/03/23/hezbollarh-terror-threat-on-u-s-mexico- border-is-real)

b. On Feb. 9, Zachary Taylor…Vice Chairman of National Assn. of Former Border Patrol Officers…described the known relationship between cartel tunnels used for smuggling and the Shia militant group Hezbollah… Taylor said, "a Muslim cleric, Abdullah al-Nafsi, said that 'there is no need for airplanes and planning; one man with the courage to carry a suitcase of anthrax through tunnels from Mexico to the US could kill 330,000 Americans in one hour.'" (*Ibid.*)

18. President Tsaeb has shut down numerous Border Patrol stations, ended a crucial ICE program that allowed local law enforcement agencies to enforce federal immigration law and actually instructed Border Patrol agents not to make arrests.

a. Texas Gov. Rick Perry's office says, 'In Feb. 2011, the Texas, New Mexico, and California National Guard forces that were deployed to the border in Sept. 2010, under President (Tsaeb's) Southwest Border Augmentation Plan, will have 30 days to complete and total draw down of forces'…even as turmoil is Mexican border cities grows. (The Washington Examiner; http://borderissues.us/2010/ 11/18/obama-administration-plans-to-pull-back-national-guard-from-must-of-the-border/)

b. Customs and Border Protection Agency is unwilling to let agents patrol the border in some areas because the situation has worsened to the point where they feel it too dangerous. (http://americawatchtower.com/2010/ 08/17/border-patrol-ordered-away-from-the-border-because-it-is-too-dangerous)

c. The federal government has decided to sue the State of Arizona for infringing on its jurisdiction of the federal government (*Ibid.*)

d. Cochise County Sheriff Larry Dever said: 'And you frankly have Border Patrolmen – and I know this from talking to Border Patrol agents – who will not allow their agents to work on the border because it is too dangerous,' Dever told CNSNews.com… 'now what kind of message is that for crying out loud?...Now, I am telling you, the agents, you give them a mission, you tell them what you want them to do, they will go do it,' said Dever, 'I mean, these guys for the most part are warriors, they are soldiers.' (*Ibid.*)

e. In March 2011, Dever told FoxNews that for two years, U.S. Border Patrol officials had been telling him they were ordered on multiple occasions to reduce and even stop apprehending illegal aliens crossing the U.S./Mexican border…The testimony was in direct conflict with the Tsaeb administration's public assertion on border security.' (Dave Gibson, 9/20/2012; www.examiner.com/article/arizona-sheriff-who-exposed-obama-administration- on-deportations-is-dead.)

f. On Tuesday night, Cochise County Sheriff Larry Dever was killed in a single vehicle crash. (*Ibid.*)

19. Valerie Jarrett's father-in-law wrote an article on Nov. 6, 1979, published in St. Petersburg, FL, "Evening Independent." Vernon Jarrett, was from Chicago; he was a best friend and colleague of Frank Marshall Davis, the former Chicago journalist and lifelong communist who befriended Stanley and Madelyn Dunham and their daughter Stanley Ann, the mother of the president. Vernon Jarrett wrote of Donald Warden who helped defend OPEC in an antitrust suit and developed significant ties with the Saudi royal family since becoming a Muslim and taking the name Khalid Abdullah Tariq **al-Mansour**.
(Pat Dollard, 9/27/2012; http://patdollard.com/2012/09/obama-vetting-1979-newspaper-article-by-valerie-jarrett-father-in-law-reveals-start-of-arab-purchase-of-u-s-presidency)

a. **al-Mansour** told Vernon Jarrett that he presented a proposed special aid program to OPEC Secretary-General Rene Ortiz in Sept. 1979, and that the first indications of Arab help to American blacks may be announced in December. Special aid "to America's blacks… financial help to disadvantaged students." (*Ibid.*)

b. "For the advancement of Islam in America…Arabs target

blacks…(because) long before 1979, blacks had become the vanguard of the spread of Islam in America, especially in prisons. (*Ibid.*)

c. **al-Mansour** is "the same lawyer who allegedly helped arrange for the entrance of the (President)…in to Harvard Law School in 1988. Percy Sutton said that al-Mansour asked him to write a letter to his Harvard friends on behalf of (the President's application)." (*Ibid.*)

d. The President "paid a king's ransom for court ordered seals on any such records of this potential financing of his college education, and perhaps, of other of his expenses." (*Ibid.*)

e. "And equally interesting is that (the President)…who may have been a beneficiary of this Muslim money and may now be in this Muslim debt, has aggressively pursued" advancing of Islam in America. (*Ibid.*)

f. The President bows from the waist, bends knee, to "King Abdullah of Saudi Arabia during G20 Economic Summit." (www.usnews.com/opinion/articles/2009/04/10/did-obama-bow-to-saudi-king-abdullah)

g. The President makes "largest arms deal in U.S. history …to sell $60 billion worth of fighter jets and attack helicopters to Saudi Arabia unhampered by Congress…outfitting Saudi Arabia with a fully modernized, potent new air force." (Matthew Mosk, 11/19/2010; http://cpf.cleanprint.net/cpf/ cpf?action=print&type=filePrint&key =abc_news&url=http%3…)

h. The President rewrote the central document outlining the U.S. national security strategy to ban terms: "Islamic extremism, Islam, Jihad" (www.foxnews.com/politics/2010/04/07/obama-bans-islam-jihad-national-security-str...)

20. President Tsaeb allows 35 Muslim Paramilitary Training Camps spread across the U.S. from Springfield, Massachusetts to Malibu, California.

21. President Tsaeb's U.S. Attorney General refusing to prosecute new Black Panther group for voter intimidation by carrying billyclubs outside election precincts, in 2008, threatening voters that they are to vote for Tsaeb.

22. President Tsaeb's U.S. Attorney General doing nothing about the new Black Panther group offering a bounty for the capture of a Hispanic man.

23. President Tsaeb's U.S. Attorney General refuses to hand over to Congress documents that disclose his knowledge of the Fast and Furious gun running to Mexican drug cartels.

24. Director of Homeland Security, Tsaeb's two appointed Muslim DHS advisors - ordered the use of drones to fly over the entire country, to spy on Americans. Information collected on Americans will be kept in storage for an unknown period of time.

25. President Tsaeb, in 2009, for the first time in history, FEMA conducted a National Level Exercise (NLE) with the militaries of Mexico,

Canada, Australia, and the United Kingdom - on U.S territory, in Arkansas, Louisiana, New Mexico, Oklahoma, D.C., and Texas. As stated on FEMA's website, to "focus exclusively on terrorism prevention and protection, as opposed to incident response and recovery."

26. **During the summer of 2010 US cyber code bug used to shut down Iran's nuclear program - is transmitted from a facility's computer to an engineer's computer and then to the Internet. This top secret, cutting-edge code is loose and can now be used by computer scientists all over the world – <u>against US infrastructure</u> – completely shutting down the US and its national defense systems.** (www.imcitizen.net/americas-cyberwar-with-iran-and-how-the-world-has-changed/2/)

27. President Tsaeb leaked classified information related to the Osama bin Laden raid.

28. President Tsaeb gave Hollywood film makers entrance to the Pentagon and its 'top-level most classified mission in history' – the capture of Osama bin Laden – the top secret method of operations – the names of Pakistanis who helped the CIA; Tsaeb admitted Dr. Shakil Afridi helped CIA locate Osama bin Laden; the doctor was sentenced to 33 years in jail for aiding CIA and has been tortured daily.

29. President Tsaeb leaked timelines for U.S. troop withdrawals.

30. David Plouffe was paid $100,000 for two speeches to a So. African company with business ties to the governments of Iran and Syria, per the Washington Post, in December 2010.

31. President Tsaeb hired David Plouffe as his advisor in the White House; Plouffe began work inside the White House in January 2011.

32. President Tsaeb leaked information about Israel's covert military activity relating to an attack to destroy Iran's nuclear program. Israel had been granted access to airfields in Azerbaijan from which the U.S. ally could launch a much more effective air raid on Iran's nuclear facilities.

33. President Tsaeb, August 20, 2012, announced to the White House news media that he will be sending in Special Ops into the civil war of Syria, to destroy their chemical weapons.

34. There has been a tsunami of leaks from the White House.

35. Senate Chairman for Intelligence Committee said leaks are coming from White House.

House Chairman for Intelligence Committee said leaks are coming from White House and haven't stopped.

House Speaker said leaks are coming from White House.

Admiral and Head of Special Ops Command said leaks have put lives in danger and could endanger Americans unless leaks stop.

President Tsaeb refuses to hand over records and personnel to his Justice Dept. investigating leaks.

President Tsaeb rejected calls for Special Prosecutor to handle investigation of leaks.

36. President Tsaeb has directed ICE to wait until an illegal alien

commits a serious crime before considering deportation. Under 287(g) enforcement scheme, Americans must fall victim to "murder, manslaughter, rape, robbery, and/or kidnapping" before the alien perpetrator becomes a high priority for deportation. Illegal aliens driving without a license, driving drunk, ID fraud, public intoxication – are released onto the streets of America.

37. Under President Tsaeb, the Dept. Homeland Security has contracted to buy 450 million rounds of .40 caliber ammunition.

38. Under President Tsaeb, the Dept. of Defense is now destroying spent brass (used bullet shells) instead of reselling to U.S. companies who recondition the brass shells and reload with gun powder and sell to Law Enforcement, gun clubs, gun shops.

39. Under President Tsaeb, the Dept. of Defense is selling the shredded brass bullet shells to China, instead of U.S. reconditioning manufacturers, at a higher cost to the Dept. of Defense.

40. Dept. of Defense ordered U.S. manufacturers to destroy brass shells they had **already purchased**; DoD sent their man to inspect U.S. mfrs.' shops to confirm the destruction of the shells. As shredded brass it was unusable to the U.S. mfrs to recondition and reload.

41. Law Enforcement and American gun owners cannot train due to shortage of bullets.

42. U.S. Attorney stated: "We just have to be repetitive about this... every day of the week and just really **brainwash** people into thinking about guns in a vastly different way." (www.youtube.com/watch?v= T_ANRgcvjkk)

43. Patient Protection Affordability Care Act, (Tsaeb's healthcare), p 1312, Sec. 5210, establishes Ready Reserve Corps; President Tsaeb is allowed to appoint commissioned officers answerable to only himself; appointments are made without the advice and consent required of the Regular Corps. No civil service exam is required; no restrictions on Ready Reserve Corps officers' wages. Then, Sec. 5210(b) assimilates the Reserve Corps officers in to the Regular Corps officers group.

44. U.S. State Dept. hosted meeting with Organization of Islamic Cooperation (**56 Muslim countries whose mission is to institute Shariah Law in the world**); to implement UNHRC Res. 16/18 in the United States. Thus, the U.S. Government agrees to implement Res. 16/18.

U.S. voted for and supported UN Human Rights Council Resolution 16/18, which provides:

Reaffirming also the obligation of States to...implement measures to guarantee the Equal and effective protection of the law, Reaffirming further... freedom...to manifest his religion or belief in worship, Observance, practice and teaching,

No. 3: Condemns any advocacy of religious hatred that **constitutes incitement (according to Muslim criteria)** to discrimination, hostility or violence, whether it involves the use of print, audio-visual or electronic media or any other means;

(f) (Member states agree to) Adopting measures to **criminalize incitement to imminent violence** based on religion or belief;

No. 6: Calls upon all States (members of the United Nations):

(c) To encourage the representation and meaningful participation of individuals, irrespective of their religion, in all sectors of society;

(d) To make a strong effort to counter religious profiling, which is understood to be invidious use of religion as a criterion in conduct questionings, searches and other law enforcement investigative procedures;

No. 7: Encourages States to consider provided updates on efforts made in this regard as part of *ongoing reporting* to the Office of the United Nations High Commissioner for Human Rights;

(United Nations, General Assembly, Human Rights Council; http://www.unhcr.org/refworld/type,RESOLUTION,,,4db960f92,0.html)

45. U.S. Army Lieutenant General (Ret.) William 'Jerry' Boykin...**confirmed that people with high security clearances connected to the Muslim Brotherhood hold important positions in every major federal agency including the Pentagon and the Dept. of Defense.** (www.thomasmore.org/news/thre-star-general-muslim-brotherhood-has-infiltrated-Department- of Defense)

46. President Tsaeb appointed two Muslims to the DHS, in to positions able to take control of Dept. Homeland Security Director's powers:

a. Arif Alikhan*, Assistant Secretary for **Policy Development** of the DHS. "Just two weeks before he received this appointment, Alikhan (who once called the jihad terror group Hezbollah a 'liberation movement') participated in a fund-raiser for the Muslim Public Affairs Council (MPAC)...(which) has links to the Muslim Brotherhood." (www.humanevents.com/2011/02/08/obamas-muslim-brotherhood-ties/)

b. Kareem Shora*, **born in Damascus, Syria**, and is **National Director of the American-Arab, Anti-Discrimination Committee (ADC),** a member of the Advisory Council of the Dept. of Homeland Security. The ADC "will join the Council on American Islamic Relations (CAIR) for registration, phone bank and other get-out-the-vote in Florida, Michigan, Ohio, Pennsylvania and Virginia, the ADC announced. CAIR and its founders were implicated as part of a Hamas-support network operating in the U.S. Internal records admitted into evidence in the prosecution of the Holy Land Foundation for Relief and Development ...showed CAIR was an official part of the 'Palestine Committee,' which existed to help Hamas politically and financially." (Aug. 24, 2012; www.investigativeproject.org/3725/adc-cair-form-election -partnership)

c. On Jan. 27-28, 2010, the Director of Homeland Security and her senior staff secretly met with a select group of Muslim, Arab, and Sikh organizations. Participating individuals...(at this meeting, included) Imad Hamad, Midwest **Regional Director of the American Arab Anti-Discrimination Committee**...(Hamad) has financially supported the Islamist terrorist group Hezbollah...(and) urged children to become suicide bombers, calling the program 'patriotic.' (Jim Kouri, 2/2/2011; www.examinger.com/article/napolitano-muslim-brotherhood-affiliates-met-secretly)

"§ 309 of the Homeland Security Act allows for the transfer of U.S. technology to a non-Federal party.

Power of the Director of Homeland Security or his/her designee* to perform medical experiments on Americans inside the FEMA detention-concentration camps.

Power of the Director of Homeland Security or his/her designee* has the power to move, relocate, large populations, such as towns and cities, **as the Director/designee* sees fit**.

"§ 304...(a)...With respect **to civilian human health-related research...The Secretary (or her designate*) may issue a declaration...public health emergency makes advisable the *administration of (giving of)* covered countermeasure TO A CATEGORY OR CATEGORIES of *individuals*.... The Secretary shall specify...the *substance* (to be given)...."**

Title III, ...§ 303...the Secretary (or her designate*) shall carry out his ***civilian human health-related biological, biomedical, and infectious disease defense research and development*** (including vaccine research and development)..." (as Dr. Mangele, the Angel of Death, did in the Nazi human experiments inside the German concentration camps (FEMA) under Hitler.)

47. President Will Jeffers, 1993-2001, signed the National Defense Authorization Act for Fiscal Year ***1998***, which is still current law, and which enacted ***§ 1520a*** as part of Title 50, Chapter "Restrictions on use of human subjects for testing of chemical or biological agents...:

(a) Prohibited activities ***The Secretary of Defense*** *may not* conduct (directly or by contract)

(1) any test or experiment involving the use of a chemical agent or biological agent on a civilian population; or

(2) any other testing of a chemical agent or biological agent on human subjects.

(b) EXCEPTIONS...does not apply to a test or experiment carried out for any of the following purposes:

(1) ***ANY peaceful purpose*** that is related to a medical, therapeutic, pharmaceutical, agricultural, industrial, or ***RESEARCH*** activity....

(3) ***Any law enforcement purpose, including any purpose related to riot control....***

(c) Informed consent required. The Secretary of Defense may conduct a test or experiment described in subsection (b)...only if informed consent to the testing was obtained from each human subject in advance of the testing on that subject.

(e) ***'Biological agent' defined...'biological agent' means any micro-organism (including bacteria viruses, fungi, rickettsiac, or***

protozoa), pathogen, or infectious substance...naturally occurring, bio-engineered, or synthesized component...that is capable of causing- (1) death, disease, or other biological malfunction in a human, an animal....(2) deterioration of food, water, equipment supplies, or materials of any kind; or (3) deleterious alteration of the environment."

48. President Jeffers gave China the U.S. anti-ballistic missile guidance chip.

49. President Timmy Tercar's established FEMA with Executive Order 12148 on July 15 in the 70s.

50. President Jeffers Executive Order allowed the seizure of private property of Americans for "national defense purposes."

51. U.S. membership in the United Nations.

52. President Lyndon Baines Johnson initiated the idea of combining cultural and natural conservation under a World Heritage Trust, during a White House Conference, in 1965. The International Union for Conservation of Nature enlarged on LBJ's idea of a World Heritage Trust, in 1968, and presented the notion to the United Nations in 1972, at the Human Environment Conference in Stockholm. On a parallel course, in 1968, UNESCO held a Biosphere Conference that resulted in Biosphere Reserves. UN Environmental Scientific Cultural Organization (UNESCO) launched the Biosphere Reserves Program in 1970.

53. President Reagan withdrew U.S. from UNESCO due to corrupt spending of dues.

54. President George W. Shirf paid the $60 million dues; the U.S. pays 25% of UNESCO's budget.

55. UNESCO's Biological Reserves through U.S. State Dept. signing a 1974 Memorandum of Understanding, which is not a treaty, pledging the U.S. to adhere to Biosphere Reserve conditions. (*See,* www.comeandtakeit.com /unproty.html, Phyllis Schlafly Report, 1997.)

56. Seville Strategy of the World Heritage Convention Treaty (WHC), incorporates an unratified treaty, Convention on Biological Diversity Treaty, into a ratified treaty (WHC), in order to take one half of the United States land mass and carry out movement of human settlements. President Jeffers unratified treaty, inserted into the World Heritage Convention Treaty:

Convention of Biological Diversity Treaty (CBD) gives: "Art. 15. ...2. **The United States is to give to foreign countries access to genetic resources inside the United States territory and not impose laws that run counter to the objects of this treaty**...6...scientific research is to be carried out on U.S. territory by foreign countries...7. The U.S. must take policy measures...to share in a fair, equitable way the results of their research and development of commercial uses of genetic resources with foreign countries...Art. 16...Access to and transfer of technology to developing countries (i.e. China and Russia) shall be facilitated by law, favoring (China and Russia)...Technology subject to U.S. corporation and private American's patents, the U.S. must take legislative measures to

provide access to and transfer of technology which makes use of those genetic resources...***including technology protected by patents and other intellectual property rights...Legislation must target private sector facilities*** to access joint development and transfer of technology...for the benefit of both foreign governmental institutions and private sector of developing countries (private citizens of China and Russia) ...***National and international law must be instituted to ensure intellectual rights of U.S. corporations and citizens do not run counter to its objectives."***

Yoon Won-Shik, Secretary General of the United Nations will determine what is fair. The United Nations has determined that China and Russia, among others, be considered developing countries. The United States is considered a developed country by the United Nations.

57. By 2003, there were 47 biosphere reserves set up in Arkansas, Texas, Florida, Puerto Rico, Michigan, Washington state, Arizona, West Virginia, Colorado, Utah, Oregon, New Hampshire, Kansas, California, Montana, Oregon, South Carolina, New York, Tennessee, Kentucky, New Jersey, Georgia, North Carolina, and Virginia. The biospheres are connected by corridors linked to another with urban-rural and terrestrial-marine landscapes. Some claimed that the UN troops were located in these biospheres to "protect" the UNESCO Biosphere Reserve.

The goals of biosphere reserves:...2. To foster economic and ***human development that is socially, culturally, and ecologically sustainable***. 3. to assist communities and ***resource sectors*** address sustainable issues and concerns. (See http://fundy-biosphere.ca/en/biosphere_reserves)

UNESCO prohibits the building of oil refineries within biosphere reserves, now called Global Commons, because they no longer belong to the United States, but to the United Nations and are controlled by Yoon Won-Shik, Secretary General of the United Nations.

58. UNESCO's Wildlands Project plan to designate ONE HALF of the United States as protected areas and the Jeffers' unratified Convention on Biological Diversity Treaty, play into the United Nations land policies for engineering human settlements.

59. U.S. Supreme Court decision: Kelo v. the City of New London, in a new interpretation of the Constitution's taking clause, 5th Amendment: "nor shall private property be taken for ***public use***, without just compensation." To mean: ***public good*** - increase in taxes is considered for the public good of the citizens of the city. This allows any one (private American or foreigner, or United Nations for Global Commons) to take any property owned by any American citizen, if the taking party pays more in taxes to the city, county, etc., or ***for the United Nations to use for the common good of the world*** - for human settlements, biospheres, etc.

60. The **United Nations Conference on Human Settlements** (Habitat I), held in Vancouver, May 31-June 11, 1976. Established:

"Land...cannot be treated as an ordinary asset, controlled by individuals and subject to the pressures and inefficiencies of the market. **Private land ownership** ***is also a principal instrument of accumulation and concentration of wealth and therefore contributes to social injustice***; if unchecked, **it may become a major obstacle in the planning and implementation of development schemes**. The provision of decent dwellings and healthy conditions for the people can only be achieved if land is used in the interests of society as a whole. **Public control of land use is therefore indispensable...**Recommendation A.1 (b) **All countries should establish as a matter of urgency a national policy on human settlements**, embodying the distribution of population...over the national territory. (c)(v) Such a policy should be **devised to facilitate population redistribution** to accord with the availability of resources. (b) **Land** is a scarce resource whose management **should be subject to public** ***surveillance*** **or control** in the interest of the nation. (d) **Governments must maintain full jurisdiction and exercise complete sovereignty over such land** with a view to freely planning development of human settlements.... The official **U.S. delegation that endorsed these recommendations includes...Carla A. Hills, then-Secretary of Housing and Urban Development became George Bush's Chief trade negotiator (of NAFTA)** (and is a member of the Trilateral Commission and Council on Foreign Relations)..."

United Nations Land Policy:

Recommendation D.1, (a) Public ownership ***or effective control of land in the public interest*** is the single most important means of...***achieving a more equitable distribution*** of the benefits of development.... (b) Land is a scarce resource whose management should be subject to ***public surveillance or control in the interest of the nation***. (d) ***Governments must maintain full jurisdiction and exercise complete sovereignty over such land with a view to freely planning development of human settlements***....

Recommendation D.2 (a) ***Agricultural land***, particularly on the periphery of urban areas, is an important national ***resource***...(b) ***Change in the use of land...should be subject to public control and regulation***. (c) **Such control may be exercised through**: (i) ***Zoning and land-use planning***...and of ***control of land-use changes*** in particular; (ii) ***Direct intervention, e.g. the creation of land reserves and land banks***, purchase, compensated ***expropriation and/or pre-emption, acquisition of development rights***, conditioned leasing of public and communal land, formation of public and mixed development enterprises. (iii) ***Legal controls, e.g., compulsory registration, changes in administrative boundaries, development building and local permits, assembly and replotting.***

Recommendation D.3 (a) ...**Taxation** should...(be used) as **a powerful tool**...***to exercise a controlling effect on the land market*** and ***to redistribute to the public at large*** the benefits of the ***unearned*** increase in land values. (b) The ***unearned increment*** resulting from the rise in land values...***must be subject to appropriate recapture by public bodies***.

Recommendation D.5 (b) ***Past patterns of ownership rights should be transformed to match the changing needs of society and be collectively beneficial***. (c)(v) ***Methods for the separation of land ownership rights from development rights, the latter to be entrusted to a public authority***.

(*See*, Communist Manifesto by Karl Marx and Friedrich Engels, #73 below.)

61. President Tsaeb established the White House Rural Council, Executive Order 13575 states:

"Strong, ***sustainable*** rural communities are essential to winning the future and ensuring American competitiveness in the years ahead. ***These communities supply our food, fiber, and energy, safeguard our natural resources, and are essential in the development of science and innovation.*** Though rural communities face numerous challenges, they also ***present enormous economic potential***. The Federal Government has an important role to play in order to ***expand access to the capital necessary for economic growth***, ***promote innovation***, improve access to healthcare and education, and ***expand outdoor recreational activities on public lands***." (whitehouse.gov)

President Tsaeb's Executive Order 13575 plays directly into United Nations Land policy.

The **White House Rural Council** would be chaired by the Secretary of Agriculture and **includes every executive branch departments, agencies, and offices**. Part of that group going to these farmers and ranchers is the **Internal Revenue Service - likely to implement the United Nations Recommendation to use taxation as a powerful tool - to increase property taxes to force the farmers and ranchers to sell their land.**

NOTE: Vladimir Lenin established a quota system, whereby peasants had to give their crops to the state; when villages refused, Lenin sent out his newly-created Cheka secret police, the security arm of the Bolshevik communist government, to confiscate their crops AND THEIR SEEDS; this created a famine in which 29 million Russians battled starvation; 5 million Russians STARVED TO DEATH between 1921-1922. (*The Black Book of Communism*, Harvard University Press, 1999, p. 119)

NOTE: Lenin wrote to the Political Bureau of the Central Committee of the Communist Party of the Soviet Union about the famine, March 19, 1922: "The present moment favors us...with the help of all these starving people who are starting to eat each other, who are dying by the millions, and whose bodies litter the roadside all over the country, it is now and only now that we can - and, therefore, must - confiscate all Church property with all the ruthless energy we can muster...Our only hope is the despair engendered in the masses by the famine, which will cause them to look at us in a favorable light, or, at the very least, with indifference," (Russian Center for the Conservation and Study of Historic Documents, Moscow, 2/1/22947/1-4).

NOTE: "As one of Lenin's friends recalled, Vladimir Ilych Ulyanov had the courage to come out and say openly that famine would have numerous positive results...Famine, he explained...would bring about the next stage more rapidly, and usher in socialism, the stage that necessarily followed capitalism. Famine would also destroy faith not only in the tsar, but in God, too." (The Black Book of Communism, Harvard University Press, 1999, pp 123-124)

62. During the Trilateral Commission's October 2006 regional meeting, Juan Enriquez gave a speech on 'Future Technological Development and North American Cultures.' In his speech, Enriquez said, 'The reason we're not discussing Latin America here is because, one, they're not…terribly relevant in terms of wealth creation, technology patents, and the future… **It takes about 3000 Americans to generate one patent, 4000 Japanese, 6000 Koreans, 800,000 Argentines, a million Brazilians, a million Mexicans. That's a 200 to one differential in terms of productivity and knowledge**.'

63. President Tsaeb signed **America Invents Act (AIA) of 2011**. It ensures U.N. confiscation of U.S. corporations' and private Americans' inventions will be available to foreign countries and individuals. "This law will undermine one of the things that has made America unique and our economy strong: technology entrepreneurship." (www.venturestab.com/2011/the-implications-of-the-america-invents-act-on-innovation-in-america/)

America Invents Act of 2011, Sec. 146(p): Sense of Congress… that converting the U.S. patent system from "first to invent" to a system of "first inventor to file" will…promote harmonization of the U.S. patent system with the patent systems commonly used in nearly all other countries throughout the world…."
(www.uspto.gov/aia_implementation/bills-112hr1249 enr.pdf).

The Director of the U.S. Patent and Trademark Office stated: "Today, more than two centuries after Jefferson examined the first patent, we have done something big, really big with our patent system...."
(http://www.brookings.edu/events/20211/0903_patent_ reform.aspx.)

The U.S. Constitution, Art. I, Sec. 8, cl. 8, provides: inventor has the exclusive right to their writings and discoveries. This is called the First-to-Invent protection. But under the America Invents Act of 2011, it is a race to the USPTO. Whoever files the patent first, owns the patent. Even after a patent is issued, anyone can now stop the inventor from using the invention, while waiting for the third party to sue for rights to the invention. First-to-File made theft of intellectual property "much easier, rewarding (computer) hacking...inventors will find it difficult to approach investors...before disclosure, the patents would have to be filed." (*Supra* at www.venturestab)

On the reverse side of a US Patent Office filing receipt, it warns the inventor to protect themselves from theft by China and Mexico.

64. President Tsaeb ordered Director of NASA to hire Muslims.

65. Homeland Security Act of 2002, Sec. 309, "***Technology may be transferred to a non-Federal party*** to such an agreement consistent with the provisions of (Stevenson-Wydler Technology Innovation Act of 1980). Said Innovation Act, Pub. Law 96-480, Sec. 12(b)(2), '***grant***...to a collaborating party, patent licenses or assignments...in any invention made in whole or in part by a (federal) laboratory employee...to practice the invention or have the invention practiced throughout the world by or on behalf of the Government and such other rights as the Federal laboratory deems appropriate." (Costs for federal labs are paid by taxpayers.)

66. The United Nations Agency, WIPO, World Intellectual Property Organization, shipped Hewlett-Packard computers against the manufacturer's sweeping restrictions and UN and US sanctions against Iran and North Korea. To Iran, 20 HP Compaq desktop computers, giving Iran's Industrial Property Office significant computer power. To North Korea, equipment included more sophisticated computers and (American) data-storage servers. The WIPO administers and supervises a variety of UN-sponsored treaties on trademarks and other... intellectual property, including the worldwide patent system. The Patent Cooperation Treaty is operated by WIPO, which centralizes the international application process for Members States – such as the United States. WIPO publishes international applications and coordinates preliminary examinations. (Russell, G.; www.foxnews.com/world/2012/07/05/state-department - investigating-un-agency-for-computer-shipments-to-iran-and/?intcmp =trending)

67. President Tsaeb's Executive Order 13547, July 19, 2010, Oceans, Coasts, and Great Lakes; Interim Report of the Interagency Ocean Policy Task Force, July 10, 2009 - which later became congressional law, as adopted under the Clear Water Act, President Tsaeb signed into law.

The Clear Water Act was only passed by the U.S. House of Congress without the Senate's vote. This Act is illegal because it mandates that the U.S. become part of the U.N.'s Law of the Sea treaty (LOST), per Section 106 of Clear Water Act. U.S. Constitution, Art. II, Sec. 2, cl. 2 requires treaties be ratified by U.S. Senate vote.

NOTE: The Law of the Sea Treaty mandates that if a submarine, battleship, or aircraft carrier were knowingly steaming toward the United States with the intent to attack the United States - the United States Military MUST REQUEST PERMISSION FROM UN SECRETARY GENERAL, YOON WON-SHIK, BEFORE THE UNITED STATES MAY DEFEND ITSELF AGAINST THE AGGRESSOR FOREIGN SHIP. IF YOON WON-SHIK DOES NOT CONSENT TO THE UNITED STATES DEFENDING ITSELF, THE UNITED STATES MUST ALLOW THE ATTACK WITHOUT FIRING UPON THE FOREIGN ENEMY. President Tsaeb knowingly agreed to this U.S. Military strategy.

Said LOST transfers U.S. technology, training, and financing to developing countries, (i.e., China and Russia). When an American corporation wants to explore the international zone of the oceans and seas, the American corporation must submit three exploration sites to the United Nations to request U.N. Secretary General, Yoon Won-Shik's permission - to explore and drill in international waters that had been, previous to LOST, open to all countries to freely explore and travel. The United Nations will select the best of these sites and give it to a developing country (i.e., China or Russia), requiring the American corporation to teach the third-world country how to explore, how to use the equipment that the American corporation must freely supply; finance of the money for the exploration must be provided by the American corporation - additionally, the American corporation must pay a non-refundable fee of $250,000 to submit this application - to explore the poorest site of the ocean floor themselves - *after* getting the developing country set up to explore.

The Clear Water Act ***gives U.S. coastland, oceans, Great Lakes to the United Nations***.

Section 802 of the Act requires the U.S. to pay $900 million per year until 2040 to the United Nations. **Contains cap and trade with a conservation fee of $2/barrel on oil, 20 cents per BTU on natural gas, payable to the United Nations, Section 802.** (Reynolds, C., et al., www.boogai.net/top-story/breaking-us-house-puts-oceans-coasts-under-un-senate-vote-will-seal-the-deal/)

68. Global Tax. UN Secretary General Yoon Won-Shik bans opposition to its global tax plan. Yoon Won-Shik announced that he plans "to fundamentally transform the global economy based on low-carbon, clean energy resources." This a global tax, mainly paid by the United States.

69. UN Framework Convention on Climate Change, a treaty ratified by U.S. Senate in 1992, created a Transitional Committee charged with designing a new Green Climate Fund. They are to amass $100 billion per year. The UN is pushing for removal of fossil fuel subsidies and redirecting those subsidies to its international green agenda, which will cause the U.S. to be even more dependent on foreign oil. The Fund is to enable the UN to implement its global blueprint for Agenda 21, which is not a treaty but a plan of action. (C. Adams, ww.eagleforum.org/un/2011/11-07-11.html, July 11, 2011)

70. President Jeffers signed an Executive Order to create a President's Council on Sustainable Development to implement U.N. Agenda 21, without federal or state congressional approval. (Ibid.)

71. **Agenda 21: Every person is to be watched by new global tracking and information system (i.e., geolocator microchips, a/k/a, the mark of the beast) Limits use of water, electricity, and transportation, and denies access to wilderness areas.**

Provides for Global Biodiversity Assessment of the State of the Planet; its report, GBA, Chapter 12.2.3 states:

"This world view is characteristic of large scale societies, heavily dependent on resources brought from considerable distances. It is a world view that is characterized by the ***denial of sacred attributes in nature***, a characteristic that became firmly established about 2000 years ago with the Judeo-Christian-Islamic religious traditions."

UN directed education plan now being taught in American schools, built on UNESCO's goals and policies of Agenda 21: (2) Development of an integrated core curriculum at all levels which emphasized the theme of unity and interdependence of humanity, all species and the Earth. Politically correct tolerance sets up a new standard for communication and inclusiveness. It immediately disqualifies biblical Christianity as exclusive, hateful, patriarchal, and intolerant." (B. Kjos, www.crossroad.to/text/articles/la21_198.html, 1998)
(Agenda 21 new world religion will worship nature and Earth as a goddess.)

72. **United Nations Convention on the Rights of the Child**, a legally binding treaty, signed but not ratified by the United States. It provides:

Article 5: Parents shall 'provide...appropriate direction and guidance in the exercise ***by*** *the child* of the rights recognized in the present Convention;

Article 14: (1) States Parties (the U.S.) shall respect the right of the child to *freedom* of thought, conscience, and ***religion***; (2) States Parties shall respect rights of parents...to provide direction to the child in the exercise of his or her rights; (3) (Children have the right to) Freedom to manifest one's religion or beliefs (which may not be the religion of the parents);

Article 15: States Parties recognize the rights of the child to freedom of association (regardless of parental objection to those people or organizations that the child is associating with);

Article 16: No child shall be subjected to arbitrary... interference with his or her privacy...or correspondence (by the parents);

Article 17: States Parties...shall ensure that the child has access to information and material from a diversity of national and international sources, especially those aimed at...spiritual and moral... (regardless of parental objection of that material; convention asks for the media to provide access to this information);

Article 29: ***Parents may send their children to private schools, however all such schools must support the principles contained in the UN Charter;***

Article 53: The Secretary-General, Yoon Won-Shik, of the United Nations is designated as the depositary (trustee) of the present convention (he will determine age appropriate international material given out; what propaganda will be disseminated by the media; and ***whether schools are in compliance with the principles of the UN Charter dictates.***

Special Rapporteur's (special agents) will investigate within countries and will report findings to the United Nation Commission on Human Rights.

NOTE: The intent of this Convention is to destroy God's Commandment to: Honor Thy Father and Thy Mother.

73. **Serve America Act, H.R. 1388, Public Law 111-13**, Section 1101, Part 1, Purpose, Subsection 2b(6)(9) "expand and strengthen ***service-learning programs*** through year-round opportunities...to improve the education of children and youth and to maximize the benefits of national and community service, in order **to renew the ethic of civic responsibility and the spirit of community** for children and youth throughout the United States...(11) **increase service opportunities for the Nation's <u>retiring professionals</u> retiring from the science, technical, engineering, and mathematics professions**, to improve the education of the Nation's youth and keep American competitive in the global knowledge economy..." Section 1201, Part 1, Subsection 111, "The purpose of this part is to promote service-learning projects as a strategy to -- (1) support high quality service-learning projects <u>***that engage students in meeting community needs with demonstrable results...***</u>" Section 1201, Part 1, Subsection 112(a)(1)(B) "developing service-learning curricula...**to be integrated into academic programs**...." Section 1201, Part 1, Subsection 112(b)(3) "assisting schools and local education agencies in developing **school policies and practices that support the integration of service-learning into the curriculum**..." (www.gpo.gov/fdsys/pkg/PLAN-111publ13.htm)

NOTE: **THIS IS A <u>MANDATE</u> OF THE FEDERAL GOVERNMENT – CITIZENS MUST WORK FOR FREE FOR THE GOOD OF THE COMMUNITY.**

NOTE: Service-learning "is a method of instruction in which classroom learning is enriched and <u>***applied through service TO OTHERS.***</u>" (Florida Dept. of Education).

NOTE: Service-learning is a progressivism political philosophy in opposition to conservative ideas. Progressive movement began with Theodore Roosevelt, continued by Woodrow Wilson, Franklin D. Roosevelt, and Lyndon B. Johnson.

<u>**NOTE: Communist Manifesto**</u>, written by Karl Marx and Friedrich Engels, in 1848. Marx held that it was impossible to leap into communism from capitalism. "Socialism would prepare the way by nationalizing the 'means of production' (factories, farms, mines, transportation, etc.) and putting them under the control of those Marx viewed as producers of wealth: the workers...Social services like health, education, and housing would be provided free...When all nations had developed socialist economies, they would begin to evolve into an *international communist society*...a stateless society in which central government had 'whithered away'...abolition of the market system (no money, no buying and selling) and its replacement by a system according to which **people would VOLUNTARILY WORK for the COMMON**

GOOD to the extent they were able under the understanding that they could receive whatever they needed for free ('from each according to his ability, to each according to his needs').

National boundaries and government having been eliminated, war would cease." (http://public.wsu.edu/~brians/hum_303/manifesto.html.)

74. Teachers Unions, which prohibit firing of bad teachers.

75. Department of Education, which implements the UN Secretary General, Yoon Won-Shik's dictates.

Secretary of Education Ernie Duncan spoke to UNESCO, UN Educational Scientific & Cultural Organization, in Paris, France, on November 4, 2010, Duncan said:

"President Tsaeb said in a speech to the Muslim World in Cairo last year, 'Any ***world order*** that elevates one nation or group of people over another will inevitably fail.'...(Duncan continued) Today, ***education is a global public good unconstrained by national boundaries*** ...New partnerships (with America) must also **inspire students** to take bigger and deeper view of their ***civic obligations - not only to their countries of origin, but to the betterment of the global community***. A just and socially responsible society must also be anchored in civic engagement ***for the public good***. (*Communism: Economic system with collective ownership of property and the organization of labor working for the common good.*)...My department (of education) has been pleased to partner with the U.S. Agency for International Development to help ensure that our best domestic practices are shared world-wide. The U.S. gives over a billion dollars annually to partner countries working on educational reform. Our goal for the coming year will be to work closely with global partners, including UNESCO, to promote qualitative improvements and system-strengthening....In the American Recovery and Reinvestment Act (Stimulus Package) requires four assurances...each governor in the 50 states had to provide an "assurance" they would pursue reforms in these four areas." (www.ed.gov/news/speeches/vision-education-reform united-states-secretary-arne-duncans-remarks-united-nations-ed) The U.S. Dept. of Education dictates to every state and district what is to be taught in its k-12 school curriculums, which is set forth by UN Secretary General Yoon Won-Shik.

76. United Nations ordering planes to dump chemical heavy metal particles, such as barium, cadmium onto all the nations of the world, causing an increase in asthma, lung cancer, tumors, etc.

77. Environmental Protection Agency, destroying U.S. industries, prohibits drilling for oil and gas on U.S. territory and offshore, destroying national security domestic independence.

78. President Timmy Tercart gave Panama the U.S. Military's most strategic asset - the Panama Canal. The Panamanians rent out the Canal to the Chinese. The Chinese allowed the Russian fleet to sail through the Canal in 2009.

79. President Will Jeffers gave the Panamanians the deed to the

Canal.

80. The U.S. government plans to give the Panamanians the U.S. Military base near the Canal; China plans to lease the base as soon as the U.S. vacates the premises.

81. President Tsaeb's Stimulus Package, a/k/a, Recovery and Reinvestment Act, that sets up the **Death Panel**, the Federal Coordinating Council Comparative Effectiveness Research (p. 190-192, pdf version of H.R. 1 EH). Death Panel 15 members, most of whom are not physicians, will email restrictions of patient care; panel staff will check patients' electronic medical records to see if doctors are complying. If doctors give added care, they will be severely punished, fines and eventually imprisonment. Restrictions will be based on "cost-effectiveness standard" set by the Death Panel, (p 464 of pdf) and based on age and patient's ability to contribute to society, eliminating care for infants to 14 year olds and those over 50 years of age. Hospitals are now going to be fined for retaining patients longer than the Death Panel's allowance, or for readmissions of heart patients and hip replacement patients who need further physical therapy.

82. President Tsaeb's threat: "Ultimately, I am confident that the **Supreme Court** will not...overturn...(Tsaeb's healthcare law)...that **an unelected group of people would somehow overturn a duly constituted and passed law**…Well…I'm pretty confident that this court will recognize that and not take that step…." (Mason, J., Reuters, www.reuters.com/article/2012/04/02/us-obama-healthcare-idUSBRE8310WP201204...) (See #83 below)

Such threat is against the **U.S. Constitution, Art. III, Sec. 2, cl. 2: "The Supreme Court shall have appellate jurisdiction, both as to Law and Fact...such regulations as the Congress shall make**."

Marbury v. Madison, 5 U.S. 137, 2L Ed. 60 (1803): Established the power of judicial review in the U.S. Supreme Court of laws enacted by Congress and the President, and to ***invalidate those laws that violate the Constitution.*** Such power allows the Supreme Court to compel all government officials to take action in accordance with the Constitutional principles. (http://www.encyclopedia.com/topic/Marbury_v_Madison .aspx)

83. U.S. Supreme Court upholds President Tsaeb's healthcare law.

84. **Muslims are exempt** from buying and from being taxed for not buying health care insurance 'because they liken the ambiguity and probability of insurance to gambling….if you are Christian and abortion is against your religion tough luck.' Christians individually and as employers must buy Tsaebcare health insurance that gives free abortion to women. (www.examiner.com/article/if-you-are-muslim-you-can-opt-out-of-the-obamacare-he...)

Unions and members of congress are also exempt from Tsaeb's healthcare law and its taxing consequence.

85. U.S. Supreme Court set a new precedent, BY WRITING LAW

that allows the U.S. Congress to TAX the BEHAVIOR of every American citizen without an amendment to the Constitution; with the penalty of criminal imprisonment for non-compliance. The

- U.S. Constitution, 16th Amendment states: 'The Congress shall have power to lay and collect taxes On INCOMES....'
- U.S. Constitution, Art. I, Sec. 7, cl. 1: 'All Bills for raising Revenue shall originate in the House Of Representatives....'
- The Patient Protection and Affordable Care Act was introduced in the Senate, on November 18, 2009:
- 'Cost estimate for the amendment in the ***nature of a substitute*** To H.R. 3590, as proposed in the Senate on November 18, 2009' (Congressional Budget Office, www.cbo.gov/publication/41423)
- 'The Senate has introduced their OWN legislation... healthcare." (President Andy Stern, SEIU, www.seiu.org/2009/11/seiu-introduction-of-the-us-senates-patient-protection-and-affordable-care-act-puts-america-one-step.php)
- 'Proposed by Reid, Baucus, Dodd, Harkin 'as a ***substitute*** to H.R. 3590' (http://democrats.senate.gov/pdfs/reform/patient-protection-affordable-care- act.pdf)
- 'Reid Unveils Final Senate Health Care Bill, December 19, 2009' (www.reid.senate.gov/newsroom/121909_finalbill.cfm)
- The bill then went to the House of Representatives and was passed on March 21, 2010.

Therefore, the Patient Protection and Affordable Care Act VIOLATES U.S. Constitutional stipulated ***process***.

The U.S. Supreme Court VIOLATED its Constitutional constraints by ***re-writing*** the Patient Protection and Affordable Care Act. The U.S. Constitution, Art. III, Sec. 1, gives to the U.S. Supreme Court, 'judicial power of the United States....'

- Judicial Power: The authority vested in courts and judges to hear and decide cases and to make binding judgments on them; the power to construe (translate*) and apply the law.' (Garner B., Ed., *Black's Law Dictionary*, 7th ed., West Group, MN, 1999; **American Heritage Dictionary*, 2nd College ed., Houghton, Boston, 1976)

The legal precedent established by the U.S. Supreme Court permits the U.S. Congress to legislate all behavior – including the taking of the mark of the Beast, Satan, or pay a tax, and

failure to pay that arbitrary amount of tax, each citizen faces imprisonment.

Dissenting Opinion of U.S. Supreme Court Justice Scalia:

"But we cannot rewrite the statue to be what it is not... perverting the purpose of a statute..." or judicially rewriting it.' For all these reasons, to say that the Individual Mandate merely imposes a tax is not to interpret the statute but to rewrite it...the Constitution requires tax increases to originate in the House of Representatives. See. Art. I, Sec. 7, cl. 1....The Federalist No. 58, 'defend[ed] the decision to give the origination power to the House on the ground that the Chamber that is more accountable to the people should have the primary role in raising revenue.'... Imposing a tax through judicial legislation inverts the constitutional scheme...."

Internal Revenue Code Sec. 6011(a), 6012(a), et. Seq., and 6072(a): 'The requirement to file an income tax return is NOT voluntary. "Failure to file a tax return could subject the noncomplying individual to criminal penalties, including fines and imprisonment..." 26 U.S.C. 5671, 5673, 5684, 6651, and 6656; 27 CFR 25.177 (www.irs.gov/businesses/small/article/O,,id= 106502,00.html)

In the U.S. Supreme Court's decision to uphold the healthcare bill as a tax on behavior, the ***U.S. Government now completely owns the American citizen; owns their food, owns their water, owns their land, owns their income, owns their defense, owns their medical care, and owns their behavior.***

86. $50 billion of U.S. taxpayer dollars is given every year in foreign aid, even to countries that hate the United States, while we have a $1.7 trillion deficit.

87. And because of the Total War Tactics against the sovereignty of the nation of the United States and its citizens by its U.S. Presidents, its U.S. Congress, and its U.S. Supreme Court, and the enslavement of the American people.

By the instruction of the U.S. Constitution, Art. I, Sec. 10, cl. 3: "No State shall...engage in War, **UNLESS**...in such imminent Danger as will not admit of delay."

End of Intermission

Chapter 14

The first thing he noticed was the smell of rotting garbage. The next thing was the clutter, the undisciplined chaos of clutter. To the invader, the conditions were unthinkable. How does he find his way out of it, he wondered? The room had a soft green glow that reached up from the neon sign on the street below and seemed to emphasize the odor of rotting food. Where the hell is that son-of-a-bitch!? His temper was peaking. If he couldn't find him soon, he would resort to some drastic measure. But just then, he noticed a long bent form over in the corner of the room. Could it be him?

He approached cautiously, nudging aside objects on the floor, empty cans of soda, paper coffee cups, large pizza boxes, plastic trays of half-eaten sandwiches, clothes that from their odor had been worn for three months before being tossed on the floor. Books, stacks of books filled every corner of the room. In the dim green light, the bottom of his boot found the remnants of a piece of pizza with anchovies. He muttered obscenities, as he kicked it away. Then taking another step, he stood beside the single bed and looked down at the form cuddled up against several pillows, his arm wrapped around what looked to be a large stuffed animal. The invader sighed heavily at the thought of having to work with this geek.

How do I do this, he wondered, as he rubbed his chin. He seems to be too fragile to handle the usual introduction. Maybe I'll enter his dream. So, there inside, he asked the question, how do I design an etheron gun? And then he answered the question; with the help of the greatest general. The invader smiled, pleased with the appellation. Just then the form moved, grabbing the stuffed animal closer to himself as he rolled onto his other side. The invader sighed, but thought, at least I've moved him. He spoke to his dream, again. What if you were given the chance to save your country? Would you do all that you could do? Would you work with someone from the 11th dimension? Do you want to talk to someone from the 11th dimension? The answer came, as the form rolled back and opened his eyes to the ghost standing over him.

The geek rubbed his eyes, first thinking the green vaporous figure was only from the light of Helena's all-night deli neon sign reflecting off the cloud of cigarette smoke still lingering in the air from his evening study. Then he realized that the green figure had a face. A face that clearly looked like General Patton. "What the fuck!" he gasped.

"Don't worry, Charlie. I'm not really green. By the way, you ought to pull your shades at night to shut out the light of the deli sign. I don't know how you can sleep with that glowing in the room like this."

"Holy Shit!" Charlie cried as he scrambled back against the wall on the other side of the bed. The feel of its hard surface at his back made him feel less vulnerable. Grabbing the stuffed animal to himself, the covers up over his bare chest, "Get out! Get out!" he cried; his body trembling. "Leave me alone!"

"Now, Charlie, I'm not here to hurt you," Patton comforted. Pausing a moment, then putting his fists on his hips above the pistols that hung at his side, sighing as he mumbled to himself, I always hate this part of interacting with the fourth dimension. There has to be a better way to begin communication.

"What are you!?" Charlie trembled, still pressed against the wall, still grabbing the stuffed animal to himself.

Patton gestured with his hands, "Just calm down, Charlie. I'm a spirit from the 11th dimension. You know about the 11th dimension. I know you've studied it."

"But it was all conjecture, hypothesis, theorems! There is no proof that it exists!" Charlie cried.

"Well, as you can see for yourself, it does exist," Patton assured. "And we need your help. You need to get yourself together, here. What I'm going to do is fully materialize so you won't be so upset."

"Materialize? You aren't materialized yet?" Charlie asked, still pressed against the back wall.

Patton sighed, "We waste so much time with this." His patience wearing thin, Patton suddenly took on a solid form and turned on the light next to the bed. "Hi, Charlie. I'm General Patton. I'm a ghost. An 11th dimension ghost. I'm here to get your help. Now, get hold of yourself, son. Your country needs you!"

"Oohhh," Charlie moaned. "I feel....ah, I...." Charlie's body began to slide down the back wall.

Patton grabbed his shoulders and sat him up. "Charlie! Charlie! Pull yourself together. I'm not here to hurt you. Charlie! Get hold of yourself!"

Charlie looked at Patton's face, as solid as any other face, looking at him. He felt his strong hands on his shoulders. As the ghost had become solid, less foreboding, the room stopped moving in Charlie's mind. He began to accept what still seemed to be a dream. There stood General Patton, bent over him, holding his shoulders. His breath had a sweet smell. His hands a comforting control. Charlie began to realize that whatever was going on, he wasn't going to be hurt.

"I, ah, I think I'm going to be all right," Charlie whispered. Now, sitting up on his own, he looked more closely at Patton. Instinctively, he slowly pulled away and reached a hand up to hold onto his head, as though in the shock of seeing General Patton before him, he would lose his mind. His long brown hair curled around his fingers.

"Charlie, I came here because we need your help."

"We? Help?" Charlie repeated in a foggy state.

"Come on, Charlie. Wake up. It's reveille time! Or would you like me to screech it out for you?"

"No, no. I'm awake," Charlie rubbed his face and then his hair, trying to regain his senses from the dream he left behind on the pillow.

"Get up, Charlie. I expect my men to stand at attention when they speak to me."

"Whaaa? But, ah, I, ah, I'm not in the Army," Charlie argued. He gestured with his long hand, "But I'll get up; I'll get up." As he stood, he adjusted the sweat pants higher around his waist. His bare chest was flat, as though incapable of taking a deep breath; his thin long arms and legs evidenced that eating was only a function of survival.

General Patton shook his head, "You don't do much weight training do you, son?"

"If that's what you're looking for, you can fly up the street to Harvard. It's only 20 blocks way," Charlie defended.

"Sorry," Patton said. "No. I came to you and your muscled brain power."

"I need to use the bathroom," Charlie announced, as he began to wade through the garbage and clothing, kicking as he walked.

"By all means, son. Go right ahead. I forget the call of bodily functions. I no longer have cause."

"I gathered that," Charlie responded as he flicked on the light inside the bathroom and shut the door.

Patton turned to take in the room in full light. The clutter was even worse than first revealed by Helena's green neon sign. He looked over the room, at the large, curved pane of the corner window and the two large windows that flanked it and opened the room to the street below and the alleyway intersecting it.

Charlie soon emerged more awake after splashing cold water on his face. The door of the bathroom slowly opened, as Charlie looked around to see if it had all been a dream. But there at his desk was General Patton in his WWII field helmet with its four-stars, his brown waist jacket, his pearl-handled Colt and .357 hanging at his sides, his riding breeches, long leather boots, with the strap of a riding crop hung around his wrist. Charlie stood in the doorway, taking in the sight of a real 11th dimension spirit and whispered to himself, "Shittttt...."

Patton turned around, "Now son, I'm the only one allowed the use of profanity on this team. If you're going to work with us, you need to conduct yourself with respect for your commanding officer," Patton admonished. "It doesn't matter if you aren't in the Army."

"Yes, sir," Charlie responded, as he slowly walked toward Patton. "What is it that you want with me? Sir."

"We need you to design an etheron gun. We need it to kill evil spirits. For the war that's about to begin. And we need it today!" Patton instructed.

"The war? There's going to be a war? You mean, between the spirits? A war in the 11th dimension spirit world?"

"Well," Patton paused, "yes, and no. There's going to be a revolution that will begin on June 6th, with the invasion of the White House by patriotic Americans. The 11th dimension spirits are going to help them, but we need to scatter the ether of the evil spirits who will try to stop us from helping Americans."

Charlie's brain was gearing up, "The 11th dimensions are going to interact with the live Americans!?"

"Yes. That is, when they all become aware of us. It's a timing thing. A matter of networking. But eventually, yes, the 11th dimensions will be fighting with the live Americans."

Charlie took several more steps towards Patton, his hand raised, his finger pointing, "I know about the etherons. Is that how you work in the 11th dimension? You guys manipulate your ether, don't you!? I knew that! I knew that!" Charlie grew excited. "I read about Podkletnov's etheron gun. It discharges 2-10 million volts through a superconducting disc to a copper anode. It produces a columnated gravity wave impulse. It works by propelling the ether along its line of fire and because of this the gravity wave impulse is able to achieve speeds of up to several thousand times the speed of light. I read this in Paul LaViolette's book, *Secrets of Antigravity Propulsion*. It's in chapter 6." Charlie looked at Patton, "Have you ever seen this guy's website, etheric.com. This guy is a genius!"

Patton was impressed, here was a genius praising the genius of LaViolette. This LaViolette guy must have an astounding mind.

Charlie continued, "He's a systems physicist - Paul LaViolette – he discovered subquantum kinetics, or SQK. LaViolette said that SQK proposes the existence of a primordial transmuting ether composed of subtle "etheron" particles. These etheron particles continually react with one another in prescribed manner and also diffuse through space...only a few of subquantum reactions may be important for describing the origin of the fields composing the matter and energy of our universe. This relevant subset of ether reactions is described by just five kinetic equations. They describe recursive conversion of X etherons into Y etherons and Y etherons back into X etherons. Under certain conditions, this continually operating cycle spontaneously forms wave patterns composed on reciprocally varying X and Y ether concentrations, the concentration of the third ether variable, G, varying in step with that of X. The X and Y electric potential fields and G ether concentration variations waves comprise the subatomic particles and energy waves that form the basis of the physical world.

The transmuting ether is the wellspring of Creation. If this continual activity were to diminish, your physical body, your house, the Earth, the Sun, the countless planets and stars filling the vast expanse of space, in fact, all the subatomic particles and energy waves composing our physical universe would gradually dissipate, dissolving into a state of uniformity. What would remain would be the ever-present, vast, and unfathomable multi-dimensional consciousness, of which we are a part, and whose now featureless calm "surface" had once generated our beautiful physical universe."

Charlie continued, "You can find this on his website:

www.etheric.com/LaVioletteBooks/ether.html.

Patton grunted, "Yeh, well, son. I'm going to depend on you to understand LaViolette's genius and interpret it for me."

Charlie replied, "Let me put it this way. SQK leads to a view of God that He is not separate from the Creation. He's not off somewhere spending His time contemplating Himself. He's with us! He is the Creation as it evolves. LaViolette is saying that Creation of the material universe includes the levels of Creation that we have no direct knowledge of. That Creation is unfathomably immense and beyond our understanding, and hence God is All that Is!"

Patton smiled, "You mean that man should stop trying to figure out who God is – just accept that He's with us. Have faith. Stop thinking we have a godlike ability to understand His nature."

"That's exactly what I'm saying," Charlie replied.

The two men nodded to each other, realizing each had the faith that God required of them.

"We need the etheron gun. We need to scatter the evil spirits' etherons, so they are unable to function."

"We can do that," Charlie said, "Okay, let me explain, with subquantum kinetics, light loses energy, in the voids between galaxies, and leaves the physical universe. For a ghost to appear or disappear depends on change in gravity potential. When gravity is lighter, the ghost dematerializes; when gravity is made heavier, the ghost reappears. The open system of subquantum kinetics is a chemical-like feeding, and if the feeding stops, waves disappear - and the physical universe would dematerialize.

Patton nodded, "Yes. We do control our soul's matter through gravity. That's how we materialize and disappear."

"You look so real!" Charlie reached out and touched Patton's shoulder. "You even feel real! This is unbelievable!"

Charlie smiled, "You know they don't teach this at MIT, or anywhere else, for that matter. But since I read LaViolette's book, I've been dying to work on something like this!"

He quickly sat down at his desk in front of the alleyway window, pulling out a long yellow pad from under a small stack of books. He rustled around until he found a pencil under a stack of papers on the side of his desk and began to write out a formula.

Patton paced around the room, kicking away the plastic container with the half-eaten sandwich, an empty paper cup, a soiled sweat shirt lying in a heap with MIT peeking out from its folds, "What we need is something that can be carried, preferably in one hand. Something lightweight that even a woman could use on the battlefield," Patton instructed.

"You're going to use women to fight evil spirits?" Charlie turned and looked up at Patton.

"We're using every god-damned, red-blooded American citizen!

Every man, woman, and child, to fight wherever they are needed!"

"This is big, isn't it?" Charlie asked.

"You don't participate in physical training or in life, do you, Charlie?" Patton replied.

"I get caught up in physics and engineering. It's a nice, peaceful place," Charlie defended.

"Only in theory, Charlie," Patton argued. "Not in the real world. In the real world, it's anything but peaceful."

Charlie began to draw from memory Podkletnov's etheron gun. When he finished he turned to Patton and handed him the design with the instruction, "You need to develop an interference device. If you want to manufacture these weapons in someone's basement or garage, they'll need to insulate their houses with aluminum oxide sheeting to prevent Black helicopters from using their equipment to see through walls, roofs, of houses. I mean, they hover over a house and can look right down into the basement! That is, I expect that the patriots will be manufacturing these guns."

Patton smiled, "To fuck up their spying on Americans! I like that! Good thinking, son."

"The easiest method is to use aluminum-backed bubble wrap sheeting," Charlie said. "They use it as insulation. They can buy it in a hardware store. They can staple it to the ceiling of their basements and walls. For that matter, Americans could even make a battle uniform out of the aluminum sheeting, using aluminum tape on the seams, to avoid heat-sensing detection on the battlefield. Or to repel microwaves back to its source. That way, Americans could even destroy the microwave guns."

"Another words," Patton said, "instead of Special Ops covering themselves with the plants of the environment in order to blend in, today Americans need to cover themselves from being detected by heat-sensing devices."

Patton paused a moment, he sighed, "That's why they are flying the drones above all of America – they use cameras that can read a license plate. That means live Americans can only move at night." Patton suddenly laughed, "So, that's why they have car head-lights that the driver can't turn off. And why they've put GPS in cars – so they can track Americans. They told us it was for safety. Humph! Yes, their safety – by detecting us."

Patton shook his head, "They've thought of everything. So they think."

Charlie had turned back to his desk, then realizing what he had just said he looked back to Patton, "Oh! General. I just remembered. The US government has microwave guns. They have them mounted on jeeps. They use it for crowd control, rioting. If you say that revolution is about to break out, it's likely they're planning on using microwave guns against Americans taking to the streets in revolution. What it does is hit people with microwaves; you know, well, maybe you don't know. It works like a microwave oven. It heats up the water in the skin of a human to the point of burning the human." Charlie shook his head, "If they hit Americans in the eyes...the eye is mostly made of water. It will boil the eyes out of their heads!"

"Well," Patton replied, "let's see Tsaeb order the U.S. Military to use those weapons against American citizens." He walked away from Charlie, "I trust that our military will take control of those weapons on our bases, and turn those microwave guns against the United Nations troops! We are fighting a 21st century war, Charlie. Microwave and etheron guns will be the weapons of this war. But just remember, Americans have a Constitutional right to bear arms. Yesterday, it was a musket, today it is a shotgun, on June 6th it will be the etheron gun. All come under the Second Amendment right to carry. The purpose of the Second Amendment was to empower Americans to revolt against their corrupted government. It's the only Constitutional recourse given to them, to bear arms. Citizens cannot impeach, they cannot try a president, and they cannot recall a congressman, as those evil traitors destroy our great country! But American citizens were given the gun to remove all of them when necessary."

Patton paced a few more steps and turned back, "We'll tell Americans not to take to the streets. This will be a stealth war. And we'll make sure there are more than the manufacturing patriots who will insulate there houses. That way the elite traitors won't know who is and who isn't hiding the manufacturing of the etheron gun. There's no way that the government can openly demand that Americans not insulate their homes with aluminum oxide! After all," Patton smiled, "They're only being energy-saving green!"

"Otherwise," Patton complained, "that would be saying that the right to privacy in a privately-owned space where Americans have the expectation of privacy is no longer legal! They can't openly admit that without declaring war against Americans. Up to now, they've attacked the United States through quiet encroachment through illegal legislation under the guise of keeping Americans safe. What they are doing with the Black helicopters is illegal, but how many Americans even know that their privacy is being unconstitutionally violated by those Black helicopters?"

"With all respect, sir, if the government finds out that people are insulating their houses to prevent detection, the government will stop all manufacturing of the aluminum sheeting. They'll attack the supply of the aluminum sheeting, instead of admitting that they are denying Americans their right to privacy. You should notify Americans as soon as possible before the government knows what's going on; before manufacturing of the guns begins. Otherwise, there's no use in my designing anything, if the government is going to know about the gun and take it away," Charlie said. "And besides, is any of this going to work? We'll be up against the U.S. Government and the United Nations! Aren't we wasting our time? Haven't we waited too long? Aren't they too powerful to defeat? Aren't we just going to be rounded up and jailed for this?"

Charlie paused a moment, "General, I'm not so sure that I want to participate in any of this. I think it's too late to stop them."

"Remember, Charlie, the government works for you and all Americans. You have to change your mind set; Americans are the boss, not a herd to be corralled. Be aware, Charlie, that the elite's weapon of political correctness was designed to shut down dissenting minds and speech of every American. Silence divides, and thereby, conquers; thereby, shuts down action of patriots! Thus, being silenced, many Americans have developed a mindset that they have no right, no ability, to control *their* government. That they have no say in what the government is doing to this country. Silence prohibits learning that others think as they; prohibits our countrymen from calling to arms to overthrow the elite's tyranny! And contrary to political correctness, the Constitution does not provide the right *not* to be offended! Free speech actually provides the right to offend others!" Patton laughed, "That's the best part of the Constitution, my right to offend others with my speech!"

Patton continued, "You've been taken in, Charlie, by the idea that the elite control you. That they know best and that you're an idiot, if you disagree with them," Patton charged. "The first paragraph of the Constitution states that 'We the People of the United States...secure the blessings of liberty to OURSELVES and our posterity....' *We* the *People* 'do *ordain* and *establish* this Constitution.' The U.S. Government is OURS, Charlie, and our children's! There's nothing in that document that hands ownership of our government over to the elite traitors as their own. *We* created *them*!"

"Regardless of what the Constitution says, they have conquered us!" Charlie defended. "So, what's the use? That is, if they take away the etheron gun and put us in jail? Then they'll pass a law saying we can't have an etheron gun, just like we can't have a machine gun. Their laws prevent citizens from carrying weapons of equal capability as government forces. I mean, have you thought this through? They're too big to fight! Tsaeb controls the U.S. Military. The healthcare bill gave him his own personal army; he doesn't need permission from Congress. The healthcare bill requires Christians to pay for abortions – where's the Constitution 1st Amendment – Congress shall make no law prohibiting the free exercise of religion! Where was the Constitution when that bill was passed by Congress?! They have United Nations troops here on our soil! They have NATO allies. How can we defeat them? Just go up the street to Harvard and look at the biowarfare they're cooking up there!"

"You've just proven my point, Charlie." Patton countered. "They developed a fear in you by the implication inherent in the political correctness weapon. It was designed to do just that. Those shitheads got that political correctness weapon from psychologists! Those who studied the mind; those who know little minds and how they work. Through the function of mob control. The implication of political correctness is that if people's reputations are destroyed and they suffer societal ostracizing for expressing their differing opinion, what would they do to a person taking action against their tyranny? The political correctness weapon is directed at the titillation of those lesser minds, those who seek a pat on the head because the idiot, the traitor, shut down someone's speech by calling them a *name*! A name that the elite's propaganda has decried was the worst of abominations! The ultimate sin! Then came another pat on the head for the little mind, if they reported a fellow countryman for smoking in an open-air smoke-free zone. Then the little mind became a member of the elite, a noble good-doer. They had obeyed the elite when they *approached a stranger* to tell them to stop smoking; obeyed the elite by curtailing their use of salt; they obeyed everything on the list of demands set forth by the elite, so that they finally became a member of the elite class with their own subjects, those who they could intimidate by calling them a name! Each name that the little mind affixed to his countryman was a step for the elite to encroach upon the ultimate control over citizens' everyday action."

Patton grabbed hold of the back of Charlie's chair turning it quickly, violently, so that Charlie faced him, eye to eye. His other hand leaning on the desk, trapping Charlie, as he bent close to his face. Patton's voice sounding his rage, "The little mind did what the government asked him to do! He used the political correctness weapon to silence dissenters. Therefore, the little mind is given the respect of always being right! Even though the little mind can be easily outwitted by a better thinking mind like yours, Charlie. But with the political correctness weapon, the little mind stands above you, Charlie! For the one thing that the little mind understands is that the political correctness weapon gives them the power to silence the opinion of a critical thinker like you. You make them feel inferior, Charlie! They can't reason like you. So, they pull out the weapon that raises them above you. And from that elevation above you, they get a titillation, Charlie! A titillation right down to their very cocks! Down to their very pussies! They devour the power it brings to their useless, simpleton lives! They don't know how to fix their own sorry lives, but the elite gave them a weapon to control your life, Charlie. That political correctness weapon is aimed at you, Charlie – and every Christian – telling you that you will not dissent against a Black president when he tells you that you will pay for the abortion-murder of an infant! You must obey the Black president when he tells you that you must disobey YOUR GOD! Because it's NOT NICE to criticize whatever the fuck the BLACK president tells you to do! They have enslaved you, Charlie, by controlling your mind, therefore, your bodily functions. Today, the Black president told you to disobey your God. Tomorrow, he will tell you what kind of toilet paper you can use to wipe your fuck'n ass! Leviticus 20:1-5, informs you, Charlie, 'And the Lord spoke to Moses, saying: Thus shalt thou say to the children of Israel: If any man of the children of Israel, or of the strangers, that dwell in Israel, give of his seed to the idol Moloch, dying let him die: the people of the land shall stone him. And I will set my face against him. And if the people of the land neglecting, my commandment, (and leave alone) the man that hath given of his seed to Moloch, and will not kill him: I will set my face against that man, and his kindred, *and all that consented with him*, to commit fornication with Moloch.' Abortion is giving your seed to Satan!"

Finally, Patton backed off, "God is going to get all of them, Charlie. He's going to get them in a way that our minds could never conceive."

Patton sighed heavily, walking away from Charlie, slapping the riding crop onto the palm of his hand, "It's just another step leading to the next, to the government installing thermostat controls inside citizens' houses; controlled from outside the house, by the government. They don't give a shit about the energy, it's only to control the mindset of every American - how much more can they fuck up your mind but through controlling whether you are too cold or too hot in your own home? That physical control they have over your own body impacts your mindset! But you are already mind-fucked, Charlie!"

Patton turned back to Charlie, "You fear they will come and put you in jail for fighting to keep our country free! You are FUCKED, Charlie! If they find out what you are doing to help stop them, they will cut the breaks in your car; they will throw you in front of a train, onto a subway's third rail. Charlie, they aren't going to put a mind like yours in jail - they are going to MURDER YOUR ASS!"

Patton frowned, "But I can't blame you. You suffered the first attempt of their announcing their tyranny. A little toe-tickle at the water's edge. The first official White House attempt to shut down free speech. The Office of the Presidency, the most powerful man in the world, asking for names and email addresses and websites of those who had the temerity to speak out against his healthcare legislation. For what reason!? What is Tsaeb going to do to those Americans who spoke out against his policies!? Tsaeb and his Chicago thugs are using Hitler's Nazi-Kraut playbook! I'll tell you what they are going to do - quietly murder every fuck'n one of them!"

Sean McSham put forth the Unprivileged Enemy Belligerent, Interrogation, Detention, and Prosecution Act - automatic imprisonment for being suspected of being a belligerent. The synonym for belligerent is quarrelsome! McSham wants Tsaeb to have that power! No trial, no Constitutional right to habeas corpus! No right to a lawyer. No Miranda warning. They don't even have to charge an American citizen with a crime! Just put away for life! Sean McSham, a Senator and member of the Foreign Affairs Private Council! Calling for Tsaeb to have this power, against every notion of what the United States of America stands for! They couldn't get that bill passed because too many Americans knew about it. So, they tucked it into the National Defense Authorization Act of 2012, Subtitle D, Counterterrorism, Sec. 1021(a). Let me recite it for you Charlie, 'Congress affirms that the authority of the President to use all necessary and appropriate force including the authority of the Armed

Forces of the United States to detain covered persons – defined in (b): A covered person under this section is: ANY PERSON WHO HAS COMMITTED A BELLIGERENT ACT AGAINST THE U.S. OR ITS COALITION PARTNERS. *DETENTION IS WITHOUT TRIAL* UNTIL THE END OF THE HOSTILITIES.'

Patton smiled, "So! You might ask, why hasn't President Tsaeb arrested himself? He continually gives aid – to the Muslim Brotherhood, $1.5 billion, at latest count – who are crucifying Christians in Egypt! The Muslim Brotherhood works with Iran in their attempt to blow the Zionist Israelis – allegedly a U.S. coalition partner – off the face of the planet. Tsaeb continually announces when and where he is about to send Special Ops, and what their mission will be – destroy Syria's chemical weapons. He gave the name of the Pakistani doctor who helped the CIA in finding Osama Bin Laden. Now, Charlie, should Tsaeb be arrested by the military as a belligerent for exposing to the world, and thereby our enemy, our top secret military missions? Is that an act of belligerence? Or perhaps, tried for treason. What do you think, Charlie?

While he's doing that, Tsaeb is asking Americans to turn in other Americans who speak out against his healthcare legislation. Tsaeb wants names and addresses of anyone who speaks out against his policies!"

Patton sighed, "Charlie, I led men in battle. I saw how Americans fought on foreign soil to defeat communism," Patton sighed, "but this war! This war will be different. This will be fought on our own soil, against our own traitorous leaders! Americans will fight with their hearts, every last one of them! That is their greatest weapon! Their heart! Nothing! Nothing! Will defeat the Americans! The elite will be torn limb from limb; burned at the stake; hung from every tree! And do you know who they should fear most, Charlie?"

Patton's voice lowered, "The mothers. The mothers will skin them alive, Charlie. The elite fucked with their children; they poisoned their children with their chemicals, destroying their brains with Autism. The elite's media pushes sexual behavior onto their elementary-aged children; they destroyed their children's Christian values through programming and ads. They've addicted their children to drugs. May God have mercy on the elite, because the mothers will show them none!"

Patton walked over to the corner window, his hands clasped behind his back, looking up at the stars and the heavens beyond, he said, "Remember, Charlie, the mandate given to the American people by unanimous Declaration, on July 4, 1776, written by a Founding Father and third President of the United States: When, in the course of human events, it becomes necessary for one people to dissolve the political bands which have connected them with another, and to assume among the powers of the earth, the separate and equal station to which the laws of nature and of nature's God entitle them, a decent respect to the opinions of mankind requires that they should declare the causes which impel them to the separation. We hold these truths to be self-evident, that all men are created equal, that they are endowed by their Creator with certain unalienable rights, that among these are life, liberty and the pursuit of happiness. That to secure these rights, governments are instituted among men, deriving their just powers from the consent of the governed. That whenever any form of government becomes destructive to these ends, it is the right of the people to alter or to abolish it, and to institute a new government, laying its foundation on such principles and organizing its powers in such form, as to them shall seem most likely to effect their safety and happiness. Prudence, indeed, will dictate that governments long established should not be changed for light and transient causes; and accordingly all experience hath shown that mankind are more disposed to suffer, while evils are sufferable, than to right themselves by abolishing the forms to which they are accustomed. But when a long train of abuses and usurpations, pursuing invariably the same object evinces a design to reduce them under absolute despotism, it is their right, it is their duty, to throw off such government, and to provide new guards for their future security. --Such has been the patient sufferance of these colonies; and such is now the necessity which constrains them to alter their former systems of government. The history of the present King of Great Britain is a history of repeated injuries and usurpations, all having in direct object the establishment of an absolute tyranny over these states. To prove this, let facts be submitted to a candid world."

Patton sighed heavily, "My God! No one was more inspired by our Heavenly Father than Jefferson when he wrote those words."

Charlie quietly listened. It was as if he had never heard the words before and their newness struck his heart with a heavy blow. The words being spoken so passionately, even lovingly, by such a man as Patton who had fought so hard to overthrow Hitler's tyranny touched Charlie's heart like nothing he had ever experienced. His chin quivered; the pain built in his throat, as he fought to hold back tears that refused to obey him. His chest heaved, his lungs poured out his sorrow, his pride, his fear of what was to come. But he knew he must follow Jefferson's mandate that tyranny might be stopped, today. He knew that he would become part of the history of America; for he understood now that America's history lived in the actions of its citizens; not just of yesterday's citizens, but today's, and tomorrow's. The cry for action against tyranny would always live in the hearts of patriots, as it had more than 200 years ago. Those patriots won independence in the distant past, and Charlie knew that it was his duty to carry on that honor, that magnificence of bravery. He owed it to those who died in the past to give him freedom; and now it was his turn to fight so that he could hand freedom over to those who will come in the future. Honor was at his door and he would not shut it out. He would welcome it in.

There was silence in the cluttered room while the men contemplated what was before them.

Finally, Patton turned back to Charlie, "What do you say, my son, will you accept God's mandate?"

"YES!" Charlie cried out, as he wiped the tears off his cheeks. "This is the complete design of the etheron gun. Here's a list of supplies that the gunsmiths will need."

"Are you sure this will work?" Patton asked.

Charlie thought for a moment, "This gun in the hands of a live American patriot against a human that is a descendant of Satan, will not only vaporize the body, it will also scatter its soul, so that it can't become an evil spirit of the 11th dimension."

"Perfect!" Patton said, as he pounded Charlie's shoulder.

"But you must remember one thing," Charlie interjected.

"What's that?" Patton sighed, not liking Charlie's tone.

"There will be a sound-barrier aftershock. A sonic boom. This is going to be one hell of a light and sound show, the likes of which have never been seen before. The shock and awe of the Iraq War will be a whimper compared to this weapon."

"More than I could ask for, Charlie, more than I could ask for!" Patton replied.

Charlie stood up next to Patton, as they looked at the design. Charlie tapped the yellow pad, "At this point here, you can hook up leads that feed to a computer. Now, let me take a few more minutes to finish writing you a computer program that will fire this baby."

"I have ten minutes, son, take your time," Patton said.

Charlie pulled up a software program from his computer, typing furiously he wrote the last stages of the code. He saved the program to a disk, pulled the disk out of the computer, and while handing it up to Patton, "I'm giving you my invention. I've been working on this for years. I was hoping that it would make me a billionaire one day."

"Better than that, Charlie, it will give you a place in the Kingdom of Heaven."

Charlie smiled.

Chapter 15

It was late in the evening, Maggie's usual time for checking in with other patriots from around the country. She had read her emails and was posting the new information on patriotic websites when her landline rang, "Hello."

"Well, hello there!" came the melodic voice.

"Hey, Ken! What's going on? I was just thinking of calling, but it's too early for you. What are you doing up, it's only 11:30 pm."

"I had a doctor's appointment for my back this afternoon. I'll go to bed around 4:30 am. My wife has tomorrow off, so she'll get up at 4:30 and let me sleep in, but I'll go back to my nightshift after tomorrow. Maggie, they're coming at night. That's why I stay up all night. They're not going to take me by surprise."

"I know, Ken.

For a moment there was silence on the line.

Finally, Maggie asked, "Did you see Farkin's YouTube radio broadcast, where he is warning Tsaeb that the America people are getting ready to revolt? He warned Tsaeb that they want him to be replaced because 'they don't want no Black face in the White House.' Farkin evidently doesn't know that it took the White vote to get Tsaeb into the White House. Or maybe he knows that the voting machines were tampered with and that the Whites actually voted was against Tsaeb in the first place!"

"Yeah," Ken replied, "I saw that video. Farkin warned Tsaeb to be careful how he handles this situation because 'the Libya uprising is coming to America.' He said that the 'American people are rising against their own government; it's not Muslim, it's not Black people, it's White Militia that are angry with their government and they are well armed.' Farkin asked Tsaeb, 'are you going to tell them to put their arms down and let's talk it over peacefully, I hope so. If not, America will be bathed in blood because of the dissatisfaction in America has reached a boiling point!' He's talking about White dissatisfaction, not Black or Muslim dissatisfaction. The Blacks and Muslims are satisfied with Tsaeb's communism, in other words. Farkin also warned Tsaeb, 'be careful how you manipulate the dissatisfaction in Libya and other parts of the Muslim world.'"

"That's the one!" Maggie cried. "That tells me that they fear a Christian White and Black Muslim war, with the Whites highly motivated to kill Muslims and Blacks. The last part of his warning about Tsaeb's treatment of the Muslim world, is telling Whites that the entire Muslim world will aid Tsaeb, if Whites try to take him down. In a round-about manner, Farkin is telling us that Tsaeb is a Muslim and part of the worldwide Muslim Caliphate!"

"Well, the American people are waking up," Ken replied. "Everywhere I go people are talking about it. And if they aren't, I bring the subject up to them."

"I know," Maggie said. "I was talking with Eddy the other day. He said that last month when he was visiting family in New York, standing in line at the grocery store, the people started talking to each other while waiting to check out! And these people were strangers to each other! If it's that common a topic of discussion among Americans, then you know that Congress knows that Americans are about to bring war on their doorstep!"

"You got that right!" Ken responded. "Americans are calling them every day with complaints."

"Oh! Before I forget to tell you, Quinn and I are getting married!" Maggie announced. "We want to marry before hell breaks loose and in case we get rounded up and put into FEMA camps."

"Well, I wish you two the best of luck. I wish we weren't half way across the country, so we could come to your wedding. With gas prices at $4.00 and rising, we just can't make it."

"Well, that's why we're only having close family and local neighbors. We plan on two weeks from now. May 15th. We don't want to take any chances that things will hit sooner than expected. It's only going to be immediate family, at my son's house in Rockport."

"I think Americans are bringing family together all across the country," Ken added. "Look at Helen, she moved back home to New York. I don't agree that New York is a safe place. She was safer here in North Carolina."

"Well, she wanted to be closer to her children," Maggie explained. "She knows that she's headed into the storm. But she doesn't want to survive in the hills of North Carolina while her kids are being killed in New York. She moved there to die with them. By the way, did I tell you that her son the cop knows for a fact that war is coming? He implied that the city of New York is in preparations. He wouldn't tell her the details, but he just told her to prepare. You wouldn't believe all the guns and ammo he has stocked piled."

"Everybody is stockpiling weapons and ammo, Maggie. And I think that they're preparing to set off a false flag, soon."

"I hope I get a chance to set up my ham radio before they strike us."

There was silence on the line.

"What's wrong?"

"Someone just rang my doorbell!" Maggie answered.

"At this hour?!"

"Yeah! I don't think I like that!"

"Do you want me to hang on?"

"No. That's okay. It might be Quinn. I'll talk to you later."

"All right. You take care."

"You, too! Good night."

Maggie got up from her desk and walked to the front door of her apartment. Looking out the peephole of the door, she couldn't see anything. She paused a moment, considering whether to open the door. Maybe someone is hiding against the wall next to the door. As she was thinking of what to do, she heard a woman's voice coming from behind her call her name.

"Oh God!" Maggie gasped. Too frightened to turn around, her body froze facing the door; her hand still clutching the door's handle, she thought of opening the door and fleeing out to the hallway and down the stairs.

"Be not afraid!" the woman's soothing voice said. "Maggie, I'm ye ancestor. I came ta help ye, not ta hurt ye."

Maggie's heart pounded in her chest, her breathing was rapid and irregular.

"Maggie, you need ta calm yourself before ye faint," the woman's voice instructed. "Take a deep breath and let it out slowly. Relax your body."

Maggie did as her ancestor advised until the dizziness went away. She slowly turned around to find a woman standing in the middle of the long dim hallway, a few feet away from her. She stood next to her mother's buffet, holding the hand of the statue of the Virgin Mother atop the buffet. But what was more surprising to Maggie was that it seemed as though she was looking in a mirror, of herself in her salad days. It was all stunning to her mind.

The woman smiled, "Greetings, Maggie."

"Hey," Maggie choked out.

"I'm going ta back away. Why don't ye step forward so we're in the light of the living room where we can sit and talk."

"Okay," Maggie replied, but her body wouldn't move. Finally, she groaned, "I don't like this!"

"Relax. Don't fight it. I am the ghost of ye ancestor, Queen Macha."

"Ah, gees," Maggie sighed. "I don't like this kind of stuff."

"Yes. I know, but we need ta talk. You and I have a war ta fight."

"Yeah. Okay," Maggie whispered, as she inched a step forward toward the living room.

As the two entered the light of the room, Maggie looked more closely at Macha. "You're really beautiful! It's strange to look another woman in the eye. I mean, we're the same height. It always throws me when I meet another woman who is six feet tall. I'm not used to it; it's rare. And it always scares the shit out of me. I'm used to a man being taller, but not a woman. I find a woman as tall as me more dangerous than a man! I can't believe that, but I do. I don't know why." Maggie couldn't stop rambling on, until Macha interrupted her.

"Because we are more dangerous, Maggie, both of us are more dangerous than a man our same height."

"Ahh, would you like to sit at the dining table, or the living room?" Maggie asked.

"What would be more comfortable for you, Maggie?"

"I'd like to sit at the table," Maggie replied and took a seat.

But as Queen Macha began to sit at the table, Maggie jumped up, "Ah, would you like a cigarette? I have cigarettes over there," Maggie pointed to her right, to the short hallway. "I'll just get the cigarettes over there," she said as she walked briskly toward her desk.

"No, but you have one."

Maggie walked over to her desk in the alcove outside her bedroom and grabbed the pack of cigarettes, lighter, and the ashtray and brought them back to the dining table where Queen Macha was now sitting.

"God. I feel as though I'm in the twilight zone. And I think it's because you look so much like me. It's blowing my mind!"

"Well, where do ye think ye got ye genes? From ye ancestors! Why would ye look so different?"

"Yes. Yes. I guess you're right, but you look so much like me when I was young. It's just unbelievable!"

"We need ta talk about attacking the Muslim Training Camps."

"The Muslim Training Camps? You and me and the Camps. Sure!" Maggie took a long drag on her cigarette.

"Ye and I are going ta lead American women inta the camps and kill all the Muslims training there before they attack the United States."

"How do you expect me to do that? I have no military training!"

"Quinn taught ye how ta cut the throat of the enemy. Did he not?"

"Well, ah, yes, he did. But I never thought I would actually have to do that. I mean, walk into a camp to find someone and slice open their throat! That's a horse of a different color. That's a different ballgame! I was thinking defense, not offense. Although a good offense is the best defense...."

"Don't worry. Ye are not going ta walk into the camp, ye going ta fly in!"

"Whhaatttt?!" Maggie choked on the smoke she had just inhaled.

"Maggie, ye need ta stop resistin' this. Ye know war is about ta break," Macha argued. "Ye know of astral projection; ye have done it before. Toughen up, Maggie!"

Maggie still coughed the last of the smoke out of her lungs.

"Toughen up," Maggie choked out. "Okay. Okay. I'm toughened. Just give me a second to wrap my head around this!"

Queen Macha got up from the table and walked around the apartment. "Why don't ye think about it while I look around."

She opened the china cabinet that had belonged to Maggie's grandmother. "Ellen Catherine," Macha said, as she pulled the photo out of the back of the cabinet. "She was a very kind woman, Ellen Catherine was. These are her crystal goblets. But the Irish Belleek pieces are ye's, are they not, Maggie?"

"Yes. I love Irish Belleek. The three thinner pieces on the right are my grandmother's, though."

Macha walked across the room to the other mahogany china cabinet, "And this was ye mother's cabinet, her wedding dishes, her crystal. The soup tureen is your great-great-grandmother's, is it not?"

"Yes," Maggie replied.

"Ye cherish the heritage that these women left with ye, do ye not, Maggie?"

"Yes."

"Ye want ta leave that heritage with ye daughter, and the daughter she will have after the war?"

"She's going to have a daughter after the war?"

"If ye fight, Maggie. But only if ye fight!"

Maggie stood up from the table, "What do I have to do?"

"I'm going ta take ye ta meet the Amazons of Greek mythology, who in fact, did exist. They fought with men in battle just as the Celtic warriors of Ireland. The Amazons were from the northern coast of Turkey and up ta the north of the Black Sea, in the Ukraine."

"Turkey? Anatolia? Where the Garden of Eden is and the messa where the Semites settled after the Ark landed on Mt. Ararat? On its northern coast?" Maggie asked, but before Macha could answer, Maggie whispered, "My God!"

"Before we leave, ye need to know. 'Tis a war for the souls of mankind that we will fight. Not men v. women, not country v. country. 'Tis the war against Satan's descendants for all our souls, until Jesus returns and judges the living and the dead."

Maggie nodded. "I understand."

"There are thousands of Muslims in those 36 training camps across the country. The Amazons will lead the American women who will be astral projecting with us. That's why Congress refuses to close the border; it's why President Tsaeb had told the Border Patrol to stop arresting illegal aliens – so more Hezbollah and al Qaeda can cross over and get to the camps."

Suddenly, the spirit of Will Booker appeared in Maggie's living room holding the hand of a female spirit dressed in anti-bellum costume.

"Will!" Maggie cried.

"Ma'm," the spirit of Will Booker greeted, as his spirit form took on a solid appearance. He looked at Queen Macha, and smiled. "She does look like you, ma'm, your Highness."

Will turned to the woman standing next to him. "Maggie, this is Belle Boyd. She aided Stonewall in the Shenandoah conflict. She is going to watch over your body while you go with Queen Macha."

Maggie looked at Macha, somewhat leery of Belle's past endeavors of spying for the Confederacy. "But I'm a Yankee," Maggie whispered.

"Remember what I said," Macha assured, "'Tis not a conflict between country v. country, north v. south, but a fight between Christians and Satan's army – for our souls against the evil trying ta take 'em. She was not your enemy, but her country's patriot, the Confederacy. Now, she 'tis a patriot of Jesus Christ, as you, as Will, as I am."

"All right," Maggie nodded.

"Shall we begin," Macha held out her arm, pointing in the direction of Maggie's bedroom. Maggie led the way into the darken room, lit only by the dim glow of street lamps below and the light of a full moon low in the night sky.

Maggie pulled the shades and turned on the light next to her bed. She turned to the three spirits and asked, "Okay, what next?"

Will stepped forward, "Don't worry, Maggie, Quinn did this, too. And he returned. Remember when you watched over his body? Belle is going to do the same for you, now. Leave your clothes on and get under the covers to keep your body warm while you're gone."

Maggie did as Will Booker instructed. Queen Macha walked over to the side of the bed. "I want ye ta take my hand and close ye eyes. Relax, even try ta fall ta sleep."

Belle walked over next to Macha and sprinkled Holy Water on Maggie's body, as she whispered, "May the Lord Jesus Christ protect your spirit and body and bring your soul back to your body safely. May the Lord Jesus Christ keep away all evil spirits from your body while your soul is gone."

Maggie closed her eyes and soon felt her body go in to a deep state of rest. And as her mind drifted in to sleep, she began to dream that she was flying. She looked about the sky, clear with countless stars shining bright as she had never seen them before. The full moon's light lit up the earth beneath her, as she looked down upon the tree tops in first breath of bloom, she thought of the Bible passage, Matt 24:32-34, "And from the fig tree learn a parable: When the branch thereof is now tender, and the leaves come forth, you know that summer is nigh. So you also, when you shall see all these things, know ye that it is nigh, even at the doors. Amen I say to you, that this generation shall not pass, till all these things be done.'

Finally, Maggie realized that she wasn't dreaming. She felt Macha's hand holding her's and she looked over to her and smiled. She knew that she was astral projecting and they were on the way to meet with the Amazons. She wasn't sure where they were going, except that they were heading south, for there below them was New York City.

Beyond the city they turned slightly westward, inland. The lights of civilization became fewer and fewer still. Maggie looked at the magnificence of the world, the universe, as she reached her hand to touch the stars that seemed so close to her now. If only, she thought, it were possible.

Suddenly, there were no lights below, only the tall trees of forests and mountains that stretched for miles below. Macha slowed the speed of their flying as they descended closer to the trees. In the dim light of the moon, Maggie could see the outline of a long ridge of a rugged, tree-covered mountain below. As they descended further, she could see outcrops peeking out between the trees and bushes. Macha pointed as she pulled Maggie down between the ridges of mountain peaks, lower into the valley. They hovered outside the entrance to a cave where Maggie could see round orbes of light dancing nearby. Macha brought Maggie down, till finally they stepped onto the lip of the cave's entrance.

"Tis the Brown Mountain ridge of the Blue Ridge Mountains," Macha told Maggie. "There are no roads or homes, just complete wilderness."

They turned to look out to the peaks of the range and the narrow valley that dropped thousands of feet just inches from their feet. Macha stretched her arm out over the landscape, "They call it the Garden of Eden. 'Tis why we come here. 'Tis coming home, again, ta the northern coastal mountains of Anatolia and the Black Sea. That was our beginning; this is where we will plan for the end."

Maggie was speechless at the beauty of the sight, and stunned that such a place was here in America and she had never thought to visit. What a terrible waste of beauty, not to be seen, she thought to herself.

As she looked out, Maggie saw other orbes of light streaking in, drifting, whirling like pin wheels, and moving toward her. There has to be one hundred of them, Maggie thought. As the dancing lights headed closer to Macha and her, Maggie stepped back in fear. But Macha reassured, "They are the spirits of the Amazons coming for our meeting."

Macha took Maggie's hand, "Maggie do ye not know these women are your ancestors. The same blood, the same genes flow through your veins as theirs once did."

Just then the lights drew closer, hovering only feet from the edge of the cave's entrance, moving two and fro and around one another, as if in curiosity trying to get a better look at Maggie. "Come, Maggie," Macha instructed, "let us go in."

As they entered, Maggie saw a fire pit at the rear of the cave, its gentle flames licked the granite wall sprinkled with mica that reflected light throughout the cave. Large rocks had been placed on either side of the deep cavern, in two rows, the back row higher and to the side of the rocks of the first row. It was primitive and efficient, at once.

Macha instructed Maggie to sit next to her on the rocks of the first row. The orbs of lights outside the cave entered one by one, and as they did the round light elongated as the Amazon's apparition became solid. Maggie was in awe of so many six-foot tall women in one place and by the weapons they carried. They were truly an impressive army. Their brown tunics were tied at each shoulder and hung to just above their knees, gathered at the waist by a leather belt. Their bare arms and legs were muscled; their skin pure white. Some carried spears, others had swords tucked in a leather sheathe hanging down the center of their backs that were held by a strap of leather fastened around their neck, another around their waist. And all carried a dagger tucked in the leather belt on the side of their waist. They walked with both grace and the confidence that comes from fearing no one.

Maggie felt a confusion of emotion that oscillated between great fear and absolute safety. She decided to deal with it later. Now was not the time to freak out, she thought to herself.

The Amazons smiled and nodded at Maggie, as they made their way deeper into the cave to take a seat on one of the rocks. That is, except one. She was Queen Penthesilea. She had led the Amazons against the Greeks, and was killed in battle by Achilles.

Maggie leaned toward Macha and whispered, "She's so young! How can she lead the invasion of the Muslim Training Camps?"

"Have faith, Maggie," Macha replied. She waited awhile, giving Maggie a chance to take in the sight of her ancestors for the first time.

"Maggie," Macha said, "these women are your kin. Throughout the Bible you can read of your genealogy. You are descended from Abraham, Jacob/Israel, King David, down through the Khazars – 'tis in your genetics. Look at them! Look at yourself, we're all over six feet tall, we all have blonde or red hair, blue or green eyes, we all have white skin, hair on our arms. We were built for war, just as King David was built for war, 1 Kings 16:18. Only 1-2% of the world's population has red hair; it results from combing two recessive genes – which was done throughout the centuries. That's a miracle in itself! The Khazars have these same genetics; they were the most potent martial power at the time in that region north east of the Black Sea. They are not related to the Ashkenazi; the men don't share the same Y-chromosome. The Khazars are from the Ten Lost Tribes of Northern Israel. The Ashkenazis are descendants of Japheth, Gen. 10; Japheth begot Gomer; Gomer begot Ashkenaz.

Maggie listened closely, "I was always led to believe that short, dark haired, dark skin people were the Israelites. I never expected any of this, or that I was related to it all.

Queen Penthesilea nodded to the Amazon guarding the entrance of the cave, "You may begin." The Amazon nodded to the Queen and walked out to the small cliff and stretched one arm towards the sky and the other down towards the valley, and pulled the electromagnetic fields together in unity, until a great mist appeared outside the cave. The Amazon repeated the stirring of the electromagnetic plasma, until the mist grew larger. Then suddenly the Amazon flew off the cliff and up high above Brown Mountain, pulling the electromagnetic field with her as she flew in swirls, until the mist covered the mountain. She clapped her hands and created a spark that lit up the cloud. Finally, the sound of thunder roared over the mountain as the plasma fed on itself and lightning flashed, over and over again. The Amazon flew down into the cave, leaving the mist over the mountain flashing lightning every three seconds, with the roar of thunder trying to keep pace.

Maggie was startled by the flashes of lightning and the noise of the thunder that continuously pounded the mountain. Macha turned to her and explained, "It will hide us from the evil spirits. In these mountains, these kinds of storms are normal. They won't know 'tis us who started it."

Queen Penthesilea placed her spear against the wall and walked to the center of the Amazons. "We are here to plan the invasion of the Muslim Training Camps. All of you will lead the American women joining us in this battle, some will astral project, others will be live on the ground. The battle will take place on the day that the Granny Quilt Crafters of America demonstrate against the price of cotton in Lafayette Park across from the White House."

Penthesilea walked casually up and down the center aisle of the cave as she related to the Amazons the details of events that would lead up to their killing the Muslims in the Training Camps. Her braided blonde hair was wrapped in a bun at the back of her head and held by a leather band. The light from the flickering fire caressed her hair, and shone like copper sparkles dancing about her head. Around her neck hung a leather pouch that contained the bronze arrowhead taken from the body of the Greek soldier who Achilles had killed for the soldier driving his arrow through the eye of Penthesilea's dead body.

Penthesilea instructed, "The Quilt Crafters are a large group of American women who have decided to take matters into their own hands. We are going to help them, along with McArthur and their armies of spirits. We have been given the privilege of killing the Muslims, won for us by Queen Macha."

"Hail! Hail! Queen Macha!" the repeating echo of voices of the Amazons rang in the deep cavern, until Macha stood and recognized their tribute, nodding her head and smiling.

When their voices finally quieted, Penthesilea continued, "We must be precise in our timing. Next month, the Quilt Crafters are planning an afternoon demonstration lasting into the evening.

Someone in their group was able to communicate with a good spirit and from there they have coordinated their operations with other good spirits and with a few Culper spies inside the White House. Throughout the history of the country, new members have come in to the Culper spy ring and continued the mission of protecting the country; otherwise they would have accomplished their endgame ten years ago as they originally planned. The Culper spies are in the White House, Congress, and the Washington police department, among other institutions."

Penthesilea looked to Macha, "Would you give us your knowledge of the meeting with McArthur, Queen Macha?"

Macha stood up and Penthesilea took her seat next of Maggie. Maggie watched the two Amazons exchange places and sighed heavily, trying to take in the stunning events. How could she relate to being here, sitting among ancient Amazons, her own ancestor, talking about a killing mission in Muslim Training Camps, just a day after watching her 15-year old grandson play baseball and exchanging bubble gum for a cookie with her three-year old grandson? How does the world come together within these dynamics of ancient to present, from fourth dimension to eleventh dimension? Her mind was reeling, as she looked over at the beautiful, ancient Queen of the Amazons sitting just a foot away from her. She wondered if she was in a dream; was she losing her mind; was war just a month away? And so she sighed again, for there was nothing else that she could do. But the sigh told her that she was real, even if not attached to her body at the moment. She had decided to come to learn how to protect her family, her country, and if it meant losing her mind, so be it. She would embrace the eleventh dimension. She would learn how to kill Muslims. She would fight for Jesus and her soul.

Macha began to speak, and as she did, Maggie noticed that the light of the fire shining on her long waves of red hair created an image of fire glowing around her, as if she herself were on fire. Maggie wondered how she must have looked in battle, charging across the field on horseback with the sun's light portraying her as embraced by fire, yet still she charged. How she must have frightened the enemy facing her attack.

"McArthur has approached the spirit Culper spies and they have accepted our help. At precisely the time that the Quilt Crafters begin ta encroach upon the White House gates, just after the Congressional leaders enter the White House for a meeting, cable TV, landlines, Internet, and cell phone ability are going ta be severed. No one outside Washington is going ta know what is going on other than a power outage was caused when installers adding new lines had cut inta the wrong lines. McArthur also has prepared for possession of those who control satellite communication and NORTHCOM, ta prevent any defense jets from flying overhead. Over radio frequencies, possessed CIA agents will make visual reports of the city that everything is quiet. 'Tis a large, complex manipulation, and for us it means that we will find the Muslims sleeping without knowing what happened earlier in the evening in Washington, DC."

Penthesilea interrupted, "That is an incredible mission for McArthur and his spirits."

"I have no concern," Macha assured, "he has the greatest generals under his command."

Penthesilea rose and continued the instruction to the Amazons, "There are 36 camps, mostly along the eastern coast, and across the south to California. Each of you will lead your spirits in attacking one camp. The camps range in size between 25 to 300 acres with three to ten buildings, depending on the number of Muslims being trained on site. They let no one into the camps, so we cannot use civilians to contrive entrance. This will have to be strictly an attack through apparition. Whatever you do, don't let the Muslims escape the camp. Each of your teams must reconnoiter the premises first to locate entrance gates and tunnel escape hatches likely one or two hundred yards from the buildings. Determine how many buildings there are, how many Muslims are on site. Intel reports that they train underground with the entrance being within a house structure. Do not limit your Muslim count to just those on the ground; you must enter the tunnels and add those that you find there. Determine whether or not they have helicopters or small planes; and where and how many vehicles they have. What do they have for resources and how can they use those resources to escape?"

"Those pussies!" yelled one of the Amazons. Immediately, grumbling in agreement permeated the cavern of warriors.

Penthesilea allowed the comments without restraint, and continued on, "It will be best to attack at night when the camp is quiet and they're asleep. Note how many sentries they put in place and whether there are alarm systems, cell phone towers, or generators. Ham radio wires in the trees. Of course, you are to kill the sentries and disable the generators, alarms, and towers, first. If they have sleeping quarters set up in a house structure with three to five in a bedroom, just quietly kill them in their beds. But make sure you start on the first floor. If you start on the second floor and they wake and try to escape, you don't want them kicking the floor and waking those on the lower floor who are closer to the door.

In a barracks type of arrangement, first make sure the doors and windows are sealed from the outside before you begin. If they have twenty to forty sleeping in a room, then killing while they sleep will likely wake the others. You can begin the kill, but if others awake, go to the secondary strategy, which is materialization and hand-to-hand. But you must be efficient, the longer they scream, the more attention it will draw. If they faint, make sure you follow up with slicing their throats. Before you leave the barracks, check every body and make sure the throat has been cut. There are to be no survivors!"

With a thunderous noise, the Amazons suddenly began to stomp there feet on the cavern floor, signifying their agreement.

Penthesilea waited a moment for the Amazons to settle down and then continued, "If they conduct themselves in a military fashion of lights out at 10PM, give them 90 minutes for the last to fall asleep. In the REM stage of sleep, you have one hour to slice throats, since that is when the brain is most active while simultaneously muscle paralysis sets in, including paralysis of the chin and neck. This is the best time to slice a throat. The one-hour kill window applies to all the barracks. Reconnoiter before the night of the kill, so you bring enough spirits with you to kill in each barrack – at the same time."

"Those devils don't deserve the peaceful death of the dagger!" an Amazon yelled, "I say hand-to-hand combat!"

"HAND-TO-HAND!" shouted another. As she stood and raised her fists against the underbelly of the mountain, her voice raging, "I want to hear them scream in fear at the sight of me!"

The flame from the fire reflecting off the mica in the granite exposed the blood thirst in the Amazon's eyes. Not even Satan could defeat her, Maggie thought. Just then, all the Amazons stood, shouting in support of their sisters. "HAND-TO-HAND! HAND-TO-HAND!"

The outcry roared like thunder. Their rage beat against the granite walls in the echoing chamber of the cavern. The fire flashed higher.

"Castrate them the way they castrate their daughters!!

HAND-TO-HAND! HAND-TO-HAND!

Amazons yelling inside, thunder raging outside, it seemed that the whole mountain was trembling.

Maggie's body began to shake with fear. She thanked God that these warriors were not coming after her.

"Settle down!" Penthesilea finally yelled. "Everyone sit down!"

She paused until the quiet of order filled the cave. "No hand-to-hand, and there's no time for castration! We are under precise time restraints. If you start hand-to-hand in one barracks, you'll definitely wake the Muslims in the next barracks and they might escape the camp. This is not a combat mission, this is a killing mission. The plan is to kill all the Muslims in the shortest amount of time. And then get out of there!" Penthesilea instructed.

"You will have four hours to complete the mission, from reconnoitering current conditions, disabling security, killing the sentries, to the main kill. And let me make clear, there's no time for anything else! Slice the throats and get out. But make sure you cut to the spine!"

Penthesilea walked over to the entrance of the cave and looked out at the lightning still striking fiercely. She turned back to the Amazons, "All right. We need to end the light show soon. Any questions? No? I have a list of the camps, here, I'll pass this around for you to see your assignment. Macha, you have the camp in South Carolina."

"I thank ye for that, Penthesilea," Macha replied.

Penthesilea instructed, "Amazons, go to your camps, look them over, watch them for a couple of days and see what you're dealing with. What kind of activity is going on; does anyone train and then leave. If they leave, follow them to where they live. When you're finished in the camps, go to their homes. Make sure you do not materialize; we cannot forewarn them by any means. And no fancy orbes of light, either! Meet with the American women who will be astral projecting, train them in the use of the dagger. One thing to be careful of is the silver thread attached to the soul of the woman in astral projection. Do not cut it! This is something we have never dealt with. Orchestrate the dance of the silver cord and dagger!"

Macha stood to speak a final word to the Amazons, "There are American women, who will fight as live soldiers, but ye must contact 'em. They are spread across the country, in small towns and large cities. They are waiting for a leader. Each of ye will be that leader. Go ta these women when they sleep and speak ta their dreams. Put images in their minds of 'em cutting through the fences of the camps and killing the Muslims who escape the dance of the silver cord and dagger. Tell 'em ta make contact with other women in their towns where these camps are located, especially women who are members of local gun clubs. Women who are hunters of game must be made ta be hunters of men, an easier task. Tell the leaders when ta attack and how, so they may instruct their groups. The night of attack is the evening that the Granny Quilt Crafters of America storm the White House. The live women warriors must cut through the camp compound fencing, so make sure ye cut the electricity, first thing, ta allow them entrance ta the camp before ye begin the kill. Instruct those live women ta find a place inside the compound, ta lie low in wait for Muslims trying ta escape, and then pick 'em off like a shooting gallery. Google Earth will give 'em satellite imaging of the camps' layout."

Penthesilea pointed to one of the Amazons sitting nearest to the cave's entrance, "You may clear it, now."

The Amazon unsheathed her sword carried on her back and walked to the edge of the cliff outside the cave's entrance and flew up into the cloud, her sword slicing through the electromagnetic field of the mist that covered the Brown Mountain. Lightning flashed wildly, violently, inside the blue mist that hung protectively over the ridge. As the Amazon flew through the noise of roaring thunder, her sword collected the ions of white hot heat. She playfully flew in a swirl through the mist and down to the tallest branch of the tallest tree atop Brown Mountain. With one hand holding her sword up into the electrified mist, her other hand grabbed the branch of the tree. With a violent roar and blinding flash of light the electricity of the cloud ran down the sword through the Amazon's spirit, into the spine of the tree and down into the seismic fault of the rock below.

Chapter 16

The weather was unseasonably cool. The overcast skies and rain of April persevered into May. But as the afternoon wore on, clouds were defeated by sunshine, and a gentle, mild breeze created a perfect spring day. Quinn and Maggie's wedding day. The children had been invited along with a few friends. The wedding was planned quickly, but only the ceremony mattered to Maggie. She had found a minister to perform the ceremony on Back Beach at Rockport, across from the home of her elder son, Jacob. Quinn's friend, Jack, would be the best man. Maggie's daughter, Alexandria, would be her maid of honor. Jacob had insisted that a reception be held at his house. Quinn's friends set up their band instruments in the great room. Persian rugs had been rolled out of the way for dancing. Friends and neighbors brought dishes of food. A barbeque grill and keg were set up on the rear patio, and a bar was set up in the parlor between the great room and the dining room. The front porch was laced with tiny white lights that grew more charming as evening began to fall.

Quinn had stayed in a hotel on the beach the night before. Maggie and her children and grandchildren had slept at Jacob's house. After the reception Maggie would go back to the hotel with Quinn, to their honeymoon suite. There was no time to go away on a honeymoon.

Just as the sun began to set, Quinn, his children, and Jack arrived at the beach followed by the priest. In the moments before Maggie arrived, Jack adjusted the boutonnière in Quinn's suit jacket lapel.

"Do I look okay," Quinn asked Jack.

"You look just fine," Jack smiled.

A few minutes later, Maggie and her daughter arrived with Maggie's two sons. When they got out of the car, Alexandria handed Maggie her small bouquet of lavender flowers and fixed the pearls caught on the collar of her pale yellow silk suit. Jacob and David escorted the women down to the beach. Alexandria was the only one under six feet, but only by one inch. Each of Maggie's children had a different shade of red hair. Jacob's auburn hair, straight body, stern face, gave him the look of a serious man. Alexandria's shining copper hair and hour-glass figure were accentuated by her mint-green silk dress. David's tawny hair, mustache and beard, broad shoulders and thick arms made him look like a Viking stepping off a longship. When Maggie and Jacob reached Quinn, Jacob gave his mother's hand to Quinn.

Quinn smiled, "You look so beautiful, Maggie."

"So do you," Maggie smiled in return.

Jacob joined Quinn's son, Joe, and his wife Kelly. Joe was tall and self-assured with his father's dark hair. Kelly had the natural beauty of the Irish, with high, rosy cheek bones, fine features, and chestnut hair. Her blue eyes sparkled when she smiled at Jacob's symbolic gesture of shaking Joe's hand. For when Jacob and Joe stood as witnesses to their parents' union, it was the coming together of first-borns in approval of the union. Quinn's daughter, Kate, had honey-colored hair with her father's light-brown eyes. Her husband, Nathan, was blonde with light blue eyes, typical of his Germanic bloodline. The tall slender couple stood next to David and his wife, Sara. Not far in Sara's past were her college athletics and sky-diving hobby that still marked her body with toned muscles. Her black hair curled softly under her chin and framed her flawless skin. Alexandria's husband, Seth, his black hair beginning to gray, had large blue eyes, and although somewhat shorter than the other men, he had strong broad shoulders.

Jack looked at the two families and then up to the passers-by on the sidewalk above the beach, stopping to look before continuing on. He understood that these two families could not be ignored.

The smell of the salt air, the sound of the waves gently lapping the sand, brought a peace to the occasion. Maggie and Quinn turned toward the priest and the ocean behind him. But they couldn't take their eyes off each other; to turn away would break the intertwining of their souls. And each wanted that intertwining. It had seemed that all that each had lived through had been in preparation of their souls' awareness of the other. It was as if God's hands had carved reciprocating planes within their hearts and instilled the knowledge in their minds that they belonged together. All were the steps coming up to this moment in time. And each was grateful for the other. Maggie saw a steadfast ability in Quinn's eyes. A quiet serenity that experience rendered from skills mastered, from the fulfillment of responsibility, from passing through the portal of pain, coming through the other side aware of life's purpose. Quinn had lived a self-examined life, the good life. He bowed to no one but Jesus Christ. And, now, he came to take Maggie as his wife. He was the most sensuous man Maggie had ever met, and she came to take him for her husband.

The priest began the ceremony with prayers, and then he asked, "Do you Quinn take Maggie to be your lawfully wedded wife, to honor and cherish, in sickness and in health, forsaking all others, till death do you part?" Quinn looked at Maggie and said, "I do." The priest asked, "Maggie, do you take Quinn to be your lawfully wedded husband, to honor and cherish, in sickness and in health, forsaking all others, till death do you part?" Maggie said, "I do." Jack brought over the rings for the priest to bless. Quinn placed his ring on Maggie's finger and Maggie placed her ring on Quinn's finger. The priest said, "I now pronounce you husband and wife." Maggie and Quinn looked at each other and kissed.

Maggie turned to her children as they came over to wish her well and hug her. Tears welled in their eyes, each telling her, "You deserve this." "You were a good mother; I know you will be a good wife." "Don't forget us!" Then Maggie turned to Quinn's daughter, Kate, and his son, Joe. Each hugged her and said, "Welcome to the family." "Take good care of our father." Quinn hugged Maggie's children as they welcomed him to their family. "Be good to our mother!"

Quinn teased, "I hope all you kids will get along!" Jacob turned to Joe, the two smiled at each other, "It's good to have a brother," Joe said, as he hugged Jacob. Alexandria hugged Kate, "It's nice to have a sister!" "Me, too," cried Kate. "Well, I'm still the baby," David said, "that makes me special!" They all laughed at the absurdity of the statement in reflection of their ages. "No, that means we get to pick on you!" "Look at it this way; I'm bigger than all of you, so I'm special!" David smiled, as he hugged each of his siblings.

Jack was more than a ceremonial best man; he had been Quinn's best friend for the past 30 years. They had met in Special Ops training, yet assigned to different teams. Jack had been with Quinn when his wife died, and each were at the weddings of their children. Both had become grandfathers at the same time. Every season, they hunted together. Jack knew Quinn had loved his wife, but he could see that nothing had captured Quinn's heart the way that Maggie had.

Both Jack and Quinn had kept up weight training throughout the years. They didn't have the muscles of their Special Ops days, but they were trim and strong. Jack's eyes now needed glasses, his hair had thinned and grayed, yet those were the only features that noted his age. He walked up to Maggie and as he bent to kiss her, said, "God bless you both."

Quinn hugged Jack, "Let's go celebrate!"

At Jacob's house, neighbors were lighting up the barbeque out back and putting a tap into the keg of beer. Dawn was putting ice cubes into a container for the bar in the parlor. Janet and Phyllis were putting out dishes of food on the dining room table. Quinn's friends, James and Rudy, finished plugging in guitars, setting up the drums, and moving furniture around in the great room to make way for dancing.

As the wedding party walked up toward Jacob's house, the tiny white lights wrapped around the columns and railings of the long front porch greeted them with festive enchantment. Maggie looked up at the dining room window. The chandelier reflecting off the orange Venetian walls gave the room a warm glow. Maggie remembered all the hard work of plastering and sanding the walls, but thinking now that it was all worth it. Quinn and Maggie walked up the steep granite steps to the porch. The neighbors sitting at the garden table stood and began to sing to them. After one chorus, Jack interrupted, "Okay. We'll be doing that throughout the night. Right now, let's have everyone congregate in the great room."

As everyone entered the house, the grandchildren were running through the rooms, discovering a circular path from the great room into the parlor, then into the foyer and dining room beyond, and into the kitchen, and back into the parlor – it was an endless game of hide and seek. Their little voices screeched when then ran in to each other again in the parlor. In the foyer, the smooth, mahogany banister that circled to the floor was too much fun to resist for Quinn's six-year old grandson. From the second floor hallway, he flew down just missing his little sister running through, heading for the dining room.

Jack called out, "Let's get champagne into some glasses!" He looked around the great room and into the parlor, "Where are the bar maids!" The wedding guests echoed his cry, "Where are the bar maids!"

Jacob's neighbors, Phyllis and Janet, yelled back, "We're coming! We're coming," as each brought a tray of glasses filled with champagne.

"Thank you, ladies!" Jack cried. "I would like to toast Maggie and Quinn. I'll wait for everyone to get their glasses ready." Jack watched as Janet and Phyllis walked through the crowded room and glasses were taken off the trays by reaching hands.

"Maggie! Quinn! Yours is a rare relationship. You knew the first time you met that you would love each other for all time. That is a gift. May you always have your love and each other, no matter what may come." Jack paused a moment, then lifted his glass, "To Maggie and Quinn!" and drained the champagne. The guests cheered, "To Maggie and Quinn!"

"Now, for some music!" Jack announced, taking off his jacket, as he walked over to his guitar, calling James and Rudy - "Let's tune it up boys!"

Quinn turned to Maggie and asked, "Could I have this dance," and finished by singing, "for the rest of my life?"

Maggie smiled and took Quinn's outreached hand, and whispered, "You may, my dear husband." Each smiled at hearing Maggie call Quinn her husband for the first time.

The slow waltz swayed gently, naively, and unsophisticated. The guitars twanged soulfully, their notes softly caressing. As they danced, the two melted in to one, comfortably, safely, and sadly. Quinn whispered into Maggie's ear, "Will you be my partner, for the rest of my life?" Both knew that this would be the last time they would dance, for the war was just three weeks away. Neither were certain that they would survive the battles ahead of them. And should either die, the other would be alone, pining the rest of their life for the other. A tear slowly rolled down Maggie's cheek, but she said not a word to Quinn. The moment, the music, being in Quinn's arms, were all too precious to be interrupted by silly crying. But a little quiver of her breath escaped. Quinn felt it and hugged her closer still, lovingly wrapping both his arms around her as they danced. Maggie had never been so sure of her love for Quinn than she was at that moment. She thought to herself, life is so tender, love so precious. How does it survive in a world filled with such evil. She had no answer.

Over by the large window at the end of the great room, Maggie's 3-yr old grandson danced with Quinn's 2-yr old granddaughter. But soon their attention was taken by the Tall Ship replica on the window's sill. Michael knelt down in front of it; Erin sat down on the sill and watched patiently, as Michael pointed to the parts of the ship, even though the music was too loud for her to hear his lecture.

Couples filled the dance floor, surrounding Maggie and Quinn dancing in the center of the room. Jack sang as he played his guitar, knowing how much the song touched the hearts of the bride and groom, for he too, knew of the war to come. But tonight was for merriment and love, and talk of war was pushed away. At least for the moment.

Phyllis and Dawn went out to the back patio to check on the barbeque that Gary was tending to. "Gary, what will you have? Hard stuff or beer?" Phyllis asked.

"I'll have another beer, if you don't mind, Phyllis," Gary replied. "Here, you can refill my glass."

"Those ribs smell luscious!" Dawn remarked, as she walked over and checked the platters of potatoes and corn that had been roasted.

"It's my special marinade," Gary whispered, leaning toward Dawn. "I came over last night and made it. The ribs were soaking in it all night."

"How would you like to come to my barbeque next week, after the sailing races, and cook for me?" Dawn grinned.

"Don't let Barbara hear you say that, my wife is very possessive," Gary joked.

John walked out, "Hey, Gary! Are those ribs done yet? I can't wait to sink my teeth into them. Did you use your recipe on them?"

"That I did, John, that I did. Just another minute and you'll be in heaven!"

After their dance, Maggie and Quinn had circulated among the guests. At the garden table, Maggie sat down and lit up a cigarette. Quinn followed with drinks for both and sat down next to her. The porch soon filled with neighbors asking if it was the smoking section. Laughter and talk, and ice cubes clinking in glasses were wrapped in the tiny white lights of the porch railings. Music drifted out the screen doors and windows of the great room. While Jack sang inside, the neighbors on the porch sang in harmony to Irish Eyes Are Smiling, "Sure they stealll your hearrrrt awayyyyy."

Quinn leaned toward Maggie, "I hate to leave the porch, but we have other guests, too."

"I know," Maggie agreed, "We can come back." The two went into the great room and found Maggie's son, David, and his wife, Sara, dancing a polka all around the great room. Others, sitting on sofas that had been moved up against walls, clapped their hands in rhythm. Guests standing in front of the fireplace tried to talk to each other above the gaiety.

"Better watch out!" Quinn laughed, "They'll run you over!"

As they entered the parlor, Janet was tending bar and called Maggie over. "Is there anything I can get you, Maggie?"

"No, but how about you? Do you need a break?"

"No, no. I'm havn' a fine time. Really a LOVELY time," Janet began to giggle.

"That's good," Maggie laughed in return. "I'm having a lovely time, myself!"

When the two women recognized the silliness of the moment,

they laughed even harder.

Quinn interrupted, "I'm going into the dining room and get a plate of food. Do you want some?"

"Oh, yes. That would be lovely, too," Maggie said and turned to Janet; the two began to laugh, again.

"Can I get you something to eat, Janet?" Quinn asked.

"Yes! That would be lovely," Janet grinned. Maggie bent in laughter.

"Oh, gees!" Quinn moaned. "Maggie, why don't we go sit in the dining room and have something to eat."

"Okay!" Maggie grinned. "I'm sorry, Quinn," Maggie whispered, "I was okay when I was sitting down. When I got up, it just hit me. But it doesn't take much to get me inebri inebiiii...drunk!" She straightened her body, "Maybe I should have warned you about that sooner!"

Quinn's children were in the dining room with Maggie's, feeding the grandchildren. When Maggie saw them, she suddenly stood at attention and then turned to Quinn, "Pisst! Don't let your children see you drunk!"

"No," Quinn whispered, "I won't let them. How would you like a steak? They just brought some in from the barbeque."

"That would be lovely," Maggie said and immediately began to giggle.

Maggie sat down at the long table and watched Quinn prepare her a plate of steak, salad, and a roll. "I'm so lucky I married you, Quinn," Maggie smiled, "You are such a great cook!"

Quinn couldn't keep from laughing. "Yes. I am quite a cook, aren't I?"

Jacob leaned toward Maggie and whispered, "How much have you had to drink?"

Maggie realized Jacob was cautioning her not to have any more. "I'll be all right, just as soon as I eat this steak. Quinn cooked it for me." Maggie grinned.

"Leave her alone," Kate quietly instructed Jacob. "This is her wedding. Let her have some fun." It was a disconcerting instruction coming from his new stepsister.

As the evening went on, Kate and Alexandria brought the grandchildren upstairs to bed and closed the doors to the ante-rooms and the outer bedrooms to further quiet their sleeping. As the two young women met in the upstairs foyer, one comment led to a discussion.

Kate asked Alexandria, "So, do you think your mother is going to fight?"

"She only mentioned that she and your father were going to be busy on June 6th. But that she'd explain later. Do you know what's going on?"

"Not really, but I know they're up to something," Kate replied.

"All I know is that there's something palpable in the air,"

Alexandria said. "Have you noticed Jack, James, and Rudy? They look as though they're hiding something. I'm mean. They look upset, but smiling in spite of whatever is making the three of them upset. They're Quinn's best friends. He must have said something to them. Why don't we see that the band takes a break. The keg is out on the back patio. Let's get them out there. Maybe we can pry information out of them."

But when the two women got downstairs, the band had already stopped to take a break. Going out to the front porch to have a drink and a cigarette, the men found one of the neighbors yelling at another. Jack nodded to James and Rudy, and the three listened quietly from the other end of the porch. The neighbors were unaware of the danger that lies within the dog that doesn't bark.

"Tsaeb is going to use that UN Arms Treaty to take away our guns! You idiot!"

"I don't care! We need gun control!" the other neighbor yelled back.

"We need to get guns out of people's hands to stop the crime across the world," a third neighbor joined in.

Phyllis sat listening for a while and then added, "Tsaeb knows what he's doing. Give him a chance to prove himself." The old woman saw herself as a righteous liberal and anyone who disagreed was wrong. "You people are listening too much to Fox News."

"Fox News is a joke! Rupera Mudick owns it and he's a member of the Foreign Affairs Private Council. How bias do you think that news is? I don't get my information from them! I listen to the Senate floor speeches. The UN speeches!"

"Well, I don't think anyone but the government should own guns," Phyllis declared.

"Phyllis! Take your communist ways and dump them at sea! It's right over there!" Janet pointed at the ocean a few hundred feet away.

"I'm telling you," John warned, "Tsaeb will take our guns away through the UN treaty. And Phyllis, you don't know what you're talking about. If you don't see that Tsaeb is an enemy terrorist of our country, then your ignorance makes you an enemy, too!"

James looked at Jack and Rudy; then took a sip of his whiskey. Each thought that John might be a contact, if needed later in the war.

"The treaty requires a UN gun registration. What the hell business is it of theirs?" a neighbor cried.

"I agree! What the hell business is it of the UN, if I own a gun? Why do they need to know my name and address and the serial number on my gun? I don't answer to them! They have no jurisdiction over me!"

"They want your name and address so they can come and take your gun from you! That's why. That is, unless the treaty's requirement for stricter licensing requirements keeps you from getting a renewal."

"Well, they're goin'a ban private ownership of semi-automatic weapons. It's the right thing to do. It'll bring peace to the world! There's too much war!"

"War between two countries is not started by its citizens; it's started by their government leaders!"

"They won't be satisfied with citizens owning rocks to throw at their lousy UN troops!"

"That's not the worst of it," John interrupted his neighbors. "What that treaty will do is destroy American sovereignty. It's a major step in ending nationhood. We'd say good-bye to our Constitution and helloooo to the New World Order! After they take our guns, the New World Order can set any law they want. How could we stop them?"

John took a sip of beer, "The difference between the WWII Germans and Jews is that neither thought to violently overthrow their government. Americans have! Most Germans didn't even own guns. BUT! Here in America!" John lifted his glass in gesture, "More Americans own guns than any other people in the world. America manufactures more guns than any other country. It's a $55 billion industry and we export to the world. When it looked as though Tsaeb would win election, gun sales here in America shot up 400%. Ammo has tripled in price. Supply and demand! They know we aren't going to let the Congress dictate gun restriction. So, they're going to have the UN do it for them. We're a member of the UN. The elite will get the majority of UN member nations to require an international registry and a ban on semi-automatic weapons here in America. And no state law can override that treaty!"

"Wait a minute!" Jacob interrupted. "Reid v. Covert, 1957, the U.S. Supreme Court established that the Constitution supersedes international treaties. The UN Arms Trade Treaty cannot ban our guns."

Kate's husband, Nathan, countered, "But Congress can REGULATE the sale of semi-automatic guns to the point that only a handful of Americans can buy them. They'll give us shotguns, give us revolvers, and claim that the right to bear arms has not been compromised by the treaty. But those kinds of guns won't stand up in battle against AK-47s or the other guns that the military has. It's a false interpretation of the right to bear arms."

"That's right!" John said. "The Second Amendment right to bear arms does not state what kind of guns. Congress can, again, falsely interpret the Constitution. If you consider what guns the citizens had versus what the military had back in 1776, they were the same type. The farmers brought their own guns to the revolution! Therefore, the Founding Fathers didn't think to categorize which guns citizens can carry. Congress has, in the past, intentionally, erroneously interpreted what the Constitution means by 'to regulate.' It legally means to make sure that commerce flows between the states. In other words, no state can ban another state's citizen from buying their goods, bar their college entrance, bar eating in their restaurants. That's the limit to Congress' commerce power. But Congress intentionally misuses the commerce clause power, to dictate.

Remember Senator Chuck Schillmer saying, 'We can do anything we want!' Hence, they strategized, let's not call this a treaty as in an agreement to take guns away from our citizens; the Second Amendment would prohibit that. Let's call it the UN Arms TRADE Treaty. Therefore, as a trade treaty, Congress can regulate it. Congress can restrict semi-automatic ownership for some contrived commerce reason. Congress can tax the sale of semis out of the hands of the average citizen. They can restrict purchase because of age, because of health issues, vision, jobs, or require military training. They can, as Chucky put it, do 'anything' Congress wants to do! And if they can get the other member states of the UN to all agree on the specific language of the trade treaty that speaks to Congress' commerce power, then the UN, by administrative authority of that treaty, can take and destroy all 'unauthorized' guns from Americans. FDR required that all Americans turn in their gold coins!

The treaty's international gun registry will tell them who has the semis and where those Americans live. As a UN member, the U.S. will be forced in to compliance. The US Supreme Court cannot stop Congress' commerce trade power with foreign nations. Art. I, Sec. 8, cl. 3. Nor can the American people, prevent the Senate from ratifying the treaty. As long as Tsaeb gets two thirds of the Senators 'present' to concur, Tsaeb can sign the UN Arms Trade Treaty. Art. II., Sec. 2, cl. 2. And there go our semi-automatic guns. Our 9mm. And anything with a magazine even though you have to pull the trigger for every shot."

When John finished, he turned, "Phyllis, I give you the real terrorists destroying the United States of America and its Constitution: its Congresses and its Presidents. They are a cancer within. And if you think for one minute that revolution is not around the corner, you're deluding yourself. The American people will not hand over their guns without a battle. I certainly won't!"

Again, James looked at Jack and Rudy, but this time he nodded. Jack and Rudy understood that they could trust John, if need be.

"So, is that why Jillary demanded a consensus decision in negotiating the text of the treaty?" Sara asked.

Jack added, "Yes. And some NGOs are demanding that the treaty bar transfer of weapons, if it substantially risks or seriously impairs poverty reduction or socioeconomic development. You know what that means? The NGOs are going to force American manufacturers to give their resources and teach their manufacturing skills, to third-world countries, so they will prosper in competition with American gun manufacturers. It was the same with the Law of the Sea Treaty!"

"But they couldn't pass the Law of the Sea Treaty, because everyone knew about it," David interjected, "so they did it through the Clear Water Act. Quickly and quietly. Most Americans don't know what it provides. It gives the UN control over all American in-land waterways and both the east and west coastal waters. That got passed, but unconstitutionally, because the Senate did not give its advice and consent as a treaty. The Clear Water Act is unconstitutional!"

"The bottom line is," John concluded, "they are going to try to take our guns to keep us from revolting against the deepening of their enslavement of us!"

"Let them come and take them!" a neighbor quietly interjected.

"Molon Labe," David said.

Alexandria's husband, Seth, listening to the discussion, asked David, "What does molon Labe mean?"

"King Leonides replied 'molon Labe' to the Persian's demand that the 300 Spartans hand over their weapons before the Battle of Thermopylae. It means, 'come and take them.' There was a movie about the battle," David explained.

As Maggie listened to the discussion on the front porch, Kate called from the great room's screen door, "Can you help me with something, Maggie?"

"Sure, Kate," Maggie replied, as she got up from the garden table. She followed Kate out to the back patio where Alexandria waited.

"What's going on," Maggie asked. "Is everything all right? Are the children okay?"

"Yes, they're in bed," Alexandria answered. "But that's what we want to know, Marm. We know that something is wrong. Kate and I were just talking about the concern that seems to be prevalent under all the smiles between you and Quinn and Quinn's friends. You all know something."

Maggie turned away from Alexandria and walked over to the stone wall. She looked at the yellow flowers growing on the sloping hill and then up higher, to the granite outcrop a hundred feet above. She wondered if she could, if she should, say something now. She and Quinn had discussed what to say to the children, but wanted to wait until after the wedding. The reception would be their last time for lightheartedness. All their children had prepared for war, finally, after a year of preaching to them. There was nothing else that they could do to protect themselves or the grandchildren that they hadn't done already. That is, except what Quinn and Maggie would ask of them after the guests had left the reception.

"Come on, Marm," Alexandria demanded. "You know I don't ask questions of what you do, but something is about to happen, and I think we need to know what that is. And it seems to involve both you and Quinn. So, Kate wants to know, too."

Maggie turned around and looked up at the open, upstairs windows where the grandchildren slept, then said, "Okay. Let's all sit down. And keep your voices down. We don't want to wake the children. No one must hear us. As you might have just heard, a couple of the neighbors are communists – whether they realize it or not. Who knows?"

Kate and Alexandria looked at each other, knowing that they weren't going to like what Maggie was about to confide in them. Each grabbed one of the lawn chairs strewn about the patio and placed them in a tight circle. Maggie lit a cigarette and blew the smoke away from the young women.

She first looked over to the kitchen's screen door to see if anyone was coming near them from inside the house and then looked at the sides of the yard. In a low voice, she said, "June 6th. There's going to be an attack."

Kate and Alexandria looked at each other in silence and then back at Maggie.

"God, I don't know where to begin."

"Start with an outline," Kate offered.

"Inter-dimensional armies are poised to fight the elite."

"What do you mean inter-dimensional?" Alexandria asked.

"We live in the fourth dimension."

"Yesss," Alexandria said slowly, waiting for the more frightening description to come next.

"There's also the 11th dimension," Maggie instructed. Looking at Alexandria, "I've told you about the ghosts in this house. I know Jacob doesn't like to talk about them. But you know about them."

"Yes, and are you saying that the ghosts in this house are going to war?"

"No!" Maggie said.

"I'm glad to hear that because I was about to admit you to the funny farm." Alexandria smiled.

Maggie sighed. "We didn't want to tell any of you until after the guests left." Maggie paused, "Okay, I'm just going to say it. There are 11th dimensional ghosts from the different wars of this country. They are going to fight with Quinn."

Thinking she heard a noise from inside the kitchen, Maggie stood up and walked over to the windows and peaked in to see if any guests were inside, seeing none, she turned to her daughter and now step-daughter and finished in a low voice, "To overthrow the government."

Alexandria opened her mouth, about to repeat what Maggie had just told her, when Maggie put her finger up to her lips and cautioned, "Shhhhh."

Alexandria nodded. "Are you? Will you be...?"

"Yes," Maggie said, as she sat back down. "I told you about the Muslim Training Camps. Well, I'm going to go with the 11th dimensional ghosts of Queen Macha and Queen Penthesilea along with the Amazons and take out the Muslims in the camps."

Alexandria and Kate turned slowly to each other. After a moment, they burst into laughter.

Kate asked, "You're pulling our leg, aren't you, Maggie?"

"No. I'm not, Kate. I've already astral projected with Queen Macha to Brown Mountain in North Carolina and met with the Amazons." Maggie took a long drag from her cigarette, "I have to tell you, they're a scary bunch!"

"Oh gees!" Alexandria cried, thinking to herself, this is too absurd! But then, why else would Jack and the rest be so upset? She grabbed the arms of the lawn chair and leaned toward Maggie and whispered, "Are you serious! Are you telling the truth?"

"Yes, Alexandria, I'm telling you the truth! And I know how fictional this all sounds. I've lost sleep over it all. I'm scared to death. About the war, the Amazons, and the Muslims! I've never killed anyone before. And I don't know if I can do it, yet how can I not kill the enemy who are planning to kill my family?" Maggie answered. "We're raised to be law-abiding, and the same government and church that has instilled that ideal into our culture, our classrooms, is using that mindset to keep us from revolting against them while they're plotting our destruction!"

"Give me a cigarette," Alexandria demanded.

Kate got up, "I'm getting myself a drink. What about you guys?"

"7 and 7" Maggie sighed.

"Me too," Alexandria said.

While Kate went inside to get the drinks, Alexandria turned to Maggie. "I don't know what to say. How did you get yourself mixed up with these...these things...did you meet them on the Internet websites!? How can you trust them? You're too old to fight! What if you get killed!"

"No! I didn't meet them on the Internet. It was the ghost of Will Booker. And when you astral project, you leave the body; your spirit is full of energy. And I die when God says so!"

"Will Booker?" Alexandria asked, just as Kate came out with a tray of drinks for the three of them.

"Do you have any more cigarettes," Kate asked, "I gave up smoking to have the baby. But I need one, and right now!"

"Your father," Maggie said, as she looked up at Kate standing in front of her, handing her the cigarettes, "Your father and I were having dinner at my apartment when the ghost of Will Booker got our attention. He put the salt and pepper shakers up on the kitchen pass-through. Then he started communicating with us. It was the next day that Will Booker took your father astral projecting to meet the ghost of General Eisenhower and the leaders of Quinn's 11th Regiment."

Kate took a long drag from her cigarette, blew out the smoke and then swallowed half her drink. "Go on."

"After that the ghost of Queen Macha appeared in my apartment." Maggie turned to Alexandria, "You wouldn't believe how much she and I look alike. Well, when I was your age. When my hair was red. Before it turned gray, and I started dying it blonde. She's our ancestor!"

Alexandria threw back her drink and then got up, "Kate do you want another drink? I'm going for another drink."

"Yes, please! By the time you get back, I'll have finished this one," Kate replied.

"I know this is hard on both of you, Kate. Your father and I wanted to spare this anxiety that you and Alexandria are feeling right now."

The night was late, quiet. Under the patio's light, Kate and Maggie sat in silence waiting for Alexandria to bring out the drinks, before continuing with their discussion. Suddenly, the antique German clock that had been given to Jacob started to chime. Maggie turned to Kate, "Do you hear that?"

"Yes," Kate said, "What a pretty chime."

A moment later, Alexandria and Jacob were at the kitchen door, their faces white, their eyes full of fear. "Jacob! Alexandria! Are you okay?" Maggie asked. "Come out here!"

"Did you hear the clock?" Jacob asked, as he and Alexandria stepped out to the patio.

"Kate was just saying how pretty it sounds."

"Marm," Jacob said, "I never got that clock fixed. But this time when Alexandria and I were at the parlor bar, the clock started to chime. I didn't hear it when you heard it last year. But we both heard it just now. And you and Kate heard it."

Something made Maggie turn and look at the window. The ceiling light of the kitchen shone over a woman looking out at them on the back patio. When she saw the apparition, Maggie gasped softly. One by one, Jacob, Kate, and Alexandria turned and saw the woman. As they watched, the apparition slowly disappeared. Kate jumped up from the lawn chair, whispering, "What was that?!" The three grabbed at each other in fear and stood pressed together, too fearful to say a word that might bring the apparition to them.

Maggie got up and went into the kitchen, seeing no one she walked into the parlor and saw the German clock on the top shelf of the inset china cabinet. The hands weren't on the hour. There was no timing trigger that caused it to chime, regardless of whether it was broken. The guests that remained were all out on the front porch, still arguing, and unaware of the clock chiming. She walked through the foyer into the dining room, empty. She continued through into the kitchen and there on the kitchen's table was an antique box that hadn't been there when she first entered the house. Maggie walked over to it, opened the box, and saw two pistols and a small oval placard with the inscription, Dennis Townson, 1796.

"Oh, my God," Maggie cried, and carried the box outside to her son.

"Jacob, did you buy these pistols?"

"What pistols? What are you talking about?"

Maggie handed him the box, "Read the placard inside."

"Townson. That's the name of the man who built this house," Jacob cried. "Dennis Townson. Where did you get this? The house was empty when I moved in."

"It was sitting on the breakfast table. I think the ghost we saw in the window set off the clock's chimes to get our attention. So we would look and find the box."

"What is going on?" Kate asked. "Jacob, do you really have ghosts living in this house?"

Jacob looked at Maggie, at first somewhat angry that Maggie told her, but then realized that the ghost's own apparition could not be denied. "Yes. There're ghosts here. My mother saw part of a woman's skirt, as she walked pass the kitchen doorway and disappeared into the parlor's inset china cabinet. She's...there are so many accounts of her."

Jacob sighed heavily and pulled up a lawn chair to sit next to the women. "Once, I heard two children laughing; one asked the other 'should we wake him.' And one time, I was having a nightmare, and a woman called my name and woke me, but there was no one there in the room. Another time, I heard a knocking on my bedroom door." Jacob shook his head, "It just keeps going on." He turned to Maggie, "Remember you heard what sounded like the paint cans being thrown around the dining room." He turned to Alexandria and Kate, "She doesn't like the house pulled apart. It took us six months of weekends to finish the dining room, but it was after about five months that she started making noises. One night, when I was reading in my office upstairs, I heard the plaster trowel being knocked against the aluminum ladder down in the dining room. It was as though she was telling me to finish it."

"That's so strange," Kate paused, "I noticed a very peaceful feeling in the dining room, earlier."

Maggie explained, "Since we finished, there is a very peaceful sensation when you stand in that room. I told Jacob that I think the woman ghost really likes the Venetian walls."

"I don't blame her; I couldn't keep from touching them. They feel like cool, polished marble. They're really beautiful."

"Okay. Let's get back to the guns," Alexandria interrupted.

"Jacob, did you get a gun license and a gun, yet?" Maggie asked, knowing the answer.

"No. I hate guns. Besides, they'll come first to take the guns of citizens' who have registered them. That's the point of registration, isn't it, so they know who has what gun and where they can come and take it away from you."

"Well, I think your lady ghost is trying to arm you. Without registering the gun," Kate suggested.

Jacob looked at one of the pistols more closely. On the side of its grip, there was an N with what looked like a crown sitting on top of the letter. The engraved brass lock plate and barrel band was exquisitely carved. An eagle encircled by a Roman-style wreath on the pistol's butt plate indicated to Jacob that the guns were worth a lot of money. He assumed they were French pistols. But, he wondered to himself, why did she bring them out, now?

"Napoleonic Code of Law," Jacob stated, "Napoleon tried to institute it after the French Revolution. He based his code of law on

Justinian Roman Law, it's the basis of our American law. It replaced the feudal laws of Europe that existed between the 9th and 15th centuries. Feudalism was basically slavery whereby the King or Lord granted privileges and charters to certain people based on their birth, and exempted those elite from the custom, the custom being the only law. But the customs were ill defined. Napoleonic Code mandated clearly written and accessible law without granting exemptions for the elite. Napoleonic Code made uniform the civil law of France. It specified that government jobs go to the most qualified. It allowed for freedom of religion. It influenced the whole world!"

"The Congress of Vienna," Maggie cried, "it declared Napoleon an outlaw. That Congress was the precursor of the League of Nations and later the United Nations. Austria, Russia, Britain, Prussia Germany were the four big leaders that came up with the Treaty of Paris, the Charter of 1814. It restored the Bourbons of France, Louis XVIII to the throne of France. The Charter held that Frenchmen were equal before the law, but restored the King and nobility, based on birth, giving them substantial and exclusive rights and privileges above the law. The King proposed laws, appointed ministers, which were only men of large property holdings, and only one per cent of the people could vote. Otherwise, the Napoleonic Code was kept intact."

Maggie looked at each of her children and Kate, "And what were the causes of the French Revolution? It was hunger and malnutrition from poor harvests; the national debt; growing commercial dominance by Britain that drove down the French economy, and taxes. The King was isolated and indifferent to the poor. He was also indecisive and backed down against strong opposition. Must I do a comparative analysis with the U.S. - or will it suffice to say that while similar our causes for revolution outnumber the French."

Maggie turned to Alexandria, "It matters not whether I fight, whether you hide or whether you all ignore what is going on, war is coming!"

Jacob sighed, "I remember reading about the Papacy during the Medieval period, 800-1500 A.D. Napoleon wanted to free the citizens of Rome from the Medieval tyranny of the Papacy. Torture was used by both government and religious officials under the feudal system. The Spanish Inquisition was begun with a Papal Bull in the 12th century. That Charter you mentioned, Marm, the Treaty of Paris, also restored the Pope, Pius VII, who had been elected after Napoleon's General Berthier arrested Pius VI, who died shortly afterwards. Pius VII was elected in 1800, during papacy exile in Venice. The defeat of Napoleon restored all the kings to their thrones, including the Pope to rule over the Papal States and Rome, against the wishes of the people. And Pope Pius VII restored the Jesuits on August 7, 1814. The Jesuits are headed by the Black Pope; today, Adolfo Nicolas Pachon. Some say he is the Anti-Christ. One of the trinity with Satan."

Maggie pushed, "If the ghost is trying to tell you something, will you listen to her? God knows, I've tried to get you to buy a gun. You stocked up on food and gold, why stop at getting a gun?" Maggie became irritated, "None of you seem to accept the fact that there is going to be war! They are planning on attacking us! The best defense is a good offense! We're going to attack them before they institute open slavery."

"I'll talk to John tomorrow," Jacob replied.

"Who's John? Is that the John from the front porch, just now?" Kate asked.

"Yes. John lives across the street and both he and his wife own numerous guns and rifles. He knows a lot of people. He can probably get me a license by the end of the week." Jacob sighed, "I'll go the next day and buy some guns and ammo."

"Lots of ammo!" Maggie demanded. "We're no longer debating what might happen. It's going to happen!" Maggie looked around to see if they were alone in the yard. "June 6th," she whispered.

"What?" Jacob cried. "What's going to happen?"

"We need to wait until all the guests are gone and have a family meeting about all this," Maggie replied.

Jacob remained silent in response, looking over the gun case, "There's no ammo for these pistols."

"Keep it handy, anyway," Alexandria warned, "just in case John can't get you that license. You won't be able to buy a gun without a license to carry."

Maggie noted that the box was deeper than required by the pistols. "Look to see if there's a drawer."

Jacob closed the box and turned it upside down. There on the bottom was a separate, rectangular piece of wood. Jacob pressed on it and the bottom of the box slid open. In a pouch, were balls of lead. In a tin, black powder.

"Let's go back to the porch," Maggie said, "other guests might be leaving and want to say good-bye."

Jacob closed up the box and carried it inside to the kitchen; putting it on the top shelf in the pantry, he closed its door. He followed his mother and sisters out to the front porch. Jack and James were carrying the band instruments out to their cars. Quinn had been trying to calm the atmosphere of the heated discussion of Tsaeb and Jillary taking away Americans' semi-automatic weapons.

"With what they leave us with, we'd never be able to fight them!" John charged. "Which is the intent behind the Second Amendment. It's the duty of every American to over throw our government when we think it's necessary! And it has become necessary! The enemy is in control of our government! Without firing a shot, they have successfully passed legislation that has and will destroy all our freedoms and our country."

"We're not going to solve the problem tonight," Quinn smiled, "And tonight is my wedding night!"

John looked up at Maggie coming through the door, "I don't blame you, Quinn, you married yourself a beautiful woman."

"Thank you, John!" Maggie smiled.

"Let's get going, Janet," John said, then looking at Dawn, "Can I drive you home, Dawn?"

"No, thanks, John, I drove my car. I had the extra glasses and a casserole to carry," Dawn said.

Maggie hugged Dawn and Janet and thanked them for all their work. "It was wonderful, more than I had expected. I really appreciate all your work. It's nice to know that Jacob has such good neighbors like you."

"Phyllis?" John called.

"I'm only next door. You know that; you're just across the street!"

"We'll walk you down the steps."

"I would appreciate that," Phyllis moaned as she got up from the lawn chair. "I'm getting old for those high granite steps. Jacob, when you are going to do something about them?"

"One of these days, Phyllis," Jacob answered, as he hugged her goodnight.

Maggie hugged John, whispering, "I loved what you said about the UN, John, keep it up. We can't let them take our guns!"

"Good-night, Phyllis, thank you, for all your help. Make sure you get some rest," Maggie said, as she hugged the old woman.

"Quinn, you're a lucky man!" James said, "I wish you the best!" He grabbed Quinn and hugged him good-bye.

"He already has the best!" Rudy said, as he hugged Quinn.

"I want to thank you guys, you did a great job."

Jack hugged Quinn, whispering in his ear, "I'll call you next week for that meeting with the militia. And don't forget to tell the kids about the mountains." Quinn patted his back, as he whispered back, "Maggie and I are going to tell them tonight. And I'll see you next week."

After everyone left, Maggie told Quinn how Kate and Alexandria had asked about what was going on. "They sensed that we all seemed upset. I know it's late, but I think it's time for that family meeting before we leave for the hotel."

"All right," Quinn agreed.

The boys replaced the Persian rugs and the sofas in the great room. Kate made coffee and Sara cut up pieces of the wedding cake for dessert. Alexandria went upstairs and checked on all the grandchildren. When everyone was finished they collected in the great room, far from the children's ears.

When everyone was settled, Quinn began, "We've been telling all of you individually that revolution was coming and have warned you to prepare for it. You shut out our words for a long time, but then you came around, seeing that it was the only way to stop the elite destroying our country. We told all of you to make plans - escape plans; where you would go and how you would get there? Well, war is going to break out on June

6th. So, let's look at those plans, again.

"Wait a minute," David asked, "how do you know for sure that war will begin on the 6th?"

"I know. We'll talk about that later," Quinn replied.

"David," Quinn began, "you told your mother that you didn't want to leave your house, but your town is highly populated with illegal aliens. You need to get out well before June 6th. You have three weeks to move all your food, guns, other valuables. You'd be better off camped out in the mountains of New Hampshire. The illegals know you are White and a citizen. Believe me; they've been noticing you and what you have. They've been waiting for revolution, too. Their numbers will quickly overrun your house and take everything, including your wife."

David sat back and looked at Sara, "Actually, I've been thinking a long time about all this, Quinn. As many guns and ammo that we have, it's not going to protect us from mobs running wild in the streets. Not over any length of time. I didn't want to say anything to you, Sara, but I don't think we should stay in our house."

Quinn continued, "What all of you need to ask is, how defensible is your house? What town are you located in; do your neighbors have guns, too? Have they stocked up on food, or are they going to come after your food?" Quinn laid out his strongest argument. "First comes your immediate families, then the larger family. Then the starving neighbors. And that's the way they're going to view things, too. They'll kill you and your family, so that they can give your food to their family. I can't make it any more real than that."

Quinn paused a moment, "Should you all collect in one house and collectively defend it? Jacob's house is the biggest; it could hold all of you. And you have that large outbuilding with a woodstove. It alone could hold one family. But defensively, the main house, you have that huge window," Quinn pointed to the window at the end of the great room, "once the antique panes are knocked out, several men can step right through it, all at one time. Then there's the hill out back. The enemy can stand high on the slope and see you crawling across the floors on the second story. You'd have to defend the front and back of the house and this south end of the house. There's an exterior stairway up to the deck outside the master bedroom. There are windows all across the front of the house. And that wrap-a-round porch will give them the footing to climb through those big dining room windows."

Jacob argued, "But Rockport is an island. They can shut down the bridges and keep troops out. We have the sea right out front; we can fish for food!"

"Not for long. All the fishing boats of Gloucester and sailboats of Rockport will all be taken to fish and feed the UN troops. There are too many big resources here. The docks of Gloucester will be used for foreign navies controlled by the UN. It'll be one of the first places they will seize. Especially since the communists control the Commonwealth of

Massachusetts."

"But I can't leave my house," Jacob defended. "It's my home. I won't leave it!"

"I'll come back to you," Quinn replied.

He turned to Maggie's daughter, "Then there's Alexandria's house. It's located in a small town in the middle of nowhere; her house, her land abuts the Hocomock swamp. You can escape into the swamp without being seen, if need be. There are enough animals in the swamp to live off of, but how safe are the children living long term in a swamp? There are trees on her land to cut for firewood; she has a generator. The house won't hold all of you; but most of you."

Quinn looked at his son, Joe, and his daughter, Kate. "You both need to move! As soon as possible. Joe, you're living in a house that invites invasion. It's big and covered with tall, thick shrubbery. You'd never be able to see who is storming into your yard, whether it's your neighbors seeking shelter or UN troops. You can't even see if there's a silent SWAT team out there. They'd be in your house before you knew it. Kate, your house is located half way down a street that has only one exit, onto a highly travelled road. If you tried to escape, you'd never get your car out of your street. You have trouble now at rush hour. Your backyard abuts a cemetery; the headstones will provide cover for troops trying to invade your house."

"What you have to understand is that even if the invading UN troops don't hurt you, they will take all your food and your ammo," Quinn warned. "You could. Your children could starve to death before it's all over. And you'll be defenseless against illegal aliens, Muslims, or just lawless thugs."

After a moment, Quinn sat back, "Everyone, I want you to think about this for a moment. Sara, think about what your mother and sister and her family are planning. Alexandria, what about Seth's family? Nathan and Kelly, what about your families? Where are they all going? If these people aren't listening, refuse to see the signs, you need to separate yourselves from them and leave your homes."

Maggie got up and walked out to the front porch; the tiny white lights still looking festive. The night was quiet of people and cars, and all she could hear was the ocean's high tide smashing against the rock walls of Back Beach, erasing footsteps of their evening wedding. Quinn followed her and lit a cigarette for her and himself. "I don't mean to scare everyone, Maggie, but none of them are truly safe, if they stay where they are."

"I know Quinn, and I'm so grateful for you directing all of us. I thank God for you! I couldn't go through any of this without you. I just hope they can separate from family who refuse to see what's going on. The whole thing will divide families just like the Civil War, but this time it'll be those who fight and those who will die because of their ignorance."

When they went back inside, they heard Alexandria and Kate telling the rest of Maggie fighting with the Amazons and Quinn fighting with the 11th dimensional spirits. When they saw Quinn and Maggie come in, they stopped talking.

Maggie sat back down, as Quinn continued to advise the family. "There's a place up north, high up in the mountains. Originally, there was one lodge that Jack, James, Rudy and I used for hunting. Jack owns the property. There's a lot of wild game. Last year, Jack and James and I built two more lodges, big enough for all our children and grandchildren. It's at the end of a long dirt road in the middle of a forest. We even rented backhoes here in Massachusetts and hauled them up there, so they'd be no local record of digging a septic system. James is an electrician and wired the place, hooking it up to a street pole several miles away. He carefully hid the wires through the trees to the lodges. But there are gas-generators for each lodge. There's a lake for fishing. It has a dock and a row boat, and we brought up another ten canoes. There's a barn. This week Jack and Rudy are buying some cows, chickens, turkeys, and a small herd of cattle. They're renting a couple of U-Haul trucks to bring them up to the property. James is buying four ton of feed and chicken wire and hauling that up, too. Now, Jack has invited all of you to take refuge there. He's sending up his two kids and their families, and his wife. They're moving in by the end of next week. James is sending up his son and his family and his wife. Rudy doesn't have a family. You'd live in a communal setting with assigned tasks for the whole group. You men will have to build chicken coops. But we brought up the lumber and nails last summer. You'll find hammers and stuff. We figured we'd wait until we bought the chickens and turkeys before building the coops. We focused on building the lodges. But now, we don't have the time. I know it's going to be difficult since you all have your own homes and are used to being independent, but you will live. It's your best chance to survive. For your kids to survive. And Jacob, you don't have a family, but you have nephews to protect. The best way to protect them is to be with them up in the mountains."

They all looked at each other. Finally, Jacob said, "I'm not going to try to talk my mother out of fighting; I know that would be useless. But what about us fighting? Here, or with you! Wherever you and my mother are going to fight. Have you thought of that?"

"Yes," Quinn answered. "But only if we fail. Then you men will have to come down out of the mountains and finish what we started. You, and others like you, will be the second wave defense of the country." Quinn paused.

"For now, think in terms of rudimentary tools that you have that you can bring. Like an axe to cut down a tree for firewood, even though you have a chainsaw, it could break. The property is 700 acres of mostly wooded land. Hilly on parts. And about a mile away from the lodges and barn is a small cabin. If you had to, you could escape to the cabin."

David offered, "We have a gas-powered generator. And a portable 50 gal. gasoline pump. Then five or six, 5 gal. gasoline containers. In fact, I bought a small wood stove that I haven't gotten around to install. We could put in the barn in case we need it, too, for sleeping, if Sara's family wants to come. We have a canoe, too. Tents and sleeping bags."

"Good, bring all of it. But there's a shed with two 250 gal. tanks, filled with gasoline. Use it all sparingly," Quinn noted. "You could be up there for a couple of years."

"We have snow blowers," Seth said. "David has one and we have one. In the winter, we can make a road system around the lodges, barn, and the small cabin. I have a chain saw for firewood. David, we can bring our table saws, drills. All that stuff."

Nathan, offered, "Kate and I have kerosene lanterns left over from camping with friends. About a dozen of them."

"We started to build bunk beds," Quinn said, "but we ran out of time. There's lumber for you men to finish them. You should bring mattresses, no springs. It's a waste of room on the trucks. There are garbage disposals in the kitchens. But when we had the backhoe up there for the septic system, we dug an area for trash. Take trash out once a week to the pit and bury it, to keep down bugs, disease, and the animals from getting into it. And when you take the trash out to the pit, take a shotgun with you. Don't let the kids or women near it.

This Thursday evening, rent trucks and get your stuff up there. Besides that kind of necessity, you'll have valuables that you'll want to bring. Hopefully, there will be life after the war. But don't expect that your cars or SUVs will fit everything. Rent the truck, park it somewhere away from your house, then at 1am, go and get it and load it up. Before day break, leave for the mountains. When you get back, go directly to return the truck. Don't bring it home, again. This way, few, if any, of your neighbors will be aware that you've moved anything out. By May 23rd, no later, call in sick with a bad case of the flu. Call any schools and tell them the child has the flu. You don't want people looking for you. On the morning of the 23rd, leave at the same time you leave for work, leave any yard gate closed or open, however you normally leave your house and yard when you go off to work. Get timers for your lights; make it look as though you're home at night. Even if there are no cars in the driveway, people seeing the lights going on and off will make them think you're still there. Time the lights to turn on in the kitchen, then off when the bedroom light goes on. Get my drift? And a few miles from the camp, stop and fill up your gas tanks, and make sure you pay cash. If you see one another at the station, do not speak, do not indicate in any way that you know each other. Don't wear clothes or hats with any markings.

Oh. And one more thing. You need to take out all your money, but don't close the account, leave ten bucks to keep it open. Make arrangements to buy at least $10,000 in quarter ounce gold coins. Or whatever you can afford to buy, just make sure you get ¼ gold coins, not one ounce coins. Cut up all your credit cards after you've made your purchases; throw them in public trash barrels outside of a fast food place.

Cut through the names, mix cards together, divide the pieces into several groups and dispose each group in a separate barrel."

Before anyone realized it, the question to move up into the mountains, lock, stock, and barrel by the end of the week seemed to have been decided. Quinn drew up driving directions for each family. Maggie called Alexandria aside, "I've packed up grandma's wedding dishes and crystal. I'll bring them to your house on Friday. Wait for me to get them to you. I want you to take them up to the mountains. Promise me!"

"I will, Marm," Alexandria promised. "And I'll pack up the platter from great-great-grandmother."

"Good!"

"Everyone," Maggie called. "I want us to break from the meeting. Walk around, have a drink, get some coffee, but break away and think about everything Quinn told you. I'm sure you'll think of questions and we need to take the time, now, to answer them."

Quinn walked over to Maggie, "How would you like to take a walk to the scene of the crime?"

Maggie smiled, "I'd love to!"

After Maggie and Quinn left on their walk to the beach, and after their silent thoughts considered what Quinn had advised, the children held their own meeting.

"I can't believe this is happening. I was supposed to grow up, find a husband, buy a house, have children, and then live happily ever after, and all of that actually came true. I knew I was a very fortunate woman," Kate cried. "How can I just pack up and leave all that behind me." She turned to Nathan, "We may never get it back. We'll lose our jobs!"

"I have everything I ever wanted, an education, a husband, children, a home, a career. We're all healthy and happy. We have a great life," Alexandria said. She turned to Seth, "I don't want us to leave it, either."

"They kept us busy, working toward those ideals, so we wouldn't notice what they were preparing for us and our children," Sara added.

"I want to kill those bastards!" Jacob yelled. "I worked hard to get my education, my job, my home. I don't want to leave it!"

"Do you know how to shoot a gun, Jacob," Joe asked, "because that's what you'll need now to keep it. Along with an army! Do you have your own army?"

"I'm not so sure about all this mountain talk," Seth argued, "Alexandria and I have built a life, a happy life together. There's no way I'm going to give that up."

"I know what you'll all saying," David interrupted, "and maybe Sara and my house isn't the asset your houses are, and a year ago I had decided to stay and defend it. But now that we've all looked at what we're going to lose as far as property and career are concerned, the thing is, we are parents with small children. Small, White, Christian children. And if this Satan and his descendants thing is true that my mother has been nagging about for the last year, I don't think we have any choice but to go to the mountains. I love my mother, but sometimes she can be a pain in the neck with all this political propaganda. But I've found that when she is pounding the table over an issue, she's right. She has always been right. And our first priority is our children. I have to say, if they mess with my kid, I'll explode. I'd rather run to the mountains and lose my career, my house, but have my children survive. If we stay home, and we find that we made the wrong decision, we will lose our children. They will kill Christian children. The price for the wrong decision is too high."

Nathan leaned forward on the sofa, resting his elbows on his knees, "Have you read about the UN troops, they're called Beast in Blue Berets. They're the dregs of third-world countries. They go into a country to put down conflict and end up killing more than the warring factions. They rape the women, prostitute the girls, and two of them held a 10-yr-old boy over a campfire to entertain themselves. They put another young boy into a metal barrel, in the hot sun for days; they kept water from him. He died! There's no way I'm going to chance the UN troops getting their hands on my family!" Nathan looked at Kate, "We're going to the mountains! End of discussion."

In the moments following Nathan's declaration, the group remained quiet, thinking of what David and Nathan had said. In the quiet, the sound of a woman weeping could be heard. Husbands and wives turned to each other, "What's that?" At first, it came from off in the distance, but then the sound quickly grew in the present, as the ghost appeared in the great room. In full apparition, standing in front of the large window of antique panes, the ghost of a young woman appeared. She was tall and slender with a regal bearing. Dumbfounded, the group sat transfixed on the ghost. Suddenly, the room, its grandeur, its antique architecture seemed to come to life with its original mistress standing before them in a deep gold Victorian dress. The woman's light-brown hair was softly tied up in a bun. Her face of perfect features was framed by the high choke collar of her dress. Her upper arms were hidden under puffy sleeves; her cinched waist was made to look even smaller by the soft folds of gold lace sitting on her hips. The long skirt flowed as she stepped towards Jacob. The shock of her apparition made the husbands and wives realize that it was they who were the strangers in a house that belonged to a distant era.

Finally, Kate broke the silence, "Jacob? Is that your ghost?"

"I think so. Her dress is exactly as my mother described seeing disappearing into the parlor china cabinet."

The ghost stopped crying and looked at Jacob, "You must take my children to the mountains. Satan is after their souls. You must hide them in the mountains. My husband and I will stay and protect the house. No one will enter. Your things will be safe. Jacob. Promise me you will take my children with you to the mountains!" Just as the woman spoke those words, the ghosts of two children materialized. The boy seemed to be 11-

years old, the girl 8-years old.

The mother presented her children, "This is Dennis Townson II." The boy was dressed in knickers and suspenders over a white linen shirt that was buttoned to his neck. His jacket was a darker brown than his pants. He wore argyle socks that came up to the hem of the knickers. "And this is Julia Rose Townson." The little girl wore a pink silk dress and white pinafore. Her blonde hair curled to her shoulders with a pink ribbon holding the curls off her pale white face. "And I am Penelope Townson," the woman said.

The little boy cried, "Jacob, we won't wake you, again, we promise."

"It was you talking!" Jacob cried.

"Please, Uncle Jacob!" The little girl cried.

"My God!" Alexandria cried, "They're really ghosts! She grabbed Seth's arm, "They're ghosts!"

The woman stepped toward Alexandria trying to reassure her, but stopped when Alexandria screamed. Seth stood up, prepared to somehow defend his wife from the ghost.

"Please. Please, don't be upset," the woman cried. "We will not hurt you. We've been among you every time you visited. We never hurt you then. We only ask for your help! We have been waiting for Jesus to come to judge the dead. But Satan's descendants are on their way here, to Rockport. He is bringing his troop, Tsaeb's Federal Civilian Police Force. They are the descendants of Satan. Jacob you are not safe here, either. You must leave this house. My husband and I will protect the house, but you must leave or they will murder you. We beg that you take our children to the mountains with you. We beseech you, Jacob!"

Jacob felt sick to his stomach with fear. He thought of what the woman spirit had said; it was the echo of what his mother had told him about Satan's descendants living among us, today. But the whole idea of war between the dimensions, revolution against the government, was so difficult to register as reality. Yet it all demanded his immediate acceptance. From all the chaos swirling around him that he had no control over, his mind could easily spin in to hysteria and shut down, but he chose to stay calm. He needed to make an immediate decision that meant life or death, and the ruination of years of building up his career, his home. He had chosen to ignore the ghosts existence because he loved his house so much. And they had left him alone, for the most part. He knew he could not go back to just a few hours ago. If he said no to this mother, he would never know peace in the house, again. He knew that he had to take the ghost children to the mountains and protect them from Satan, if that was possible. The facts made his decision for him.

"I will take your children to the mountains," Jacob told the woman. "I will make preparations to go. You will know when. They can come with me in my car. Sometime at the end of this week. I have to figure out what I have to do."

"Thank you, Jacob. Thank all of you," Penelope looked around at Alexandria and Seth, Joe and Kelly, David and Sara, Nathan and Kate. "Please do not be afraid. I can see the fear on your faces and I don't mean to cause you such consternation, but I had to ask Jacob in front of all of you. So that all of you would know his decision. So you would know that my children will be with yours. But I promise you, they will not hurt your children. They will protect them."

Sara held tightly onto David's arm, breathing in gasps, "I don't want ghost children around our child. This is too much. A war. We have to flee to the mountains. Now take ghosts with us! I can't handle this!!"

"It's okay," David comforted. "You have to calm down."

Penelope pleaded, "They have been playing with your children all day."

"Ohhh!' Kate cried. She jumped up, but didn't know where to run. Nathan stood up and took her into his arms. Kate cried, "Do something! Stop all this!"

"There's nothing that I can do," Nathan said, "just hold on to me. Try to calm down. Our daughter is all right."

"When you were down at the wedding," Penelope explained, "they played upstairs together. Dennis taught them a song."

Sitting on the sofa, Kelly was curled up into a ball tucked under Joe's arms, as he comforted, "It'll be okay. She's asking for our help. She's not threatening us. She seems like a nice lady. I don't think she'll hurt any of us."

Jacob stood and turned to everyone, "These are strange times. We're seeing things that we never thought we'd ever see outside of a science fiction movie, but this is real. Our mother astral projected to Brown Mountain! Quinn astral projected to meet with the ghost of Eisenhower! Ghosts exist! They are souls! They are among us all the time. I've lived three years in this house with these ghosts. They could have hurt me a thousand times. You've stayed as guests. Marm has stayed as a guest. They tried to communicate with her, but they didn't hurt her. Get over it! We don't have the time for hysteria!" Jacob's voice raised against the sound of the women crying, "We don't have time for the shock! Get hold of yourselves! The kids would have been hurt by now, if they were going to do anything to them."

"Jacob is right," David said. "You need to get hold of yourselves and accept that this is part of life. I know it's hard, but we don't have the time for anything but acceptance. We need to protect our children. And if Penelope is scared about her children's souls, then it's a warning that we have to protect all of our children's souls."

Jacob agreed, "And as their uncle, and now step-uncle, I need to help you to protect those children. So, we need to make plans to move to the mountains." He turned to Penelope and her children, "Would you mind disappearing so we can get used to all this. I will take your children to the mountains. I promise."

"Yes, and thank you, Jacob," Penelope said, as she and her children slowly dematerialized. Now unseen, they went to the corner of the room and listened.

Leading the group out of the shock of the moment, Jacob changed the topic. "I have a question for Quinn. What about a radio transceiver, Morse Code, a police scanner? Can we run our computers from there? Use the Internet, or will it allow them to find us?"

"My question is, how will we know we should come down from the mountains? How will we know that we have to fight a second wave? Or when?" Seth said.

They all sat down; the women looking at each other, shaking their heads, as the men began to discuss a second wave attack.

Alexandria said, "I have a question for the ladies, if they will come out to the kitchen." Sara, Kate, and Joe's wife, Kelly, followed her. "Let's make some more coffee; I think it's going to be a long night."

When they got out to the kitchen, Kate asked, "So, what's your question?"

"I didn't want to listen to them talk about the second wave attack. I don't want to think about us women staying alone in the mountains while they go down and fight." Alexandria confessed. "I just wanted to get us out of there. Away from it all. Do something routine to get our bearings in all this life's other side."

"Well, I have a question," Kate sighed, "it seems that we're all going to the mountains. With ghost children! Get used to it. So, what about our periods? How many women will be at those lodges who have menstrual cycles?"

"Well, I heard Jack tonight; he said that he has two daughters-in-law. James' son has a wife. Rudy has no family. Then there's you, Kate, and Sara, and you, Kelly. And me. That makes 7 women having menstrual cycles. Why?" Alexandria asked. "What about our periods?"

"If we're going to be hiding up in those mountains, let's say, at least for six months, maybe years, what are we going to use for feminine pads?

"Wow, what a bloody mess that would be," Sara began to laugh and started the other women going. Their laughter continued for several minutes, as they walked around the kitchen, sometimes bent in laughter, some slapping the shoulder of another, wiping tears from their eyes. It was an acceptable method of catharsis after seeing Penelope and her two children. Finally, all the excess emotion was drained from their bodies and one by one they sighed heavily a last good-bye of their fear.

"Oh, gees," Alexandria started, "well, what did women do before Kotex? We won't be able to buy any once we're secluded in the camp! Likely, stores will be cleaned out during the war. Remember Katrina?"

"Well, either we buy a truckload, or we buy rags," Kate offered.

"Ohhh, so that's where they get that disgusting phrase, 'on the rag.' I never knew what they were talking about, but the way they said it, I knew it wasn't good," Kelly said.

"So, what do we do?" Sara asked, "It's going to be extremely expensive buying a year's supply for seven women! And what about disposal? It'd be an environmental nightmare!"

"What about animals? They'll think they're smelling a wounded animal and might seek it out for food." Kate cried.

"Eeeoooh," the women cried in unison.

"Not only that - who is on the pill?" Alexandria asked. "You won't be able to get refills. What about a diaphragm?"

"That seems to be the best idea. You can wash it out and reuse it, instead of Trojans. And we can't buy a truckload of Trojans, either," Kelly added.

"There's always abstinence or the rhythm method," Alexandria said.

The women looked at each other and laughed, "Yeah! Sure!"

"But you know what," Kate interrupted, "we should plan on taking something. We should bring cloth diapers, infant blankets, and whatever medical instruments are needed to deliver a baby in case one of us does get pregnant. Unless one of you is pregnant, already?"

"No. No. No." They all answered.

"A textbook on delivery," Kelly added. "We should bring all the equipment and keep it as a dedicated baby-delivery kit."

"I think we should go for buying rags that we can wash out," Sara voted, "I remember my mother telling me about her mother telling her that women used to soak the rags and then wash them out and boil them for the next month."

"Okay," Alexandria said, "we go buy rags. And some sort of thing...Oh, yeah, I remember my mother telling me when she was a kid and had to buy a sanitary belt for her mother, and she was embarrassed because the son of the storekeeper was behind the counter that day. So she asked her friend's younger sister to buy it. But when the boy asked - wide or narrow, the girl turned to my mother and asked her which one she wanted. And the boy laughed. But I don't think they sell those belts anymore."

"Buy under pants that are two sizes bigger than you normally wear," Sara said.

"We need a book on identifying herbs and plants in the woods. There'll be some that we can eat. We need to know which are medicinal and which are poisonous. And I'm buying vegetable plants. Honey! Honey is good for cuts, infections."

"Coffee's done, let's bring the pot out to great room for the guys," Alexandria said.

Down at the beach, Maggie and Quinn stood on the sidewalk overlooking Back Beach. The tide was still high enough to slap against the rocks. Quinn wrapped his arm around Maggie's waist as they watched the lighthouse off in the distant water. "It'll work out. We've done all we can, with our children and with the ghosts. I think we answered God's calling to us."

"Yes. I think the children will listen to you. They know your background, your military training. And I know God is with us. Whatever might happen, I accept His will to be as it will be."

"Me, too," Quinn said, "Come on, we better go back, it's getting chilly."

Just as Alexandria was putting the tray of coffee and cups on the table, Maggie and Quinn walked into the great room.

"Marm!" Alexandria cried, "She was here! She wants Jacob to take her kids with us to the mountains!"

Maggie walked over and held Alexandria, as she stood crying. When Sara began to cry, "They had been playing with our children all day!" Maggie reached out an arm to hug her, too. Kate walked over to the women and put her arms around them, "Oh, me, too!"

Maggie looked at Quinn, "She must be the woman in the kitchen window that I told you about. The one that left the pistols out."

Quinn held up his hands to calm the women, "It's okay. The children are all right. You put them to bed after they played with the ghost children. It's the soul in the 11th dimension. Both Maggie and I have been with them. They were, they are people, just in a different form. And they're appearing so they can help us. It's all part of what needs to be done to save our country."

Maggie patted Alexandria's back, "I know you hate ghosts. I know this is upsetting. I was scared, too. But you must go right to acceptance of the abnormal. You can't allow yourself to emotionally collapse in fear. Reject the fear. It'll be easier on you if you're strong, and fear won't stop them. There is no stopping them or the war. Acceptance will allow you to think of what you need to do to protect your children. Do you understand? Reject the fear."

Maggie looked at each of the women and reached out for Kelly and hugged her, "I want all of you to White Light yourselves and your children in the Holy Ghost. Jesus' spirit will protect you from all harm."

The women pulled themselves together in a group and quietly prayed.

Jacob stood up, "We told them to just accept it. And they were okay until they saw you, Marm."

"Well, that's what mothers invoke in their children, no matter what their age. There is no safer harbor than a mother's arms. Sometimes, the adult has to become a child, again, to be comforted and have the harshness of the world shut out. But it's only temporary. They'll be okay. It's the proper way we develop, from the time we take our first step away from mother we must be able to return to her arms. To the safety of where we were before we ventured in to the unknown world. That way, we learn that the venture did not sacrifice the safety. Throughout our lives the pattern is the same. And as the child grows older, each move is farther away from the mother, but returning is key to finally walking away in to adulthood and total independence." Maggie looked at the women, "Why don't we sit down and have some coffee. Normal activity is the best way to handle the abnormal."

"Ladies," Quinn announced, "I'd like to have a last drink with the gentlemen, if that's all right?"

"Absolutely," Maggie agreed. "We'll be fine."

"Gentlemen, if you'll follow me," Quinn said.

On his way through the parlor, he stopped at the bar and picked up a bottle of whiskey and glasses and handed them to his son, Joe, and waited for the men to continue on to the dining room. He walked back to the great room door and closed off the ladies now settling in on the sofas. He followed the men into the dining room, closing the door behind him.

"What's going on," Joe asked. "When I got married, I couldn't wait to leave for my honeymoon!"

"Well, son, it's time for the men to have a little talk about a different kind of fact of life. Will you pour everyone a glass."

"Oh, I don't want a glass," Jacob motioned with his hand, "I'm all set."

"Yeah, me too," David echoed.

"Suit yourselves," Quinn said, knowing that they'd change their minds later.

Quinn took out a piece of paper from his suit jacket pocket and unfolded it and laid it out at the end of the dining room table. "I want you all to gather around me on each side, so you can see this map of the camp. The property is close to Maine's western border, here. Jack specifically chose it because it's so far from Interstate 93 that runs up through New Hampshire and off into Vermont and then Canada. It's also far from Interstate 95 that runs along the coast of Maine before it turns inland and up into New Brunswick. The property is a bitch to get to, but that's the point. They won't be transporting troops nearby. Other than a few campers in the Wildlife Refuge, the greater area is very isolated. Go up past Berlin, on Rte. 16 to the junction of Rte. 26. This is where the two roads cross, one heading east into Maine, the other heading west to Vermont's border. If you head towards Vermont, catch Rte. 3, it'll take you into Canada. Rte. 16 will take you into Maine and hook up with Rte. 27 that goes up into Canada. But stay off these roads during winter. Other than Rte. 3, there are no other roads north from that junction; it's all mountains. To the east of the junction is Lake Umbagog, here. Jack's property is nearby. You need to know these roads in case you have to escape into Canada. If necessary, you can canoe southeast into Lower Richardson Lake and escape into the wilderness of Maine from there."

Quinn began to explain what the cryptic notations on the map meant. "This is the intermediate road that takes you from Rte. 16 to the road leading into Jack's property. As you can see, it circles back onto the highway up here. But if you note what looks to be a coffee stain on the map is actually a marker that you're to look for after coming off the highway. The intermediate road is a dirt road through the forest, so you have to look hard for the marker. It's a medium-size boulder, and next to it is what looks to be bushes. The bushes are what we created, a hunting blind. Remove the bushes and you'll see the dirt road you are to take to the lodges. But you must return the blind into the position you found it, even if you know one of you is following 30 minutes behind. Don't wait on this intermediate road, not even for five minutes! You're to get off it as soon as possible. This is key to your being found. If you do nothing else right, be sure you replace that blind so that the road is undetectable. Even to the point of sweeping tire tracks with a branch of pine needles.

Quinn looked at each of the young men, demanding an individual answer.

"You have to drive a mile down the dirt road before you get to the lodges, here. Look around, reconnoiter the place as soon as you get there to be sure you're alone or with other family. Since you never met Jack's or James' sons, we created a code word for all of you to identify yourselves to one another. The one entering the camp must be the first to say the code, and the one at the camp will respond with another code. The code, if you're the one entering, is '11th dimension' and the response code is 'Patton.' You got that?" Quinn, again, looked at each man for an answer. If you don't, you could be shot!"

"What's this all about," David asked. "Hidden roads, code words? This place is in the middle of nowhere!"

"This is about your survival, in every sense of the word, including your soul. Sloppiness will get you and everyone else killed! You damn well better pay attention. And ask questions! Because this, right now, is the last time you'll get to ask them. You'll soon be up in the mountains away from civilization, and hopefully the war."

The young men looked at each other in recognition of their fear that Quinn had invoked. First one, then another, "Joe, I'll have that drink now," Jacob said. "Yeah, pour me one, too, will ya?" David asked.

"As I said in front of the ladies before, there is lumber for chicken coops - build them. While some are building, the others are to go out, three at a time, out to this small clearing, here, for martial art training. Tell the children that you're going hunting. But always leave the majority of men with the women, just in case. Never leave the families unattended. Not for one minute!"

Quinn took a swig of whiskey, wiping his gray mustache afterwards. "Now, I've trained Joe on all the martial arts the Army taught me. He's going to train the rest of you. Jack trained his two sons, and James his son. So," Quinn pointed to each man, "Jacob, David, Seth, and Nathan are the only ones who haven't had any training. You all need to learn how to kill with your hands. And with this. It's called the Columbia." Quinn took out a small three inch knife, its handle had round openings for finger leverage. "Joe will show you how to use it. Make sure you all buy one before you leave. David, you belong to the gun club, but

Maggie said that it's been a long time and you haven't shot all the guns. So, Joe, I want you to teach them how to shoot defensively. Make sure you clean the guns regularly. After a week, when the families are settled in, you can each start teaching your wives how to shoot and teach them martial arts. It's a contact sport, so only husband teaches wife. But each individual adult must be able to defend the camp and fight invaders."

"Gotcha," Seth said, while the others nodded their agreement.

"Now, over here, is the small cabin. I said earlier that it was for sleeping, escape-to-cabin. But that cabin is full of military-issued rifles, machine guns, sticks of TNT, boxes of grenades, rocket launchers, and all the ammo your guns can handle. None of the children are to go there. Each of you are to spend 30 minutes every evening playing a game, throwing a baseball through a small hole in a piece of plywood. We have it all set up. There are orange balls at the camp that are the same size and weight as those grenades. You need to learn to throw with precision. Move your distances back from the target as you successfully throw through the hole. Every day, you and your wives are to weight train for one hour. There's a weight room, stationary bike, in the main lodge. Jacob, work up a schedule of these activities for all the adults."

"Will do," Jacob replied.

"In every lodge there is a safe room in the basement. If you find yourselves suddenly surrounded, put the kids down in the safe room of your lodge. There's food and water, a battery-powered lantern, extra batteries, a first aid kit, and a 9mm with plenty of ammo. There are air vents that go to the outside; they are hidden by bushes. During the fighting, one woman from each lodge is to go down there with the children. You are to have drills once a week with the women and children going down into the safe room. Close the door; let them get used to it. Tell them it's a game. Those who are the quietest are the winners of the game. Give 'em a treat."

Quinn pointed to the map, "Over there, to the north, and here to the south are hunting blinds with a bright orange ribbon tied to a limb. When you get up there, look for these immediately, and memorize their location. Use natural land markings to find them, again. Then take down the orange ribbons. Inside the blinds are MREs, two shotguns and ammo. In case one place or another is over run, seek shelter in these blinds. Two of you at a time are to patrol the camp every night, including the small cabin. You need to learn every inch of this property like you know your cocks!"

Quinn took a sip of his whiskey, wiped his mustache, "Okay. Now. Listen up! Sam Houston defeated Santa Anna because Santa Anna didn't post sentries. Santa Anna and all his men were asleep, siesta time. They were tired. Houston had 918 men against 1200; he lost 9, 30 wounded. Houston lost two horses and was shot in the foot, but he got that murdering prick! They found Santa Anna hiding in the bushes the next day. George Washington defeated the Hessians at the Battle of Trenton on

Christmas Day because they didn't post sentries! There was a cold snowstorm. And they were hung over from Christmas Eve celebration. King Leonides posted sentries at his rear, but they fell asleep, so the Persians were able to surround him. All these battles were won and lost because of SENTRIES. You are to post two SENTRIES every night! SEPARATE from the patrol. Is that clear?!"

"Yes, sir!" the men responded in unison.

"On the road leading to the camp, here, half way to the lodges is a tree house that we built. It's camouflaged. You post one sentry there. There's a bird call hanging inside the house that sounds like a night owl. If that sentry hears or sees something coming, he's to blow that call two times, count to five and blow it one time. Got that? He then descends the tree house and runs to the camp."

"Yes, sir!"

"On top of the barn is a watch tower. That sentry, if he hears the owl call, is to warn the others. We set up a silent alarm that leads from the watch tower into the adult bedrooms and the common rooms of the three lodges. You are to drill on this after everyone has gone to sleep. Make sure you respond. You are to keep loaded guns in your bedrooms at all times. They're already in place. And, yes, there are closets for the guns right next to the door to the bedroom. They have latches on them that are too high for any of the kids to reach. During the drill, both the men and the women are to muster outside. Depending on the threat, you either kill the few intruders and bury them in the trash pit, or you get the kids and go to the small cabin. If they're moving too fast, take the kids down into the safe rooms. Half the men stand and fight from the camp, the other half to the cabin and get the rocket launches and grenades and head back to the camp."

Quinn straightened up and looked at the men, "We've done all that we can do to provide a camp where you can survive. It's up to all of you men to work as a military unit and do what you have to, to protect yourselves and your families. To do that you need to select a leader and a chain of command to follow, and once you've made that decision, you must stick with it, otherwise you won't survive. Tasks must be assigned and completed. Talk to each other, and learn what skills you bring to the group. Teach each other your skills. Work in pairs, letting the others know where you are going and when you'll return. But you need to rotate the pairing. Because you're a small unit, you must all learn how each other thinks, acts, handles pressure, how physically agile each is, and how well you can trust each other with your life. Each of you must step up to the plate and provide that leadership and back up. Anyone who slacks off will cost all of your lives. Understand? Any questions, so far?"

There was a collective sigh as the men took it all in, stepping back from the map. "Anyone want another shot?" Quinn asked.

"No. I'm good," each answered.

Jacob asked, "What about Internet, transceiver, police scanner?"

"The very safest way to hide is to make no contact, whatsoever, with the outside world. Use no radio or electrical signals. Whatever you do, shut off your cellphones! Before you leave home, shut off your cellphones and cover them *completely* with aluminum foil. Even if turned off, they can be tracked. The aluminum will block that tracking. All U.S. Passports must be covered in aluminum foil, too.

Bring a three-year calendar with you. Nathan, why don't you take care of that? Make sure you mark off each day. On July 4th, there is likely going to be a lot of communication, attacks. On July 4th go up here," Quinn pointed to a ridge of outcrop. "It's four miles from camp. Only two men are to go. You'll find camouflage fatigues, flak jackets, boots, and helmets in the small cabin. You'll also find a transceiver and a key. Don't wear the fatigues in front of the kids, you'll scare them. Go to the cabin, first, suit up and then to the outcrop, return to the cabin, stow the gear, and then return to the camp. Maggie gave me your sizes. You'll find canvas bags with your stuff inside. Jacob, David, Seth, Nathan, you go with either Joe, or one of Jack's or James' sons. They've been taught how to work the transceiver. They will teach each of you. Joe knows Morse Code; he's the only one who will send messages, but only if absolutely necessary. You got that, Joe?"

"Got it, Dad."

"From the top of that outcrop, you can see for ten miles in clear weather. If you hear any noises, engines, shooting, go to the outcrop and scout the land. There are binoculars in the radio equipment case. Everything is stored in an aluminum-covered case that has been covered in camouflage material. To find it, look for a large, old tree; put your back to it and count ten paces north, then ten paces east. Remember moss grows on the northern side of a tree."

"Okay, just one more thing," Quinn said, "at night, sound carries. Or let's say, it's noticed more readily, when during the day it wouldn't be. No guns at night. Mid-day is best for practicing your shooting. And the first thing you're all to concentrate on is target practice. People will just think you're hunting. Then practice running through the woods, ducking, weaving, jumping over fallen trees. Run as if Satan were after you!"

Suddenly, a man's voice was heard from the other end of the dining room table, "Beware the northern passage!"

Quinn and the young men looked up to see who had given such a warning. Slowly, the apparition of Dennis Townson appeared. The collar of his shirt with a wide bow tie came up to his chin. His black vest had a gold chain that crossed his mid-section to a watch sitting in a small pocket. He looked no more than 40 years old. A refined man with dark wavy hair, blue eyes, he announced, "I am Dennis Townson." Gesturing with his hands, "I built this house. You spoke moments ago to my wife. We have placed our children in Jacob's charge."

As the ghost walked around the table, the men leaned toward Quinn, who stood steadfastly at the other end of the dining table. Seeing the men's reaction, Townson turned, instead, toward the fireplace and placed his boot on the hearth, a hand on the mantle, "There was a time when I fought for freedom, too. I envy your duty, Quinn. But my place is here, in this house. There are thousands of ghosts that haunt these old Rockport homes. We will counter the NATO troops. Should they dare come marching down South St., it will be to their terror." Townson smiled eerily, "It should be a bloodcurdling, spine-chilling good time for, as you said, Nathan, the dregs of third-world countries! In my day, I fought against the Papacy's army under Napoleon when he invaded Rome, in 1796." Townson waved a hand toward Jacob, "You may take my pistols with you to aid in protecting my children. But I warn you all, beware the northern passage. The Chinese are in Canada and will send troops down Highway 87 into New York, for they too, want to rid this land of the God-forsaken elite, so they may take charge of our country. Other Chinese troops will go down Highway 91. The highway that runs down the eastern boundary of Vermont, down into western Massachusetts. These latter troops are the ones that will be your greatest threat. Along the way, they plan to rendezvous with the Muslims in the New Hampshire and Springfield, Massachusetts, training camps. Then they will take the turnpike to Boston. They will use Total War tactics, destroying everything they don't take for their own survival. They will hand the port of Boston over to the NATO troop ships."

"Jacob, will you hand me that bottle of whiskey," Seth asked, matter of factly.

Quinn looked at the young men and smiled, "This never gets easy. Seth, when you're through." Quinn took the bottle and poured a shot out for each of the men.

Quinn turned back to Townson, "I wish that you could drink with us, sir."

Townson smiled, "Indeed, the pleasure would have been mine."

"Do you have any other warnings for us?"

"Quinn you and your 11th dimension regiment cannot fail. For in the end, if you understand me, Satan would win all our souls." Townson did not wish to scare the young men with the details of torture and decapitation that Muslims had centuries ago inflicted on those they had defeated in battle. The coming revolution, if the Muslims win, would see a torture of Adam's descendants until they accepted Satan.

"I understand," Quinn replied, "The best generals of the United States are leading the attack. And we have Jesus Christ on our side, how can we lose?" Quinn paused, "But rest assured, we will not falter in our resolve to win. Nothing will be taken for granted, sir."

"Very good, Quinn. Jacob, thank you for taking our children to the mountains."

Jacob nodded his head, "Yes, ah, you're welcome."

"I then bid you gentlemen, goodnight," Townson said, as his apparition disappeared.

Quinn turned to the men, "Just accept it. It's part of life. Look at it this way our souls survive our body's death. You've just seen the proof of it."

"Okay, Dad," Joe said, "What was he talking about envying your 'duty'?"

"Why don't we all sit down," Quinn said and proceeded to tell the men about the 11th dimensional generals and their strategizing an attack against the communist government of the United States.

In the great room, Maggie was instructing the young women. "I brought up children's books for various ages; writing tablets; pens; pencils. Make sure you bring their favorite toys, blankets, whatever will bring them comfort. There's also a chalkboard and chalk hanging in the main lodge. You must keep the children occupied, and there's no better way than teaching in a classroom setting. One adult must be with the children at all times; they are never to leave the campsite, unless you take them all at one time swimming or fishing in the lake. You said you already figured out what to do about your menses and so forth. There are plenty of canned goods and MREs, bags of rice and barley, in each of the lodges, but take every bit of your food from home. There's a kitchen in each of the lodges, but no one, of course, is to go hungry. And keep track of the expiration dates; I marked them on the shelves of the food we stored there. The chickens are for eggs, the cows for milking, and the turkeys for butchering. When needed, the cattle are to be butchered. But first try to breed the animals to maintain a food supply. You'll find freezers in the kitchens; they're full of frozen meats. Make sure you heat the milk to pasteurize it. You can make cheeses from the milk. I left a book up there and the implements needed to do that. I brought up all my knitting and crocheting needles, several pattern books for sweaters and Afghans, and lots of yarn. I know I have to knit something during the winter months. But I also left journals for each of you. Write to let out your private emotions."

The women were quiet, letting Maggie gather her thoughts. "I think that's about it, except for prayer. I left a Douay Rheims Bible in each lodge. I recommend that you pray every day for an early end to the war. And you need to think of yourselves as pioneers. Americans lived with less than what you will have at the camp. Don't compare the camp to your homes, you'll only become embittered. Be thankful for every day that all of you are healthy and alive. Every one of you is to do her share and help other families, not just your own. And please do not complain; understand that this is stressful on all of us. And I recommend that you get to know one another. Have coffee together once a day. Be a sounding board for each other and your husbands. Pull your own weight, but forgive each other's weaknesses. We're human, not saints."

Maggie paused, "Are there any questions?"

"Just one," Kate looked at the other women and then back to Maggie, "when are you going on your honeymoon?" The women all smiled, "Yeah! When?"

Just then the men came walking into the great room, finished with their meeting. Fear had drained the color from their faces. Their minds exhausted.

Quinn said, "Ladies! I bid you good-night. I am taking this woman, my wife, to let her have her way with me!"

"Ahh...just a minute. We're her sons," David cautioned, "we're going to pretend that you're just driving her home and dropping her off. We don't want to hear otherwise. We're just going to live in our own little fantasy land. But, it's okay, you can take her home, now."

Quinn walked over to Maggie's baby, now 6'3" tall and 35 years old, "David. I want you to know that I dearly love your mother. You have to see that God has brought us together as husband and wife. She will always be your mother. I will never take that away from any of her children." Quinn lowered his voice as he wrapped his arm around David's broad shoulders, "Let her be a woman to her husband. It's what she wants. Let your mother be human. A woman. Not just a mother."

"I know," David said quietly, "it's just that I'm her protector. She was always there for me, my wife, for our child. She's never gone out with a man before you. And I don't remember her being with my father before their divorce. She's always been alone. Our mother. I hope that you cherish her as much as her children do."

Quinn looked David in the eye, "I do cherish her. I do."

Chapter 17

The Alamo. It was a Roman Catholic mission and fortress compound, Mission San Antonio de Valero. Between February 23rd and March 6, 1836, a 13-day siege of the mission took place, during which an estimated 187 Texian and allied American militia fought for Texas independence against 5400 uniformed Mexican soldiers led by the Mexican Republic President General Antonio Lopez de Santa Anna, a descendant of Japheth, when admittedly 1500 Mexicans were killed by 187 militia. Santa Anna ordered the firing of 21 cannon that blasted iron balls against the walls of the Alamo and two forward strike attempts that failed. It took a third forward strike in which the Mexicans revealed themselves to be the screaming banshees from hell, scaling walls and overwhelming in numbers of hand-to-hand combat, before the last of the Texians fell. It was at the Alamo that Davy Crockett fought, they say, like a ferocious bear, requiring 20 Mexicans to bludgeon his body before they took him down. His blood soaked the Mexican-banshee uniforms. Jim Bowie, ill and dying on a cot, fought against the Mexicans only to suffer the same unmerciful butchery that was the Mexican intent to cause the greatest of pain before death, as is the lust of Satan's children in killing Adam's descendants. The ghosts of those who died at the Alamo still haunt, still protect, the want of independence and freedom from Satan's children.

Today, twelve militia generals from across the United States met in secret to strategize their effort in the coming revolution. And the ghosts of McArthur and Eisenhower were there to greet them.

They came to the Alamo. For in the American psyche, nothing represented the steadfast belief in freedom and the courage to fight in the certainty of death for it, as is the legacy of the Alamo. The militia generals needed that joining of faith, knowing they, too, would rather die than be the slaves of Satan. But there was more to the story than the courage of the Texians and Americans, as Texas fought for her independence from Mexico. It had been a battle between Satan's descendants and the followers of Jesus Christ and the descendants of Adam and Eve.

As they gathered within the open expanse of the main room of the Alamo, the twelve militia generals began to see the ghosts of Davy Crockett, Jim Bowie, Col. Travis, and the others who died at the Alamo, walking toward them. It was a terrifying sight of bloodied faces and bodies, and ragged clothes that had been sliced by Mexican bayonets. One militia general elbowed another, pointing to the apparitions of six monks over near the chapel's door. The militia knew they were to meet with the ghosts of McArthur and Eisenhower, but were not expecting to see these other ghosts of the bludgeoned Texians and Tennessee frontiersmen, who now surrounded them. These ghosts were heroes to the militia generals, but they were ghosts, first. Should the generals run from or greet their heroes? They decided to wait to see what the apparitions would do. They had already decided, as Jim Bowie had, to die for freedom; did it matter that they would die at the hands of the ghosts? The fear from seeing so many spirits suddenly appear as vapor and then materialize into live, ordinary human appearance made some of the militia generals tremble involuntarily. But still, each nodded to the other that they would remain in place. Then from the old jail off on the right of the open expanse came the ghosts of Generals McArthur and Eisenhower.

McArthur reached the group of militia generals, first. He smiled, "Gentlemen, I can see by your faces that you recognize all the ghosts."

The militia remained silent, fixated on one face or another of the ghosts. It was the beginning of an era looking at the end of an era; those who had and those who would, die for freedom. Each of the militia wondered if they would have the same valor, now questionable when seeing such satanic-inspired wounds the men of the Alamo had endured.

"Gentlemen?" McArthur asked, attempting to rouse them from their fear.

"Yes, sir!" Pete finally responded. "I, ah," Pete choked, "I am Pete, General of the U.S. Militias."

"Yes," McArthur said, "I spoke to you in dream. I suggested that your militia join our spirits in fighting this revolution."

"I remember, sir. I called all the militia generals and told them of our, ah, discussion. I told them that you wanted us to join forces. And they all agreed. Sir."

As Pete was talking, the ghosts of Crockett and Bowie came closer, looking over the militia generals. Some were dressed in Bermuda shorts and t-shirts with Harley-Davidson logos, some with long hair tied up at the nap of the neck. Their appearance so removed from Crockett's buckskin shirt that was sliced to shreds, or his moccasins rather than the sandals of the militia. Crockett carried a flintlock rifle and Bowie wore a long, wide knife at his waist. He looked at Crockett and snorted a sarcastic laugh. The militia at first embarrassed began to challenge the ghosts. "Don't let the shorts fool you, Bowie," Paul countered Bowie's laugh. "We couldn't wear our fatigues into this place, we'd be arrested! This is a historical monument."

"I understand," Bowie smirked, "but couldn't you wear pants?"

"We needed to look like tourists," Steve interjected.

"This isn't productive," Eisenhower said, "let's move on with our plans. Now, Pete, since you're the leader, why don't you introduce your generals to us."

"Yes, Sir," Peter replied, snapping into attention. As he walked up the line of his militia generals, he announced their name and state. "This is Paul from Nebraska, Matt from Michigan, Philip from the state of Washington, Jimmy from Kentucky, Andrew from California, John from Virginia, Mickey from Massachusetts, Bart from Alabama, Luke from Texas, Thad from Arizona, and Simon from Wyoming."

McArthur and Eisenhower grinned as Crockett cried, "Sounds like you men are the twelve Apostles come back to life!"

Pete smiled, "It is strange, isn't it? We don't understand how it all happened. We all have our own stories as to how we came to be generals of the militias in our region. One story is different from another; unexpected turn of events; and all very strange. We decided to just accept it."

"Well," Bowie replied, "Except for Mickey! Mickey wasn't an apostle."

Mickey stepped forward, a large man, even taller than McArthur, with white freckled skin, red hair and beard, "Michael Thomas, Sir! My Christian name is Michael, after the Archangel and Thomas after the Apostle!"

"I stand corrected," Bowie responded coolly. "I expect that you're Irish parents nicknamed you Mickey?"

"Yes, sir, they did," Mickey replied and stepped back into the informal formation of militia generals.

"All right," McArthur intervened, "We're here to strategize our plan for war. The first step is educating you generals and make sure you have an overview of the attack. Then we'll take up the individual local plans. Gentlemen, if you'll follow me over to that display case, we can use it as a table for the maps."

As the militia generals followed McArthur's and Eisenhower's materialized spirits, Crockett and Bowie flanked them. But as they walked, more and more spirits of Texians and Americans began to appear. First, as shadows, then in full materialization, with some floating overhead, all trying to get a once-over of the militia that they would be fighting with. The great expanse of the room opened up to the ceiling high above. It was as if they had built the second story walls with windows, and later decided not to build the floor. No one could reach the windows to look through, except the ghosts, who now sat on the window sills. They were lookouts, there to warn of the coming of evil spirits of Mexicans who had fallen at the Alamo. If they came, the ghosts of McArthur and Eisenhower would immediately disappear, and Crockett and Bowie would fight them again, as they had every time they showed up. The insanity of fighting the Battle of the Alamo over and over again had been witnessed only once by a park ranger, for it usually began at 3am, when the world slept and the evil spirits haunted the night. It was the time of morning the Jesus was arrested, thus gave a sense of excitement to the evil spirits.

McArthur opened up a map of the United States and spread it across the glass top of the display case. "As you can see, there are markings of the military bases, naval ports, coast guard, border stations - they're marked in green. The Muslim training camps are here, mostly along the eastern coast, marked in red. The Muslim sites will be handled by the ghosts of Queen Macha, Queen Penthesilea and her Amazons. Washington, DC, is marked in black. It will be handled by the Granny Quilt Crafters of America and the ghosts of the Civil War. General LeMay and his ghosts will be going into Israel and flying home our F22 Raptors, landing on US Air Bases, here, here, and here." McArthur pointed to the map. "These sites marked in blue. Admiral Nimitz will command the Navy, including the ghost ships, the carriers USS Hornet in California, and the USS Intrepid in New York Harbor. General Eisenhower will be commanding the Army, including your militias." McArthur paused and turned to Eisenhower, "General."

Eisenhower took over, "The Army ghosts of Patton, Bradley, and the spirits soldiers of WWII, Korea, Vietnam, and the Gulf Wars will fight with your militias. Our first priority is the underground labs that are located here in Langley, Virginia, and inside the mountains of North Carolina. There's a Rocky Mountain lab, here, in Hamilton, Montana. And Harvard University, also, has a lab that needs to be closed. They've been cooking up a lot of crap for decades. Simultaneously. All action will take place simultaneously; they won't know what hit them. Now, there's a highly restricted air base, Tonapah Airfield, they call it Area 52. There are elevators that go deep, deep underground, but these elevators are the kind used on aircraft carriers, very heavy duty. There are all kinds of new experimental planes kept there. It was where they housed the F-117A stealth fighters, before the Pentagon disclosed their existence and moved them to Holloman Air Base, New Mexico, in '92. It was a quick turnaround, making way for the latest experiment. They specialize in top secret defense systems. So it could be anything! Our intel isn't sure what the hell it is. The 7th CTS 'Screamin Demons' serves as a transition training unit, prepping experienced Air Force pilots on flying the F-117A Nighthawks. There are only two units, the 8th Black Sheep Squadron and the 9th FS Flying Knights that fly the Nighthawk. But they have a maintenance crew that is deployed with them on every mission that has any duration. They take their orders from the National Command. We need to get inside those underground facilities. But LeMay will take care of the aircraft we might find here and the F-117As at Holloman with his spirit pilots taking possession of the bodies of the trained pilots.

"I am sure you are aware of it, but let's review. Dan Rummysfield, a member of the Foreign Affairs Private Council and former Secretary of Defense, established the USNORTHCOM - a/k/a NORTHCOM. After 9/11, it was set up to watch Americans. They know that Americans will find out what they are doing to our country. They know Americans are going to revolt. Attached to NORTHCOM is the Consequence Management Response Team (CMRT), about 800 strong, so far. Their commissioned officers were established as the Ready Reserve Corps, through Tsaebcare. This CMRT is prepared to take over in national emergencies from local and state authorities. NORTHCOM is headquartered at Peterson AFB, Colorado Springs. Now, the US Supreme Court 2008 decision, found them to be unconstitutional, but they're moving forward with it anyway. The Military Commission Act of 2006 lifted restrictions provided by the Posse Commitatus Act that prohibited US Military from having direct contact, arresting or searching American citizens. They're not only going to unconstitutionally assist local authorities in fighting, arresting, and searching civilians, they will take complete control. All under the Muslim officers of the Ready Reserve. They'll be moving populations into FEMA camps. Each president has declared or renewed the status that the United States is living under a national emergency. They've done this so that Tsaeb only needs to take the final step in declaring Martial Law. Congress cannot do anything for six months once Martial Law has been declared. Tsaeb has direct command of the Ready Reserve Corps and the CMRT as his private army. He'll be able to do anything he wants.

Besides illegal legislation, the other weapon they've been working on is weather control. The technology to control the course of hurricanes has been patented. They've also been chemical dumping all over the world. But you can rest assure, they will be dumping chemicals onto towns, or places where they think the militia are camped. You need gas masks and clothing that covers every part of your body. They will bring on a monsoon of rain and winter storms upon you. These weather control centers are what need to be attacked, immediately. Part of your units need to assist LeMay in gaining control over the airbase at Lincoln, Nebraska. That's where the chemtrail planes fly out of. Those planes need to be grounded and the chemicals disposed of. At the beginning of the war!"

Eisenhower stepped away from the display case, looking at the militia generals, "Now, Bradley has been coordinating transport of arms, ammo, food, gasoline and other supplies, to make sure we're able to arm and feed the militia all across the country. This isn't going to be easy. Tsaeb stopped all drilling by withholding permits, except for the Brazilian oil company owned by Egroeg Rooss, a key player in their New World Order scheme. Tsaeb has begun to release the emergency gas reserves, allegedly to bring down gas prices for Americans, but he's really using up the supply so the militia and the U.S. Military won't be able to drive their trucks, tanks, in revolution against that Muslim invader! Tsaeb wants the U.S. Military to be unable to move their vehicles in defense of the foreign troop invasion they have planned against this country. But Bradley has been redirecting gasoline into our own emergency reserve stations.

And Patton has developed a weapon that will destroy evil spirits, but it will also annihilate the human body. A larger version is being manufactured for installation on pickup trucks. These are being made in a factory in Massachusetts, and handheld size are being made in the homes of Americans all across the country. Patton and Bradley are coordinating their efforts to bring those guns to the supply depots that Bradley has set up. Bradley's mission is to make sure that those supply lines are not broken. They have been directing supplies to twelve main depots stationed in grid formations across the country, with the largest in the mid-section of the country. We're expecting the Russians, Iranians, Hezbollah, Hamas, and the Mexican Militaries to come up across the southern border, while the three million Chinese now in the Canadian woods will cross down over the northern border. But local police have also spotted the Chinese on the southern border. Their plan is to surround us; trap us in the middle without access to gasoline or food, so that's where we've put our greatest amount of supplies of ammo, guns, and gasoline. Tsaeb has been training Saudi Arabian Muslims to fly F15s; they've been training over Idaho. Right now, we're not sure where they will be launched from when they attack. They have UN and NATO troops stationed in national parks, as well as on our American bases. President George Erbert Wake Schirf brought them in during his regime for training purposes, and they never left. And by the way, 90% of UN troops are Muslims.

Now, Generals Lee and Sherman are reconnoitering the bunkers of the elite. Many of the elites have already left the country; they've brought their entire families to China. Other elites have had old silos remodeled as underground bunkers; some have built their homes into the sides of mountains. There's one bunker in D.C. that can hold 5000 people for two years. When the time comes, Lee and Sherman and his bummers will seal up these places, sealing the death tombs of those who make it inside, and sealing out those who didn't get there fast enough. At the Denver International Airport in Colorado is a troubling mural, The Children of the World Dream of Peace. It depicts a large, demon-faced soldier wearing a green uniform, carrying a 9 mm at his waist, an AK-47 in his left hand and an Islamic scimitar sword in his right. The sword's point is stabbing the butt of a white dove, the symbol of the Christian Holy Ghost. This is a death message; I don't care what the artist claims! Sherman's bummers are checking out the underground tunnels, trains, and whatever else they have there. It's suspected that the elite and government figures have prepared an underground city there. It's the largest international airport in the U.S., at 53 square miles. Regardless of anything, we need to shut it down. We're going to put the Vietnam War veteran spirits in charge of that airport. They're a group that's really pissed off! They earned the privilege of shutting down and controlling the elite planning to use that airport."

Eisenhower frowned, "These preparations that the elite have been making over the last decade can be found in the Bible." He picked up a Douay Rheims Bible from the display case that McArthur had earlier set down beside the maps. He opened the Bible to The Apocalypse, Ch. 6:15-17, and read, 'And the kings of the earth, and the princes, and tribunes, and the rich, and the strong, and every bondman, and every freeman, hid themselves in the dens and in the rocks of mountains: And they say to the mountains and the rocks: Fall upon us, and hide us from the face of him that sitteth upon the throne and from the wrath of the Lamb: For the great day of their wrath is come, and who shall be able to stand?'" Eisenhower looked up from the Bible, "Now, if we're not in the end times, why are the elite preparing such accommodations for themselves?"

He closed the book, "Gentlemen, we are, indeed, in the end times."

Eisenhower walked away from the display case and turned back to the militia generals, "Now, gentlemen, I know that most of you have had U.S. Military training, which is the best in the world, but the US has been ordered by its presidents to train those who will be fighting us. As I said, UN and NATO troops were unconstitutionally brought onto our military bases to train with our military. President Schirf has allowed illegal aliens, South American SM-31 gang members to join the U.S. Military; he and Jeffers also allowed over a million South American and Mexican gang members to set up shop here in the cities of the U.S. Tsaeb is training the Iraqis and the Saudi pilots to fly our planes. Those who you will be fighting are in your neighborhoods and have been trained for combat by your federal government with your tax dollars. The thing to remember, the Alamo fell because they couldn't regroup fast enough, before the onslaught of the third-wave attack. Keep this uppermost in your minds when on the battlefield. Before you strike, have a second and third fallback contingency plan that you may utilize immediately and effectively. Have at the ready a second unit of infantry that replaces the frontline.

As I noted before, Tsaeb is going to continue to withhold oil drilling and release the emergency gasoline supplies that have been marked for defense, only. What Tsaeb is doing is trying to get all Americans to surrender, so that the Zionist Jews and Muslims can take our country fully intact, which is best for them. All they have to do then is ship White Christian Americans off to the FEMA camps where their vaccines will kill all of them. This is why we have no time to delay our attack. Make no mistake; this is a war between good and evil, the followers of Jesus Christ and the descendants of Satan. Which means that even if a person was born with the genetics of Satan, they still have free will to follow Jesus. But know this, the culture taught through the *Talmud* and the *Qur'an* is one that forbids Zionist Jews and Muslims from defecting and becoming Christian. So, you must be weary, the children of Satan are the best of liars, the greatest at deceit and sleight of hand. If any want to join forces with you, don't trust them."

Eisenhower paused, "Do you understand! Deceit is their ONLY power! There is nothing god-like in Satan's power or his descendants. They can control the weather only by the technology that humans have invented, most of them Christian inventors, who were overpowered by the money used to buy the company who owned the technology, or paying the thieves who stole the technology, or by killing the inventor. They didn't invent it or create it!

They enslaved us with the Federal Reserve Act, but only because they got corrupt politicians to vote for its passage. They don't have supernatural powers! Why do you think they are building bunkers or fleeing to China? If they had supernatural powers, or if Satan was going to come and assist them, they wouldn't need bunkers. In fact, if Satan had any power, he would have taken over the world centuries ago. Michael the Archangel defeated Satan and his angels in their battle in Heaven and God sent them down into the bottomless pit. Deceit is their game - getting you, the American citizen surrounded by corrupt people, their Satanic bloodlines, to eventually wipe you off the planet - through human methods - not by some magic trick! They have succeeded only because the American people have allowed themselves to be controlled by them. But that has come to an end. And their end!"

Eisenhower wiped his mouth with the back of his hand, as if trying to wipe the filth of Satan's name from his lips. "Now, there are Christian Americans out there that have been unknowingly working for satanic bosses; they know them, who they are and where they live! These American Christians are the ones who actually have been keeping this country going; inventing its technology, designing its computers, and operating America's military. You need to tap into these Christians, this insider knowledge base. These people have the ability and access to communications and computers; they can call in air strikes using NORTHCOM to strike UN and NATO troops! Use this American know-how!"

Eisenhower paused as he tugged at the waistband of his brown field jacket and changed the subject of his instruction to the militia generals. "On the battlefield, you have to first know your enemy's strengths and weaknesses, his vulnerabilities. And always know his numbers before striking. And at every turn possible, throw a kink into his strategy. The psychological effect is enormous. Don't waste your men or resources trying to take a whole town. Hit and retreat, hit and retreat. Never in a consistent pattern. Never use the same number of men. Make precision strikes. Set up units whose only mission is to target their supply lines, take what you can of their supplies and blow up the rest. Throw heavy debris, fell trees, along their pathways to hamper their travel. You want to irritate them like flees torture a dog.

And when possible draw out their soldiers and ambush them. The important element of this war is that we will strike all at once, all over the country, and on our borders. We're going to spring up from every wood, every field, every neighborhood, every town, every state, and we're going to come out blasting!

They'll be in such chaos they won't be able to communicate with each other. And even if they can, they won't be able to rescue each other. It will be an overwhelming surprise attack. The shock and awe of it all will make the Iraq war look like a whimper. And we need to end this revolution as quickly as possible. We know that their strategy is to outnumber us, using military-trained Russians, Iranians, Mexicans, Chinese coming across our borders, and with the UN, NATO troops, and South American gangs already dispersed throughout the country.

But Americans fight with heart, just as 187 Texians and Americans did at the Alamo during that 90 minute final battle. And we have Jesus on our side. We have ancient prophecy on our side. They know our civilians are armed but untrained; many are elder vets, some not in good health. They've poisoned our foods and made Americans fat from viruses that supersize fat cells. They've given Americans cancer; the way they do their own political rivals. They've put millions of Americans out of their jobs, so they are unable to store up food and ammo. All so that Americans will surrender to them and leave their homes and towns intact for them to move in to."

Eisenhower put his fists on his hips, his anger increased at the thought of what he was about to disclose, "The U.S. Military takes blood samples of soldiers before they send them out. They require them to take oaths to fight for and take orders from the UN! Christian soldiers are sent out on the frontlines, the satanic bloods are kept here, those that pledged to take orders from the UN. When the shit hits the fan, fighting will begin on our home bases among the U.S. soldiers - between the Christians and the Muslims and Zionist Jews. Your militias need to stand ready to take those bases - either joining the U.S. Military Christians, or to defeat the U.S. Military Muslims that took control of those bases."

Eisenhower continued, "Their plan is to have Israel strike Iran. With all the Middle Eastern countries, instigated by CIA, Muslim Brotherhood, and Code Pink, uprising in Libya, Egypt, Syria, all those countries will attack Israel, along with Iran. The plan is then to send our aircraft carriers, US Military, and all our fighter jets to rescue Israel. Once US Military, ships, and equipment are locked inside the Mediterranean Sea, the Red Sea, and the Persian Gulf, THEN China, Russian, Iranians, Mexican Military, UN and NATO Troops, SM-31 gangs will attack America. We need to be pro-active and put a kink into their strategy. Now, the intel has it that Israel plans to attack Iran in November. That's why we're moving against them on June 6th.

Eisenhower paced back and forth, his arms interlocked over his chest, "What you need to do is to meet with your militia officers, let them know the general strategy of the entire war, so that if you generals are killed, they can carry on. But, first, you need to go out into all your troops, at every level, and find the spies among you. They are there, as sure as rats are in abandoned buildings. Find out who they are to report to; what they have reported to the enemy, so far. Find out code words. Then kill them immediately and dispose of their bodies; bury them in deep graves in the woods or out in the desert."

Eisenhower paused, looking at each face of the militia generals, "The most important thing you must do, first, is seek out the spies among you. And before we leave here, I'm going to instruct you on that a third time. No army will stand if there are spies among its ranks!"

He paused, again, to let his warning sink in and then continued, "What you generals must excel at is knowing when to fight, and when not to. Leave nothing to chance, be sure that all preparations have been made. Know your enemy's numbers and capabilities before you strike. It's better not to engage and encounter them on another day, when you and your men are ready. Keep your men healthy at all times. You can't send sick soldiers into battle, you'll only be sacrificing the entire unit. Above all, you must constantly have men looking out for troop movements and enemy vulnerabilities as they happen. Take advantage of their vulnerable areas. And if you're going to shit in the woods, bury it! It's as much of a trail as a neon sign.

Now, it's best not to communicate electronically, or by radio, you'll be immediately spotted by satellites. All your men must wear uniforms that are insulated or covered by aluminum to prevent their detection from heat-sensing equipment, whether from helicopters, planes, or satellites. We won't last a day unless your men are covered with aluminum foil. This is a new era of war. We must adapt to the enemy's capabilities and technology. The best way is to use simple, creative methods to hide and attack and communicate with command center and other units. Use the natural surroundings to cover yourselves. You've all seen the movie, The Shooter. The Patriot. Red Dawn. Learn from these movies!

You must strike quickly, efficiently, and then get the hell out of there. Keep your militias fighting in the locality they originated from. Each man knows the woods and mountains, marshes and swamps better than the enemy. That is your greatest military asset - hang on to it. Don't bring your militia into strange places. Not if you can help it. This is where this war will be different from the Civil War. In the Civil War you had the northern armies against southern armies. This war is against every American citizen, and once it begins, every person able to fight, in some fashion or another, will fight - all over America. All at the same time. Let me tell you, there are millions of Americans just waiting to hear that fighting has broken out, and they'll come out blasting themselves, even though they're not connected to your militias.

Your hardest decision is knowing whether to go to rescue another unit, leaving your base unmanned and vulnerable to attack, or stand fast and let the other militia unit fall. This is the kind of decision that you must discuss among your generals before the shit hits the fan. But all this means that you need as many active volunteers as possible. The elder civilians can work as local spies; they can maintain the fort while you send out precision strikes. Your greatest problem is if they send out large forces against a town and outnumber the local militia. It's better not to engage; let them take the town, then come back and eat away at them, bit by bit, from the outer edges. Find out where these large gangs of SM-31, UN/NATO troops are camped and assess where they might attack, and move out all civilians and militia from the town, taking all their food and water with them. But this has to be accomplished through stealth, at night. Commandeer buses. If you allow civilians to be taken, they will use those captives to get you to surrender. It's better to bomb the place that civilians or family are being kept, than to allow their torture or your surrender. Rescue only when you have absolute certainty that you will succeed."

Eisenhower realized the difficulty in accepting such instruction, but he had to say it. He needed it on the back of their minds, in case the situation arose. The militia was the only real chance of America getting back its freedom. A family member couldn't stand in the way of that victory, not against the chance that the world would be lost to Satan. If America falls, so falls the world.

"If you strike in the morning, your enemy will be at his sharpest, strongest, fastest. Around 3pm, his body will start to break down. If you wait for night, he won't have any energy at all. If you divide your men into two groups, one to fight at night, the other to fight in the morning, put your best men out in the morning. But dividing your troops for day and night combat is the best way to keep the enemy from getting any sleep; it'll screw with his mind and over a short period of time, disorient him. Psychology is a key weapon in war. Remember that! Use it as a weapon, and defend yourself against it. I know you have Americans who can play trumpets. Before your night attacks, play those trumpets into loudspeakers, close to their camps, let them think that Jesus Christ Himself is descending from Heaven just to send them, personally, into hell! The trumpets will announce the King's entrance into their camps.

I want you to keep in mind that you are never to fight going uphill, only downhill. Whatever the field might be, a building, mountain, a rise on a field. Always be on the top bunk. And whatever you do, do not be taken in by a false retreat. They are baiting you. Don't follow them, you'll all be ambushed. Only send your best men to take on the mercenaries they have. And look for booby traps, poisoned food, poisoned water. If they were left it behind, it's a good chance that they've poisoned it all. Remember Crzezinski's warning of their use of biowarfare to make the enemy sick before attacking him. The US Military used it in Desert Storm. You want to steal food from an active camp."

Eisenhower was silent for a moment, "As I told you boys earlier, this is a war between Satan's descendants, the evil of the world, and the descendants of Adam and the followers of Jesus Christ. You cannot let the enemy live to fight you another day. Military training teaches that you must give a way out to a surrounded army, otherwise they will fight to their death, and you're apt to lose the battle. The truth is, like a cornered rat, they will jump at your throat. They have nothing to lose. Give them an opening, but as they retreat, you need to kill them all. I don't care if they're being carried away on a cot, make sure that enemy soldier is dead!

And if they are allowing you a way out, expect them to ambush you on your retreat.

Always keep the sun at your back, or a tree at your back, or a foothill. Patrol regularly the local swamps, rivers, ponds, and marshes. These are excellent natural covers for the enemy to use while moving in on your territory. But never fight in these places. Prepare your militia to greet them when they emerge from the swamp.

The best part of keeping your militia in their local areas is that they know how to read the birds and animals. Watch them closely, they are your forward gatekeepers. I repeat: watch the animals and birds! They will tell you when the enemy is approaching. And if you're good enough in reading the behavior of the birds and animals, they'll even tell you how large a troop movement is coming at you. But set up lookouts, using the natural terrain to hide your location. Use bird calls to signal to your other troops.

Organize Christian nurses and doctors so that they know they are to respond when this all comes down on June 6th. Have them set up hospitals in the homes of Americans wherever you can, perhaps in the homes of senior citizens, out in the suburbs and especially nearby likely battlefields. They converted private homes into hospitals during the Civil War.

Once the enemy has crossed deeply over the southern and northern borders, they will be emboldened. They will become intense, nervous about being caught and excited about killing you. Their senses will be heightened. Either you strike them before they get too deep into the United States, or you wait until you can surround them. You must heavily outnumber them to surround them. And you're apt to have friendly-fire kill when you surround the enemy. I prefer hitting them as soon as they cross the border and then drive them back. Think speed and efficiency, maintaining your soldiers and resources for another battle, if possible. You don't want to surround and attack the enemy, if it's going to bog down your troops and use up all your ammo. If you have no resources left after that battle to fight another, you've lost the war, even if you won the battle.

Key to fighting them at the border is that the UN and NATO troops, the Latin gangs, Muslims in the U.S. Military - will attack your rear. Because our presidents have unconstitutionally peppered the entire country with these foreign armies, any large scale battle that your militias engage in must be fought back to back. You are actually wedging your militia between the camps of the enemy that are inside and outside the country. The U.S. is not clear territory with the enemy only on the border. You're fighting on a checkerboard and must zigzag between the enemy's troops. We're not defending America, it has already been conquered, the enemy has already set up their camps inside our country - all across our country. We are fighting to take back America from the enemy!"

Eisenhower walked up to the display case, picked up the marker next to the map and began to draw on the corner of the map, "Now, the Romans used the square formation when they were surrounded, two parallel lines of men on four sides, the commanders in the center, and they moved forward on the corner of the square. So that the square moved as a wedge, connected to a rear wedge protecting the front. In a large attack, this is the best formation. And it's best when moving troops near or between enemy outposts. But in daily routine, set up your men so that at any time, if hit by a surprise attack, the rest of the line is able to circle around to rescue your men and strike the enemy. Never bunch up your men in a single camp, string camps out like a pearl necklace.

When the enemy is attacking on a frontal assault, put your infantry on the front line, behind them a large reserve infantry. On either side are auxiliaries flanking the front line, with Calvary behind the auxiliaries. Now, a lot of Americans own horses, if you haven't by now, talk to them about using those horses in a Calvary charge - a surprise attack into a camp with the infantry following - to steal food, destroy equipment. Then get the hell out of there. Everything depends on the terrain, the number of enemy, and the type of equipment they have. You must be flexible to handle all scenarios. Once you have determined where you can use a Calvary attack, advertise a horse show on June 6th or a horse auction. It'll provide cover for moving large numbers of horses into the area of attack."

Eisenhower picked up a large envelope on the display case, opening it he pulled out photos attached to documents. "We brought photos of the leaders of the Russians and Iranians. The Chinese. The Mexicans. The leaders of the SM-31 gangs. Along with their profile. Use their personal life experiences against them. There is a synopsis on how each think, how they fight. This is their vulnerability, our knowledge of their leaders. But it's your strength that they don't have this information on you militia generals. They don't even know who you are! And even if they do, they don't know how you think under pressure. They don't know what kind of leaders you are or whether your men will follow you into hell. Use that anonymity. Don't wear any insignia on your clothing to signify your rank. Don't let anyone call you by your last names. If you have two Pauls in your unit, the leader should be called "Paul." The second Paul, "Little Paul." Your men should know you and your officers by facial recognition. When reporting the death of any commander, just say that the boss went to a meeting.

You need to set up a spy ring before the shit hits the fan. You need the intel of what your enemy is up to. Send out men to scout out their encampments, find out who comes and goes. Try to hook up with a U.S. soldier on each of the bases that will feed you intel."

Eisenhower's anger re-emerged, "But do not bring that U.S. soldier into your camps. Each Special Ops Forces has been injected with a microchip, so they can be tracked. These are the elite soldiers of the world, and they are highly feared by the U.S. Military top brass and the federal government, Dept. of Homeland Security. While the microchips will respond to a frequency to give an individual identification and location of that soldier, the government can send that Special Ops soldier a deadly electrical signal through the implanted microchip. Our spirit soldiers will take care of those transponders and set those soldiers free. But in the meantime, do not physically bring them into your ranks."

Eisenhower sighed, "Our intel found that a European company located its manufacturing facility in the Silicon Valley; made billions and billions of these injectable microchips, and then shut down the facility. We know that they injected them into the Special Ops Forces. But it's likely other troops have been injected. And it's likely that every Christian soldier in every military in the world has been injected. If the chip is located in the body, cover the place with aluminum foil; wrap it around an arm or neck. It might work to block detection."

Eisenhower paced the floor inside the main room of the Alamo, thinking of his last comments to the militia generals, "Remember, no army can mobilize without supplies. Hit their storehouses, their weapons caches, their equipment. If you can get a spy into their mechanics unit, he can sabotage their vehicles. Get spies in as truck drivers, and they can drive the supplies, weapons, to a random, spontaneous meeting place. Like in a rest stop along the highway along its destination route. But when you do that, only take a percentage of the truck's load, and then send it on its way. Be creative! If there's a manifest detailing the numbers of guns, only take the amount that can be covered by the claim of a math error or typo. Claim that whoever entered the amount had dyslexia and transposed the numbers. Only take the amount reflected in that transposition of numbers. If it reads 154, you take 9 guns and claim it should have read 145. This way, you can repeat the taking. It all depends on your need, the volume of captured guns, and who they are going to. If you have a thousand guns going to UN troops - take them all. But it will be your last hijack and the truck driver needs to go with you. Be creative. Be flexible. I'm counting on American ingenuity."

Eisenhower stopped and looked at the militia. He realized that he threw out a lot of information at them. He hoped that it would all be remembered and implemented. "Do any of you have any questions?"

"Yes, sir," Bart replied with a thick southern drawl, "Are we fighting that military complex you warned about before you left office?"

"Yes, you are. They were preparing back then for this war, building up their weapons technology, the satellites, the biowarfare, communications, heat-sensing equipment, computer-controlled explosions. All of that for this war. The wars in between were to make them rich and to test those technologies. Cameras on every street. Everything has been designed so that Americans can't hide, can't defend themselves. They know Americans will be the hardest to take down, but if they take America, they control the world."

"What about the veteran spirits?" Mickey asked, "How will they be working with us?"

McArthur stepped forward, "Okay. This is the other facet of this war. There are two kinds of spirits, as mentioned, good and evil. For the most part, they will be fighting each other to keep them from interfering with your battle, but millions of good spirits will be assisting your militias. You need to listen for them, but you have to be careful.

The U.S. Government has been working on technology that can cause a person to hear words inside their heads. Not full sentences, not yet, but they're working on that. It's geared toward making people insane, push them over into the abyss. Make them robots, doing whatever the government tells them to do. The ghosts will not, I repeat, will not talk to you inside your heads. They will touch your right shoulder to get your attention, and then they will talk to you. Any words that are not your own and are inside your head, realize that they are using their technology on you. It won't sound like your thinking. It won't answer the questions you think about. If you suspect something, ask a question, tell it to repeat what it said, a fourth and fifth time. I suggest that you wrap your head in aluminum foil, and don't feel foolish about it. It will block transmission of their radio waves. Line your hats with aluminum. You've seen it in the movies and the characters were made to look like fools, crazy, for doing it. That's their plan, so you'll resist protecting yourselves. In the movies, the character doesn't want his mind to be read. They can't do that, but they can insert words into your minds. They can make you think that you are being possessed."

The militia looked at each other, not having heard of those experiments by the government. Suddenly, the world seemed to be living out the fantasies of spy novels and hero comics.

"One more thing," McArthur said. After drawing on his pipe, he warned, "Their latest technology is the creation of life. They now have the ability to create a genome and get it to operate in a cell. The new cell functions; it divides like a normal cell. If we fail to overthrow the Zionist Jews and Muslims, they will be creating genes that are computer-designed. But if something goes wrong with their cells that they plan to put into the oceans, the results will be catastrophic. The inventor bought through mail order, short sections of DNA that he put together in his lab. They took the genome that they created and injected it into a cell of the composite mail-order DNA strain of bacteria. They converted the DNA of that simple bacteria and created their own man-made strain of bacteria. From there, they are working on creating synthetic biological organisms. Right now, the technology is so new that there are no laws that regulate the lab or the inventor in its use. The U.S. Congress has intentionally delayed making restrictive laws that would prevent the inventor from making hybrids of humans or selling it to the Rothschilds or Rockefellers. No controls, but this technology allows them to turn your parakeet in to your dog! This is the step they've been looking for to inject animal DNA into humans. They'll inject fetuses inside the womb to be born with the best traits of animals; the vision of an eagle, the wings of a bird, the legs of a cheetah, the strength and aggressiveness of a Kodiak bear. It'll be their future army."

The militia generals looked at each other in disbelief. Some shook their heads; their faces showed their sense of defeat; how could they possibly fight such creatures.

McArthur continued, "But this manifold, multiple kinds of technology that they have, and this specific technology of creating bacteria, signals that we are in the true end times. The overwhelming numbers of hybrids of Satan's descendants with humans is why God brought on the Great Flood. God will stop this, again."

He picked up the Bible and began to read: "Rev. 6:2, 'And I saw: and behold a white horse, and he that sat on him had a bow, and there was a crown given him, and he went forth conquering that he might conquer."

McArthur looked up at the militia generals, then continued, "Rev. 19:17-21 ‘And I saw an angel standing in the sun, and he cried with a loud voice, saying to all the birds that did fly through the midst of heaven: Come, gather yourselves together to the great supper of God: That you may eat the flesh of kings, and the flesh of tribunes, and the flesh of mighty men, and the flesh of horses, and of them that sit on them, and the flesh of all freemen and bondmen, and of little and of great. And I saw the beast, and the kings of the earth, and their armies gathered together to make war with him that sat upon the (white) horse, and with his army. And the beast was taken, and with him the false prophet, who wrought signs before him, wherewith *he seduced* them who received the character of the beast, and who adored his image. These two were cast alive into the pool of fire, burning with brimstone. And the rest were slain by the sword of him that sitteth upon the horse, which proceedeth out of his mouth; and all the birds were filled with their flesh.’"

The militia looked at each other and at the bloodied soldiers of the Alamo. However way they looked at the situation, it was all mind-boggling. How do they relate to the historical Alamo spirits, the end times knowledge of creating life, and the Biblical account of Jesus defeating Satan? It was more than their minds could accept as reality. So far removed were all these things from the world in which they grew up in or imagined in their wildest day dreams. Yet it was up to them to save the country, to prepare the way for Jesus Christ. They decided not to try to fully comprehend, but to just accept and go home and fight.

Eisenhower stepped forward, "As I told you before, no army can stand if it is infiltrated by spies. Your first priority is to cull out the spies among your ranks. Then you simultaneously, take out these labs and take control of all U.S. Military bases. That’s the mission; how you accomplish it I’ll leave up to you."

Chapter 18

They call it the Devil's Den. Legend had carefully warned of a monster-size snake that lived among the ancient out-cropping of the battlefield at Gettysburg. A deceitful black snake that they had christened, "The Devil." But long before the Civil War, before the legend, the stratum of igneous rock of the outcrop had been eroded and broken in to large boulders, randomly tumbled, forming caves that later gave shelter to Confederate sharpshooters, into which they secreted themselves and picked off Union soldiers on the other side of the valley. The deceit of safety within the Devil's Den of boulders did not warn of ricocheting bullets that killed both Confederate and Union soldiers alike. The 5700 acres of the Gettysburg National Military Park surround the Den.

The leaders of quilting guilds from across America came to meet at Devil's Den before carrying out their plan to storm the White House and assassinate the President. But choosing to meet on this battlefield did not happen by chance. The Battle of Gettysburg was fought by 85,000 Union and 75,000 Confederate soldiers, and rendered 51,000 casualties. It was the bloodiest battle of the Civil War. These were the men for whom the quilters' ancestors of both northern and southern women had made quilted blankets. Gathered today were their great-granddaughters from both sides, grateful for their sacrifice. They came together to discuss final plans for storming the White House. But what they were not aware of was that they were brought to this battlefield to answer the pleas of the restless spirits of their ancestors, the soldiers and quilters alike. The plea could only be answered by their descendants – to kill the ancient, monster-size snake. With its death, the ghost soldiers would be released from the battlefield to fight in the Second Revolution. The request would soon be revealed to them.

At the moment, uppermost on their mind is the plan of the guild to get close enough to the White House in large enough numbers to allow a surprise invasion without triggering a suspicion of danger. The descriptive on the assembly permit, "Granny," gave them that cover. They had received a permit to demonstrate over the price of cotton, in Lafayette Park across from the White House. It all worked like pieces of a quilt being sewn together, since the reason for complaint was not completely false; the price of cotton had tripled over the last three years. The government's wrongful assumption was that a group of women, quilters, were not harmful to the corrupt, evil leaders that had taken control of America. Sun Tzu's *Art of War* spoke of the enemy providing the opportunity to defeat them; the quilters saw that opportunity and seized it.

As the guild leaders gathered, one from every state, they greeted each other with solemnity and purpose of mission. Their feelings were summarized in Lincoln's Gettysburg address. The sentiment of Lincoln's words ratified the plan in their hearts.

Lincoln's speech had once been required of every American child to memorize, but no longer required by the Secretary of Education. A cabinet position established by President Timmy Tercart, member of the Foreign Affairs Private Council, co-founder of the Triple Commission. Of late, the progressives in Texas tried to omit George Washington and Abe Lincoln from children's textbooks, and, instead, substitute them with the biography of Opal Sinfrig, a financial backer of the foreign Muslim invaded of the Office of the Presidency. Progressives, communists, wanted the role of the author of the Declaration of Independence, Thomas Jefferson, as Founding Father, to be down played. The United States educational system had been the best in the world, until the elite butchered it, piece by piece, so that the children to be born in a once-great country would not know their foundation nor become articulate, critical thinkers. So that the American children would not know their nation's tradition of individualism and self-reliance. So that the American children would only know what the UN Charter Agenda 21 dictated their education to be: teach them to be citizens obligated to volunteer for the common good of the world.

Just as slaves had been prohibited from learning how to read and write and prohibited from speaking their opinion, the elite and UN Secretary General Yoon Won-Shik, little by little, were digging a deep abyss of ignorance between the governing leaders and the citizens. President Tsaeb banned the scholarship program that allowed access to poor Washington, DC, school children to an extraordinary private academy – in the same month that his daughters were entering that private academy. It was all part of the elite's plan to effect the New World Order that they would hand over to Satan. It coincided with their Political Correctness weapon to silence speech. Dummy down and silence the populace, so the elite could argue that the high unemployment was due to the citizens' own inability, their own ineptitude. Eventually, citizens would be forced into taking the breadcrumbs thrown to the ground for them to scavenge in competition with their fellow countrymen. The essence of divide and conquer.

The mothers of America had had enough of these thugs, these communists, Satan-worshippers, Zionist Jews, and Muslims destroying their history, their culture, their country, their families, and their children. And they decided to take back their country.

The women gathered around Agnes. In representing the Granny Quilt Crafters of America, Agnes had made application for assembly in Lafayette Park under her name, and thereby, she became their leader.

In a somewhat high pitched nasal resonance, Agnes collected the women around her, "Here we are ladies, coming down to the last patches of our quilt," Agnes said. "If any of you have any doubt whatsoever, speak now or forever hold your peace!"

Flossy laughed, "We're not getting married, Agnes, we're planning a revolution! Don'tcha you know."

"I know, Flossy, but I want to make sure that everyone has fully committed themselves to this revolution. Once we step onto that park, there's no turning back. And we could fail. We could be arrested. And our own death is very likely. I want you all to think about what we are planning - the assassination of a sitting president, regardless of his being an invader. This is a turning point in our lives; after the invasion of the White House, we may never be able to return home to our families."

"Well, wait a minute," Margaret interrupted, "I'd like to say something, before anyone makes a final decision. Yes, we may not return to our children or husbands, but we cannot allow what they are doing to our children."

Margaret pulled out a piece of paper on which she had written part of Lincoln's address. "But first, I think we should say something about where we are, now. Gettysburg. You know what I mean? I know that we were coming here to talk to a female ghost, but, first, I think we should say something about what happened here. I'd like to read the last paragraph of Lincoln's address. Then we can make our final decisions. Is that okay with everyone?" Margaret looked around at the group of women, each nodding their assent to her agenda. "That's a nice gesture, Margaret." "Yes, I think we should do that." "We probably should have planned some sort of ceremony."

"Okay. Let me read the last paragraph of his address." Margaret took off her sunglasses. "Just give me a minute, here," she said, as she fumbled through her purse. "Here they are," she announced, as she pulled her reading glasses out of the case and put them on. "Oh, by the way," she said, looking over the rim of the half glasses, "the battle took place on July 1 through the 3rd, 1863. The heat must have been awful!" Margaret sighed at the thought. "Oh, and Lincoln came here by train on November 19, 1863 to give this address. Okay? And this is the last paragraph. She cleared her throat and began:

> It is rather for us, the living, we here be dedicated to the great task remaining before us -- that, from these honored dead we take increased devotion to that cause for which they here, gave the last full measure of devotion -- that we here highly resolve that these dead shall not have died in vain; that the nation shall have a new birth of freedom, and that government of the people, by the people, for the people, shall not perish from the earth.

Margaret folded the paper and took off her reading glasses and carefully tucked both into her purse. "Do you remember when - those of you 60-somethings," Margaret chuckled lightheartedly, "when we were required to memorize that entire address? I do! When I first saw how long it was, I thought that I would never be able to do it. But just for the fact that my teacher thought I could, told me that brains have that kind of ability. It challenged me to memorize it, just to see if my brain was as good as everyone else's. I remember stumbling over the words; I remember feeling the sentiment." Margaret laughed, "I remember wanting to recite it like a great orator, you know, emphasizing the words like they do. OF THE PEOPLE! BY THE PEOPLE! Reading it over and over to memorize it, it made me wonder how our ancestors gave up their lives for our country. The Civil War, the American Revolution. Being taught back then of how important it was to memorize this speech, made me think I was special, living here in America and having the brave ancestors that we had. I looked at my neighbors differently. Those who fought in WWII. I looked at them with new respect. I became in awe of them. To be an American meant that you were brave. Those who died here were just, just, incredibly brave. The American Revolution and the Civil War were such magnificent examples of Americans' resolve to be free. Memorizing Lincoln's address made me ask questions. Aren't other countries free like us? Why not? Why don't their citizens do what our citizens did for us? You know? I mean as a kid, you don't think of anything except play. It was in the classroom that brought my attention to these larger questions. Why isn't the whole world free?"

Margaret looked at the women's faces, "I remember feeling a sense of pride for the soldiers, for their bravery. I wanted to be like them, saving our country. What a noble, romantic death."

"That's my point," Agnes cried. "We can't fight this revolution from the standpoint of a child's idea of a romantic death! We have children to raise! They need us to nurture them. Have we provided for them? In case we don't return. We talked with each other about this on the phone. Have you done that?"

"We have," Carol answered. "My mother and father-in-law have agreed to share the burden. They're too old to physically fight. They both see raising my children is their military effort in this revolution."

"Just how bad are your kids?" Megan asked. The women laughed.

"I'm sorry, Carol," Kim said, trying to hold back her laughter, "but I wondered the same thing."

"That's enough," Carol smiled. "You know what I mean! We all step in to the role that we are able to fulfill. Each one is important. We can't do this alone. Each role brings success to the revolution."

Agnes held up her hands to silence the laughter and comments. "This is what I'm talking about! Do you all have the support of those around you, at home, that will allow you to carry out your mission?"

"I think we settled that issue before we got here," Grace intervened, "The question is, has anyone else stopped the elite's destruction of our children, of our country? We need to view it from the standpoint of what they have accomplished, so far, in conquering America. I want to reinstitute the American culture of Mom and Apple Pie. That culture was about the respect of family and country! Love of neighbor. It was a Christian culture. The elite purposely set out to destroy it, so they could bring in their communism. They did it through the sexual revolution. And who started that revolution? Well, I'll tell you!"

Grace pushed her way through the crowd of women, until she was out in front. She turned to face them, "It was with the open approval of the birth-control pill by President Lyndon Baines Johnson! That's who! And I might add, a member of the Foreign Affairs Private Council. The pill was pushed by physicians in league with the quiet approach to population control, and by the left-wing progressive groups like the SDS rebelling on college campuses against the traditional values of our Christian nation. But the pill increased sexually transmitted diseases, teen pregnancy, out-of-wedlock births." Grace's voice raised in anger, her arm reaching out, her finger pointing, charging, "Marriages declined! The divorce rate doubled! They intentionally cut deep in to our culture! Destroying our Christian morals!"

In support, Margaret walked over to stand next to Grace, addressing the quilters, "Women were encouraged by false feminism," because the pill was available and pushed by Margaret Sanger. You've all heard of Sanger. She was an atheist! She's the one who wanted the sterilization of the "unfit." Especially Blacks. Sanger used the pill to push her agenda to purify civilization. I read an article about her online." Margaret's voice became sarcastic, "She said, 'Only upon a free, self-determining motherhood can rest any unshakeable structure of racial betterment.'"

As if giving a political rally speech, Grace picked up Margaret's argument, her voice still raised, "Sanger was an avowed socialist! The American Humanist Society gave Sanger the Humanist of the Year award. Those people believe that there is no God! They think that everyone should live their lives for the greater good of humanity! They are Communists! They throw God and individualism out the window!"

Grace turned to Margaret, "Margaret, I read that same article that you are talking about," and turning back to the women, she added, "Sanger said that 'THINKING PEOPLE'! should mandate the registration of individuals with venereal disease and that 'THINKING PEOPLE' should have the power to select those individuals who should be sterilized. Sanger said, 'Apply a stern and rigid policy of sterilization and segregation to that grade of population whose progeny is already tainted....' That witch was working toward the elevation of the elite to the position of GOD!"

Margaret put her hand on Grace's arm, "Sanger was just the first step. You know what I mean? What about 'humanitarian' medical missions to Africa? Do any of you really believe that AIDS started from a monkey's bite of a human in Africa? The South American Amazon jungle is more suited to growing bacteria, fungi, and viruses than Africa!"

Shifting her weight from one foot to the other, holding a hand to her heart, Margaret charged, "In my opinion, the elite of the U.S. government developed that virus. Remember how they asked homosexual men to participate in a drug experiment in San Francisco and New York. And was the third location in Philadelphia? I don't remember, now. But those are the first cities that broke out with AIDS only among gays twenty years after those experiments. Okay," Margaret gestured with her hands, pointing at the women, "Now, think a minute of the Hitler experiments on homosexual men in concentration camps. They even castrated them to see if they would no longer be homosexual. From those experiments, they learned the only way to get rid of homosexuality is to kill homosexuals. Who were the most effected by AIDS, homosexuals and Africans. They targeted these two groups. They took literally Sanger's words: that 'THINKING PEOPLE' should have the power to select those individuals who should be sterilized.' Who would live or die."

Margaret turned to the different women as she spoke, "Sanger wanted to sterilize blacks. Billionaires Willy and Missy Shakes, go on a big medical vaccine mission in Africa, as though they were some kind of saints. At the TED conference, Shakes said that if we really try, we can bring down the population through vaccines, healthcare, and reproductive health services. The only way you reduce population using those methods it to sterilize with vaccines, and 'reproductive health services' means tying off fallopian tubes and vasectomies – and forced abortions. He's a lone knight on a killing mission! You know what I mean? In my opinion, I think that these kinds of 'mercy missions' that others had done years and years ago in Africa were to exterminate Africans. Look at all the cases of AIDS in Africa! Now, look at all the natural resources that continent has. The Chinese are buying up those resources from African kings to the detriment of their people. Just like African kings sold their people into slavery to Europeans and Americans, to get rid of their over-flowing populations!"

Grace interrupted, "I'll give you a better example! Remember the U.S. Public Health Service's Tuskegee syphilis experiment on Black men? They didn't give them the syphilis, but they told them that they were treating it when, in fact, they were only monitoring its effect on the human body. There was a cure! There was a cure!" Grace's voice sounded her empathy. "But the U.S. Public Health Dept. withheld it from those men! How unconscionable! Who the hell did those people think they were! And they didn't tell those men to stay away from their wives. So then their wives got syphilis! And some gave birth to sick infants. All the men and their wives died! They knew that they would die! Of a horrible death! The point is, the elite are trying to kill us through stealth. Most of us here are White, but it doesn't matter. Their current extermination plan is aimed at age, not race. That strategy will exterminate greater numbers. And the Stimulus Package's Death Panel and Tsaebcare are the final steps to our extermination!"

"The Death Panel!" Joan cried out among the group of women, "It is in the Stimulus Package! The Recovery and Reinvestment Act of 2009. It's called the Council for Comparative Effectiveness Research!"

"That was clever of them not to put it in the Tsaebcare legislation," Megan charged, "so they could claim that it's not in there where it should logically be, only to lead people to believe that it doesn't exist." Megan looked at Agnes, "For that reason alone, their deceitful tactics, I want to exterminate THEM!"

Margaret cried out, "Abortion is legal in this country. The Death Panel decides cost-effectiveness medical treatment. Well! Put the two together – and what have you got? It's cheaper to abort a baby than provide the mother with prenatal treatment and delivery. The Death Panel has the law and authority to FORCE women to abort their babies!"

Joan yelled out, "It's the priority curve of treatment," as she eased her way through the crowd of quilters. "Going back to what Grace said – she's right, their plan targets age." Reaching Grace and Margaret, she turned to the women, "Those between the ages of 15-40 get medical treatment because their age bracket makes them able to serve the state. The elite need people to service them. They developed robots to do most of the manufacturing of appliances and cars. Robots can serve as maids. Robots can even perform surgery, but the elite also need soldiers to protect them. When you think about it, 15-40 year olds are the ripe age for combat. Then the elite looked at the ages that will drain resources and have planned for their extermination. But the only way they can get away with that is by stealth. How will the collective nation of citizens know of the individual withholding of medical treatment from the infants and children up to 14 years? Or withholding from their grandparents? The media will soon bury talk of Tsaebcare's limitations; its withholding of treatment. It's Tuskegee on a grand scale! Any suspicion will be blocked. They own all the media! We get only the news that they want us to hear. They can claim that the mothers didn't look for medical treatment, during pregnancy or afterwards. Or the mothers were on drugs. Or were alcoholics. It's the mother's fault that their children died! People already accept death at 65 as normal. The government can claim that they didn't live an active early life the way previous generations did. Their diets were bad. That THEIR research shows that longevity is receding due to lifestyle. It's a planned attack on family on both flanks. The use of the priority curve is advocated by Death Panel member Ezra Samuel, MD, brother of Ron Samuel, Tsaeb's former Chief of Staff. And doctors who don't do what the Death Panel dictates are penalized! Repeat offenders are imprisoned!"

"The way I look at it," Alice charged calmly, her arms folded in front of her, "the problems with the greatest healthcare system in the world could have been fixed by providing portability of coverage, tort reform, prohibit sick people from being thrown off insurance company's coverage, stop denial of coverage for pre-existing disease. They could also have established, and I think they might already have it, but establish a fund to cover catastrophic illnesses. And prosecute doctors who are stealing from Medicare. And other than the last two, none of these changes would have cost a cent in taxpayer money, yet would have fixed all the ills of our healthcare system. Ya notice how they minimized those elements, claiming healthcare had to be changed because it didn't cover enough people. It didn't cover the illegal aliens who were using emergency rooms! First, they changed the laws to mandate emergency room care be given to them, instead of preventing them from invading our country! This is why they refused to secure the borders. They wanted the hospitals to fail, so it would make their argument that the entire healthcare system needed change! There are so many hospitals closed along the border because they weren't compensated for the mandated free illegal alien healthcare! Now Americans along the border have no hospitals to turn to! Step by step, each law gave them the excuse to destroy us! That's their bottom line! What they intend to do is destroy the economy through Tsaebcare! Exterminate us through Tsaebcare and the Stimulus Package!"

"Chain migration!" Sally called out, "If they stop the legalized chain migration of extended families of legally admitted immigrants!" The woman turned to listen to Sally at the periphery of the crowd. "That would solve the Social Security and Medicare problem! There wouldn't be twenty aunts, uncles, cousins and their spouses and their children claiming benefits of Medicare, Medicaid, Social Security, welfare monthly payments, food stamps! They wouldn't be taking up the public housing apartments from poor Americans. The twenty relatives collecting off of the one working legal immigrant paying taxes into those programs has been calculated to destroy those programs for Americans who have paid into the system. They use that tactic, and on top of it – they rob Medicare of $716 billion to pay for Tsaebcare!"

"What was accomplished by throwing out the greatest healthcare system in the world," Margaret asked, "when it could have been fixed without taxation? And let's put Sally's claim into the mix. How do we save Medicare and Social Security - cut out the chain migration immigrants from draining a system that they never paid into and that their one relative can never make up for! And Sally, it's also the illegal aliens who are getting those low-income apartments and welfare checks in sanctuary states like Massachusetts!"

Margaret looked around at the women, "So, what was accomplished by these laws?"

"It all increased our national debt!" Megan cried out. "It increased our taxes. It lowered the standard of living for Americans. It gave the Federal Reserve, taking our taxes, more wealth and power. Congress made the American people slaves to the private owners of the Federal Reserve central banks! The elite's intent is to minimize Americans' independence. Break our economy. Create job loss. They want us to be dependent on government handouts! They want us so weakened that we have to accept their New World Order!" Megan took a momentary pause, as she looked around at the women, "I say we cut them up into pieces and dump them into our food processors!"

"We're going to need those tree mulching machines!" Marie cried out. "I'm with the revolution!" The women suddenly broke out with jeers of rage. "Let's crucify them!" "Let's hang them!" "No, No! Mulch their sorry asses and spread it on the lawn of the White House!" "Yeah, mulching the lawns of Washington! That has my vote!"

Agnes raised her hands, trying to shout louder than the outrage of the quilters, "Ladies! Ladies! We're getting angry. And please keep your language civil. We are Christian women!"

"Agnes," Kim asked, "How can you worry about our language? We're talking about assassinating the President!"

"We can still be ladies!" Agnes asserted.

"Agnes, are you sure you can do this?" Alice asked. "Can you kill another human being?"

Agnes thought about the question, then finally, in a low voice, "I must. It's my duty. I'm a mother. And the way that I look at all this, motherhood is less about the giving of birth, and more about the loving and patient forgiving of the child, as he or she develops. It is the mother living a Christ-like life in encouragement of the child to find its way to Jesus. She can only show the way through her living. I mean," Agnes hesitated, trying to find the words to explain her feelings. "God is the essence of individualism, the free will to choose to follow Jesus or not. Isn't that the nature of individualism? I teach my children individual self-control. I teach them to assert themselves, but with respect for their elders. I teach them that they will never regret an act of kindness. I observe them to determine what their God-given talents and abilities are, and then try to encourage those abilities. I see that as my daily task of motherhood. Any woman that provides that to a child is a mother. That is God's calling to some women and to some grandmothers. Not every woman is able to give that to a child."

Agnes looked down at the boulder under her feet just protruding above the soil. "A mother who forsakes her daily task commits the greatest of abominations against a child of God. Think about that! A child of God!" Agnes waved her hands and shook her head, "Don't look at that phrase as a trite, false religious slogan. That babe that came out of your womb that they placed in your arms - it has a soul. God placed a soul into that babe. Women who adopt children, they are given another human being whose soul was given to them by only God. What a tremendous responsibility for that mother. She is holding God's child in her arms. When she betrays that child, she is the greatest of traitors, for that babe, that child is absolutely helpless. When a mother betrays the greatest of trusts, she commits the highest of treasons. I have no fear of being arrested for revolution. No fear of the enemy who has laid siege to our government charging me with treason. How could one disobeying the Constitution charge me with treason when I fight to uphold the Constitution? It doesn't follow reasoning." Agnes paused a moment, "I fear only God. I am for revolution to protect His children. I fight to bring Jesus back to our country. And I have prepared a safe harbor for my children, if I don't return from Washington. I'm ready to die. Let that also teach my children that I chose Jesus, by fighting Satanists. I chose not to become one of them."

The women were quiet for a moment until Marie spoke, "Agnes, we all feel that way. All the women back home have said or indicated that same sentiment. To the quilting women, true feminism is God's calling to motherhood. Through mothers, God's hand nurtures the growth of His creation of souls. We see ourselves as the frontline of protection of His children. We know that without mothers, there would be no civilization, and all humanity would die out in a generation. While we're trying to be honest in our caretaking, we are deeply angry, but we have reason. You feel that anger, too, Agnes."

"But we need to keep our heads," Agnes warned. "We're talking about taking control of our nation! Destroying the entire government that we live under. What kind of chaos is going to result when there's no federal government? And if we act through our emotions, we're going to fail."

"But, here in this place, it's okay," Sara said, pausing to consider how to put everything in to perspective. "Think of being in the locker room before the big game. You played sports in high school, didn't you Agnes? In the locker room, your coach charged up the team with her words. The blood needs to speed faster through the veins to give the players energy. Focus. The drive to win."

"I did play basketball," Agnes admitted, "and I remember one particular game. Throughout, the girl guarding me kept taunting me, close to my face, 'Go ahead and shoot!' She got me so angry by the end of the game, when the score was tied. And that one last time she yelled in to my face, 'Go ahead and shoot! I thought to myself, 'Okay, I'll shoot! And I'll show you!' But I missed. I didn't focus my eyes on the rim or how far I was from the basket, or the angle of the shot. I just threw the ball with all my anger, just to show her. They got the ball and scored and won the game. I learned never to become angry during competition. And I don't want any of you to become angry on the battlefield, either."

Carol reached out to Agnes and pattered her back to reassure her. "We're here, today, in the locker room, but in Lafayette Park, we'll be without emotion facing only the task at hand, kill the President!"

"We're between the feelings that you just expressed," Marie argued, "and the knowledge of the elite's planned, intentional destruction of our families. When we talked with each other at our meetings, we learned how our families are suffering. The mortgage foreclosures. The layoffs. We noticed the increase in autism in our children; the drug addiction among our teenagers. We complained of the TV ads that stripped women of our dignity. Of ads that make our husbands look stupid and incompetent. The ads against our husbands, especially White men, creates in the family's' mindset, especially wives, that we can't depend on them. It's a form of subliminal propaganda that wives, mothers, can only - should only - rely on the government. We discussed this. Everyone sees it. And we didn't talk about our menses to anyone but our husbands! Okay, maybe a best friend. We certainly did not discuss it with our children! But the ads show diagrams of sanitary pads. These are ads that teenage boys are seeing. How can we expect them not to say something about menses to our daughters! The TV ad says that the topic is up for public discussion. How do we teach our daughters to have modesty around boys, if the TV ads are stripping them of their natural sense of modesty? Those ads allow boys to mentally invade our daughters and once inside that intimate space of the mind, how do our daughters argue against further, physical, invasion by the boys? This is an intentional strategy of the elite. It's the elite who own these radio and TV stations. They own Madison Avenue who produce these ads. How can they not know of their invasion? Not know of their destroying the morals of our children? And have you seen the latest ads? Children turning in their fathers to government officials, for stealing a fork of macaroni off their dinner plates! It's the wedge between parents and children. It's a destruction of the father as head of household. It's putting the child as the authority figure in the family unit. It's a precursor to Hitler's Youth Movement. To a time when those children reported their parents to government officials, if the parents disagreed with Hitler putting teenagers in adjoining summer camps and telling them it was for the good of the country to become pregnant at 14 and 15 years old and unmarried. Proliferate the superior German race! All guidance and control of parents over their teenagers was taken from them. Our kids have Al Gordo telling them to instruct their parents on government issues because the children know more about the world than the parents do. They are indoctrinating our children with communism and the New World Order. And no one is stopping them! How insane is that!"

Megan finished the discussion, "Agnes, this is something that we must stop. The elite are evil. There's no other word for them. They are true evil in every sense of the meaning. And no one else is stepping up to the plate to stop them! It's significant that we are here, representing the mothers of America, on the bloodiest battlefield. We could have met at Boston Harbor, where the first revolution began, but the Communist completely control the Commonwealth of Massachusetts. It is the Petri dish of all their socialist legislation from gun control to Tsaebcare. They've allowed 250,000 illegal immigrants into their state! It's a sanctuary state. The governor is a friend of Tsaeb! What does that tell you? They targeted the state that began the first revolution. Where the shot fired was heard around the world! How very symbolic to turn the Sons of Liberty in to communists!"

"All right," Agnes agreed, "but let me say it this way. When we arrive at Lafayette Park, think of sewing a quilt. We get out of the buses just as we select our quilting fabric. We move toward the south end of the park just as we lay out those quilt squares in a pattern. We wait for the signal just as we pin the pieces together. And then move on the White House just as we begin to sew those squares together. Everyone should be mentally focused on the incremental steps that will lead to our finished blanket, the assassination of the president, and not about why we are sewing a quilt. All the why questions should be answered before we step onto Lafayette Park. All emotions are to be left at home! We only think of what step we need to take next."

"I think that's a good idea, Agnes," Margaret agreed. "Ladies," Margaret turned to the guild leaders, "When you go home, make sure you tell all your quilters to think the way Agnes just laid out."

The leaders nodded quietly, as they stood on the pathway in front of The Devil's Den. Then one after another of the quilters noticed four women walking out of the Den, until finally all were turned facing the strangely-dressed women. Agnes walked over to them, to one in particular, and asked, "Are you Earth Woman?"

"Yes. You are Agnes?" The petite woman asked.

"Yes. I am." Agnes held out her arm, "And these are the leaders of the quilt guilds."

Earth Woman turned to the three women standing next to her. "This is Rose O'Neal Greenhow, Mary Elizabeth Bowser, and Harriet Tubman. Rose spied for Confederacy. Mary and Harriet spied for Union. I am a Ojibwa, a Chippewa. I fight beside my husband against the White man. I am the ghost who spoke to your dreams, Agnes."

Rose asked the quilters, "Have you made your final decision to fight?"

Agnes had told the quilters that they would be meeting a ghost, but these women looked alive, real. But in listening to them, knowing who they are, the reality of actually seeing a materialize ghost who talked to them overwhelmed the women. And now there were four ghosts. Fear rose up from the core like some slow-moving volcano. In the quiet of the two groups of women looking at each other, one quilter suddenly cried out, setting off the others. "Oh, my God! They're ghosts!" "I think I'm going to faint!" "Oh, dear, Jesus!" "I think I'm going to throw up!" Trembling women grabbed hold of fainting women to keep themself steady and the other from falling. Others turned away; walked a few feet away, pacing, chanting low, "I don't know if I can do this. I don’t know if I can do this." “I know I can’t do this!”

Finally, Agnes turned to the quilters. "Ladies. We need to do this. They aren't going to hurt us. They are here to help us with our plan at Lafayette Park." Women blessed themselves and asked God to protect them. They took hold of each other's hands to strengthen their resolve, and then turned back to Agnes and the four spirits standing next to her.

The quilters looked at Agnes and nodded, then watched anxiously as Agnes answered the ghost of Rose, "We have made our final decision to fight the evil elite."

"Good," Rose said. "We will each speak of what needs to be done." As she stepped closer to the women, the women grabbed more tightly to each other's hands, whispering a gasp and rearing backward. But their feet were planted firmly on the ground.

The ghost of the tall White woman of wealth and refinement took another, smaller, step toward in the quilters. This time, the quilters didn't gasp, instead became fascinated by Rose's appearance. In mourning of her widowhood, she wore a black silk and lace dress. The antebellum design was nothing the quilters had ever seen, not so close or as beautiful. Her black hair was parted in the middle and tied up in a bun at the back of her head. Sloping shoulders belied her courage. The long oval face with full lips and soft, sad eyes, stirred everyone's heart. Her name was Rose O'Neal Greenhow, a mother of eight.

Rose instructed the guild leaders. "On Monday, June 6th, D-Day, at 3pm, you will gather on Lafayette Park. You will not be alone in the park."

The quilters looked questioningly at each other, but before they could ask what she meant, Rose continued. "Groups of women from across the country will drive in cars to several parking lots, leaving one woman to drive the car to a different rendezvous parking lot. After leaving the cars, get on the buses waiting in the parking lot. The buses will take you to Lafayette Park. They will pull alongside the park's northern entrance, on the far side of the White House. Have your women get out quickly and fill the southern end of the park, facing the White House. There will be 700 quilters. Once you are dropped off at the park your mission lies before you. When you have completed your mission, you must walk out of the city. Scatter in all directions. You will have several miles to walk. You are to plan with your driver where you will meet her, a Home Depot parking lot or a restaurant parking lot outside the city's limits.

The only identification you are to have on you is a pin, a quilted American flag. Attach these pins to your clothing in such a way that they do not come off in battle. If a woman joins your group and is not wearing a quilted pin, she is a spy. She must be killed with a knife, immediately. Lay her body out as though she is sleeping on the lawn. Place women sitting and talking on either side of her body as though part of her group. Create laughter and focus attention onto the quilts that you'll be bringing. There will not be any metal detectors or searches, but be sure to sew metal rings along one edge of the quilt to show cause for the quilts setting off a metal detector that you might be subject to. You have prepared quilts with trapunto pattern under which you have placed Tasers, 9mm, .38 cal., ammo, and knives. The batting should cover these objects, if a D.C. policeman that is not with us looks over the quilts. Be ready to answer that the hardness of the trapunto pattern keeps the shape of the design and that the quilt will be used as a wall hanging and not as a blanket. Lay the quilts on the ground and sit on them, as if at a picnic. Bring picnic baskets with you. Begin to eat. All will let you hide your cutting into the trapunto patch to retrieve the weapons. Make sure you wear clothing with pockets to slip the weapons into. Make sure you bring infra-red lenses.

By 12pm, all the buses will be emptied and on the move toward the city streets they are assigned to block. Post women in pairs on the east and west sides of the park near trees or close to bushes that they can crawl into when the battle begins. They will provide cover to those quilters leaving the White House, after the assassination. All your snipers must have silencers on their guns. The streets on the east, west, and south sides of the park are used by only government vehicles, so any car driving by once the attack has begun must be stopped. Aim for the drivers and tires. Post snipers along the street facing the White House, to kill guards secreted away on the White House lawn, bushes, and trees. Guards also have trained dogs. Bring mace for the dogs; clip the mace to your belt for fast access and repetitive use. Again, have your snipers take up positions close to objects that will provide cover once the battle begins. Look up into the trees! There are sniper nests up in the trees. Have your snipers take them out. There are also NASAMS, Norwegian Advanced Surface to Air Missile System set up around the White House, to protect the airspace above it. The missiles are not of concern. But the men guarding them will have sidearms; your snipers need to look for these people and kill them. Slitting their throats is the best way. We don't want gun shots before you get inside the White House. Send your tallest women after these guards, as soon as the women begin to encroach upon the White House."

"Oh, God!" Kim moaned, in the silence of the quilters. Being one of the taller women, she knew that she would be selected to cut the throat of a guard.

"Just think of it as killing a chicken for dinner," Flossy laughed. "Remember, Kim, knife into the side of the neck and slice outward, to silence the gurgling." It wasn't a taunt, but an instruction, for the task would fall to Flossy, too.

Kim felt sick at the thought of blood gurgling. She grabbed hold of Megan standing next to her. Megan could see the queasy look on her face, and whispered sternly, "Stop it! Stop it! Women deal with blood all the time! The guard protects those killing your child! He doesn't give a shit about slicing your child's throat!"

But Kim was focused on the image of gurgling blood pouring out of the throat of the guard and started to faint. Megan grabbed her by the shoulders and shook her in to awareness, "Stop it! What are you, a wimp! Are you going to fall in cowardly surrender?! Are you going to let this evil get away with what they're doing! This isn't murder! This is WAR! People die in war! This is a righteous kill! This is grow-up time! Be a WOMAN! This is the world and only the strong survive! Your children will only survive if you stand up and do this!"

Kim was jolted awake and found herself looking into Megan's eyes. Eyes that pierced deep inside her. Their incredible power was all Kim could think about. Finally, she began to hear the words, "This is a righteous kill!" Kim repeated them over and over to herself, this is a righteous kill. Then whispered, "Only the strong survive." Kim stared at Megan yelling at her just inches from her face, "Only the strong survive."

Finally, Kim came around, "I'll be all right. I'll be all right, Megan."

But the other women heard Megan and some began to cry. Others began to laugh hysterically. They held each other. But as Megan's word penetrated, 'This is WAR! Be a WOMAN!' they straightened themselves.

After the women quieted themselves, Harriet stepped forward. "I know this ain't easy for you women. None a you was born in ta slavery. You didn't even witness mine. But you need ta think differently than ever b'fore. Slavery existed b'fore and it will again, if we don't stop 'em. Theys must be stopped!"

The quilters watched the Black woman and listened intently. They knew that they needed to hear from one who had suffered the way the elite planned to make them suffer. The woman's sturdy build appeared larger under her battle uniform of a dark, three-quarter length wool coat and full skirt that hung to her ankles. She wore black shoes that tracked her slavery. Her narrowed black eyes, broad cheeks and pouty lower lip below her knitted brow was the physical manifestation of Megan's words. The task ahead was grim. It was nothing they could avoid or escape. The elite had been attacking America for one hundred years. But now, Americans would fight back. Before it was too late.

They could see it all in the face of Harriet Tubman as she spoke, "We need to create chaos! Loud enough to split de attention of de Secret Service. But Tsaeb, he has himself de Farkin's Muslim brotherhood as bodyguards that will be at de White House, too. So, we is goin' ta have a party at Lafayette Park. Spirit singer and a band will set up at de south end of de park. Theys gonna be loud and gay. When the battle begin, talk on walkie-talkies between de Secret Service and D.C. police will be drowned out. De partying in de park will be loud and noisy as can be."

Harriet looked around at the women and smiled, "I done this b'fore. At Combahee Ferry in South Carolina. I know how ta do this. We done free 750 slaves on that raid. I know how ta do this."

The women stood silently, taking it all in. History and every day stuff and their possible near-future deaths were all colliding before their eyes. Their minds couldn't catch up with the collision of all that was, is, and will be.

When Harriet stepped back next to Rose, Mary, stepped forward to speak to the quilters. She was a tall Black woman, standing straight with a primly appearance in a white dress that hung over narrow hips. At her neck was a buttoned choke collar. A hat sat squarely atop her pulled back hair; her young face had even features. Her refined appearance should have informed her boss, Jefferson Davis, that this woman, albeit once a slave, had been educated enough to read his plans.

Mary Elizabeth Bowser stood and looked at the guild members for a moment and then said, "You heard that dur'n the American Revolution, George Washington was one of the Culper spies. They only knew the next spy, those who gave 'em information and those they passed information to. Not even Washington knew all of 'em. Culper spies still protect this country and will be help'n you at the house."

The quilters began to mumble among themselves, "Culper spies!? Some had heard about them spying for the colonies during the Revolution. And for some of the quilters, to hear that they would assist their mission to kill the president made them feel safer. Yet others felt vulnerable that other people knew of their mission.

Mary continued, "They will be drugg'n the coffee of the sharpshooters that stand guard on the roof. A slow act'n elixir, but they be asleep after 30 minutes. The Culper spies among the D.C. police will be on the road between the White House and the park. They will allow women to slowly move closer to the gates of the White House. Mind you! You do it slow like. Keep smil'n and talk'n nice. Laugh'n among yourselves. Like you so interested in each other that you don't know where you are awalk'n. Talk about your chill'en or the price o' cotton, noth'n else. Give certain women the task to watch the White House, and tell all the other women not to look at it. The women who do the look'n will be covered by one or two women, no more. Tell those cover women to put their backsides to the White House while talk'n to the one look'n. When the look'n woman is face'n the house, she can see the congressional leaders arrive at the house for the meet'n with the president. The code to signal that the congressional leaders are enter'n the house is 'trapunto' stitch. It will signal the time is come to move on the house. The look'n woman can't tell what she is a see'n 'cause they be spy'n on y'all with listen' machines. The one see'n must cover her mouth when she speak the code. Either with a hanky, or with a c'gar."

The quilters looked at each other, questioning, "What woman smokes a cigar?"

Mary smiled, "Just use a hanky. Pretend to blow your nose. When the look'n woman says trapunto stich, the cover ladies will soon disappear into the crowd of quilters that are talk'n in groups, and make her report to 'em. Another woman in that group will walk on to another group of women and tell 'em the code word. No woman is to walk from group to group. Understand? Mind you! When each woman tell the code, they are to put their head down. And cover her mouth. Keep her voice down. To keep mouth readers look'n at 'em through spyglasses. Or hear'n them through listen' machines.

The soldier spirits here will be among you. Unseen. But when all is ready the spirits will fly above the city and bring down a great fog. It be the fog o'war! The fog will blind ever'body. The guards at the gates of the house will try to see if people be mov'n against them. So, you must wait 12 minutes before mov'n to the house. Laugh and cry like foolish, helpless women scared of the fog. The guards will think it just nature be'n its nature. When you cry'n out, put on your infra-red lenses you brought in your picnic baskets. They be lettn' you see through the heavy fog. But when you approach the gates of the house, be silent. Take the guards by surprise."

The quilters nodded at Mary to show their understanding. Mary walked back to stand next to Rose, and Earth Woman stepped before the quilters. The petite woman was without the appearance one might expect of a warrior. Her movement was gentle, almost submissive. Her hair was braided behind each ear and lay upon her chest with animal fur caught up at the end of each braid that hung down to her waist. The ceremonial dress was of softened white leather, with red, orange, and blue decorations that matched the white leather boots that came up to her knees. Her soft voice instructed that the spirit soldiers of Gettysburg surrounding them now will be in the city of Washington.

The quilters had not noticed any other spirits. But as Earth spoke, out of curiosity, the women began to look around. Those on the outer rim of the group turned to look behind them across the vastness of grass-covered outcrop and boulders that strewn the battlefield. And there they stood, thousands of ghosts dressed in Confederate butternut and Union blue Army uniforms, torn and bloodied. The Army of Northern Virginia Confederate soldiers were dirty with full beards; many were barefoot. They carried their rifles down at their sides in one hand, and in their other hand they carried their equipment rolled up in a blanket. They hardly looked like the greatest army of all time, such as they were known. The Union soldiers were bearded also, but their blue uniforms sharper, albeit bloodied. A more disciplined and better outfitted regimen, their polished boots cried out from under the dirt and dust haphazardly earned before the wearer's death. They carried their ammo and equipment in backpacks. Their rifles were slung over their shoulders.

In their sudden awareness, the women cried out, "Oh, my God! Oh, my God!" Alerting the other women in the group to turn around. "There's so many!" They grabbed at each other in fear. Their knees buckling under them. They grabbed for safety, but there was no defense. "There're thousands and thousands of them!"

Agnes stepped next to Earth and called out to the women, "Do not be afraid! Keep hold of yourselves! They are your army, fighting with you!" The women grabbed each other's arms, whispering reassurances to each other. "But I don't think I'll ever get used to this!" "We have to. We can't do this alone." "They're here to help, not hurt us." "God, most of them are so young." "Just think of them as your sons."

"Well, I would like to do that, but some of them are women!" Alice replied.

"What!" Carol cried.

"There are women. Look!" Grace ordered, her finger pointing.

As the quilters looked closer at the ghosts on the battlefield, they began to realize that there were many women. In dazed confusion, they looked at the spirits; their hair, no longer hidden under hats, hung down over their shoulders. They stood in tattered uniforms of butternut and blue that curved over their breasts and hips. Their cheeks were smooth.

Megan asked Earth, "Who are those women? There must be a hundred of them!"

Earth Woman explained, "Their numbers are many times a hundred. They were with the Confederate and Union armies. They were caught up in the chance meeting of the two armies. They chose to live with the armies to lay with the men. They do not belong to one man, but to the whole. These women understood man. To lay with woman is man's first craving. And his last. When man knows woman, he fights as a man. She renews him like the water renews the earth. Without woman, there is no man. All would be thrashings of foolish boys. Some of the soldiers were very young, but they fought as men. Some women are called to be mothers. Some women are called to bring a boy into his manhood. You are the mothers. These women brought the boy into manhood. In this way, these women fought for their nation.

The quilters looked at each other. They understood what Earth Woman was saying, for they weren't just mothers, but wives. They knew what their caress meant to their husbands.

Earth had waited for the quilters to think about what she had told them and then said, "In D.C., the spirit soldiers on the field will block passes. Roads will be filled with broken cars. Other spirit soldiers will go and take the Capitol. They will kill the evil Congress they find there. Others go to find the tents of Congressmen and women and cut them down. Others will scout out men and women of the mighty court. Before the Sun rises again, all the branches of the tree will be broken. When you are finished at the house, you must leave the city at great speed. Scatter in all directions away from the city. Some of you will walk north, some to the east, some to the west. From there head to your own tents. There will be great confusion over the city. The people will hide you on your journey. Those of you that were in the house are to walk south toward the Eclipse. Then southwest, to the Memorial for Signers of Declaration of Independence. From there walk southwest to Lincoln Memorial. You must reach the Potomac River on the far side of the Lincoln Memorial. Walk across the Arlington Memorial Bridge and up into the cemetery and pass through to its other end. Your spirit army here will protect you with heavy fog closing over the city, over the great confusion that will follow your work.

Do not leave your quilts in Lafayette Park. Do not throw them by the side of the road. If one is left by a dead quilter, pick it up and carry it out of the city with you. And take her pin off her, too. When you get home, burn the quilts and bury the ashes along with the pins into a river or lake.

Earth Woman looked at the women's faces. "Others prepare to finish what you begin."

The women were relieved to hear that they could go home after killing the president, but interrupted Earth Woman, "What do you mean 'others are preparing to finish'?" "What are you talking about?" "What others?" "Yeah. There's only us?" "Don't forget the Culper spies." "Okay, but she means more than them."

Rose stepped forward, "We have met with McArthur after his meeting with the militia generals. Eisenhower will lead the live militias' and veteran spirits' attack against the United Nations troops here on our soil and the Russians, Chinese, Iranians, and Mexican Militaries on the southern border. And the Chinese on the northern border. Queen Macha will lead the attack on the Muslim Training Camps. Nimitz will lead the naval battle; LeMay the air battle, including the commercial airports. Nothing will fly into or out of the United States. Patton is to produce and manufacture the weapon that will destroy the evil spirits. Bradley is setting up the supply lines for the weapons and food, gas, and ammo. Lee and Sherman are locating the bunkers of the elite. Our job is to cut the head off the snake; all of these others will destroy its body."

The women were taken aback. They thought they were the only ones fighting. But more than that, the names that Rose spoke were icons of military history. The women stood in shock. Their minds stopped functioning for the moment when they heard names like McArthur and Nimitz and the rest. And who was Queen Macha? "Well, wait a minute," Grace cried, "those people are dead! Many years, dead!" "How can they fight?" Margaret asked. "How do they know of us!?" Sally asked. "Wait!" Alice demanded, "What do you mean EVIL SPIRITS!?" The others heard her question and became frightened. Kim ran from the group then suddenly bent over and began vomiting onto the grass. Megan and Sara went over to her, one holding back her hair, the other rubbing her back. "Let it out, Kim."

Sally began to cry, "I don't think I can handle all this." Carol wrapped her arm around her. "She said that they have a weapon to use against them. I mean, it's General Patton! He knows how to fight!"

"I figured that I could talk myself into killing a human being, but there are so many ghosts getting involved in all this!" Sally cried.

"What the hell is going on," Megan demanded. "Where are all these ghosts coming from?!"

"We've always been here," Rose replied. "We've been waiting for live Americans to do something. We were just about to start something ourselves when we heard of the Quilters making plans to invade the White House. So, we decided to go with your plan and help you carry it out."

Margaret turned away immediately, "I need to sit down." She walked over to a boulder and sat down. Taking a Kleenex from her purse, she blew her nose, and when she finished, she started talking to no one. "God, it's strangely cool. It's May. It's Pennsylvania. I thought it would have been warmer."

Flossy walked over to her, "How'ya doin' kiddo?"

"Oh, I'm fine. I'll be all right," Margaret answered, as she returned the tissue to her purse.

Flossy sat down next to her. She looked back at the women,

crying, trembling, vomiting. She looked over at the four women spirits and then across the battlefield and the thousands of spirits of the Northern Virginia Army and the Union Army of the Potomac. She thought of the evil spirits that Patton had developed a weapon to destroy. She took a deep breath and thought to herself, I knew there was more to life than what we saw. What we were told. She took another look around and nodded. I knew it!

Agnes went to each woman, trying to calm them. "I told you that we would be meeting with a ghost, a spirit. I'm sorry, I didn't know there would be soldiers. I didn't know that other spirits were going to finish the war. But look at it this way, we get to go home to our families once we finish killing the president! That's a good thing!" She kept moving from one woman to another, "Kim, I'm so sorry about the evil spirits. I didn't know there were evil spirits. I didn't know that Patton was involved, let alone making a gun to destroy the evil spirits. You need to think.... You need to be grateful for the weapon. They can be stopped!"

The women were still in shock. Still trembling over the thought of so many spirits fighting. "What have we started, here!?" "We just wanted to keep it simple." "Yeah. Just kill the president, maybe a few congressmen." "Enough to shut down the government. That was all." "This is turning in to something that we can't handle." "We have lost complete control of this situation!" "What the hell are we going to do?" "Is it too late to stop all this?"

The women were exhausted with the stress and the awareness of starting an inter-dimensional war. They began to walk over towards Margaret and Flossy sitting on the boulders nearby. They sat down wherever they could find a boulder to sit on. They became quiet, pensive. "We live our daily lives in and around other people that we don't see. How weird is that?" "It's like a science fiction movie!" "So those ghosts were thinking of taking action, too? Before we came up with our idea." "How many others are out there.... I mean, live Americans who are planning on doing something?" "She said that Eisenhower was going to lead the militias. So, I guess the militias have been planning something." "Some Queen is going to fight the Muslim Training Camps!" "We knew about those camps." "Yeah. And if the ghosts knew what we were planning, they must know that those Muslims are planning something, too." "I guess they're going to get them, before they get us!"

The women threw out their thoughts, randomly. No one expected an answer. No one tried to answer. And as the cool, May morning air soothed the exhausted women, they sat quietly for a long time. Occasionally, looking at the soldiers standing on the battlefield; occasionally, looking at Rose, Harriet, Mary, and Earth Woman, as they talked with Agnes. After the long silence, Megan suddenly cried out, "Patton! Lee! McArthur! Son-of-a-bitch!" "I know!" Alice smiled, nodding her head, "How can we go wrong with them?" The other women began to smile at each other. "We're going to win!"

In the different perspective, the women became accepting. Slowly, one by one, they got up from the boulders and began milling around each other, talking, pulling a leaf from a shoulder, patting a back, hugging Kim and Sally, whispering reassurances.

As they began to relax they moved around, taking in the entirety of the scene in which they had been actors. "It has been one incredible adventure," Megan said to Alice. "One incredible adventure!"

"Indeed," said Alice. But hearing a noise behind her, she turned and saw seven spirit soldiers coming up the pathway, marching in two-column formation. Just a few feet from the quilters they stopped. The soldier in the front saluted the quilters, and Agnes specifically, "Ma'm. I am Joshua Lawrence Chamberlain, Commander of the 20th Regimen of Maine."

Agnes nodded acceptance of the Commander's salute. But then confusion filled her mind. "Commander. You didn't die on this battlefield. Why are you here?"

"For the men, ma'm. I came to be with my boys. But I'm not the only one, ma'm. Union Maj General 3rd. Corps Commander Dan Sickles came back, too, ma'm. His guilt brought him back to his men. He put them in harm's way, so he condemned himself to be trapped here with them. He positioned them out in front of the Union Army like a sore thumb. At times, they were surrounded by the Confederate Army in the middle of the peach orchard. His line extended out into the wheat field. He lost half his men; 9,000 are captives here. He was on horseback when his leg was cut off by cannon fire. But he sat up; propped himself up against his horse and lit a cigar to assure his men that he was still alive, so they would keep fighting. When they carried him off, a cloud of cigar smoke wreathed his head. But his men were driven back to the Union line along Cemetery Ridge."

After a short pause, Chamberlain continued to explain to Agnes, "Ma'm. We were not supposed to fight on this field. The south came down from the north, and the north came up from the south. The world was turned upside down, ma'm. Lee's Army of Northern Virginia was heading north in his second attempt to invade. He sent Maj. General Richard S. Ewell and his 2nd Corps to Harrisburg. Ewell was on his way to smash the rail hub there. He was at the outskirts of Harrisburg when Lee's dispatch recalling the 2nd Corps south, to Gettysburg, arrived. Jubal Early, Div. Commander of the 2nd Corps, was coming down from the north, York, Pennsylvania. Early's Div. arrived at Gettysburg on the first day of battle, The battle had been going on for five hours when his Div. arrived. Early ordered his men into battle as soon as they arrived, without formation. They appeared out of nowhere off the Union's right flank. They proceeded to smash the Union position, sending the 11th Corps of the Union Army fleeing through the town of Gettysburg. Hundreds of them took up hiding in cellars and wood rickets, attics. Most of them were captured."

Chamberlain looked across the battlefield and sighed, "This is an upside down place this battlefield. And we were fated to meet here, long before we were born."

He continued, "Lee had sent out small detachments to forage for food and supplies all over southern Pennsylvania. Lee was at a farm between his scattered armies. He heard the start of the battle in the morning and summoned his cousin Maj. General Heth, commanding a 3rd Corps Div. Heth explained that he and his men were looking for shoes that they had heard were in Gettysburg. Heth thought it would only be a small skirmish when they first ran into a small band of Union soldiers, but then the Army of the Potomac Infantry showed up. Lee tempered his irritation, ma'm, because he didn't know himself where the Union Army was located, how could he be angry at Heth. Jeb Stuart and his Calvary, the eyes and ears of the Army of Northern Virginia, couldn't get in touch with Lee. The Confederate Army was marching blind in Union territory. Neither side planned to fight here. It was just another sleepy town where the roads came together. It was a meeting engagement."

"What is a meeting engagement," Agnes questioned. Trying to make sense of what Chamberlain was saying to her.

"The Confederate and Union armies come upon each other by chance. The three days of battle were not planned by Lee or Meade. It was the deceit of The Devil. The Confederates' temptation were the shoes. The Union's temptation was to stay and fight because of the natural strength of the position from Culps Hill to Little Round Top. The Devil imprisoned the spirits of those who died here."

"The snake!?" Agnes cried.

"The snake is its deceit. His Gettysburg uniform. He is the Devil."

"But why come back to be entrapped by him?"

"These men. The Confederates and Union soldiers are my brothers. I don't know that I can say it any better, ma'm. I could not rest elsewhere knowing that they were captured here. It was better for me to be captured and be among them for eternity than never to see them again. Their wounds are my wounds; their tears my tears."

Chamberlain straightened to attention, "Ma'm, I would like to present the escort." Chamberlain turned to the six soldiers standing in column formation behind him. "Union Col. Strong Vincent, Commanding a brigade in the 5th Corp was shot in the heart when defending Little Round Top. Confederate Brig. Commander Robert Garnett was shot off his horse while leading his men marching in formation across the field, during Pickett's Charge. Confederate Brig. General Louis Armistead, during Pickett's Charge he was on foot leading his men over the stone wall at the Angle, with his hand on one of the Union cannon, exhorting his men to come over the wall, he was mortally wounded. Union Commander John Reynolds, on horseback while exhorting his men into McPherson's Woods, was killed by a Confederate Sniper. Confederate General William

Barksdale, leading his Mississippi brigade on what a Union observer called 'the grandest charge ever made by mortal man' against the Union position hole up in the peach orchard; he was unhorsed by dozens of Union bullets. He died the next day in the Union field hospital. Union Col. Alonzo Cushing commanded a 7-gun artillery battery, decimating Armistead's and Garnett's formations while they approached the Angle, trying to break through the Union line. Cushing was shot through the heart."

Chamberlain suddenly shouted, "Atten hut!" The two columns of Civil War spirits snapped to crisp attention.

Agnes nodded, "Gentlemen," and then turned to Chamberlain, "What are you going to escort?"

"Who, ma'm. We are going to escort the mother to Little Round Top. The Devil is sunning himself there."

Agnes looked at Earth Woman and then to the quilters, confused and looking for answers. "Why are you going to escort a mother to The Devil!?"

Chamberlain replied, "A mother must kill The Devil. One of you mothers. So we may be released from the battlefield to fight this revolution. So we may kill the evil that killed us before it kills our descendants. The mother must be the off-spring of Eve, to strike the head of Satan's offspring."

"Oh, my!" cried Agnes. "I didn't know about this."

The women looked at each other, one of us, they whispered. Then one by one, they all turned to Megan. After a minute or so, Megan realized her election.

"She must be a descendant of Eve!" Megan cried to the women. "That's what he said! I don't know that I'm the descendant of Eve."

Chamberlain turned to Megan, "Ma'm. You are descended from Adam and Eve."

"How do you know? I don't know! I think that I would know. Wouldn't I," Megan asked.

"We were told that she would have red hair. You are the only woman out of all of you with red hair. And these women selected you. They were directed to choose you."

Megan stood in disbelief. Finally, shaking her head from side to side, "I...ah...don't know what to say." Then looking at the women, questioningly, "Who directed you?"

The women looked at each other, "I don't know. I just thought of you, Megan, when he said a mother had to kill the snake. I just thought, Megan is the one to do it."

"Ma'm. Shall we?" Chamberlain asked.

Megan sighed heavily, emptying her lungs of the dread that passed through her body. She wondered to herself, what was more incredible, her walking away with seven ghosts or walking away to kill a monster-size snake? Quivers ran down her spine. The soft hair on the back of neck prickled. There and then she blessed herself and called upon the Holy Ghost to cover her in His protection.

As she stepped toward the ghost of Chamberlain, she forced herself to think, experience the adventure. Experience the adventure. It was the only thought she allowed to pass through her mind. At least, for the moment.

"Ma'm," the soldier saluted, Megan, "We will take you to Little Round Top where he is sunning himself."

Megan swallowed hard, "Okay."

On the way, Megan felt sick to her stomach, thinking to herself, I hate snakes! I hate them! Trying to build up the courage, preparing her mind, she coached herself, just commit to it; he who hesitates is lost. What did Mailer say, tough guys don't dance. Just walk right up to it and kill it; don't think about it; don't dance around it. Just kill it! After this, I'm going to buy myself a vanilla shake on the way home. The sooner I kill it, the sooner I'll have my vanilla shake. Keep it simple, Megan, keep it simple.

As the spirits and Megan climbed up to Little Round Top, Megan spotted a large rock. She estimated it to be ten pounds. She picked it up and tucked it under her arm as a quarterback carries a football to the goal line. She felt relief that the morning was unusually cool, for it would make the snake sluggish. At the top of Little Round Top she saw the snake. It's size caused her to involuntarily pull back. She began yelling inside her head. Don't hesitate! Don't dance! Commit to it! As she thought the last words, she walked quickly with intent up to the head of the ugly menace, lifting the rock up over her head as she walked. Now, standing over the snake as it faced away from her, The Devil began to lift its head, but the cold of the morning air made it impossible and his head dropped onto the ground. Then it slowly slithered from side to side, but it was unable to fight against the stiffness of his muscles. Again, it tried to lift his head just as Megan brought the rock down as hard as she could. She heard a crack, but she didn't want to take any chances. She moved quickly, picking up the rock, she smashed its head again, and then again, and again. She stopped for a moment to look at the ancient creature. Its head was crushed. The wounds bled. She dropped the rock at her side and she quickly backed away.

The soldiers of the Confederate and Union escort ran to the edge of Little Round Top, looked down on the Valley of Death and to their brothers waiting below. Suddenly they screamed out a rebel yell, a high-pitched yipping, while the Union escort yelled a deep-throated Hurrah! Their cries echoed across the valley below and told of their freedom and their lust for the battle to come. All the soldiers waiting below returned their cries from tens of thousands of throats. Megan grabbed hold of a nearby tree with one arm and blocked an ear with her other hand. The sound pierced every mind of the quilters below. The noise was deafening. It screeched down their spines as they stood on the pathway outside Devil's Den. As the ghostly screams continued endlessly, the women quickly closed ranks, huddling together. Their heads bowed with hands clasped hard against their ears, but still they couldn't shut out the Confederate and Union battle cries. The women began to cry and fall to the ground along with Agnes, but the screeching met them on the ground as it echoed off the outcrop. "What have we done?!" "What have we done!!"

For the first time, the spirits began to fly above the battlefield, released from captivity. They flew off beyond the battlefield's boundary just to be sure and then returned and flew over the heads of the women, gently yipping, softly hurrahing. This time it caressed the hearts of the women. And so, the women stood up and watched the soldiers flying in formation of loops and swirls, the bursts of freedom.

Chamberlain watched them flying for a moment and then turned to Megan, smiling, "Thank you, ma'm. You've given us our freedom." He then turned to the escort spirits and ordered, "Take it back to Earth Woman."

In the uppermost boulder of the outcrop, was a weathered depression in the shape of a large, spread-winged, horned bat. It was as though its image had been burned onto the boulder by the Sun, as it had flown over the battlefield. The depression was as deep as a cistern in which Earth Woman prepared a fire. From the precipice of another boulder, a second woman stood, looking out across the vast acres of the battlefield, searching for Megan. "Here she comes!"

Megan and Chamberlain led the six other spirits carrying the carcass of The Devil, down from Little Round Top across the valley and were, now, almost at the Den. As they climbed up to the highest boulder, the other women of the guilds followed them. The Devil snake was lain across the depression, next to the fire. The women formed a circle around the snake, its long tail fell beyond the boulder's edge and onto the golden grass. Earth Woman took her knife and cut off The Devil's skin starting at its nose, pulling it back to expose its crushed skull and bleeding muscles underneath. She next cut out the eyes and threw them into the fire and then passed the sharp knife to the next woman, who in turn sliced off a chunk of skin around the Devil's thick body and threw the skin into the fire, and then passed the knife to the next woman. And on it went, until The Devil was absent of any skin. Earth Woman then approached with an axe that she raised above her head and brought it down to decapitate the eyeless Devil. Then she passed the axe to the second woman who also brought the axe above her head and cut off a portion of the Devil and tossed it into the fire. When all the women had finished, the carcass of The Devil lay burning in the cistern of the uppermost boulder. The smoke arising from the ashes of the burning serpent had the odor of sulfur.

In silence, the women watched the ancient evil burn in the fire for more than an hour. As they did, the spirits of Confederate and Union soldiers walked up towards the outcrop, surrounding them in closer proximity. The women turned to face them. Seeing the young faces filled their hearts with sadness. They had died in a war over the economy, over the south being controlled by the north, over a president who promised the world to keep the union of the states. But the war that the women and the spirit soldiers would come to fight, would be for the souls of a Christian nation against the Muslim and Zionist Jews, the children of Satan.

Next to the boulder where The Devil had burned to ashes, Earth Woman took the axe and chopped the ground, until she had loosened it enough for her to open a deep hole with her hands. Then she went over to the fire in the cistern, the belly of the spread-wing horned bat, and pounded the ashes with the end of the axe's handle until the ashes of The Devil snake became small particles of dust. She took them up and placed them into the hole and buried them. She turned and raised her hands to the heavens and called upon God to send The Devil down into hell.

As the women watched Earth Woman, Megan noticed a rainbow. She quietly pointed up to the sky. When the other quilters saw it, they cried out, "But there are no clouds! There was no rain!" Megan crossed herself and began to pray, "Our Father Who art in Heaven...." The women and soldiers joined their voices with Megan's. Their prayer echoed across the vastness and blessed the battlefield of Gettysburg.

Chapter 19

Beyond all the galaxies to the outer periphery of existence, in the highest of Heavens, they gathered. The serenity among the holiest of angels was magnificent. The witnesses were brought before the gold throne to give an accounting of the matters on the lowest of Heavens, Earth.

Dwight Eisenhower and John Kennedy were dressed in long, white linen robes, barefoot, and without adornment. They stood before the large gold throne upon which God the Father was seated. His white garment of singular fabric blazed with the reddest heart of His Son and His body glowed with the Holiest of Spirits.

The witnesses waited for the Father to speak and when He spoke, His voice was deep and strong, soothing and loving. "What do you say of Earth?"

Kennedy looked at Eisenhower, to bid that he speak first. Eisenhower nodded in recognition.

"Holy Father. It appears that we must strike, now. Satan sits on the throne of Peter. Within the year, the Popes, Benedict XVI and Nicolas, will openly institute their war against your Israelites and those who believe in Your Son, Jesus. Tsaeb has signed all the laws necessary to gather Your followers into the FEMA concentration camps. The camps are now fully prepared to accept many millions of Americans. And the Dept. of Homeland Security has purchased an additional 4.5 million rounds of ammunition. The United Nations is prepared to issue the global currency, which has already been printed. The microchips mark-of-the-beast are ready to be injected. The UN will require injecting every human with a microchip in order to convert their currency to the global currency. Otherwise, no man might buy or sell, but he that has the character, or the name of the beast, or the number of his name. Each microchip has a barcode. If people refuse to take the injection, they will be put to death. The U.S. Census takers entered into their computer network system all the names and locations of your Israelites. That database of names will be cross-referenced against those who will be given the microchip through injection. All the town hall vaccine centers will be ready in four months. Through the Antichrist, UN Secretary General Yoon Won-Shik, Satan has sent warships of the United States to surround the open stargate in the Gulf of Aden, off of Yemen. Satan's angels plan to emerge through that Stargate; they will kill all the Americans and take charge of the ships. Stargates have been opened in six areas of the United States national parks that had been taken over by the UNESCO Biosphere projects, so that Satan's angels can emerge and kill millions of Americans. The Seagate portal off Puerto Rico is open; the Stargate over Norway is open."

Eisenhower continued, "Holy Father, Your four angels are standing on the four corners of the earth, holding the four winds of the earth, that they should not blow upon the earth, nor upon the sea, nor on any tree. Your angel ascended from the rising of the sun, having Your sign, and has cried with a loud voice to Your four angels, to whom You gave to hurt the earth and the sea. Your angel told the four angels, hurt not the earth, nor the sea, nor the trees, till we sign the servants of our God in their foreheads. That sign is now being put on Your servants' foreheads."

Kennedy then spoke, "Holy Father, in Rev. 17:12, it speaks of the ten kings, who have not yet received a kingdom, but shall receive power as kings one hour after the beast.' Syria is about to fall to the Muslim Brotherhood and the formation of the Arab Union will be completed. The other unions of Asia Cooperation Dialogue; Association of Southeast Asian Nations; Central American Integration System; Central Asian Union; North American Union; Pacific Union; Organization of Eastern Caribbean States; European Union; Community of Latin American and Caribbean States – are already formed and ready to be announced. The Antichrist has already chosen kings for those ten unions. The kings have promised to deliver to the beast their strength and power. The United Nations has been in power for 64 years, already, beyond the hour of the establishment of the UN seat of the Antichrist. I fear that we cannot wait for the announcement of those ten kings. The UN is moving to take guns away from Americans.

Your prophet, Elias, awaits Your Word to speak before the United Nations, which will be broadcasted out to the world. The Superwave is not far away from Earth; it will cover the Earth in an electromagnetic shield for the Chastisement.

And we are now on the eve of the mothers of America carrying out their plan to take down the White House. The spirits of Gettysburg will assist their revolution and will attack the U.S. Congress and Supreme Court. All the underground bunkers have been found and the spirit of Sherman and the 11th dimensional spirits are prepared to close the entrances, keeping the elite out. And for the elite who got inside those bunkers, the bunkers will become their tombs. They will be buried alive. As for Satan's portal under the throne of Solomon, Paton will close it, so that the Black Pope and Satan may not escape through to the other side of the universe. The way will be prepared for Your Son to battle Satan."

"Holy Father," Eisenhower added, "It did not appear that the mothers could be stopped, so Your 11th dimension soldiers decided to follow their initial assault, instead of trying to stop the mothers."

The Holy Father interrupted, "These mothers are my first line of defense against Satan. They carry the burden I placed upon them with brave hearts, and they will be well rewarded for their battle against Satan's army. I gave them the free will to choose, and they chose Me well. I will write upon them My name and I will make them a pillar in My temple and they shall go out no more from the highest of Heavens. Nor shall they shed tears from broken hearts for the sins committed against their children. I will make their children whole. I know the works of these mothers. I have given them an open door that no man will shut, because these mothers kept My Word and have not denied My name. Behold, I will bring to the synagogue of Satan, who say they are Jews and are not, I will make them come to adore the feet of these mothers. And these mothers will know that I have loved them."

"Then," Eisenhower asked, "It may begin?"

"Let it begin!"

Chapter 20

The day had come. In overwhelming forces, the American people stood up together to take back their country. Overtime, they had communicated to each other all the facts; they made their arguments; they deliberated; they prayed; they made their judgment of treason; numerous appeals were made; the judgment of treason stood; and now they were about to carry out sentencing. It would be a surprise attack, a quick and merciful kill. No hesitation. Nothing can stop them, not even the gates of hell, for the God of Abraham has willed it.

Though the sun had not risen over the eastern horizon, all over the United States, American patriots rose from bed at the same time to begin the Second American Revolution. They sat down to breakfast with their families and prayed together.

More than eight million American citizens are licensed to carry a gun. Collectively, Americans own more than 300 million guns and more than a trillion rounds of ammo. This would be a time of sharing with their fellow patriots less fortunate.

Of the U.S. Military power, there are Marine installations in 8 states; Navy installations in 23 states; Air Force installations in 37 states; Coast Guard installations in 22 states; Army installations in 48 states and Puerto Rico. Texas has 24 Army bases, training centers, airfields, depots, and a medical center. California has 40 Army installations. Worldwide: U.S. Military installations are located in 31 countries.

Of the U.S. Navy there are 11 aircraft carriers, 22 cruisers, 62 destroyers, 29 frigates, 3 littoral combat ships, 9 amphibious assault ships, 2 amphibious command ships, 9 amphibious transport docks, 12 dock landing ships, 53 attack submarines, 14 ballistic missile submarines, 4 guided missile submarines, 14 mine countermeasures ships, 11 patrol boats, and 1 intelligence ship. They are stationed on the east and west continental coasts of the U.S. and at Pearl Harbor and Guam, and on international seas. The U.S. battle fleet is greater than the next 13 largest foreign navies combined.

Of U.S. nuclear weapons, there are a total of 5000 warheads, of which there are 1737 deployed strategic warheads, 500 operational tactical weapons, 2700 reserve warheads in storage.

The U.S. Military is the largest military the world has ever known, and within the day it will be in the hands of American patriots. The men and women of the U.S. Military were coming home to fight for their own country's freedom.

At the same moment in time all over the world, the revolution began. General Bradley ordered his 11th dimensional ghosts to take spiritual possession of the bodies of the Combatant Commanders responsible for geographical theaters stationed around the world. Live, lower-ranking Colonels and Captains of every branch jailed their corrupt superiors and took control of bases and ships, killing all Muslims, SM-13 gang members, and illegal aliens in U.S. Military service. In foreign seas and lands, every ship of the U.S. Navy and Merchant Marines, and every plane of the U.S. Air Force were loaded with soldiers, sailors, airmen, Marines, Special Forces, Special Ops, bringing with them every U.S. fighter jet and attack helicopter, tank, Humvee, truck, jeep, rocket launcher, surface to air missile, rifle and ammo, computers, and medical equipment and supplies.

MacArthur, himself, took five brigades of 11th dimension ghosts from WWII and headed for USNORTHCOM at Peterson AFB, Colorado Springs and to the Commander's office. MacArthur took spiritual possession of the body of the Army Commander; his men possessed the bodies of the Joint Staff and lesser leaders and grunts. He ordered other ghosts to Washington, DC, to possess the members of the Department of Homeland Security to keep them out of the way of operations. MacArthur and his ghosts were now in control of all communications and spy drones flying over the United States. And after giving final orders to troops, Eisenhower joined MacArthur at the command center at NORTHCOM. From there Eisenhower would communicate during battle with all sectors of the Army.

Any questions that came in to the center about troop movement MacArthur answered: Simulation response training due to threats from the on-going Muslim World Caliphate and international demonstrations of hatred against the United States.

General Bradley had set up the supply lines and left two platoons in charge, and then led the rest of his WWII 12th Army Group of 11th dimension ghosts to the Pentagon. Once he took spiritual possession of the body of the Secretary of Defense, Bradley commanded Pentagon operations.

Bradley's supply platoons were headquartered in Kansas where the railway lines crisscrossed the United States, with two ghost soldiers stationed at each supply depot set up along 150,000 miles of rail where grandfathers and high school students, who couldn't fight on the battlefields, were standing at the ready. Every means of transport to get supplies to the Army and militia out in the countryside would be used, including horseback, mule pack, motorbikes, and all-wheel terrain vehicles. In other locations, row boats and pickup trucks, and even rental U-Haul trucks were waiting. They were prepared to refill ammo, food, medical supplies, batteries, boots and uniforms, and blankets wherever needed in the country.

Eisenhower had deployed the living American Militias and U.S. Army on separate missions. The Texas, Arizona, and New Mexico militias were sent to the Rio Grande. The California militia was sent to LA. Will Booker was ordered to lead the militias of Washington State, Montana, and North Dakota to the northern border. General Washington and his 11th dimensional Continental Army were ordered to cover the National Forests where UN and NATO troops were encamped in 27 states. Eisenhower ordered the live Green Berets, Special Ops, and Special Forces to set up shop in the outskirts of 42 states the day before. This morning they prepared to kill SM-13 gang members who had taken over cities and towns. Lee was deployed to Washington, DC, and the Capitol, Federal Reserve Board, World Bank, International Monetary Fund, the Supreme Court, and to the White House to aid the Granny Craft Quilters of America in assassinating the President of the United States. Stonewall was ordered to permanently seal the bunkers built for the elites in NYC, in D.C., and across the country, locking the elite inside, if necessary, as their tomb. Sherman was ordered to the city-sized, underground bunker at the International Airport in Denver, Colorado. After sealing all exits, entombing those inside or preventing the elite their refuge, he and his men would head for the underground military labs and kill all they found there. They would fly to Graveyard University in Cambridge, Massachusetts, where they would destroy every biomedical weapon cooking in its labs. Grant was ordered to kill the Antichrist, the UN Secretary General and burn down the UN international city compound. Patton was deployed to Rome to kill the False Prophet, the Jesuit General Black Pope, then on to Jerusalem to Solomon's Sepulchre to close the wormhole. Quinn and his 11th Regiment of ghosts and astral projecting veterans, headed for Jerusalem to join Patton.

LeMay was ordered to Israel to bring back the U.S. F22 Raptor jets and from Saudi Arabia, the F15s.

Nimitz was ordered to Command the U.S. Naval Fleet.

Maggie, Queen Macha, Penthesilea and the Amazons met early and split into groups, meeting up with the astral projecting American women hunters lying in wait outside the 35 Muslim Brotherhood paramilitary training camps spread across the United States. Each camp was located near critical infrastructures of power dams, Army munitions plants, military bases, and headquartered in Islamberg, Hancock, NY, adjacent to a reservoir that serves five NYC boroughs with drinking water. Before the day would break, they would kill every Muslim paramilitary soldier encamped on U.S. territory. Penthesilea had divided up her Amazons and the group of hunters to cover 34 camps, located mostly along the U.S. east coast, down across the south, out west to Malibu, California. Maggie and Queen Macha went to the largest camp in South Carolina with a large group of woman hunters.

Maggie's and Quinn's children and grandchildren had moved up to the camp in the New Hampshire Mountains two weeks before. They arose this morning, anxious, reminding each other, nothing will happen before noon. We have all morning to wait. Yeah, we'll gather at 12:30pm in the common room of the main lodge to see if we can pick up radio news. If not, Joe and Seth will go to the hill and listen to the ham radio, for just a few minutes; just to see if anything was happening. Would they broadcast any battles, strange military movements, or would all communications be shut down across the country? They wondered.

The ghost of Dennis Townson had gathered the ghosts of haunted houses of Rockport and Gloucester; they prepared to fight NATO Troops that might attempt amphibious landing.

It would begin in Washington, DC. College-aged patriots started to set up the staging for the concert on the lawn of George Washington University, four blocks from the White House. Other patriots went on to the campuses of Georgetown, Howard, Catholic University of America, and American University – to spread the word to the summer students that there was going to be free beer and concert with Stuns and Hoses at GWU – at high noon. Get there before the beer runs out! No one was told that the band of Stuns and Hoses would be materialized ghosts. Other young patriots quickly prepared to set up block parties in major intersections near the White House. Chaos was about to engulf the city of Washington.

The Granny Quilters from across America had stayed in the houses of those located closest to the target. They slept on floors, sofas, and camped out in backyards. They would ride in groups to the buses that would take them to Lafayette Park. The mothers of America would set off the Second Revolution. The 11th dimensional ghosts would finish it, with the help of the world's greatest military.

As they drove in Margaret's car, Marie turned on the tape player to hear Green Bayou by Cindy Ronnell. She remembered back to her youth when the song was popular on college campuses. To when she had met her husband. She sat quietly looking out the window as she listened to the melodic, soulful song. She longed to be home with her husband, to be wrapped in his arms, floating along the bayou, lazily drifting. She wondered if that was what life was supposed to be, or if it was supposed to be mankind slaughtering mankind, as she would do today. As her husband would do with the militia. How can the human heart long for love and turn to kill. Why was killing necessary? To survive, she told herself. We are forced to kill or accept being killed. Once the killing ended, she told herself, she could drift on the bayou, in peace, in harmony with her man and with all that God had put on earth. It felt to her as though she was back in the Garden, but instead of civilization's beginning, she was at civilization's end. But she would be true, she thought to herself. She would not be naïve as Eve had been, seduced by something evil. She wanted forever with her God, her man, and with the river. Today's killing of evil she needed to do to bring peace to her soul. And, if necessary, she would die to bring that peace to the world for her children. She asked God to forgive her for her sins and she commended her soul to God the Father, Son, and Holy Ghost.

Before long the Quilters had reached the buses, each one driven by a woman patriot. The seven hundred quilters boarded the buses quickly, carrying with them a picnic basket with small portions of food and a quilt with trapunto stitching that hid their weapons. Their snipers carried 9mms with silencers. Each quilter had a small spring-action knife; many packed Tasers. They brought infra-red glasses, and wore dark blues, browns, gray clothing with pockets and dark-colored running shoes. And each wore a quilted pin of the American flag, securely fastened to their shirts.

Agnes was in the first seat in the lead bus. As the buses pulled up to the north entrance of Lafayette Park, she stood and turned to speak to the mothers. Her high-pitched voice seemed to squeak out her words, "Remember ladies. We are preparing to make a quilt. We are now about to lay out the pieces. You all know the next steps."

She turned back to look out the windshield of the bus, as it pulled up to a stop. The doors opened. Agnes paused a moment, realizing what her step down onto the pavement meant. She took a deep breath and stepped onto the battlefield.

The women disembarked quietly, quickly; and as a group walked into Lafayette Park, the next bus immediately pulled up and the women alighted. And the next and the next, until all the buses had pulled away. Agnes had remained at the entrance, and as the last bus pulled away, she looked at her watch – 12pm. The buses headed slowly toward the intersections that they were assigned to block, precisely at 12:30pm.

As the women entered the park, they spread out, with some providing cover for the pairs of women who took up positions under bushes on the east and west sides of the park. Those snipers were to watch the streets lining the park. Other snipers set up positions at the south end of the park, near the roadway across from the White House lawn.

The mothers laid out their quilts on the thick green lawn and prepared for battle. Sitting down on their quilts, they opened their picnic baskets and took out their infra-red glasses and put them into their pockets. With a spring-action knife they cut into the trapunto stitching of their quilts and retrieved guns and Tasers; then put the knives into their pockets. Under jackets, they put their guns into holsters they had made of heavy cotton webbing. Each one took out small canisters of mace and clicked them onto the metal loop of their jacket's zipper pull. When they were finished; most got up on their feet. They were ready.

But Agnes grew concerned; the women were quiet, solemn faced. She walked among pairs and groups of women, whispering, "We're supposed to be talking about the high price of cotton!"

As Agnes walked along she noticed two women huddled together, crying. She walked over to them and put her arms around them and whispered, "This is not the time for crying. You must be brave."

"It's not about being brave. We're in the city of our government. The White House is right there! Look at it. How can we invade it? It stands for everything that means freedom. It's where freedom guides the world. I respect it too much to bring such savagery into it. I can't do this! I am a law-abiding citizen. How can I go against something that I have cherished all my life?

Agnes signaled to Margaret, motioning her to come over. As she did, Agnes whispered, "We need to sing, now. Get them all to sing. I need to talk to these women, but I don't want any listening devices to pick up our words. Cover us with your singing."

Margaret nodded and walked directly over to a small group of women, "We need to sing, now. Right now! And loudly."

The women looked at each other, "America the Beautiful. Let's sing America the Beautiful."

From deep within their souls, the words poured out, first softly, in reverence, "Oh beautiful for spacious skies, for amber waves of grain, for purple mountain majesties, above the fruited plains."

Their sweet-sounding voices, delicate and true, brought the attention of the rest of the seven hundred quilters spread throughout the park. Each turned to the small group of women, and from where they stood, joined their voices. "America. America. God shed His grace on thee. And crowned thy good with brotherhood from sea to shining sea." Their voices coalesced in a warm embrace of the images of the country for which they sang, the Statue of Liberty, the Grand Canyon, of Yellowstone, Yosemite, of the Rocky and Smoky Mountains. The images of the campgrounds that they had once brought their children, now closed to them by UNESCO. They sang of a country that had been taken from them, and they remembered their founders, "O beautiful for pilgrim feet, whose stern impassioned stress, a thoroughfare for freedom beat, across the wilderness."

The women all turned to face the center of the park where Agnes consoled the two women in tears, unable to move against the symbol of freedom. Amidst the rising, loving voices, Agnes whispered to the women. "The man in that house is not our president! He is an invading Muslim conqueror! He is the one that has disgraced Our country. He is the one, along with his executive order, who is heading to our farms, our ranches, our rivers and forests to take them from our countrymen. You are obeying the law, the one that Jefferson taught us!"

To the surprise of the tearful women, Agnes recited a portion of the Declaration of Independence that Jefferson had written:

But when a long train of abuses and usurpations, pursuing invariably the same object evinces a design to reduce them under absolute despotism, it is their right, *it is their duty*," Agnes' voice became hard, "to throw off such government, and to provide new guards for their future security."

Agnes continued in hard whisper, "Did you hear those words? It is our DUTY TO THROW OFF such government! We are NOT showing disrespect for the symbol of a free nation! We are NOT revolting AGAINST America! We are NOT revolting against the Office of the Presidency of the United States! We are fighting to SAVE both! That creep is not an American! HE is a foreign invader! WE are the conquered. HE! Is the terrorist! Hell bent on destroying OUR country!"

Agnes paused a moment, taking a deep breath to calm herself. She waited to see if the women would change their perspective. She gave them two minutes, and if they continued to cry, she was prepared to stab them in their bellies, before they could expose the plan to the security wiretaps within the park that Agnes knew were spying on the quilters.

But after a minute, the two women straightened their bodies, blew their noses, and wiped their tears. They looked around at the quilters singing and joined their voices, "O beautiful for heroes prov'd in liberating strife, who more than self their country lov'd, and mercy more than life."

All the quilters joined hands with each other, their bodies stood taller, showing their resolve to move forward with their plan. Their voices, still warm, grew louder, "O beautiful for patriot dream that sees beyond the years. Thine alabaster cities gleam undimmed by human tears. America. America. God shed His grace on thee, and crowned thy good with brotherhood, from sea to shining sea."

When the women ended, Agnes took out her Bible from her picnic basket and turned to 2 Chronicles 7:14. She read:

And my people, upon whom my name is called, being converted, shall make supplication to me, and seek out my face, and do penance for their most wicked ways: then will I hear from heaven, and will forgive their sins and will heal their land.

Seemingly taking in the beautiful day, the snipers looked over at the trees on the White House lawn, looking for the government snipers that they would have to kill. Flossy poked Kim's arm, "Over my left shoulder. You see that strange looking structure? It's hiding the surface-to-air-missiles. I counted two guards." Flossy was holding her picnic basket, trying to look as though she was searching for something buried inside. She mumbled, "Don't forget to nod your head, as though you're focused on me and not them. Tilt your head and make yourself look relaxed. And smile! For God’s sake, smile! But do you see any more than those two men?"

"Yes," Kim replied, "I see three more. That's not good."

"No," Flossy whispered, "We need women to cover them. Why don't you walk over to Agnes and let her know that we need at least two, if not three more snipers for the missile guards."

Kim turned away, looking for Agnes. When she found her, she walked toward her and put three fingers on her chin as if to rub it, indicating to Agnes: send three snipers to the south edge of the park.

Just as she was passing Agnes, Agnes nodded and continued to walk. As she did, she looked across the crowd of women, looking for the tallest women. When she located Grace, Agnes walked up to her and tapped her elbow, whispering, "Come with me." And the two walked over to Alice, Agnes tapping her elbow and tilting her head to the side. And then to Marie. They continued on toward the south end of the park. Along the pathway, Agnes stopped and turned back to face the three women, now in front of her as they faced the White House. She reached up to rub her nose, covering her lips as she whispered, "There are five armed guards on the missile site. You three need to help take them out. Flossy and Kim are over there, to your left. They will take two of the guards. When the fog comes, get close enough to use your Tasers on them and then cut their throats."

When she finished instructing the quilters, Agnes walked away to chat with another group of women. The group was charged to be look outs for the arrival of Congressional leaders and Cabinet Secretaries for the luncheon meeting with Tsaeb. As Agnes approached Carol standing with Margaret and Susan, she asked, "How are things going?"

"It's quiet. Very quiet. It seems that we might be here for a while," Susan expressed concern.

"It won't be long," Agnes whispered. "It's a sit-down lunch meeting. And the Congressional leaders are scheduled to be back on the Hill by 2pm for a vote. They have to be on time. Remember to smile, laugh a little. Make sure you talk about quilting and complain about the price of cotton loud enough to be picked up on the listening devices that the gatekeepers are using on us. Prepare your speech to use the code word." When she finished, Agnes moved on.

Inside the White House, the chefs were preparing the lunch. The Culper spy working in the kitchen had brewed fresh coffee at 11:30am. He had dumped a strong sedative into each of two thermoses, poured in the coffee and sealed them. He left the thermoses in the usual pick up spot on the counter for the White House roof sniper guards when they changed the watch at noon. He then carried out his usual duties of cleaning the pots and pans used in preparing the luncheon. As utensils and bowls were discarded by the Chefs, he quickly picked them up and put into one dishwasher and emptied the other dishwasher. Clutter was always cleaned away immediately; clean dishes were constantly added to cupboards. Everything was flowing as usual in the kitchen's organized chaos. Chefs were giving orders and staff ran to carry them out. One group prepared the first course; another group the main course; and another group prepared the dessert. The Culper spy checked the dining room to see that all was in place. As he looked over the table settings and glassware, he envisioned what the room would look like after the carnage that was to ensue within the hour. He moved about the room methodically, calculatingly, and without emotion. He adjusted the small flower bouquets sitting in elegantly etched crystal so that they were precisely equally distant from each other along the center of the table. He adjusted dinner plates to be one and one half inches in from the edge of the table. It would be a vegetarian meal; no sharp knives were required. All was in ready.

Out on the street, blocks from Lafayette Park, to the northwest and to the northeast, cable repairmen drove up to round lids on the streets. They got out of their trucks and placed orange cones around the manhole covers. They noted their watches. Each had arrived at their designated spot precisely at 12:15pm. They opened the covers and two men descended underground to the cables that controlled TV, telephone, electricity, and street signal lights. A third man stayed above and pulled cable from the truck, as if preparing to lower it into the underground cavern. As he walked over to the open hole, he looked up to see a black van driving by. He looked at the driver and nodded. The driver nodded one time and continued on. Each was possessed by an 11th dimensional ghost.

Three ghosts of Lee's Army of Northern Virginia flew above the Capitol, creating a large, dark and threatening cloud that spit electrical charges between the billows of cloud. Outages of communications would be blamed on the cloud that refused to move away from the Capitol.

In and about the city, nearby the White House and Capitol, numerous vans, both black and white, some with logos of local businesses that didn't exist, of florists, caterers, and dog grooming services. Inside the vans were the Wild Weasel radar pods that would send out bursts of energized microwaves to jam security radar detectors placed around the city. The drivers were fully materialized ghosts soldiers that had fought and died in Vietnam. The navigator ghosts operated the Wild Weasel. They were prepared to drive in and about the government neighborhoods; and during the attack on the White House, they would send out jamming signals and then quickly turn off the burst of microwave as the vans moved along. No wireless Internet services, cell phones, radio signals, or satellite signals would get through. With so many vans sending signals out in relay fashion, the backtracking of the signal would jump from the northwest corner to the southeast corner then to the northeast to the southwest corners. Pedestrians would blame the electrical storm hanging over the Capitol. Security would think, at first, that the signal came from the area of the Capitol, but in its back tracking think that it came from one neighborhood across town, and then another neighborhood nearby, and another and another. Confusion and chaos would set in; till, finally, maybe it was simply the electrical storm.

Underground, the TV cables and landlines would be cut, except for the one line to the Culper spy switchboard operator in the White House, who would answer calls that all is well at the White House. The President was at a luncheon meeting with his top staff, Cabinet, and Congressional leaders, and absolutely could not be disturbed. Other calls would be put on hold, until the caller became too impatient and hung up.

In Lafayette Park, the women took notice of the cars lined up on each side of the park belonging to employees working in the Eisenhower Executive Office Building next to the White House. If any employees came out to their cars during the battle, the quilter snipers hiding in the bushes would have to kill them. The quilters hoped that Lee's Army of 11th dimensional ghost would stir up a fog thick enough that the employees would realize that it was too unsafe to drive.

At the south end of Lafayette Park, the materialized ghosts of singers from the 1950s had already set up and had begun to sing the old songs. Agnes looked at her watch, 12:15pm, she knew underground cables had been accessed and vans were circling the city ready to turn on and off the Wild Weasels. Everything was in ready. She looked to the skies above to see if she could see a spy drone. She smiled to herself, thinking, what would MacArthur do if she waved at him. The noise of cars pulling up to the gate of the White House entrance pierced her day dream. She turned and watched as the cars of the Congressional leaders and Cabinet Secretaries pulled up to the front door of the White House; she watched as they walked inside and their cars pulled away.

She turned back to the quilters, looking them over as they talked with each other in groups, or sang along with the rock and roll music, as the lookouts nodded to them and then walked on to other groups at the north end of the park. All were in place. All were ready. The music filled the air with the innocence of rock n roll beat, to a time before drugs and abortion were seen as the new culture of America. The women began to move from the north of the park toward the south end, seemingly to be closer to the music. Within minutes, they had provided the cause for those standing at the south end to move onto the road between the park and the White House fence. And after another song played, and after the crowd grew happy with chatter of song and of quilts – and of trapunto stitches, the assault team women had moved to the outer perimeter of women closer to the gate and fencing of the White House.

It was now 12:30pm, and on cue, a fog began to move steadily along the ground and then higher to surround the White House, the Eisenhower Executive Office Building, and Lafayette Park. The Granny Quilt Crafters of America began to cry out in mocked fear of the alleged blindness that the fog brought to them. Women stationed themselves in the middle of Lafayette Park and began to cry out louder and louder as the fog grew thicker and shielded them in their strategy. They quickly pulled from their pockets infrared glasses and put them on. And as the crying women moved toward the center of the park, the sound of fear moved away from the White House, so that the guards at the gate dismissed any idea that the frightened old women were a threat to security. But as the whole body of women had drawn closer to each other for assumed safety and comfort, the ghost band at the edge of the road in front of the White House began to play louder to provide cover and signal to the 75 women assault team to rush the White House gate and the guards of the missile defense system set up near the bushes on the White House lawn.

The guards on the roof of the White House had fallen asleep from the Culper spy's drugged coffee. At the edge of the White House fence, Kim and Flossy raised their silencer guns and shot numerous rounds into two of the guards at the missile launcher. When their bodies fell, the other three guards tried to draw their weapons, but Alice standing nearby, already had one of them in her sights and zapped him with her Taser. In perfect, coordinated expectation, Marie and Grace zapped the second and third guards with their Tasers. Each woman ran over to the man that she had Tasered, as he was lying helplessly on the ground. Marie fell down on her knees next to the man. "I'm so sorry!" she cried, and slit his throat.

Grace quickly blessed herself, then cut the second guard's throat. The third guard began to get up when Grace hit him again with her Taser, yelling at Alice, "Get him!"

"No. No. I can't kill him!" Alice cried, standing next to the man as he convulsed at her feet.

"Son-of-a-bitch!" Grace yelled, running over to the man, then dropping to the ground, she slit his throat. In retaliation, his blood spurted her blouse and jacket.

"I'm sorry," Alice cried, "I thought I could." Her body trembling, "It's just… I just…"

"Never mind," Grace said, quickly jumping to her feet. "Get to the gate. Get to the gate!"

Through infra-red glasses, Marie looked down to see what the wetness was that covered her hands. Some kind a brown substance. Then she realized it was blood discolored by the infrared glasses. She looked at her knife, dripping liquid brown. She looked at Grace and cried out, "You're covered!"

"This is WAR!" Grace yelled in a hard whisper. "People die in war! What did you expect! Come on! Move!"

By the time the three women reached the White House gate, the other quilters had stunned the guards and slashed their throats. Voices urged softly, "Come on! To the House! Run!"

A platoon of ghosts from General Lee's Army of Northern Virginia had broken the necks of the guards throughout the rest of the White House grounds. Guard dogs had been enticed by thick, raw steaks to climb into their cages.

The way was clear. The band at the edge of the park played louder, the fog grew thick, and 75 American mothers closed in on the White House. Suddenly, the front door began to open. The quilters stopped short. Had they been caught? Their hearts' pounded. But there in the doorway stood the ghost of Harriet Tubman, smiling as she whispered, "Greetings ladies." The women sighed with relief, but then quickly filled the foyer and into the other rooms, finding bodies of Secret Servicemen dead on the floor. Rose O'Neal Greenhow was locking the frightened office staff in a utility room. Oblivious to what was happening, laughter could be heard from behind the closed doors of the dining room. "This way, ladies," Mary Elizabeth Bowser escorted the ladies to the dining room and pointed, "Your duty lies inside."

Agnes walked up to the door, turned back to the other quilters to be sure they were ready. She looked at the doorknob and turned it. When she opened the door, she felt a sense of shock seeing all the leaders that she had only seen on TV. Thoughts of being rude for intruding without knocking, without being invited, flashed through her mind. How odd she thought, when I'm here to kill them. She looked at the President taking a sip wine. When he saw Agnes, he lowered his glass and set it down on the table, and demanded, "Who are you?"

The President's dark, evil eyes seemed to freeze Agnes in place. She whispered to no one, "It's him. It's the President!" Suddenly, the women pushed her from behind, realizing that she was in a state of shock and they had no time for it. The women rushed into the room too fast for the diner guests to move. They had been captured. The guests looked at each other and then at the women lined up in chaotic rows several deep, just standing there for a moment, looking at their targets.

Within seconds, Grace pushed through the crowd of women, her hands and shirt covered in the blood of the guards. The guests gasped at the sight of her. Without hesitation, she raised her gun and shot the President in the head two times. The loud noise slammed against walls and stunned the senses. In its wake, for a second, there was absolute silence. No one moved. Maybe they were safe. Maybe the women only wanted to assassinate the president. No. No. That's not it. Guilty minds knew that the women had come for them, too. Suddenly, the silence was pierced by the scream of a cabinet secretary, and, as if pressing the play button of a video, the action began. The 75 Granny Quilt Crafters of America began shooting as congressional leaders, cabinet secretaries, and senior staffers scrambled to hide behind chairs and buffet and finally grabbing each other to use as a shield. Agnes stood with the women as they all emptied their guns into the wall and floor on the other side of the room, and on the way, the bullets penetrated bodies for a time, and times, and half a time.

As shots were being fired, Agnes' mind flashed to Rev. 12:14, 'The woman is given two wings of a great eagle, so she can fly in to the desert, to her place, where she is nourished for a time and times, and half a time, away from the face of the serpent.' Agnes stopped shooting, her arm dropping down to her side; she looked at the ugliness of the serpent as it lay in bullet-riddled lifeless shape of congressional leaders, cabinet secretaries, and president. The serpent had found the woman and had almost destroyed the great eagle wings that had brought her to shelter. This was a time wherein her daughters slayed the serpent to protect the woman.

Agnes walked over to the body of the President and shot him in the chest two times. "Double stitching makes a tidy quilt."

The noise of gunfire had filled the White House, but no one came to the leaders' rescue. Lee's Army had made sure of that. The switchboard operators had taken refuge in a closet, thinking that the Secret Service were handling matters. Only the Culper spy switchboard operator remained on duty, "I'm sorry, sir, the President is not available. He's in a very important meeting."

Agnes looked around the room. The white linen table cloth was hanging off the table. Expensive dishes lay broken on the floor. Pieces of crystal wine glasses were strewn about the room. Blood was splattered on the walls and floor and puddled under bodies that had tried to no avail to use another for shelter. The lifeless body of the President draped backward in his chair; underneath lay the dead body of a cabinet secretary who had tried to use his body as a shield. The small etched-crystal vases that had dressed the center of the dining table had been shattered by bullets, sending flowers in to the air. Some had come to rest here and there about the room on puddles of blood. In the silence of death, from the corner of the room, a low moan could be heard. Without hesitation, Marilyn walked up to the woman lying on the floor and shot her two times in the head.

"The quilt is finished," Agnes sighed, her body drained, "Let's go home."

They left through the front door, heading back to the park to tell the others who had provided cover for the 75 to storm the White House, "It's done. Scatter!" One quilter said to the other, "I'm kind of disappointed." "Yes, me too. I thought I was going to be able to use my gun. But it all went so smoothly. I'm a little disappointed." "Next revolution," Grace said, slowly wiping her bloodied hands on her quilt, her body exhausted, her heart still pounding, "I promise you, you can kill the president!"

The ghost band continued to play as the women quickly gathered up their quilts and picnic baskets and hurried out of the park in every direction. The fog covered their departure until all were gone. As the band played a final song, the singer looked around, noticing that the fog was lifting. She motioned to the other ghosts, "Let's go." Within seconds they and their instruments disappeared without a trace.

Overhead, when the fog was gone, MacArthur could see the White House from the spy drone and telephoned the men working on the cables underground, "You can turn it back on now." And to the college patriots, "You can finish up when the beer runs out." And to the block party organizers, "Let the traffic proceed."

In the Executive Office Building, workers looking out the windows noted the lifting of the strange fog that seemed to have a mind of its own. It wasn't the usual slow crawling fog that sometimes visited the area. No, this fog had climbed up to cover building rooftops and touched every window along the way. It's thick, soupy vapor seemed to peer inside and look at the office occupants, as if defying them to try to escape. No, this fog held them captive. And now the fog, the opaque mist, gave them their freedom. The sun came out and telephones rang and work began, again. "Maybe the fog shorted out a few lines." But no one would tell; no one would admit to the fear that had held them.

While death was meted out at the White House, Lee's Army had spread out, looking for the Chairmen of the Federal Reserve, World Bank, International Monetary Fund, and bank computers, too. When the chairmen were found, their last minutes of life were spent screaming in the horror of Civil War ghosts in bloodied uniforms that came at them slowly, giving them time to recognize what it was that was about to kill them. Suddenly, the frightening apparitions grabbed hold of skinny necks and thick and squeezed slowly but ever so steadily, till all breath was gone and bodies of chairmen fell limp. And death took over and carried them down into Hell where justice required of them to continue to scream for all eternity. For the horror of their death would be repeated over and over again.

The ghosts of Lee's Army went searching, every nook and cranny, whereupon computers were found and hard drives were fried. And the staffers quickly confessed to the determined apparitions the location of every off-site backup storage record and every book, where all were burned. The chains of economic slavery were broken. And never again would presidents, congressmen and women be able to illegally wrap those chains around the necks of every American citizen born yesterday, today, and tomorrow, and sell the American people to private foreign owners of the Federal Reserve. No amendment had ever been made to the U.S. Constitution allowing Congress to relinquish its duty to coin and regulate money. The Federal Reserve Act of 1913 was an illegal act, and therefore, had no authority of law to support it. The Federal Reserve System had been a con game, a scam on the American people, and therefore, no money was owed to the foreign owners of the Federal Reserve Banks.

Lee's Army of Northern Virginia had freed every American. The U.S. no longer had a national debt; the country and its people were given a second chance. This time they would make sure they had constitutional recourse to immediately recall their representatives; this time the verbatim language of amendments passed by every state would have to be published nationally for one year before the amendment was finalized. All citizens would have a forum to ask questions and demand answers; all questions and answers would be published, all before another vote to accept or reject any amendment.

This time every bill would have to pass constitutional scrutiny before given to the president to sign in to law. This time, any bill that financially impacted Americans would be voted on nationally by Americans and not the House, including wages and benefits of Congress. This time, all members of Congress would be limited to two terms. This time, members of the U.S. Supreme Court could only serve ten years and would be voted in to office by national election. This time, no member of Congress would be exempt from any law that they passed. This time, no bill could address more than one issue; no bill could be more than 100 pages long and must be written in plain language. This time, Congress would be forbidden to give away their constitutional duty to regulate the value of the dollar. No longer would Congress be allowed to give away or sell national parks and lands and natural resources, or prohibit Americans from entering those lands. No longer would Congress or Presidents be allowed to take land or natural resources from States or private owners. No longer would American inventors' intellectual property be taken from them. No longer would EPA and other federal agencies have any authority of law. No longer would the Secretary of the Treasury have authority to point to a business and shut them down and take their assets. No longer would the U.S. Government be able to own any share of a private business.

No longer would Congress have authority to regulate commerce. No longer would Congress and the President be allowed to dismantle the U.S. Military and national defense through any treaty. No longer would the government be allowed to make decisions on Americans' healthcare treatment. No longer would there exist a federal Department of Education. No longer would the United States of America be a member of the United Nations. No longer would Congress and Presidents be allowed to send manufacturing jobs overseas. No longer would Presidents have authority to issue laws under Executive Order. The list of widespread attack by the Communists to destroy America would be stated and worked out by the American citizens. Every law signed by Tsaeb would be deemed null and void as of this day.

The men who had gone under the streets of the city to help the Granny Quilt Crafters of America, had also turned off electrical systems of the Federal Reserve. And the ghosts of Lee's Army turned clocks and timers till vaults opened their thick doors. 18-wheeler trucks backed up to platforms; gold was loaded onto the trucks and driven back to Fort Knox. When the dust of revolution settled, the other Federal Reserve Banks would gladly surrender their stolen money.

Other of Lee's Army went to the Capitol. There they fully materialized in their rag tag, bloodied uniforms, long beards and unkempt hair, hats torn by bullets, carrying their rifles down at their sides; their boots beat heavily on marble floors, warning of their deadly approach. Staffers didn't look to see what caused the coming treachery; they had been expecting this day to come. Without a word, they jumped up from desks, hurrying to the office door to lock it shut and ran back to hide in closets. Down the end of long hallways, staffers returning from lunch suddenly came upon Lee's Army. Scream after scream echoed off marble throughout the building.

Inside the Senate chamber, all the senators waited for the momentary return of their leaders from the White House luncheon, so they could cast a vote for the next unconstitutional law that they planned to force upon Americans. When one and then a second of the senators heard the screams from the hallways, they began to yell, "Lock the chamber doors! Hurry! Call the guards!" But it mattered not. Through the locked doors came Lee's Army of Northern Virginia, bent on assassination. Fear buckled the knees and collapsed the toughest senator. Captured in the Senate chamber, Lee's Army circled the 97 men and women, and began firing large metal balls from Civil War long rifles – and as if in a turkey shoot, metal pierced the heads of traitorous senators and fell them where they stood.

In the House chamber, screams of men were louder than the congresswomen as death approached. But being a federal building, no one was allowed to carry a gun, although one cannot kill a ghost. As for the guards, Lee had already dispensed with them. They had been the first that the vaporous ghosts had killed.

The larger body of the House with greater numbers took longer, but Lee's Army persisted till the last Congressman was assassinated. The bodies lay dead under members' desks, in front of the chamber doors, behind the Speaker's desk, and on the floor of the chamber. It would take a month of restoration before the two chambers could accommodate the new Congress.

Simple, quick, and without hesitation sentencing was carried out upon the corrupt body of the House and Senate.

The easiest job was the assassination of the members of the Supreme Court Justices. The last Branch of the Communist government was expediently finished with a quick snap of necks.

By 4am, the Muslim paramilitary training camps had been shut down. While the Amazons had flown to the other camps across the country, Maggie and Queen Macha had flown to the camp in South Carolina. Outside the fenced compound, two Muslim paramilitary guards patrolled the darkness with assault rifles. The invisible ghosts of Macha and Maggie hovered above them. Macha signaled to Maggie, you take him. In a sudden burst of speed, they charged the guards, snapping their necks. The men dropped lifelessly to the ground. Maggie and Macha took their guns and flew to the center of the compound and dropped the guns to begin the heap that would later be burned. The Amazons and astral projecting women hunters spread throughout the camp. Maggie followed Macha. Inside the communes, they all found the wives and children, along with the soldiers. Maggie looked at Macha with concern. Macha whispered, "We will not kill the wives and children. They are the Muslim soldiers' first victims, held captive by Shariah Law that mandates their wives and daughters be castrated, sewn shut until the husband cuts his wife's vaginal introitus open for his sexual pleasure. If the wife goes in ta child labor while the husband 'tis out of town and not available ta give the mid-wife permission ta cut open the wife's introitus ta deliver the child, both the mother and child die a long, painful death. We will give them a second chance."

Maggie followed Macha into one of the houses and found two bedrooms full of children sleeping soundly. Macha motioned to Maggie to follow her through the wall of the bedroom, into a room where three couples slept; their beds separated by plywood walls, creating smaller cells. Macha pointed to Maggie and then to one of the cells. Maggie looked into the cell and saw a man sleeping on his back, his face covered with a long beard. She paused a moment, wondering if she could do this, actually kill another human being. Then she thought of her grandchildren and decided – before he gets my grandchildren, I'm going to get him. She flew over to the man and quickly stabbed her knife into the side of his neck and pulled it outward, as Quinn had taught her. No sound was made, no gurgling of air fighting its way through blood. Instantly, the man was dead. Maggie turned to find Macha coming from the third cell, her second kill. The wives continued to sleep, undisturbed.

Throughout the camp, Amazons led astral projecting women hunters from commune to commune, killing only the men. Maggie and Macha entered another bedroom where two beds were separated by a plywood wall. Maggie flew up to a bed on the husband's side, her knife about to stab his throat when the wife opened her eyes and saw Maggie hovering over the bed. She saw the knife in Maggie's hand and knew that Maggie was about to kill her husband. The wife said not a word. Quickly, Maggie cut the husband's throat, afterwards looking over at the wife, wondering if she'd scream and wake the rest of the compound before the Amazons could kill the rest of the foreign soldiers. To her shock, the wife smiled at Maggie. Maggie returned to Macha, whispering, "Let's get out." Outside the commune, Maggie explained to Macha that the wife never tried to stop her. "She never said a word; she just smiled. And listen, she's still not screaming for help!"

"Think about it; would you want ta be married ta a man that beat you when he's in a foul mood, and his law does not protect you from his abusive treatment? You did her a favor; she wanted ye ta know it."

On the southern border, the Texas militias came upon the Mexican Military carrying Russian AK-47s, riding in two black jeeps, at first, only detected by their headlights shining into the dark desert. They were about to cross over into Mexico. One Military jeep led and the other followed the black jeep of the drug cartel gang members on their way back from a drop-off house 100 miles inside the U.S. They carried two million dollars from drug sales in the U.S. Sam Houston and Col. Travis' Alamo spirits hovered above the edge of the Rio Grande, in full materialization, smiling at the Mexicans as they approached Houston and his men.

"Can I help you gentlemen?" Houston cried out. The jeeps stopped and the men jumped out and began firing their AK-47s at the ghosts of the Alamo. Houston moved closer, "As you can see, gentlemen, we are already dead. You waste your ammunition of us," Houston smiled. The Mexicans focused their gunfire on Houston, yet still he approached. Still he smiled. Now, they believed. Now, they knew it wasn't a trick of a moonless desert. And in great fear, they scrambled into their jeeps and started back into the U.S., but there they were soon met by the fire power of the Texas militia. Within minutes, the bodies of the Mexican Military and drug cartel gang members lay dead on the desert floor. The militia picked up the money and strapped it on to a horse and sent it back with two militia to the nearest town bank. It would be given to border ranch families that drug gang members had murdered.

In California, New Mexico, Arizona, and Texas, the militias continued on to border entry check points. They took control of checking the passports, turning back anyone who was not an American citizen. Americans who were leaving the U.S. the militia warned, "You won't be able to return. The border is being sealed." Americans quickly turned back. One called out, "Is it happening? Is the shit hitting the fan!? I want in on the action. Where do I go? Who do I report to?"

"Go back to your towns; get your guns ready. You'll know if we're not successful. But if you have horses, jeeps, motorcycles, all-terrain vehicles, anything that can travel off road, and semi-automatic guns, come back here. Bring your own food and water."

"It'll just take me two hours. I'll be back in two hours! I want in on the revolution! This is my country, too!"

"You'll have your chance," the Texas militiaman told him. "We're expecting the Mexican Military, the Russians, Hamas and Hezbollah to try to storm the border, once they know what's going on. We can use more guns all along the border. If you know others with the right equipment, bring them with you. But wait." The militiaman grabbed the drivers arm and bent down, "Listen to me. Are you listening?"

"Yeah. I'm listening. What?"

"You can't broadcast this. We need to be as covert as possible. The longer we can do this without the world knowing, the better we'll be assured of victory. We need to secure the country. You got that? Remember, 'loose lips sink ships'?"

"I remember. My father was a sailor in WWII. I heard all the stories. Trust me; I'll only talk face to face with my buddies. I've got at least 100 men. We'll be back!"

"And wrap your cell phone in aluminum foil - and wrap any other electrical device that you're carrying, so you aren't tracked by the Mexican cartels. They're heavily equipped with the latest of everything."

"Got it. My buddies and I have been waiting for this day. We're ready for this. We've been expecting an invasion across the southern border. We're all geared up."

Truck after truck arrived at border roads along with machines to lift off 42-inch high, cement Jersey barriers, as a temporary measure to block roads in all the states along the Rio Grande. The barriers were set out in rows, so if Russian tanks tried to climb over the first barrier, they would come down with their nose wedged against the second barrier, locking up the butt of the tank on the first barrier. The barriers would keep out trucks and other troop vehicles, but they wouldn't stop the foreign troops invading on foot to take advantage of America's internal chaos of war. And once all road blocks were in place, word would get out that something was going on inside the United States.

The UN had already made plans that divided up the U.S., with China and Russia getting the larger shares. Word of war would immediately raise the question, had the other ally already moved in on taking control of the entire U.S.? The militia took cover along the border and waited for a possible invasion. Their mission was to give time for the subordinate commanders of the U.S. Military to take control of California and Texas bases away from the UN troops and U.S. Communist commanders. The militia didn't know for sure, how many UN troops were living on the bases, or what kind of fighting was taking place there. They didn't know if it would take the U.S. Military coming home from foreign assignments to finally take back the bases located on US soil.

They did know that it would be another day before those troops would arrive home. They did know if the Russians and Mexicans tried to invade before help arrived that they would likely die, just as the Texians and Americans had died at the Alamo. But the militia had decided to let the Russians and Mexicans know what fighting for one's freedom was all about.

They did know that Nimitz had ordered Rear Admiral Miles R. Browning and his ghost ship, the USS Hornet (CV-12), berthed in Alameda, California, out to sea to stand guard off the northwest coast, in case the Chinese decided a naval attack.

All the Texas militia could do was wait to see who would get to the U.S. southern border first, the Russian and Mexican Military a dozen miles away, or the fighter jets from the USS Nimitz aircraft carrier, sitting off the port of San Diego. While subordinate leaders wrestled to capture control of the carrier, naval pilots were climbing the ladders of fighter jets.

MacArthur kept a close watch from NORTHCOM command center through the spy drones flying over the southern border and Mexico. He could see the Russians troops encamped nearby the border. So far, they had not made any movement toward the border. Eisenhower was ready to redeploy 11th dimension ghost of WWII, if necessary. But the Nimitz fighter jets dropping scatter bombs would be a more efficient method to end any skirmish. And what if the Russians and Mexicans decided not to invade. No one wanted to escalate an American revolution in to a foreign war.

On the northern border, Will Booker led the Washington State, Montana, and North Dakota militia to cross over into Canada. While they waited in the forest, Col. Booker and a squad of 11th dimension ghosts marched into the camp of the Chinese. In partial materialization, Booker and his men sang as they marched, "Mine eyes have seen the glory of the coming of the Lord: He is trampling out the vintage where the grapes of wrath are stored; He hath loosed the fateful lightning of His terrible swift sword: His truth is marching on."

The voices echoed throughout the forest in eerie resonance. Hearing Americans singing, the Chinese soldiers grabbed their rifles and came running from the far corners of encampment. They ran here and there but the echo of voices couldn't be found. Finally, they ran to the center of the camp. When they reached the Major General's quarters, dread washed over their bodies. There, marching-in-step two feet above the ground, were twelve ghosts soldiers dressed in the blue uniform of the Civil War Union Army, singing "I have seen Him in the watch-fires of a hundred circling camps, they have builded Him an altar in the evening dews and damps; I can read His righteous sentence by the dim and flaring lamps," the voices grew louder, "His day is marching on."

The Major General had come out to the porch of his quarters. Seeing his men at the outer edges of the buildings, hiding behind latrine buildings, and clumps of trees, he knew he had to appear strong and not cower in the face of the apparitions. Though his body trembled in fear, he remained at attention. Col. Will Booker approached as the squad continued to sing, "I have read a fiery gospel writ in burnished rows of steel: 'As ye deal with my contemners, so with you my grace shall deal; Let the Hero, born of woman, crush the serpent with his heel, Since God is marching on.'"

Booker marched up to the general and saluted, "Major General. I am Col. Will Booker of the American Civil War Union Army."

In a daze, the Chinese general saluted slowly in return.

Booker continued, "Sir, you are the Commander of all Chinese troops stationed along the U.S.-Canadian border. Is that correct, sir?"

The Major General replied, "That is correct, Colonel."

"Sir, the American people are conducting a revolution," Will explained. "I am here to advise you to retreat from Canada immediately. All foreign militaries are advised to stay out of the conflict; this is an internal matter. Besides the American people, there are one million 11th dimension ghosts who will hunt you down and kill your men. There is no use in fighting; you not win against the American people. If I may, sir, give you a demonstration."

Will gave a telepathic message for a company of 11th dimensional ghosts waiting in the forest to enter the camp. Within seconds the ghosts responded, flying over the heads of the Chinese military as they tried to hide, making sounds that terrified their minds. Yelling in Chinese, "Get Out! Get Out! Or today you die!"

A few brave soldiers began to fire their guns at the ghosts. In retaliation, the ghosts picked them up like rag dolls and flew them around the encampment, as they screamed in terror.

The squad of ghosts marching-in-step continued to sing.

The cacophony of screams and singing and gunfire soared the fears of already frightened Chinese. Soldiers ran screaming across the encampment, out from hiding places, smashing in to each other, falling over objects and running off into the forest, screaming in a terror that they had never felt before.

The 11th dimension ghosts let the rag dolls drop onto the roof of the Major General's quarters, where they slid down onto the ground in front of the Major General. The chaos was too much, too loud and the men too fearful, to control.

Will Booker waited until the demonstration was over and he could see that the Major General understood that his army would be defeated. "Sir," Will asked, "What is your response?"

The commander looked at the ghosts, hovering a foot above the ground, still marching-in-step, still singing.

"We will leave." He turned to his subordinate, "Prepare to move out immediately."

Booker offered, "We can assist you in packing up."

"No," the Major General responded, then pleading, "Please. We will move out. Please leave us, now."

Will moved closer to the Major General, then ordered, "You are not to communicate with the rest of your military units on the border or to your superiors back home what is going on in America, only that you have ordered them to leave Canada. We will hear your communications, General, and we can return within minutes no matter where you are, and we will kill your army. Do you understand, General?"

"Yes. I understand."

Will then gave the command to the militias of all the northern states to proceed to set up Jersey cement barriers on every road leading from Canada into the United States. Once the job was completed, the militia settled in, just in case the Chinese changed their mind and decided to attack.

In the U.S. national parks, General Washington ordered the five Divisions of 11th dimension WWII ghosts and his Continental Army to disperse into battalions; they covered the forests of 27 states. In three encampments they met Russians, in other camps the Germans, the Ugandans, and other UN member states' soldiers. The Continental Army ghosts swooped down from the skies wreaking havoc, overturning tents, jeeps and trucks, while WWII ghosts shot and killed the UN soldiers as they tried to escape. By the time they were through, more than half a million bodies lay dead and dying on forests floors of the national parks. As Washington withdrew his troops, wild animals moved in to lunch on the remains of the UN soldiers. Justified by the starvation that had followed their being ousted, the animals returned to reclaim their territory and the spoils of 11th dimensional war.

The two Brigades of live soldiers led by Green Berets, Special Ops, and Special Forces divided up into 42 small battalions and headed for the cities to kill SM-13 gang members who had brought drugs and fear into American neighborhoods. Eisenhower guided the soldiers' movements from the spy drones flying overhead. For all their violence of rape, mutilation, and murder aimed at the helpless, the SM-13 fell easily to the superiority of the Special Forces.

Eisenhower plugged in to the Homeland Security database of facial recognition identity, cell phone and auto GPS locator systems. The spy drone photographed license plates and passed their numbers through the database and immediately identified name, citizenship, DNA, home address, arrest records, fingerprints, and a list of associates of the car's owner. Street cameras provided gang movement from block to block. Heat seeking instruments in the spy drones hovering over cities conveyed the number, size and shape – of the gang members inside buildings. Eisenhower told the numbers and locations of gang members to the Special Forces through their headgear. The Special Forces burst through doors and shot all the occupants, except those who could be identified as civilians and children. Other buildings were hit by shoulder rocket launches and grenades. It became a mass slaughter of SM-13 gang members, forcing the Special Forces to change assault rifles when one became too hot. Within the day the Special Forces had killed the majority of SM-13 gang members throughout the United States. Others scrambled to the southern border where the Texas and Arizona militia killed them.

Grant and his Union Army of the Potomac reached the Antichrist, UN Secretary General Yoon Won-Shik. He was about to speak to the full assembly of what appeared to be some irregularities in attempting to communicate with the White House. As Yoon looked up from the podium, he noticed the representatives of the member states falling one by one, then two at a time, dead upon the conference tables. Members watched as others fell dead in quick succession and jumped from their seats and began to race for the doors leading out of the assembly hall. But there the ghosts of the Union Army caught them by the throats and crushed their necks. Bodies began to pile against exit doors. The soon-to-be dead ran anywhere and nowhere; their screams echoed in the great hall, as they looked for escape. Grant, in ghostly vapor hovered overhead, looking at the Antichrist, mumbling to himself, "This is what true evil looks like. Humph," he snorted, "Not very impressive." The Antichrist watched in confusion the members dropping in sudden death, yelling from the podium to a room of unseen death, "This wasn't supposed to happen! We serve Satan! We are *PROTECTED* by Satan!"

Just as Grant materialized he flew at Yoon and snapped his neck.

LeMay and his WWII pilots had two missions, go to Israel and capture and return the U.S. F22 Raptors and a second mission to Saudi Arabia to capture and return the U.S. F15 fighter jets, and destroy U.S. attack helicopters that Tsaeb had secretly sold the Saudi king.

MacArthur had assigned LeMay WWII soldiers to take out communication towers and block interference on the ground while his pilots took control of the jets. The Saudi pilots were being trained in Idaho, as part of the arms deal with the king. In Saudi Arabia, the F15 jets sat idle on the airstrip. As LeMay's pilots climbed into the jets and started the engines, the ground security was alerted. The WWII ghosts were waiting in control towers, and as the jets were started, the ghosts fried all communications. The Saudi soldiers ran across the tarmac toward the jets, looking for targets to shoot, but no one was in the cockpit. They turned to each other in confusion. They called on walkie talkies to the tower, but got no response. The jets taxied down the runway in close line formation, and one by one lifted into the skies. As the Saudi soldiers began firing at the jets, the WWII ghosts flew down from the towers and struck from behind, killing them. LeMay's pilots took the F15s to the skies and headed for Ireland.

At the same time, Israel's pilots were flying a training mission in preparation for war with Iran. LeMay's pilots had to possess the pilots' bodies in mid-air flight. But then they could fly directly to Ireland instead of battling for the planes on the ground.

The jets could not fly directly from the Middle East to the east coast of the United States. They had to stop to refuel half way home; LeMay chose Ireland. Once the Belfast International Airport allowed emergency landing of two planes, the WWII ghosts took over the airport and rerouted commercial flights to London. Airport bomb threat, they reported. LeMay's Raptors and F15s were the only planes landing at Belfast. And as if a pit crew for NASCAR drivers pulling in for a pit stop where the cars are refueled and four tires are changed within seconds, LeMay's men kept up such a pace. A plane landed, refueled, and took off; then the next and the next throughout the day. Each fighter jet headed for Maine where they would refuel again, and then head to air bases all over the U.S.

In the meantime, Eisenhower ordered two units of 11th dimensional ghosts to kill the Saudi Arabian pilots and the Singapore Air Force Squadron stationed at Mountain Home Air Force Base, Idaho, while it was being taken over by its live Airmen. By the end of the day, no foreign troops would be alive on U.S. bases.

MacArthur knew that these Generals would complete their missions successfully because they were the best generals that America ever had. But he worried about Patton. Patton and his men were on their own in killing the False Prophet and closing the wormhole underneath Solomon's Sepulchre – the gates of hell. It had been into this wormhole of bottomless pit that God had put Satan after Michael the Archangel defeated him, in A.D. 30. It was through these gates that the angel of God released Satan for a short time, in A.D. 1030. If Patton ran into trouble, MacArthur wouldn't hear about it until it was too late.

Before they left for Rome, Patton had advised his army of their two missions and had given them the layout of IL Gesù, the Church of the Jesuits, that was connected to the residence of the Black Pope. The compound was located five miles across the Tiber River from the Vatican. Once they were close to the target, telepathy was out of the question. Telepathic messages would give warning of their approach; only hand signals could be used. The problem Patton faced; how does one approach a scattered enemy, quietly waiting in the darkness of old Baroque buildings. They were dead; there was no waiting for a changing of the guard or bathroom breaks; they could remain stationary for eternity. In the crevices of ornate trim and high above on transept ceilings, the outer guard watched.

When Patton and his 3rd Army of 11th dimensional ghosts reached the Tiber River, two miles from IL Gesù compound, they listened for the telepathic chatter of evil. And in the midst of evil, they heard that the False Prophet, Alonso Negrete, was reading alone in his private quarters.

Each of Patton's men carried an etheron gun that would obliterate the evil spirits, but first they had to deal with the outer perimeter of spirits guarding the compound. Beyond them was an inner circle of spirits guarding the False Prophet. To annihilate the outer and then the inner circle of the enemy presented too many uncertainties. Instead of playing on the field that the enemy had provided, Patton decided to reconfigure that battlefield. Before they left for Rome, Patton planned a diversionary tactic that would corral all the spirits onto one field. A plan that would bring out the Prophet's inner guard, leaving the Prophet open to being killed.

Patton gave the hand signal to begin the diversion. The signal was picked up and forwarded from one man to another to another of a line of live Christian men who were positioned on roof tops across the neighborhood of old buildings, until it reached Via D'Aracoeli and to the man standing down on the street. He had looked at his watch; he was on time. He looked up and down Via D'Aracoeli to see that he was alone on the block. Then he looked up to the man on the roof top across the way. The man was looking toward the river and then suddenly turned and look down to the street and gave the signal – go! The man on the street took a small vial of Holy Water out of his pants pocket and blessed himself one more time then started down the empty street and up the few steps of IL Gesù and opened its heavy wooden door. Slowly, he stepped inside. He looked around the large expanse of ornate decoration and waited. The evil spirits on guard high on the transept saw the man, at once, and became angry. They could see the holy aura that surrounded him. Who was he to enter their church! They thrashed about and gnashed their teeth. They screamed obscenities down to the man, ordering him, GET OUT! The cries of the outer guard spirits, so alarming, drew in the spirits of the inner sanctum from every building of the Jesuit compound. Now, the Church of the Jesuits was filled with all the evil spirits of the compound, and were about to converge on the holy man. He stood still, holding his Rosary in his hand, he kissed its cross and blessed himself and began to pray, just feet inside the doorway. The evil spirits became even more outraged to hear his prayer and began to screech and fly in raging loops all about the church, except for two who slowly approached the man, reaching out to kill him. Suddenly, the 3rd Army burst through a wall of the church and began firing etheron guns at the spirits. The noise of screeching banshees and etheron guns blasting rebounded off the ornate walls and shattered frescos and brought down statuary. Then, at once, the deafening noise stopped. Evil had been vaporized out of existence. The holy man turned and walked out of the building and back up the Via D'Aracoeli.

Patton, alone, had gone directly to the residence of the False Prophet where he remained reading, so confident that his evil spirits could handle the nuisance that caused such a racket of noise in the church.

Patton entered the room quietly and in the quiet, in a low voice, he demanded, "Look at me you son-of-a-bitch!" In shock at the tone of insult, Alonso Negrete looked up. Patton dropped his etheron gun down at his side and pulled out his .357 magnum and shot Alonso Negrete, twice in the chest, a third time in his head. Now, his spirit would continue to exist, for Alonso Negrete's soul had a date with destiny in the pool of fire and brimstone.

Patton joined up with his 3rd Army and together they headed to Jerusalem and the Well of Spirits. As they approached the Mount of Olives, they flew in low and stopped among the trees to regroup. From the Mount of Olives, just east of the Garden of Gethsemane in which Jesus had prayed and had been arrested, Patton and his men listened for the chatter of 11th dimension evil spirits coming from the Dome of the Rock. Voices came from around and under the Rock.

The battle between good and evil over this land began 3700 years ago, about 1688 BC, when the descendants of Satan, the Chanaanites, built a fortification wall around the area today called the Temple Mount, in Jerusalem. When God led the Israelites out of Egypt, about 1500 BC, He promised them He would cast the Chanaanites out of this land that He had given to Abraham about 5000 years ago, or 1300 years previous to the Chanaanite wall. Moses' successor, Josue, granted Jerusalem to the Tribe of Benjamin 3512 years ago.

And on this land of the Temple Mount, Solomon build the First Temple about 960 BC.

Titus destroyed Solomon's Temple in A.D. 70.

Hadrian, in A.D. 135, filled in and enlarged the Temple Mount area above the ruins of Solomon's Temple. Hadrian then built the Temple to Jupiter, a six-sided building. (www.bible.ca/archeology/bible-archeology.map?245,363)

In A.D. 325, Constantine tore down Hadrian's Temple to Jupiter and built a church on the site with an eight-sided dome, as seen today at the Church of Mary's Rock and the Church of the Nativity. Constantine's dome is thought to be built on the place where Jesus was condemned at the fortress of Antonia. (*Ibid.*)

In A.D. 685, the Muslims built the Dome of the Rock over the Temple Mount, but mistook the foundational structure they built it upon as Solomon's Temple; the Dome's site is either on Constantine's octagon dome or Hadrian's hexagon Temple of Jupiter. (*Ibid.*)

In 1099, Crusaders took Jerusalem and established sovereignty over the Holy Land. The Dome of the Rock was converted into a church and the Al-Aqsa mosque was renamed the Temple of Solomon. (www.american.edu/TED/hpages/jerusalem/muslim.htm)

In 1187, Saladin recaptured Jerusalem and control over the Dome of the Rock. (*Ibid.*)

In 1517, Jerusalem fell to the Ottomans. Under Suleiman, the city walls were rebuilt as seen today. (*Ibid.*)

In 1967, during the Israeli-Arab Sixth Day War, Israel took control of the Dome of the Rock, but left it under the maintenance of Muslim Awqaf Supreme Council.

It has been claimed that on the Temple Mount, on the Rock of Moriah covered by the Dome of the Rock, is the place where Abraham was willing to follow God's command to sacrifice his only son, Isaac. But this is wrong. Abraham was living in Bersabee, the southern edge of Israel, near the Red Sea, where he had dug the Well of Oath. When God asked Abraham to sacrifice Isaac, Abraham saddled an ass and took two young men and the boy Isaac; the three of them walking. The journey was through the Negev Desert, with mountains scattered irregularly like litter on a flat plane that they had to walk around, by a young boy. The temperature was very hot. When they came to the mountain that God had chosen, Abraham and Isaac climbed up the mountain. It is highly unlikely that a very old man riding on an ass, walking his young son and two young men across a very hot desert terrain could ever have reached Jerusalem 250 miles away, in three days. (Gen. 21 and Gen. 22) After God released Abraham from His request, Abraham and Isaac and the two young men returned to Bersabee and dwelled there.

But legend places Abraham's obedience to God at the Rock of Moriah, the Holy Mount, later called the Temple Mount. Today, the Dome of the Rock covers this Rock of Moriah that allegedly has the footprint of Muhammad and the handprint of Gabriel from the night Muhammad was taken to Heaven by Gabriel.

When King David had sinned by ordering the counting of Israelites, God punished Israel with a plague. The angel of the Lord stood by the thrashingfloor of Ornan the Jebusite, ready to strike Israel a final time. David pleaded with God not to destroy the Israelites, and God ended the plague and held back the Israelite's final destruction. David was told to build an altar to the Lord God on the thrashingfloor of Ornan the Jebusite. David went up immediately, bought the site from Ornan and built an altar and made sacrifices to God. 1 Chron 21:1-26.

The site of Ornan's threshing floor was chosen by God for His altar. "A threshing floor is usually a place surrounded by a low stone wall, often where bedrock was exposed on a hill. Here, it was easy to catch the light wind necessary to blow the chaff away from the kernels of wheat that were tossed high in the air during the winnowing process. It was important that it *not* be exposed to strong winds and, therefore, threshing floors were *not* established on the *highest* point. The bedrock could be easily swept to provide a clean place to catch the falling kernels for collection and storage," (http://scottsadventures.net/Travel/Israel/Bronstein_Files/ The%20Threshing% 20Floor.pdf).

"Mount Moriah rises as a long ridge at the south end of the City of David and continues on past the present Temple Mount, and reaches its highest point outside the Northern walls of the Old City." (www.templemount.org/theories.html) The Temple Mount is higher in elevation than the City of David, and both are within the walls of Jerusalem.

There are three theories on the location of the First/Solomon and Second/Herod Temples. The first, that the temples were built north of the Dome of the Rock by 110 meters, putting them under the current Dome of Tablets.

The second theory, the temples were located immediately near the Dome of the Rock.

The third theory, is of Tuvia Sagiv, a Tel Aviv architect, who locates the temples east of the present Western Wall, with the Holy of Holies (the inside chamber of the temple) located under the existing El Kas Fountain, midway between the Dome of the Rock and the Al Aqsa Mosque.

The archeological foundation and blue prints of Hadrian's Temple to Jupiter are almost identical to the footprint of the Dome of the Rock and Al Aqsa Mosque. Tuvia's recent research suggests that the Dome of the Rock's site may have been originally a Chanaanite High Place with tomes underneath and later the location of an Ashoreh pillar, a sacred pole to the goddess of fertility. (*Ibid.*)

If Tuvia Sagiv is correct, the site of the First/Solomon's Temple and the Second/Herod's Temple sit *between* the Dome and the Mosque. It is well accepted that Solomon worshipped Satan and conjured up demons. Solomon built altars to Molech for his Egyptian wives where babies were sacrificed. Beneath the Rock of Moriah is a cave with small altars. "The entrance is on the south-east corner of the Rock. The height of the cave is six feet. Its floor is paved with marble; its sides are plastered and whitewashed. Beneath the floor of the cave is a lower chamber called the Well of the Spirits." (*Picturesque Palestine,* Vol. 1, pp 61-62; http://www.lifeintheholyland.com/dome_of _the_rock_history_traditions.htm)

"The Well of Spirits is considered by some learned men to be the entrance to Paradise, and by other equally learned, the entrance to the opposite *region.*" (*Jerusalem, Bethany, and Bethlehem,* pp. 48-51; at *Ibid.*)

Did Solomon have his temple builders dig the cave under the Rock of Moriah and dig the Well of the Spirits beneath the cave – *adjoining* the grounds of the First Temple? Did Solomon require his own place to conjure up the demons – outside the Holy of Holies where the Ark of the Covenant rested? Or when constructing the First Temple, did Solomon's builders discover the entrance of a wormhole – that led to the *opposite region* – of the universe. Or is this Well of Spirits the entrance to the bottomless pit – and are the two the same?

But no matter, for it is to this Well of Spirits, to these gates of opposite region, to the very gates of hell that Patton and his 3rd Army headed.

As they watched and listened from the Mount of Olives, Patton faced a number of problems. If he and his 11th dimension soldiers used telekinesis to move the Dome of the Rock, the evil 11th dimension spirits would detect that the 3rd Army was amassed on the Mount of Olives. If they directly assaulted the evil, the spirits would scatter and come back later with their own attack on Patton and his men. If the 3rd Army surrounded and came out blasting the trapped evil spirits, there would be cross, friendly-fire eternal annihilation of his men.

Patton had thought through these problems long before he had left for the mission. He had met with Quinn and worked out a joint tactical strategy that focused on the geography of this specific battlefield. While Patton was killing the False Prophet, Quinn and his 11th Regiment had gone directly to the northern backside of the highest peak of Mount Moriah north of the walls of Jerusalem. There, Quinn and his men quietly waited until they saw Patton and the 3rd Army coming down from the north, flying low and circling wide through the ridges of mountain to the Mount of Olives. Quinn waited another ten minutes for Patton's message. It soon came. Patton sent one of his men back to Quinn with a hand-signal message: mark the time. Quinn knew that it meant that the attack would commence in five minutes. Quinn indicated his watch and held up five fingers to one of his men who passed it on to the next man down the line, till all received the message.

On the mark, Patton's 3rd Army went flying out from the Mount of Olives, heading for the Dome of the Rock. Patton and his men withheld their fire; a horizontal attack with the etheron gun would penetrate the Dome and beyond to obliterate other non-target structures.

On the mark, Quinn's 11th Regiment soared upward, hovering high over the Dome, pulsating their etheron guns downward onto the Dome, until the entire building disappeared. Now exposed, the evil JS spirits flew up from the cave and from the Well of Spirits. They saw Patton's army coming at them from the east, but they didn't see Quinn's Regiment hovering above. They first flew west and then upward in a wide oblique angle, trying to escape.

Quinn waited until the JS spirits reached a higher altitude than his QRs. Then he raised his arm and brought it down quickly in a forward motion, signaling to his men to attack. With a sudden loud burst that thundered across the skies, they shot their etheron guns at the evil spirits, taking out a third of them in the first volley.

Confused by the surprise attack and the annihilation of their comrades, the evil JS spirits screeched, as they flew chaotically across the heavens. Evil was not supposed to end. Evil was supposed to be indestructible; they had been promised by Satan! In fear, they collected in a ball of tangled mass, trying to hide behind each other. Quinn's men annihilated another half of them within seconds. But then the spirits began to scatter, forcing Quinn to send a telepathic message to his men - two to one…two to one. In a cosmic dogfight, soaring in every direction, good chased evil. The Earth grew smaller beneath them as they soared beyond the ionosphere, but still Quinn and his regiment pursued. Using loops of flight to evade the etheron guns, the JS spirits saw the silver threads of Quinn and his men and realized that they were live, astral-projecting souls. Their weakness was their silver thread. The spirits wouldn't even need to get close to Quinn or his men. The thread extended up from Earth, from where their bodies lay. Suddenly, two JS spirits turned out away from each other in a wide circle of flight then banked down towards Earth, beneath the action of battle. One of Quinn's men saw an evil spirit heading for Quinn's thread and swooped down to engage the spirit; and just as the spirit reached out for Quinn's thread, the soldier exterminated the spirit. And quickly, very quickly, he pursued the second spirit headed for silver threads of the QRs. The JS spirit flew evasively up and down, left and right, when suddenly he turned back and reached out and caught the thread of his pursuer, slicing the thread with his sharp claws. Though he floated unattached, the soldier pursued and annihilated his killer.

While Quinn and his regiment pursued the spirits to the outer stratosphere, Patton and his men had soon reached the Rock of Moriah, now exposed. Patton immediately signaled to a squad of men to follow him down the steps to the excavated cave beneath the Rock. The other soldiers of the 3rd Army scattered about the area, taking cover and looking at the skies for signs of the QRs, looking at the cave and the Mosque nearby, watching for more evil spirits to appear. The noise of Quinn's regiment firing their etheron guns at the Dome and the fleeing banshees screeching brought out more evil spirits from the Mosque. The 3rd Army blasted their etheron guns, taking out both the JS spirits and the Mosque.

Within the sound of battle waging above them, Patton and his squad reached the cavern below the Rock. He turned to his men, holding up five fingers and then one; then pointed to the marble slab that covered the deep cavity below, called the Well of Spirits. The six men scrambled to remove the slab. Patton and three men walked over to the edge of the Well and looked down into its darkness. The pit emanated a low humming sound as though some kind of electrical energy was at work, and in the darkness, a movement of the walls could be seen. Out of curiosity Patton lingered a moment longer, trying to discern what was going on when suddenly an evil spirit flew out, screeching a blood thirsty sound that echoed off the walls of the cavern. The men in the chamber all jumped back, startled by the suddenness of it. The JS spirit flew behind Solomon's altar in the cave, taking refuge where Solomon had sacrificed to Satan. As good faced evil, the evil spirit's long thin fingers tipped with sharp claws reached around the altar's base; his hideous face looking out at Patton and his men. Its long hooked nose and hooded eyes resembled his father, Satan. As the spirit watched him, Patton moved slowly between the creature and his men. When Patton raised his etheron gun, the spirit ducked behind the altar. Quickly, Patton responded, shooting his gun at the altar and blasted the altar and the spirit into nothingness.

The noise in the cave echoed down into the Well of Spirits, calling to the nether world. Up from the Well flew a dozen evil spirits, followed by a dozen more. Like bats, evil flew around the cave, clawing and screeching at Patton and his squad. But three of Paton's men broke free of the assault and rushed toward the Well and shot down into it. The spirits screeched louder, for they knew they could never again enter the bottomless pit of the nether region. Some began to flee the cave; others tried to hide in the crevices of the walls. Others sought out a strange pillar in the corner of the cavern. The pillar of Aphrodite, who the Muslims called Koubar, Alla wa Koubar was their chant – Satan and Aphrodite! When Patton's men stopped shooting down into the bottomless pit, they saw that the mouth of the pit had been sealed closed. Patton went to the edge of the Well. He could see movement from inside; a slamming against the seal of the pit, as evil struggled to get out.

The squad chased the rest of the spirits out of the cave and quickly took cover. Once outside, the spirits were met by the rest of Patton's 3rd Army that had taken cover when Patton and the squad had entered the cave. Still some of the spirits escaped the 3rd Army, flying upward to the heavens, just as Quinn and his 11th Regiment QRs were returning from their cosmic dogfight.

Quinn sent out a telepathic message to his regiment to take evasive flight – as the evil spirits soared high and the blasts from the 3rd Army's etheron guns followed them up to the heavens. When the 3rd Army saw Quinn and his men, they ceased fire. Quinn and his men took flight after the spirits. This time they would be cautious of their silver threads; one man pursued evil, as a second man held back to protect the thread of the first. The second dogfight covered a wide expanse of outer space, as Quinn and his regiment pursued, blasting their etheron guns – this time with greater urgency, greater speed. They looped the heavens, with each silver thread protected in the flight. The banshees from hell screeched through the skies, up and down, left and right. But at each turn, Quinn's men met them and annihilated them, until there was silence in the heaven.

In the quietude of the moment, Quinn looked around until he found the soldier who had been caught by the claws of evil that had severed his silver thread in the first dogfight. He would never be able to return to his body. Quinn flew over to him. The new reality of existence was strange to Quinn, for it had allowed him to speak to the man in life and now speak to him in his death. Quinn's heart was heavy, "I'm sorry. I let you down. I should have known that they would see our weakness. I should have prepared for it in the first attack."

"No, sir, don't be sorry for me," his voice was jovial and bellowed through the silence of space; his arms gestured widely to take in the limitless boundaries of the cosmos. "It's an honor to lose my life fighting for Jesus! It was a glorious fight. It was a glorious death! And I can still fly the heavens! What an adventure!"

Quinn had no words. Flying the heavens so freely was magnificent. The battle had been like no other. But coming face to face with the idea of sacrifice of not holding Maggie and his children in his arms, Quinn found heart-breaking. Next to his men, he wondered if he had the same measure of self-sacrifice that Jesus deserved. The attitude of the soldier in death had taught him of a higher level of devotion to Jesus. It was one thing to promise God one's will to die for Him; it was another to fulfill that promise with an enthusiastic, loving heart.

Finally, Quinn ordered, "Let's get back to Patton."

Within minutes, they arrived at the cave and reported to Patton.

Patton asked, "Were your men successful?"

"Yes, sir," Quinn responded, "We chased them to the outer limits of space, but we got all of them."

"Any casualties?" Patton questioned.

"One, sir. A spirit caught hold of his silver thread and broke it. He's with us, but he won't be able to return to his body."

Patton ordered, "Tell him to fall in with my men."

"Yes, sir," Quinn said.

"All right, let's get back home," Patton ordered.

"Sir? If I may ask a question?"

"Go ahead, Quinn, what is it?"

"Did you see a pillar down under the Rock. Elias said that my men and I were to destroy it. It is the pillar of Aphrodite, a fertility goddess. The Muslims called her Koubar."

"I believe it's down there, Quinn. You have my permission to proceed."

Quinn turned to his men and motioned them to the cave. Once down the steps, the men searched around and found the pillar, its column was half buried by the walls of the corner. Quinn held up his arm to stop his men before they shot their etheron guns at it. He searched for support structures for the Rock of Moriah above them. There were only three in the small cave. He thought for a moment; then called over Scott who was a retired Vet who had served in the Army Corps of Engineers. "It looks like that pillar of Aphrodite could be a support column, keeping the Rock of Moriah from falling into the cave."

Scott walked over to the column and traced it up to the ceiling and then back down to its base. He turned to Quinn, "You're right, sir. You see how wide the footing is," and reaching up to the ceiling, "there's another plate here. You can see its edge; here, the Rock of Moriah is sitting on it. We blow out the column, down comes the Rock. We have to support the Rock or cut the Rock and let part of it fall into the cave and then destroy the plate and the pillar."

"Well, there's nothing we can easily move in here that will support the weight of the Rock. I think we should go up top and cut the Rock in to pieces until we have a clear shot at the pillar. We have to know that we're completely destroyed the pillar."

"Yes, sir," Scott replied, "I think that's the best way to handle it."

When Quinn and his QRs reached the surface, he noticed Patton's 3rd Army resting about the wide terrace that had surrounded the Dome and the Mosque that had been obliterated during the battle with the evil spirits. And beyond the terrace, Muslims slowly approached. Quinn noted that they were in shock at seeing that both their Dome and Mosque were gone. How could he now start cutting up their Rock of Moriah – without starting a war with them? It then occurred to Quinn: they couldn't be seen by the living. Quinn walked over to Patton talking to two of his men. "Sir, the natives are getting restless!"

Patton turned around and saw men coming out from hiding after the roar of battle with the evil spirits. Patton turned to Quinn, "If you're going to destroy that pillar of Aphrodite you better do it now. The whole damned countryside is going to be here in a few minutes!"

Quinn's plan to cut the Rock of Moriah would take more than a few minutes and would be loud. Their 11th dimension power allowed them to conceal their weapons, but the Rock falling in to pieces would be another matter. Then it came to Quinn – "Let's make a show for them!"

"What do you have in mind – levitate the rock!?" Patton laughed.

"Can we do that, sir?" Quinn asked. "I mean, if the entire 3rd Army and my regiment all used their powers of telekinesis, can we move such a heavy weight as the Rock?"

"Let's find out," Patton said. "Quinn, I like the way you think!"

The 3rd Army and QRs quickly encircled the Rock. Quinn picked five of his QRs, "Over here, the pillar is in this corner of the cave." They positioned themselves to have clear aim at the pillar of Aphrodite when the Rock was lifted high enough.

Moments passed and nothing happened. Patton sent out a telepathic message so that the Muslims who had been gathering on the terrace wouldn't hear his command to his men. *Focus, on my count of 3. 1, 2, 3.*

The Rock began to wobble up and then dropped. Patton ordered, again, *Stop thinking of success. Keep it moving up. On my count, 1, 2, 3!*

The Rock began to lift steadily, breaking free from the cement of thousands of years of sediment that had nestled into the crevices surrounding the base of the Rock. Quinn and his men fell to their stomachs on the walkway that was once the interior floor of the Dome of the Rock. Leaning down into the cave, they aimed their etheron guns at the pillar of Aphrodite that was now fully exposed. The blast of etherons hit the pillar from top to midway when suddenly, a horrific screech emanated from the pillar. Out flew the evil spirit of Aphrodite. Quinn yelled, "Move!" Within a second of clearing the hole, the Rock came roaring down into the cave.

The concentration of the 3rd Army had been broken by the screeching Aphrodite.

But the Muslims who had come onto the terrace and saw that the Rock of Moriah was levitating thought some miracle was happening, for they couldn't see Patton nor his army or Quinn and his regiment, nor Aphrodite. Perhaps Satan was coming up from the Well of Spirits, perhaps Muhammad was returning to the Rock that he had stepped on when Gabriel had taken him to heaven. Perhaps Muhammad was taking the Rock to heaven with him. They didn't know what was going on, but surely it was a miracle. They dropped to the terrace, bent in prayer, bowing and chanting, "Alla wa Koubar! Alla wa Koubar! Alla wa Koubar!" Satan and Aphrodite, Satan and Aphrodite!

But the spirit of Aphrodite flew low above the terrace, above the prayerful Muslims and thinking that they were the ones who had burned her face with the etheron gun, she swooped down and clawed the backs of every man of them. The Muslims rolled about the terrace in pain, leaving trails of blood as they tried to crawl away. Again, Aphrodite attacked them, slicing their faces and eyes. Each time she swooped in to attack she let out a screech from hell. The Muslims screamed in fear, screamed in pain, for they couldn't see what it was that was attacking them.

Patton moved close to Quinn, "We have to get her."

"Yes, sir," Quinn said. "I have a plan."

"It better be good," Patton replied. "And make it fast before she sees us and takes off. I think she might be a little fast for us. She's really ticked off!"

Quinn stood up and walked to the center of the terrace between the Muslims writhing on the ground.

Aphrodite clawed another Muslim as he tried to hide behind a bush, for that she clawed him twice, and then turned to come back and attack again when suddenly she saw Quinn standing, looking at her. She stopped and hovered above the wounded Muslims. Who was this thing, she wondered. He wasn't like the living Muslims who had worshipped her for centuries. She stepped down onto the terrace and walked slowly over to Quinn. Her long black hair fell over her shoulder onto her small breasts. Her red silk gown draped around her narrow waste and flowed down to her bare feet. She circled Quinn, as her black eyes tried to penetrate him. Quinn turned to keep her in front of him. "You can see me," she said to him, "that means you are not human. But what are you? You are too beautiful to be an evil spirit. And you don't seem to be dead. Are you like Solomon? Are you a living being whose soul has left his body?"

Just as she was about to reach out to the silver cord coming from Quinn's midsection, Patton yelled, "Now!"

At once, the QRs began firing at the evil Aphrodite, until there was nothing left of her.

Quinn sighed with relief. He walked over to Patton, "Telepathy is a great thing. I'm glad you were able to read the plan I had on my mind."

"Did you get enough of that pillar?" Patton asked.

"I think we got what Elias wanted us to get. But I'm going over there and blast through the Rock to get to the footing of the pillar. It's supposed to be completely destroyed. I won't feel at ease unless it is."

Patton smiled, "I can see why God chose you to lead the 11th Regiment."

The two warriors looked back at the Muslims still crying out in pain. "I think we gave them enough of a show," Patton laughed.

"It'll just take a few more minutes, sir."

"Good. Then let's get the hell out of this place. It gives me the creeps."

By the end of the day, the world knew that the Americans had begun their Second American Revolution. But by then, the major issues were settled. The government leaders were all dead, and for the time being, the U.S. Military controlled the country. Eisenhower announced to the country that within a month, elections for interim president and members of congress would be elected. The following year, regular elections would be held and would include elections for Supreme Court justices.

The world knew that all U.S. Military personnel and equipment had either reached home or would arrive within the next day or two, to support the revolution. No country was interested in trying to interfere; they were busy contending with the void left behind by the absence of U.S. forces. The UN Antichrist and General Assembly were all dead; there was no single voice to issue an order to invade the U.S. All UN troops on U.S. territory were dead. And even if the world joined forces, they were helpless against the Americans. NATO would not attempt a useless endeavor. The Russians, Hezbollah, Hamas, began to pull out of Mexico and return home. The Chinese had left Canada and were already heading home.

It had been sudden and all-consuming – and it was over in days.

Americans went to the ports, to the airstrips, and to bases to welcome back their military men and women. Christian services were held all over the country. But the non-Christians were not happy and took to the streets in America – outraged by the Christians. In foreign lands, they burned the American flag and demanded revenge. It would soon come, to the outraged.

On Sunday afternoon, while most families had gathered together, TVs and radios in homes and stores clicked on to the same station. The crackle of ham radios sounded. Display screens in the world's war rooms suddenly flashed on. Car radios bleeped a piercing pitch. Cell phones rang in unison. Kindles, iPads, and computers turned on; car navigational systems and every appliance that had a viewing screen were now displaying an ancient man.

He was dressed in a long, white linen robe. His white hair and beard gave him a startling glowing appearance that would burn onto the memory of all who saw him. All at once, the world was looking at a prophet from antiquity. He stood silently at first, waiting for the eyes and ears of the world to adjust to him. Then he spoke. His voice was powerful and foreboding. He spoke in Aramaic, but all the world's people heard him in their own language.

"I come as the prophet that the God of Abraham had promised He would send to you. I am Elias. I have come to warn you that the great and dreadful day of the Lord is at hand. I come to confirm the blood of the new testament of Jesus Christ. You must repent of your sins. If you are to have eternal salvation, you must accept Jesus Christ as your Lord and Savior. Elias paused a moment, "You have been warned for the last time. The end is nigh - the choice is yours. Jesus or Satan."

Suddenly, all transmission ended and every screen went black.

Every nation was thrown in to chaos. People prayed. People took to the streets demanding to know who was behind such blasphemy. This is the work of American technology! American flags were burned; stepped on in outrage. World leaders went on national TV, holding press conferences – yes, the old man known as Elias was an insane, delusional man. He had escaped a mental hospital. Then the quiet came.

Finally, the citizens of the world looked to the skies for a sign. Some had turned to their Bibles, to Luke 21:25-26, 28-31, 34-36, where Jesus said: "And there shall be signs in the sun, and in the moon, and in the stars; and upon the Earth distress of nations, by reason of the confusion of the roaring of the sea and of the waves; Men withering away for fear, and expectation of what shall come upon the whole world. For the powers of heaven shall be moved; And then they shall see the Son of man coming in a cloud, with great power and majesty; But when these things begin to come to pass, look up, and lift up your heads, because your redemption is at hand. And he spoke to them a similitude. See the fig tree, and all the trees: When they now shoot forth their fruit, you know that summer is nigh; So you also, when you shall see these things come to pass, know that the kingdom of God is at hand...And take heed to yourselves, lest perhaps your hearts be overcharged with surfeiting [overindulgence] and drunkenness, and the cares of this life, and that day come upon you suddenly. For as a snare shall it come upon all that sit upon the face of the whole Earth. Watch ye, therefore, praying at all times, that you may be accounted worthy to escape all these things that are to come, and to stand before the Son of man."

Chapter 21

The Watchman had been looking at the skies for more than a year, for signs that had been promised. Odd things came and went, seen only by Christian patriots - a cloud in the distinct, sculpted outline of a large white dove floated across the sky and then evaporated. Nine hundred miles away, a white dove cloud appeared to another Christian, and again, evaporated, but reassured those who saw and to those they gave their testimony that the Holy Ghost was with them and America.

The world was in turmoil, out for revenge against the Americans who had killed the Jesuit General and the U.N. Secretary General. The destruction of the Dome of the Rock was unforgiveable! Death to America! was chanted the world over and in places of their own country.

Americans settled in throughout their nation, prepared to fight any invasion. Ready to fight their own countrymen who did not follow Jesus and who had threatened and raged against them. Christians would not bow to any god, except to their God of Abraham.

Then came the first cry of the Watchman of an aurora borealis that was rapidly growing beyond the northern pole. An ionization of particles that waved across the sky in reds, blues, and greens. The Northern Lights they had been called in Alaska and in other regions of northern villages. But these, the Watchman cried, were enlarging and moving beyond the tips of Greenland, Russia, Canada, and Alaska. Now, they almost covered the northern half of the Earth - and moving still further south. Rapidly. And up from the South Pole appeared the same electromagnetic phenomenon. Moving quickly northward to meet its celestial counterpart, until the whole Earth was enclosed inside a shell of mesmerizing beautiful colors, waving across the night and day skies. The thick murky electromagnetic blanket covered the Earth and blackened the light of the Sun. Surely, it was the sign of the end times! Christians moved quickly securing livestock and pets inside shelters. They hid themselves and families inside their homes, praying and fasting. And for three days and three nights it continued. They called it the Chastisement.

Suddenly, a cosmic Gamma burst slammed hard against the earth and every living thing that was outside was instantly bombed to oblivion. It exploded planes in the skies and they fell like balls of fire all over the Earth, destroying structures below and killing all those who had rejected Jesus Christ. In underground missile silos, launches were triggered by the electrical interferences and missiles headed for pre-programmed targets. But once in the sky, their wires were fried by the Superwave that followed close behind the Gamma burst, and the missiles fell to earth in nuclear explosions upon their own lands. That is, except the U.S. The U.S. Military had taken seriously Dr. LaViolette's advice of the coming Superwave and had insulated the electrical systems of all U.S. missiles. But they hadn't insulated the launching systems because of sequestration budget cuts. The electrical interference caused spontaneous launches, but the 5000 U.S. missiles soared into the heavens unscathed by the Superwave and continued on to hit their foreign targets in nuclear explosions. Countries were decimated. Billions of people died worldwide.

All TV and radio reception, cable, cell phone, computers, electrical plants, generators, batteries, car, bus, and truck engines, elevators, escalators, factories, building and house lights, street lights, traffic lights, stoves and microwave ovens, and all electric appliances were all shorted out. Mankind had been sent back to the beginning of civilization.

At night, the faintest of heavenly shape came from the Sun reflecting off the moon that through the vagueness and ambulation of the electromagnetic waves caused the moon to look blood red. The stars were blocked out altogether. The earth was enveloped by electrical waves of color that prohibited all other thought and focus. The world could not function. Its citizens grew fearful - what did it mean? Was it a sign from God? Others were sure it was the sign of the end times approach. Others mocked the idea of God's existence; they looked to the scientists for an answer, for a solution. Communications between continents ceased. Government officials of adjoining countries ran messages to each other by horseback, questioning - what have you done!? Who is behind this? But the horses failed and the men died as the Superwave continued to pass over the world. No answers returned. Every nation, every people were alone.

A great stress fell upon all the nations of the world. The oceans and seas were caused to roar; the waves higher than ever before as the remaining glaciers were melted by the Superwave and the blood-red moon tugged at the seas, as the Superwave continued to pass over. The earth trembled and rumbled out thunderous groans, as if it were about to tear apart. Fear grabbed the hearts of men who died in the expectation of the end of the world – in expectation of judgment of their blackened souls. Above the United States a great cloud formed, covering the nation from sea to sea. And as the cloud descended, all could see the Son of man in great power and majesty. Americans looked up, knowing their redemption was at hand. They trembled and fell to their knees and prayed to be forgiven of their sins. And into the valley of Josaphat – New York City – the valley of destruction – the day of the Lord at hand – came Jesus Christ.

Jesus sat upon a precious white throne. And as He did, He was One with the Father; the white aura of His Holy Ghost radiated from His Holy essence. He summoned Satan from the Vatican where Michael the Archangel had held him captive from the beginning of the Second American Revolution. Then He summoned the soul of the Antichrist out of the ashes of the United Nations compound and the soul of the False Prophet from IL Gesù in Rome, from where Christ's angels had held them until this moment in time. And this time, Jesus, as One with the Father and His Holy Ghost, sent Satan, the Antichrist, and the False Prophet into the pool of fire and brimstone, for ever and ever.

The billions that had died from the Gamma burst and Superwave stood in the presence of His great white throne, as His angels opened books and the Book of Life. The dead were judged by things written in the books according to their works. Death and hell gave up their dead that were in them. They were judged according to their works. And hell and death were cast into the pool of fire – this was the second death.

Anyone not found in the Book of Life was cast into the pool of fire.

A great voice from the throne, said: Behold the tabernacle of God with men, and He will dwell with them. And they shall be His people; and God Himself with them shall be their God. And God shall wipe away all tears from their eyes: and death shall be no more, nor mourning, nor crying, nor sorrow shall be any more, the former things are passed away. For the God of Abraham would no longer afflict the seed of David.

And He that sat on the throne, said: Behold, I make all things new. And He said to me: Write, for these words are most faithful and true.

And He said to me: "It is done."

Rev. 21

www.ingramcontent.com/pod-product-compliance
Lightning Source LLC
Chambersburg PA
CBHW071331020726
47502CB00001B/60

* 9 7 8 0 6 1 5 7 2 7 3 2 5 *